HEARTsToPPeR

VOLUME 4

All rights reserved. Published by Graphix, an imprint of Scholastic Inc.,
Publishers since 1920. SCHOLASTIC, GRAPHIX, and associated logos are
trademarks and/or registered trademarks of Scholastic Inc.

Heartstopper: Volume 4 was originally published in England
by Hachette Children's Group in 2021.

Library of Congress Control Number: 2020946440

ISBN 978-1-338-61756-6 (hardcover)
ISBN 978-1-338-61755-9 (paperback)

10 9 8 7 6 5 4 3   22 23 24 25 26

Printed in China 62
This edition first printing, January 2022

ALICE OSEMAN

HEARTSTOPPER

VOLUME 4

graphix
An Imprint of
SCHOLASTIC

August 10th
Is it too soon to tell Nick?? We've been going out for like four months, although it feels like longer!
We decided we're officially boyfriends,
Woah
Yeah
we've been to Paris together,
and we came out to, like, the whole school year.
Me. We're dating.

No, that does make sense
You can always tell me stuff like that.
I even told him about my weird eating thing... even though I'm totally fine and he doesn't need to worry.
But should I tell him I love him?
What if he doesn't feel the same??

5. LOVE

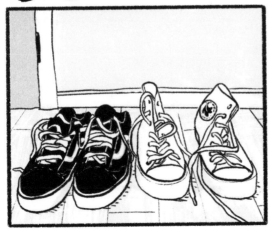

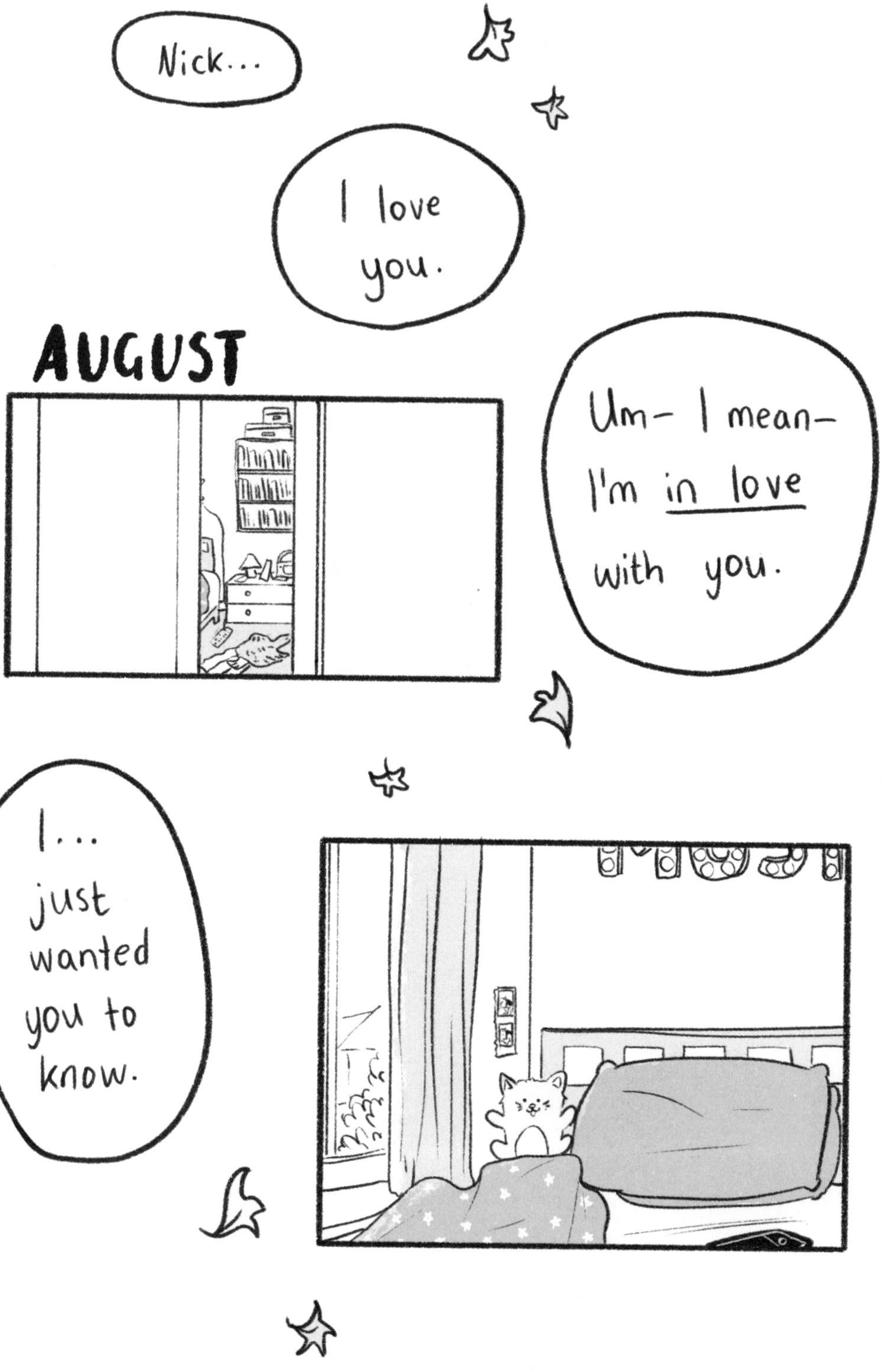
Nick...
I love you.
AUGUST
Um- I mean- I'm in love with you.
I... just wanted you to know.

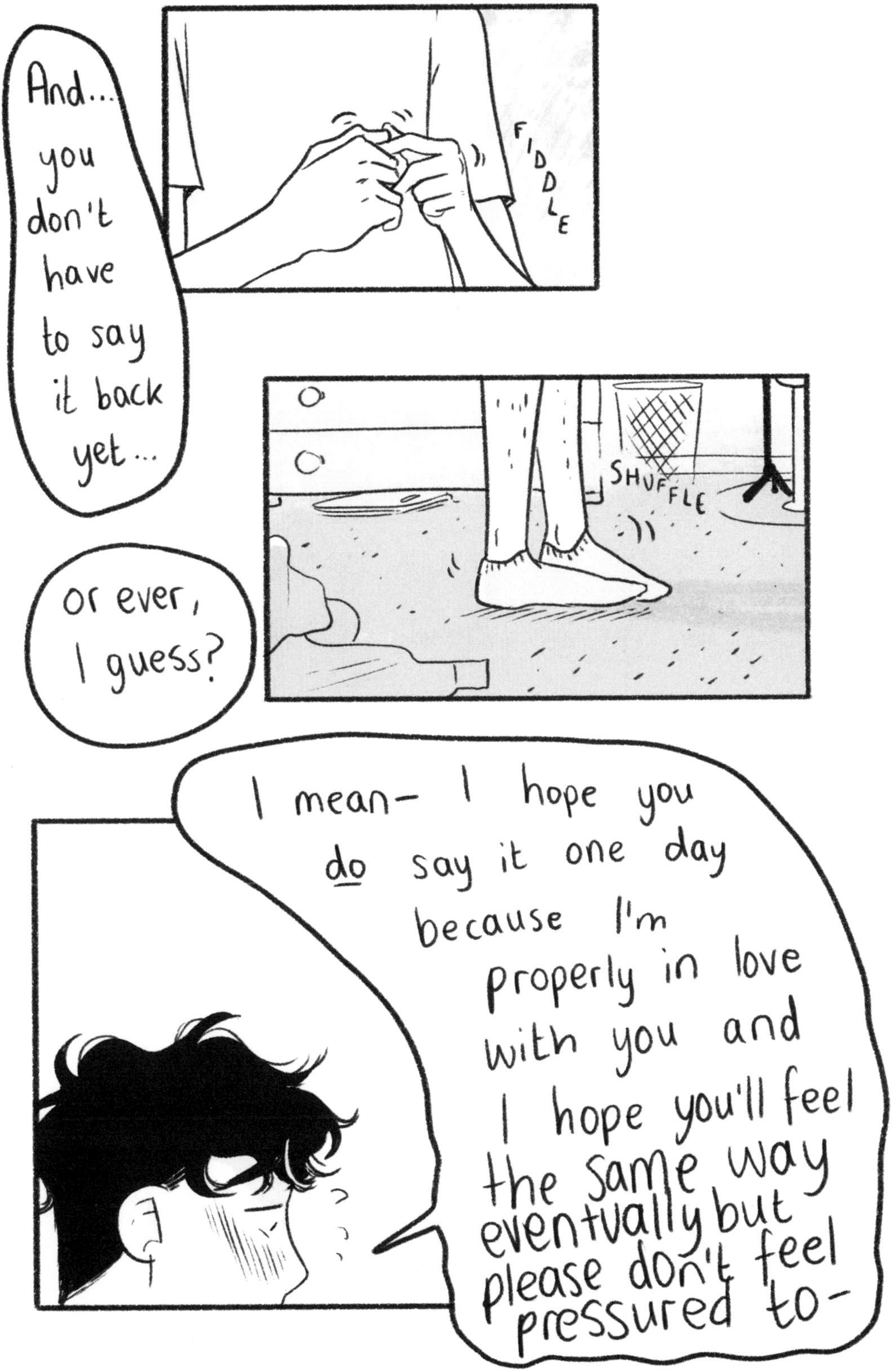
And... you don't have to say it back yet...
FIDDLE
or ever, I guess?
SHUFFLE
I mean- I hope you do say it one day because I'm properly in love with you and I hope you'll feel the same way eventually but please don't feel pressured to-

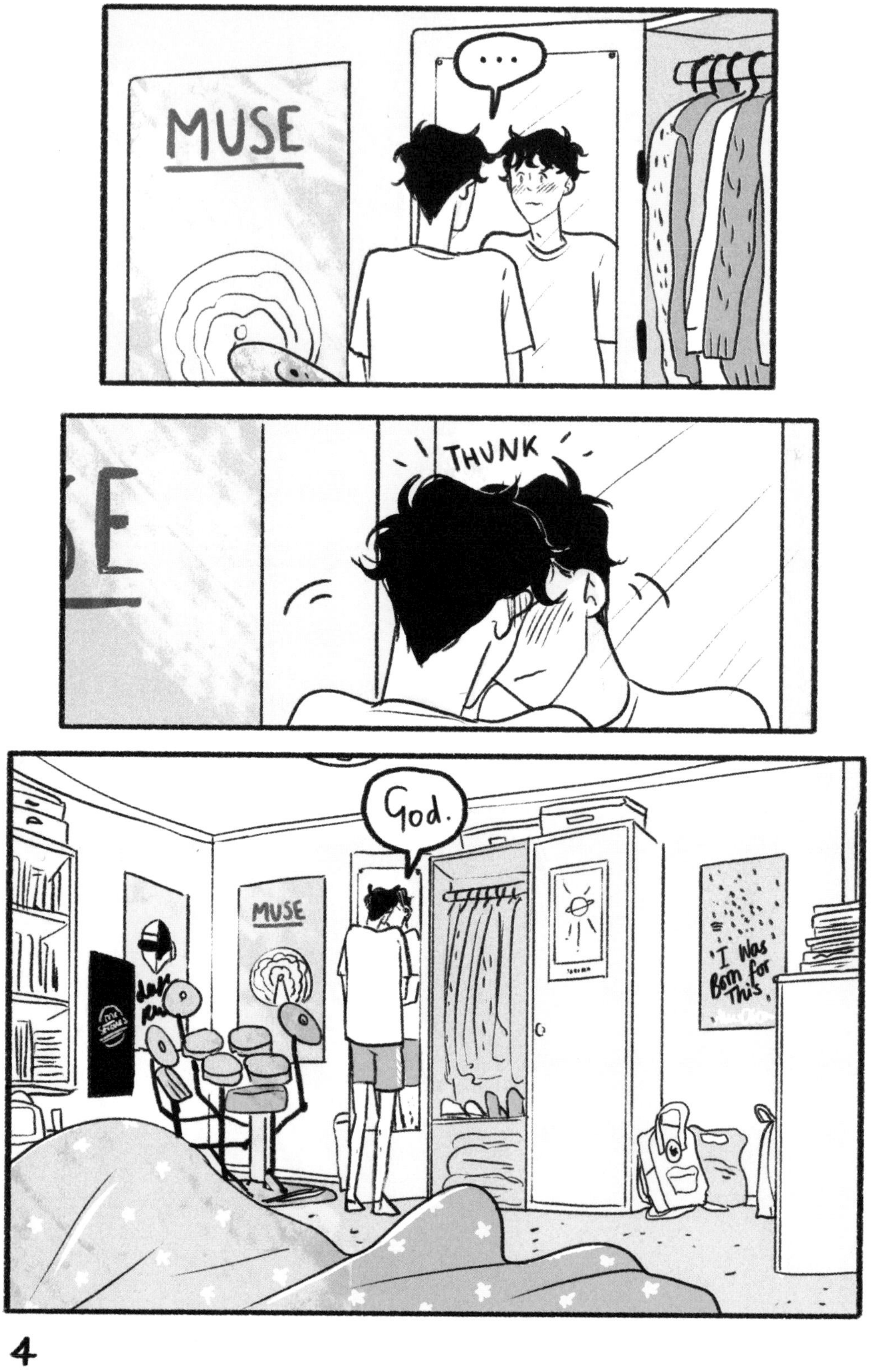
MUSE
...
THUNK
God.
MUSE
I Was Born for This

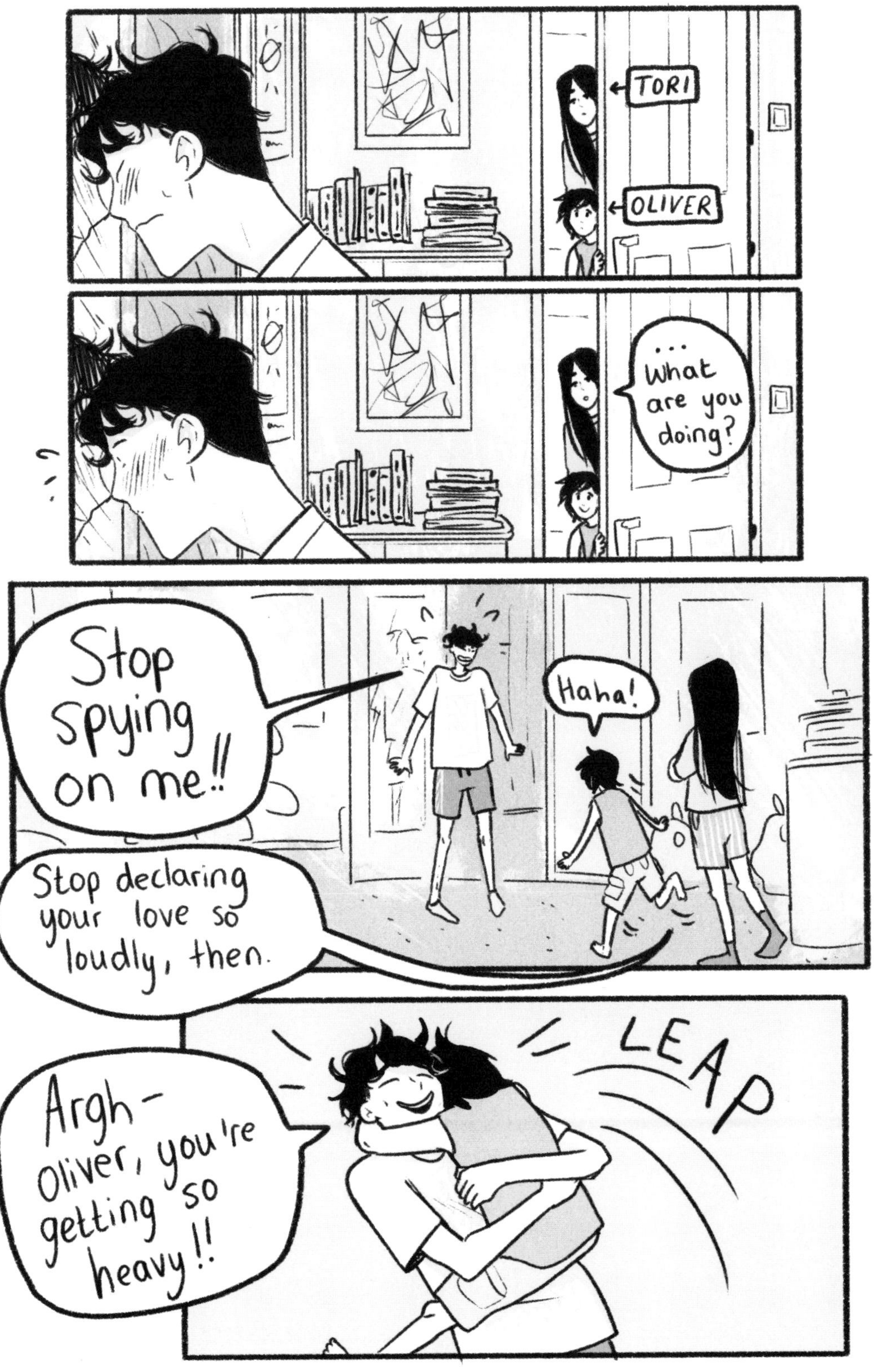
TORI
OLIVER
... What are you doing?
Stop spying on me!!
Haha!
Stop declaring your love so loudly, then.
LEAP
Argh- Oliver, you're getting so heavy!!

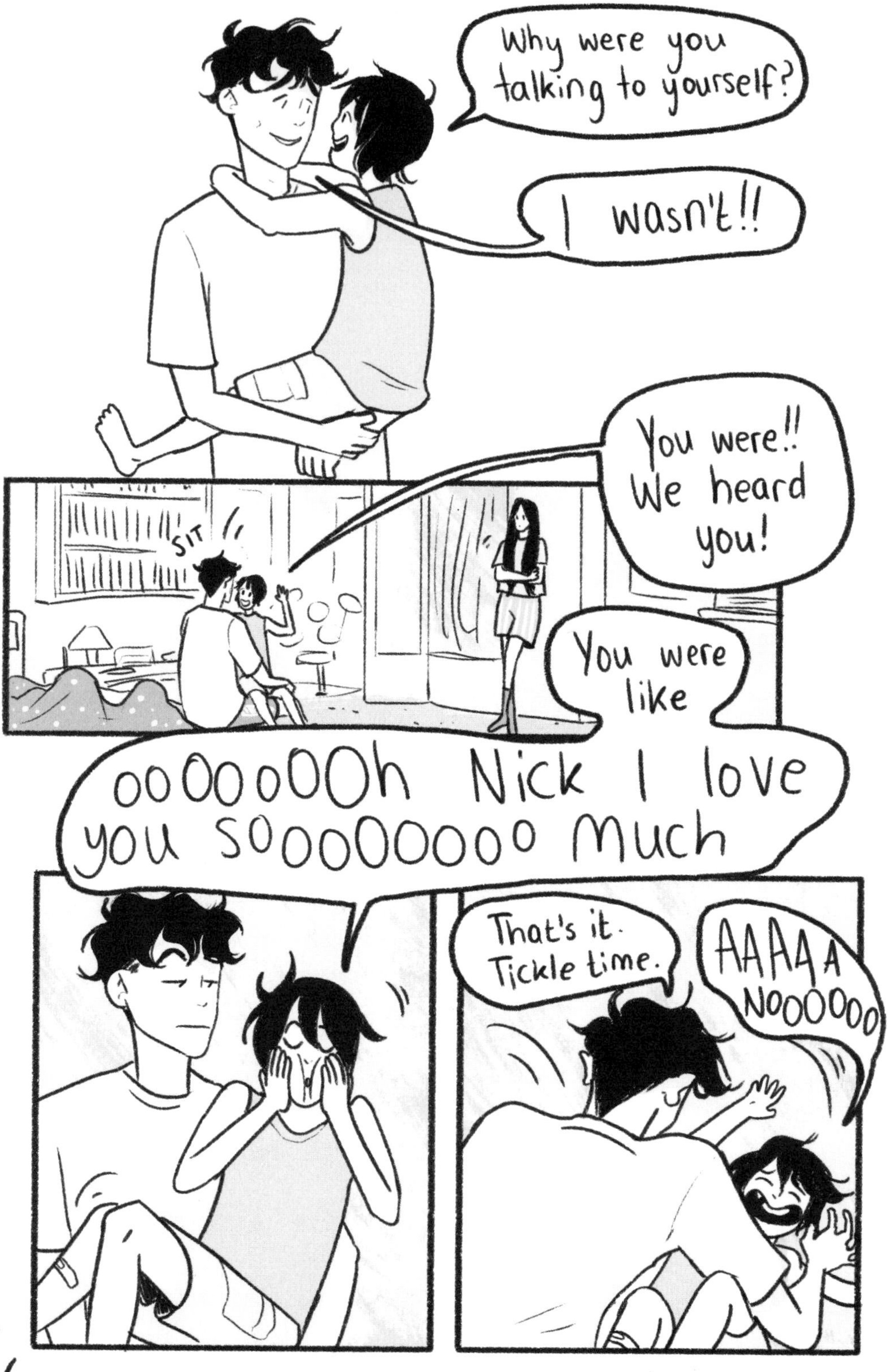
Why were you talking to yourself?
I wasn't!!
You were!! We heard you!
SIT
You were like
oooooOOh Nick I love you sOoooOOooo Much
That's it. Tickle time.
AAAAA NOOOOOO

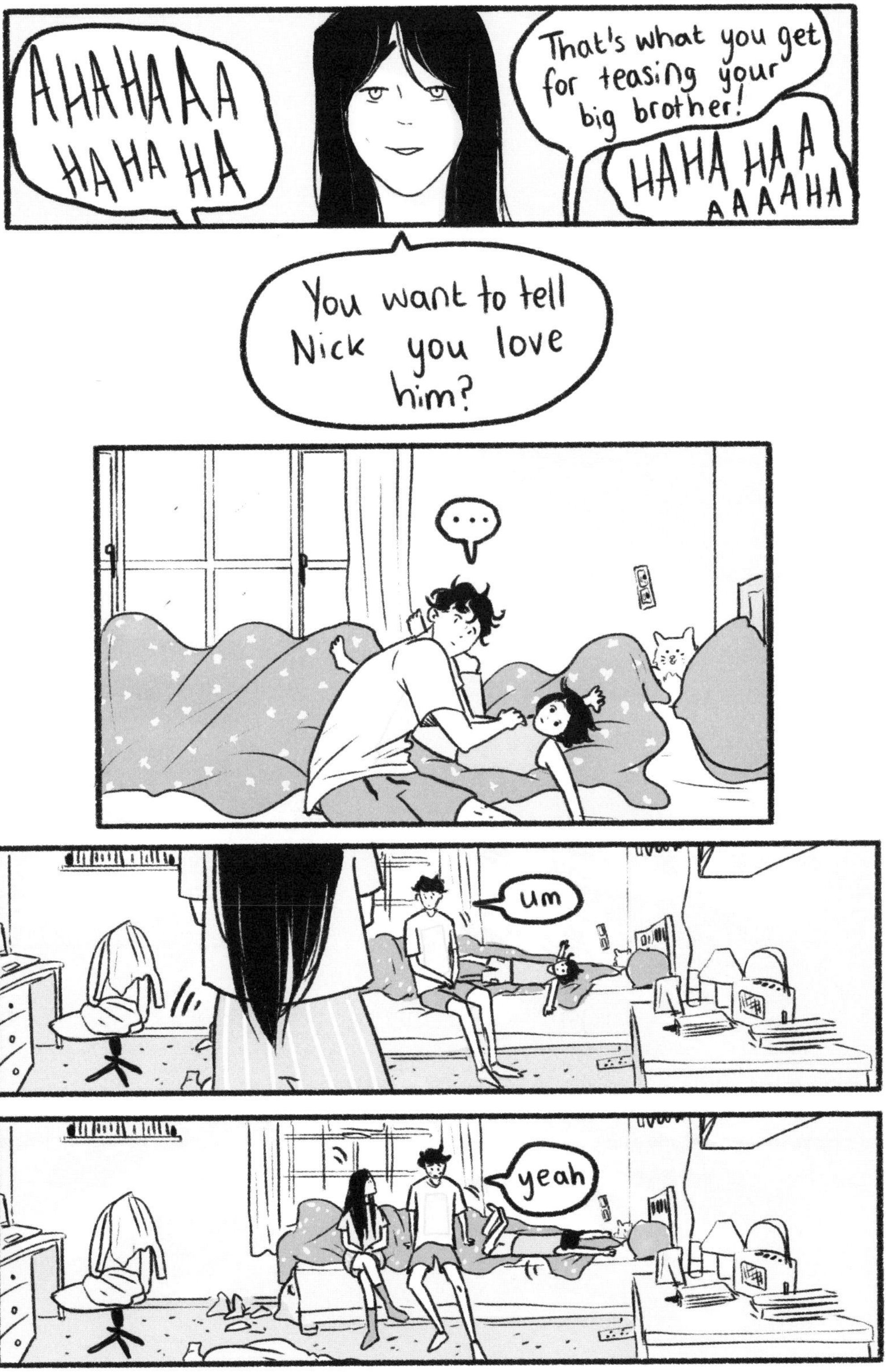
AHAHAAA HAHAHA HA
That's what you get for teasing your big brother!
HAHA HAA AAAAHA
You want to tell Nick you love him?
...
um
yeah

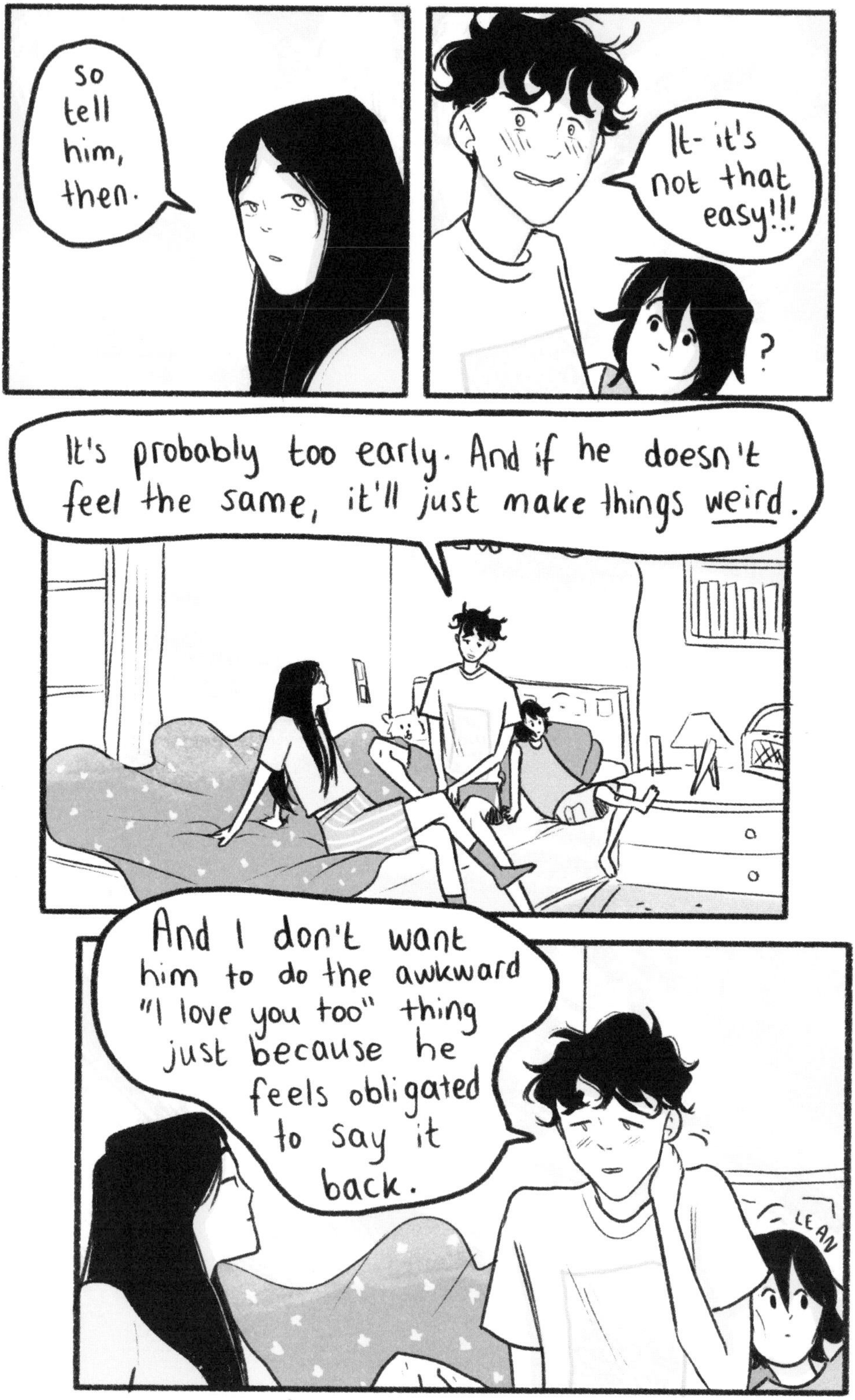

So tell him, then.
It- it's not that easy!!!
?
It's probably too early. And if he doesn't feel the same, it'll just make things weird.
And I don't want him to do the awkward "I love you too" thing just because he feels obligated to say it back.
LEAN

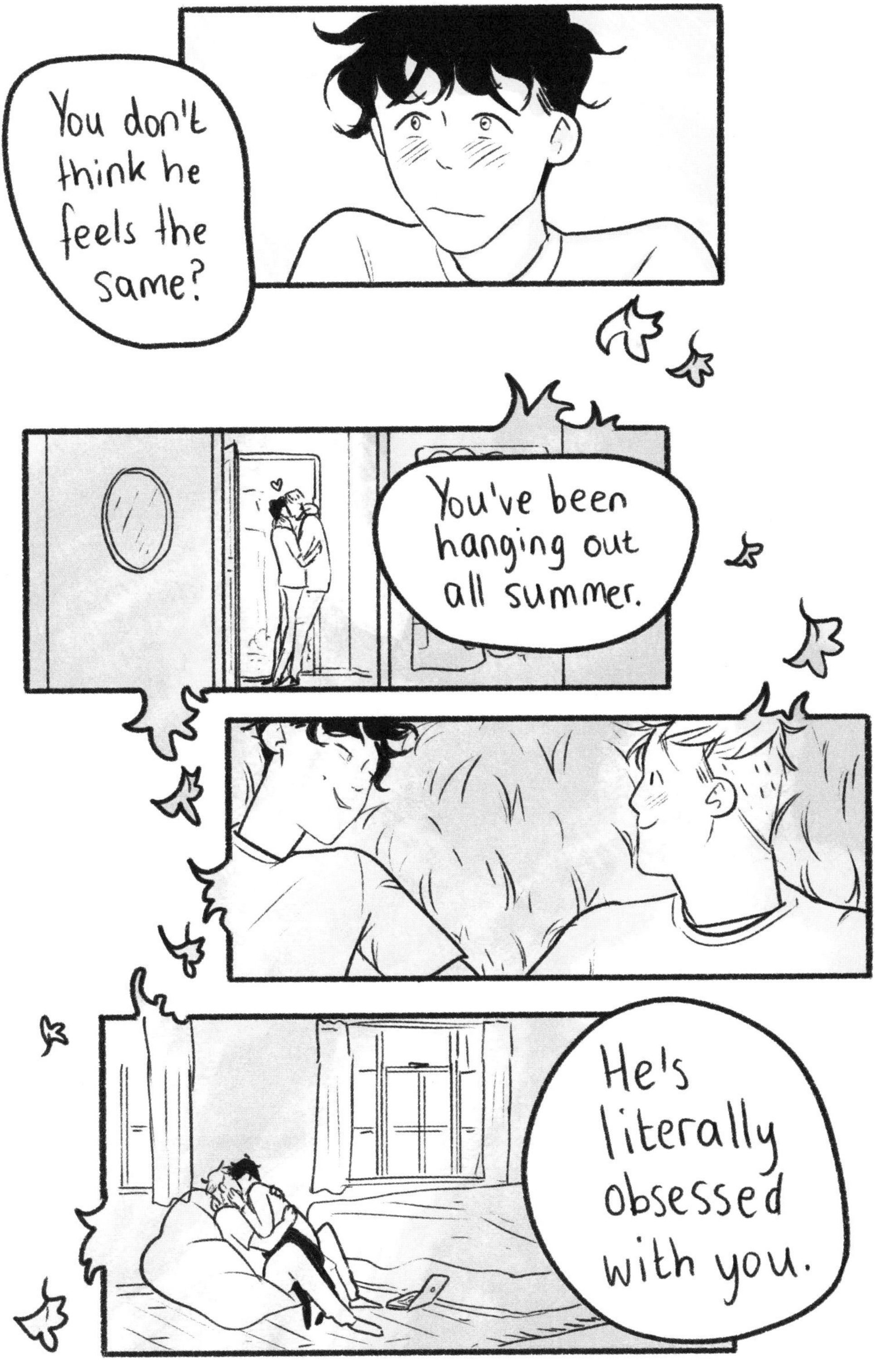
You don't think he feels the same?
You've been hanging out all summer.
He's literally obsessed with you.

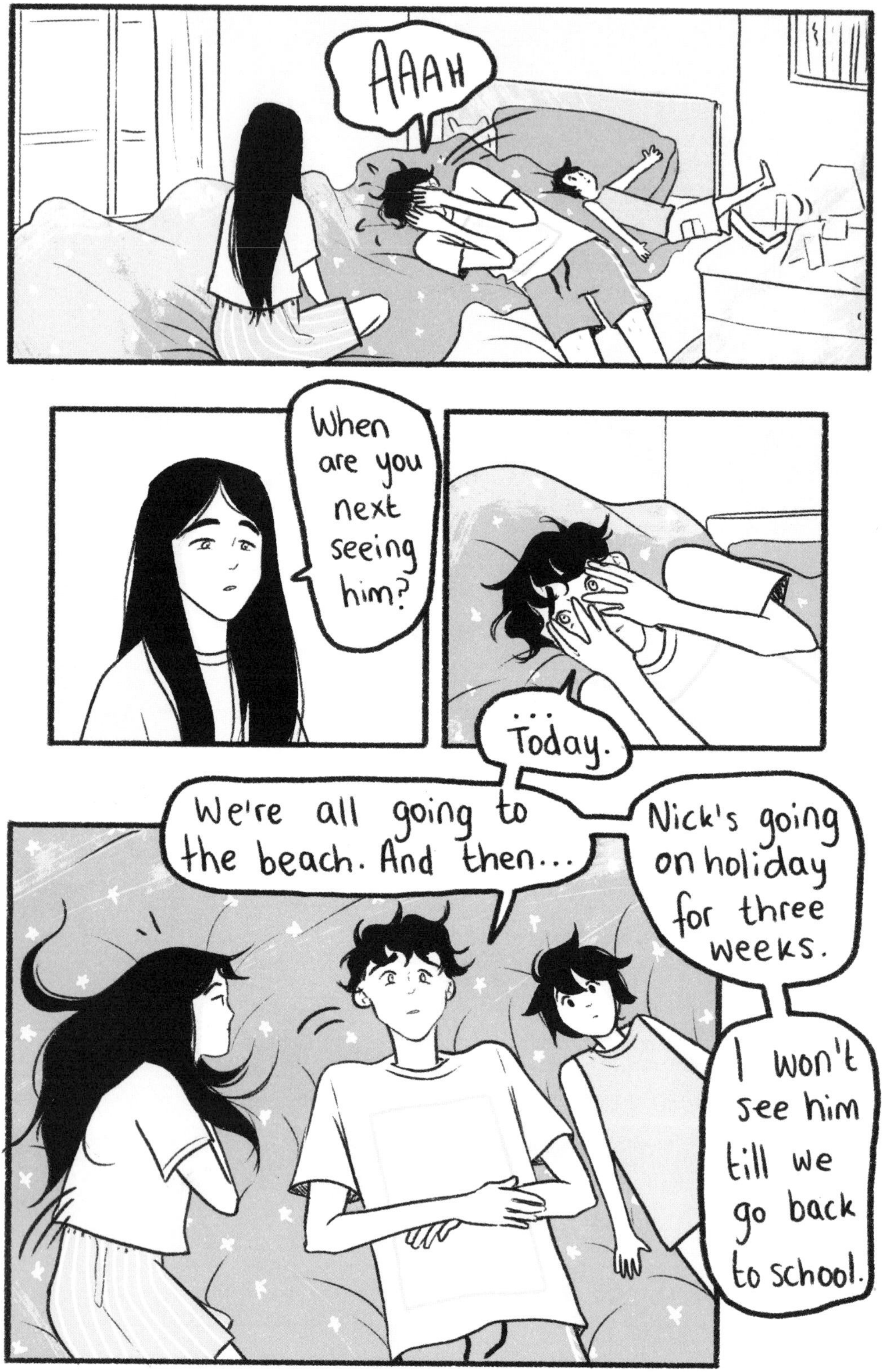
AAAH
When are you next seeing him?
... Today.
We're all going to the beach. And then...
Nick's going on holiday for three weeks.
I won't see him till we go back to school.

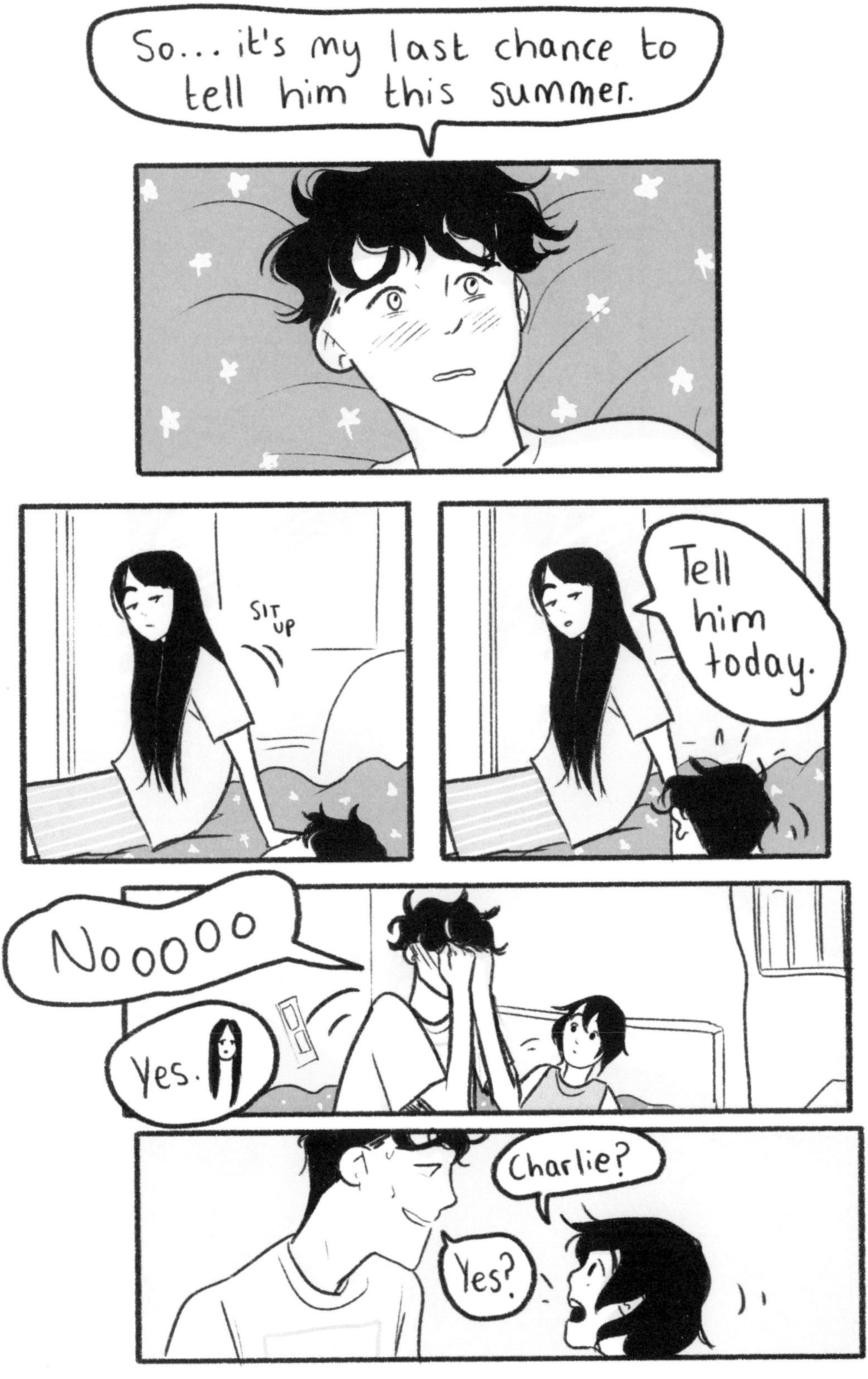
So... it's my last chance to tell him this summer.
SIT UP
Tell him today.
Nooooo
Yes.
Charlie?
Yes?

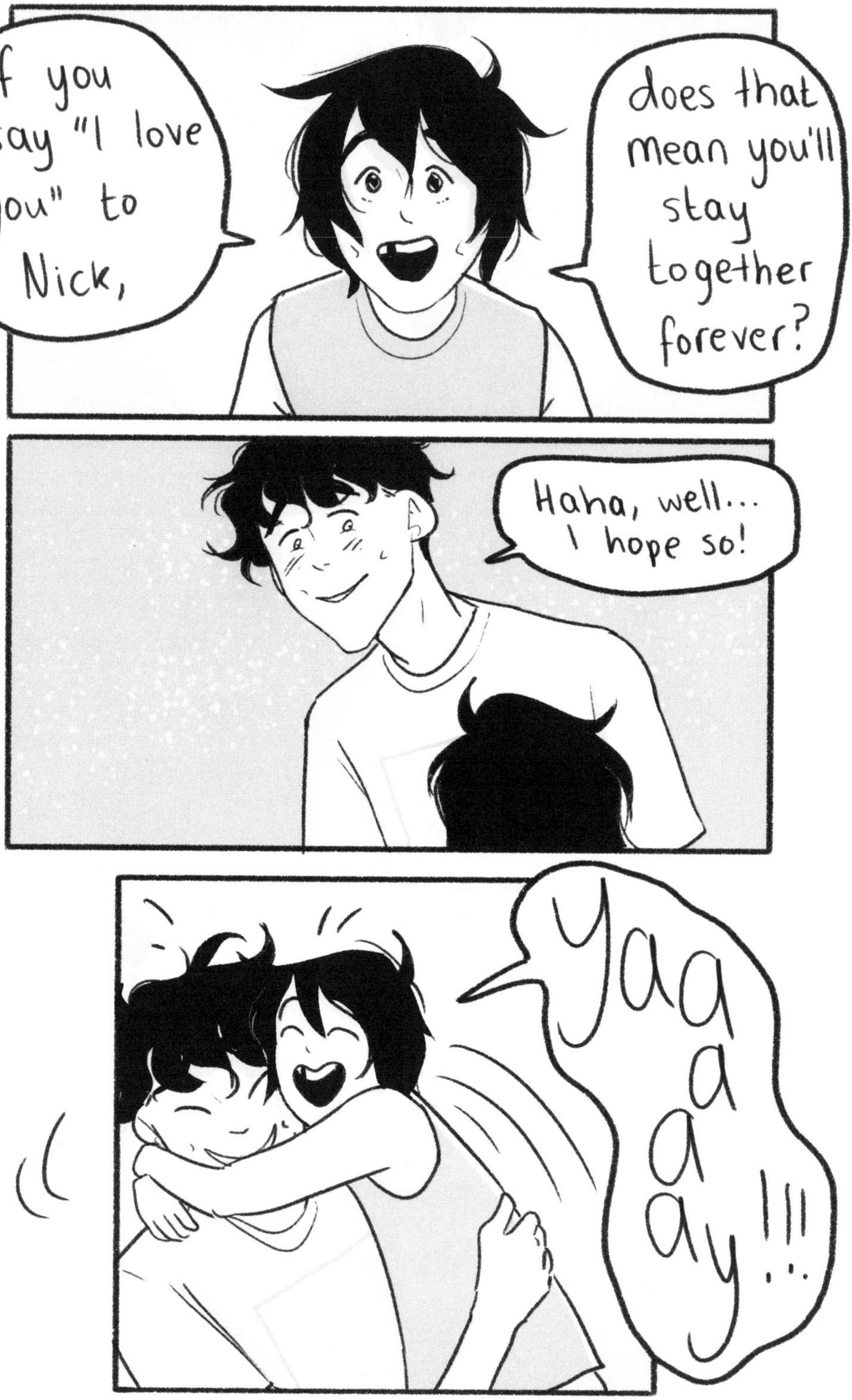
If you say "I love you" to Nick,
does that mean you'll stay together forever?
Haha, well... I hope so!
Yaaaaay!!!

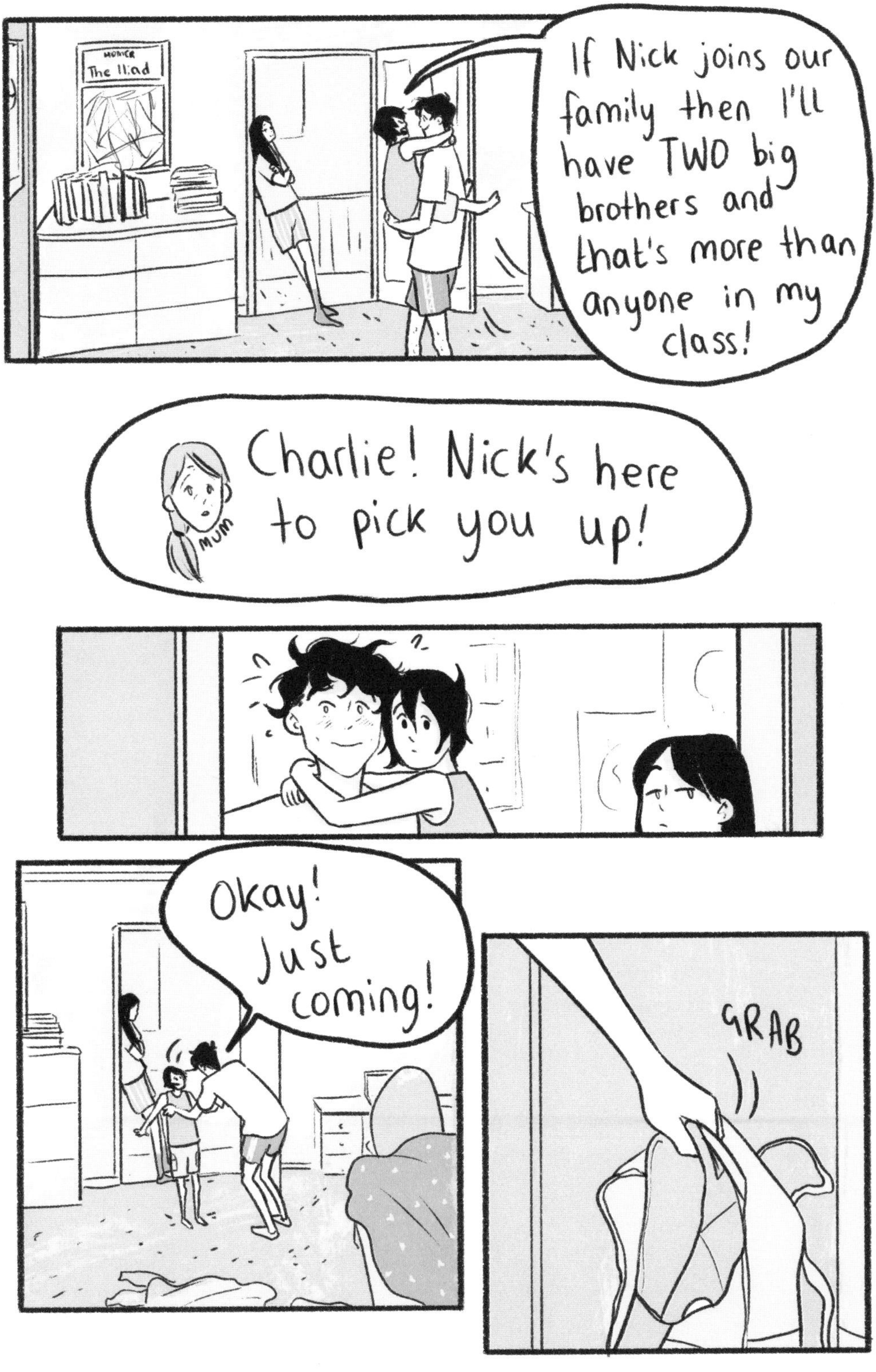
HOMER
The Iliad
If Nick joins our family then I'll have TWO big brothers and that's more than anyone in my class!
Charlie! Nick's here to pick you up!
MUM
Okay! Just coming!
GRAB

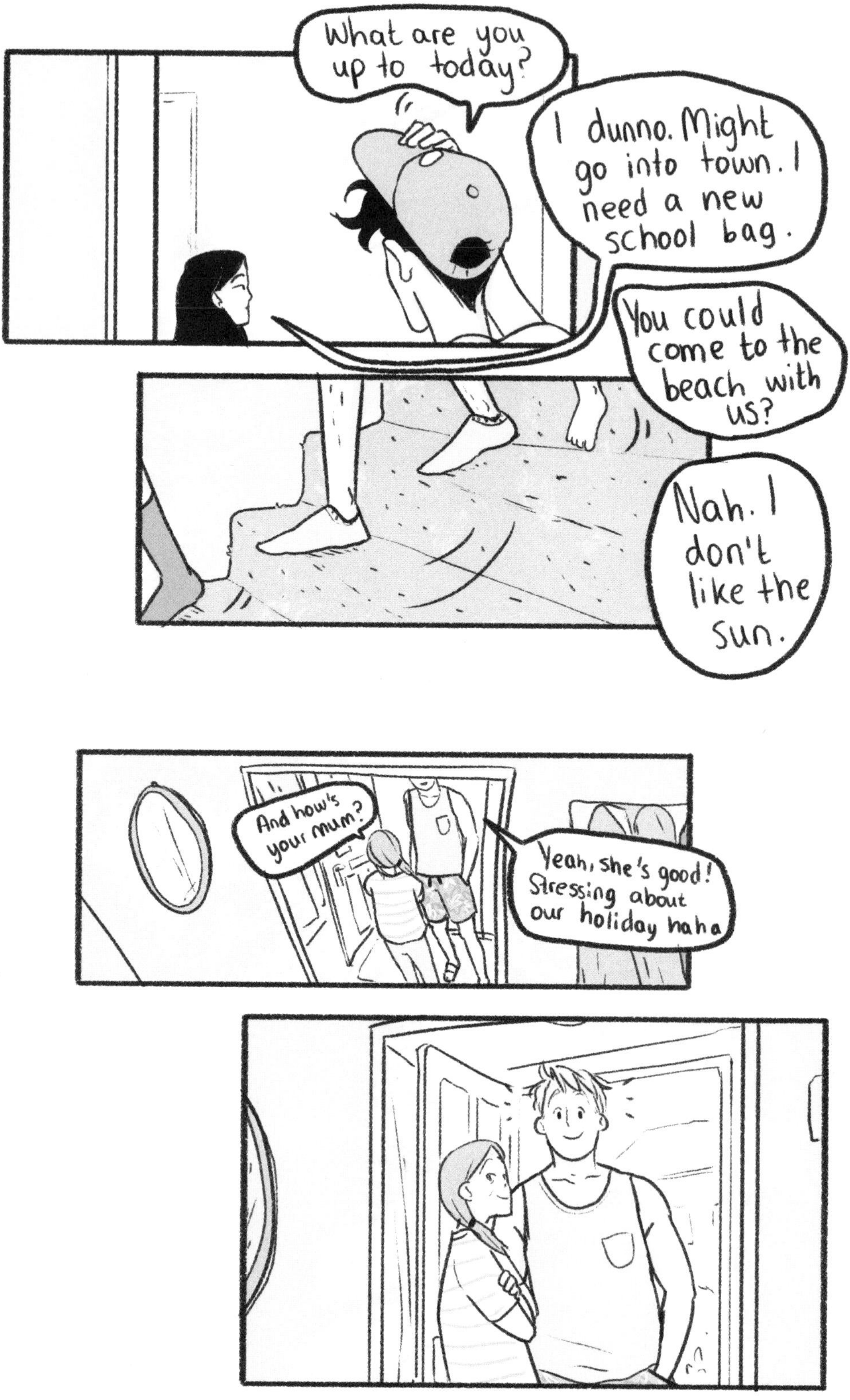
What are you up to today?
I dunno. Might go into town. I need a new school bag.
You could come to the beach with us?
Nah. I don't like the sun.
And how's your mum?
Yeah, she's good! Stressing about our holiday haha

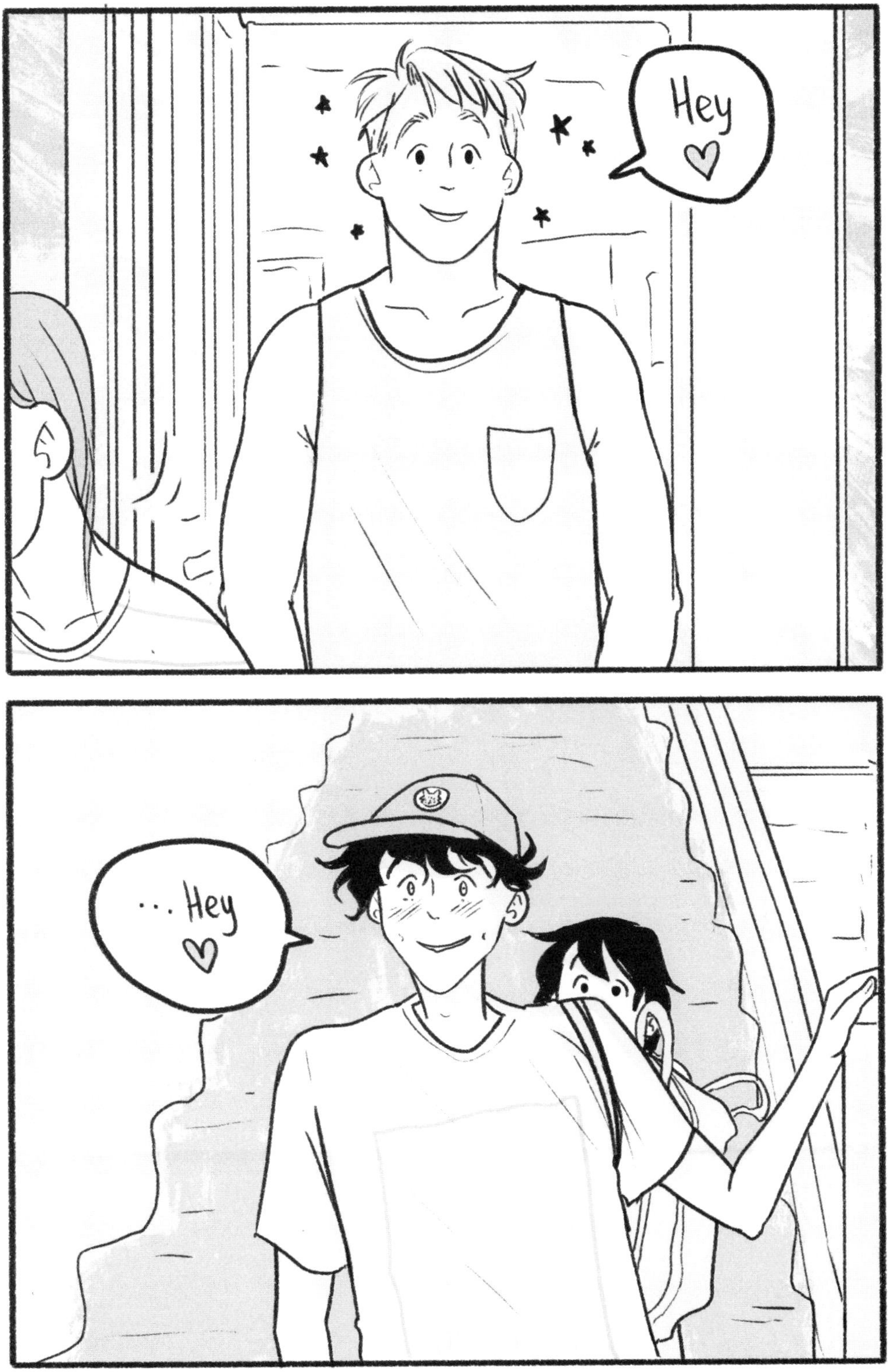
Hey
...Hey

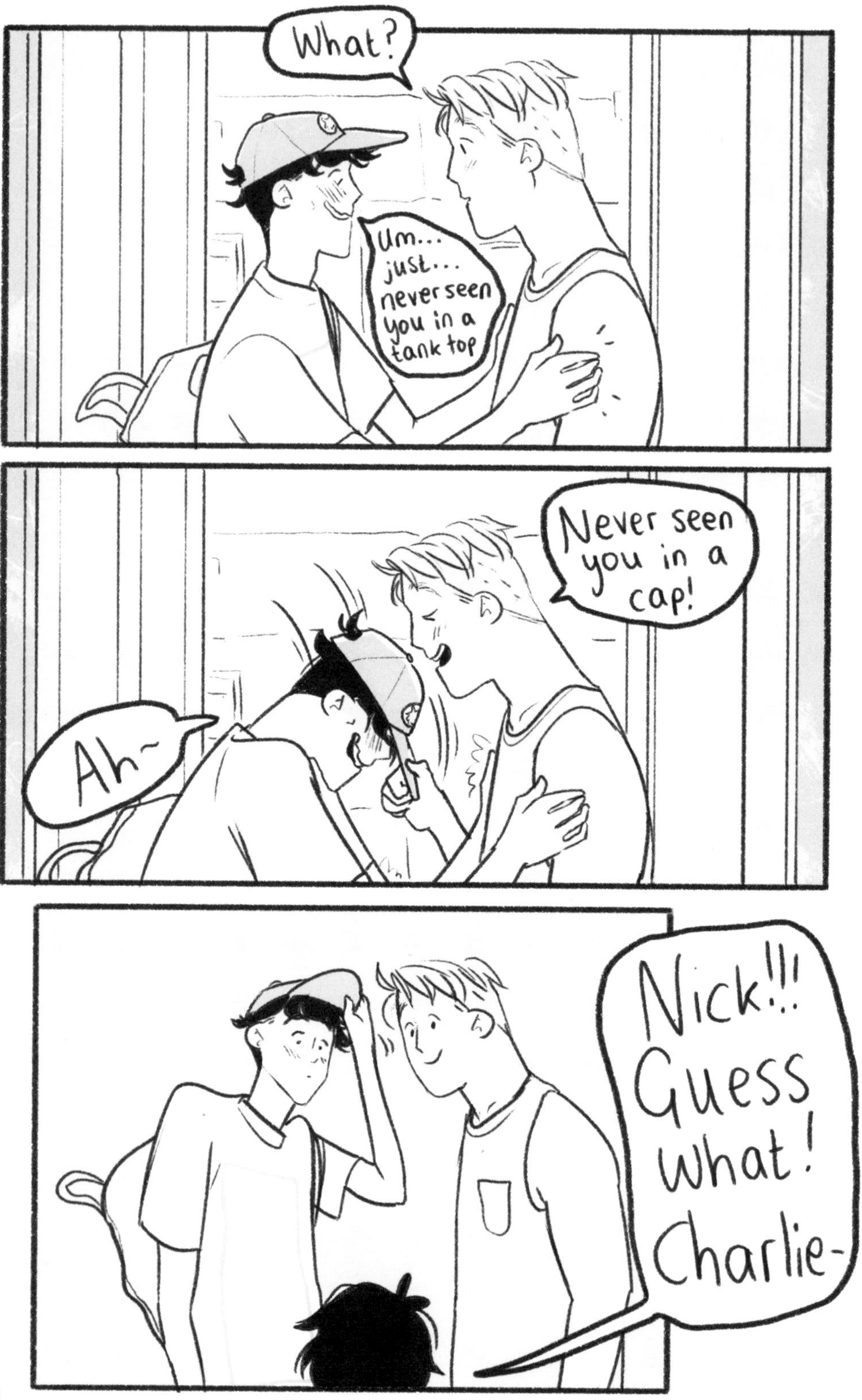
What?
Um... just... never seen you in a tank top
Never seen you in a cap!
Ah~
Nick!!! Guess what! Charlie-

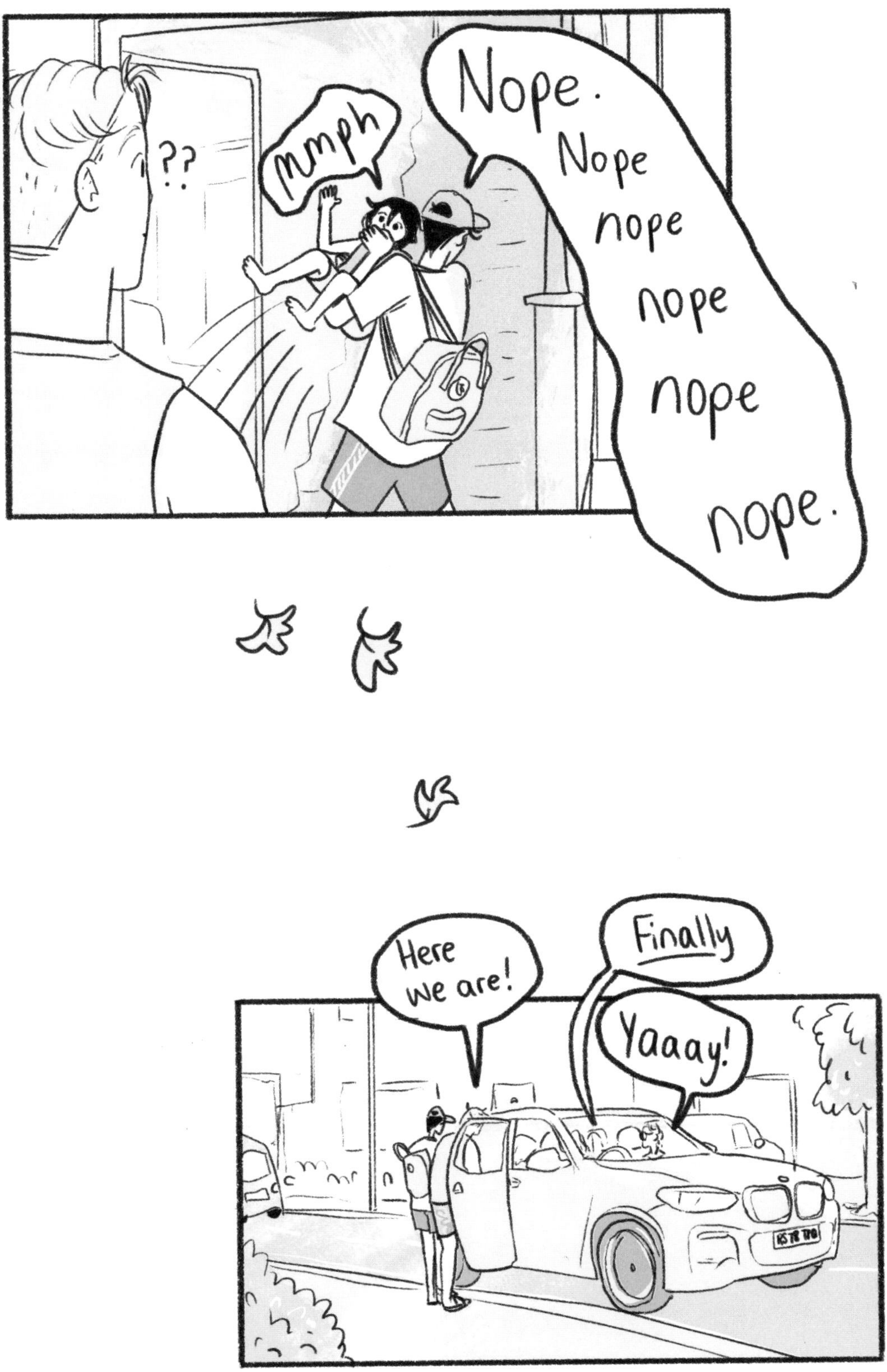

??
mmph
Nope.
Nope
nope
nope
nope
nope.
Here we are!
Finally
Yaaay!

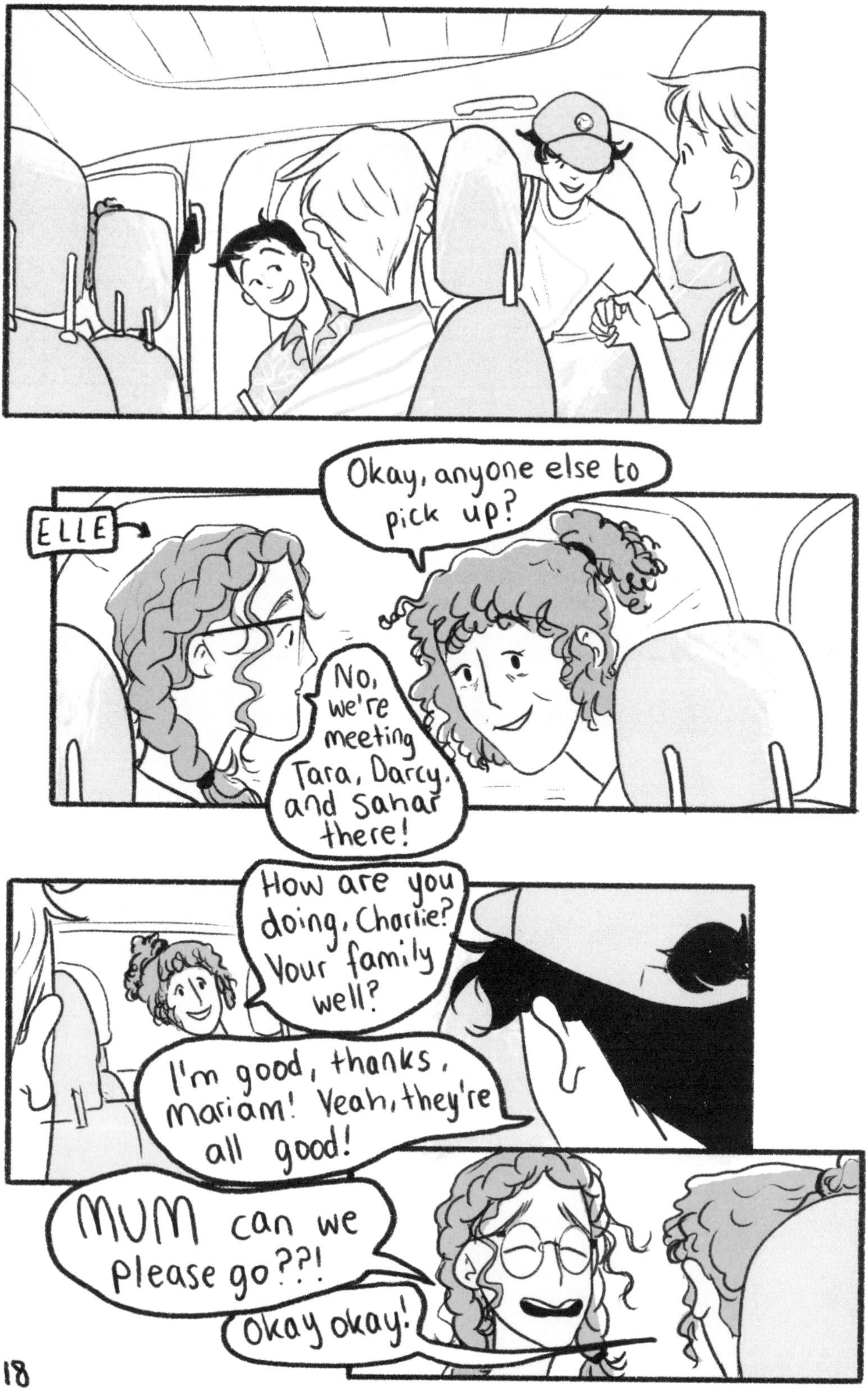
Okay, anyone else to pick up?
ELLE
No, we're meeting Tara, Darcy, and Sahar there!
How are you doing, Charlie? Your family well?
I'm good, thanks, Mariam! Yeah, they're all good!
MUM can we please go??!
Okay okay!

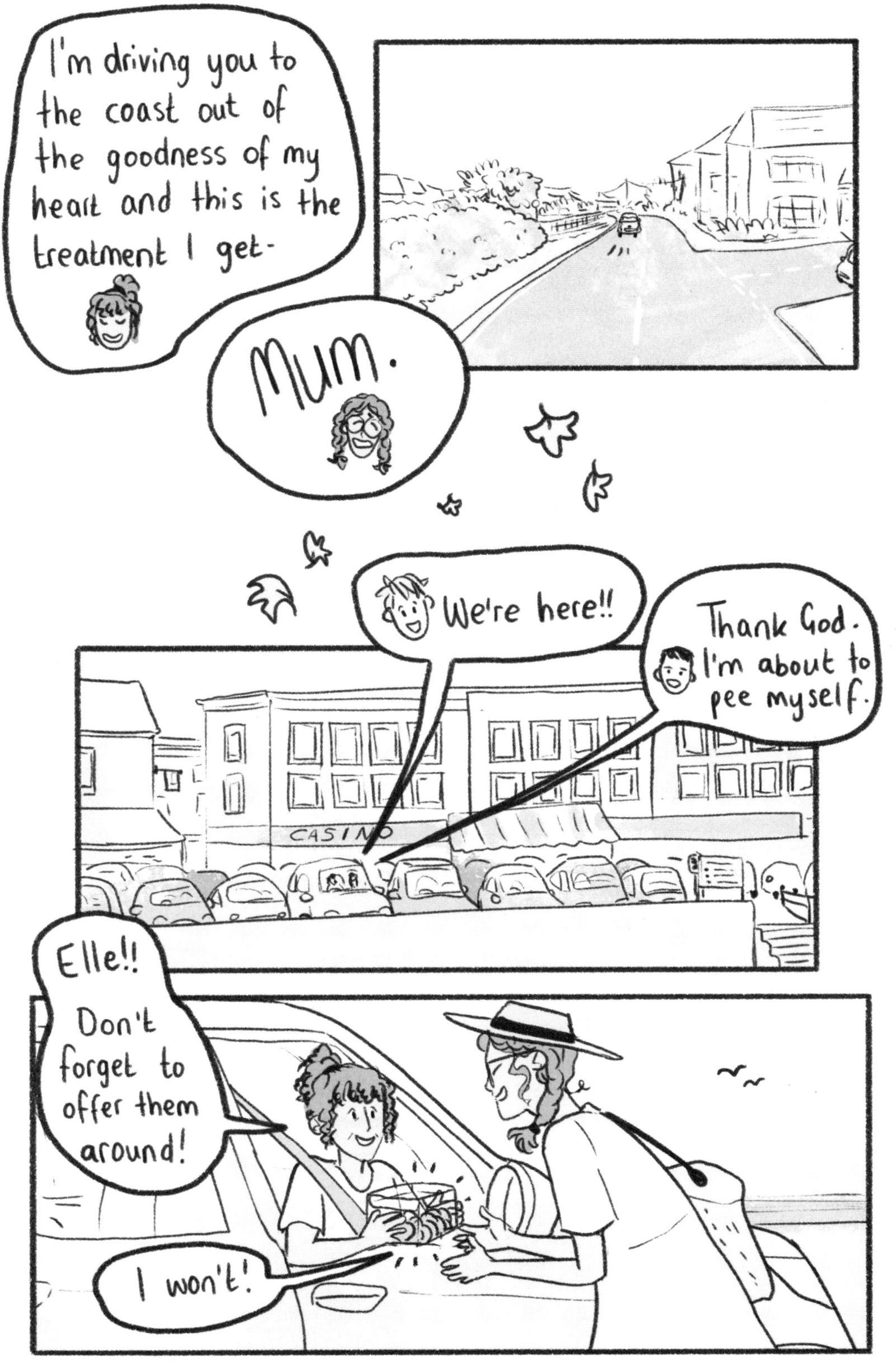
I'm driving you to the coast out of the goodness of my heart and this is the treatment I get-
MUM.
We're here!!
Thank God. I'm about to pee myself.
CASINO
Elle!!
Don't forget to offer them around!
I won't!

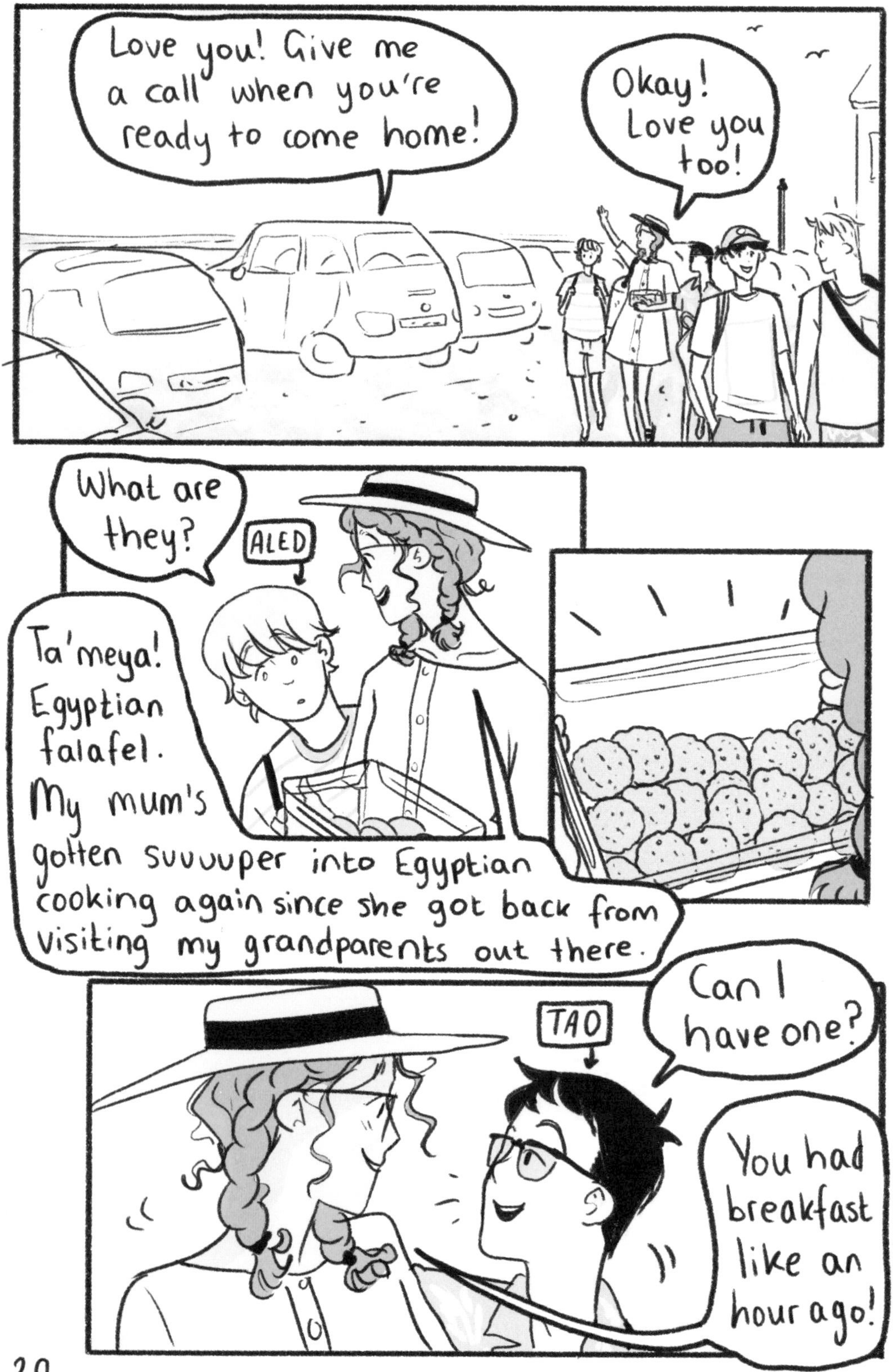
Love you! Give me a call when you're ready to come home!
Okay! Love you too!
What are they?
ALED
Ta'meya! Egyptian falafel. My mum's gotten suuuuper into Egyptian cooking again since she got back from visiting my grandparents out there.
TAO
Can I have one?
You had breakfast like an hour ago!

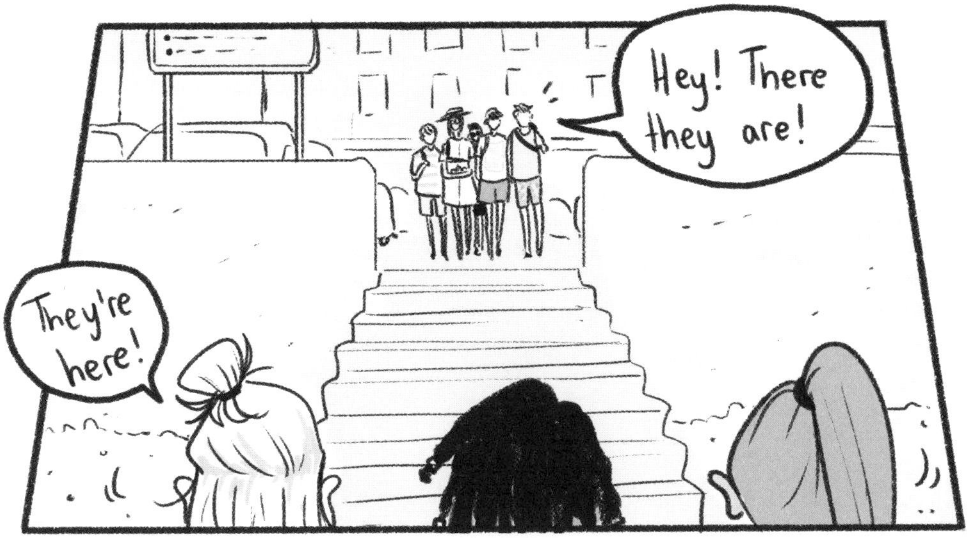
Hey! There they are!
They're here!

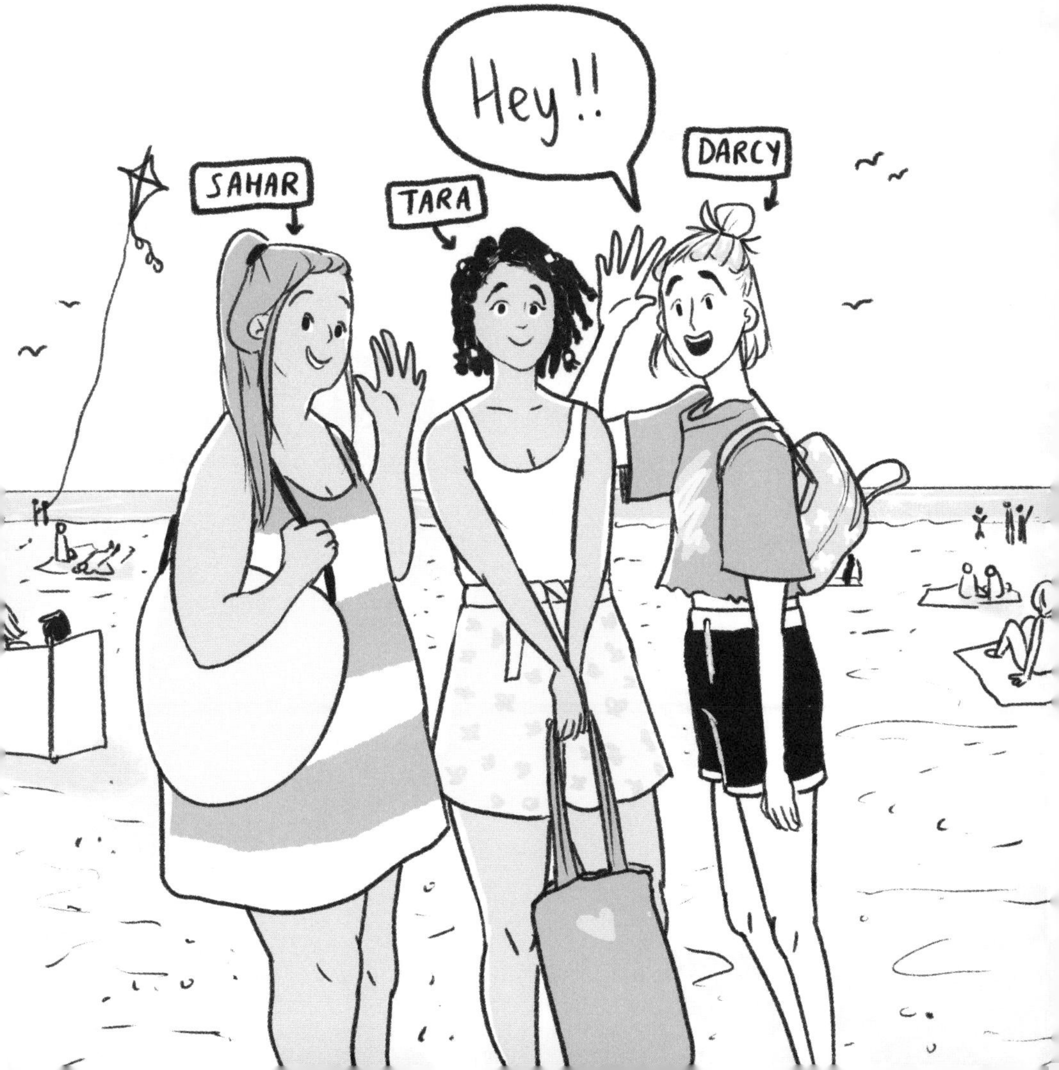
Hey!!
SAHAR
TARA
DARCY

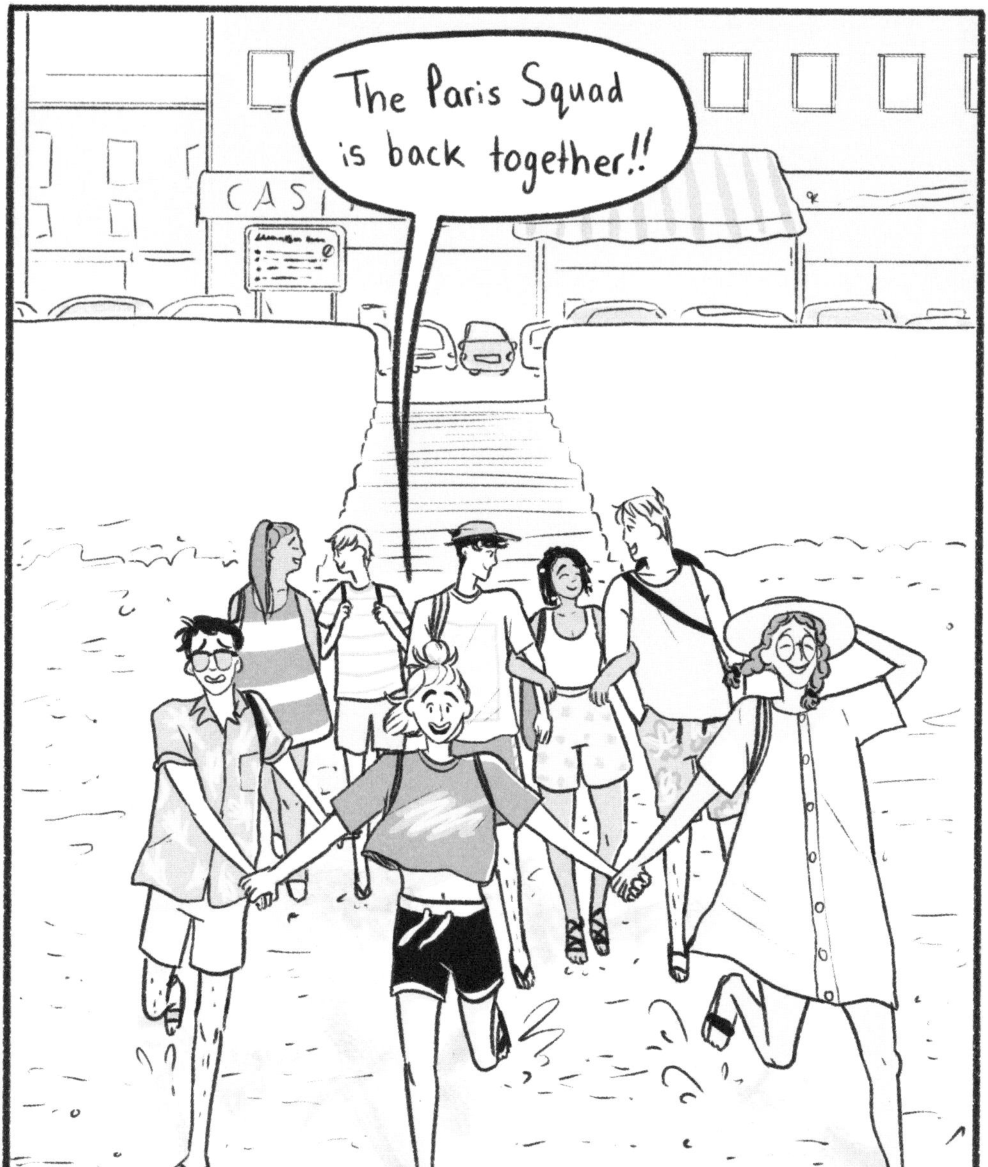
The Paris Squad is back together!!

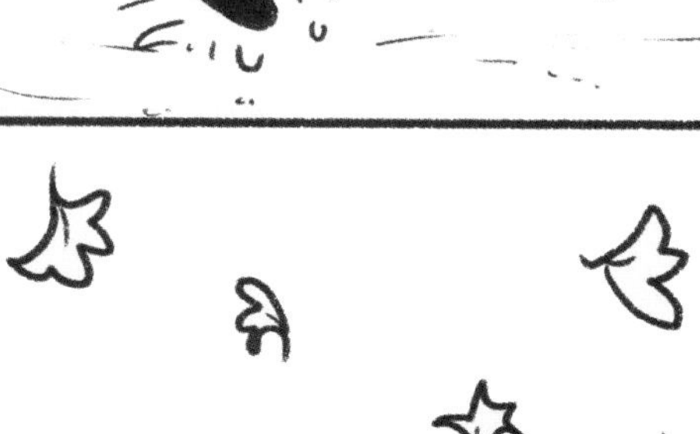

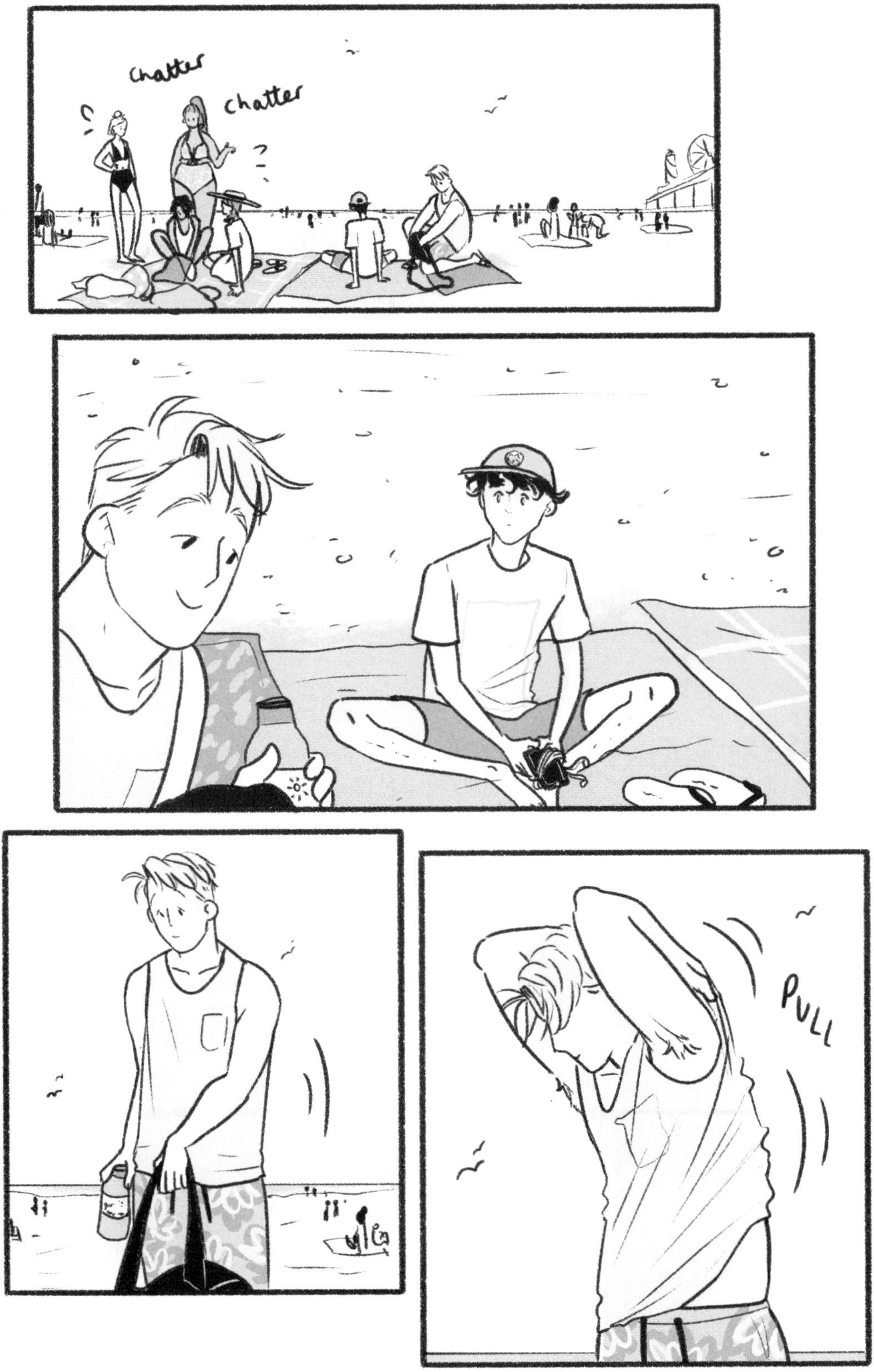
chatter
chatter
PULL

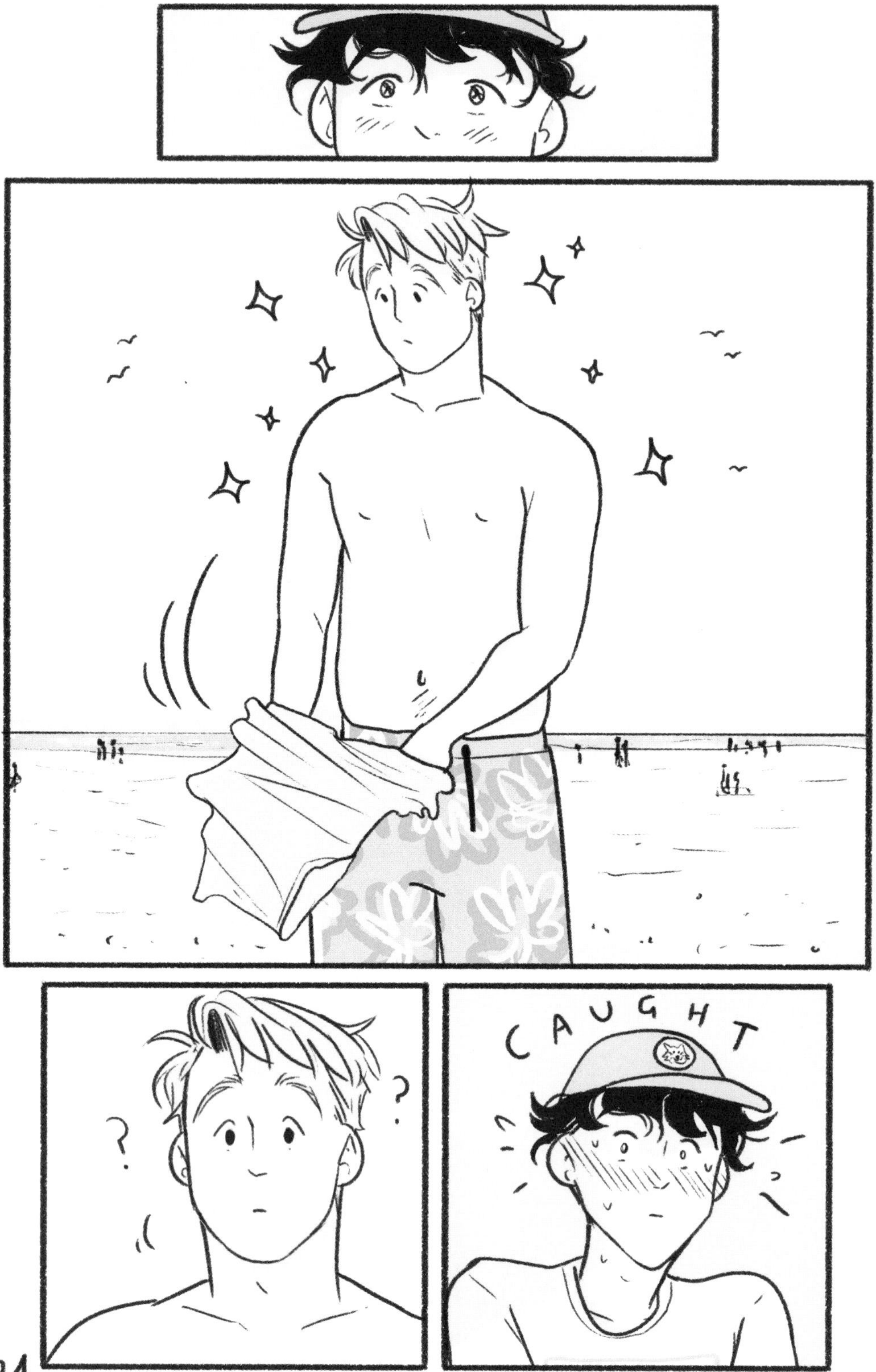
CAUGHT

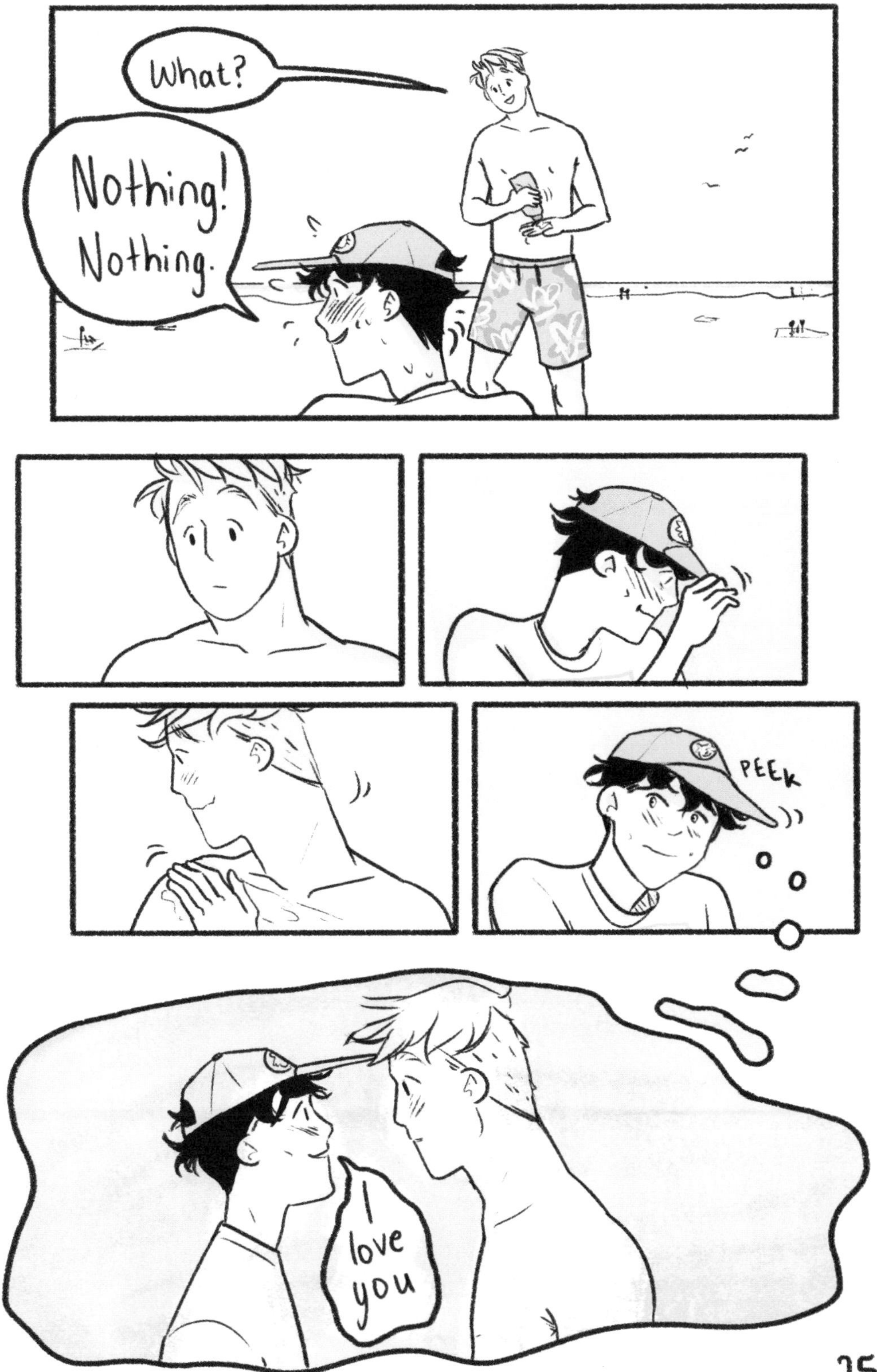
What?
Nothing! Nothing.
PEEK
I love you

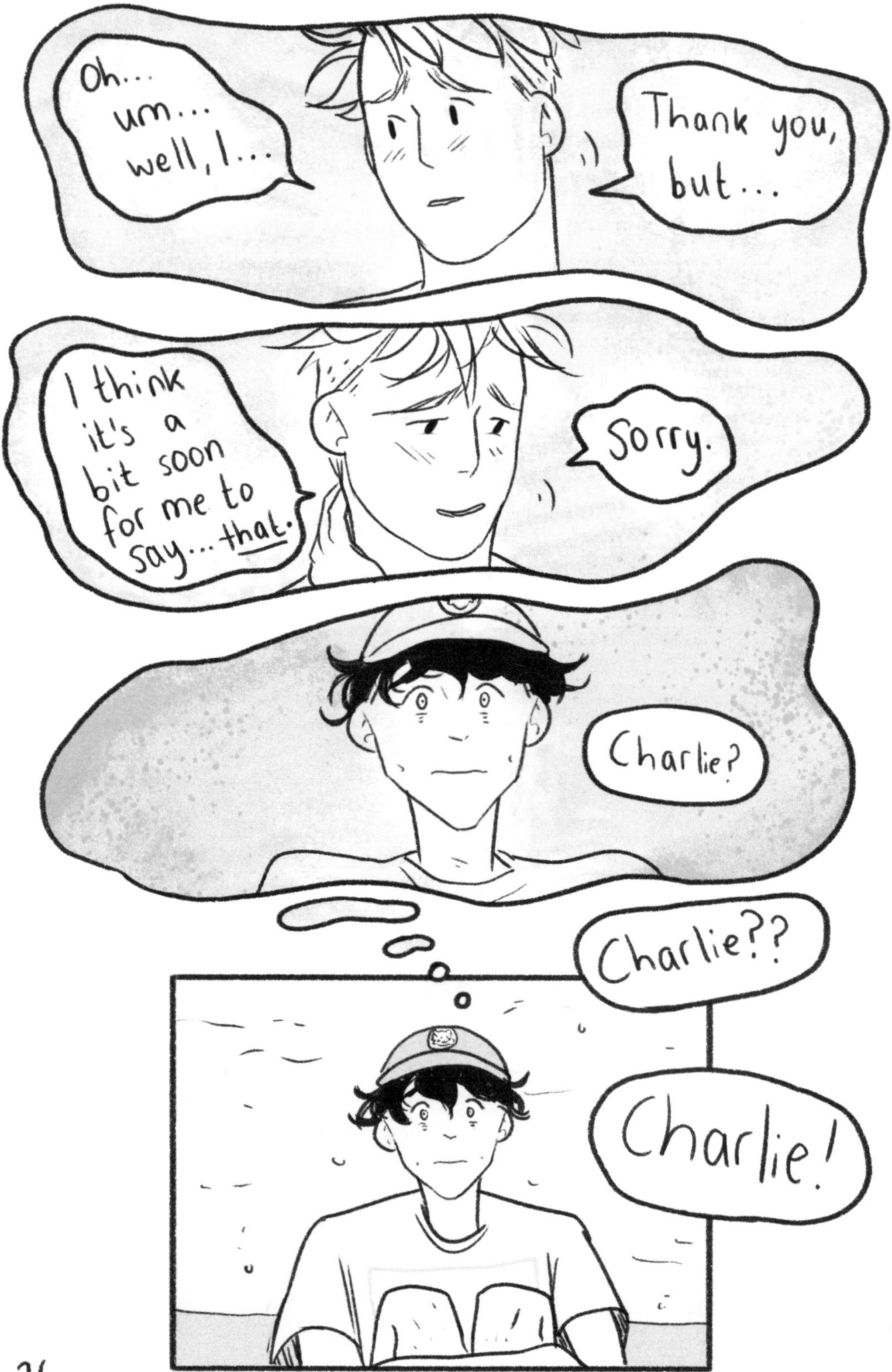
Oh... um... well, I...
Thank you, but...
I think it's a bit soon for me to say... that.
Sorry.
Charlie?
Charlie??
Charlie!

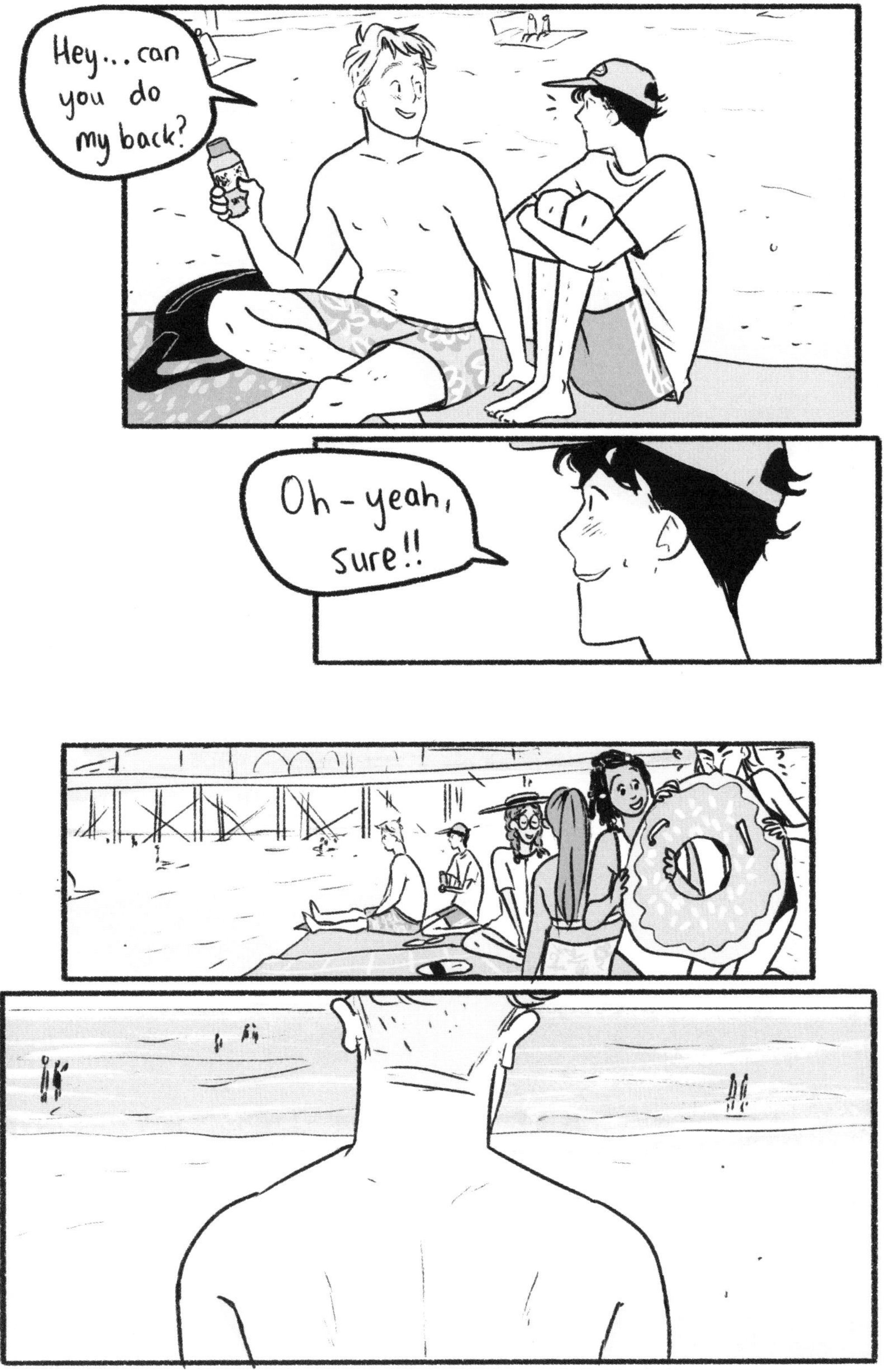
Hey... can you do my back?
Oh-yeah, sure!!

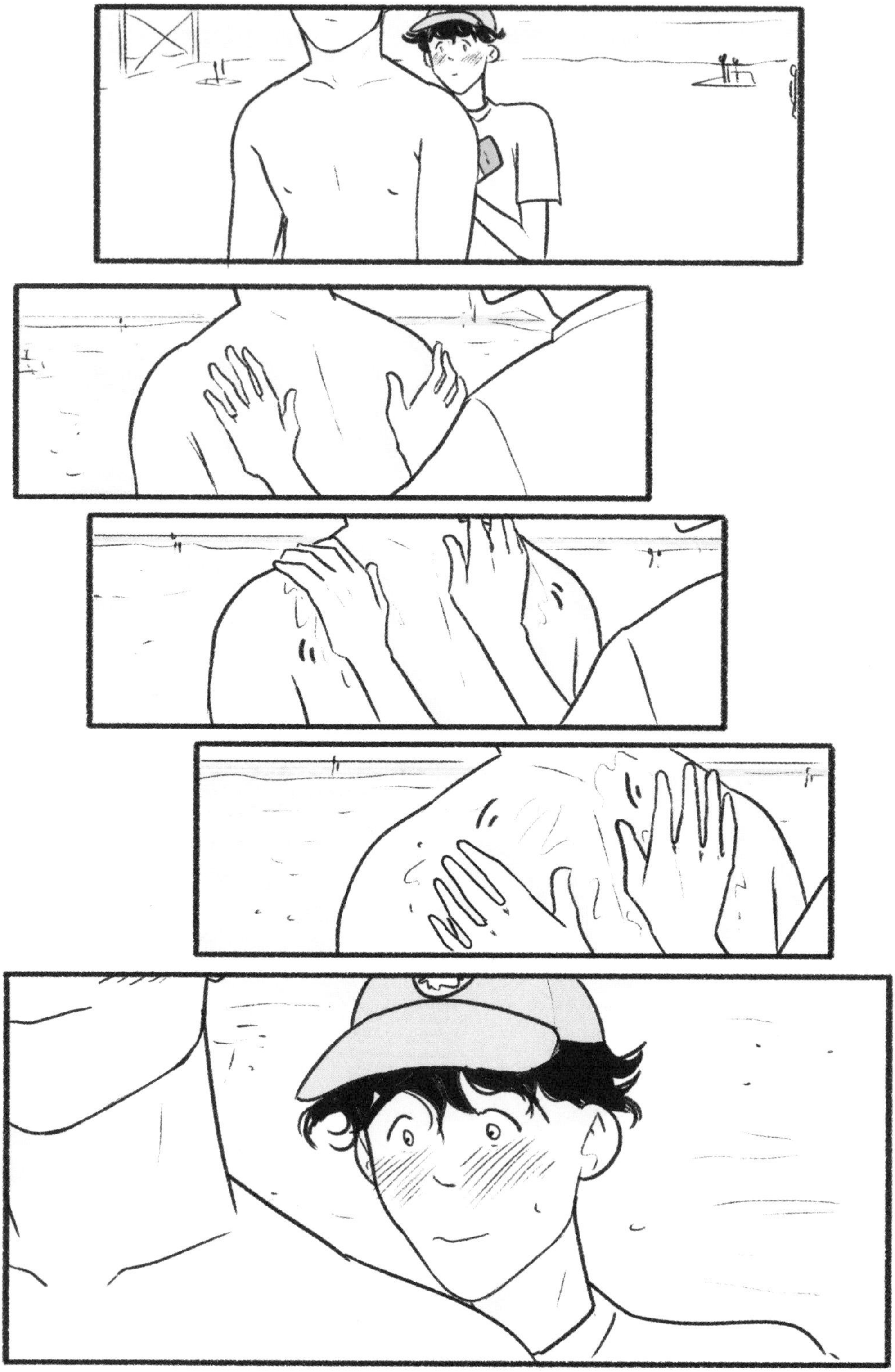

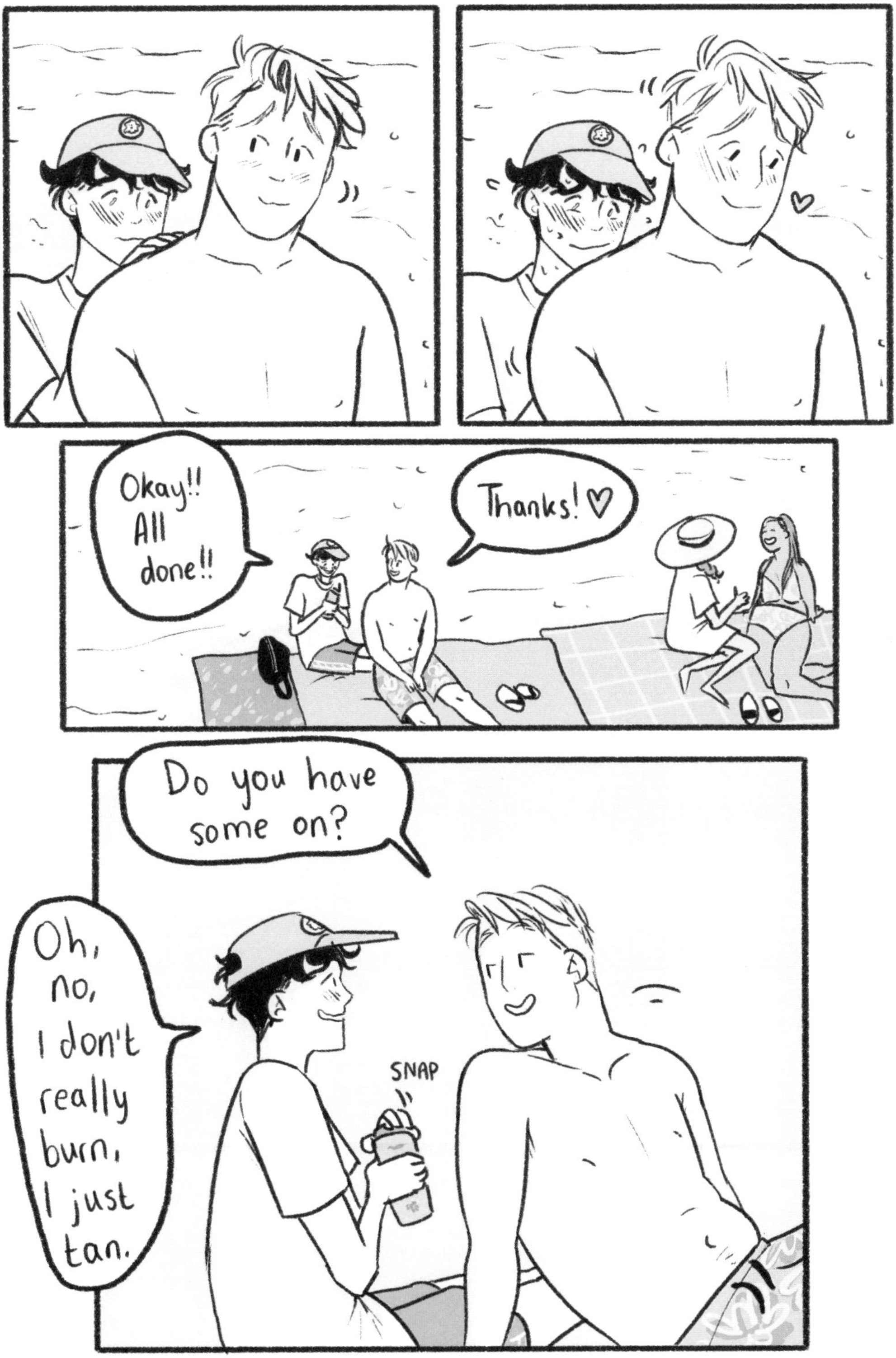
Okay!! All done!!
Thanks! ♡
Do you have some on?
Oh, no, I don't really burn, I just tan.
SNAP

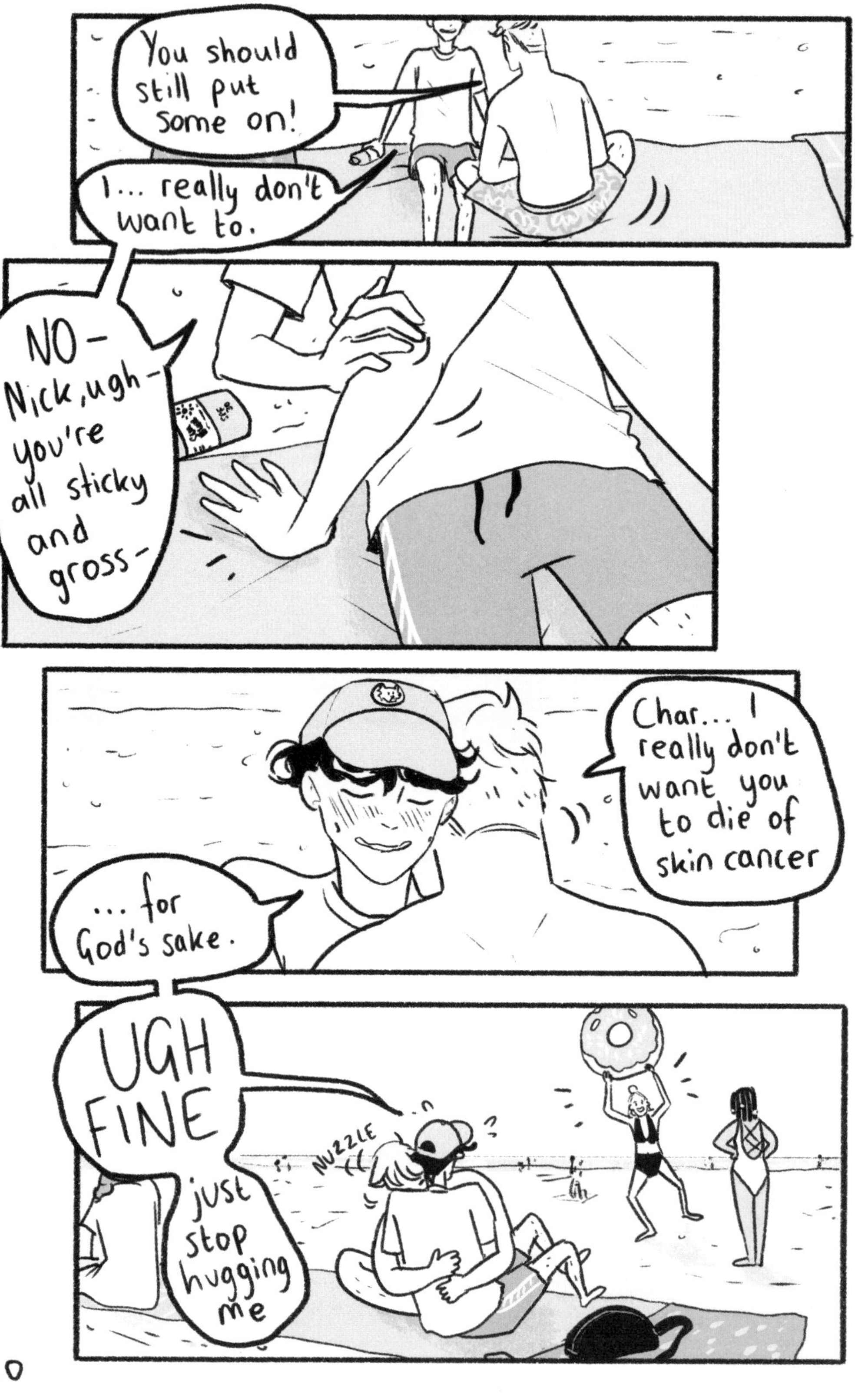
You should still put some on!
I... really don't want to.
NO- Nick, ugh- you're all sticky and gross-
Char... I really don't want you to die of skin cancer
... for God's sake.
UGH FINE
NUZZLE
just stop hugging me

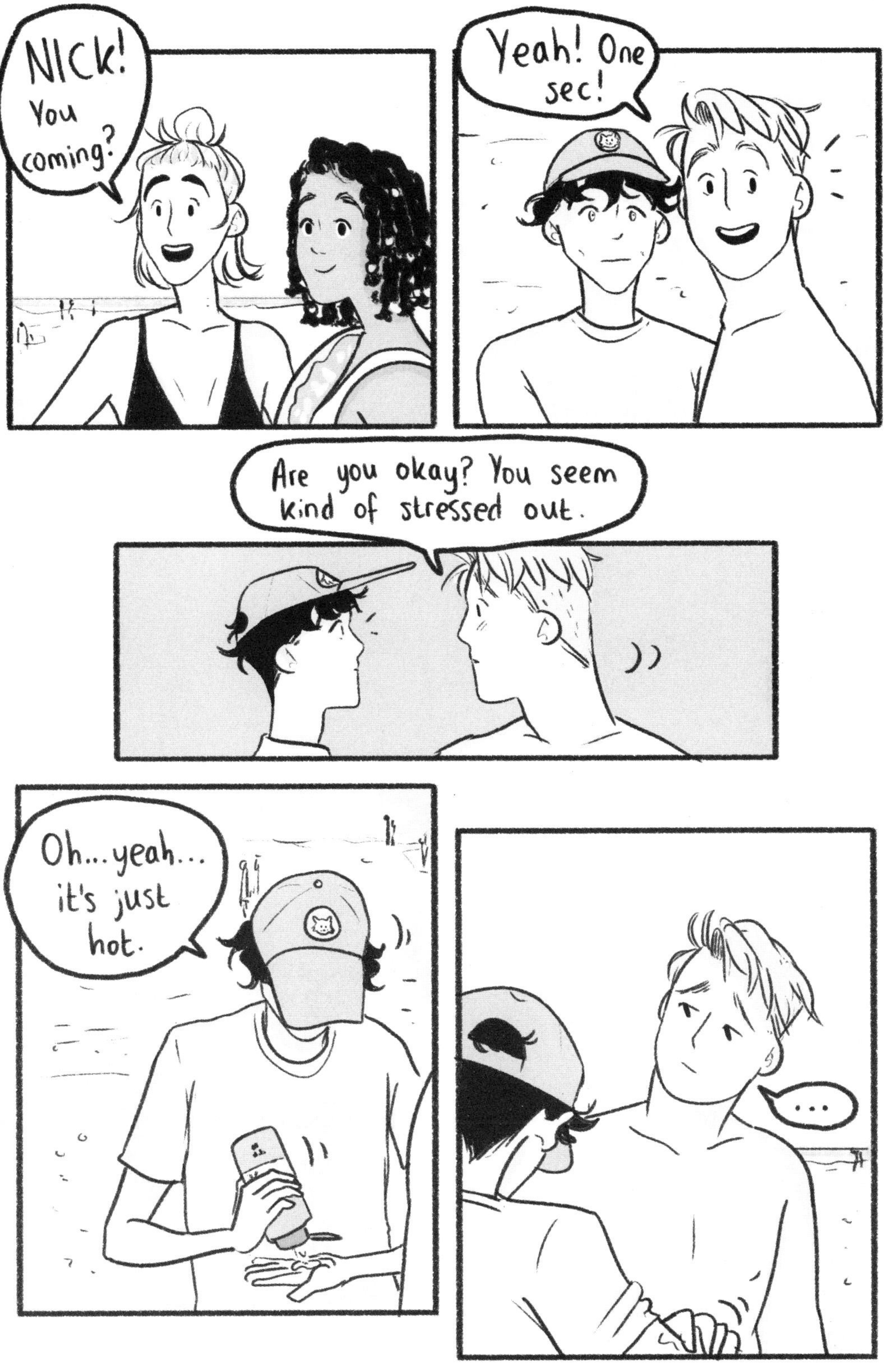
NICK! You coming?
Yeah! One sec!
Are you okay? You seem kind of stressed out.
Oh...yeah... it's just hot.
...

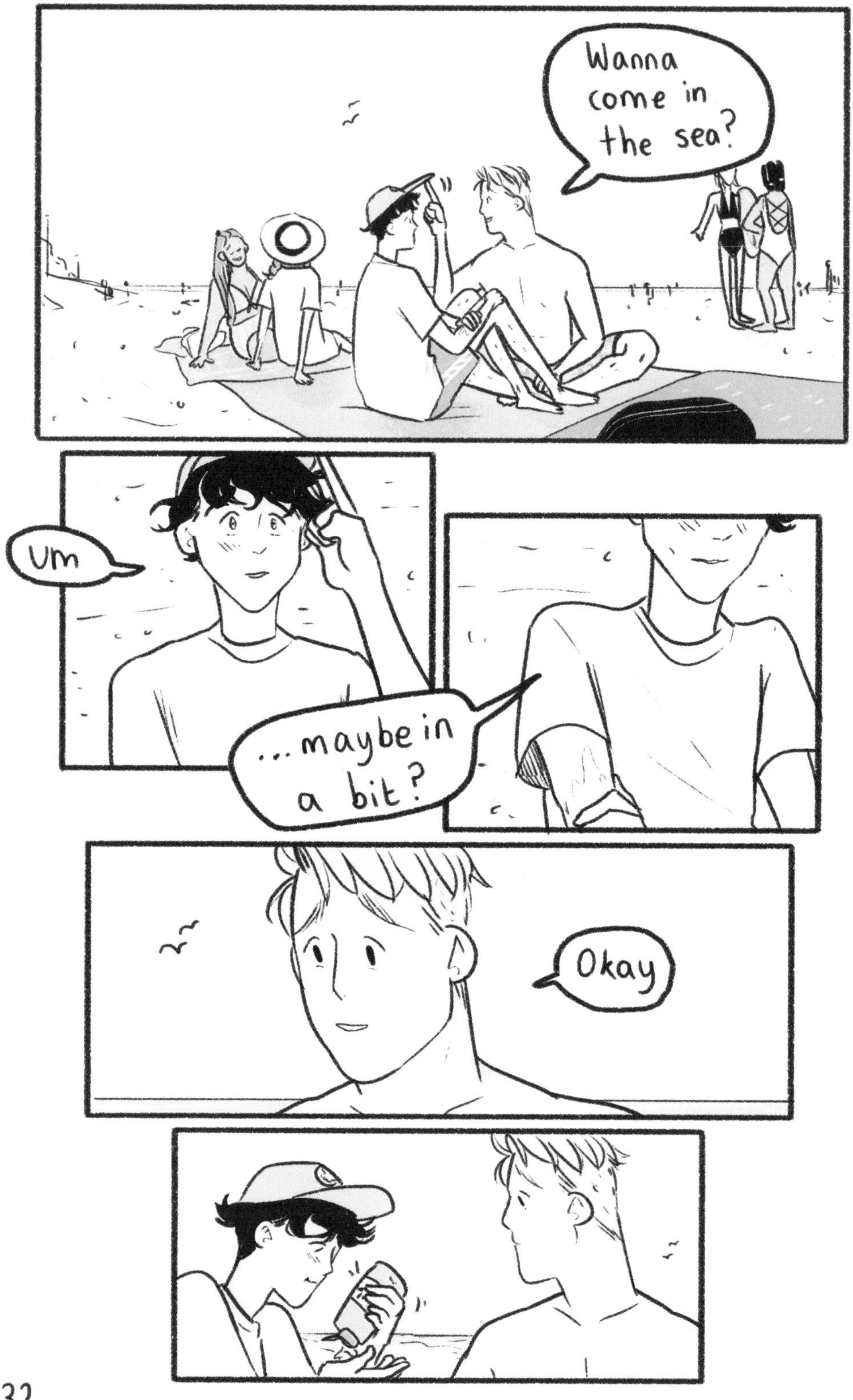
Wanna come in the sea?
Um
...maybe in a bit?
Okay

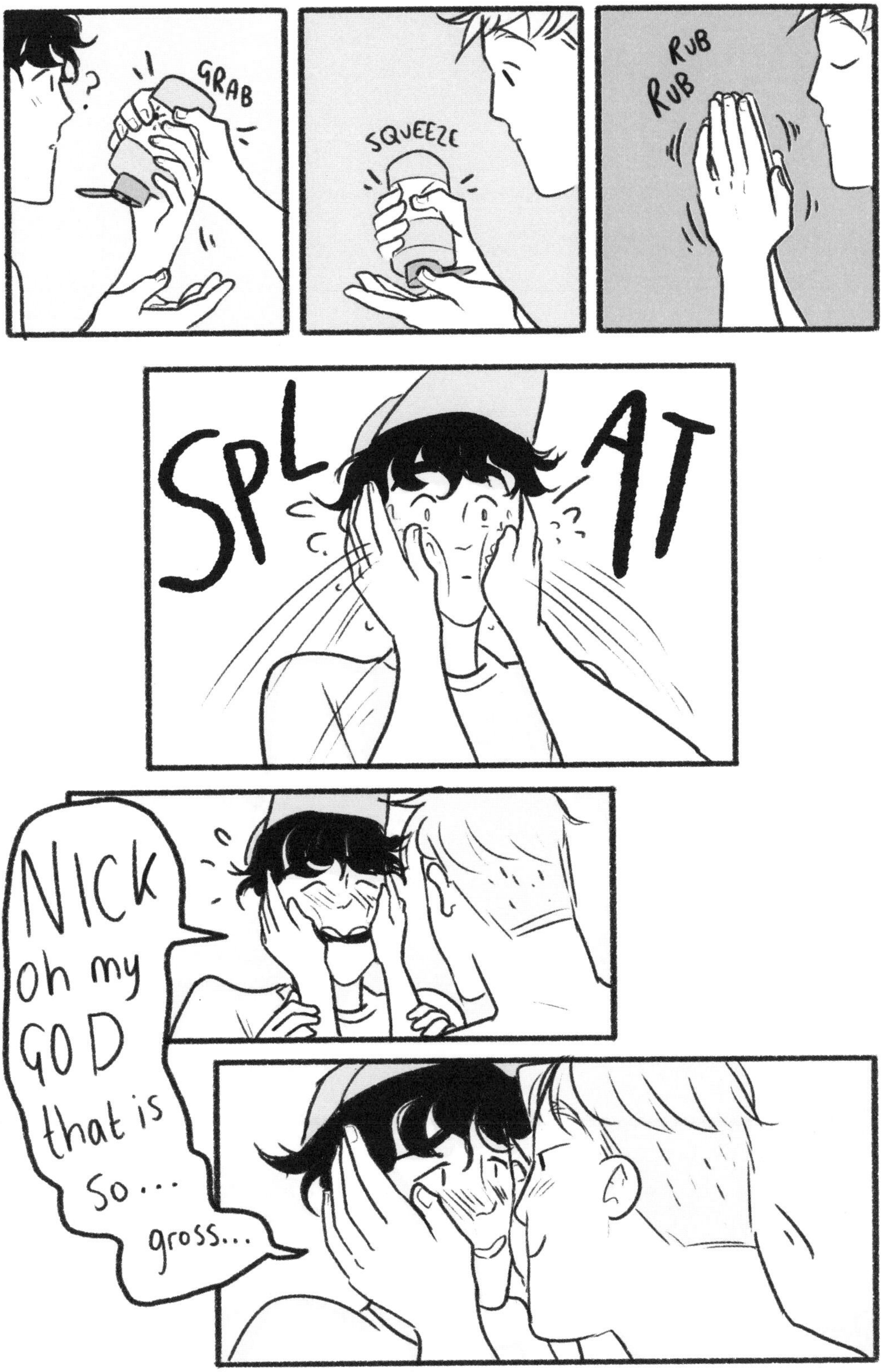
GRAB
SQUEEZE
RUB
RUB
SPLAT
NICK oh my GOD that is so... gross...

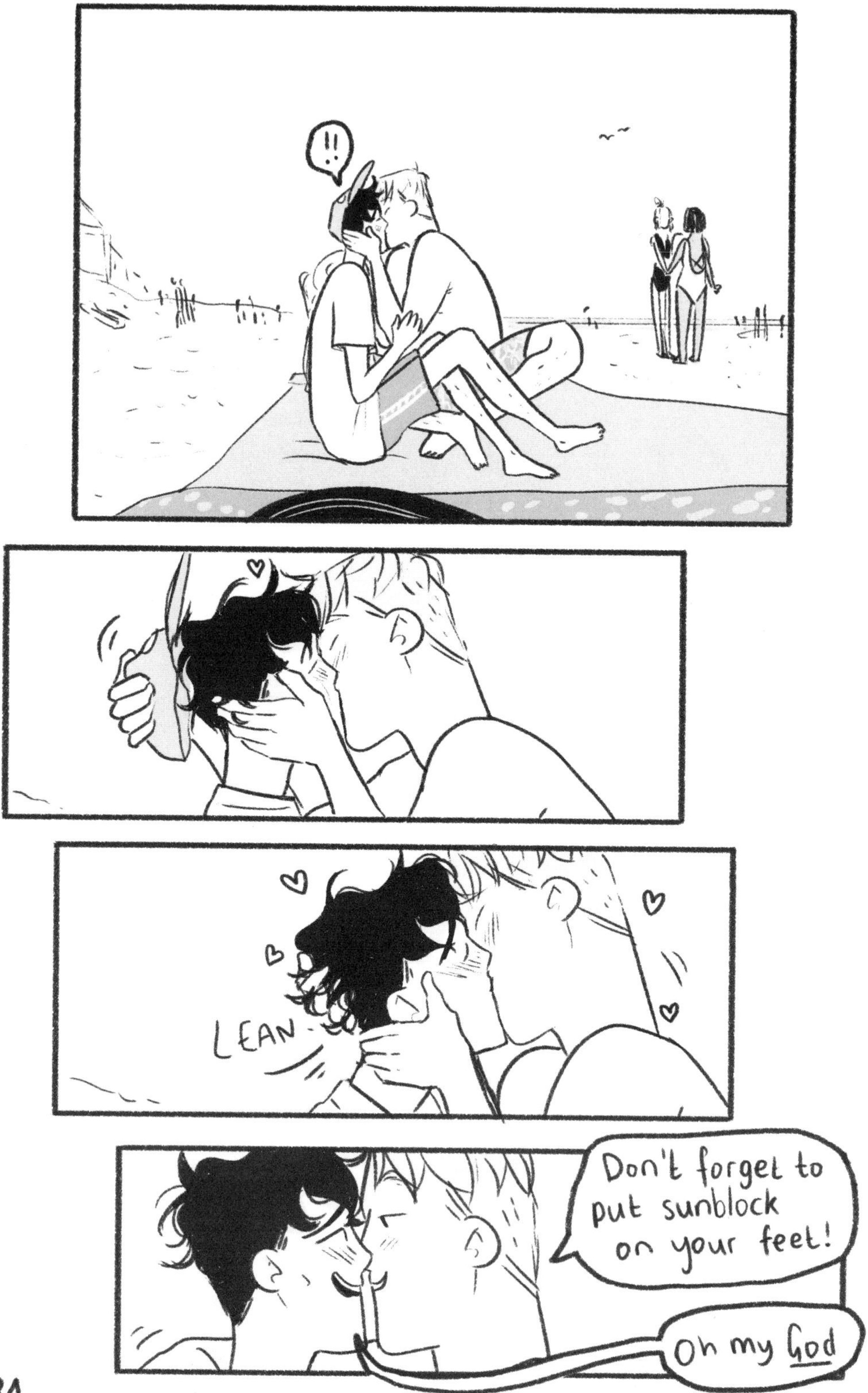
!!
LEAN
Don't forget to put sunblock on your feet!
Oh my God

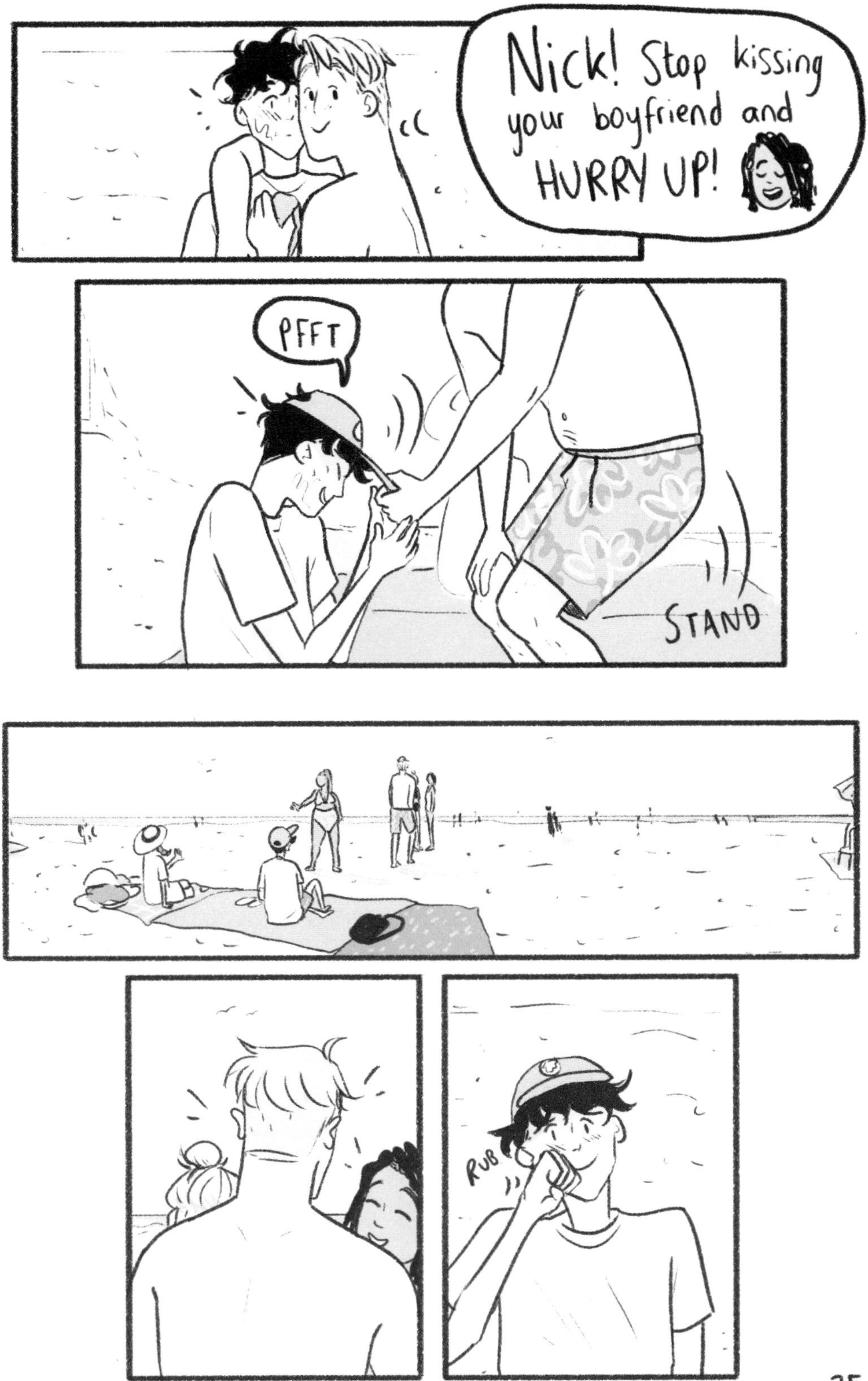
Nick! Stop kissing your boyfriend and HURRY UP!
PFFT
STAND
RUB

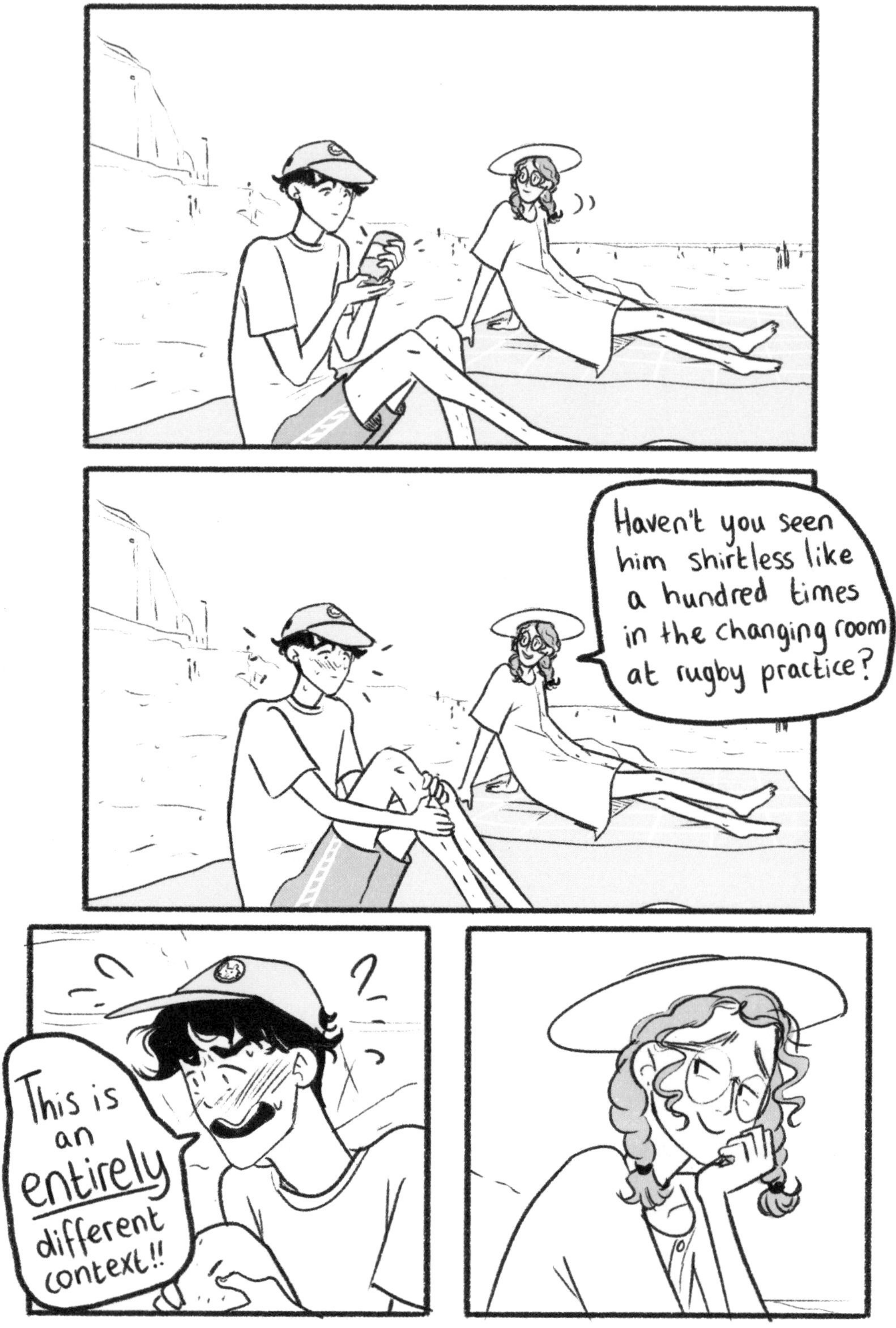
Haven't you seen him shirtless like a hundred times in the changing room at rugby practice?
This is an entirely different context!!

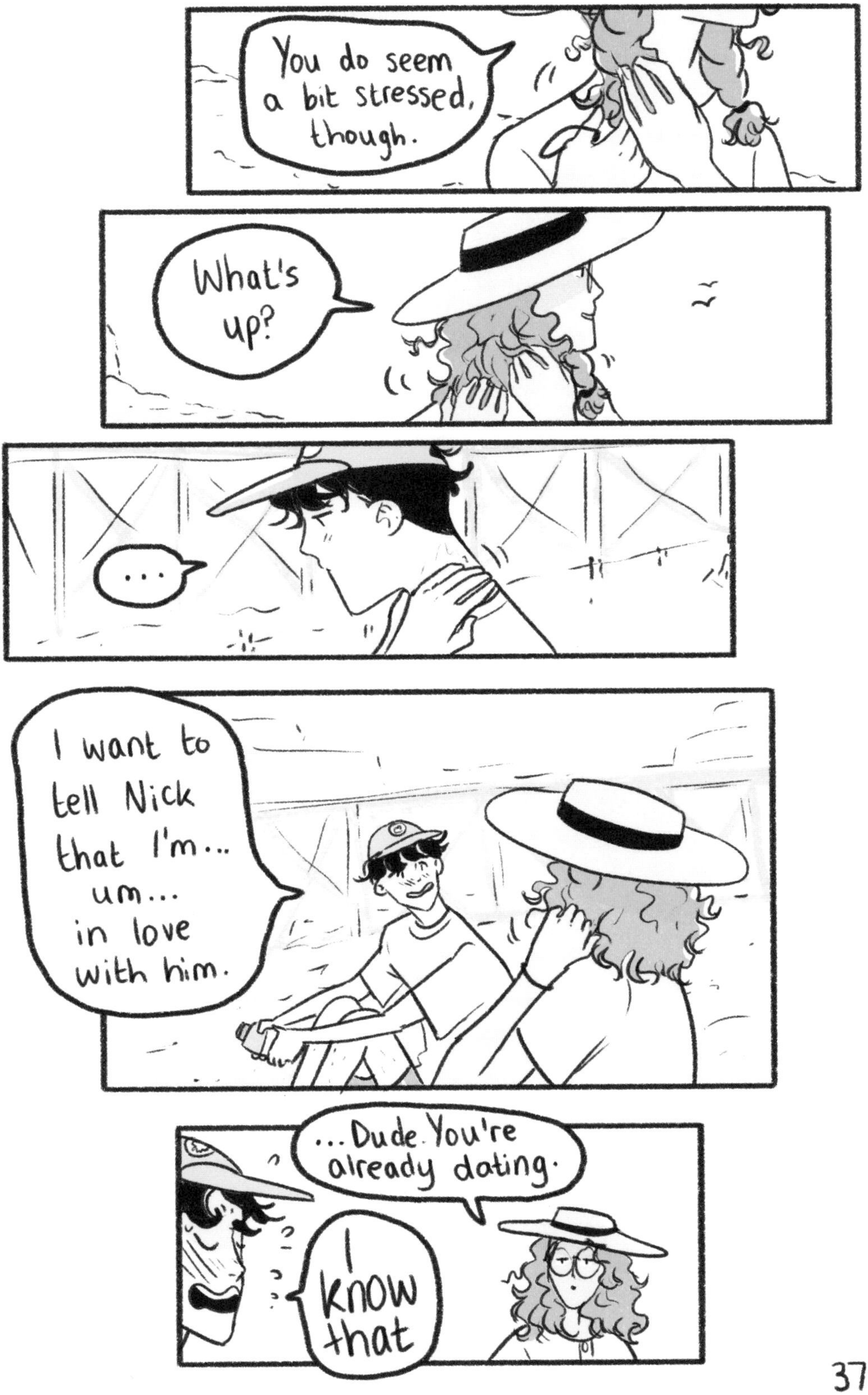
You do seem a bit stressed, though.
What's up?
...
I want to tell Nick that I'm... um... in love with him.
...Dude. You're already dating.
I know that

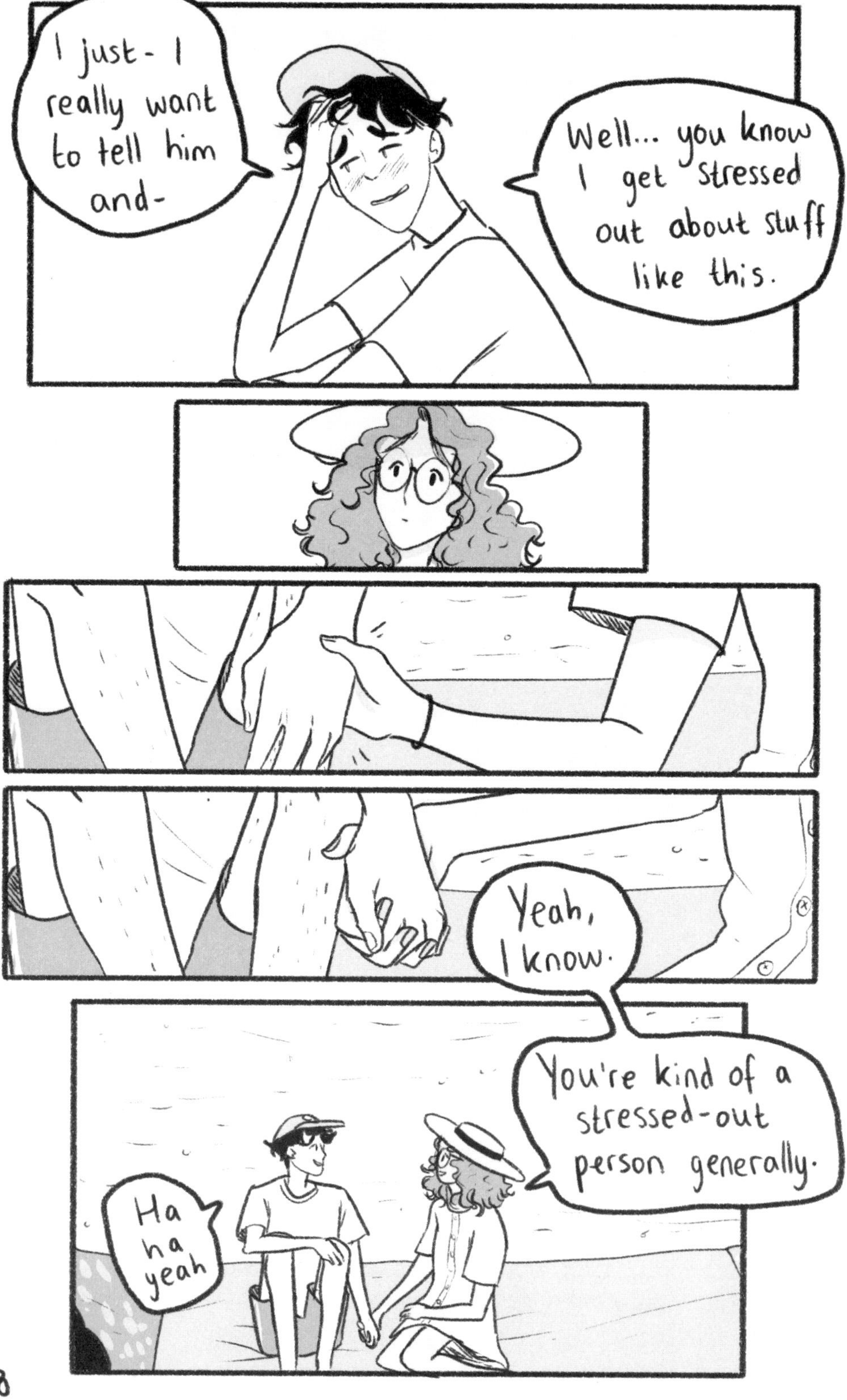
I just- I really want to tell him and-
Well... you know I get stressed out about stuff like this.
Yeah, I know.
You're kind of a stressed-out person generally.
Ha ha yeah

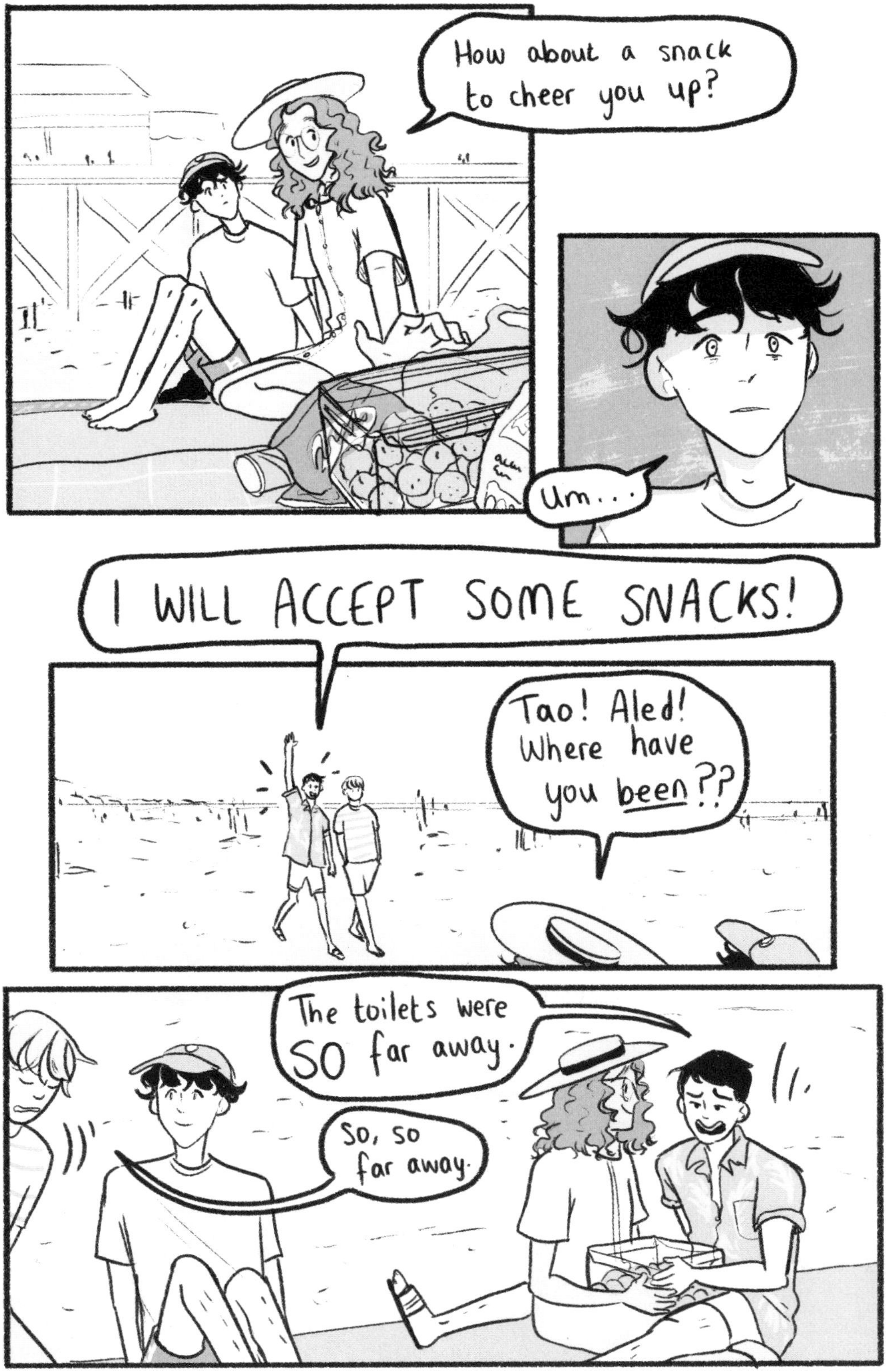
How about a snack to cheer you up?
Um...
I WILL ACCEPT SOME SNACKS!
Tao! Aled! Where have you been??
The toilets were SO far away.
So, so far away.

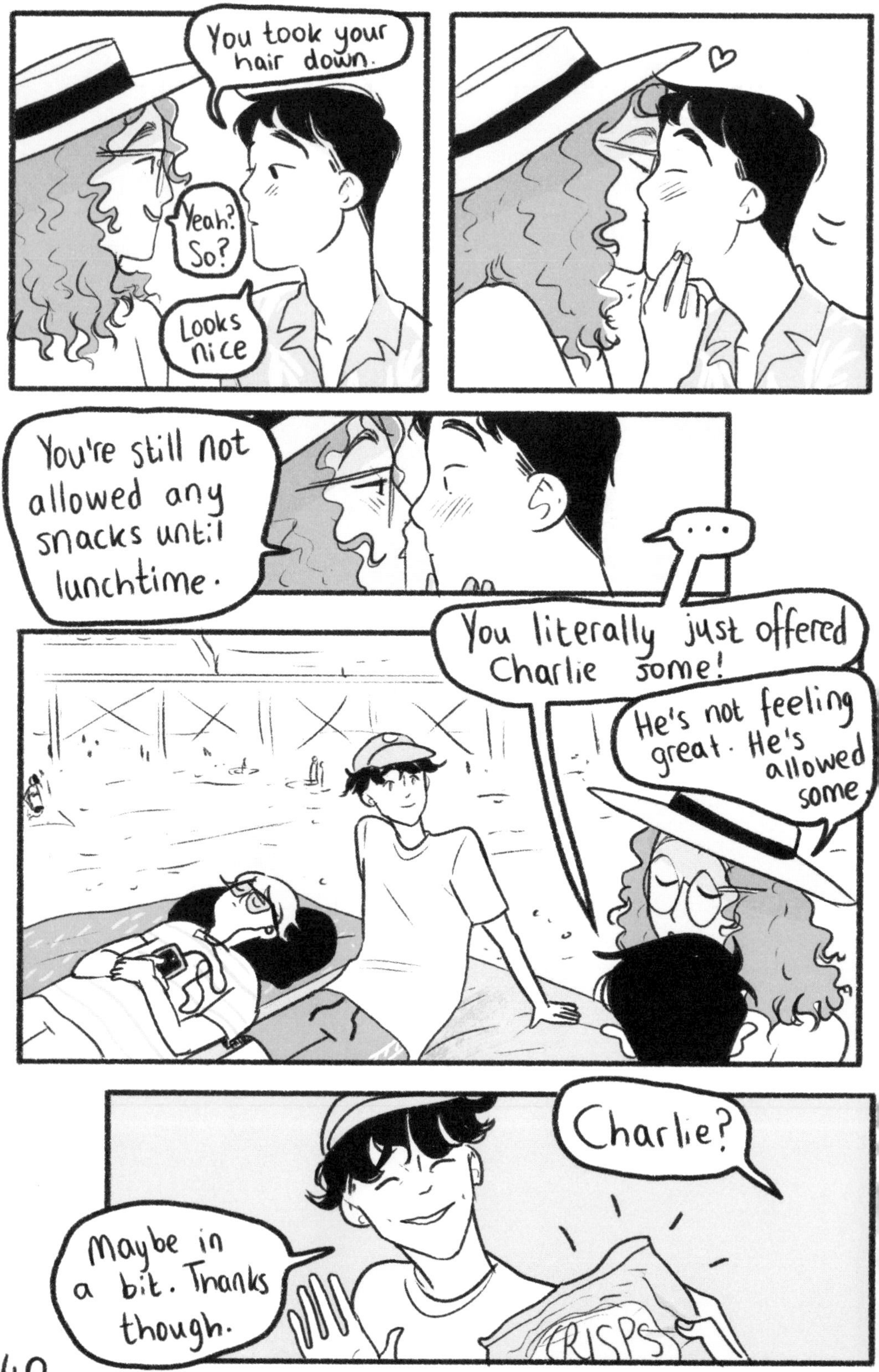
You took your hair down.
Yeah? So?
Looks nice
You're still not allowed any snacks until lunchtime.
...
You literally just offered Charlie some!
He's not feeling great. He's allowed some.
Charlie?
Maybe in a bit. Thanks though.
CRISPS

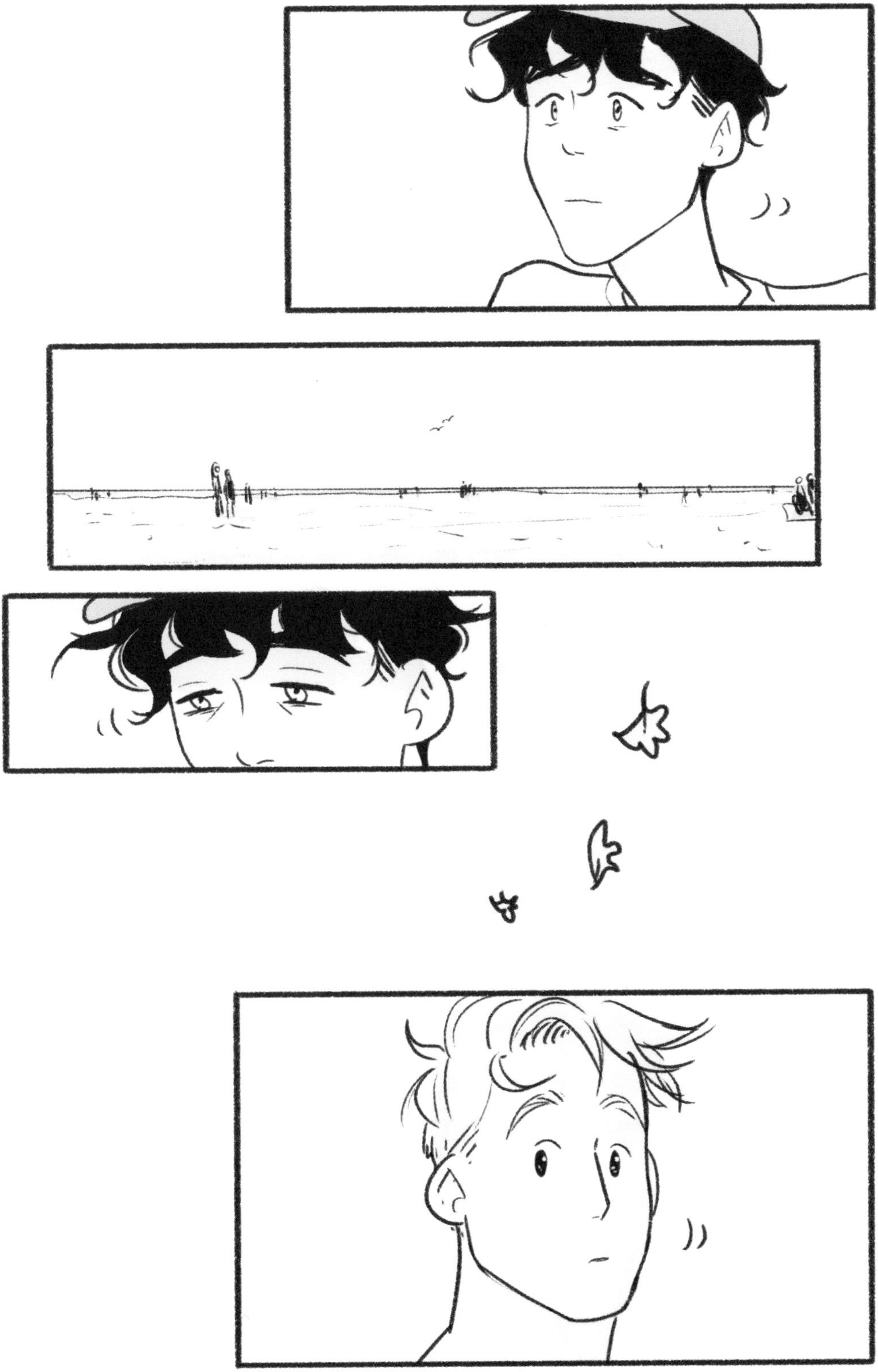

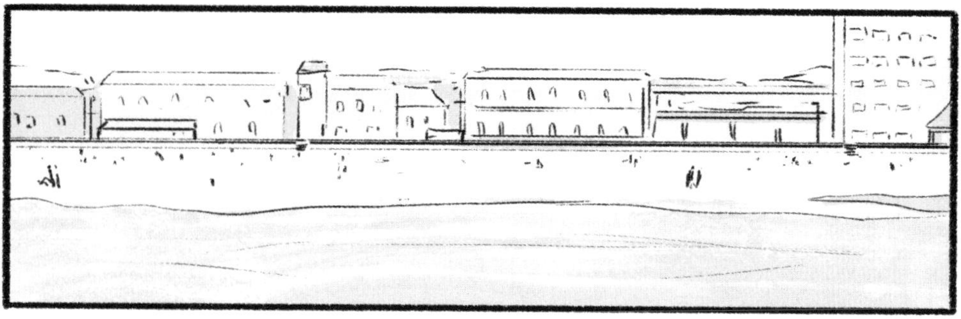

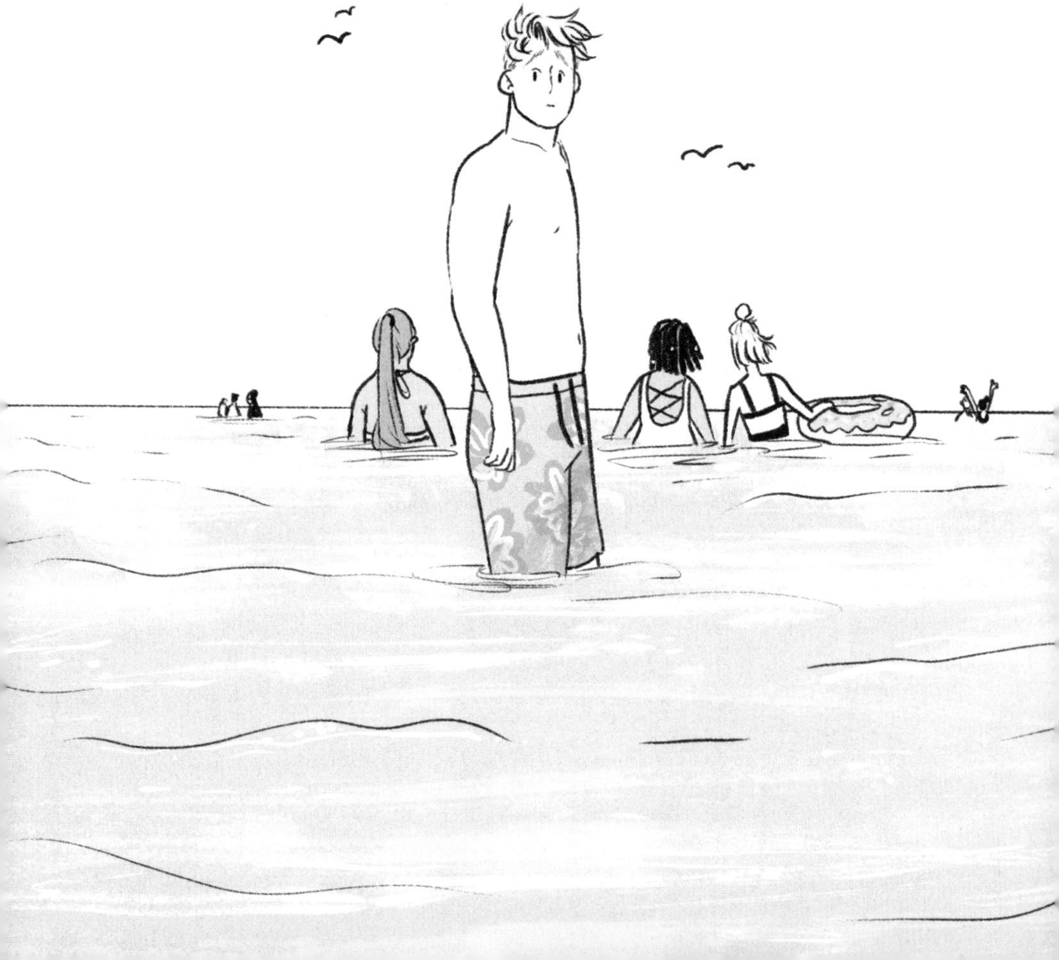

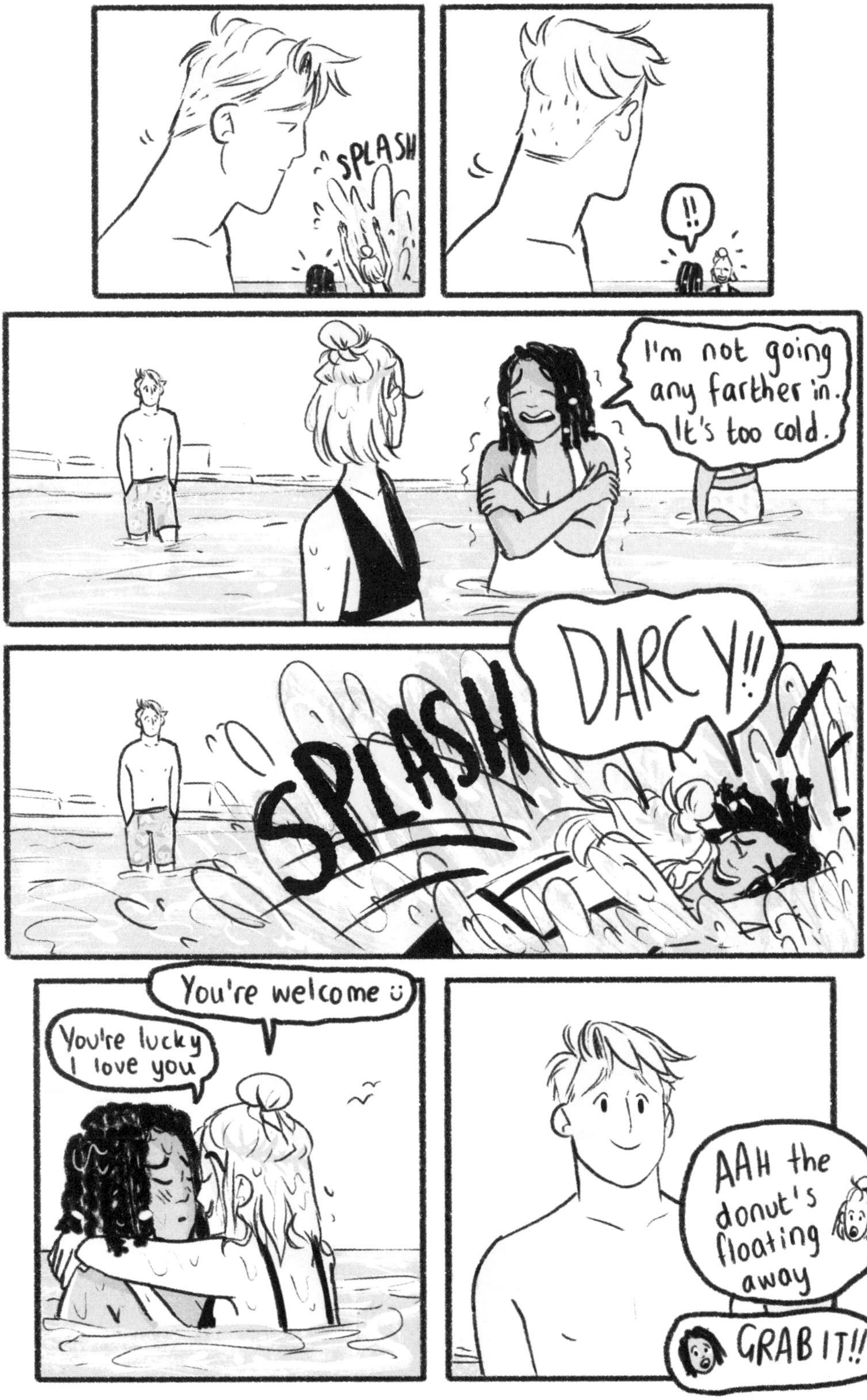
SPLASH
!!
I'm not going any farther in. It's too cold.
SPLASH
DARCY!!
You're welcome
You're lucky I love you
AAH the donut's floating away
GRAB IT!!

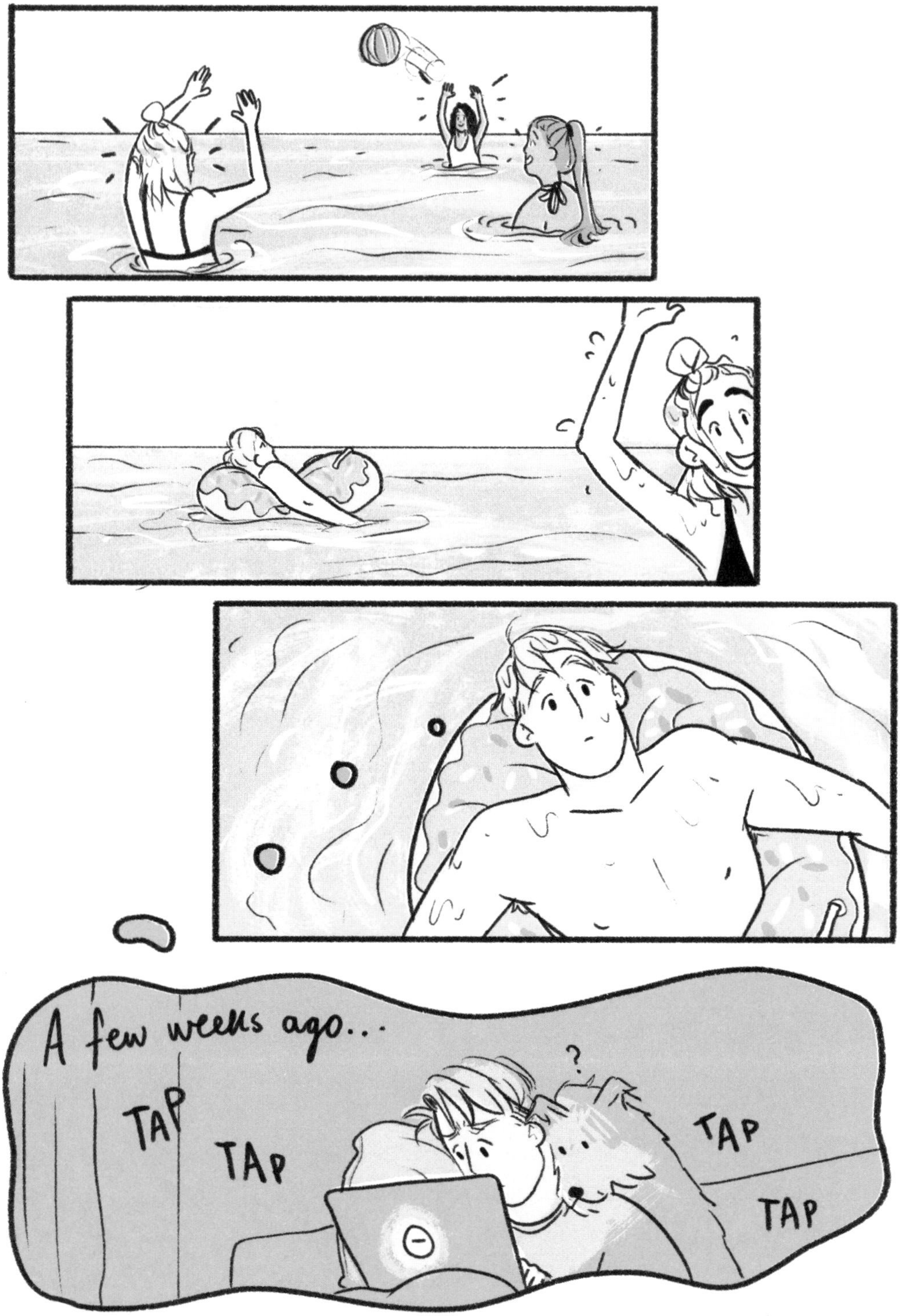
A few weeks ago...
?
TAP
TAP
TAP
TAP

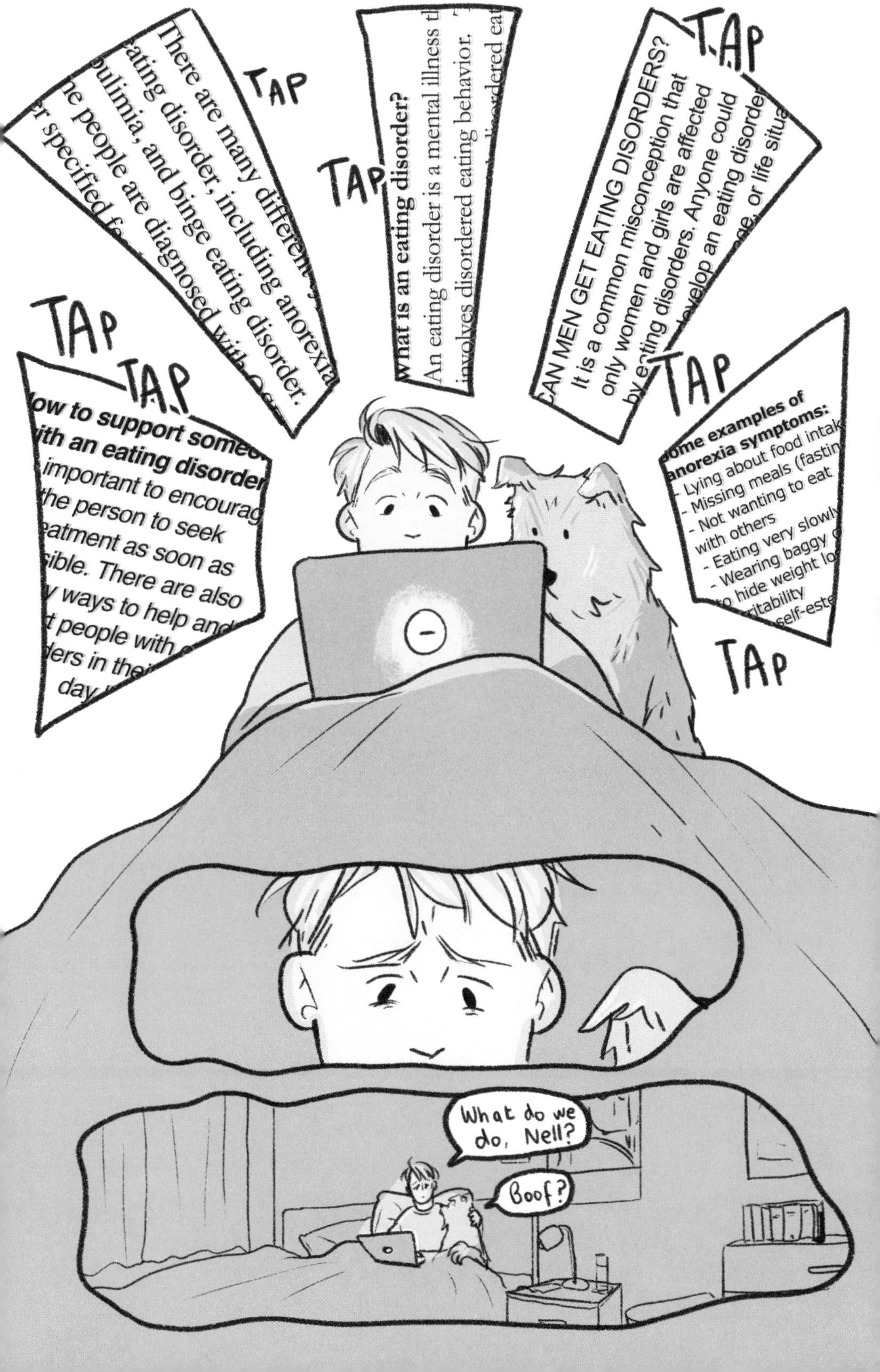
There are many different
eating disorder, including anorexia
bulimia, and binge eating disorder.
TAP
What is an eating disorder?
An eating disorder is a mental illness
involves disordered eating behavior.
TAP
CAN MEN GET EATING DISORDERS?
It is a common misconception that
only women and girls are affected
by eating disorders. Anyone could
develop an eating disorder
TAP
TAP
TAP
How to support someone with an eating disorder
important to encourag
the person to seek
eatment as soon as
sible. There are also
y ways to help and
t people with e
ders in thei
day
TAP
Some examples of anorexia symptoms:
- Lying about food intak
- Missing meals (fastin
- Not wanting to eat with others
- Eating very slowly
- Wearing baggy c
to hide weight lo
- Irritability
TAP
What do we do, Nell?
Boof?

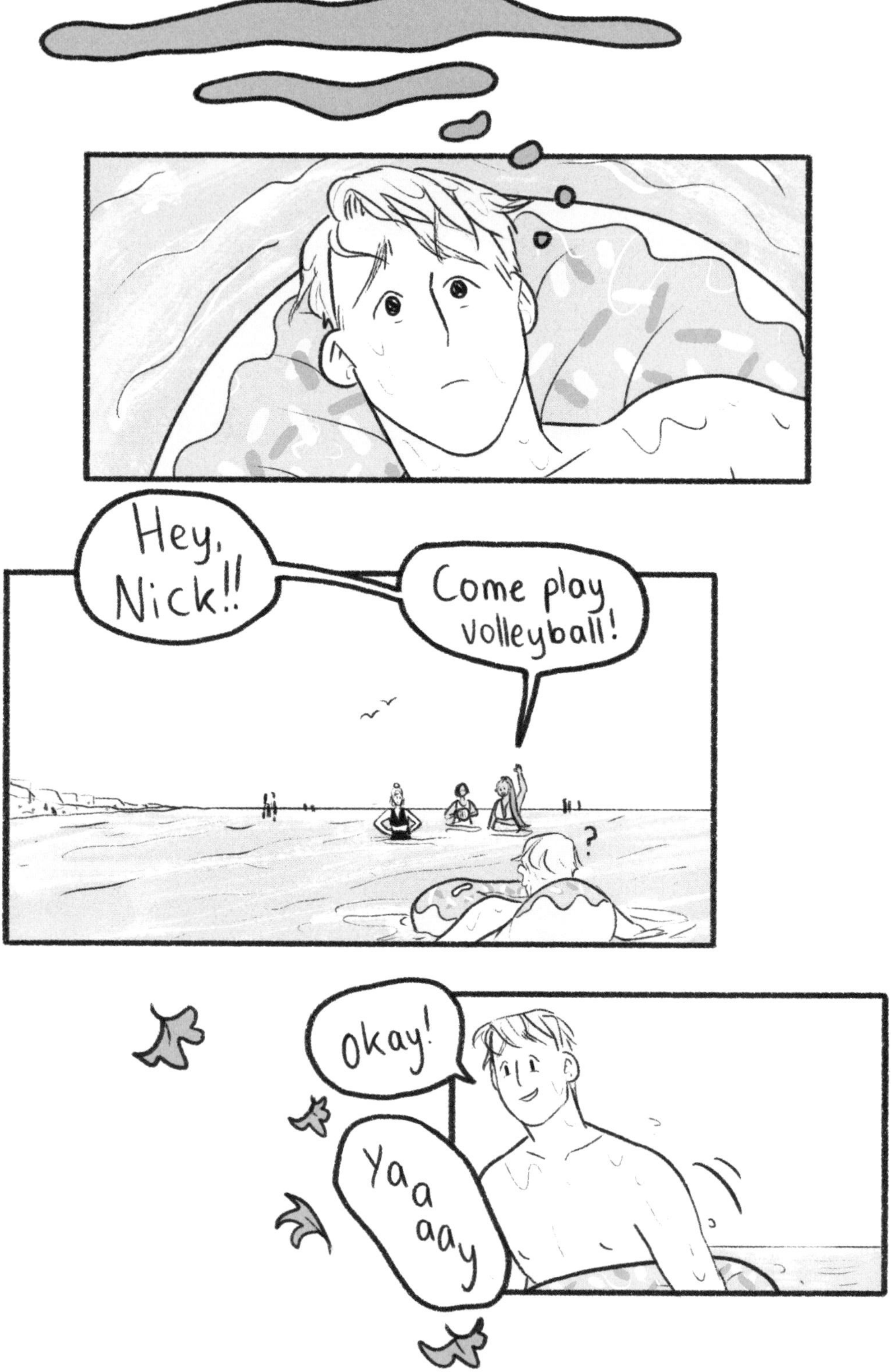
Hey, Nick!!
Come play volleyball!
?
Okay!
Yaaaaay

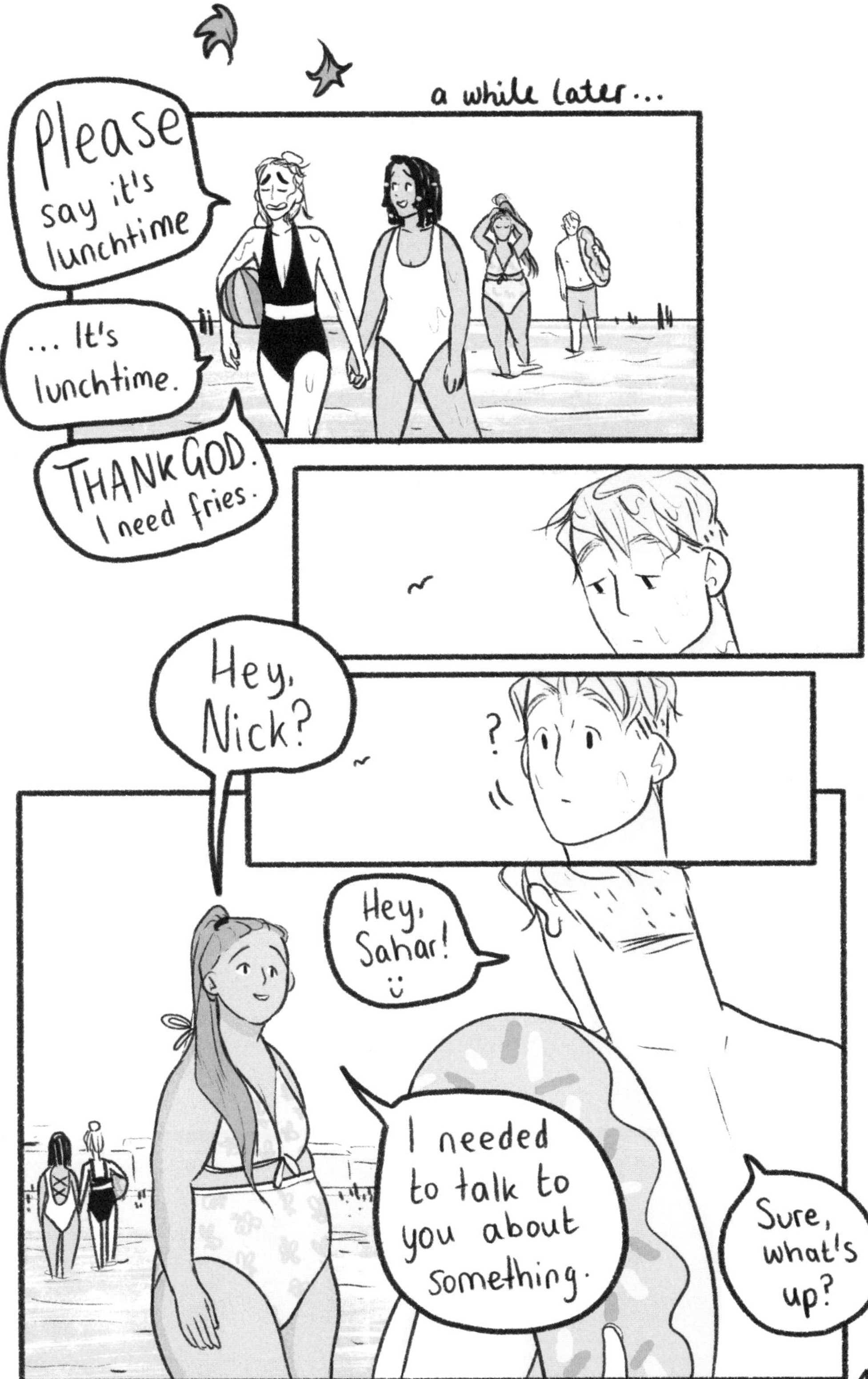
a while later...
Please say it's lunchtime
... It's lunchtime.
THANK GOD. I need fries.
Hey, Nick?
?
Hey, Sahar! :)
I needed to talk to you about something.
Sure, what's up?

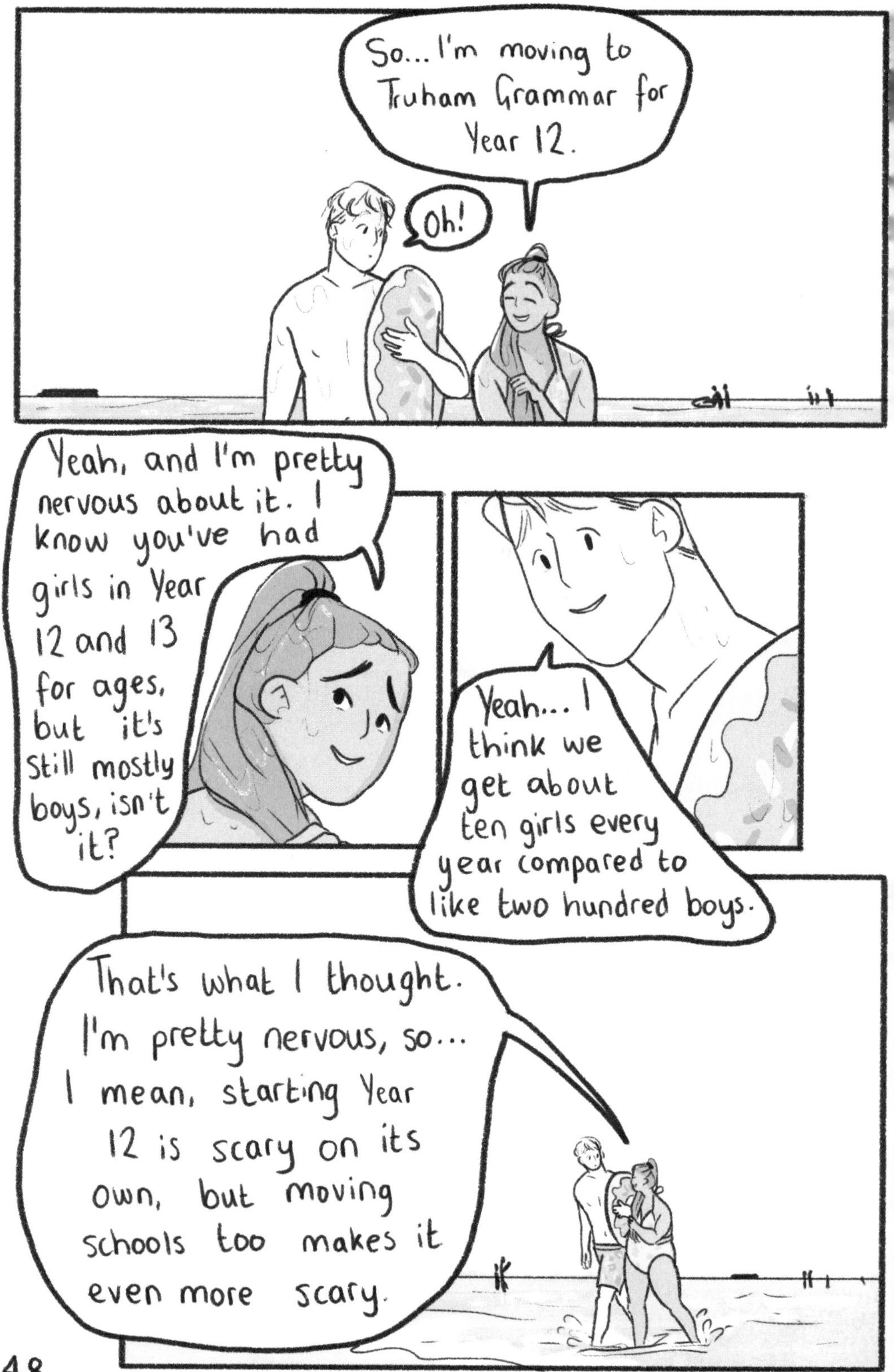
So... I'm moving to Truham Grammar for Year 12.
Oh!
Yeah, and I'm pretty nervous about it. I know you've had girls in Year 12 and 13 for ages, but it's still mostly boys, isn't it?
Yeah... I think we get about ten girls every year compared to like two hundred boys.
That's what I thought. I'm pretty nervous, so... I mean, starting Year 12 is scary on its own, but moving schools too makes it even more scary.

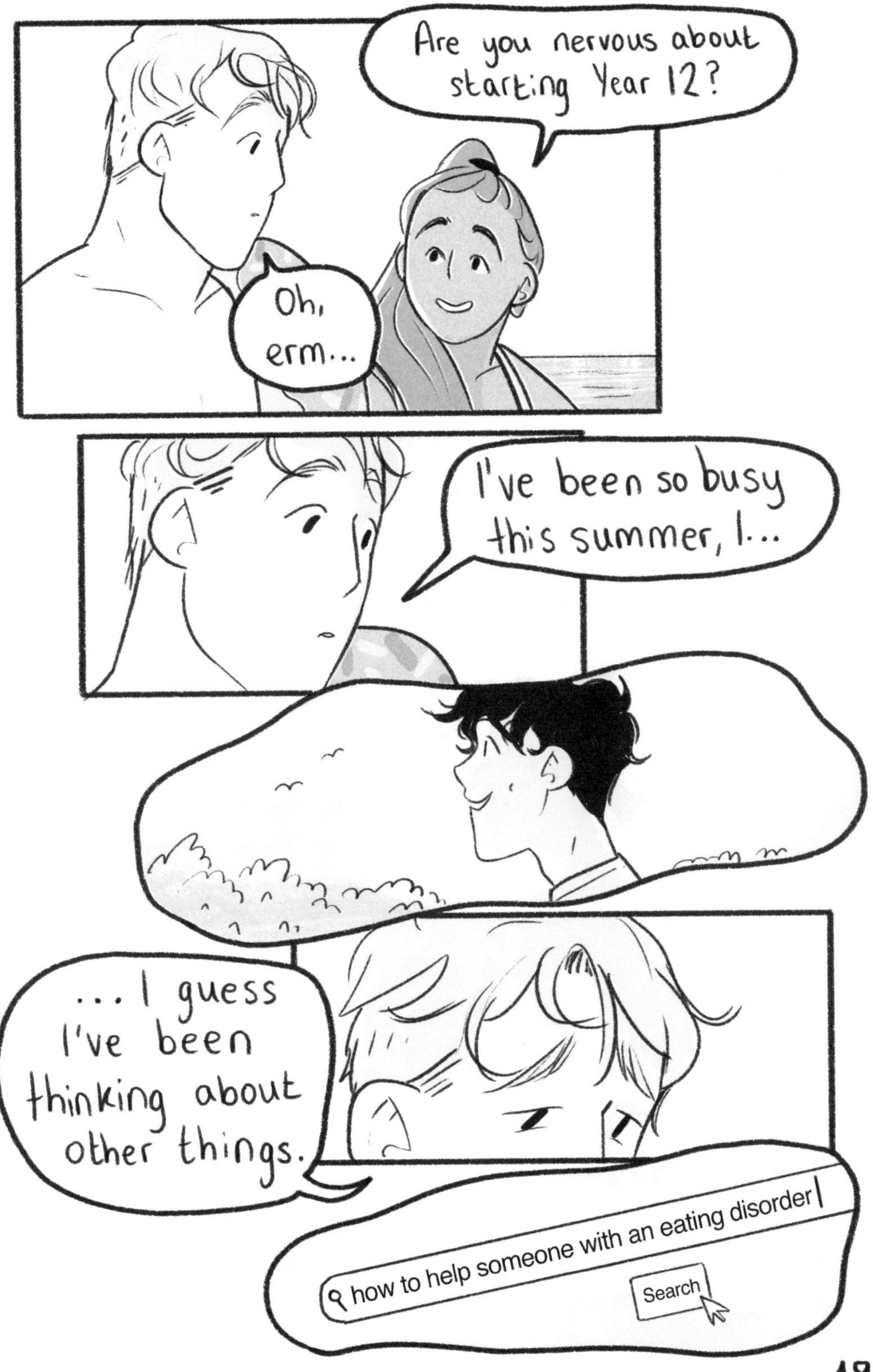
Are you nervous about starting Year 12?
Oh, erm...
I've been so busy this summer, I...
...I guess I've been thinking about other things.
how to help someone with an eating disorder
Search

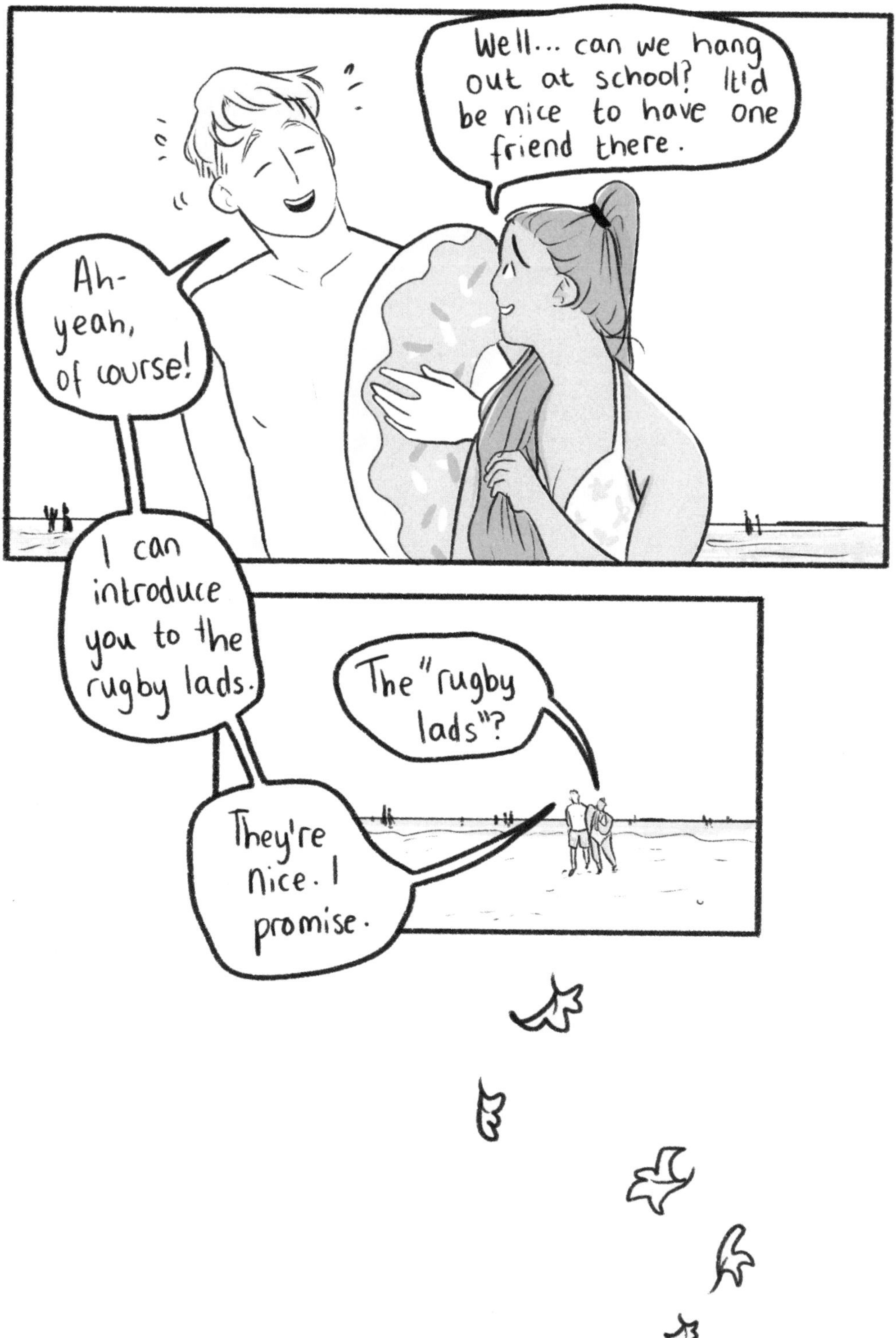
Well... can we hang out at school? It'd be nice to have one friend there.
Ah- yeah, of course!
I can introduce you to the rugby lads.
The "rugby lads"?
They're nice. I promise.

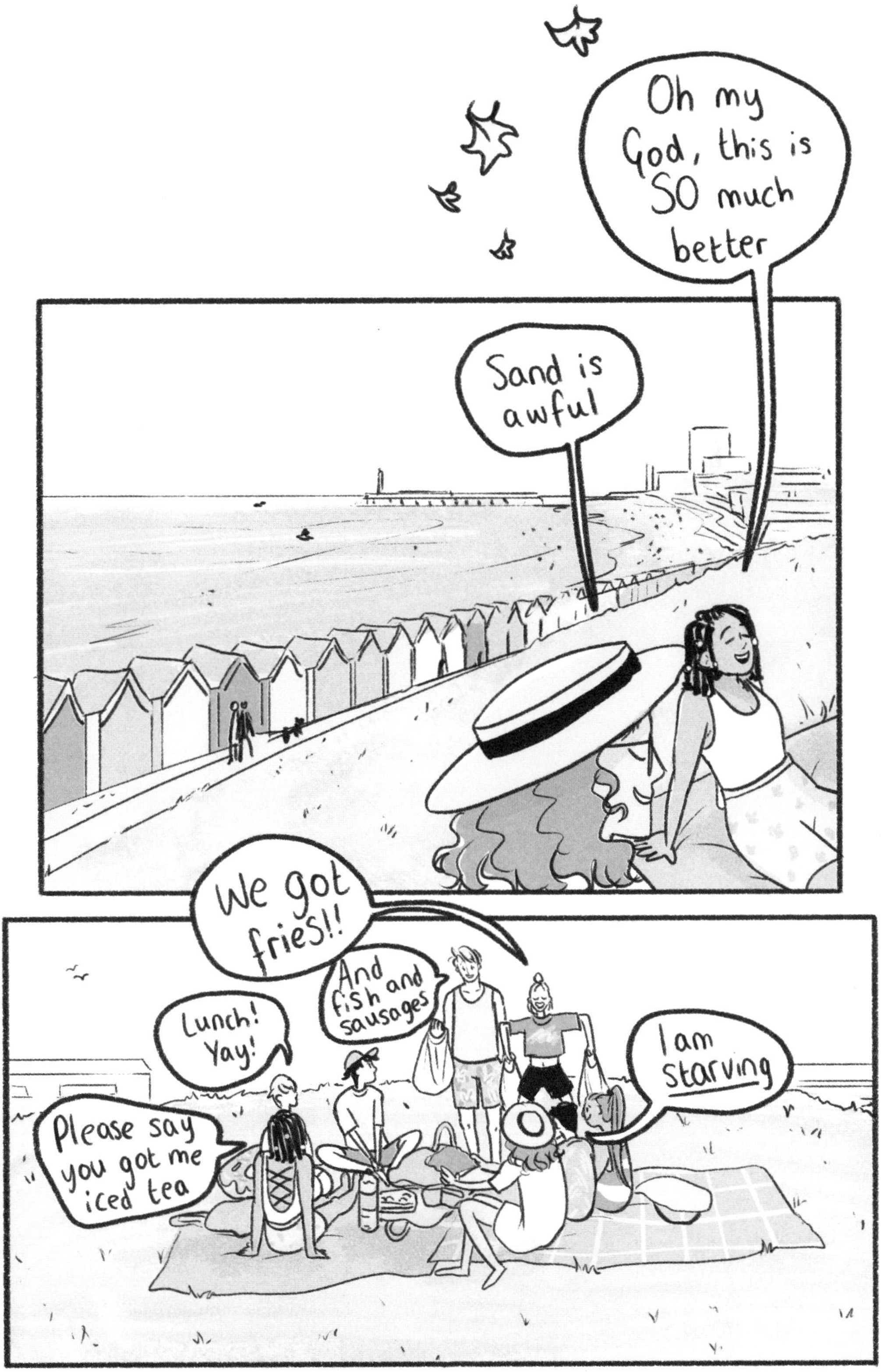

Oh my God, this is SO much better
Sand is awful
We got fries!!
And fish and sausages
Lunch! Yay!
I am starving
Please say you got me iced tea

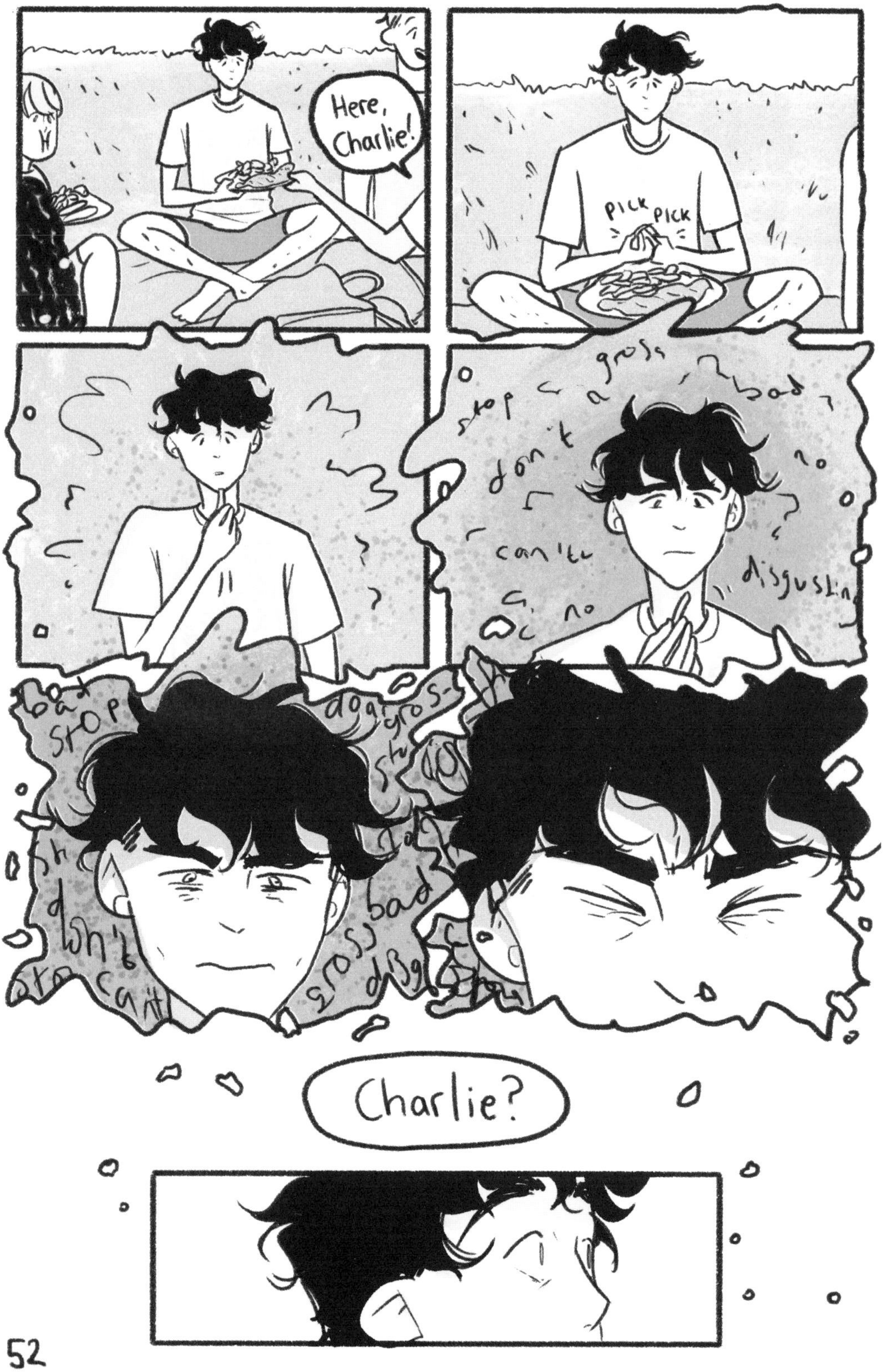
Here, Charlie!
PICK
PICK
gross
stop
bad
don't
no
can't
no
disgusting
Charlie?

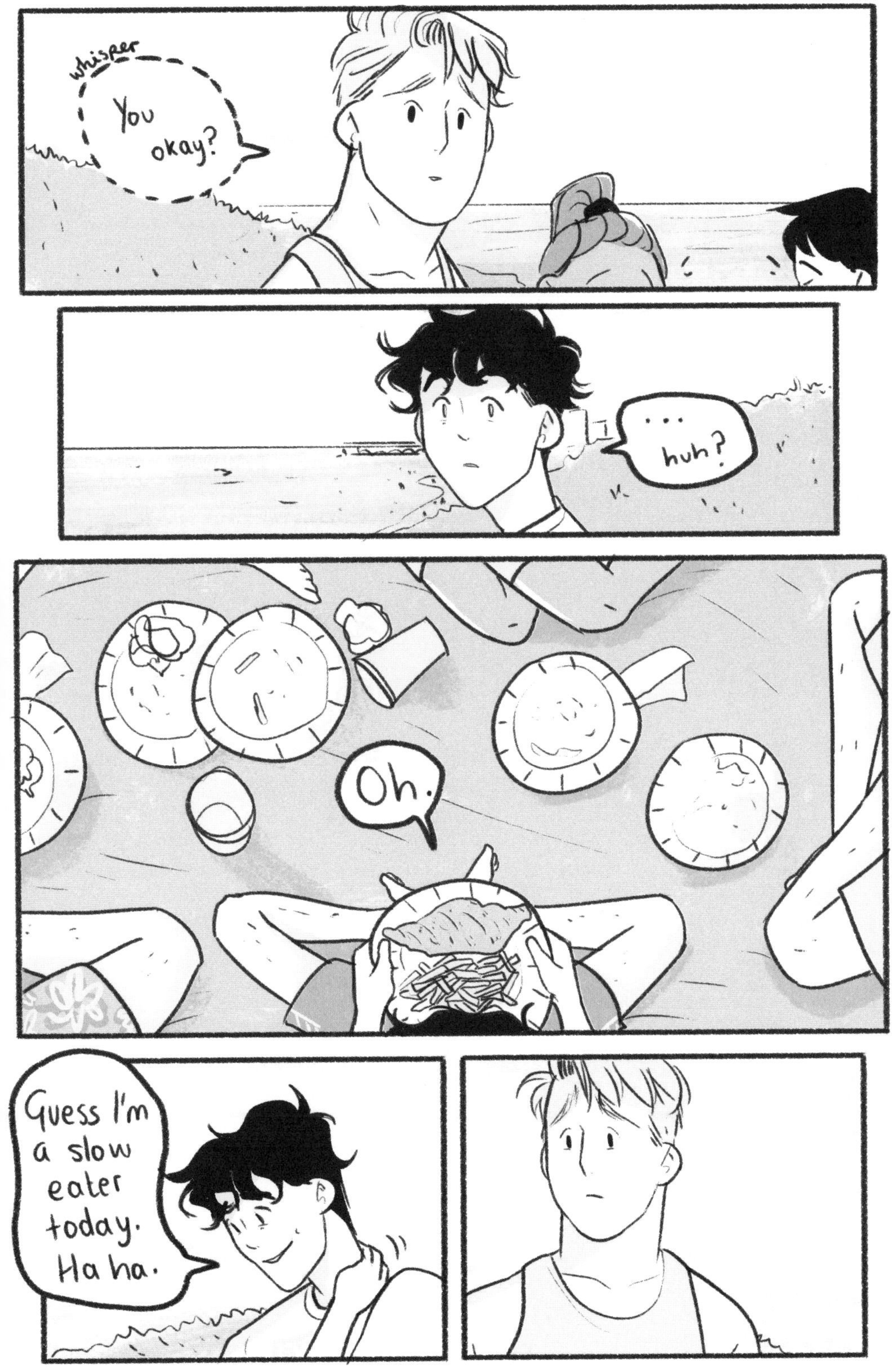
whisper
You okay?
... huh?
Oh.
Guess I'm a slow eater today. Ha ha.

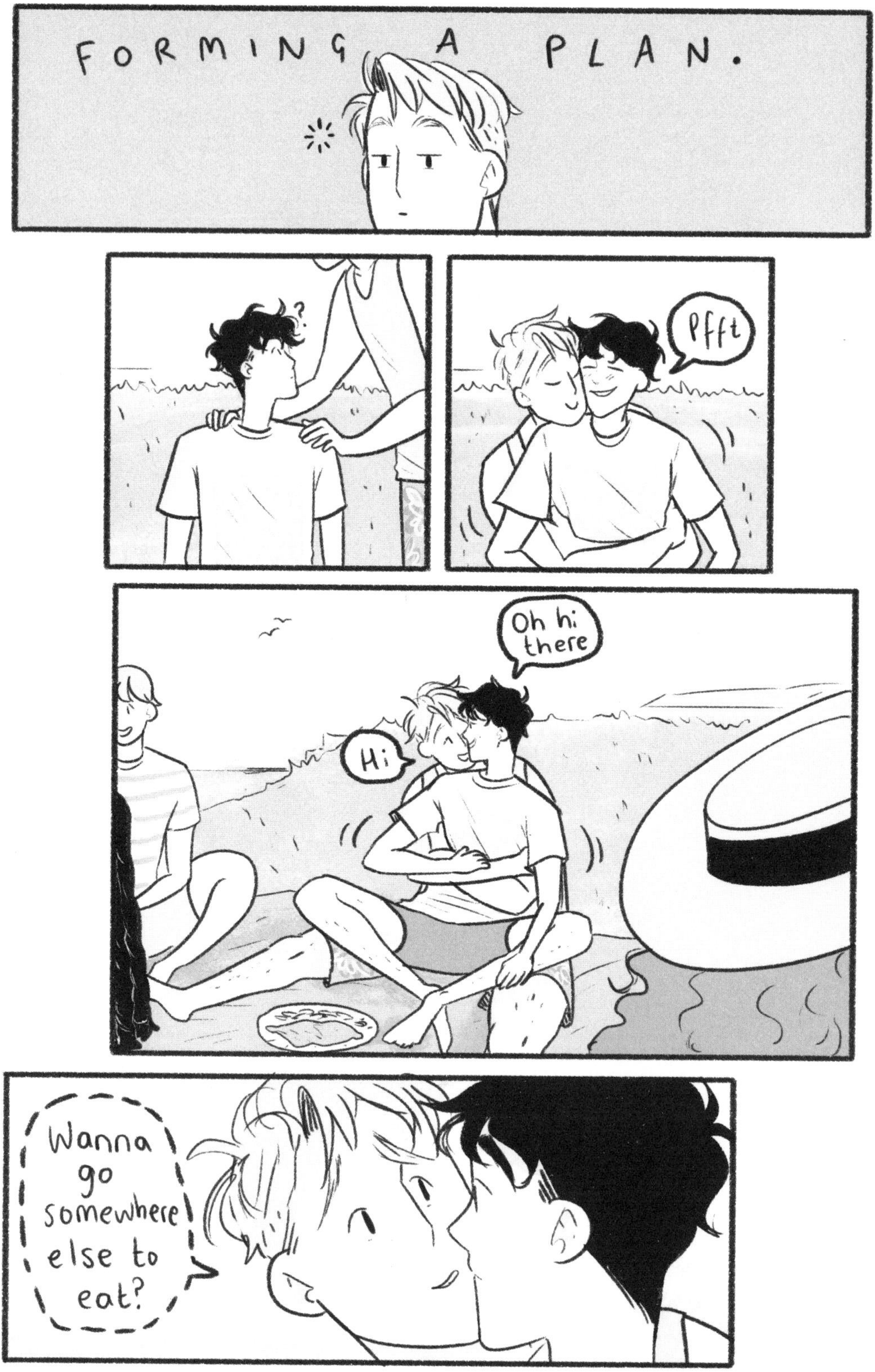
FORMING A PLAN.
?
Pfft
Oh hi there
Hi
Wanna go somewhere else to eat?

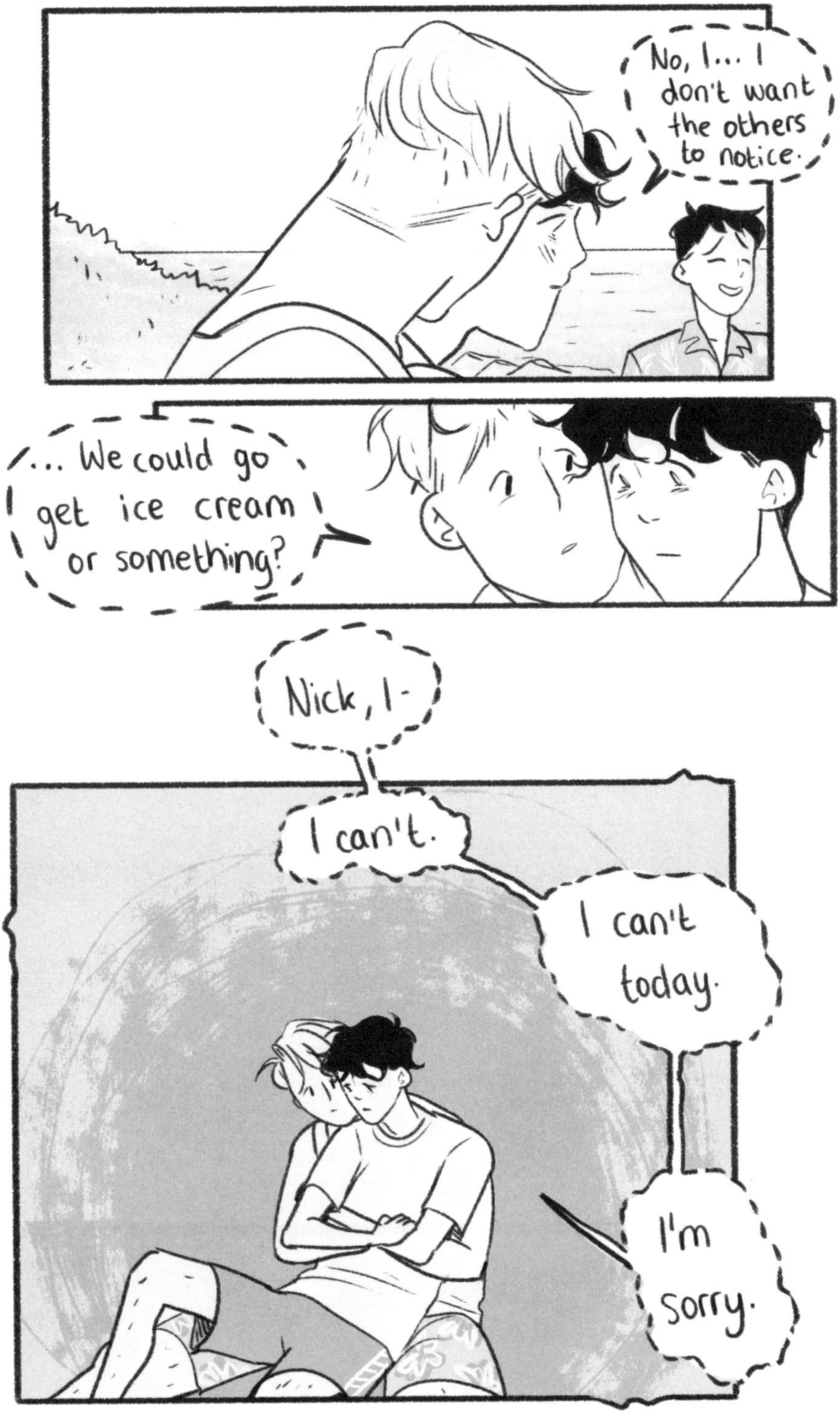
No, I... I don't want the others to notice.
... We could go get ice cream or something?
Nick, I-
I can't.
I can't today.
I'm sorry.

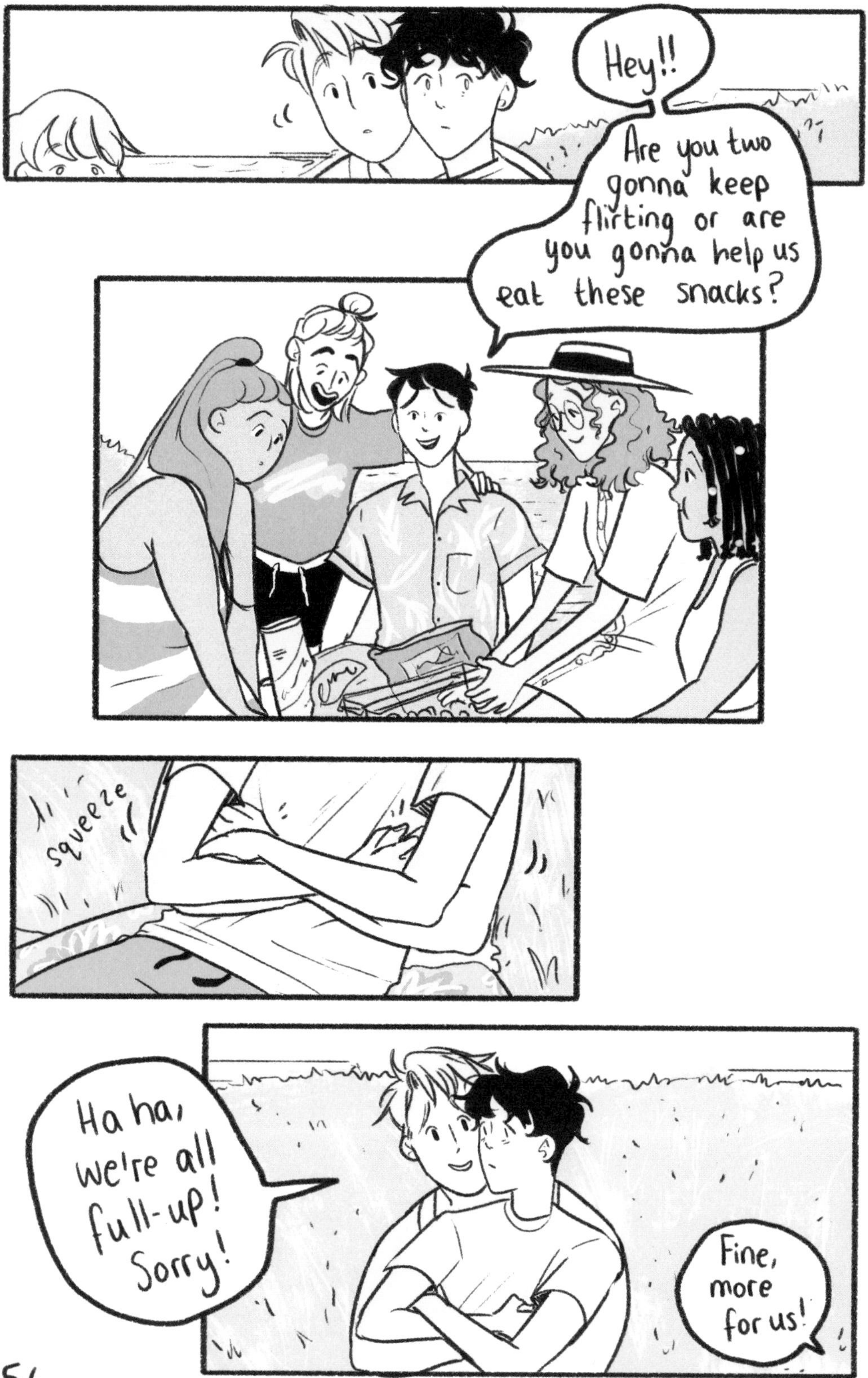
Hey!!
Are you two gonna keep flirting or are you gonna help us eat these snacks?
squeeze
Ha ha, we're all full-up! Sorry!
Fine, more for us!

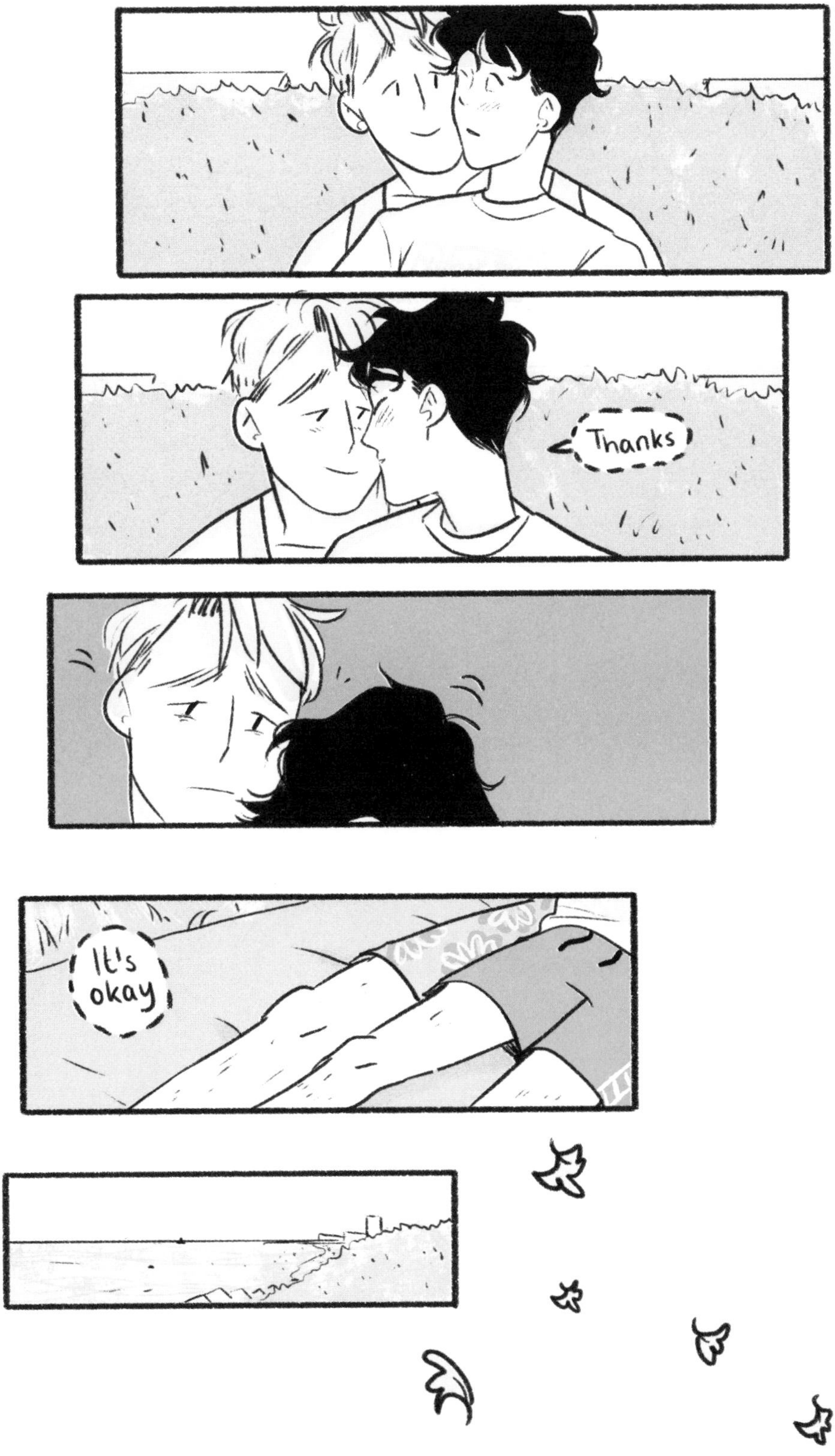
Thanks
It's okay

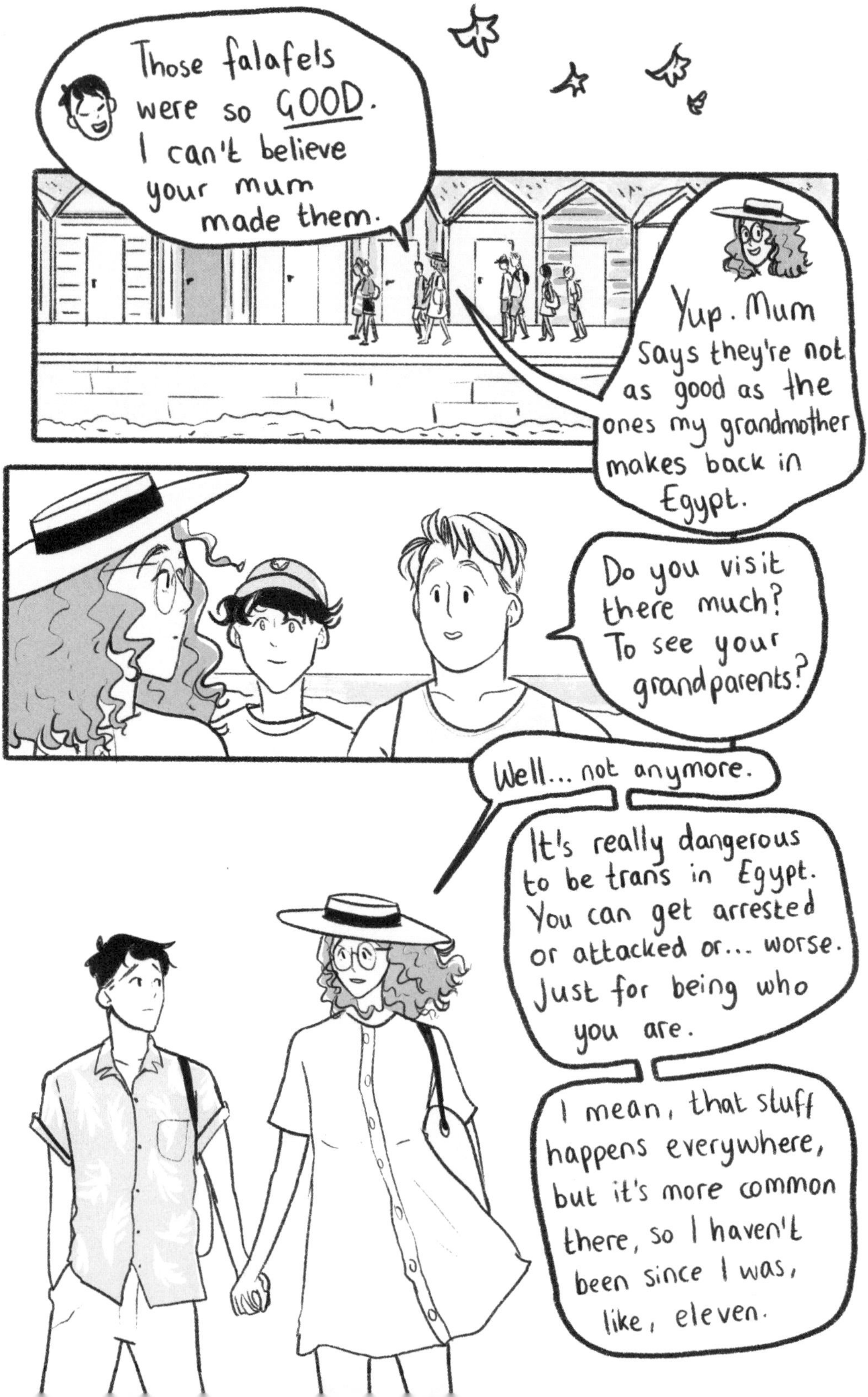
Those falafels were so GOOD. I can't believe your mum made them.
Yup. Mum says they're not as good as the ones my grandmother makes back in Egypt.
Do you visit there much? To see your grandparents?
Well... not anymore.
It's really dangerous to be trans in Egypt. You can get arrested or attacked or... worse. Just for being who you are.
I mean, that stuff happens everywhere, but it's more common there, so I haven't been since I was, like, eleven.

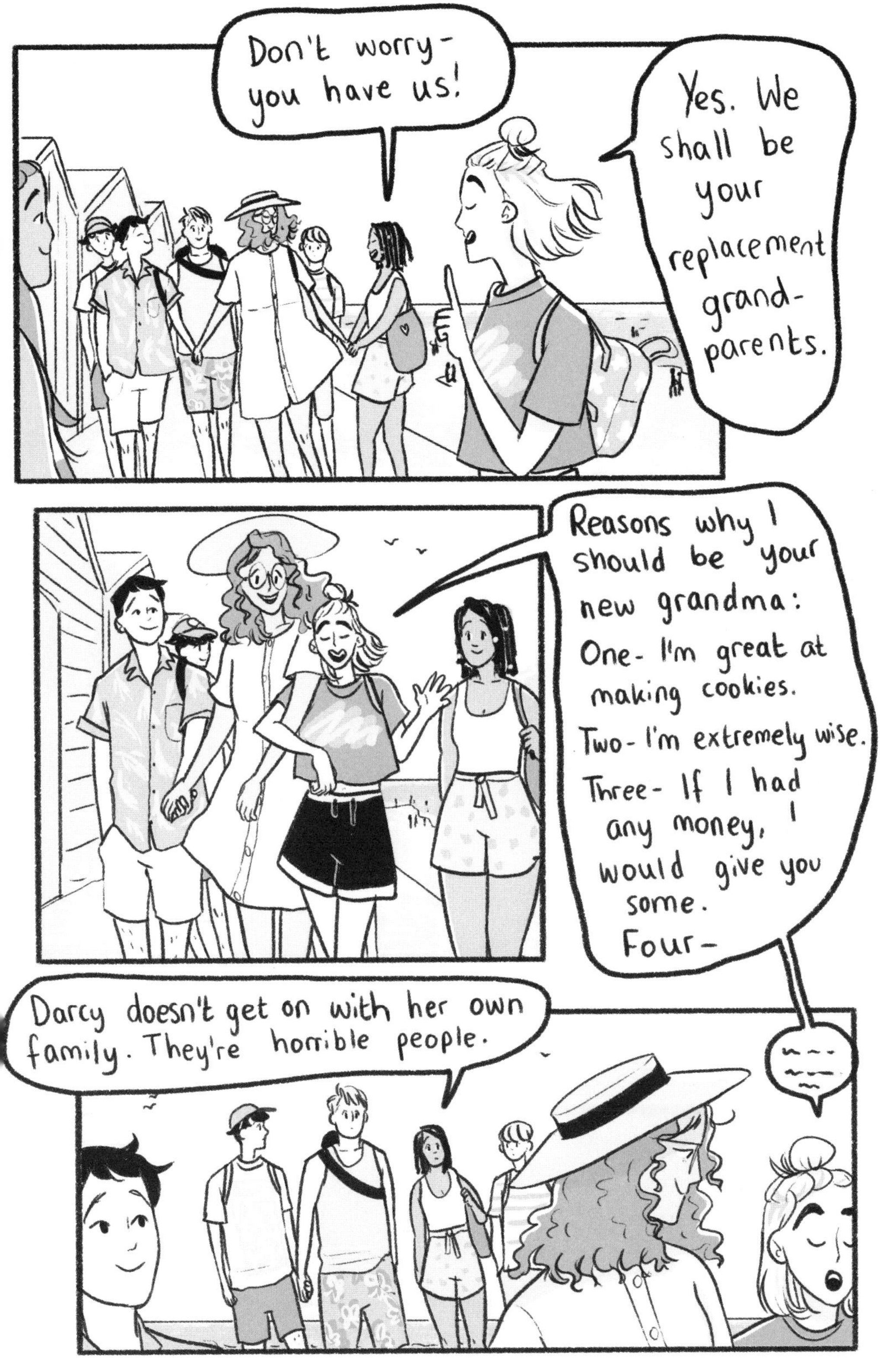
Don't worry- you have us!
Yes. We shall be your replacement grand-parents.
Reasons why I should be your new grandma:
One- I'm great at making cookies.
Two- I'm extremely wise.
Three- If I had any money, I would give you some.
Four-
Darcy doesn't get on with her own family. They're horrible people.

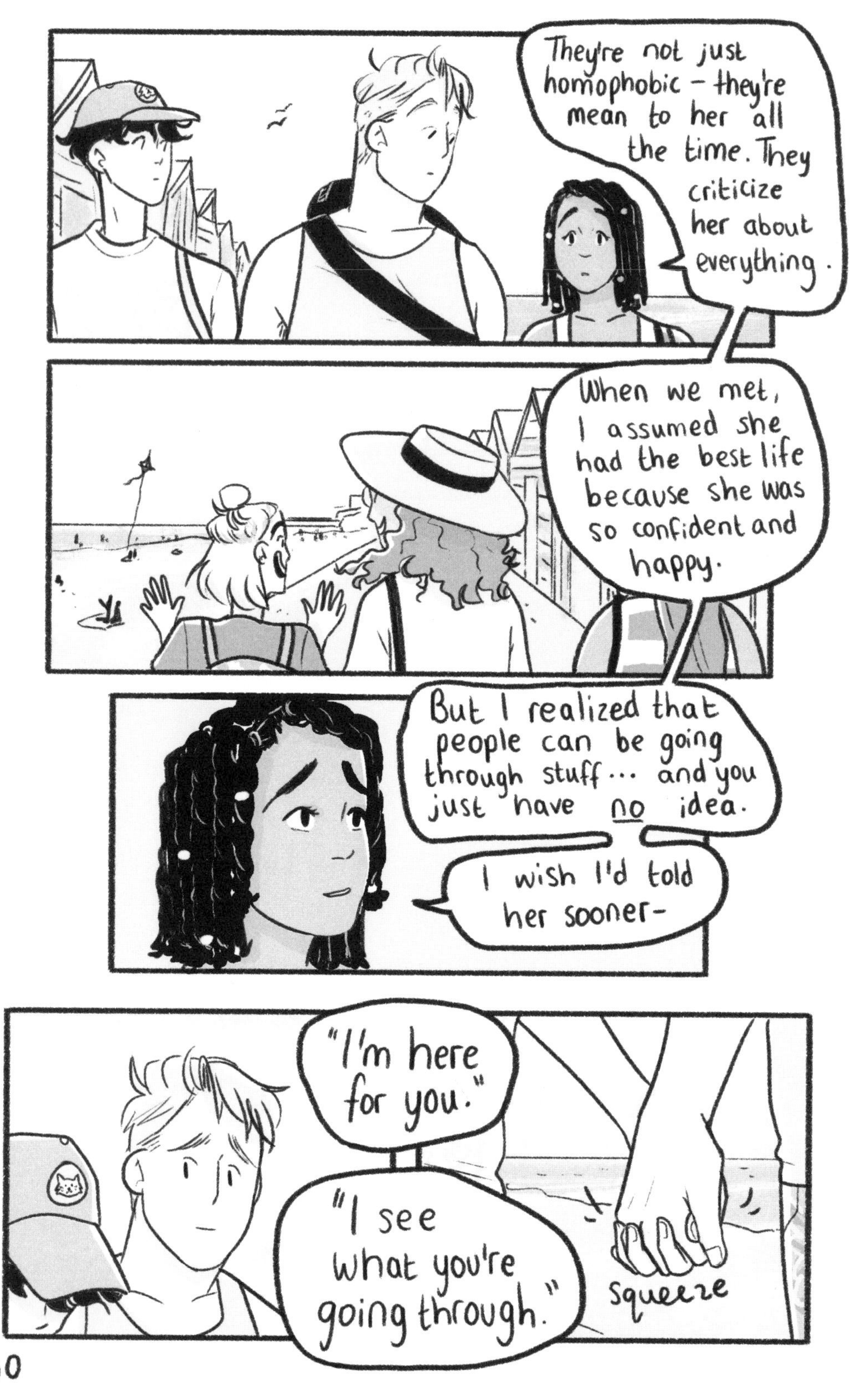
They're not just homophobic – they're mean to her all the time. They criticize her about everything.
When we met, I assumed she had the best life because she was so confident and happy.
But I realized that people can be going through stuff... and you just have no idea.
I wish I'd told her sooner–
"I'm here for you."
"I see what you're going through."
squeeze

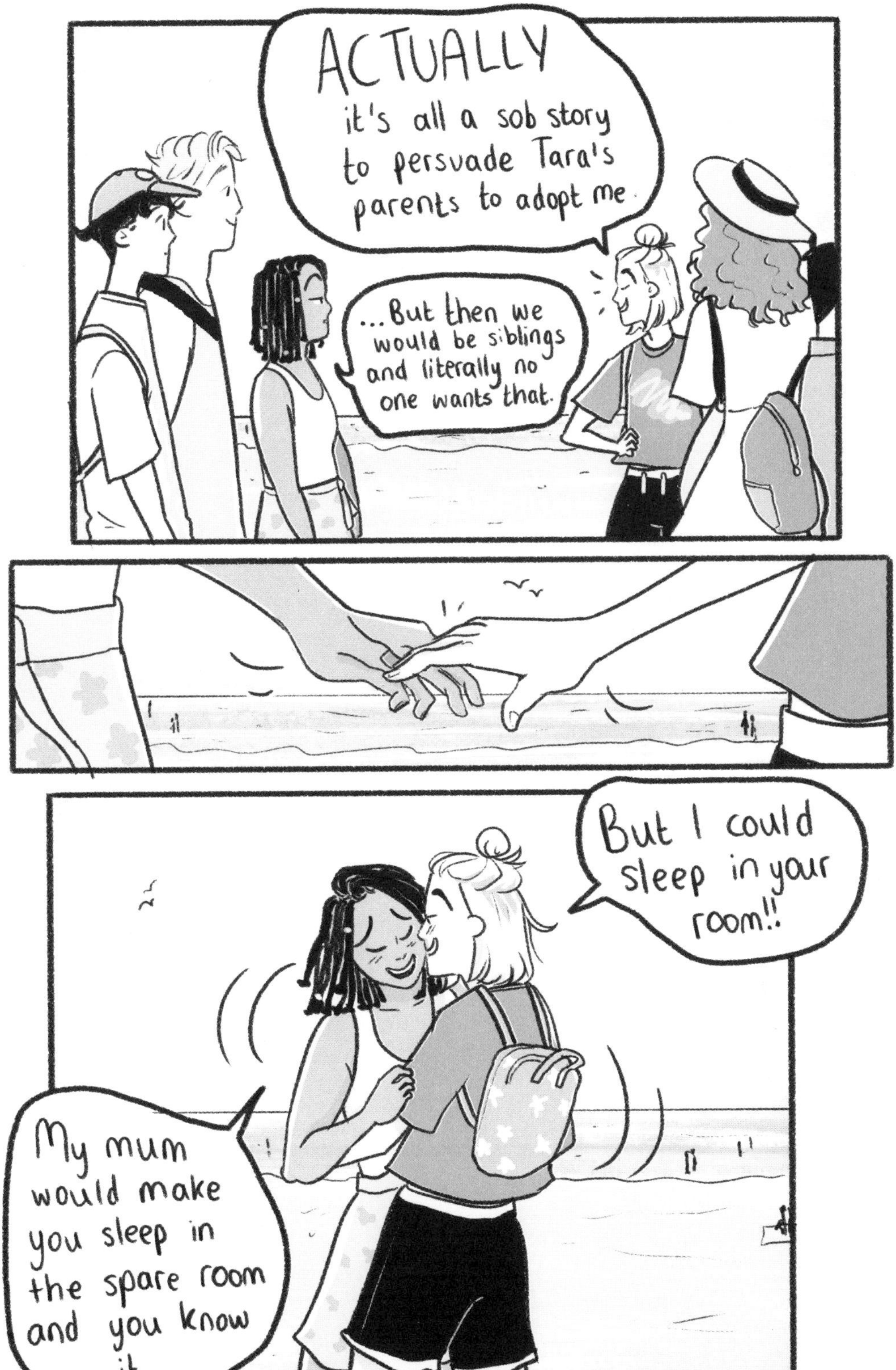
ACTUALLY it's all a sob story to persuade Tara's parents to adopt me.
...But then we would be siblings and literally no one wants that.
But I could sleep in your room!!
My mum would make you sleep in the spare room and you know it.

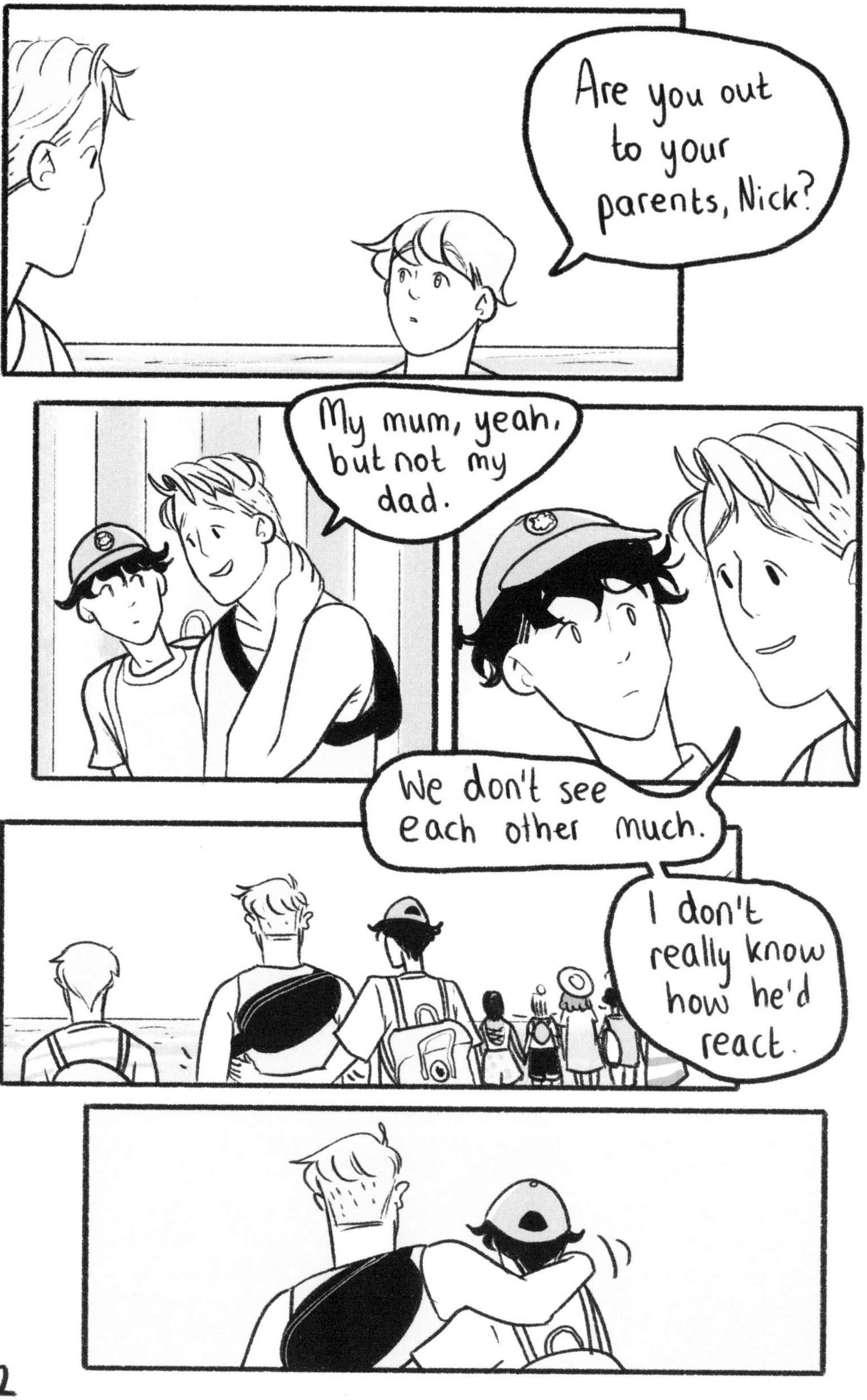
Are you out to your parents, Nick?
My mum, yeah, but not my dad.
We don't see each other much.
I don't really know how he'd react.

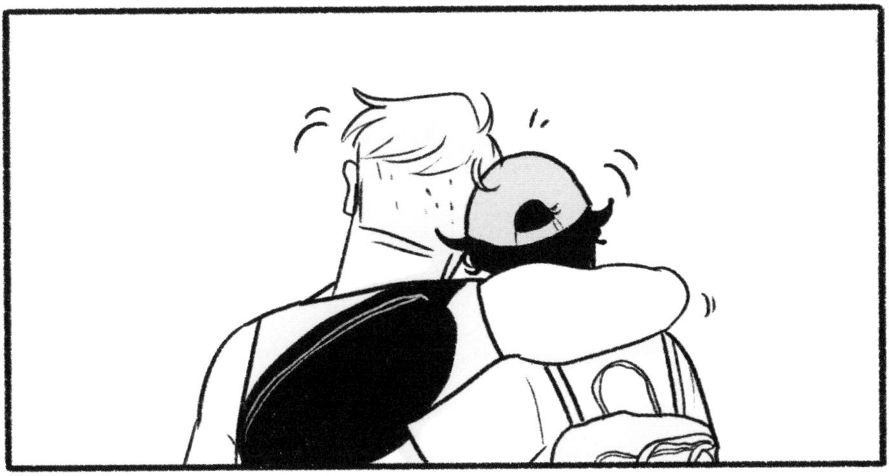

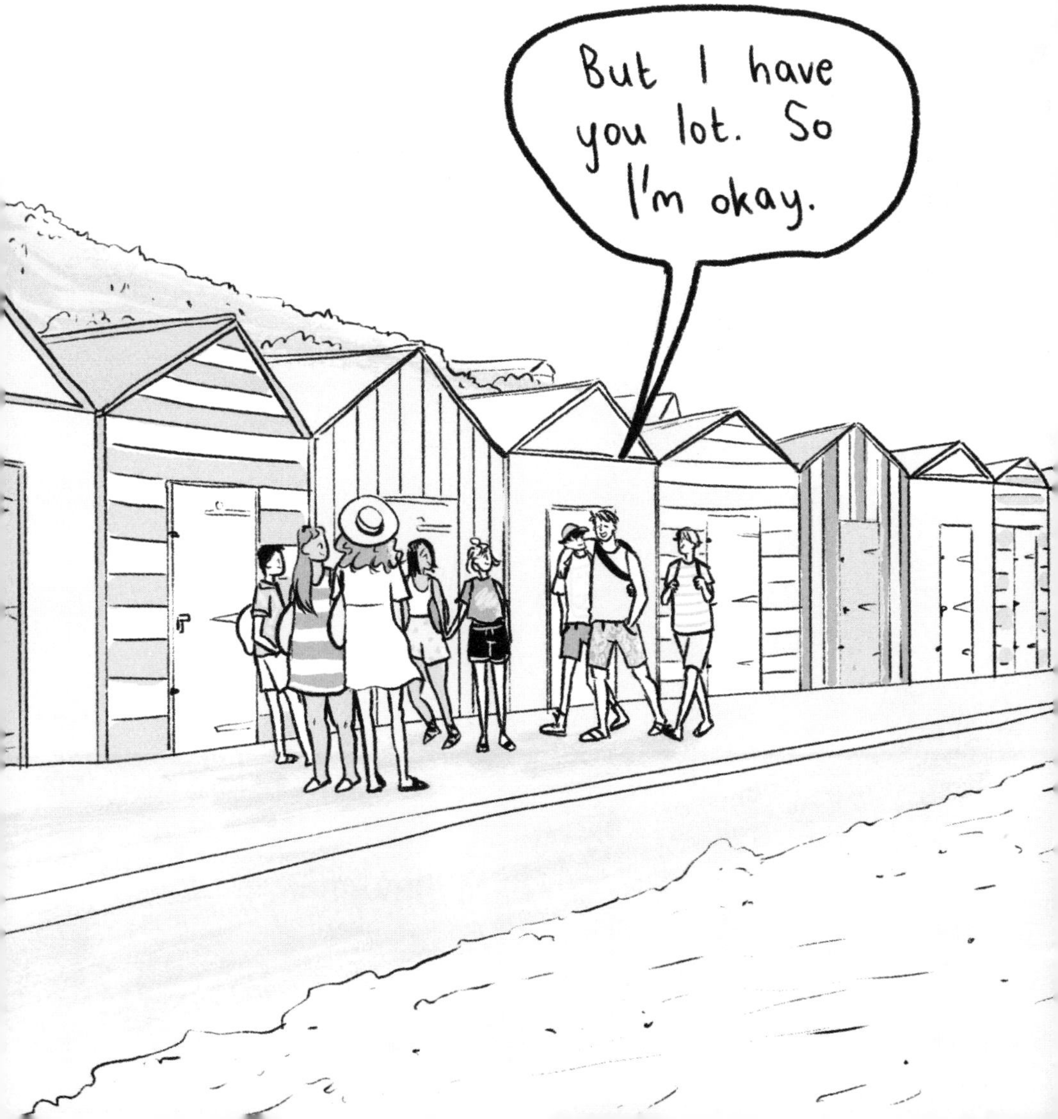
But I have you lot. So I'm okay.

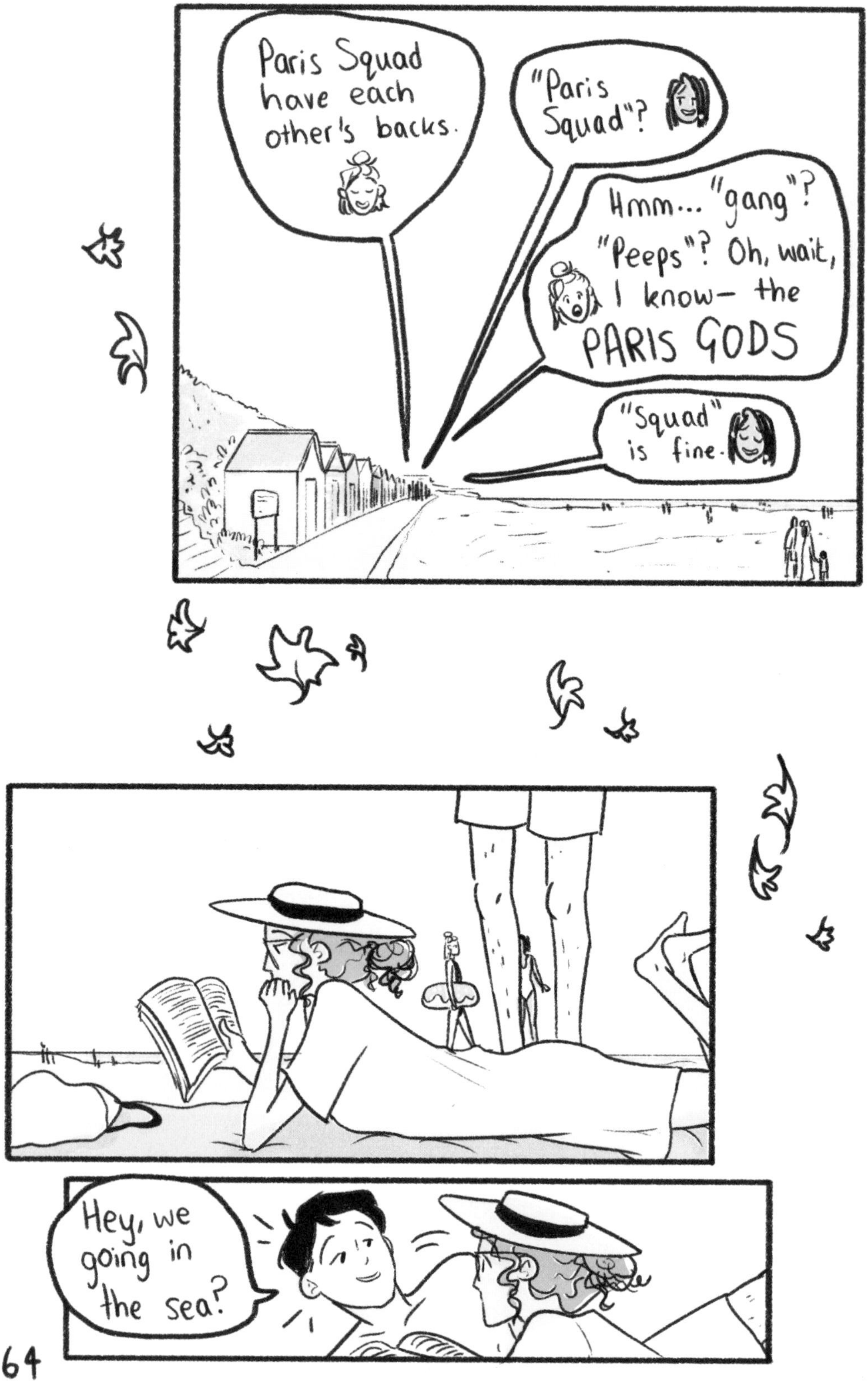
Paris Squad have each other's backs.
"Paris Squad"?
Hmm... "gang"? "Peeps"? Oh, wait, I know— the PARIS GODS
"Squad" is fine.
Hey, we going in the sea?

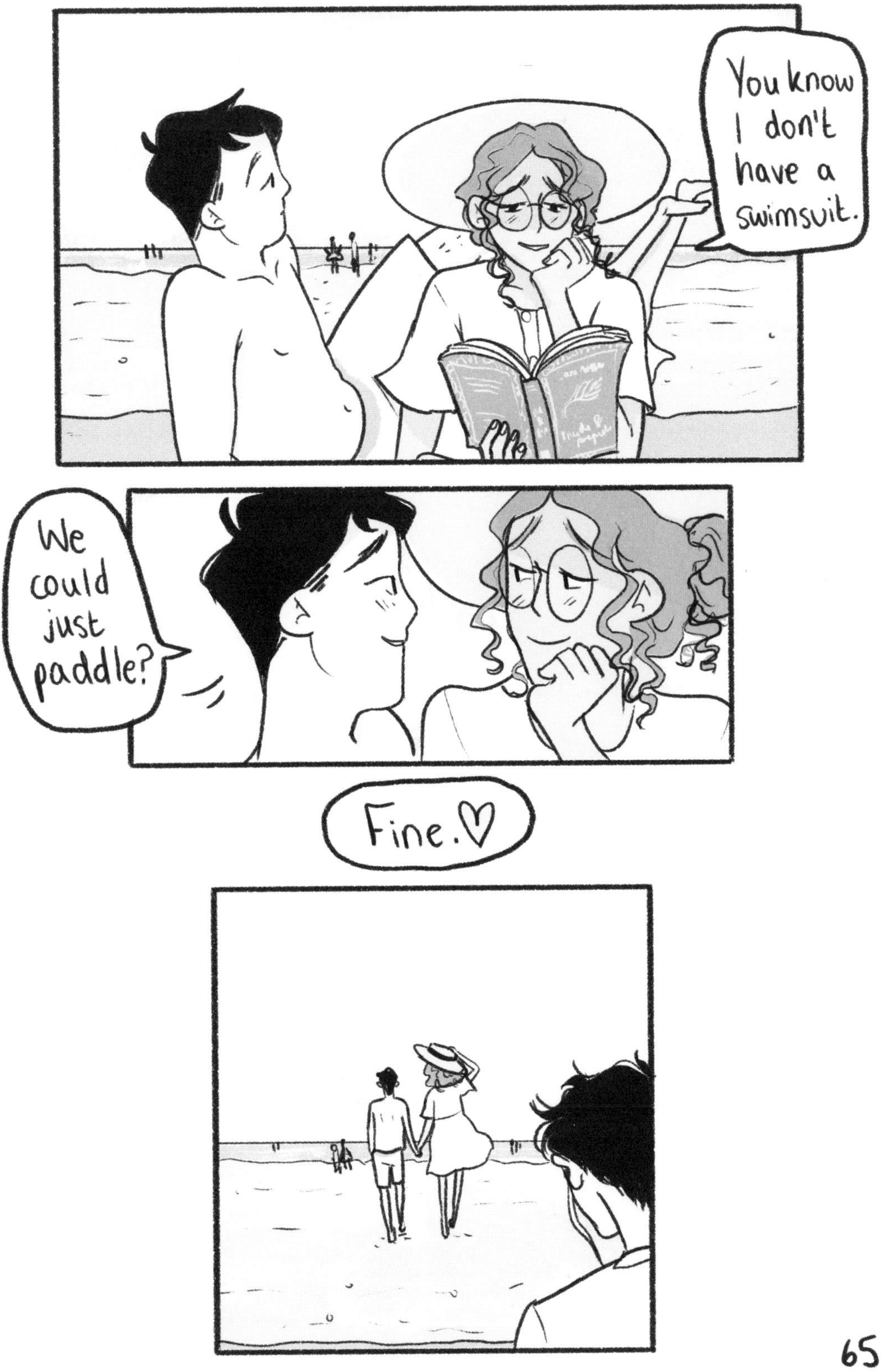
You know I don't have a swimsuit.
We could just paddle?
Fine.♡

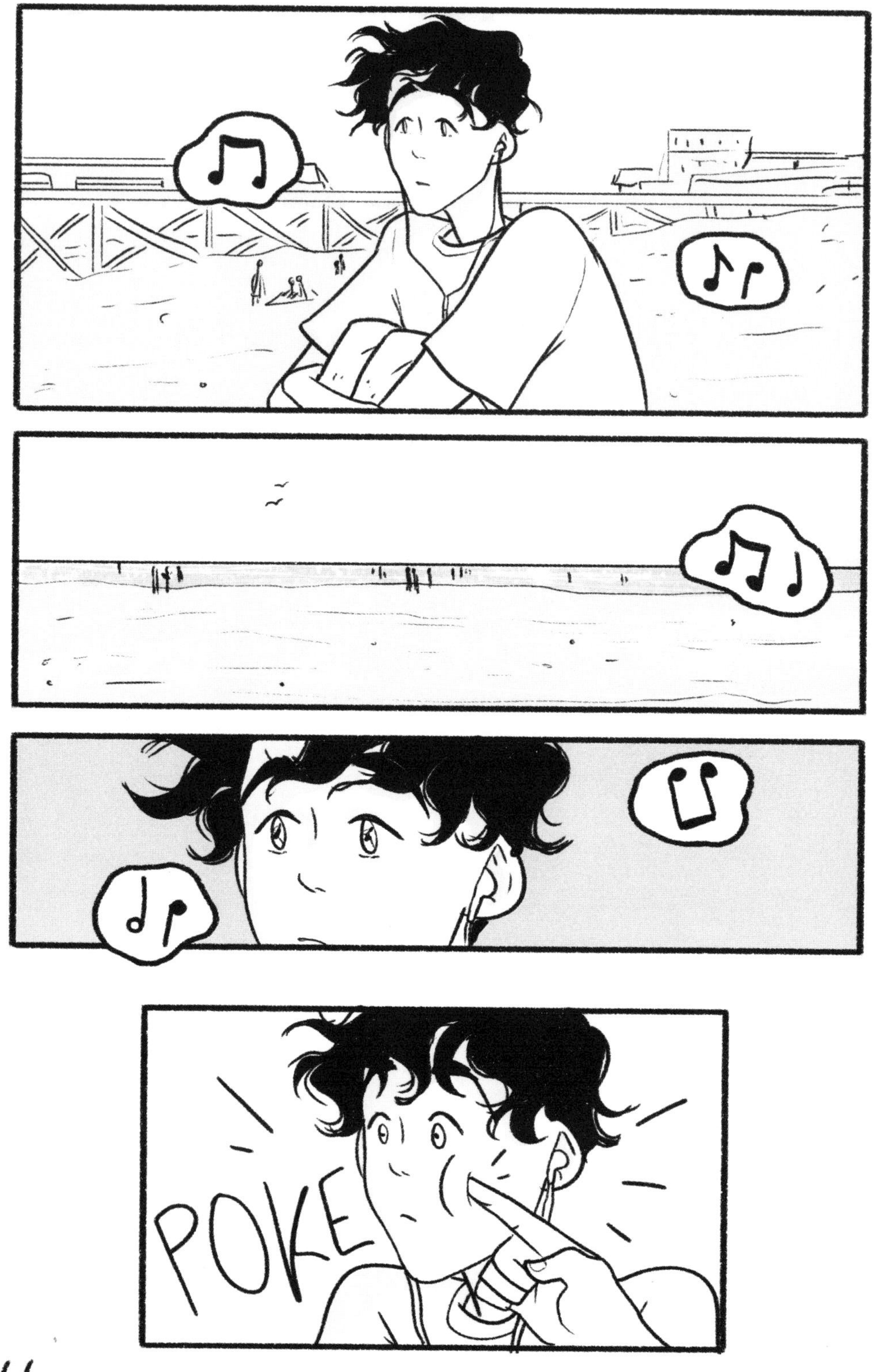
POKE

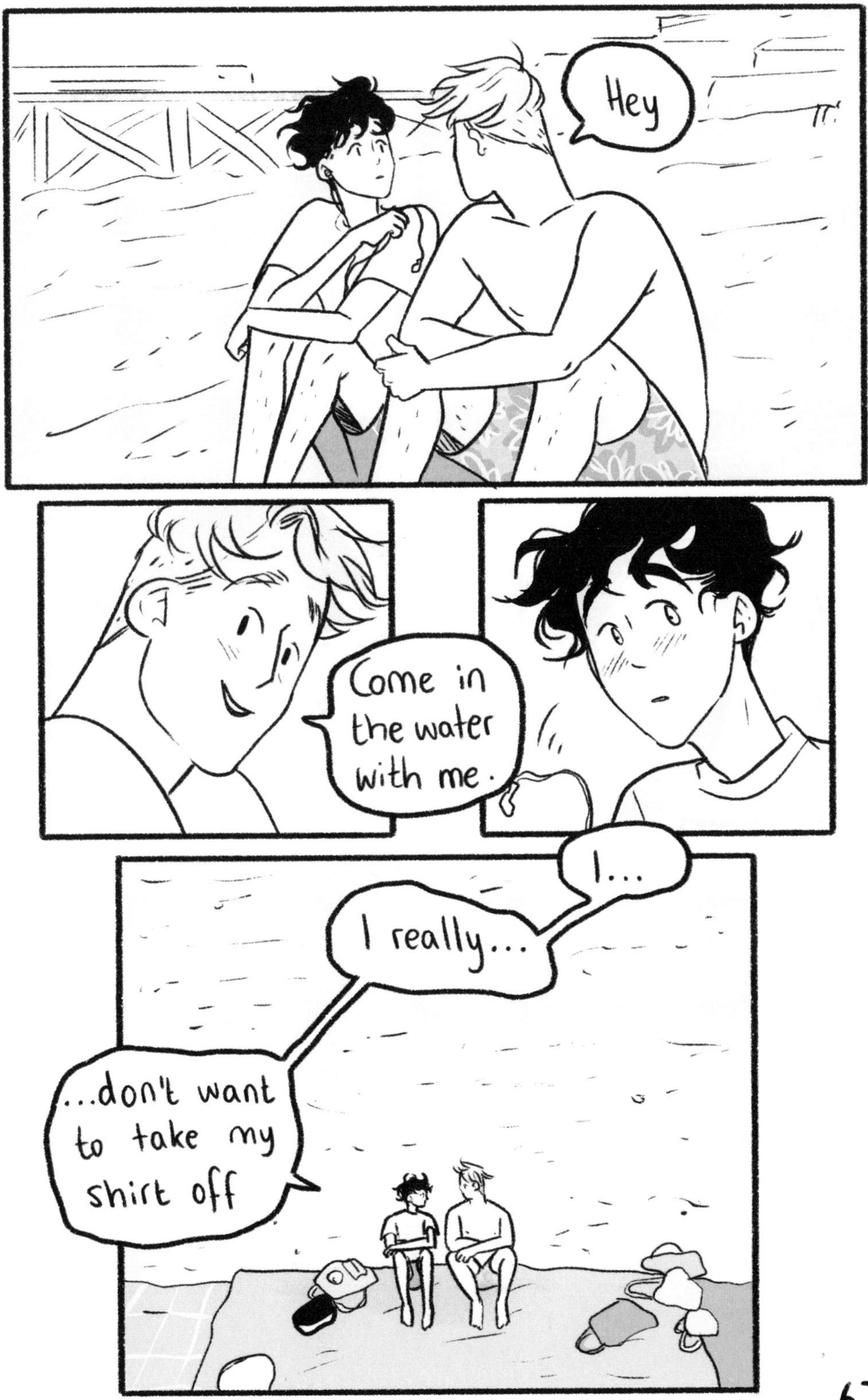
Hey
Come in the water with me.
I...
I really...
...don't want to take my shirt off

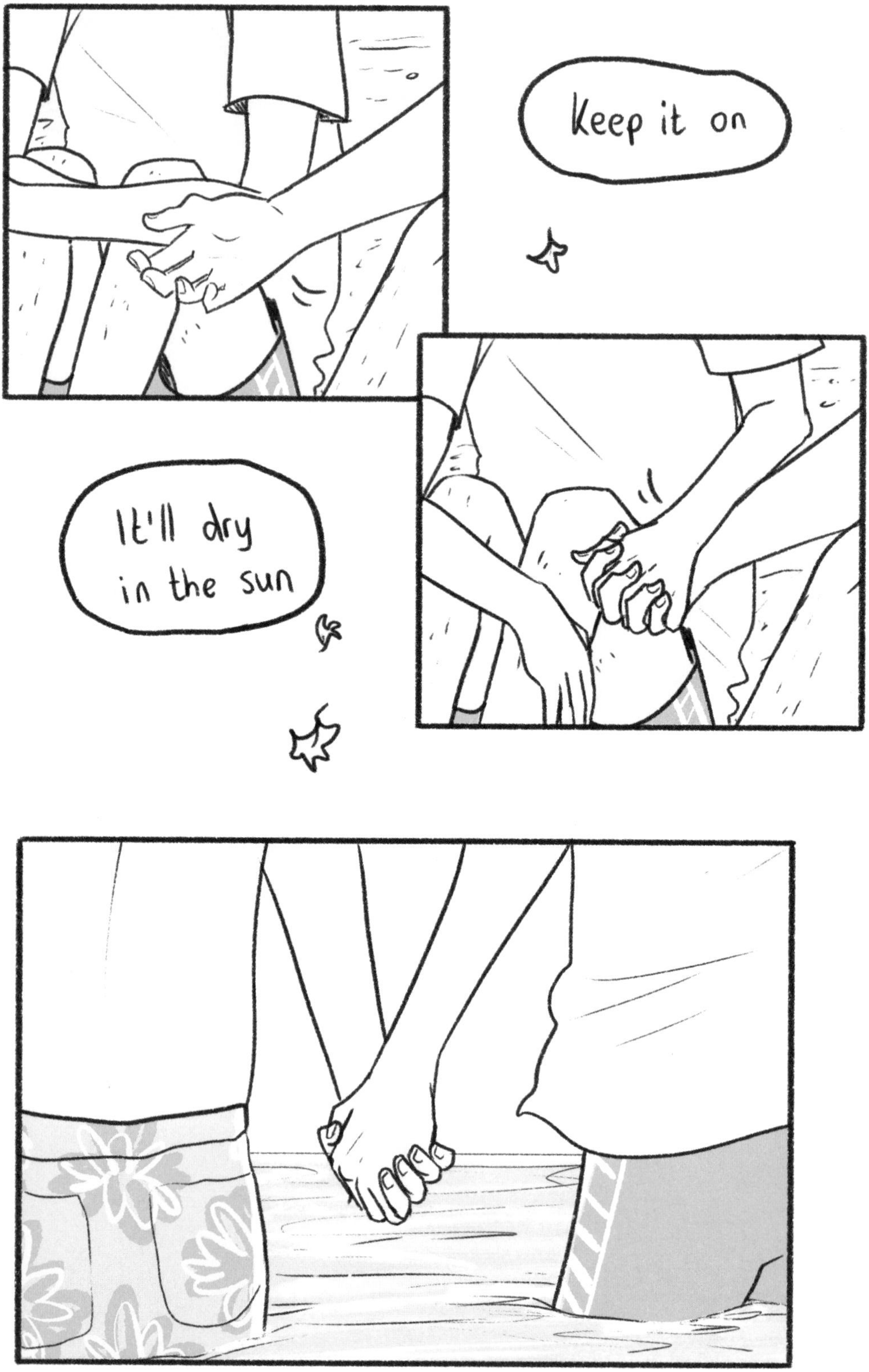
Keep it on
It'll dry in the sun

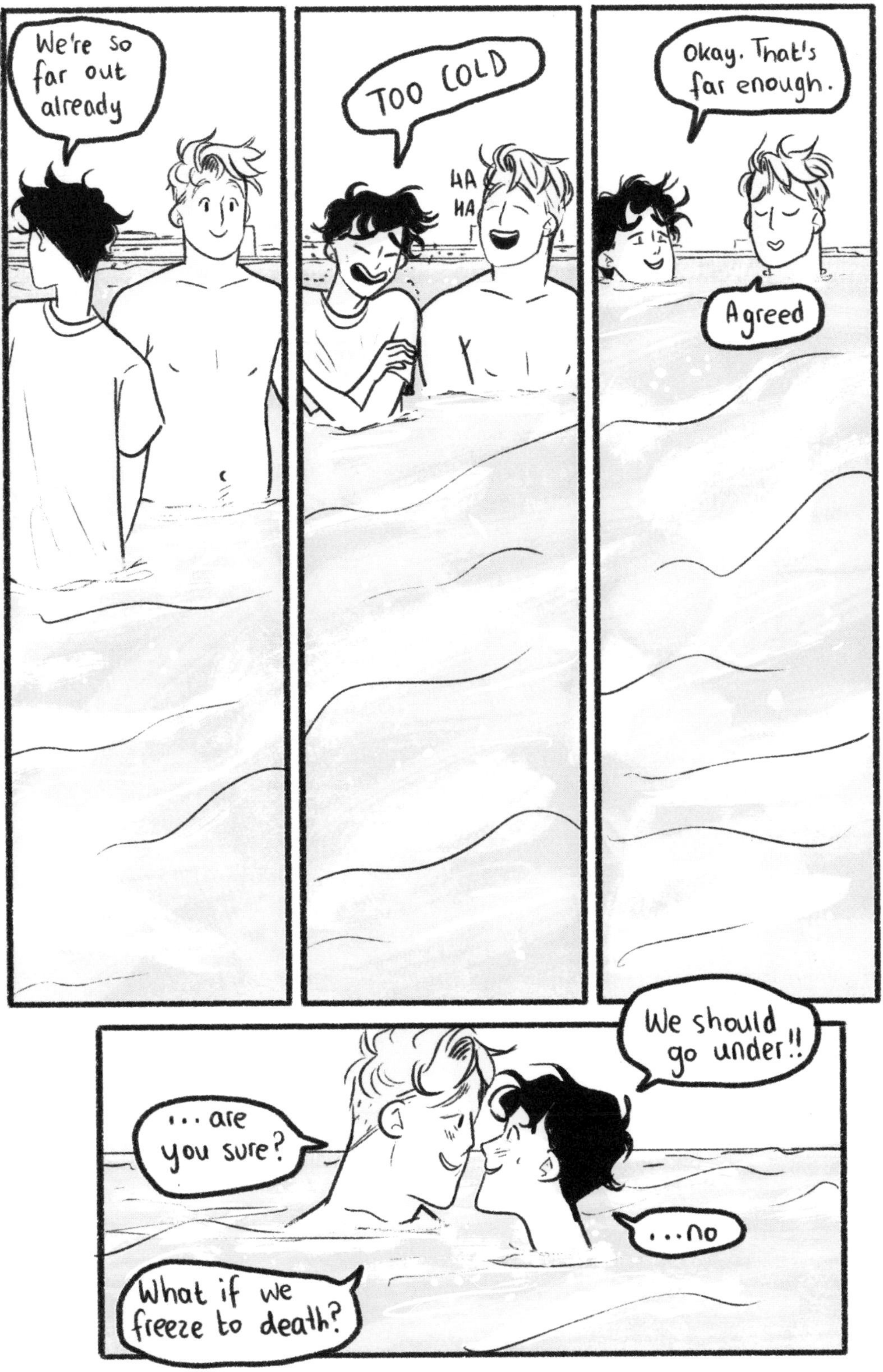
We're so far out already
TOO COLD
HA HA
Okay. That's far enough.
Agreed
We should go under!!
...are you sure?
...no
What if we freeze to death?

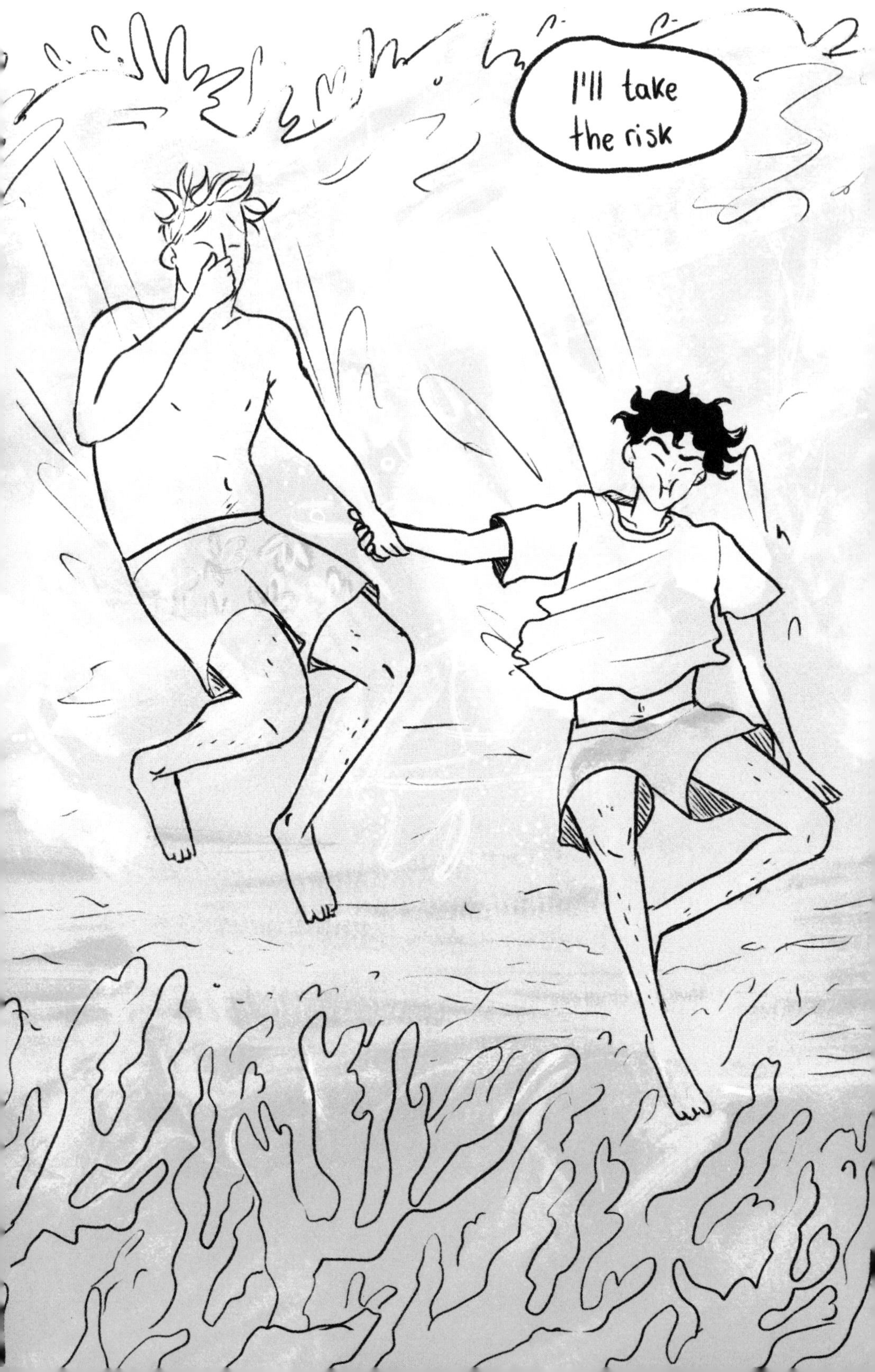
I'll take the risk

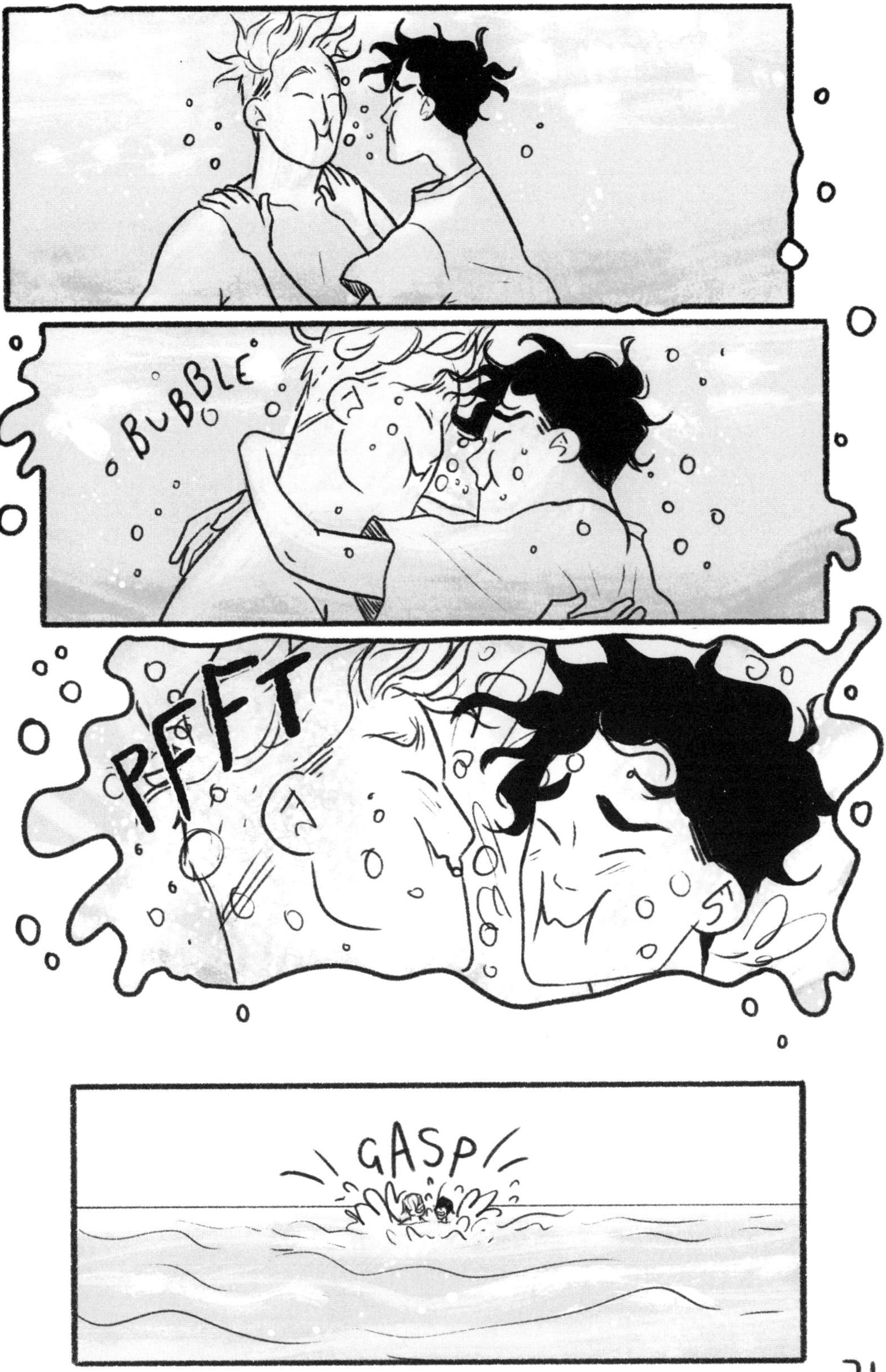
BUBBLE
PFFT
GASP

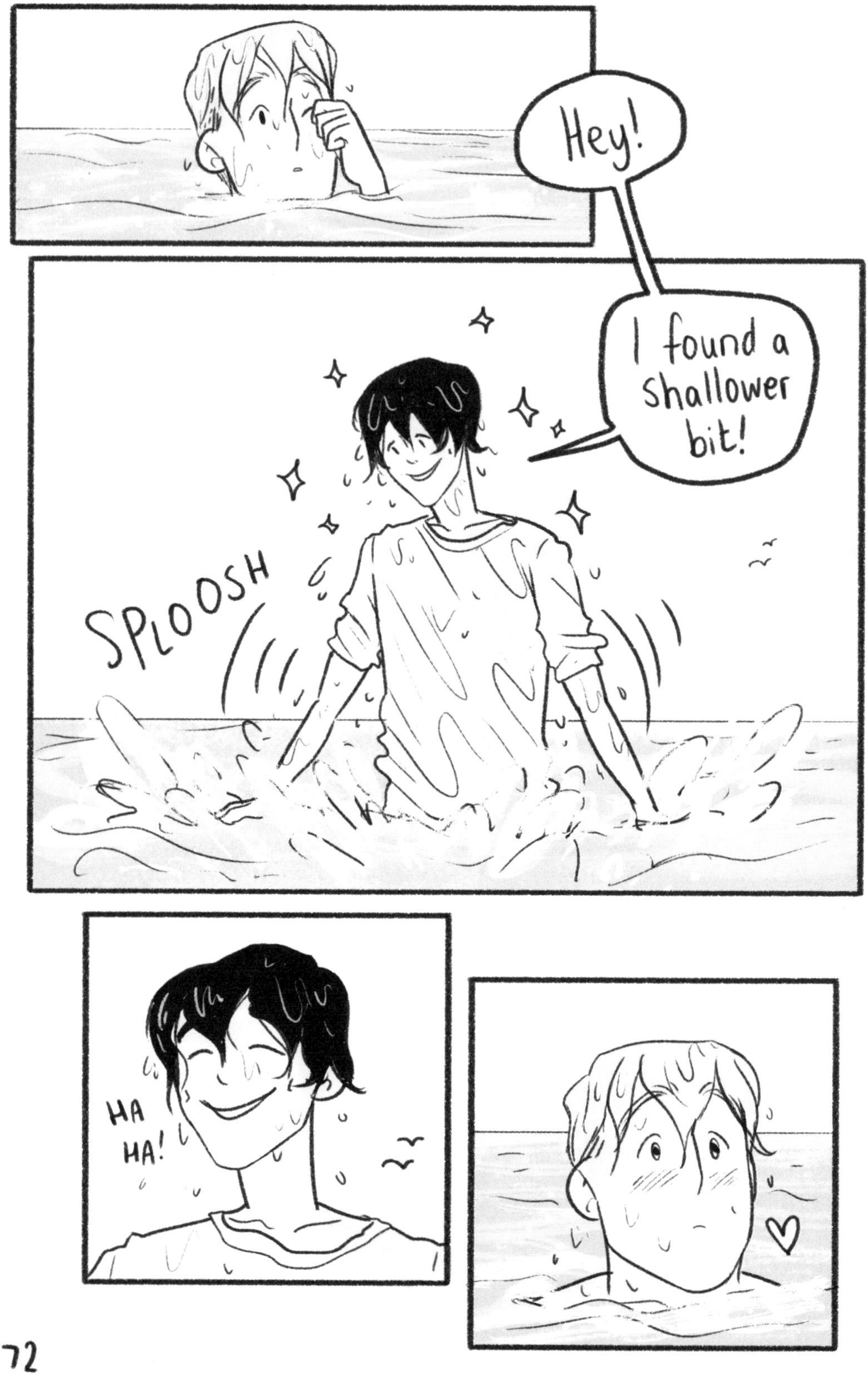
Hey!
I found a shallower bit!
SPLOOSH
HA HA!

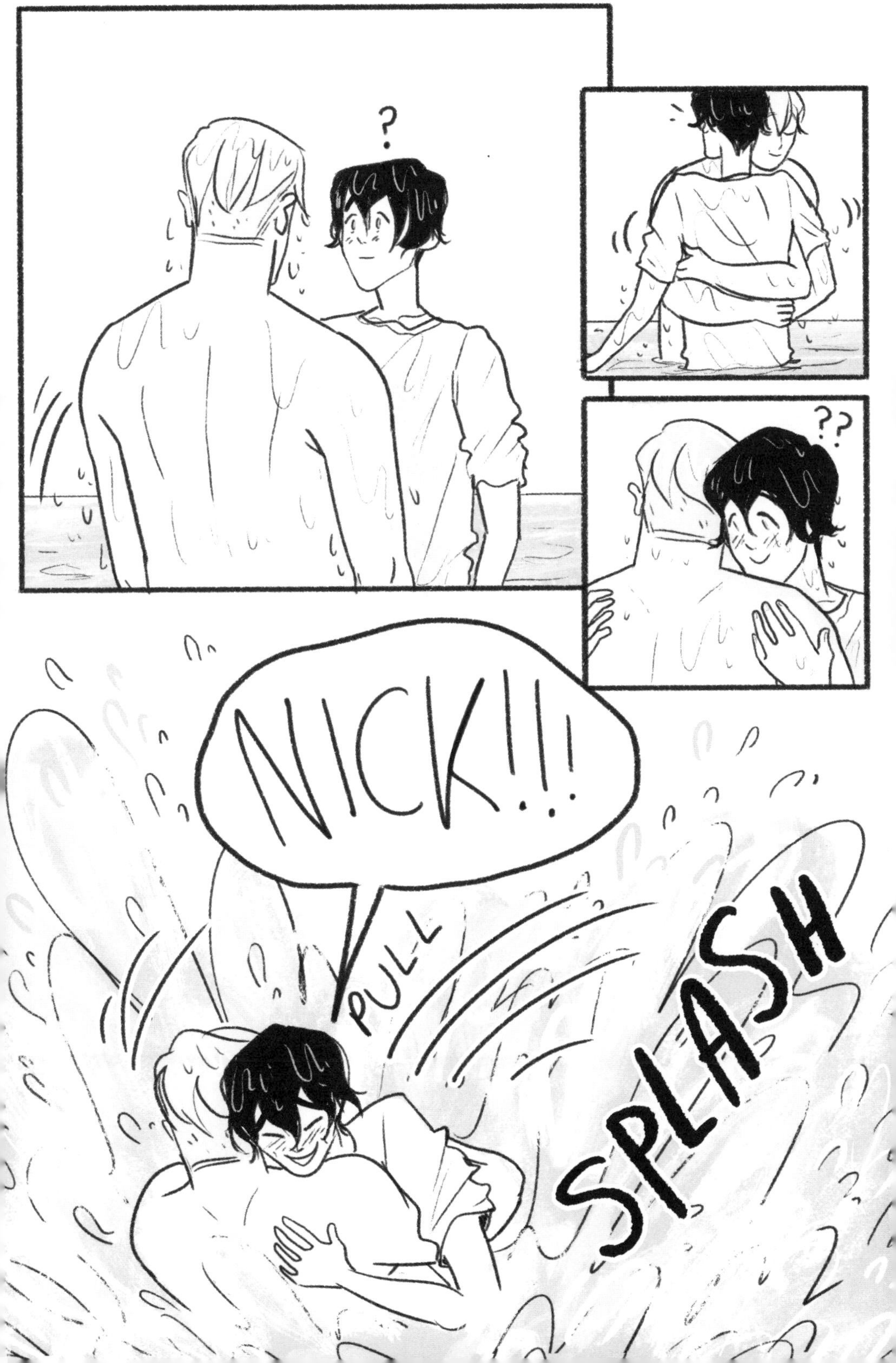
?
??
NICK!!!
PULL
SPLASH

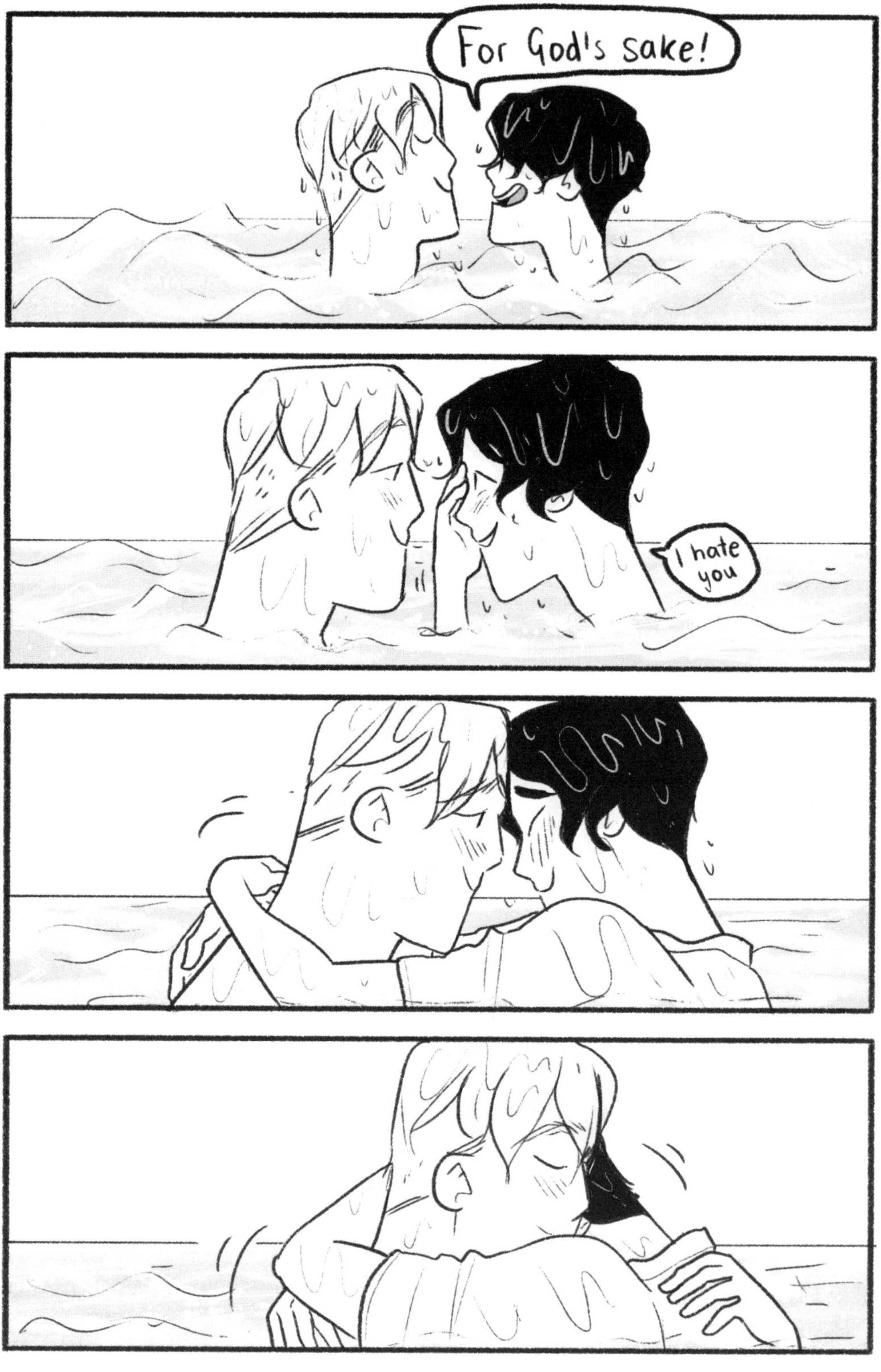
For God's sake!
I hate you

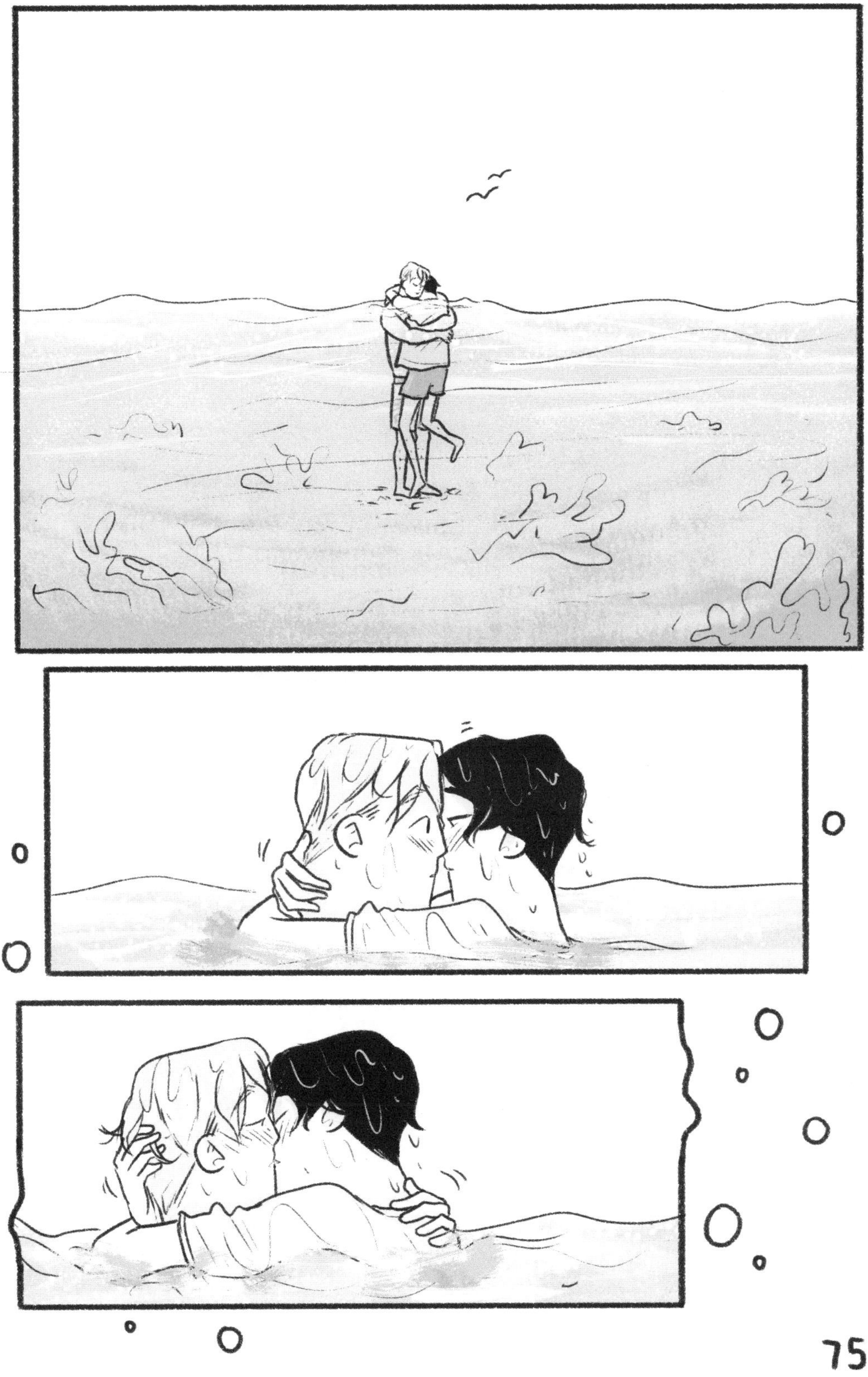

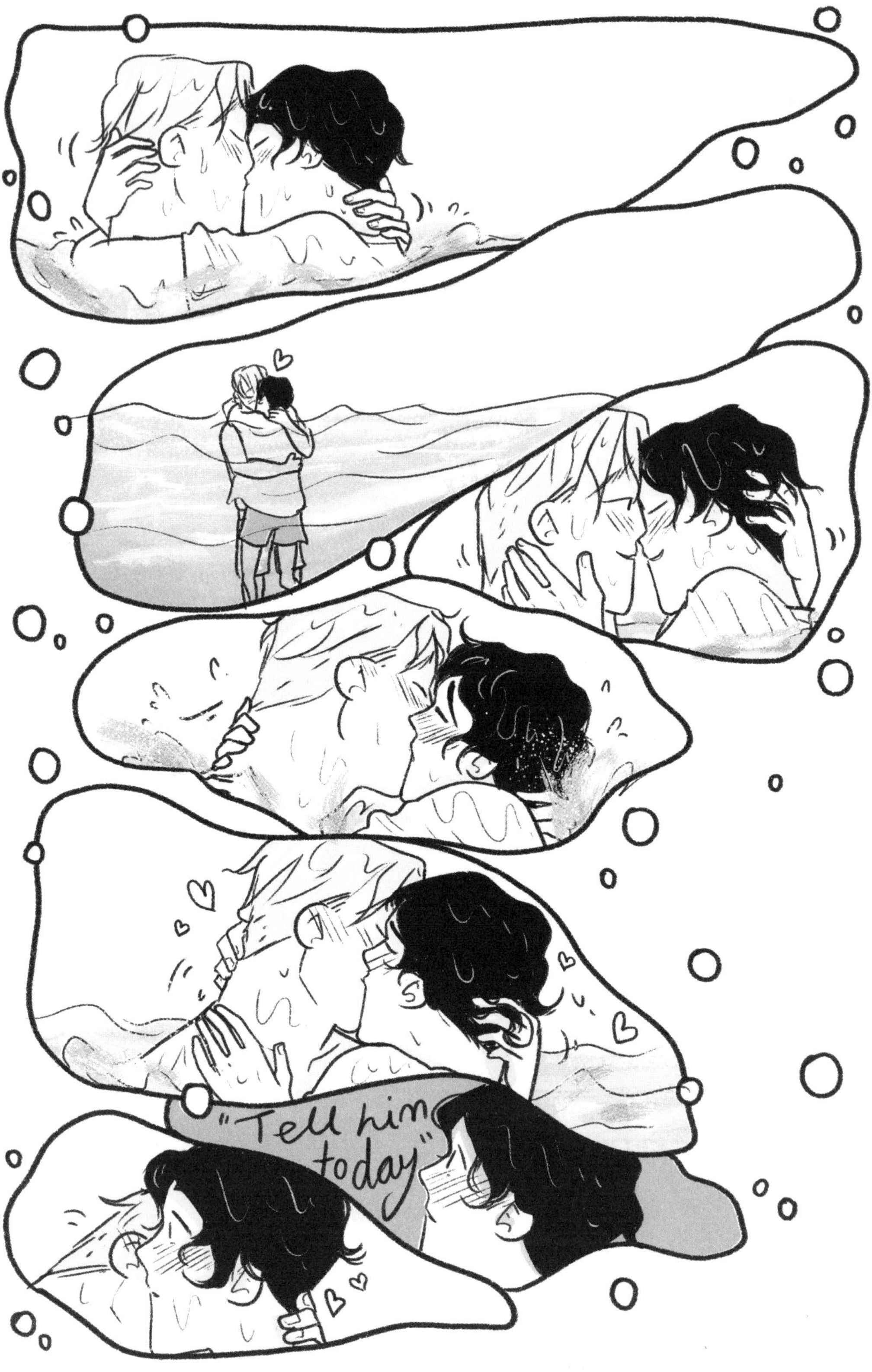
"Tell him today"

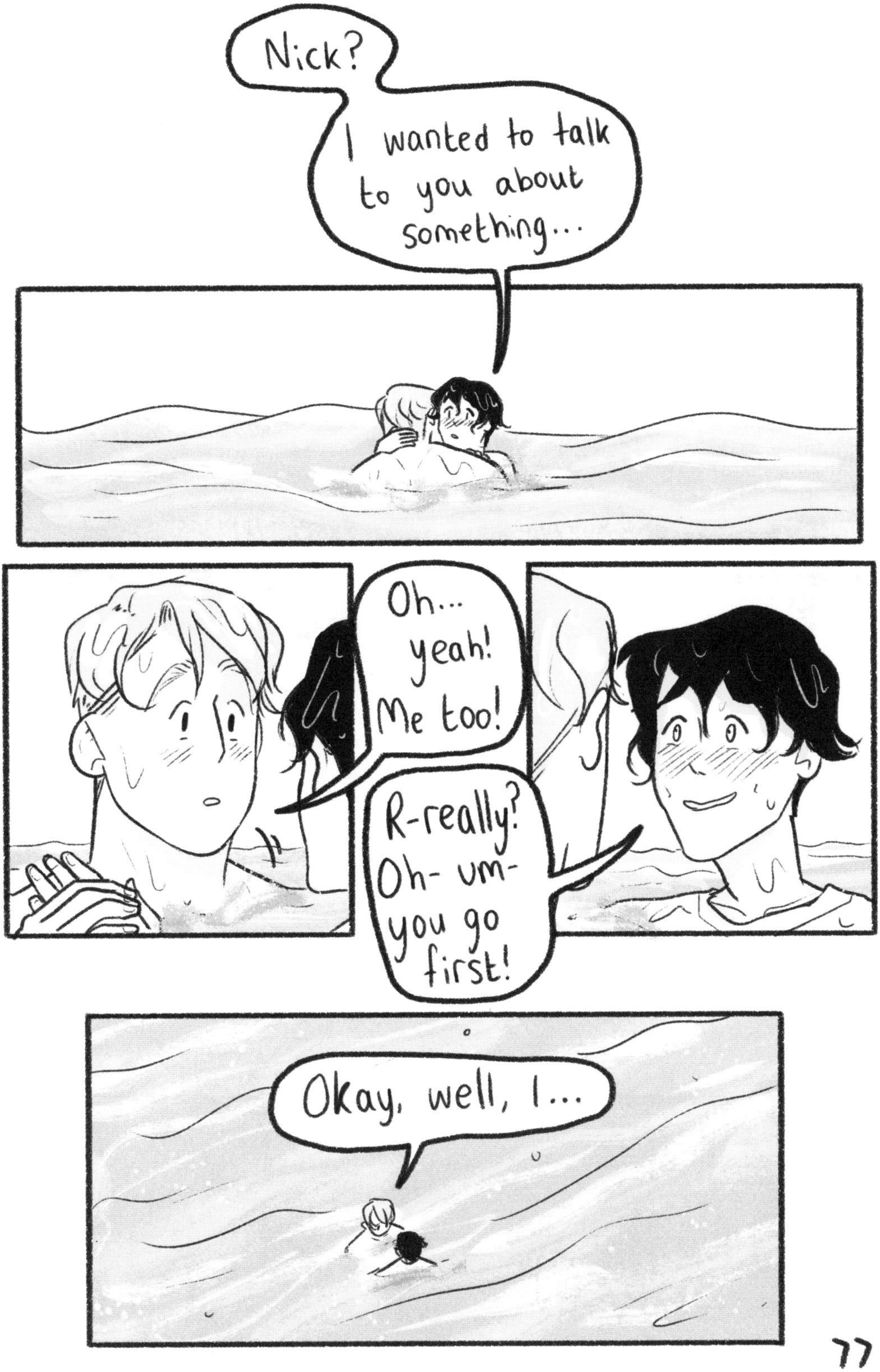
Nick?
I wanted to talk to you about something...
Oh... yeah! Me too!
R-really? Oh- um- you go first!
Okay, well, I...

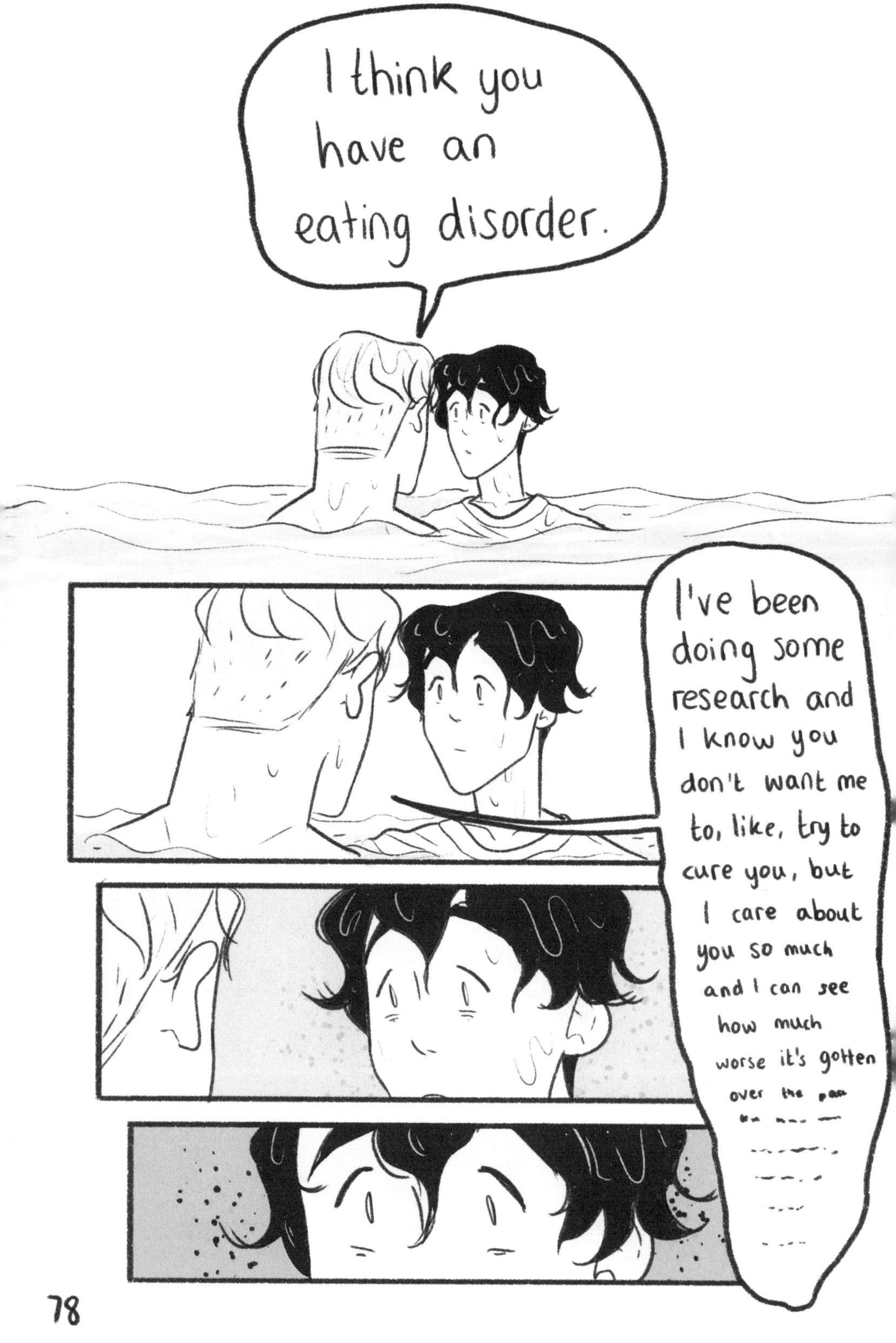
I think you have an eating disorder.
I've been doing some research and I know you don't want me to, like, try to cure you, but I care about you so much and I can see how much worse it's gotten

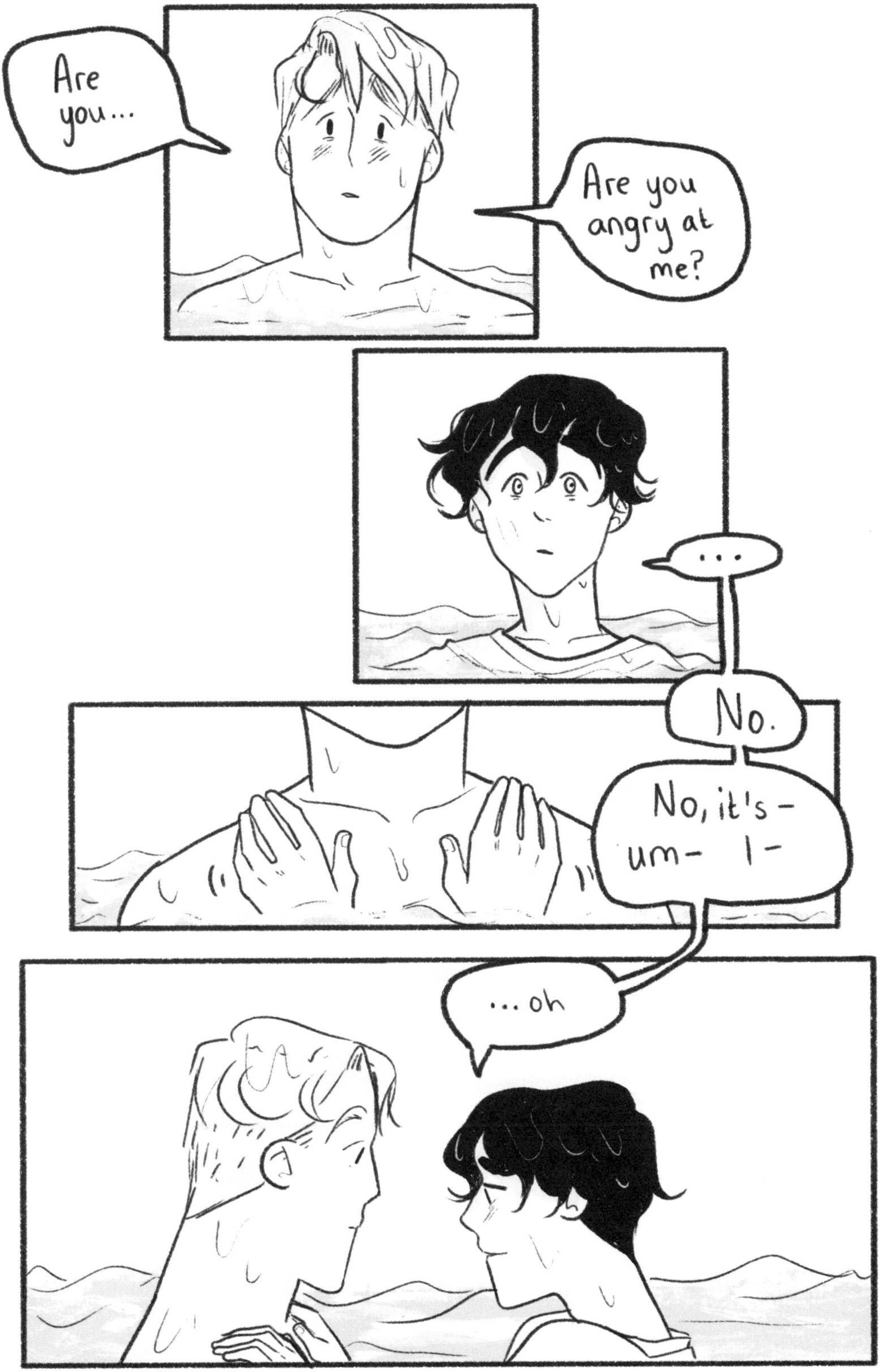
Are you...
Are you angry at me?
...
No.
No, it's - um- I-
...oh

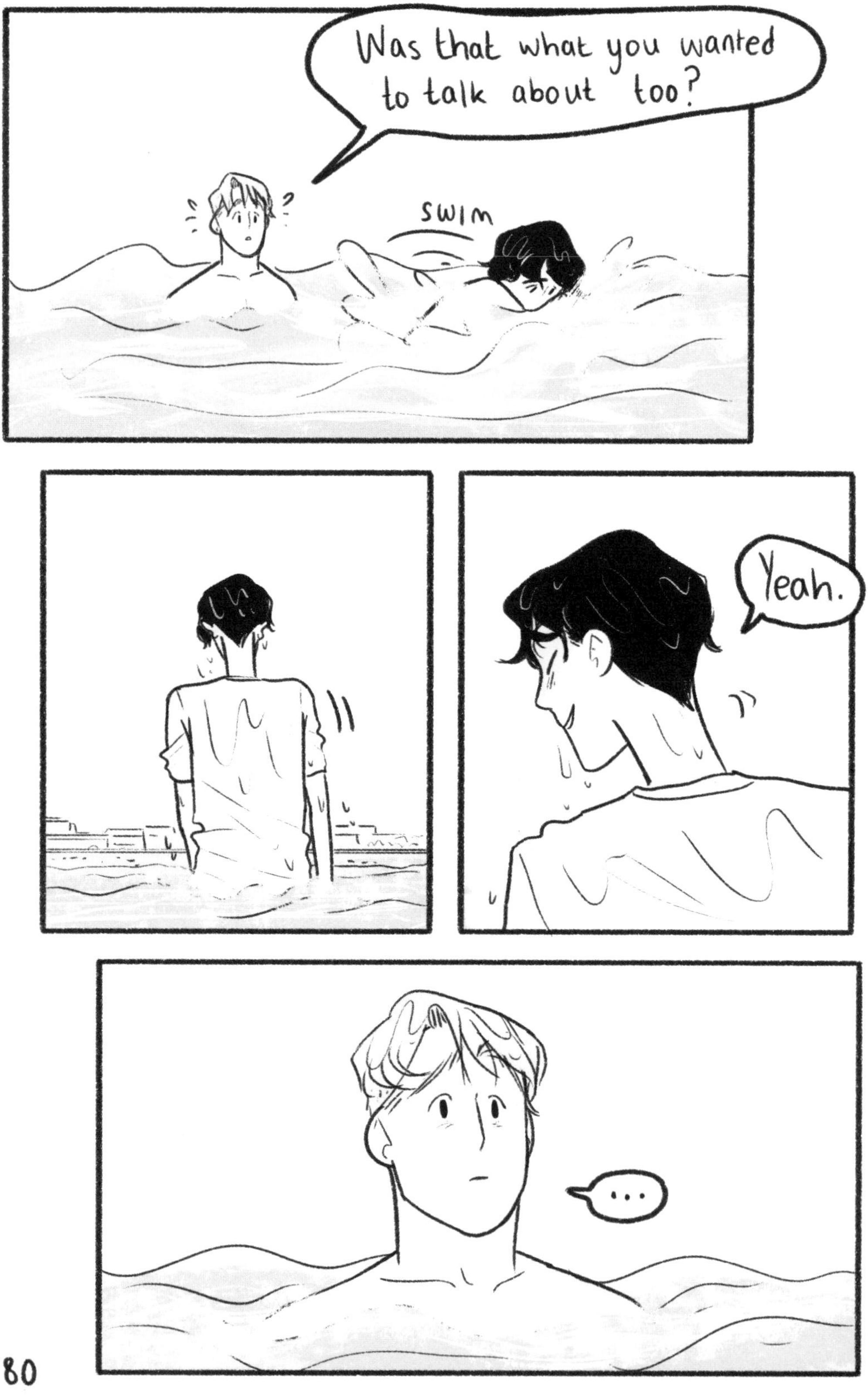
Was that what you wanted to talk about too?
SWIM
Yeah.
...

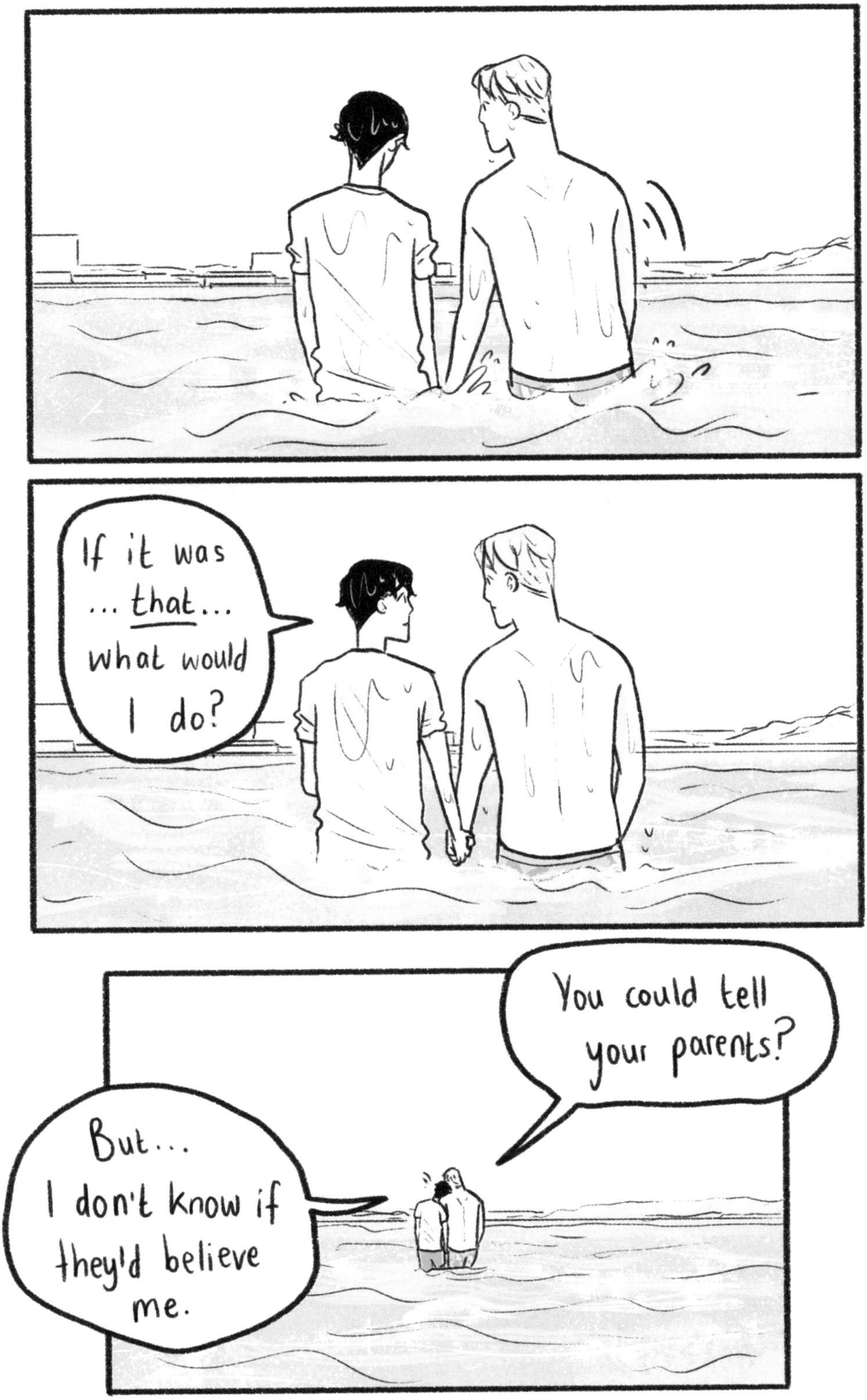
If it was ...that... what would I do?
You could tell your parents?
But... I don't know if they'd believe me.

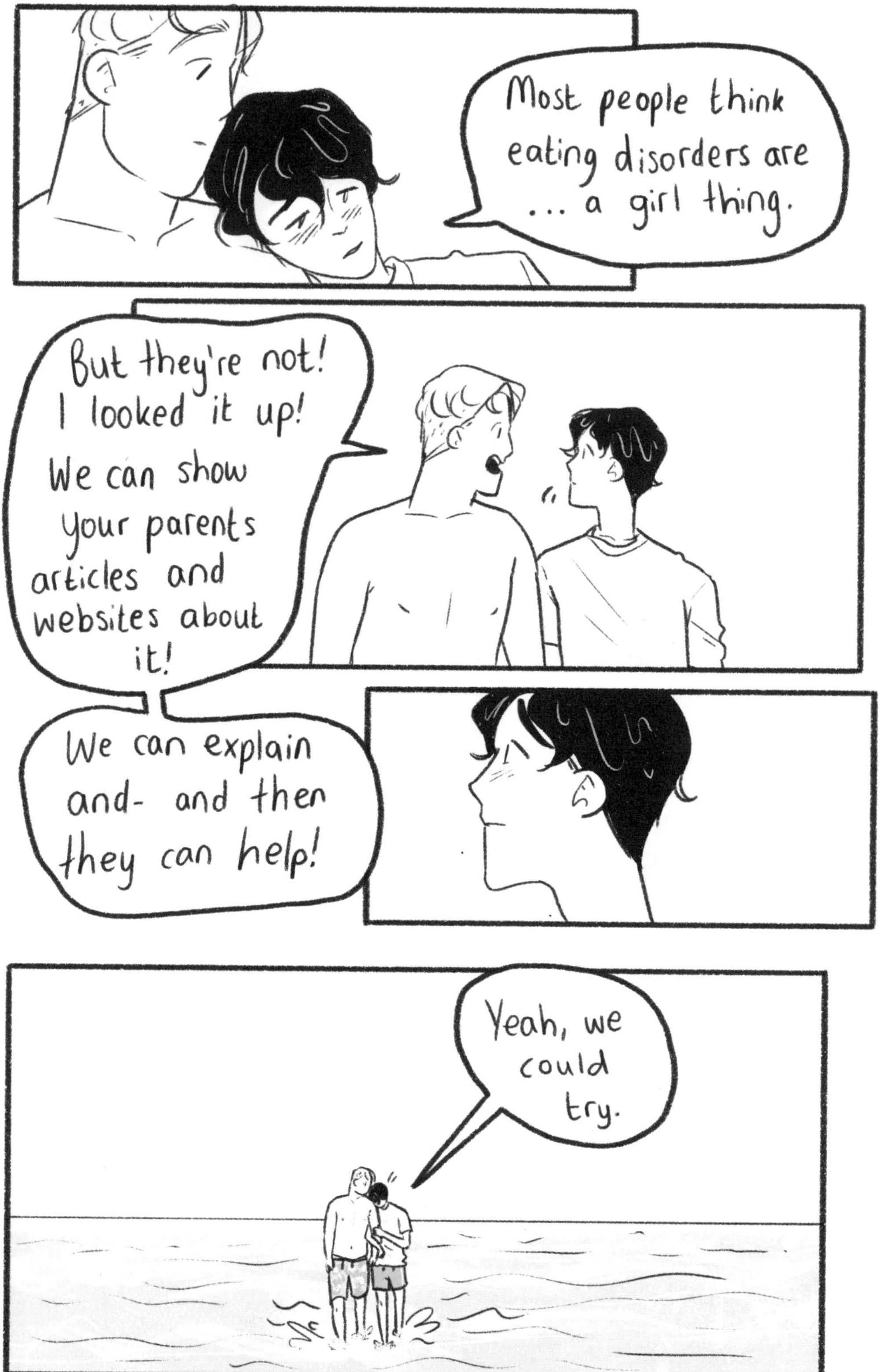
Most people think eating disorders are ... a girl thing.
But they're not! I looked it up! We can show your parents articles and websites about it!
We can explain and- and then they can help!
Yeah, we could try.

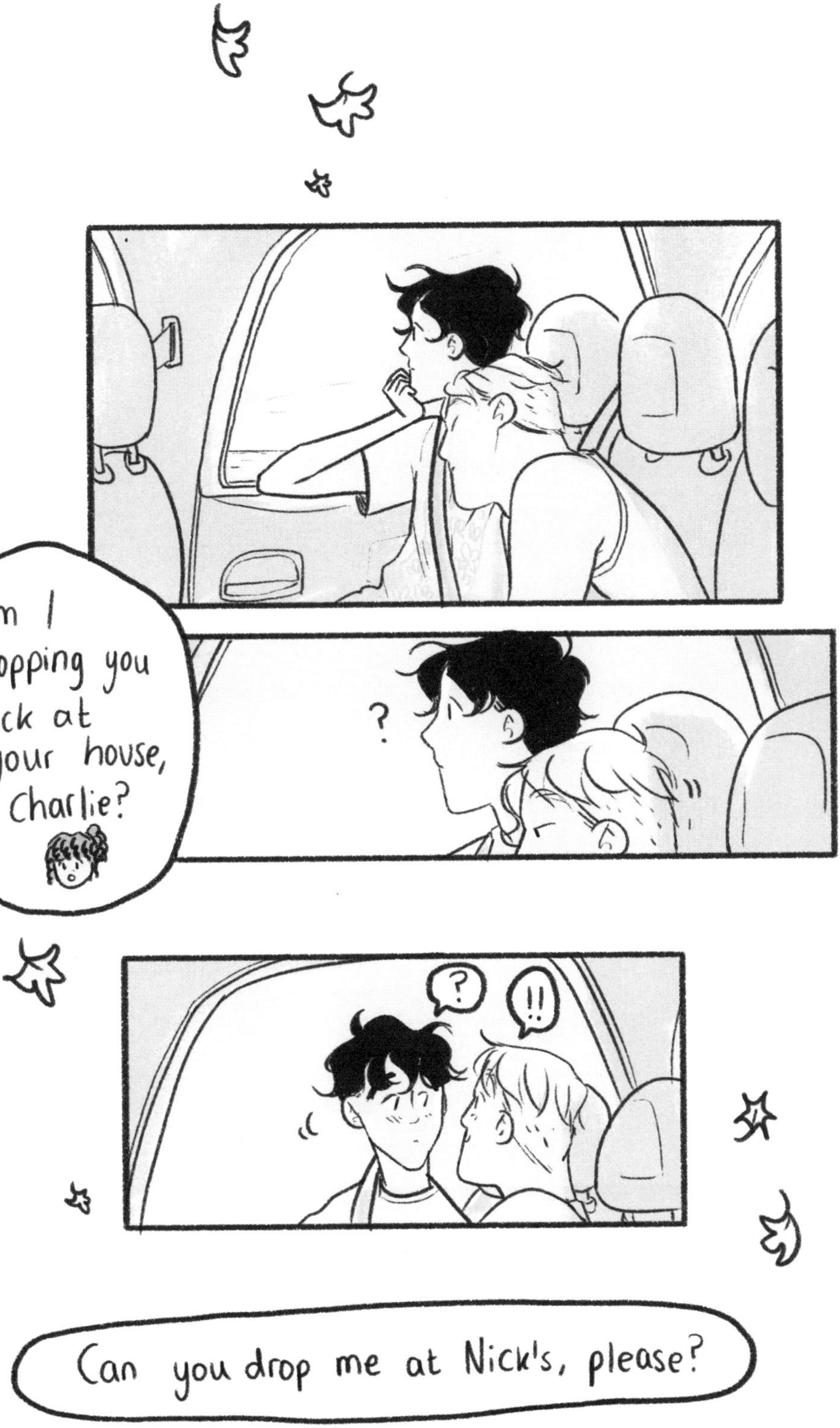
Am I dropping you back at your house, Charlie?
?
?
!!
Can you drop me at Nick's, please?

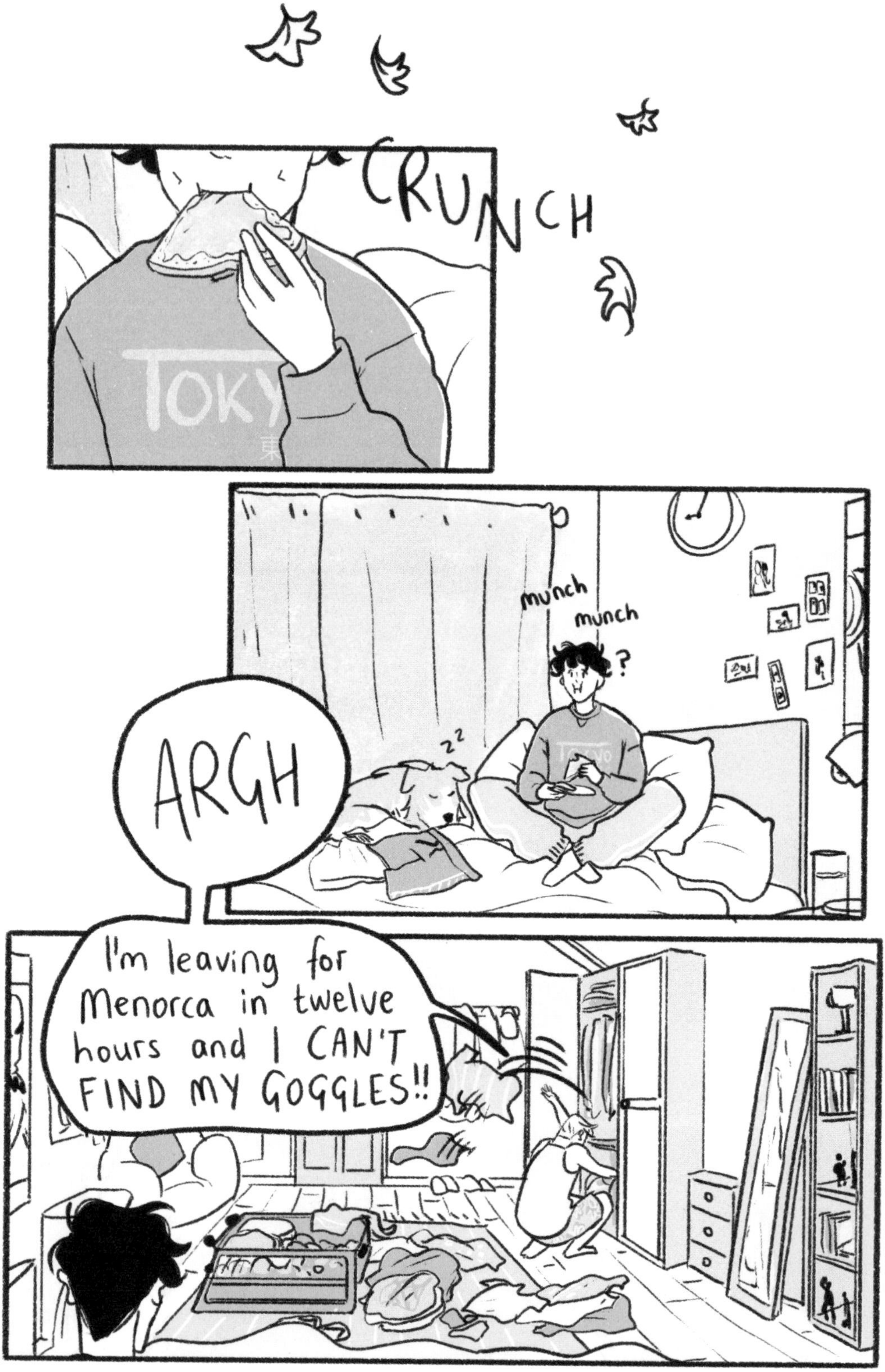
CRUNCH
munch
munch
?
ARGH
I'm leaving for Menorca in twelve hours and I CAN'T FIND MY GOGGLES!!

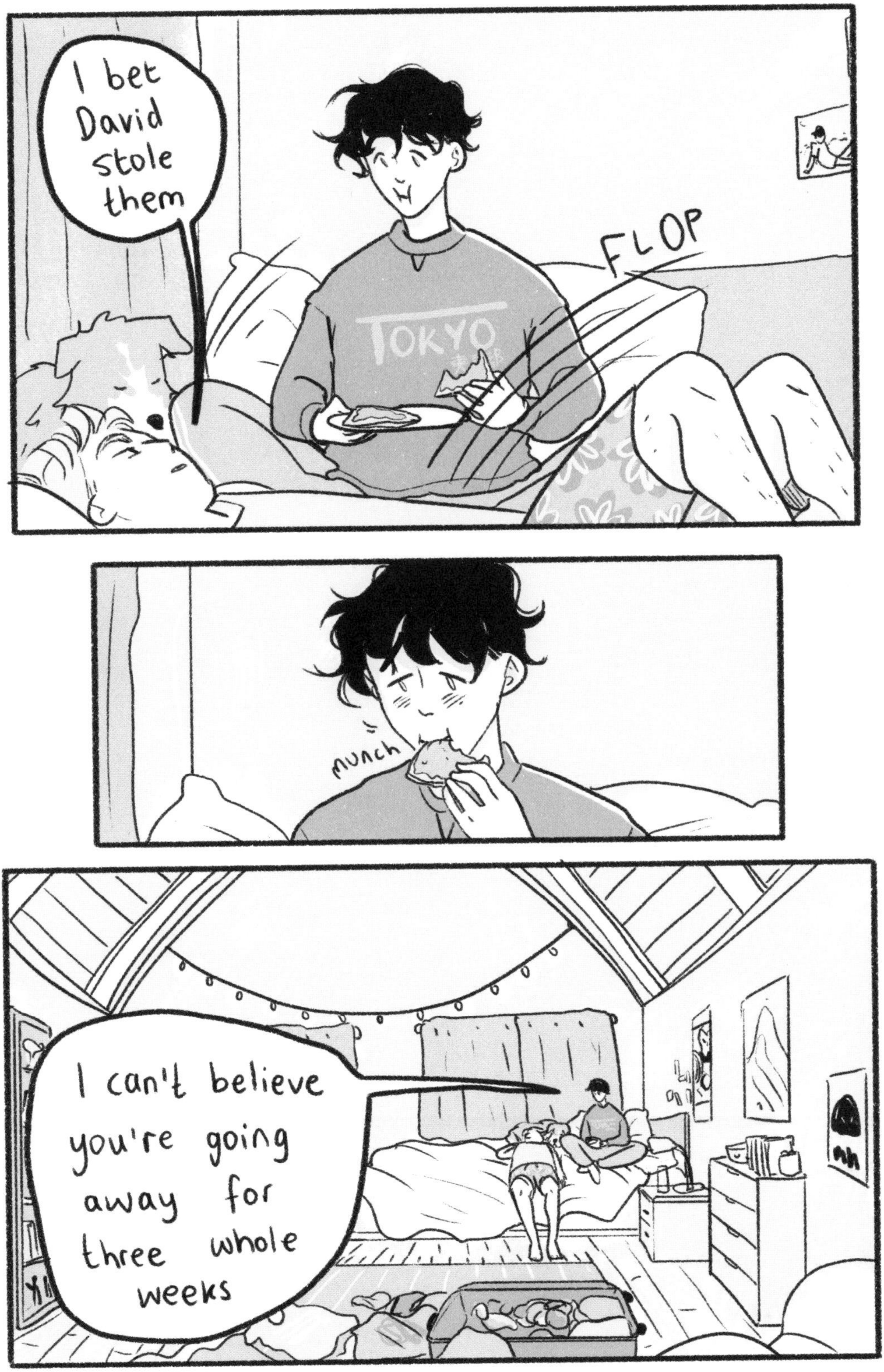
I bet David stole them
FLOP
TOKYO
munch
I can't believe you're going away for three whole weeks

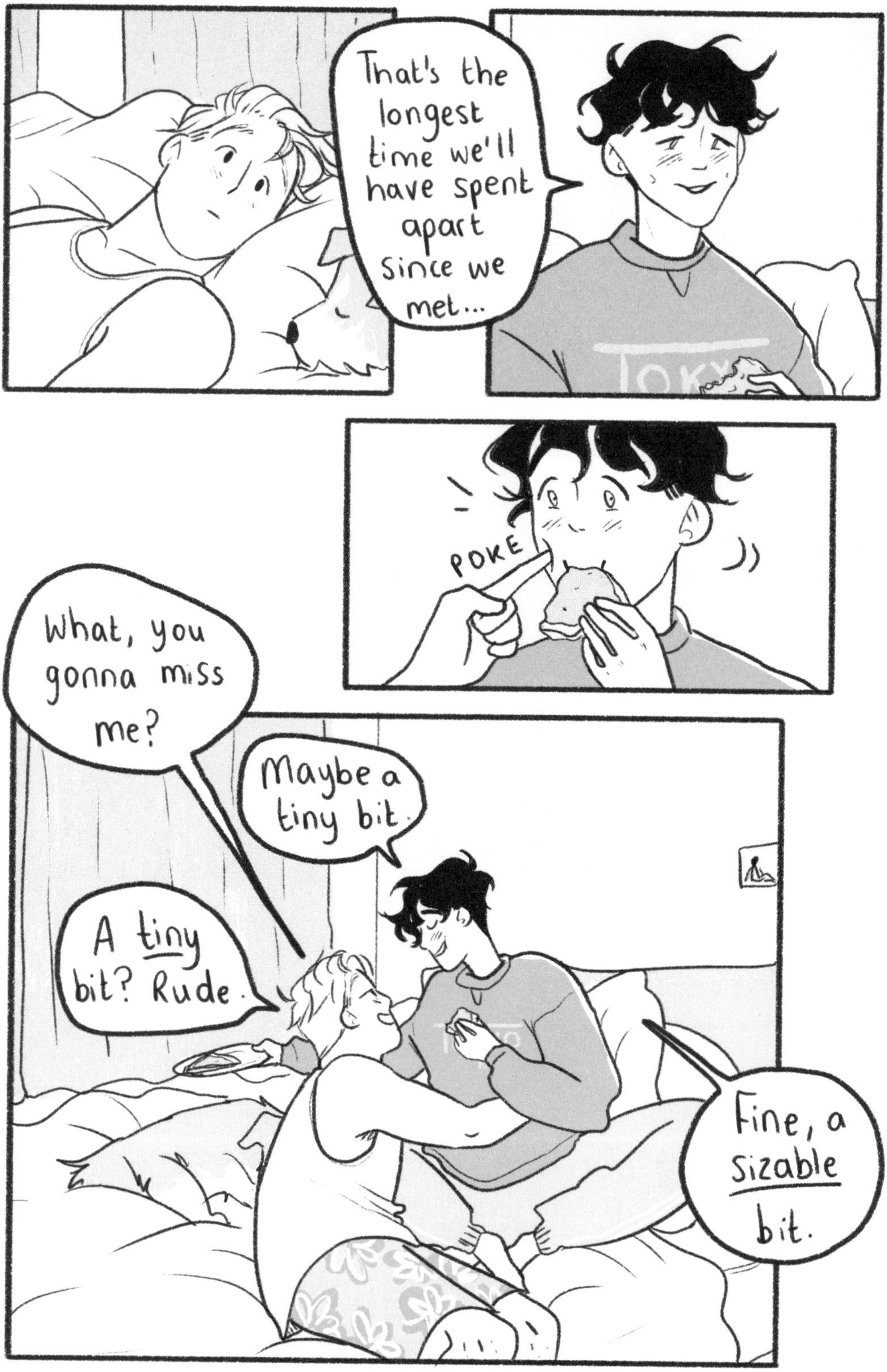
That's the longest time we'll have spent apart since we met...
POKE
What, you gonna miss me?
Maybe a tiny bit.
A tiny bit? Rude.
Fine, a sizable bit.

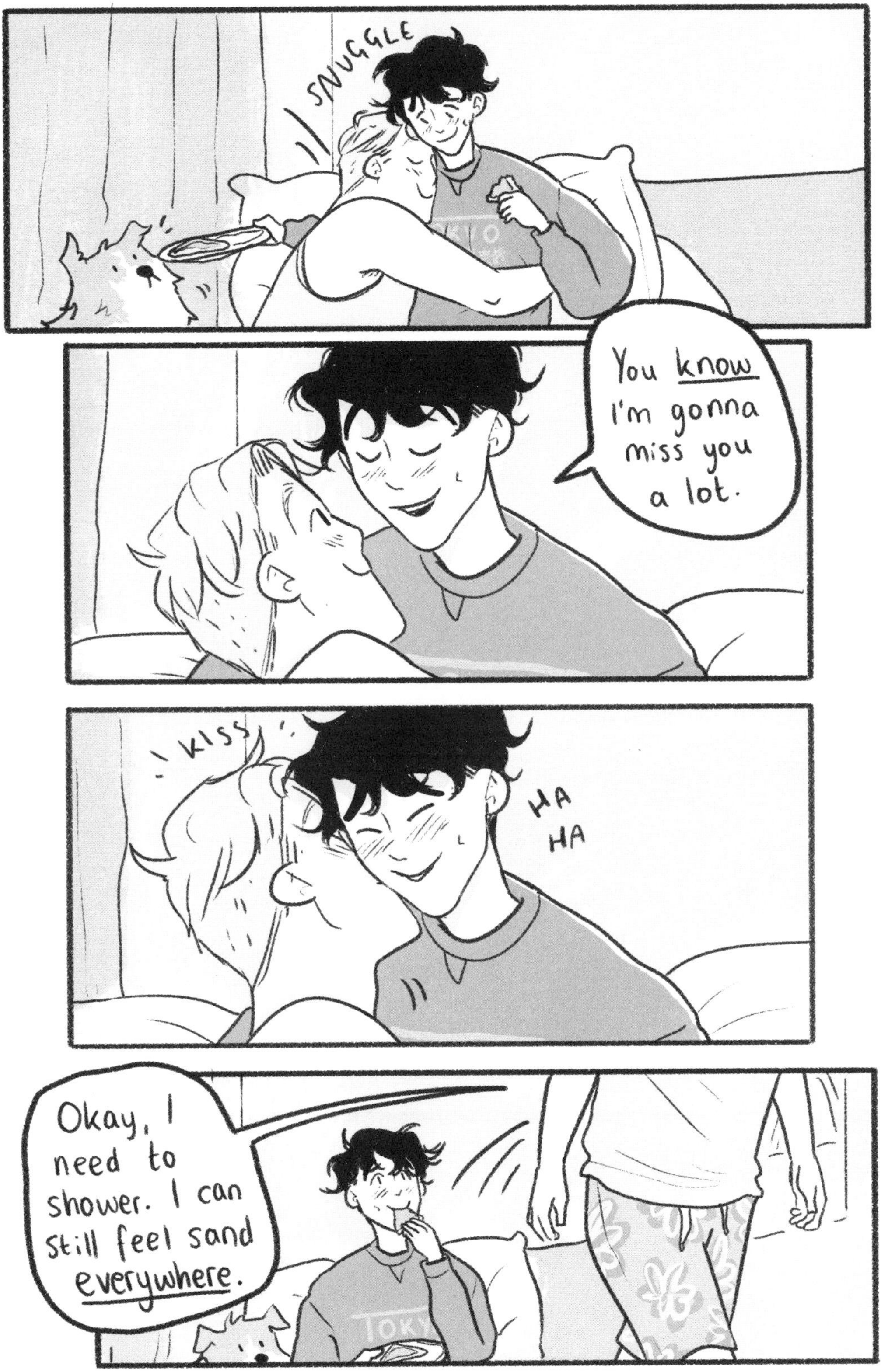
SNUGGLE
You know I'm gonna miss you a lot.
KISS
HA HA
Okay, I need to shower. I can still feel sand everywhere.

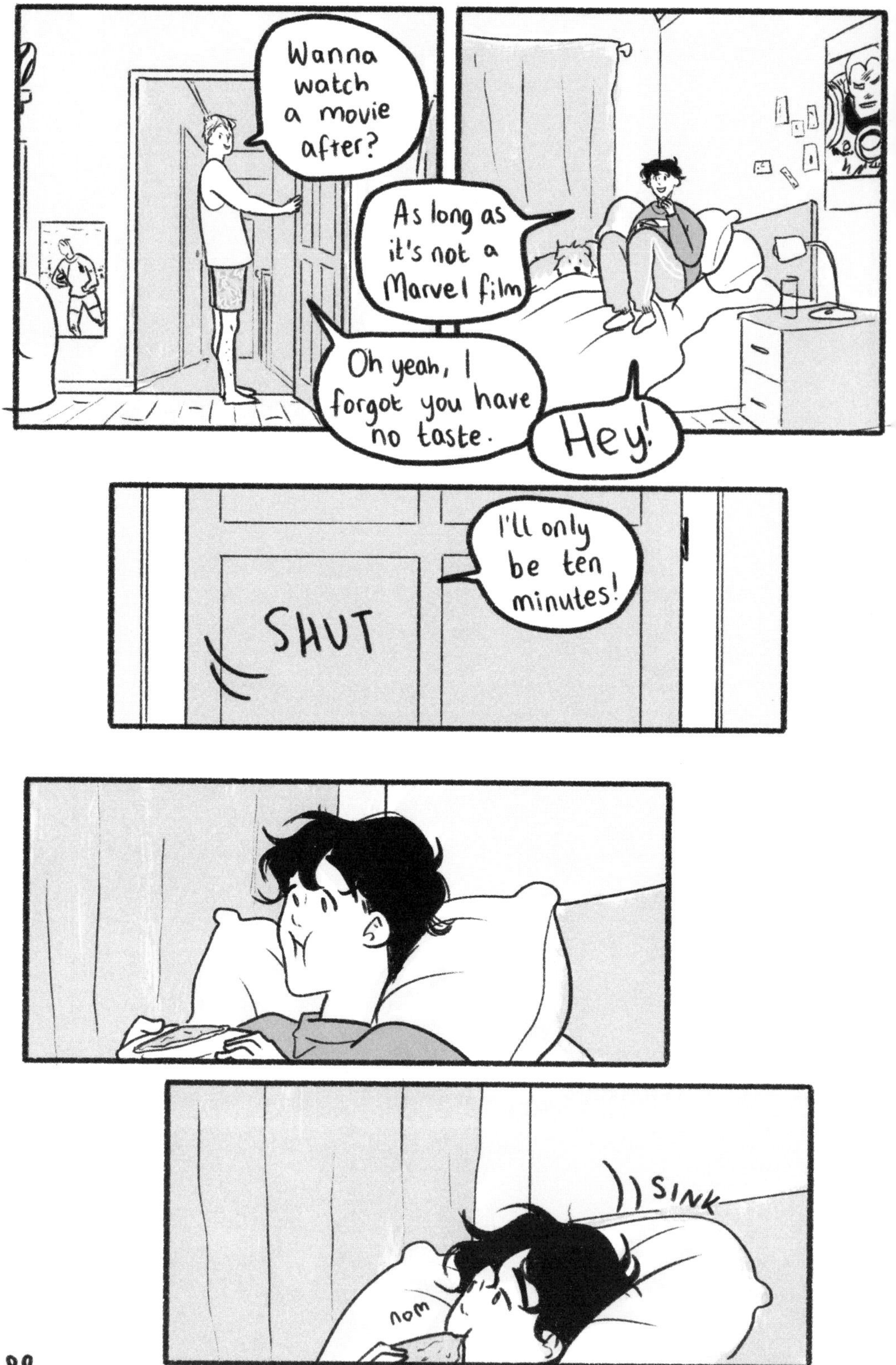

Wanna watch a movie after?
As long as it's not a Marvel film
Oh yeah, I forgot you have no taste.
Hey!
SHUT
I'll only be ten minutes!
SINK
nom

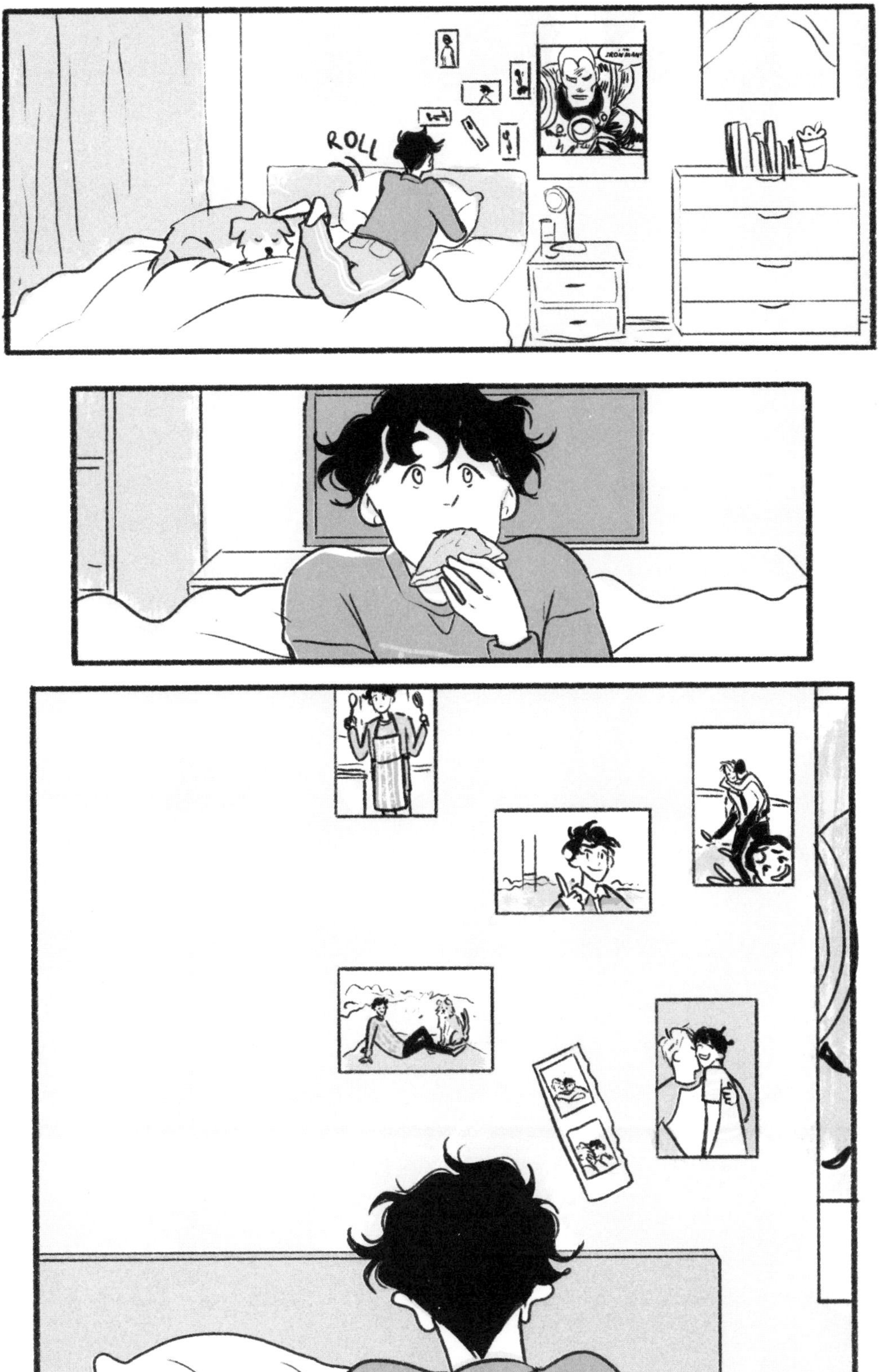
ROLL

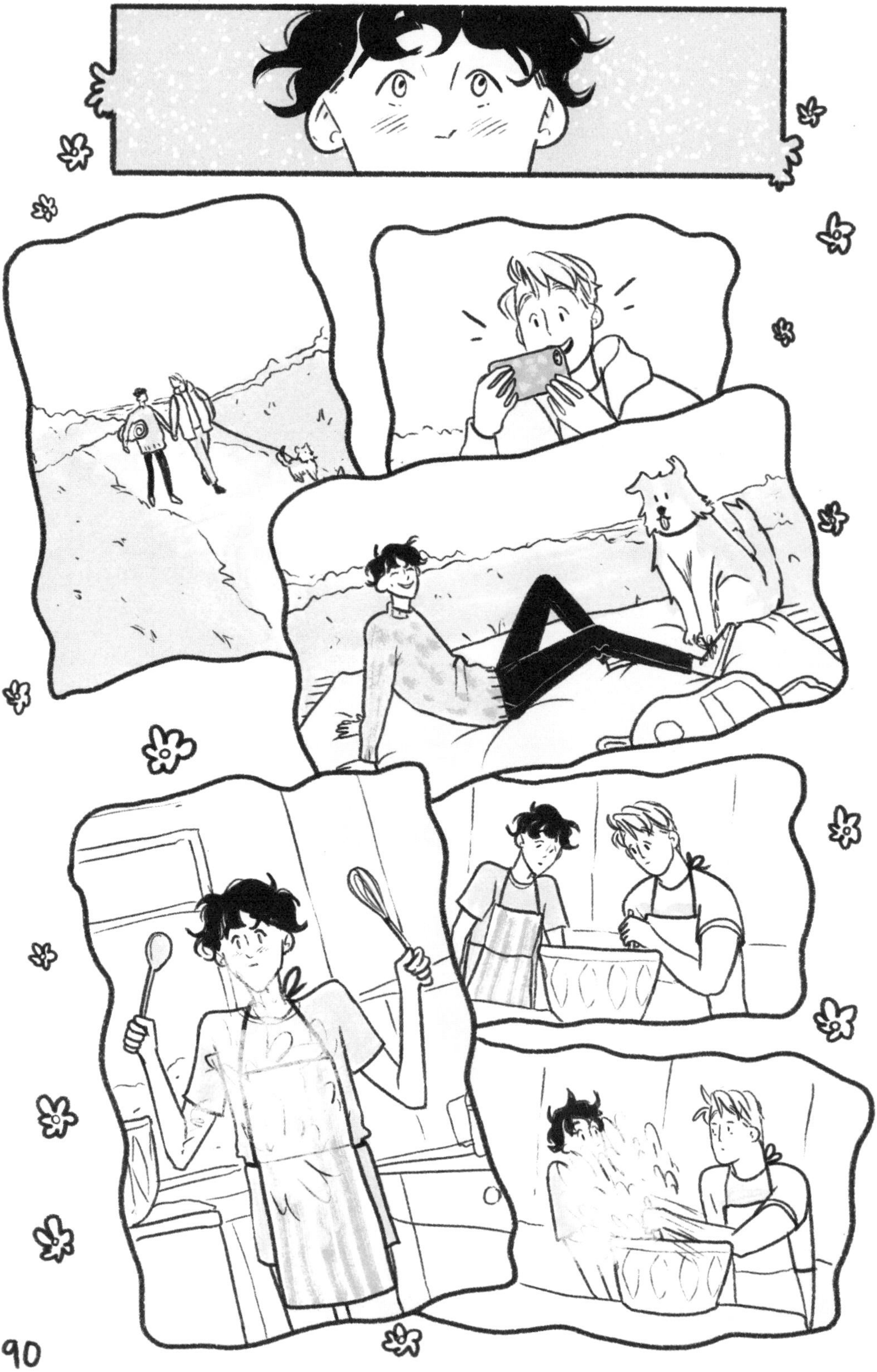

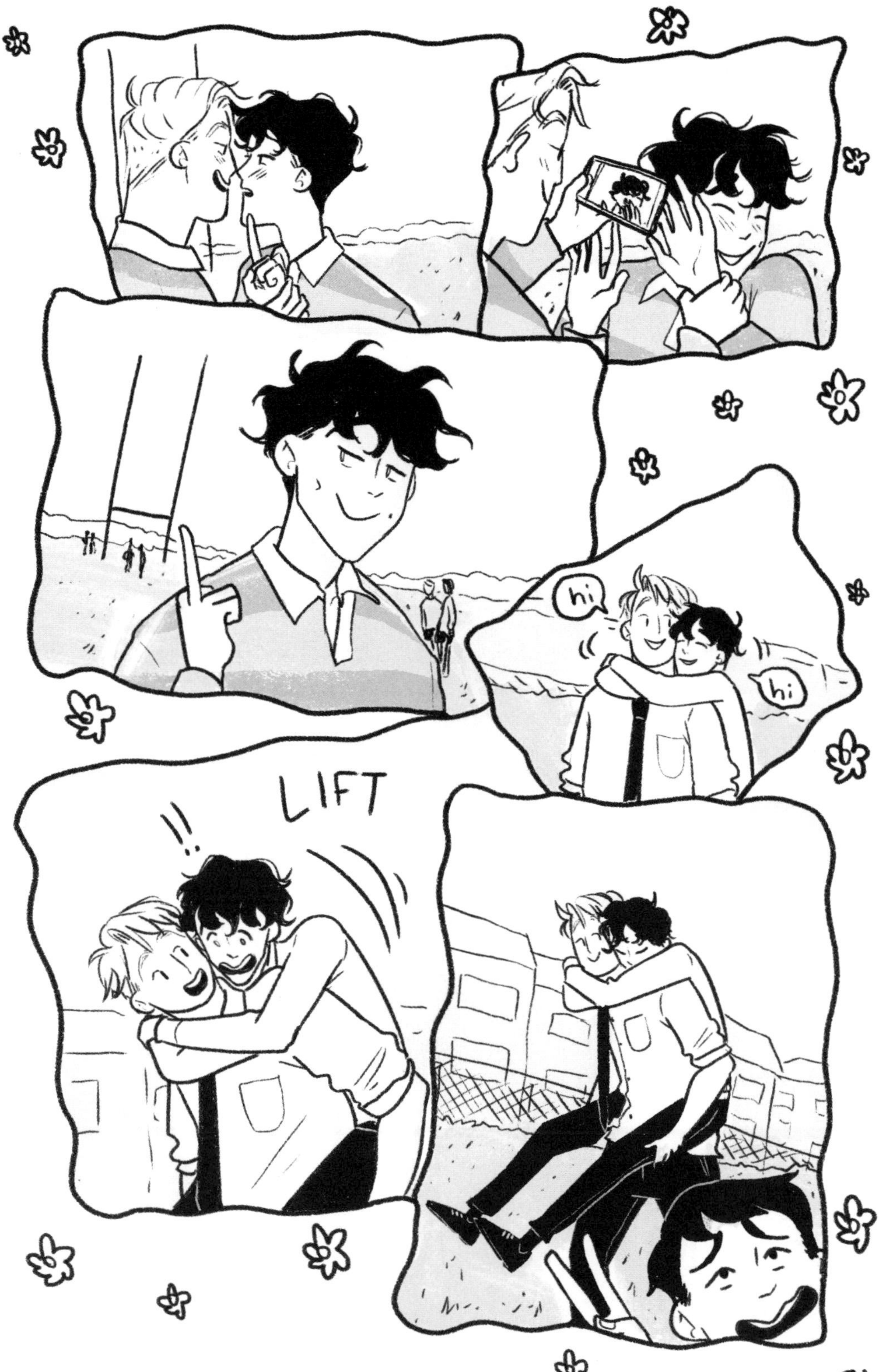
hi
hi
!!
LIFT

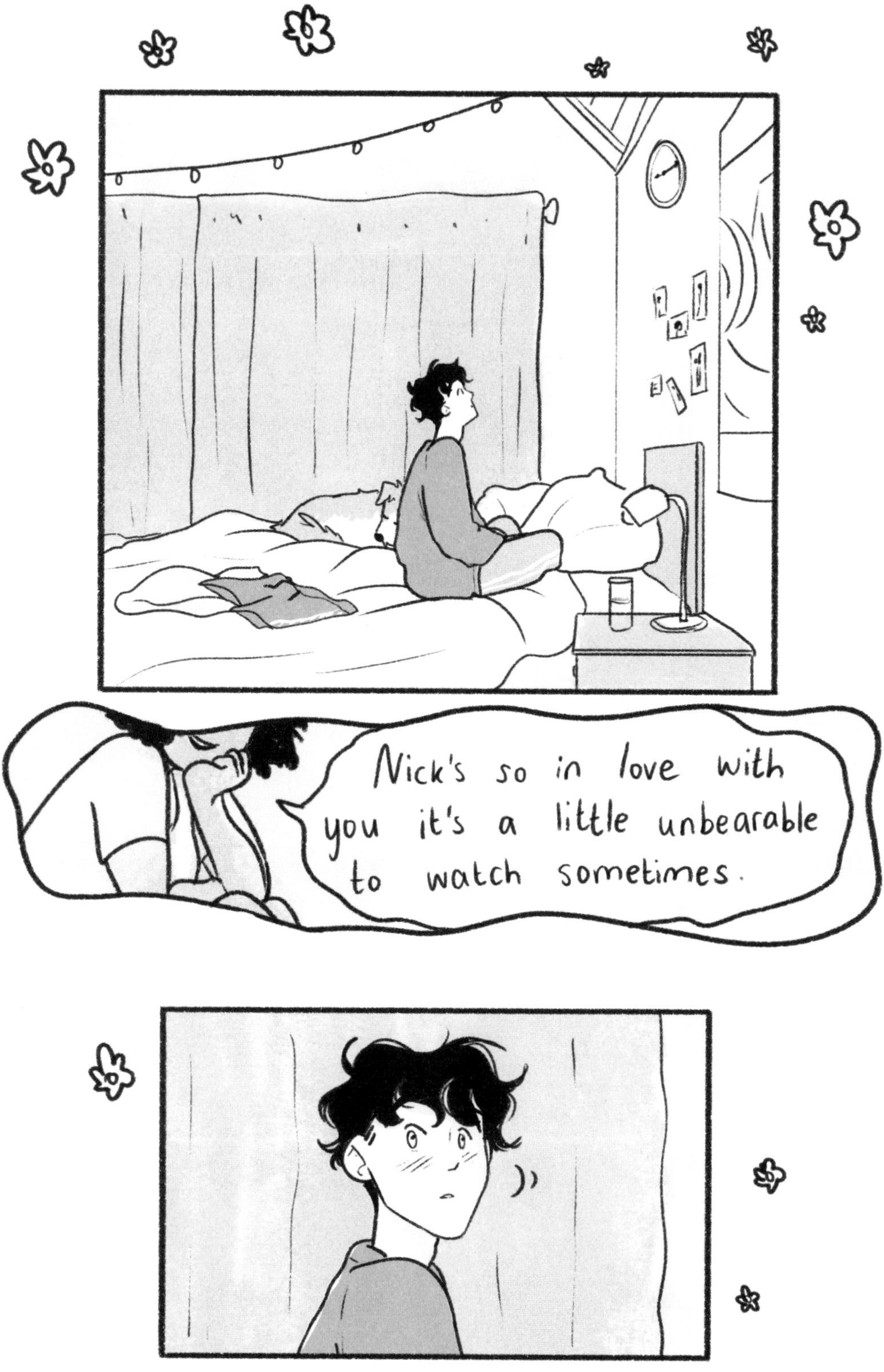
Nick's so in love with you it's a little unbearable to watch sometimes.

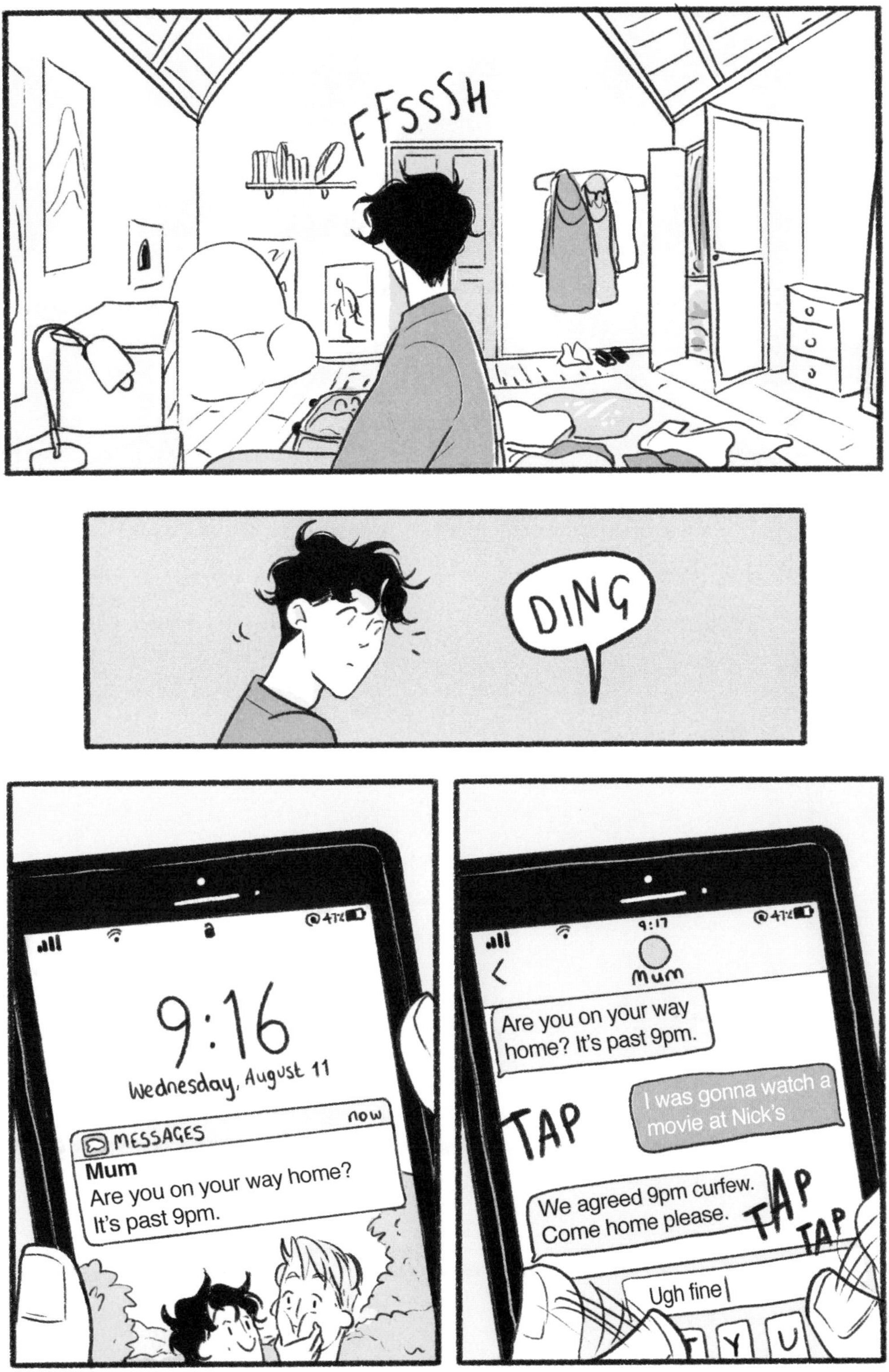
FFSSSH
DING
9:16
Wednesday, August 11
MESSAGES
now
Mum
Are you on your way home? It's past 9pm.
9:17
Mum
Are you on your way home? It's past 9pm.
TAP
I was gonna watch a movie at Nick's
We agreed 9pm curfew. Come home please.
TAP
TAP
Ugh fine

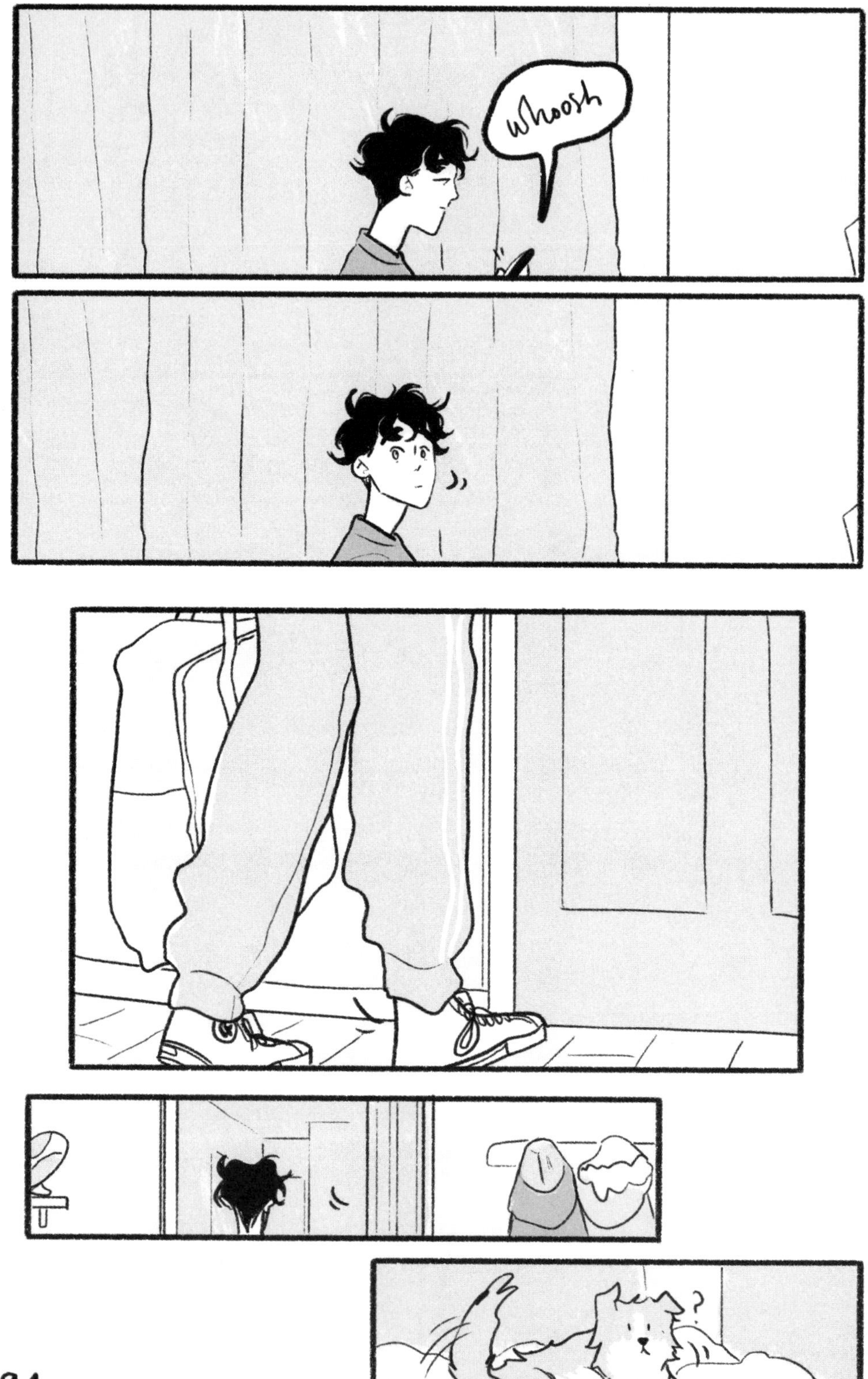
whoosh

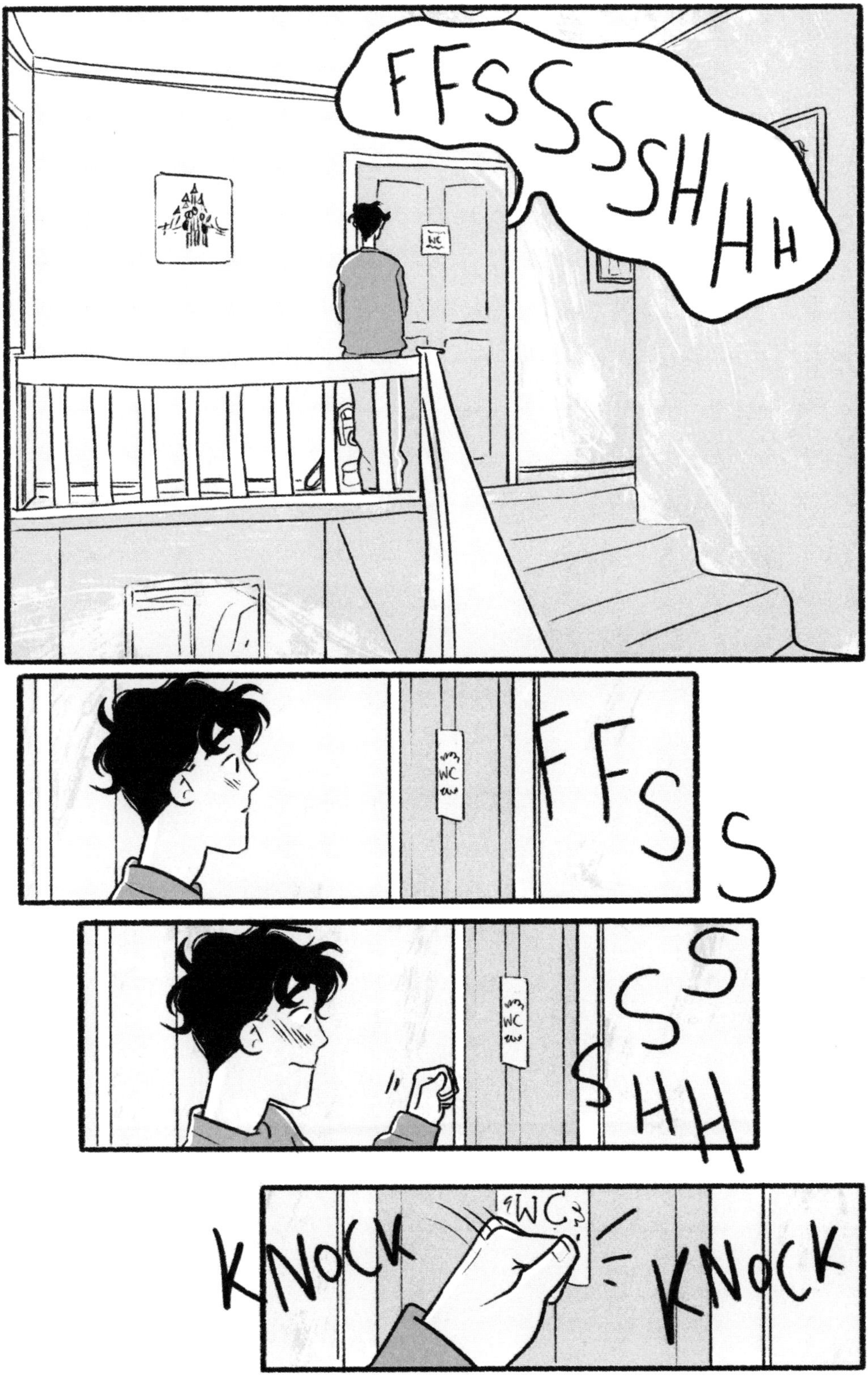

FFSSSSHHH
WC
WC
FFSSS
WC
SSSHH
WC
KNOCK
KNOCK

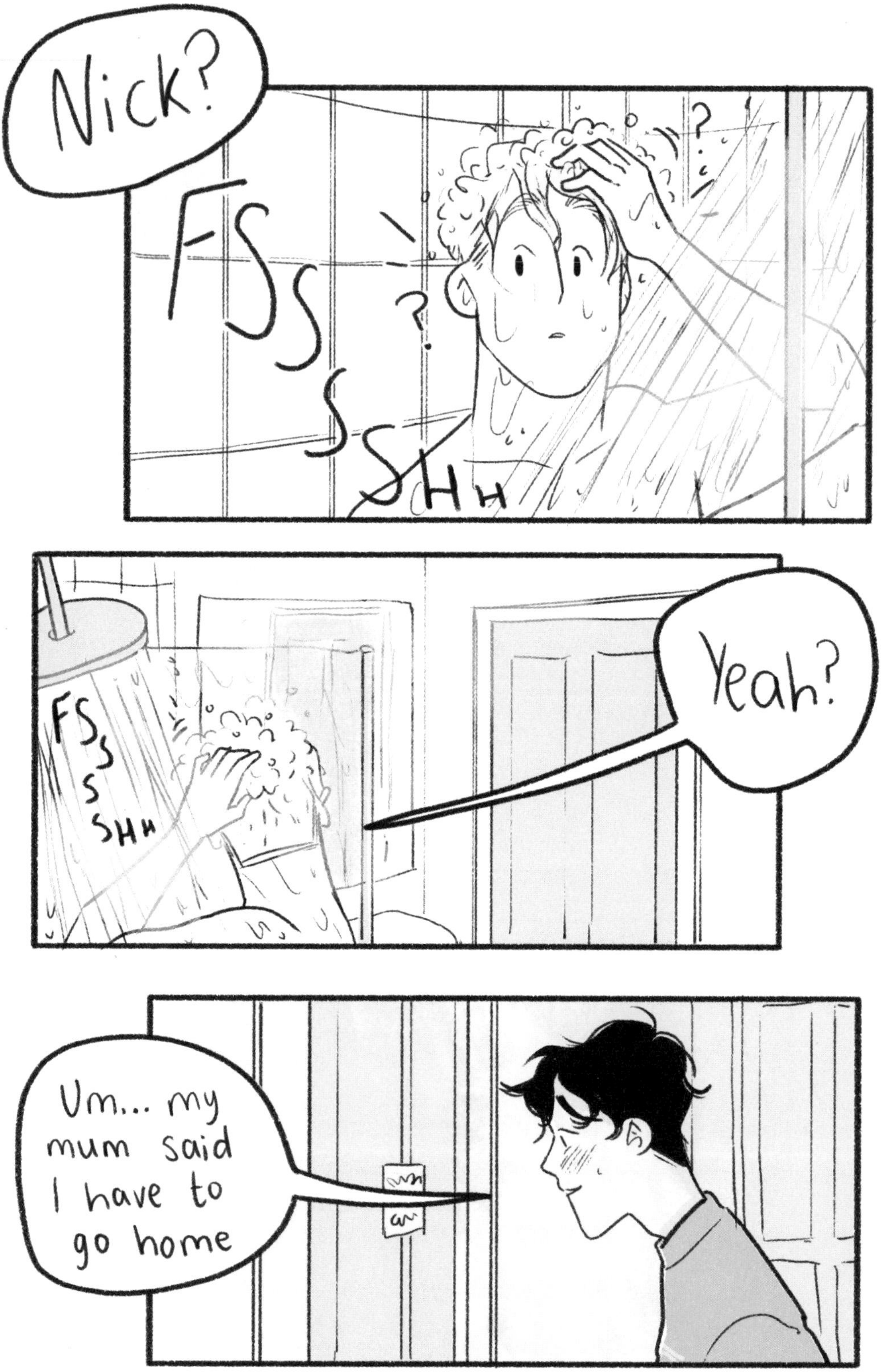
Nick?
FSSSSHH
Yeah?
FSSSSHH
Um... my mum said I have to go home

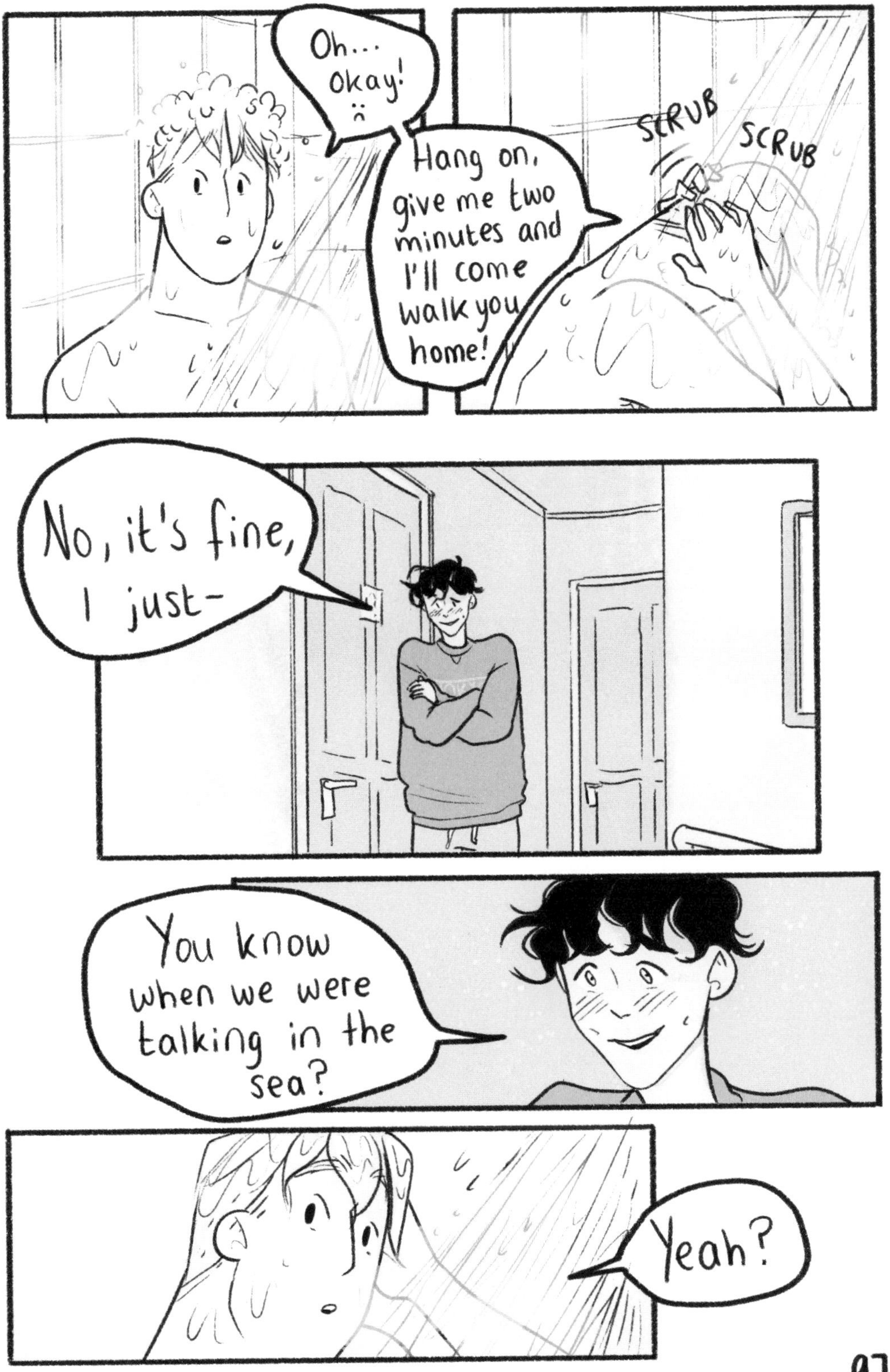
Oh... okay! :(
Hang on, give me two minutes and I'll come walk you home!
SCRUB SCRUB
No, it's fine, I just-
You know when we were talking in the sea?
Yeah?

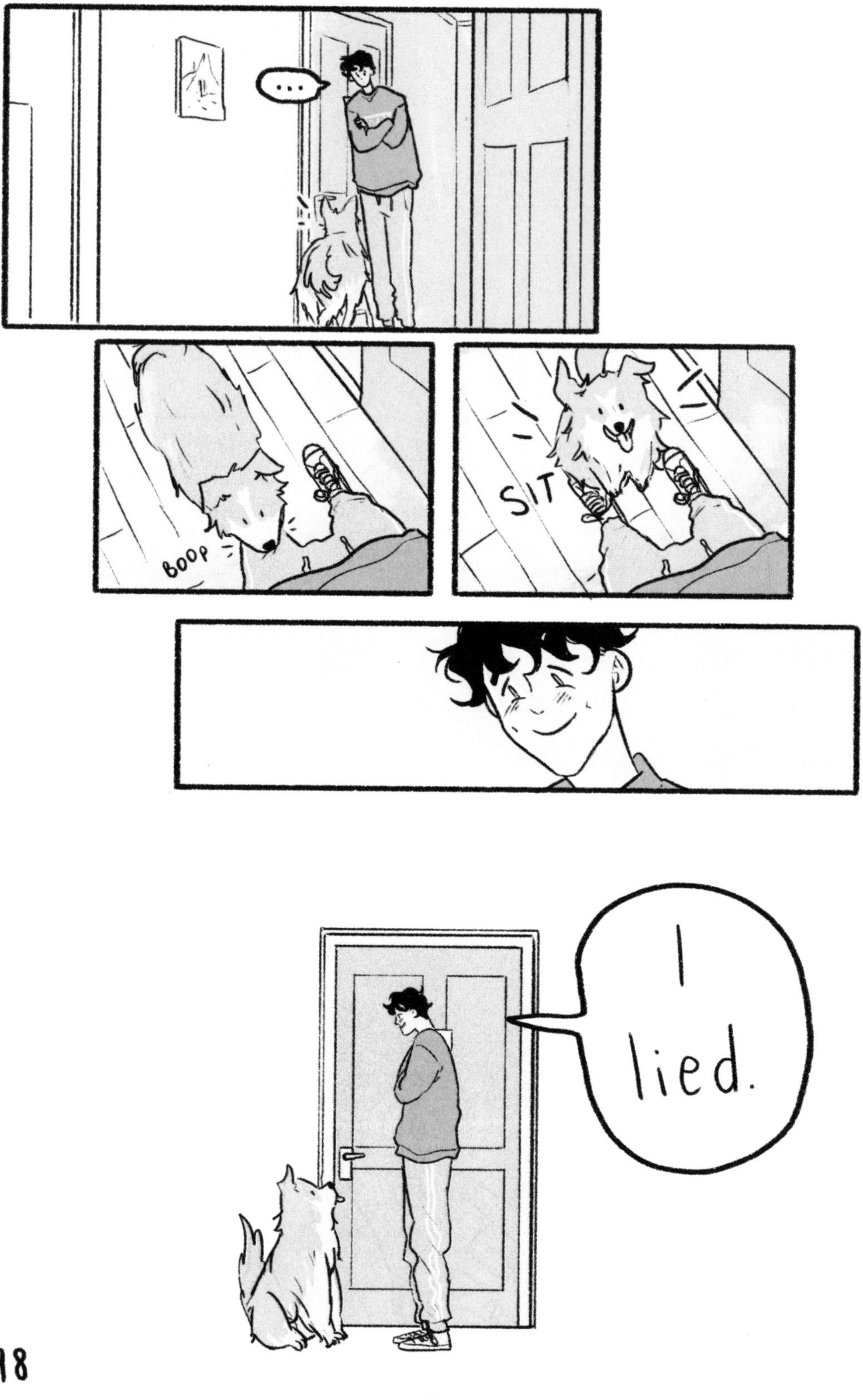
...
BOOP
SIT
I lied.

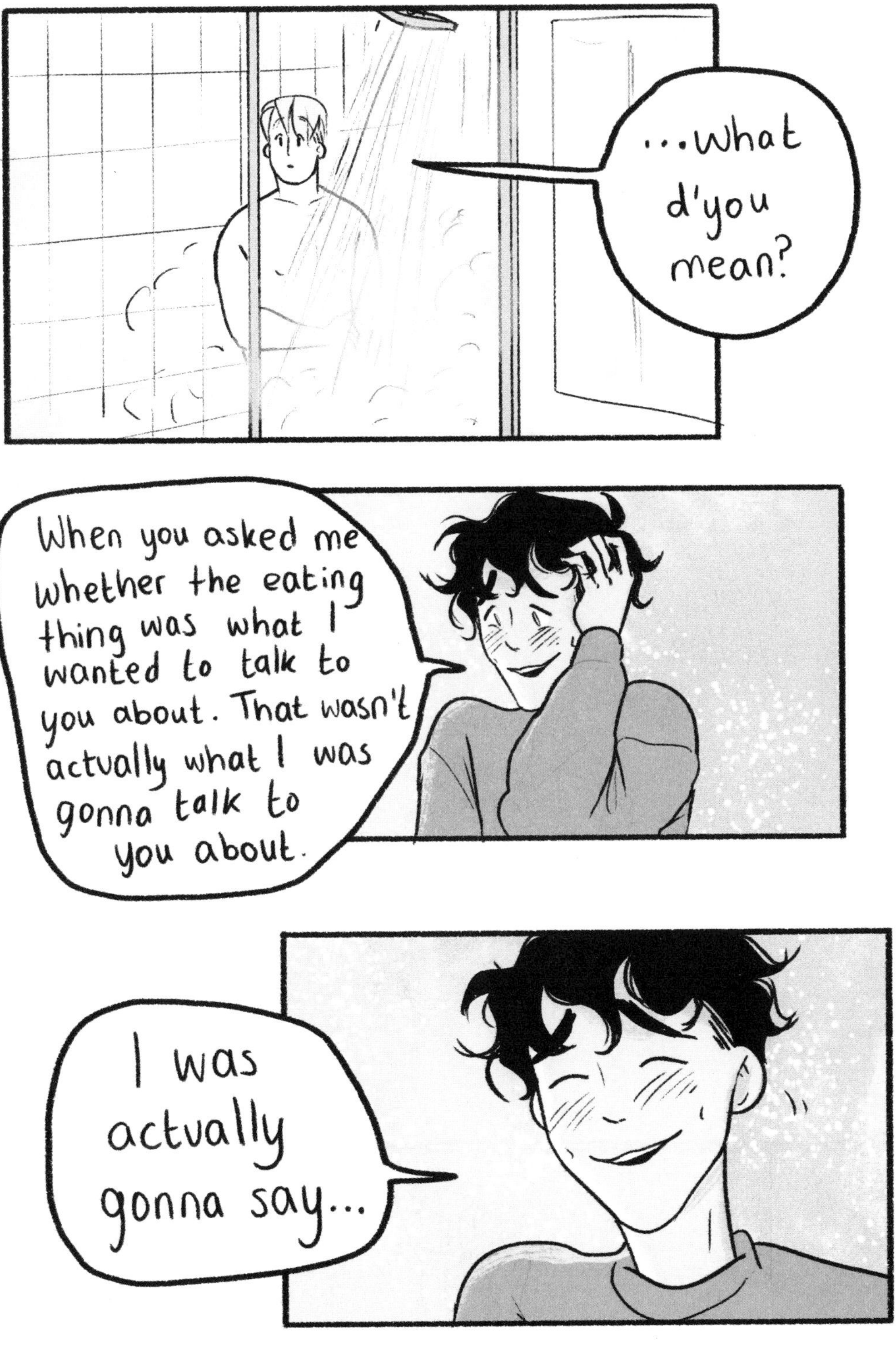
...what d'you mean?
When you asked me whether the eating thing was what I wanted to talk to you about. That wasn't actually what I was gonna talk to you about.
I was actually gonna say...

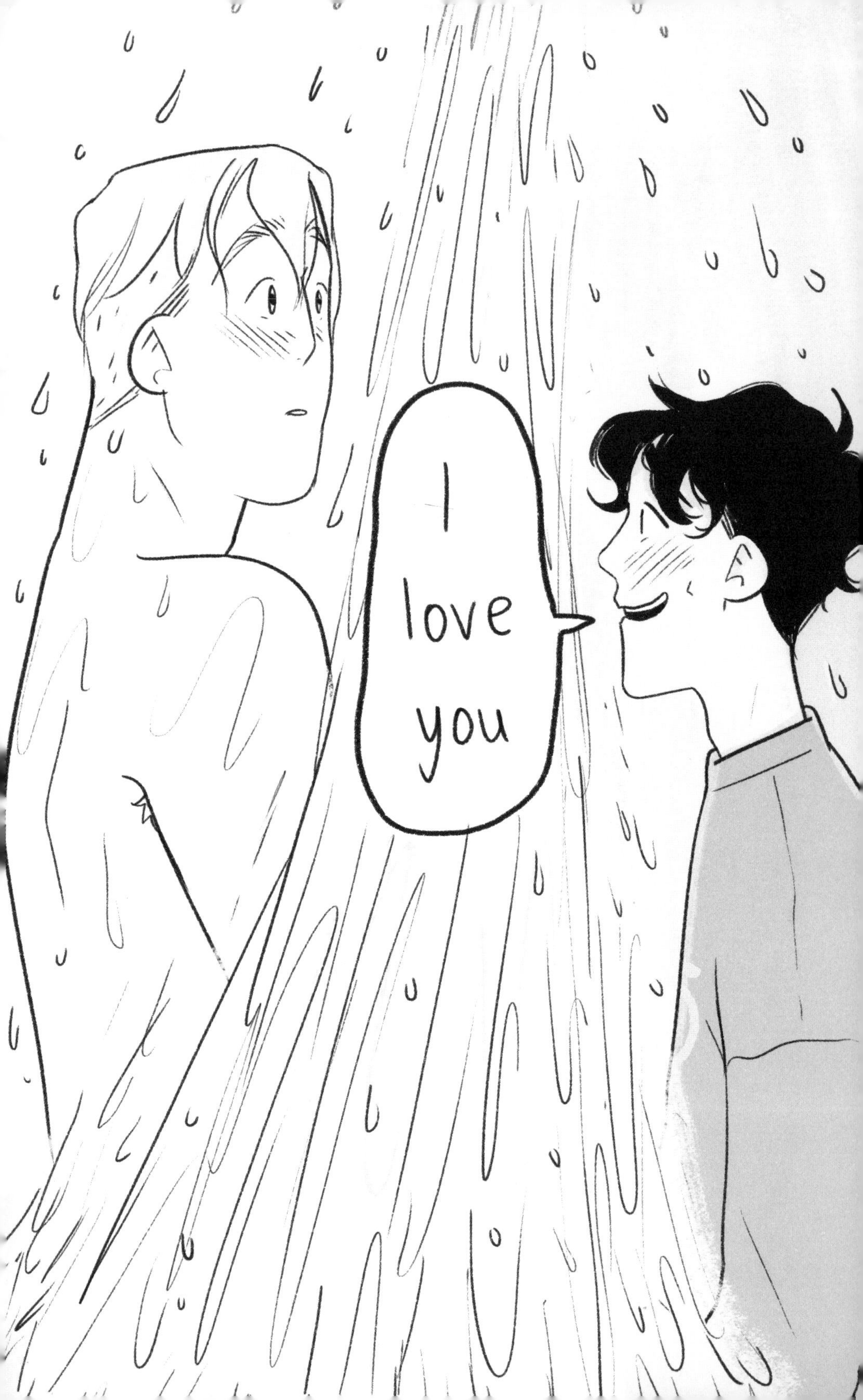
I love you

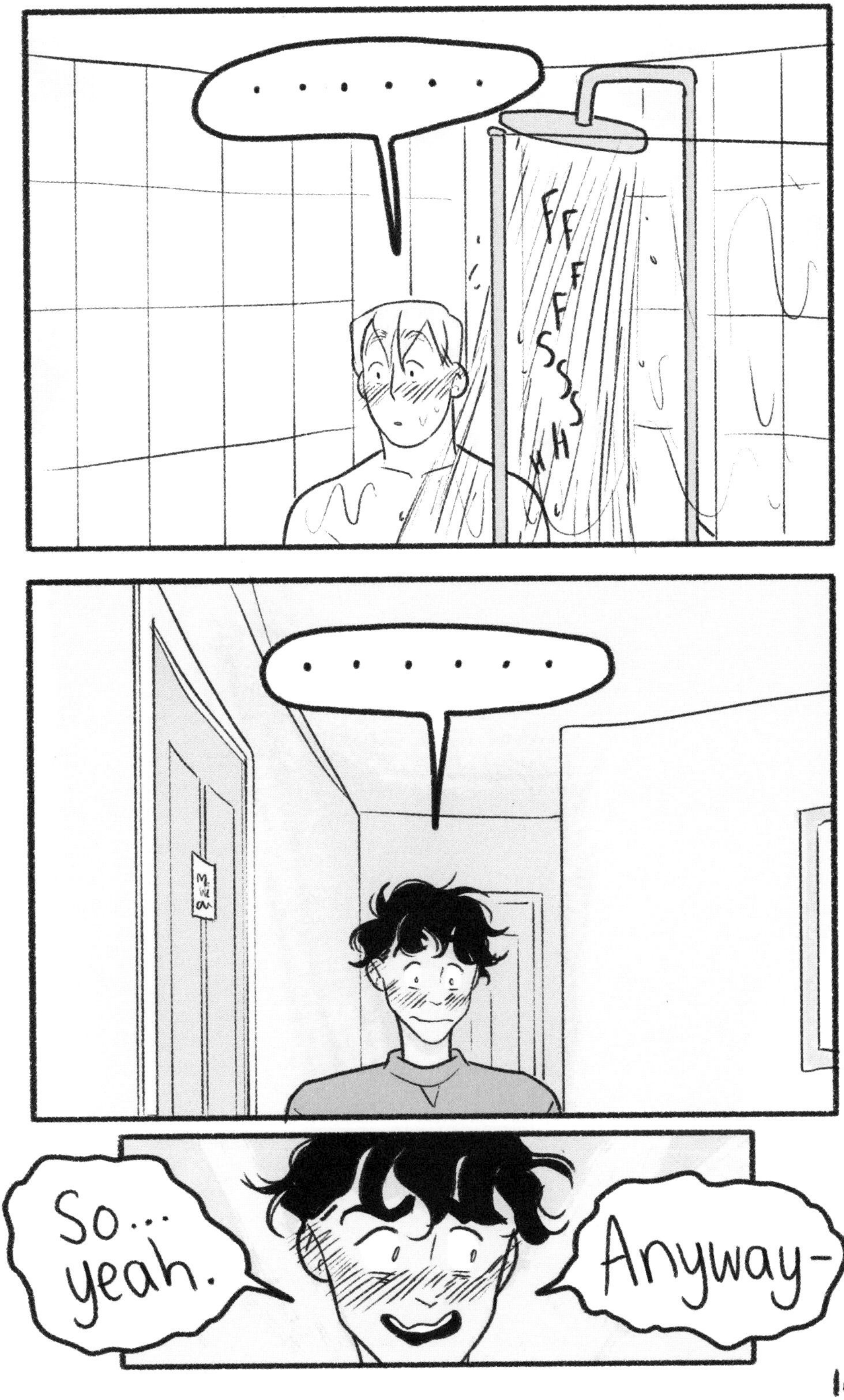
. . . . . .
FFFFSSSHH
. . . . . .
So... yeah.
Anyway-

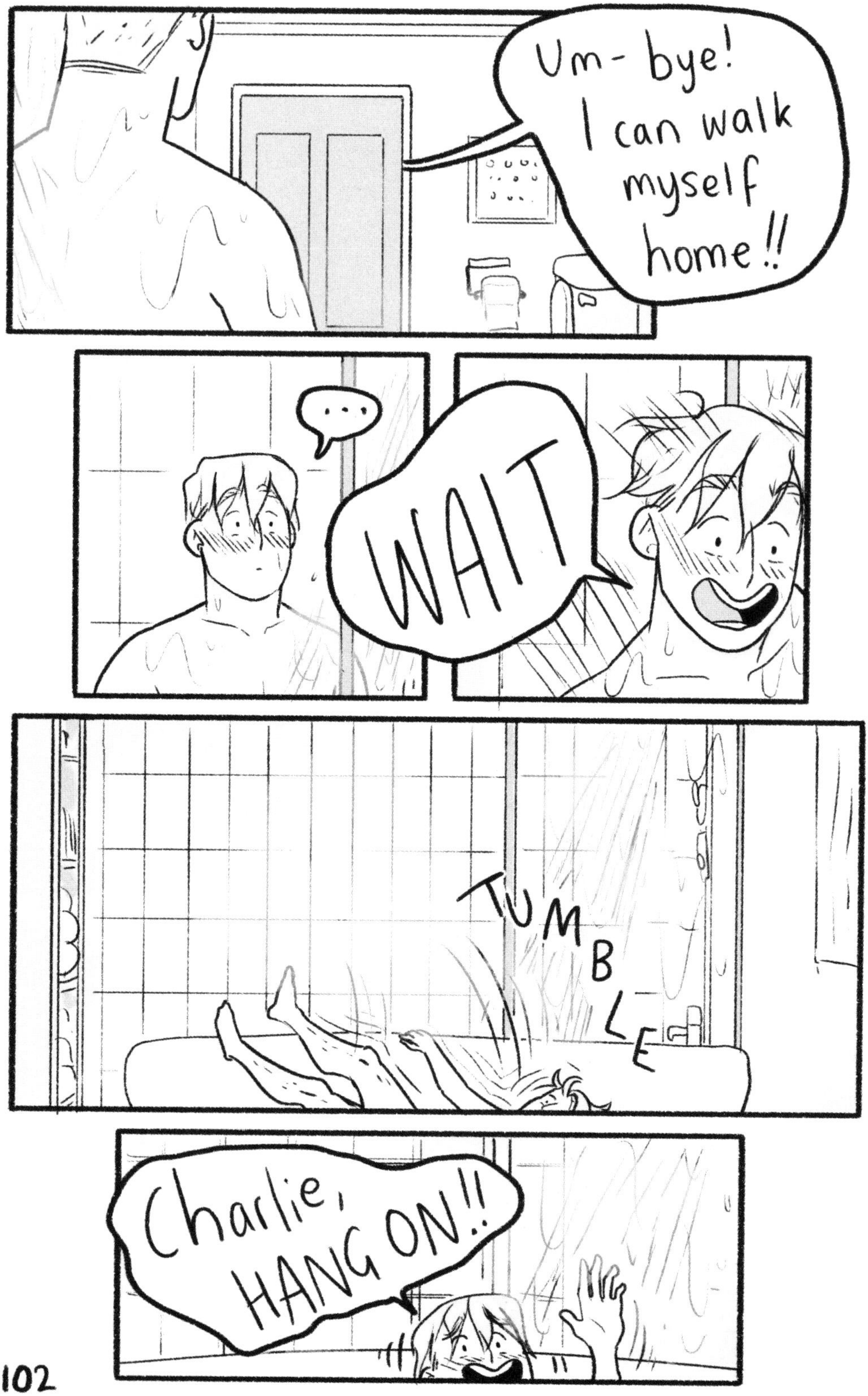
Um- bye! I can walk myself home!!
...
WAIT
TUMBLE
Charlie, HANG ON!!

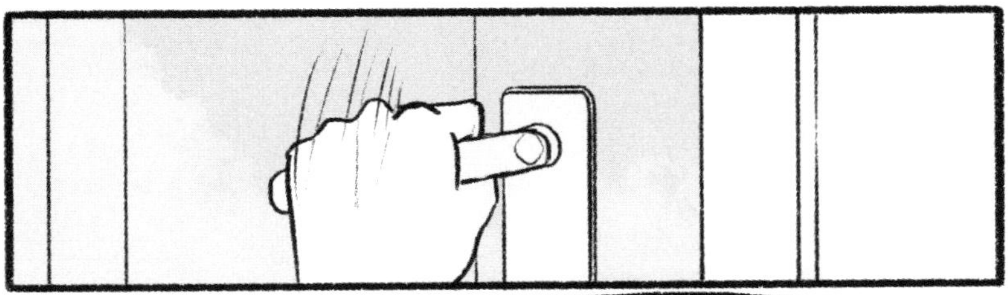

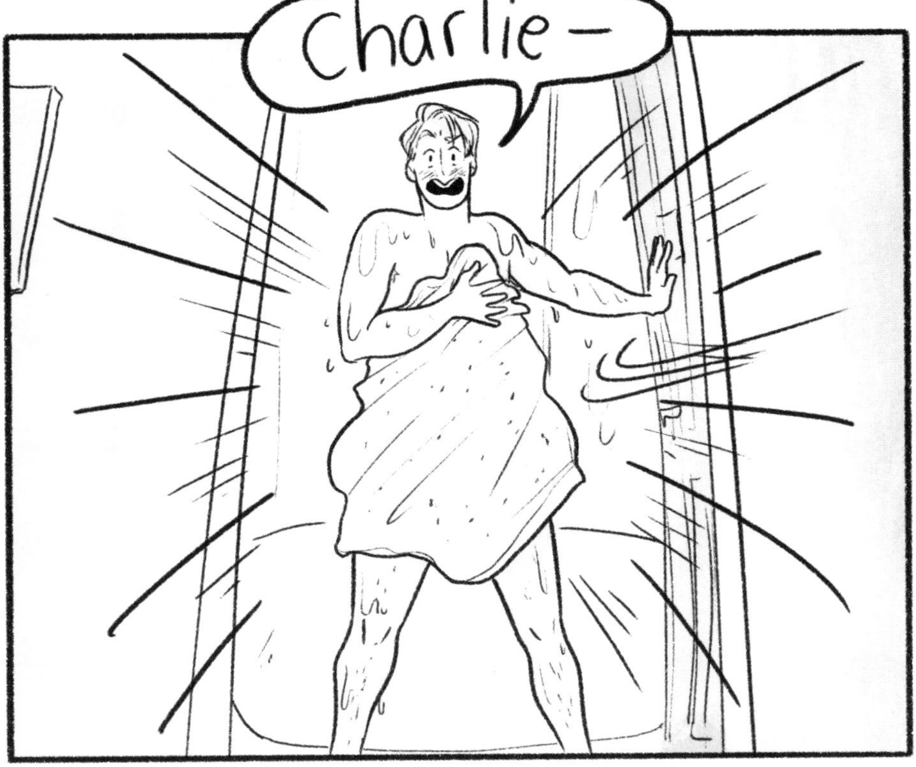
Charlie-

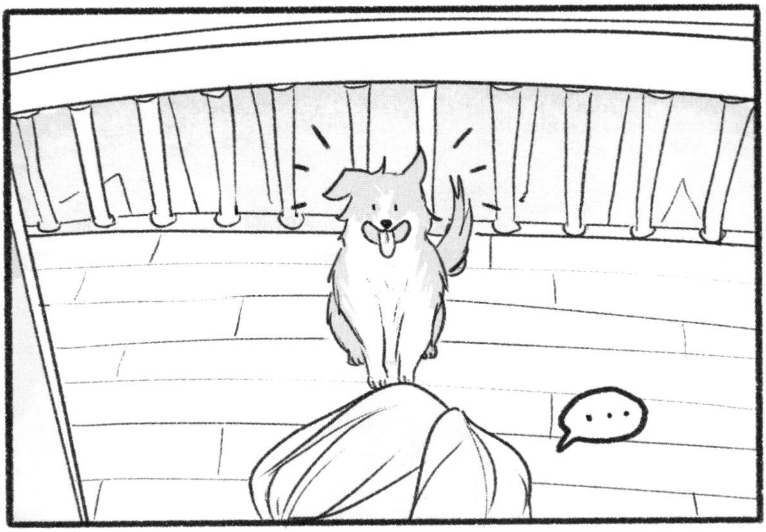
...

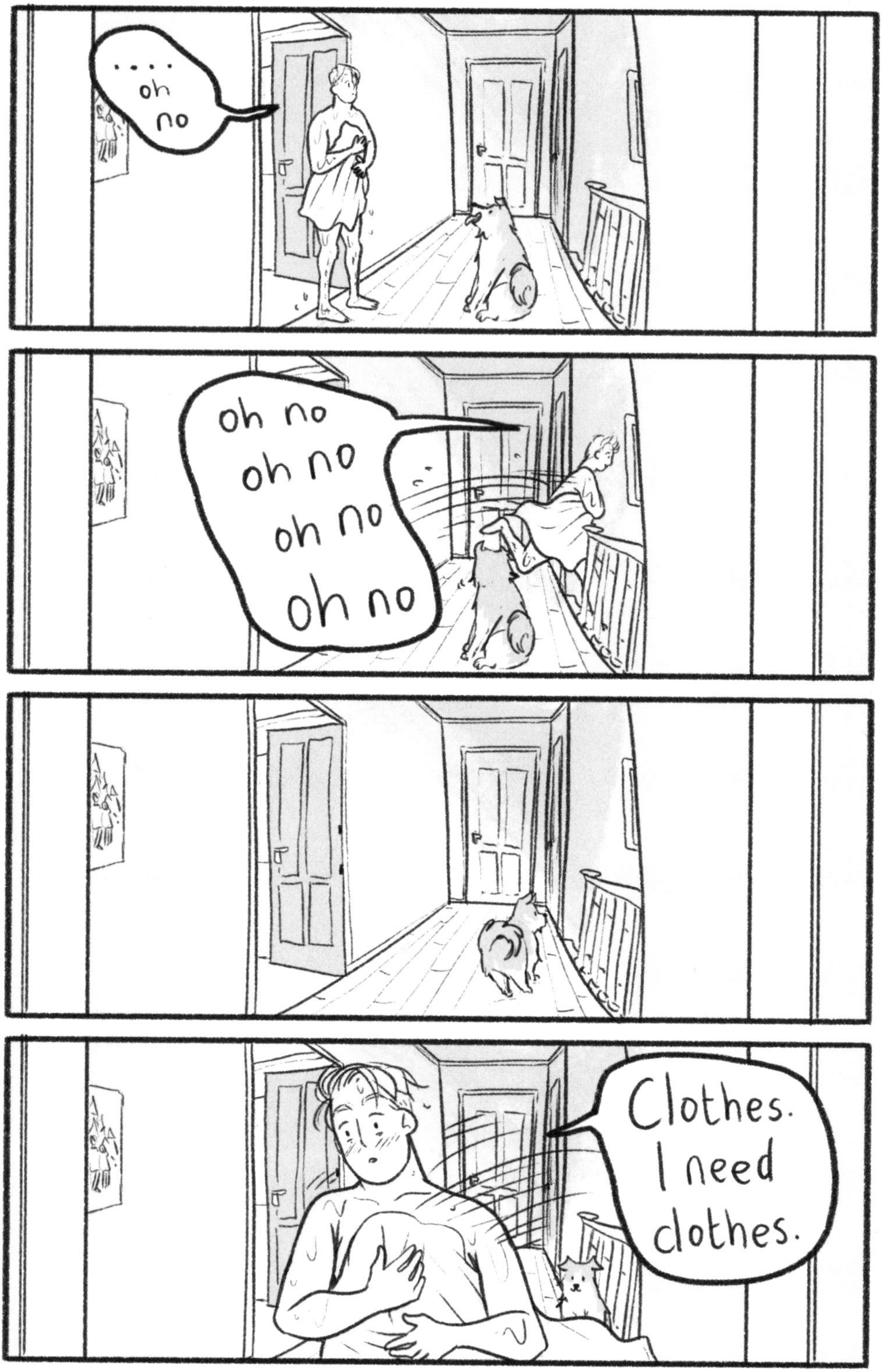
.... oh no
oh no oh no oh no oh no
Clothes. I need clothes.

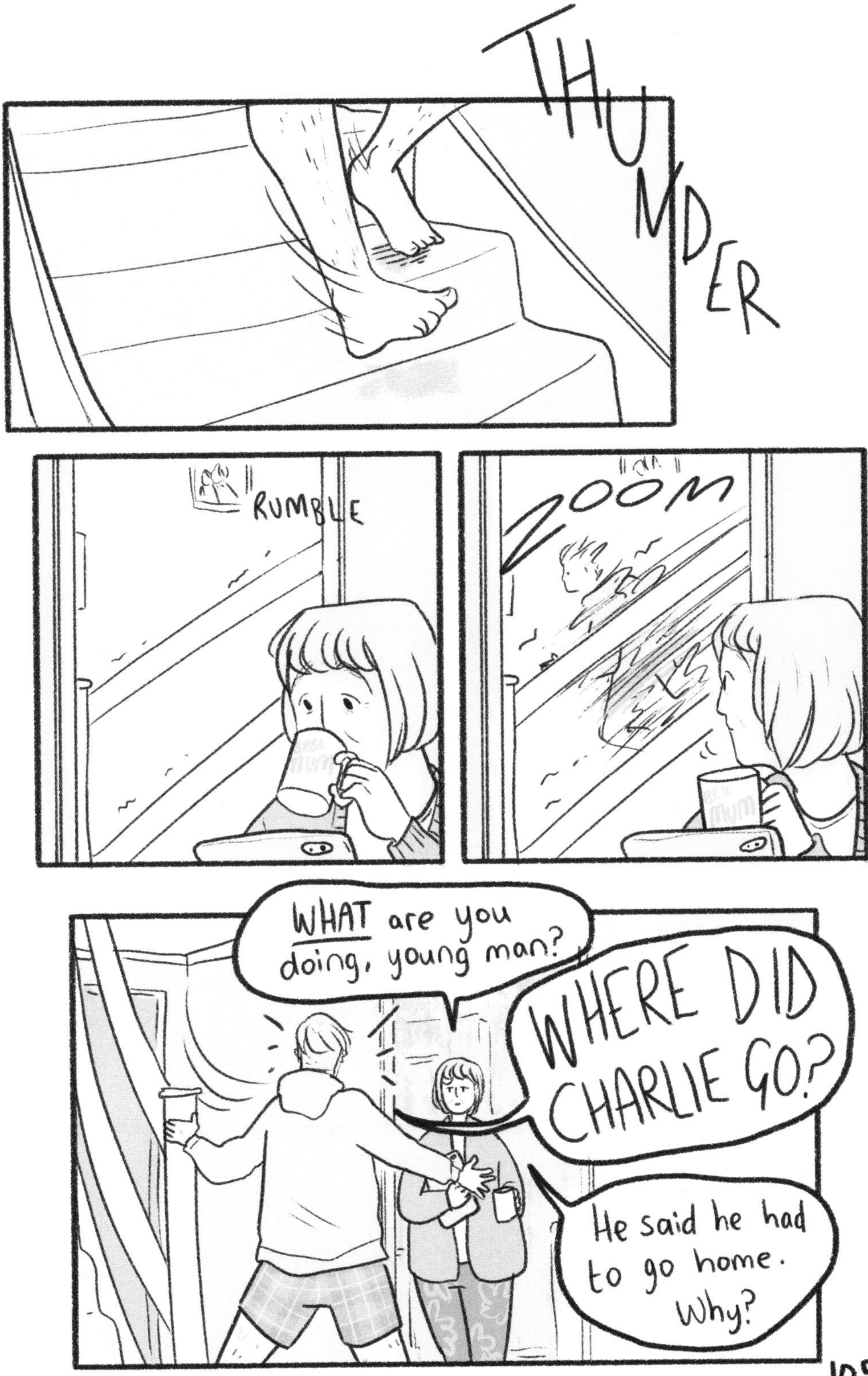
THUNDER
RUMBLE
ZOOM
WHAT are you doing, young man?
WHERE DID CHARLIE GO?
He said he had to go home. Why?

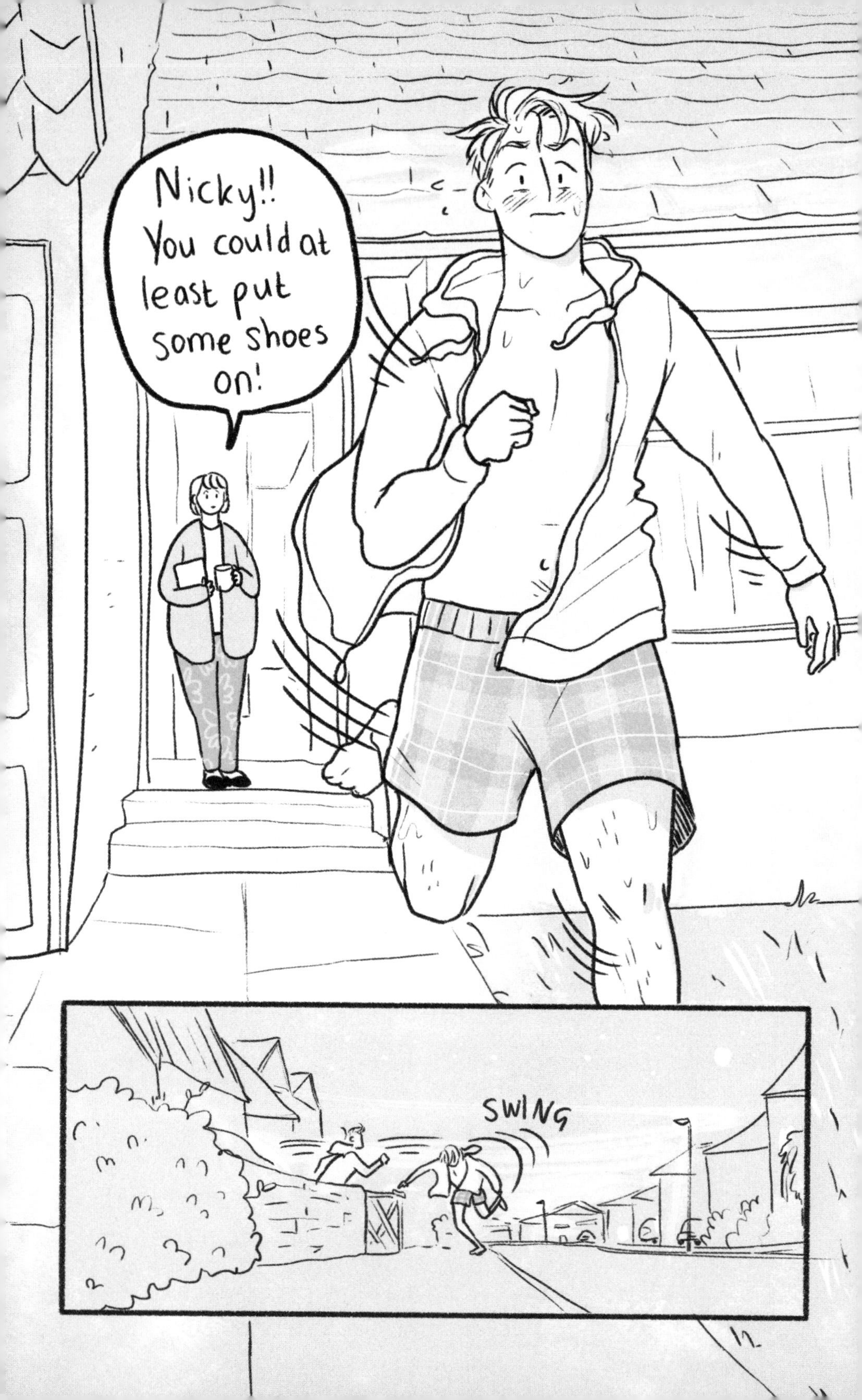
Nicky!! You could at least put some shoes on!
SWING

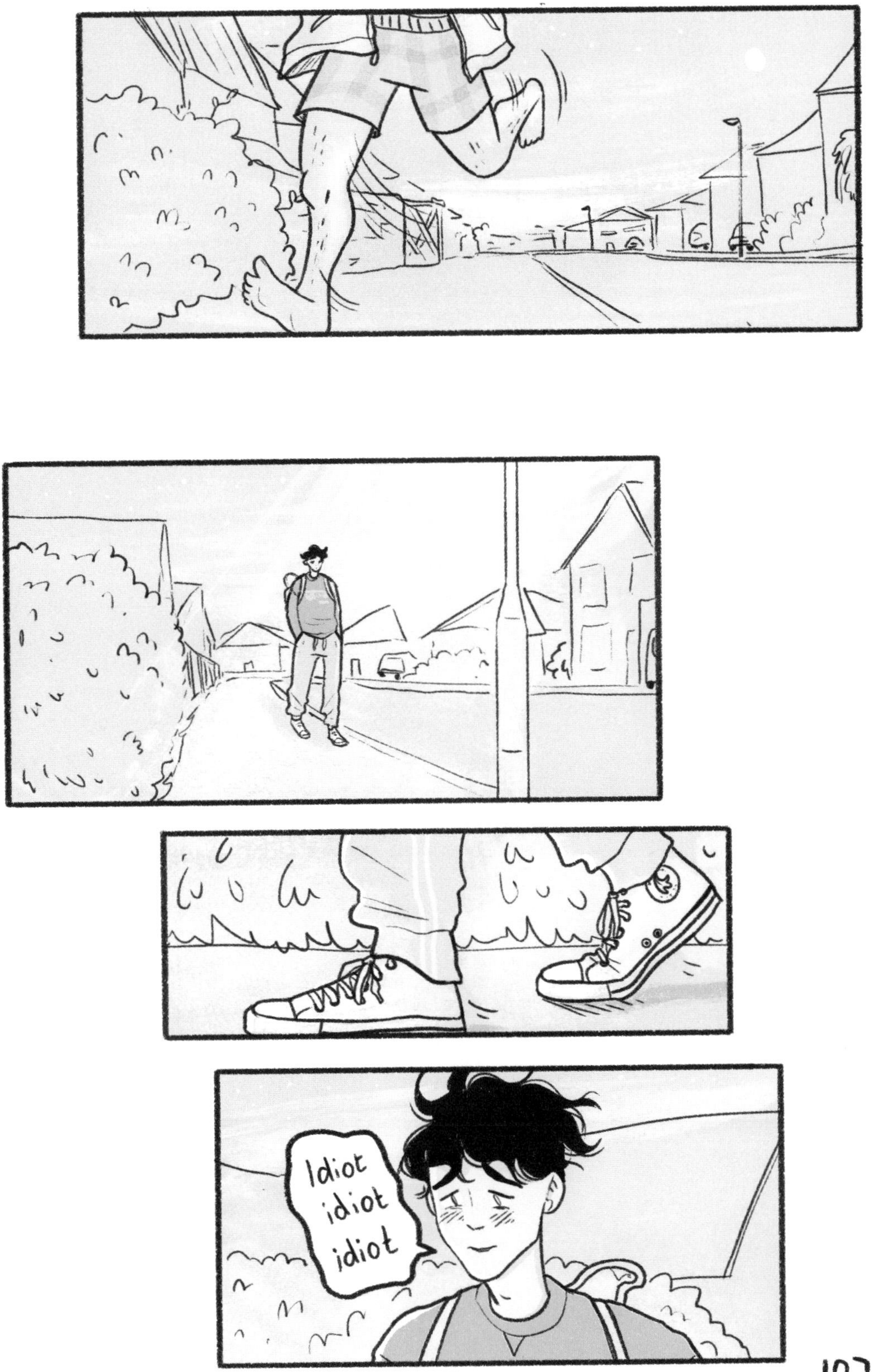
Idiot
idiot
idiot

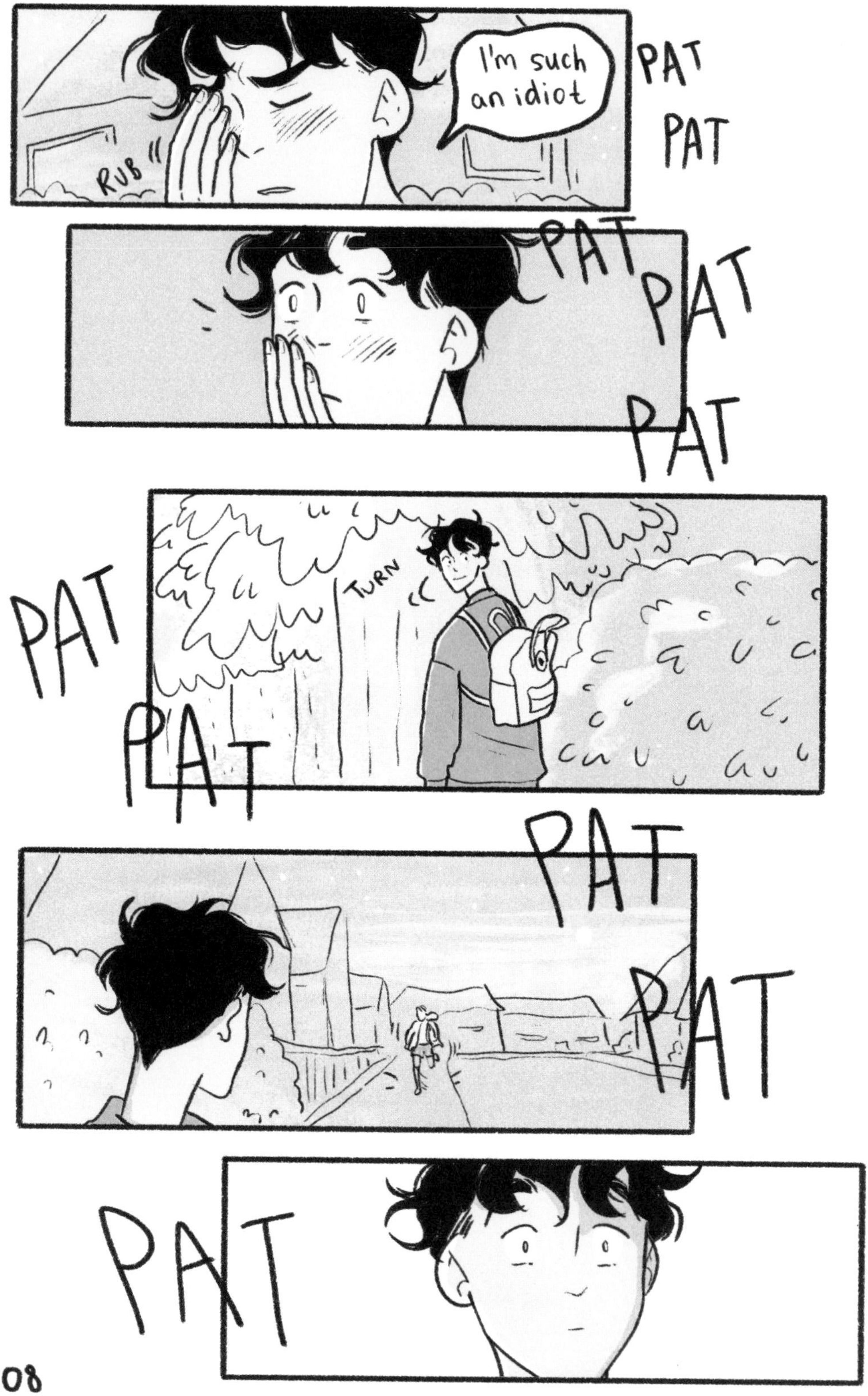
I'm such an idiot
RUB
PAT
PAT
PAT
PAT
PAT
TURN
PAT
PAT
PAT
PAT
PAT

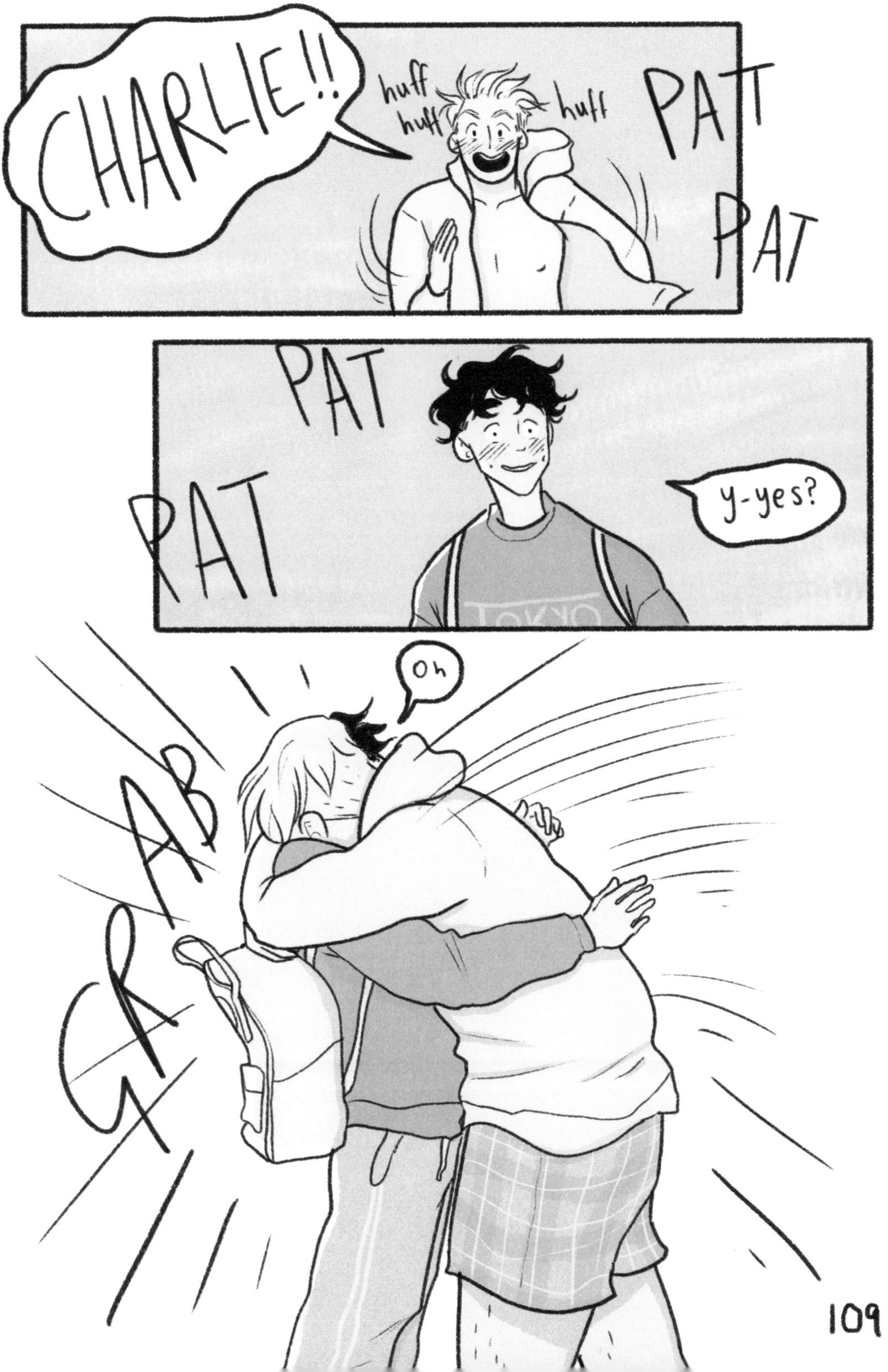
CHARLIE!!
huff
huff
huff
PAT
PAT
PAT
PAT
y-yes?
Oh
GRAB

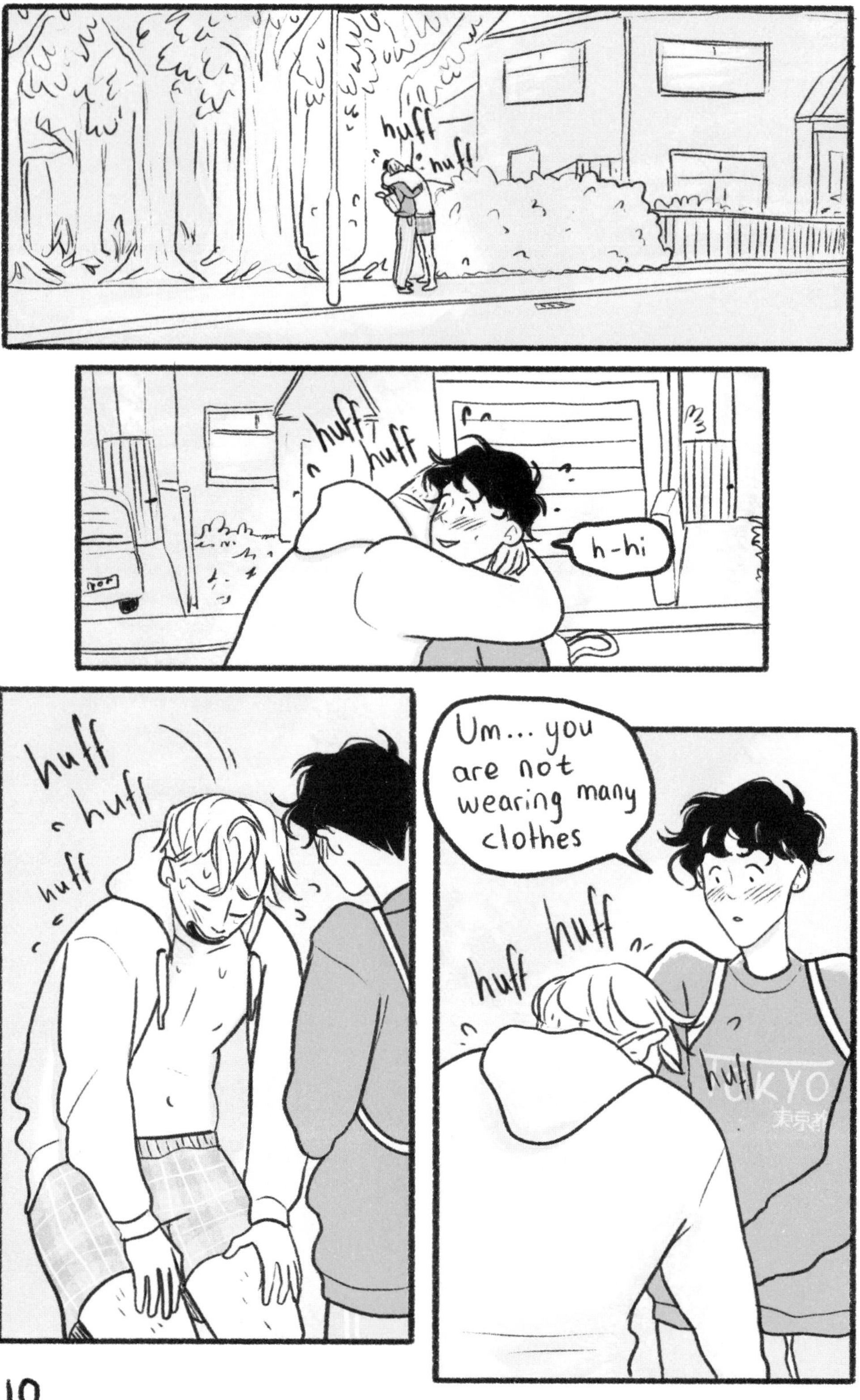
huff
huff
huff
huff
h-hi
huff
huff
huff
Um... you are not wearing many clothes
huff
huff
huff

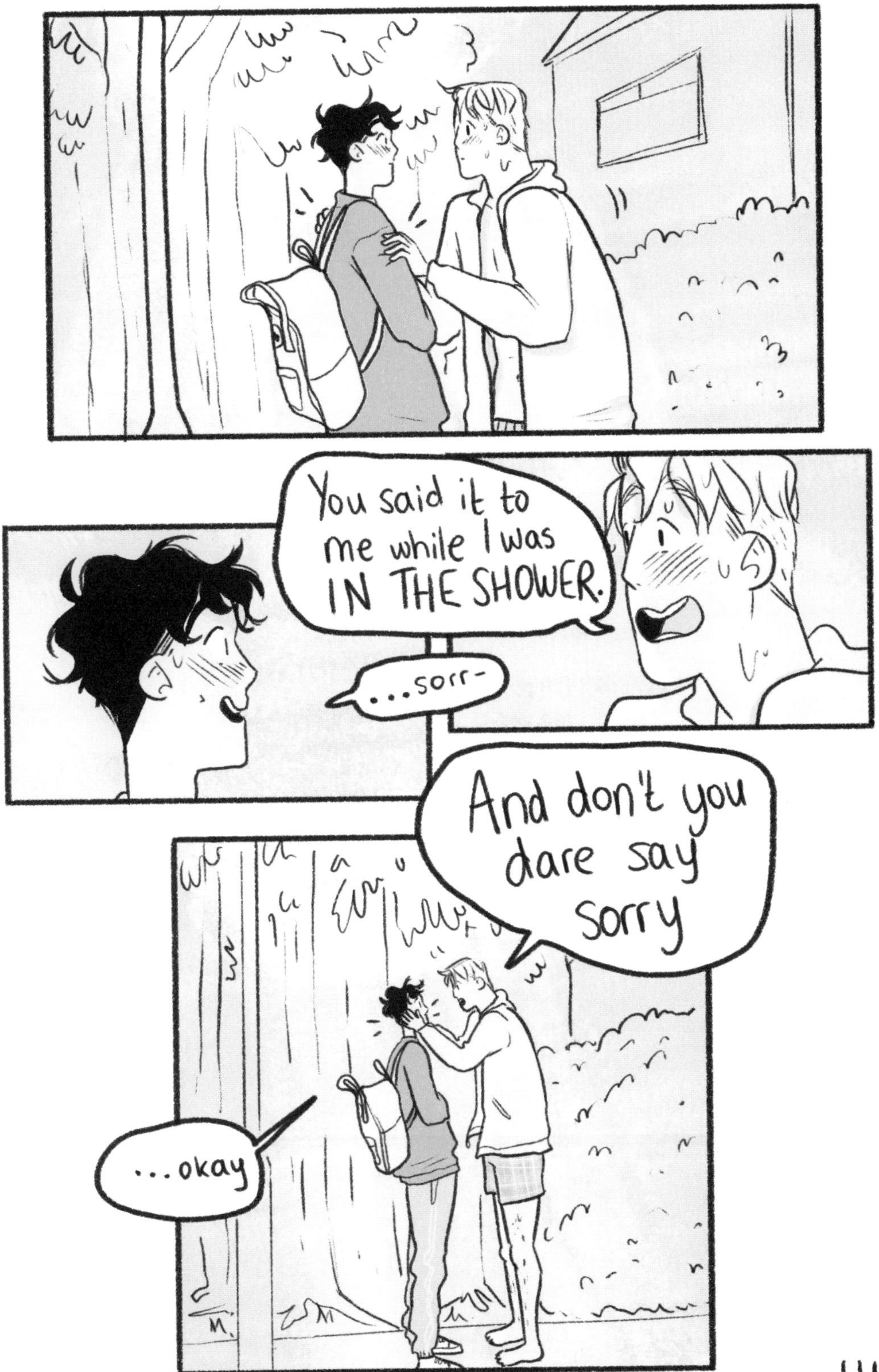
You said it to me while I was IN THE SHOWER.
...sorr-
And don't you dare say sorry
...okay

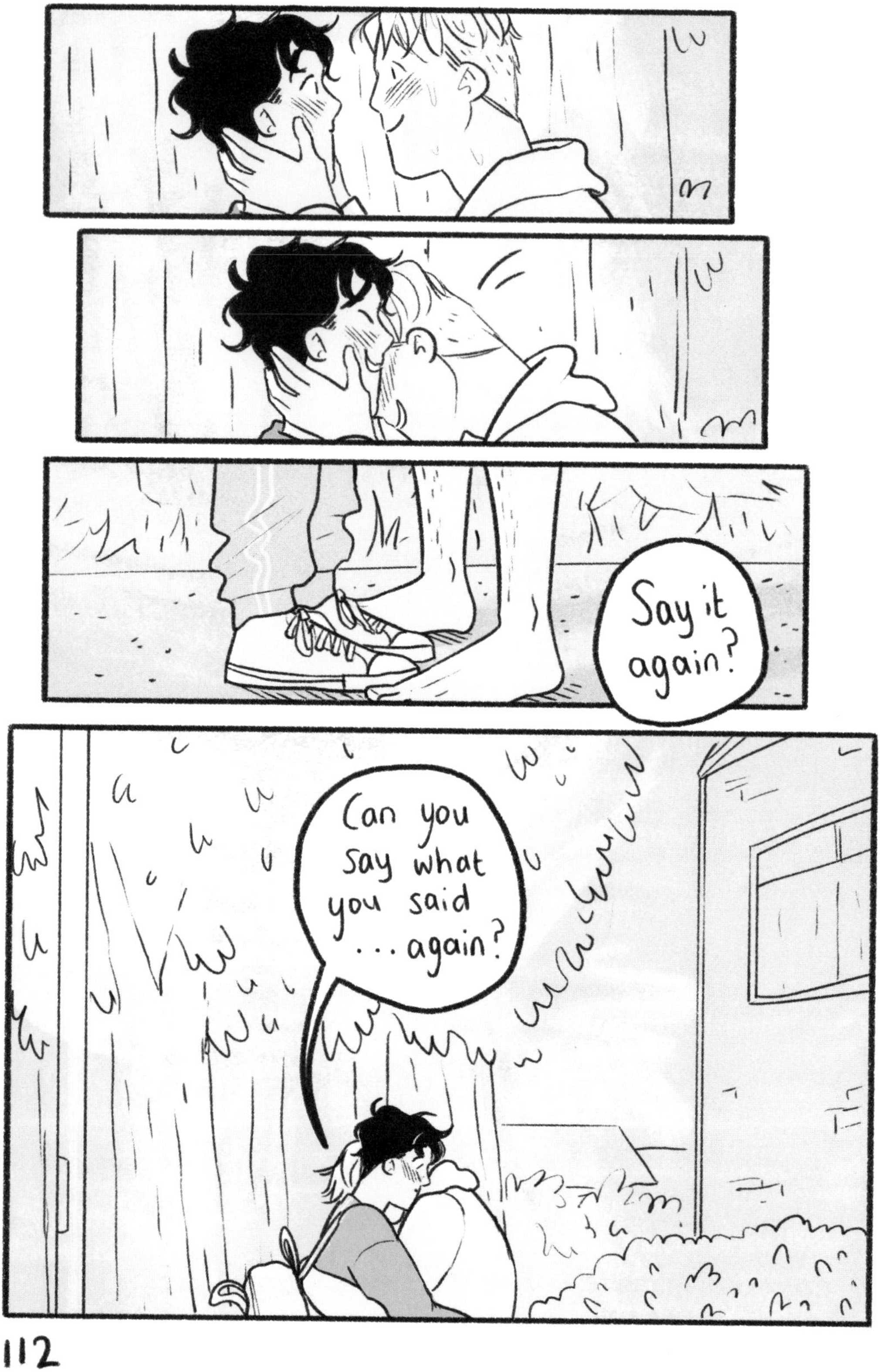
Say it again?
Can you say what you said ...again?

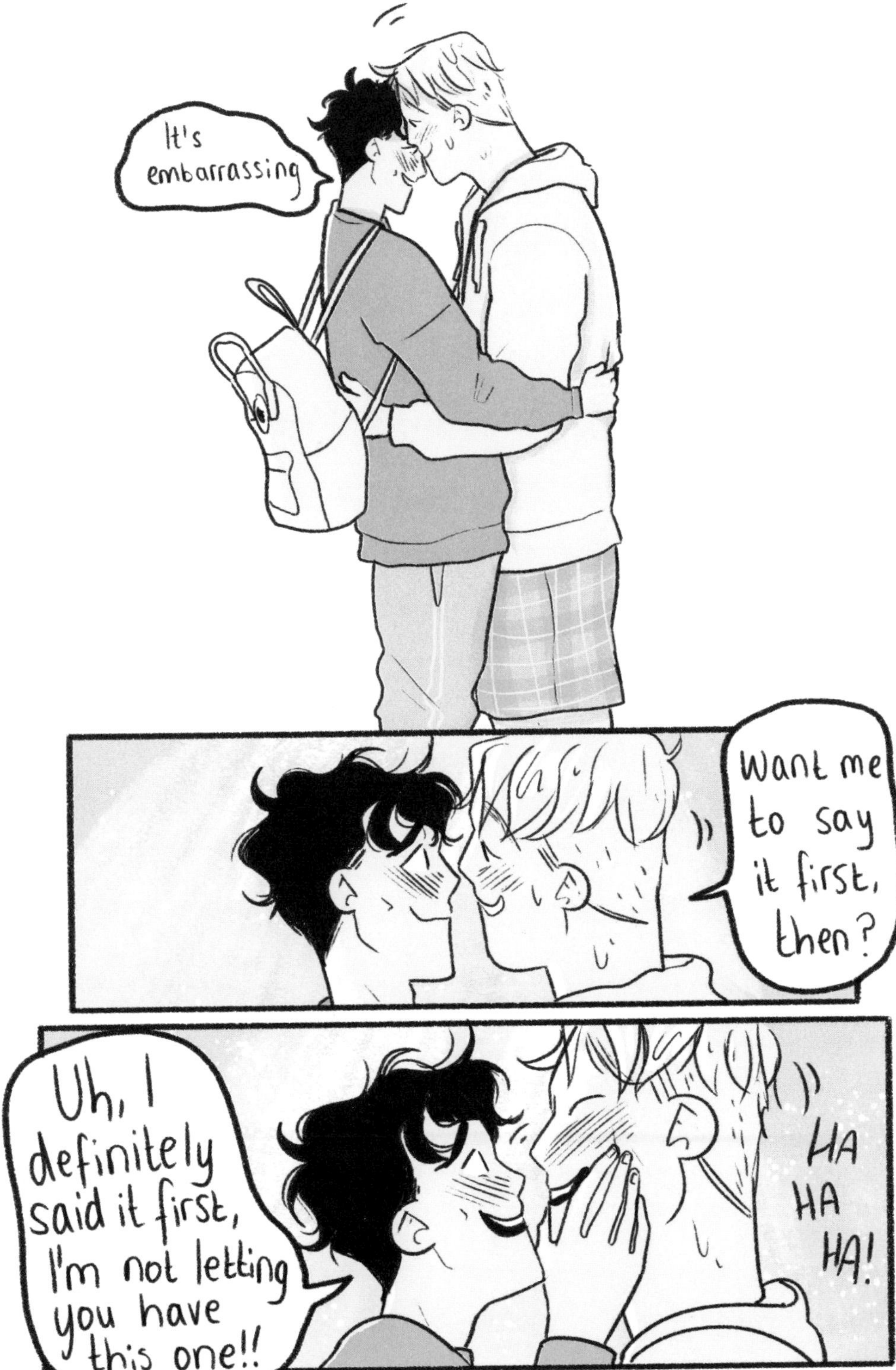
It's embarrassing
Want me to say it first, then?
Uh, I definitely said it first, I'm not letting you have this one!!
HA HA HA!

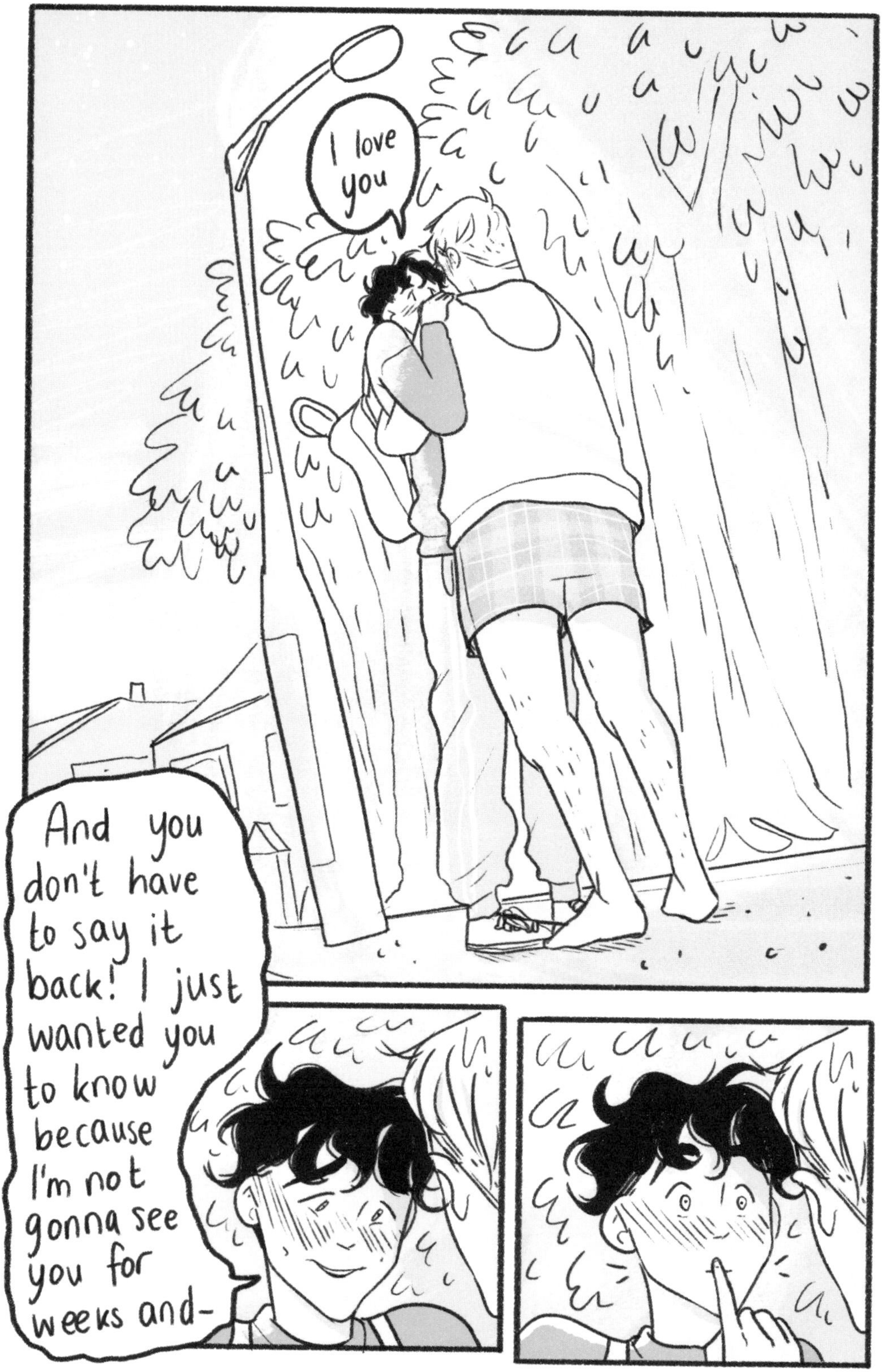
I love you
And you don't have to say it back! I just wanted you to know because I'm not gonna see you for weeks and-

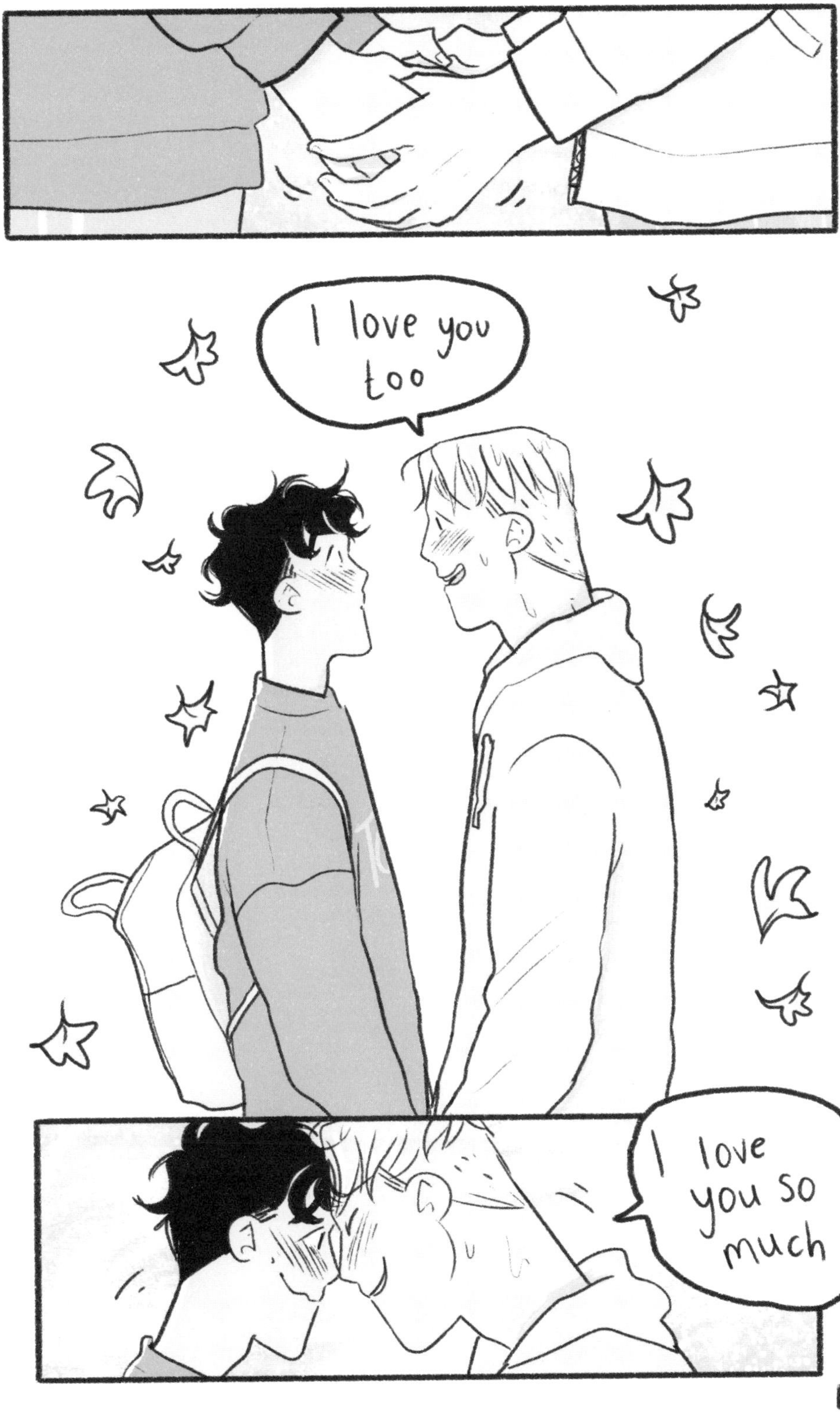
I love you too
I love you so much

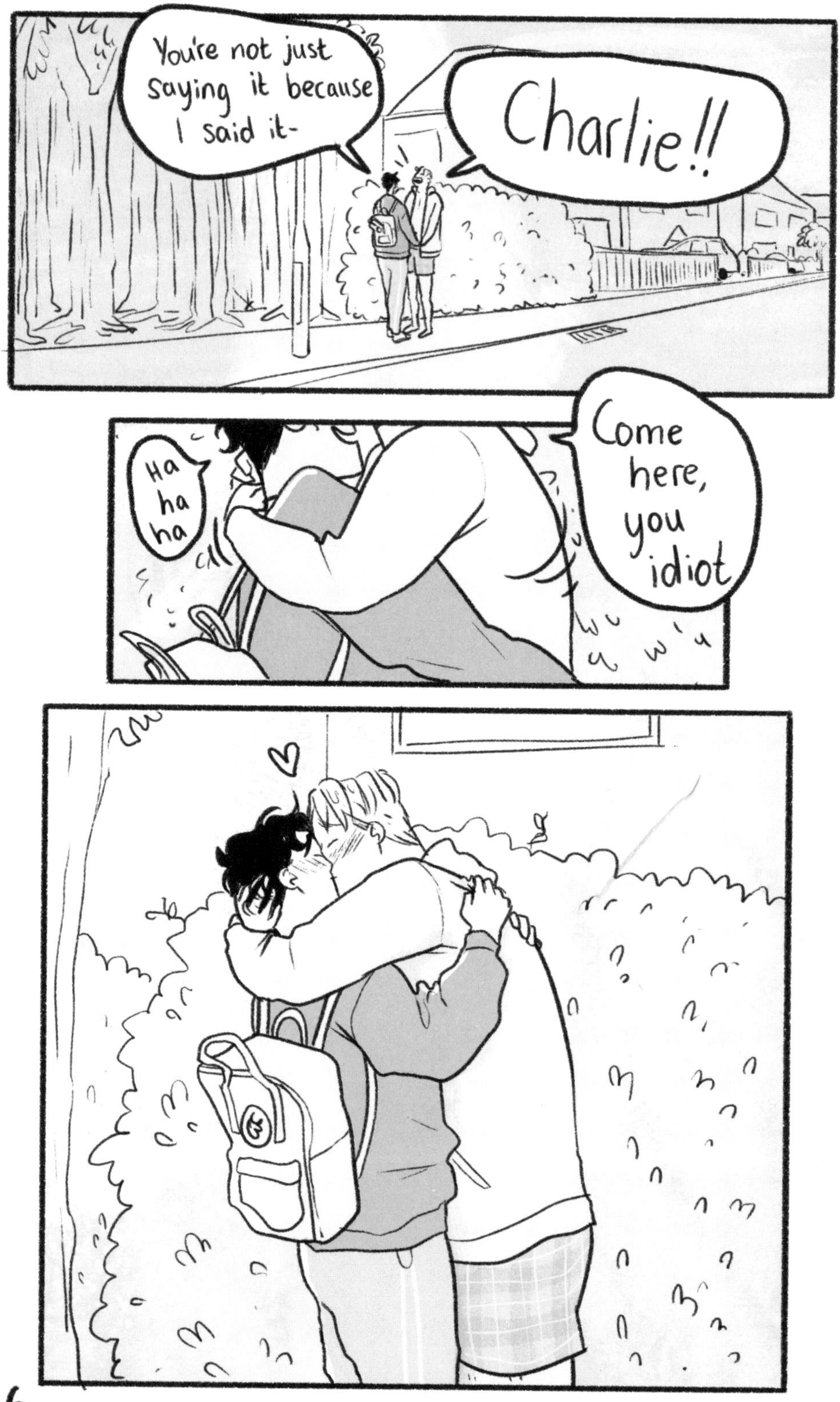
You're not just saying it because I said it-
Charlie!!
Ha ha ha
Come here, you idiot

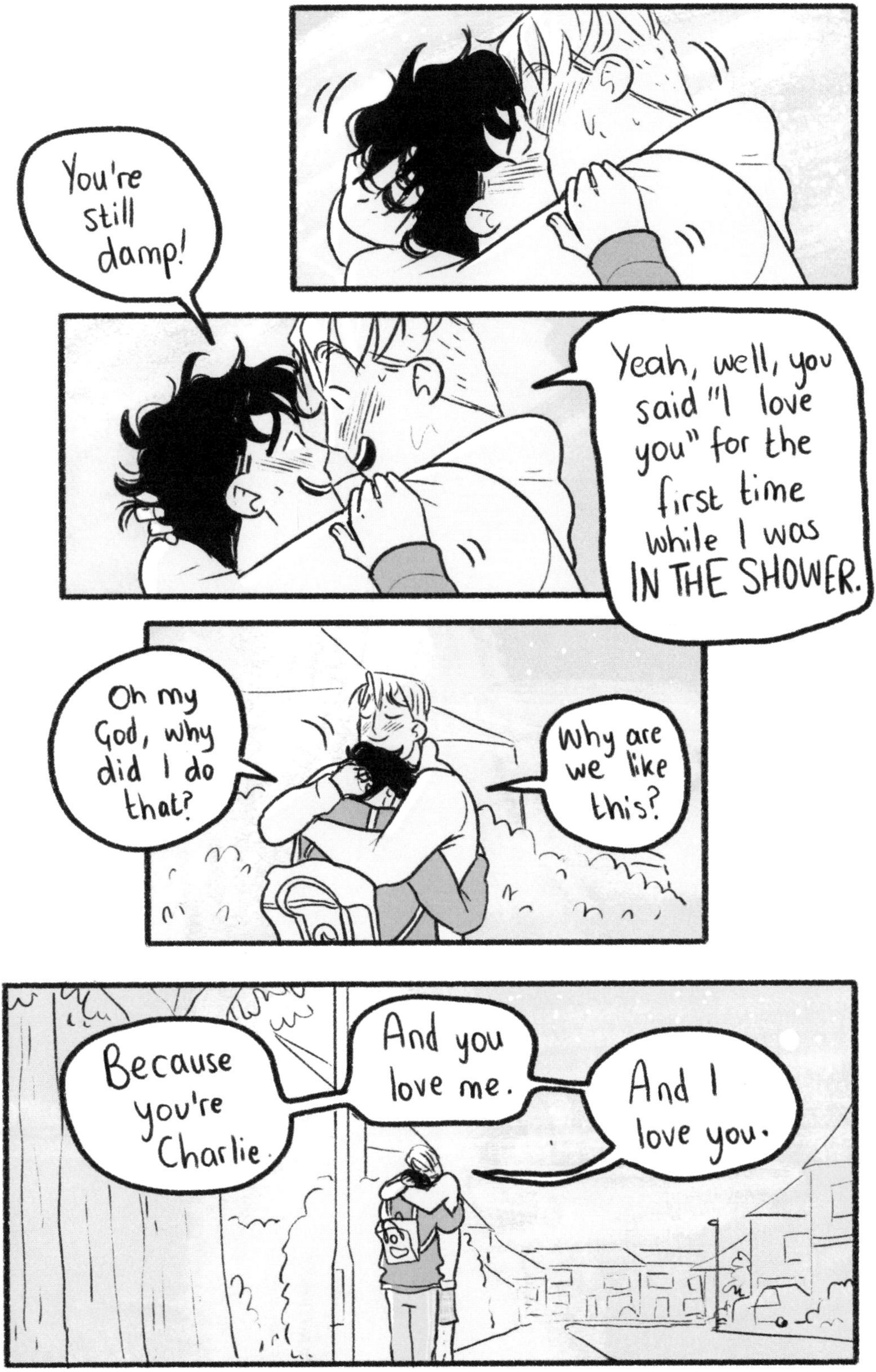
You're still damp!
Yeah, well, you said "I love you" for the first time while I was IN THE SHOWER.
Oh my God, why did I do that?
Why are we like this?
Because you're Charlie.
And you love me.
And I love you.

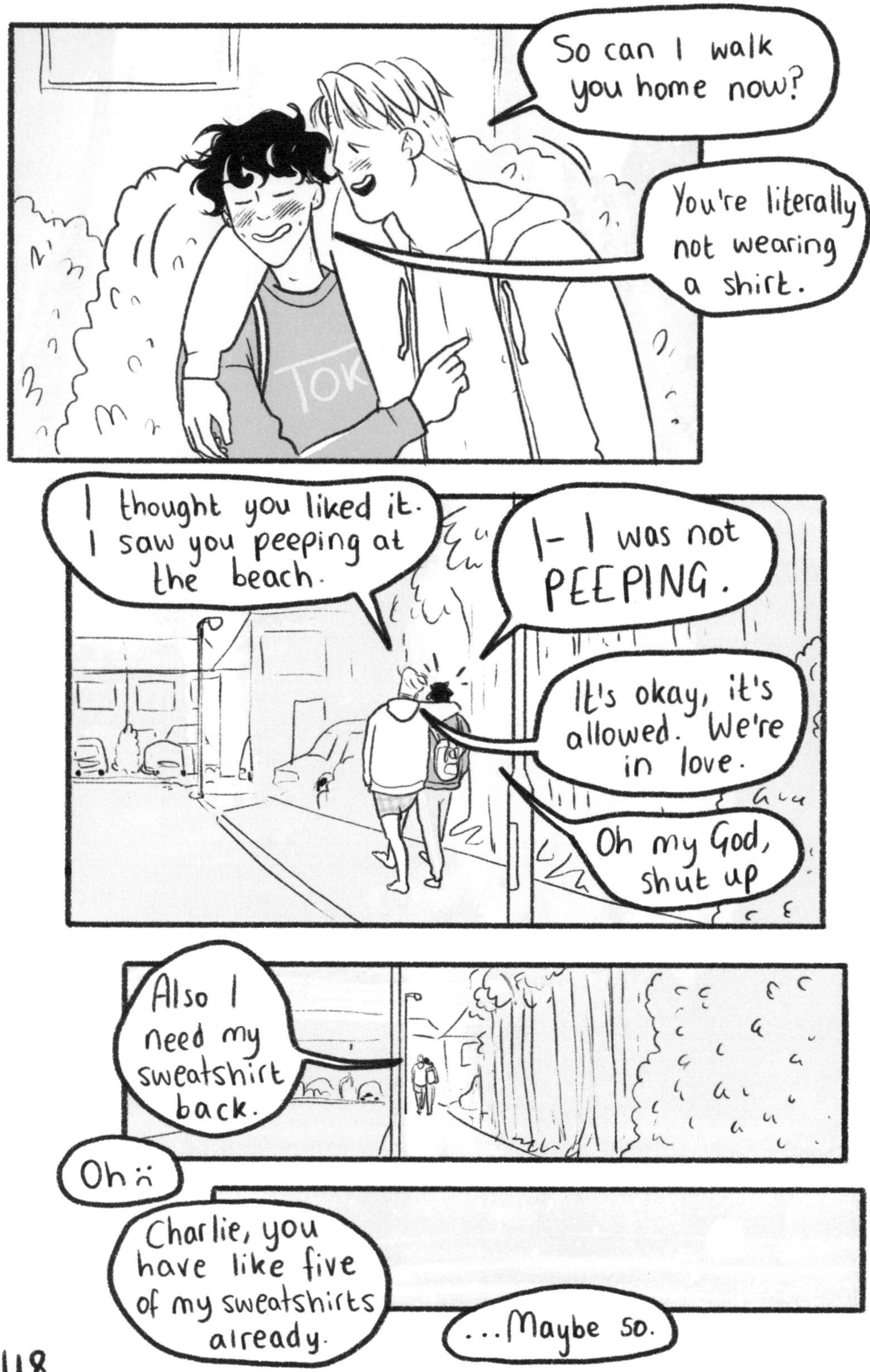
So can I walk you home now?
You're literally not wearing a shirt.
TOK
I thought you liked it. I saw you peeping at the beach.
I- I was not PEEPING.
It's okay, it's allowed. We're in love.
Oh my God, shut up
Also I need my sweatshirt back.
Oh :(
Charlie, you have like five of my sweatshirts already.
...Maybe so.

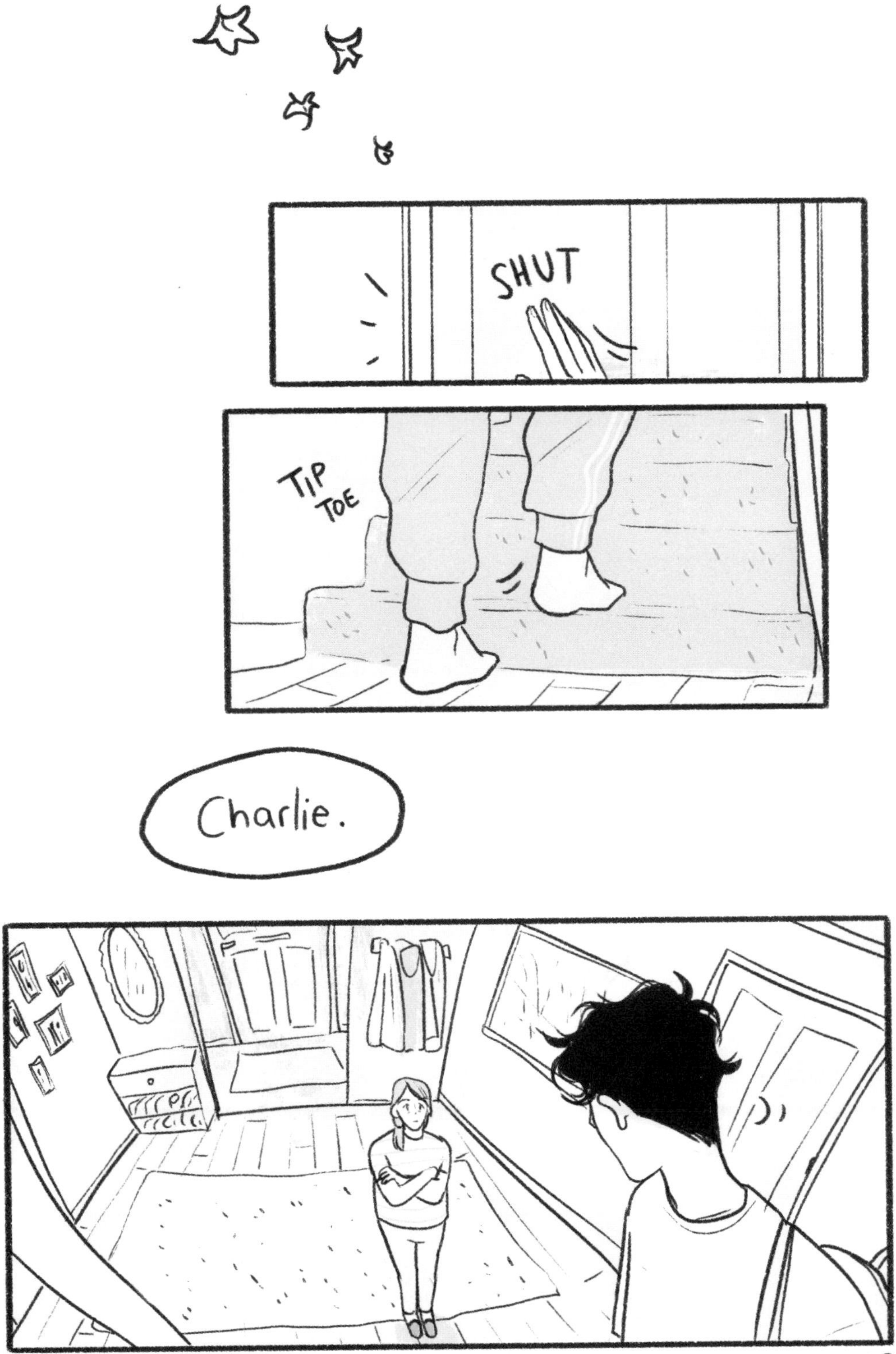
SHUT
TIP TOE
Charlie.

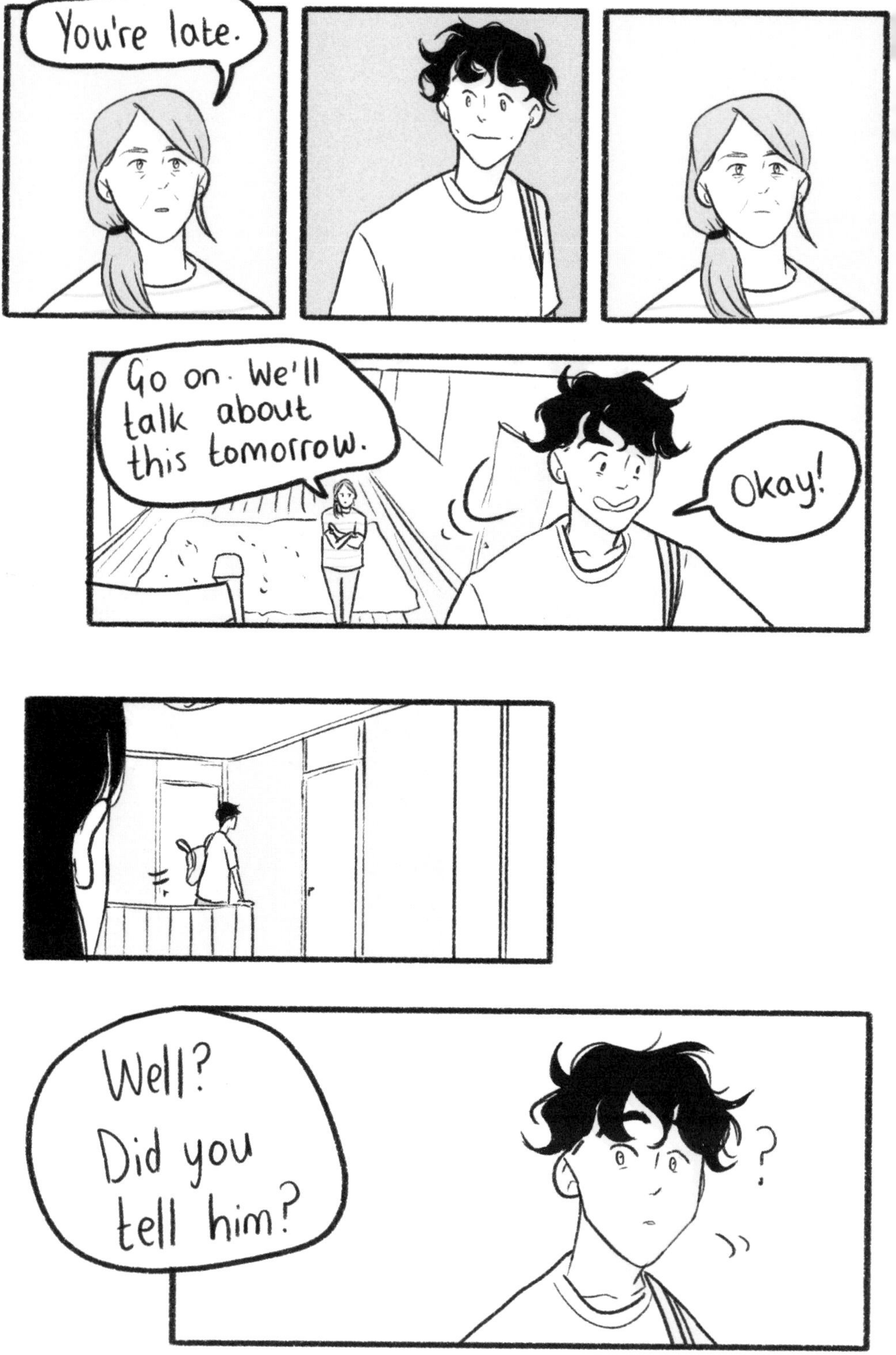
You're late.
Go on. We'll talk about this tomorrow.
Okay!
Well? Did you tell him?
?

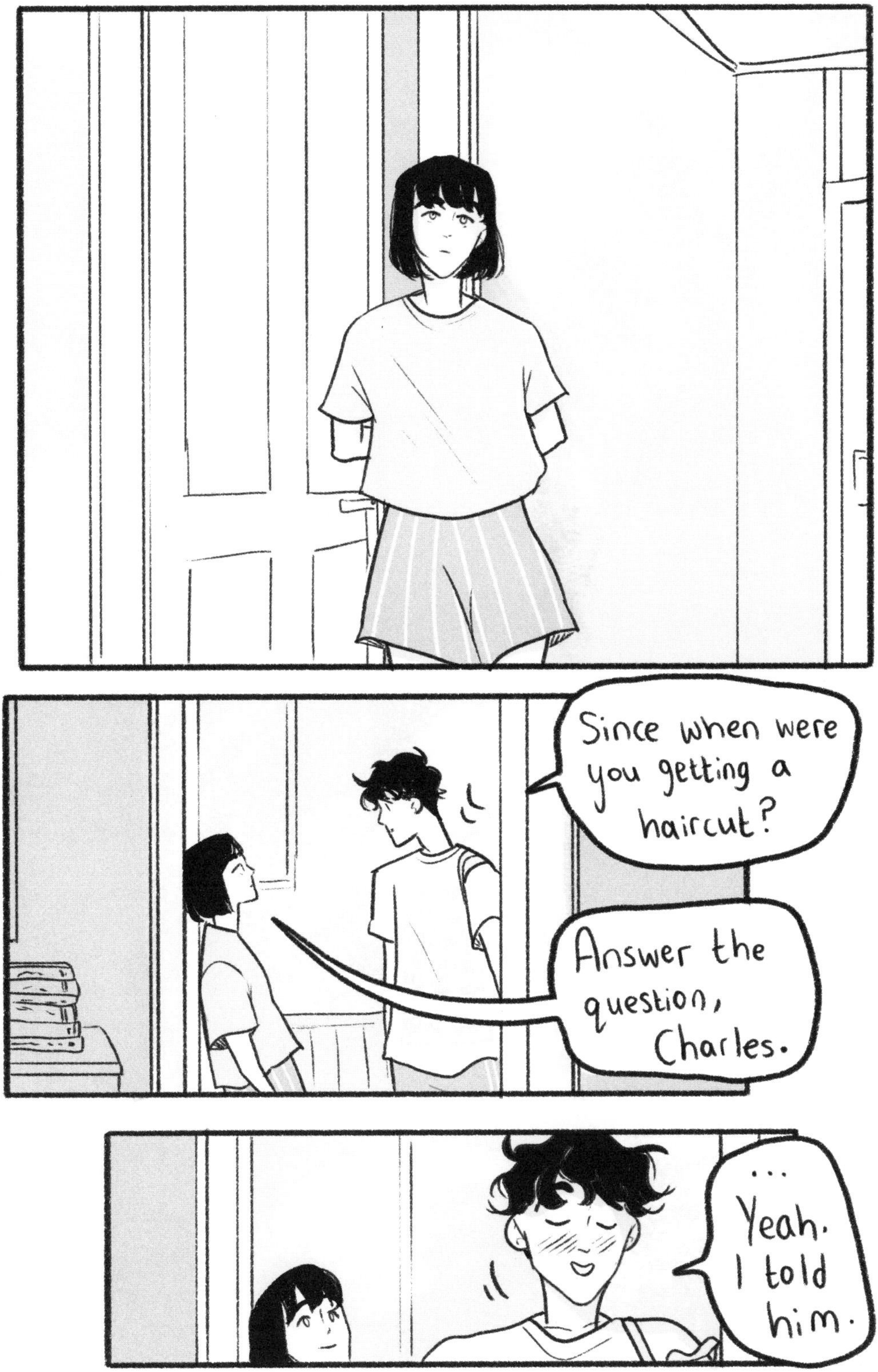
Since when were you getting a haircut?
Answer the question, Charles.
... Yeah. I told him.

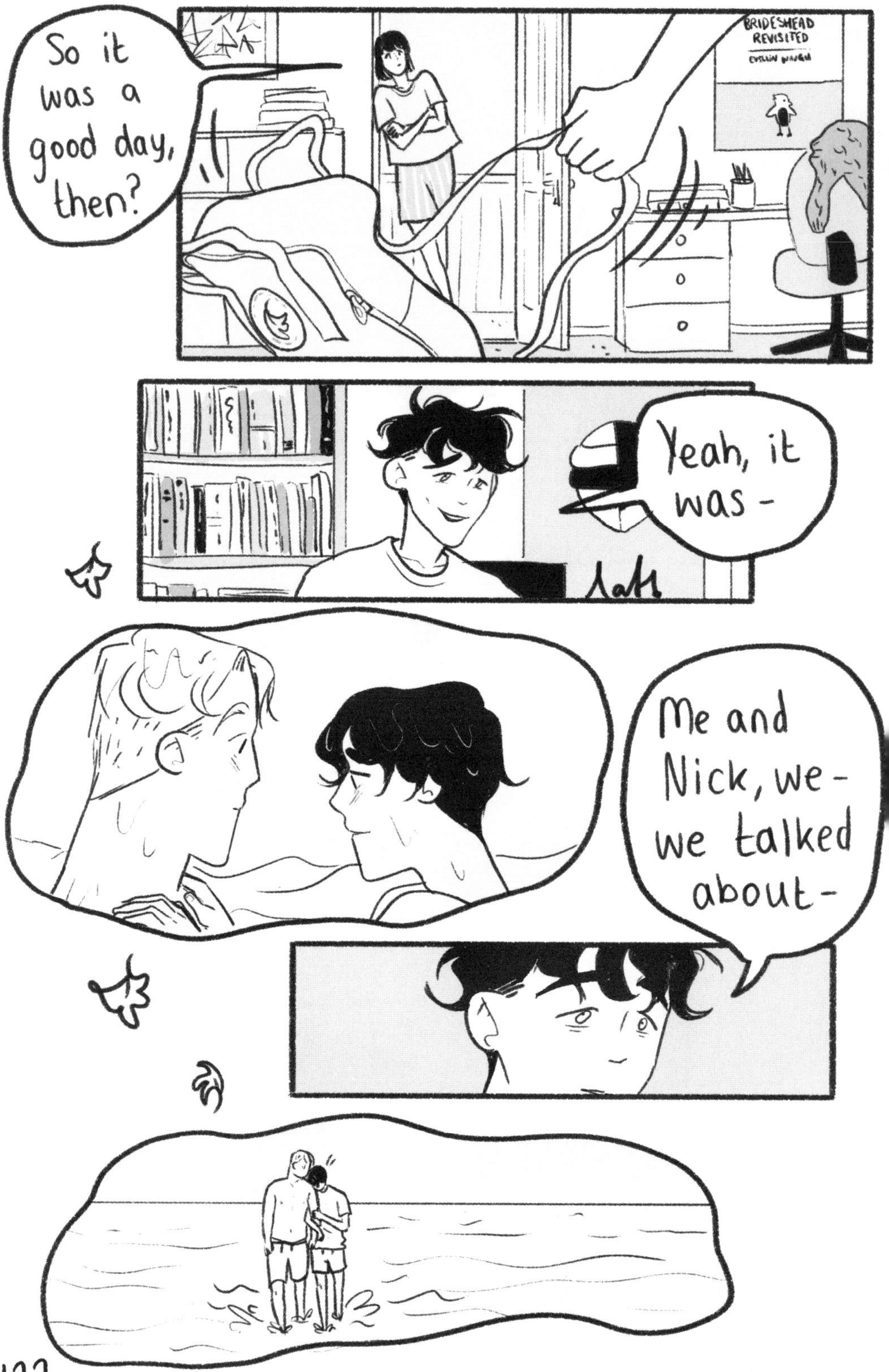
So it was a good day, then?
BRIDESHEAD REVISITED
Yeah, it was-
Me and Nick, we- we talked about-

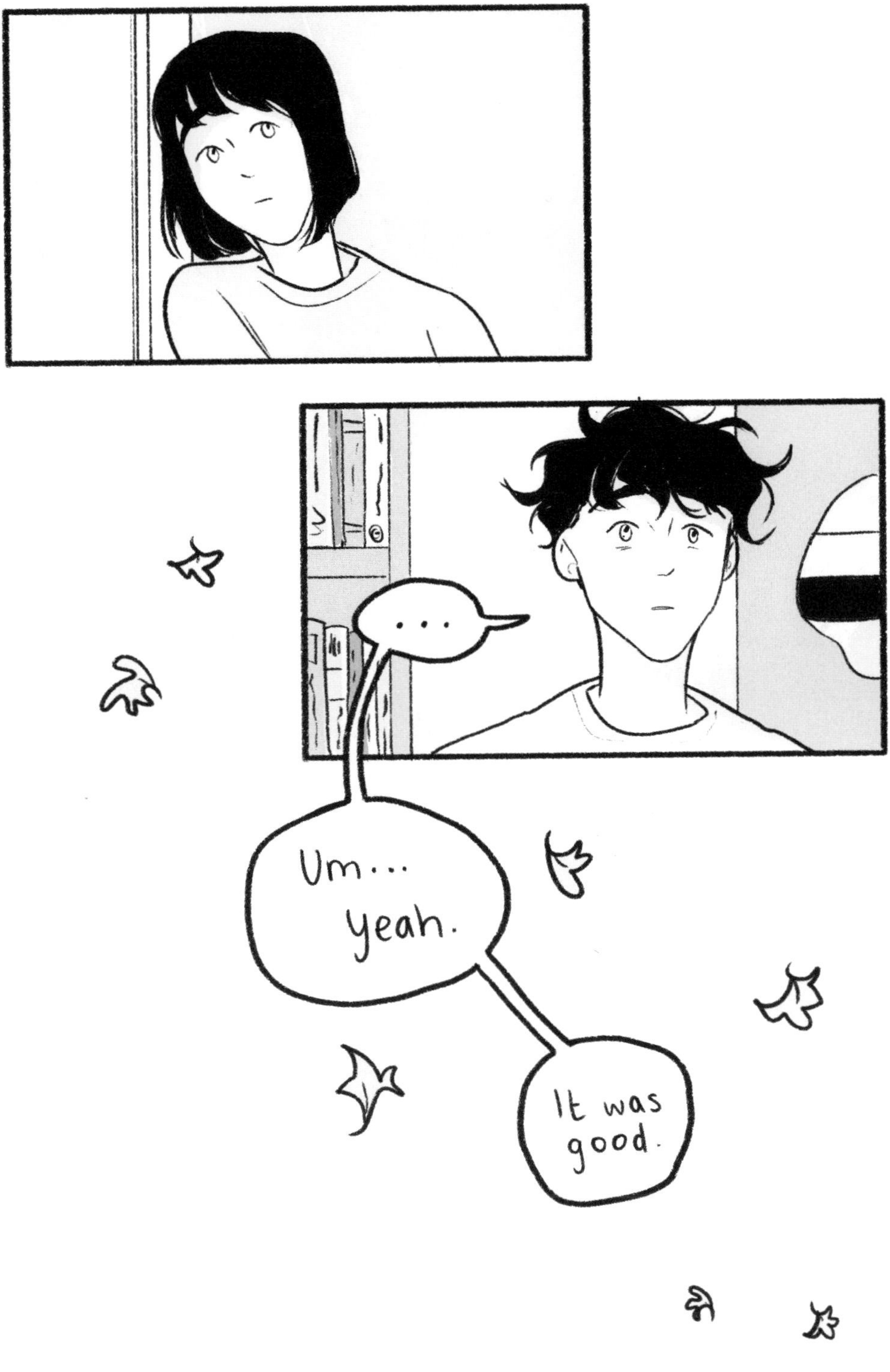
...
Um... yeah.
It was good.

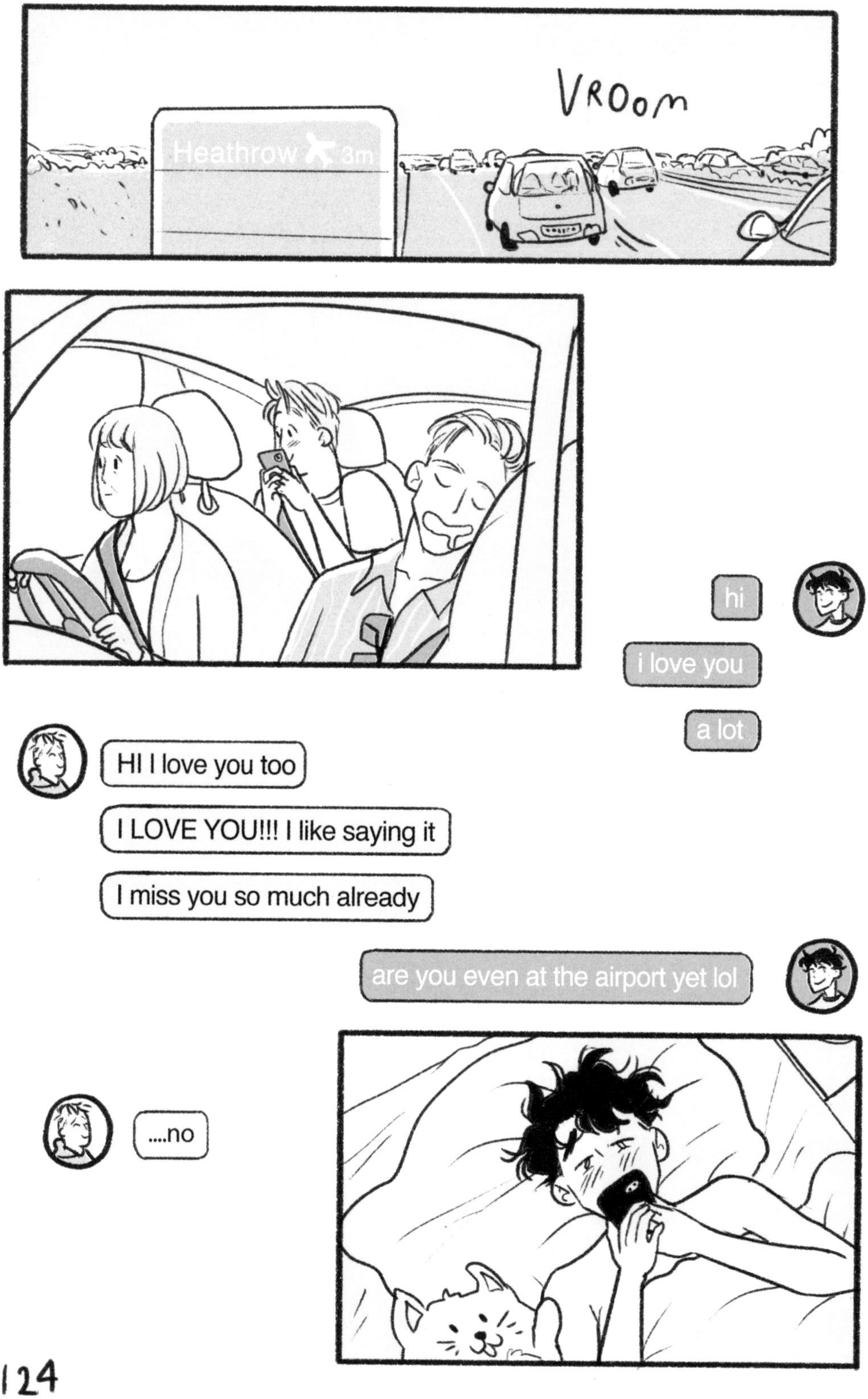
VROOM
Heathrow 3m
hi
i love you
a lot
HI I love you too
I LOVE YOU!!! I like saying it
I miss you so much already
are you even at the airport yet lol
....no

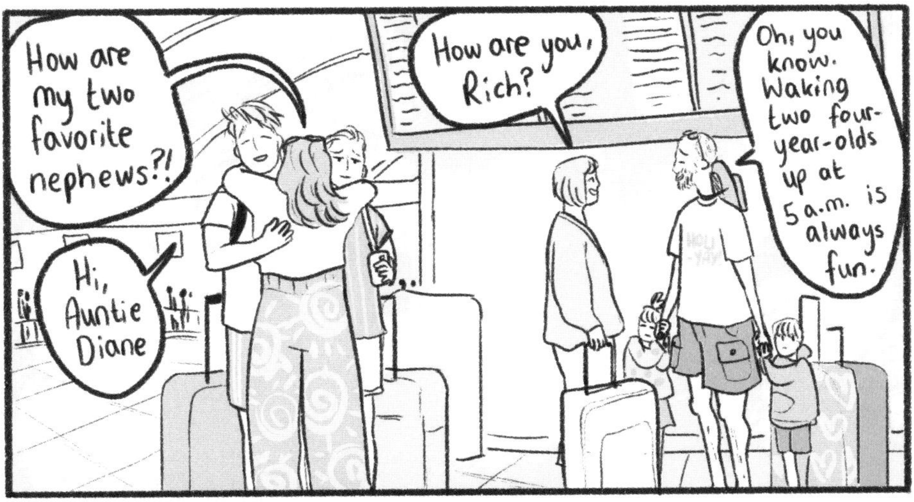
How are my two favorite nephews?!
Hi, Auntie Diane
How are you, Rich?
Oh, you know. Waking two four-year-olds up at 5 a.m. is always fun.

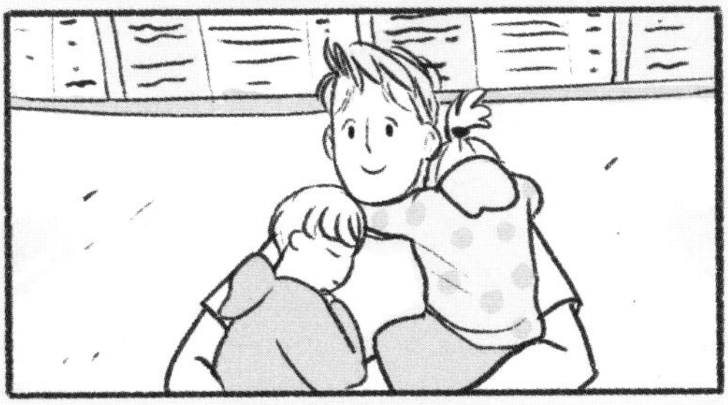

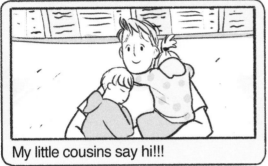

My little cousins say hi!!!

omg

can i come to menorca with you pls

Plane leaves in 90 mins!

Can you run that fast??

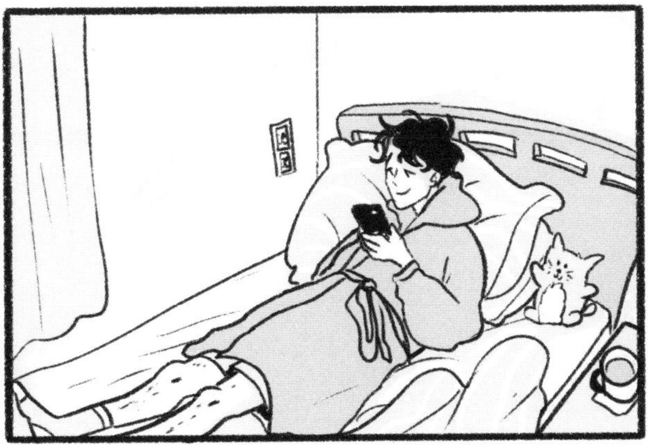

i could try

i could fit in your suitcase

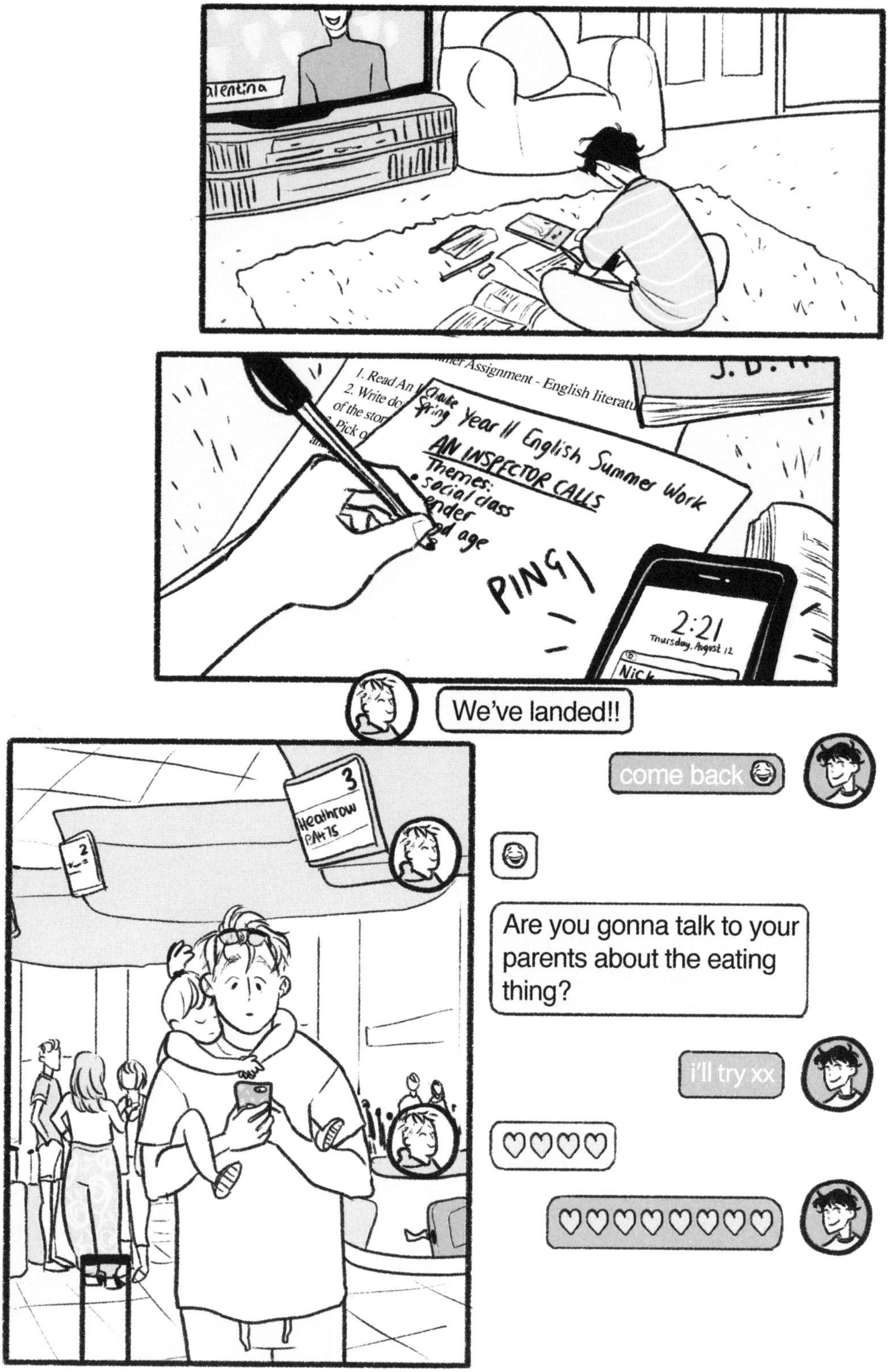

Year 11 English Summer Work
AN INSPECTOR CALLS
Themes:
• social class
PING!
2:21
Thursday, August 12
We've landed!!
come back 😂
😂
Are you gonna talk to your parents about the eating thing?
i'll try xx
♡♡♡♡
♡♡♡♡♡♡♡♡

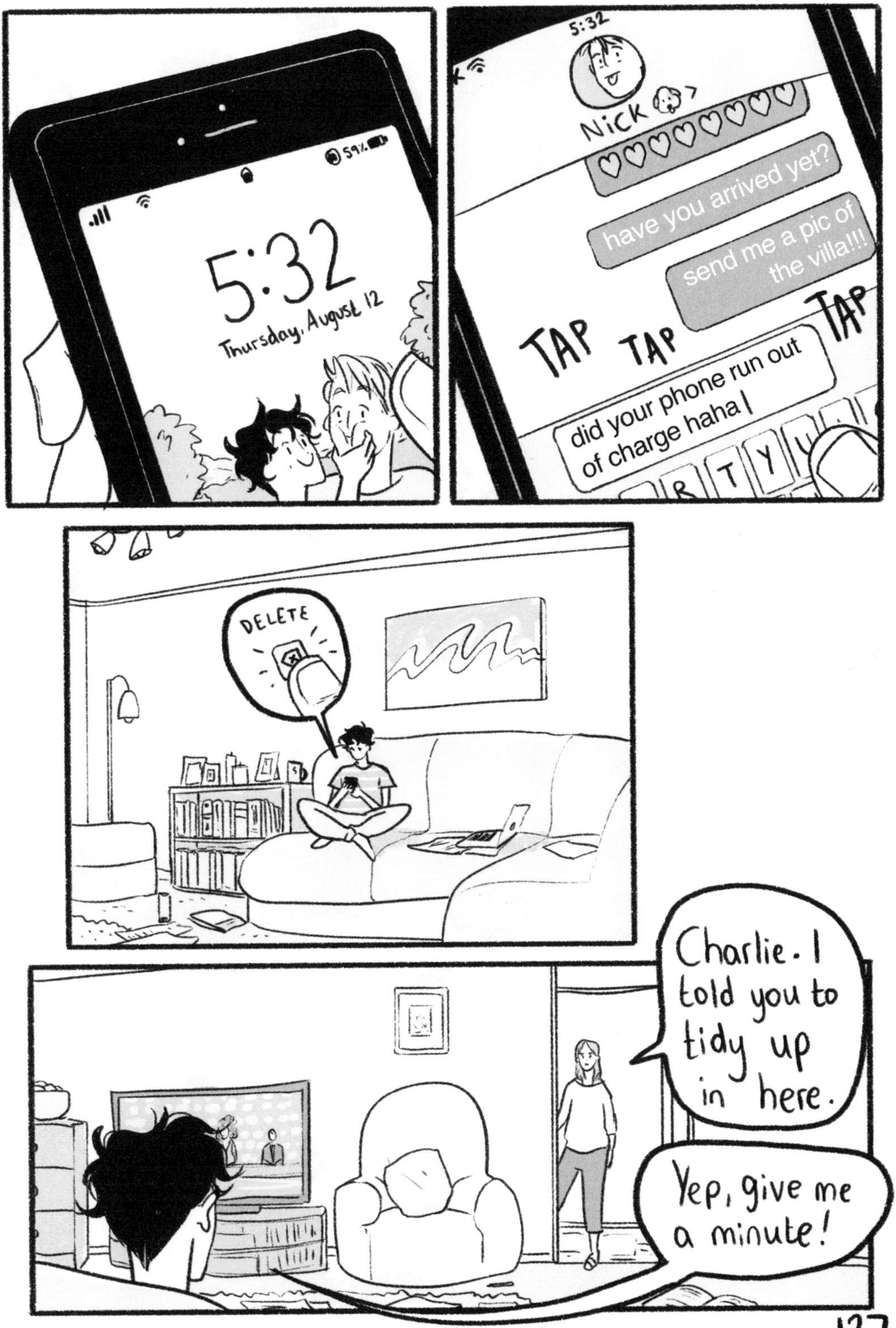
5:32
Thursday, August 12
5:32
Nick
have you arrived yet?
send me a pic of the villa!!!
TAP
TAP
TAP
did your phone run out of charge haha
DELETE
Charlie. I told you to tidy up in here.
Yep, give me a minute!

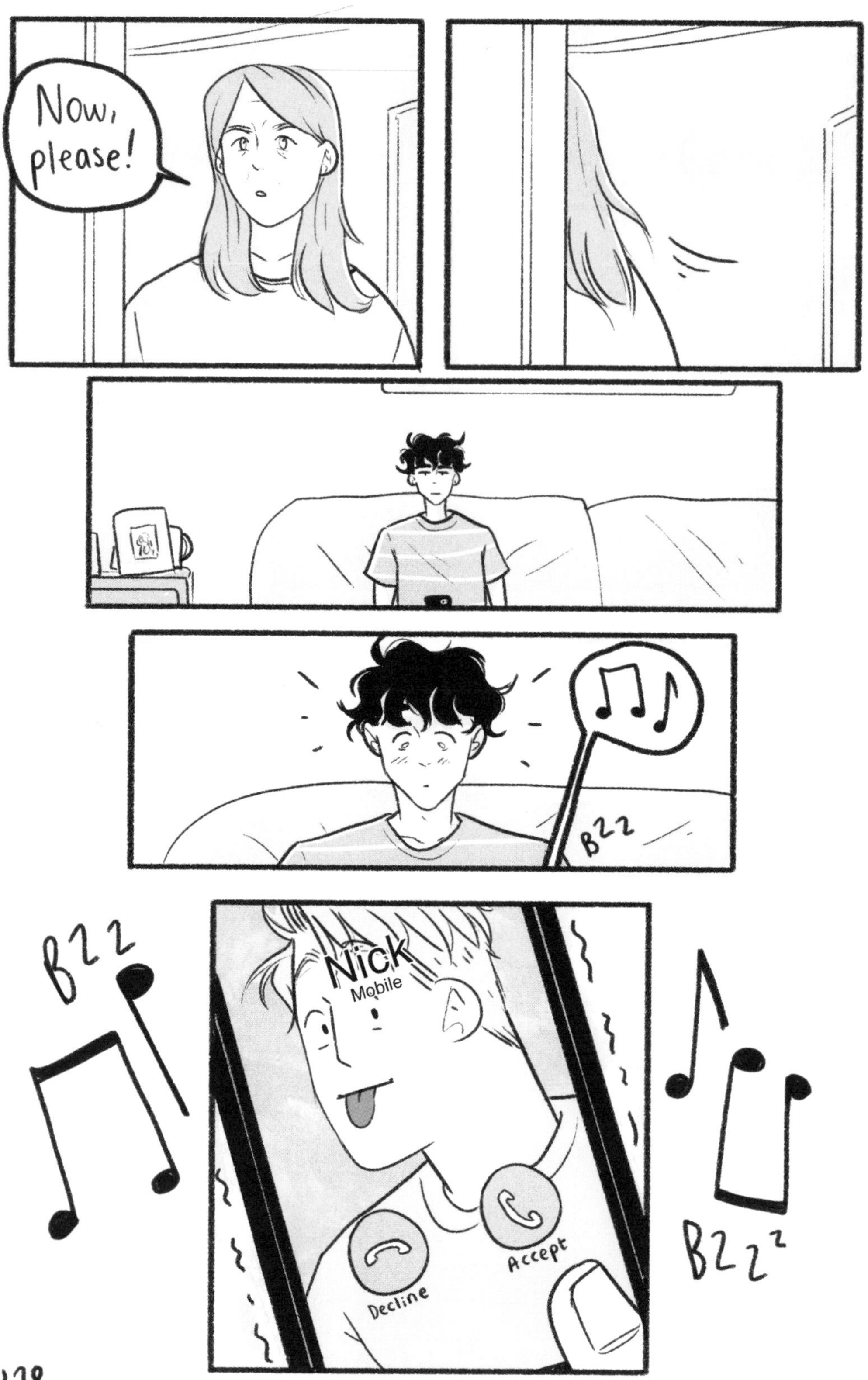
Now, please!
BZZ
BZZ
Nick
Mobile
Decline
Accept
BZZZ

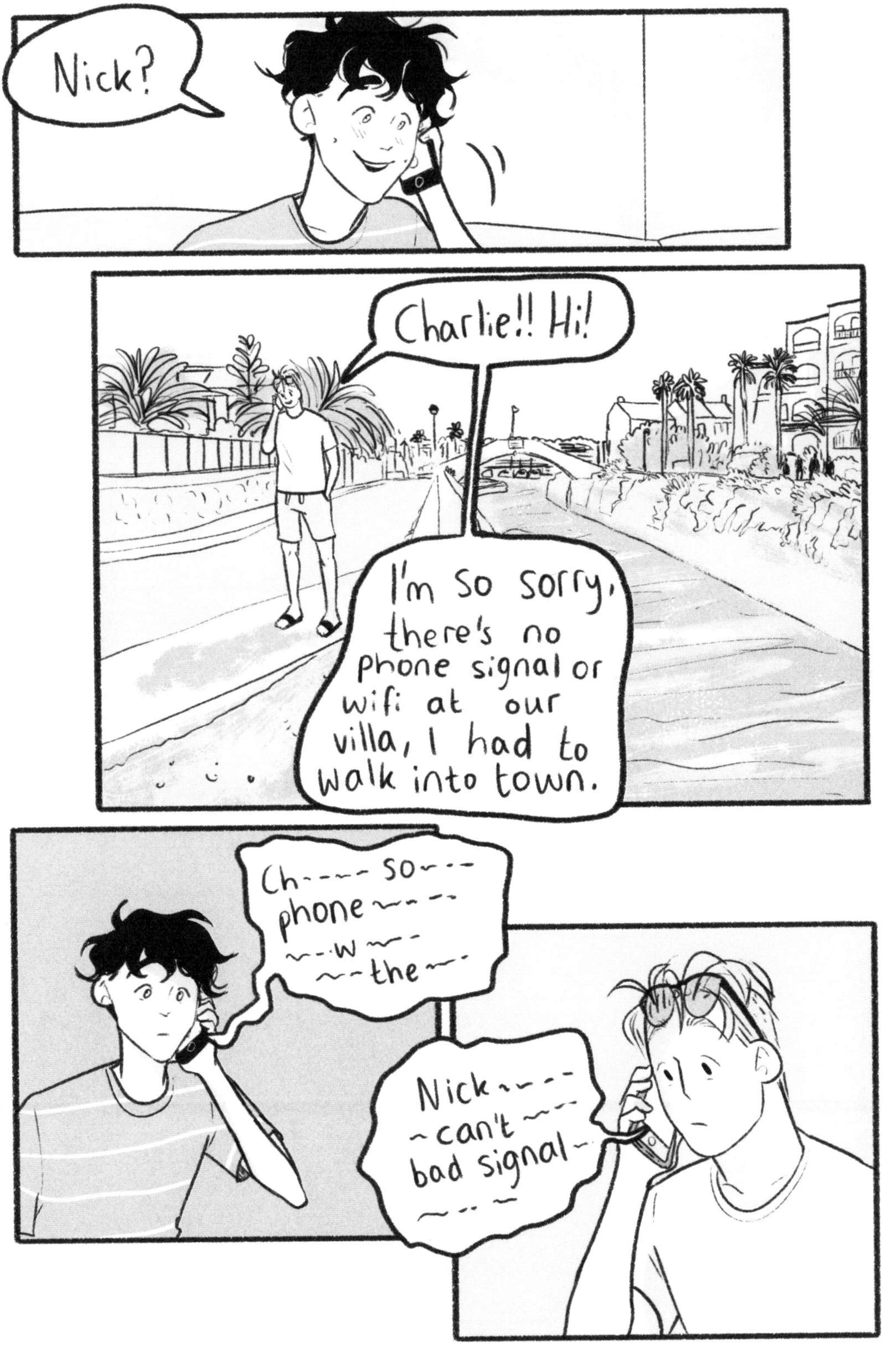
Nick?
Charlie!! Hi!
I'm so sorry, there's no phone signal or wifi at our villa, I had to walk into town.
Ch---- so--- phone---- --w-- --the--
Nick---- -can't--- bad signal--- --

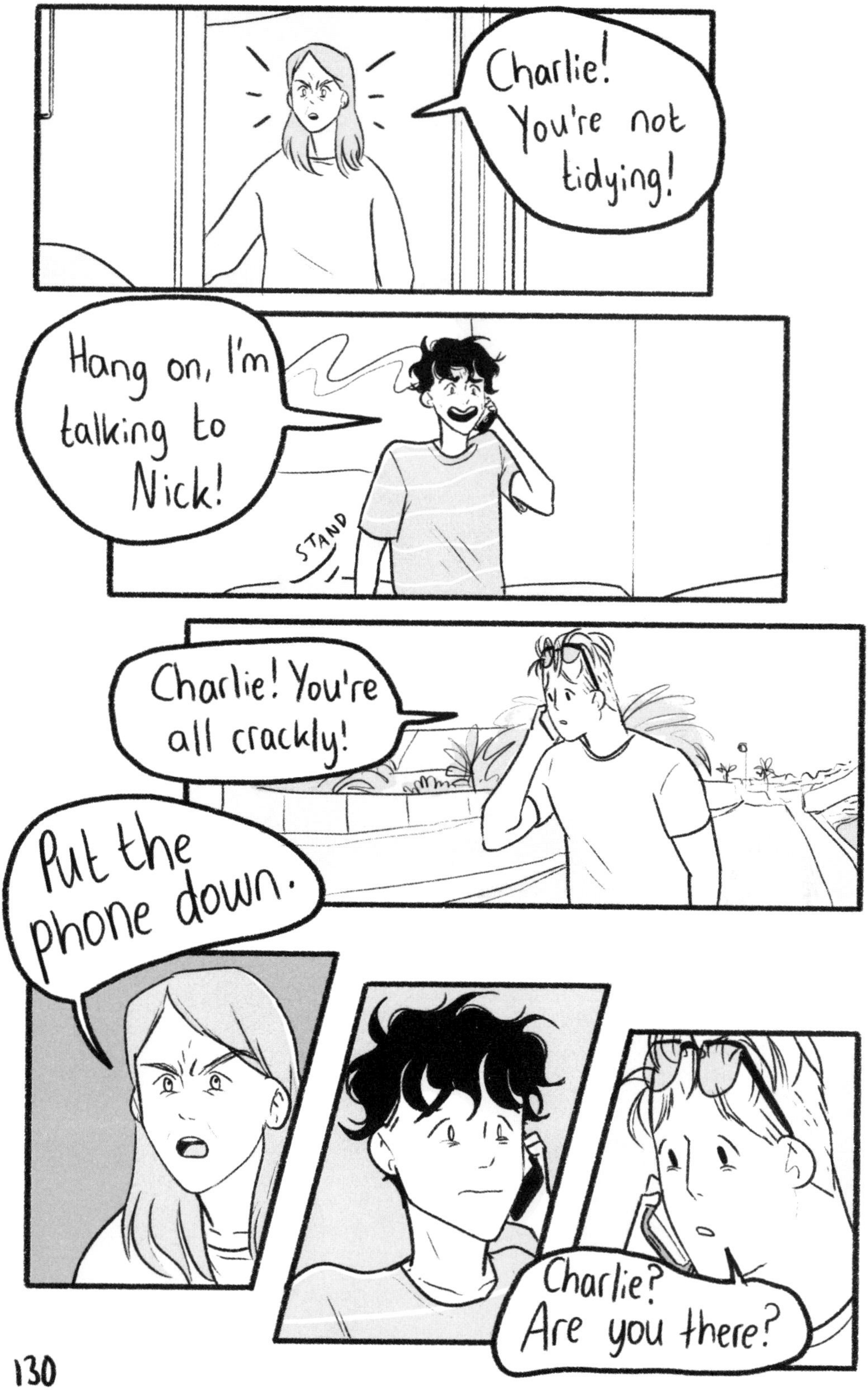
Charlie! You're not tidying!
Hang on, I'm talking to Nick!
STAND
Charlie! You're all crackly!
Put the phone down.
Charlie? Are you there?

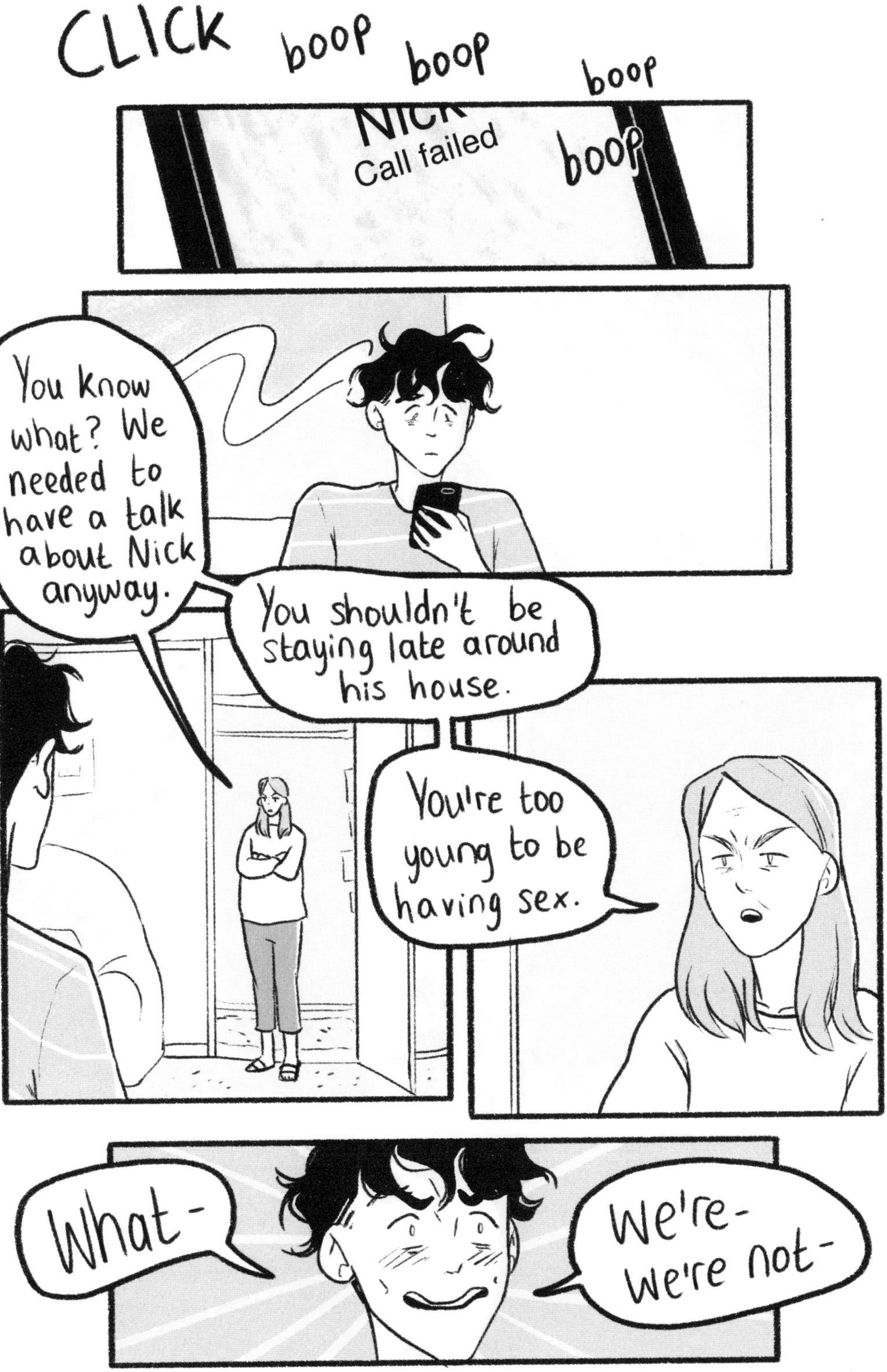
CLICK boop boop boop
Nick
Call failed
boop
You know what? We needed to have a talk about Nick anyway.
You shouldn't be staying late around his house.
You're too young to be having sex.
What-
We're- we're not-

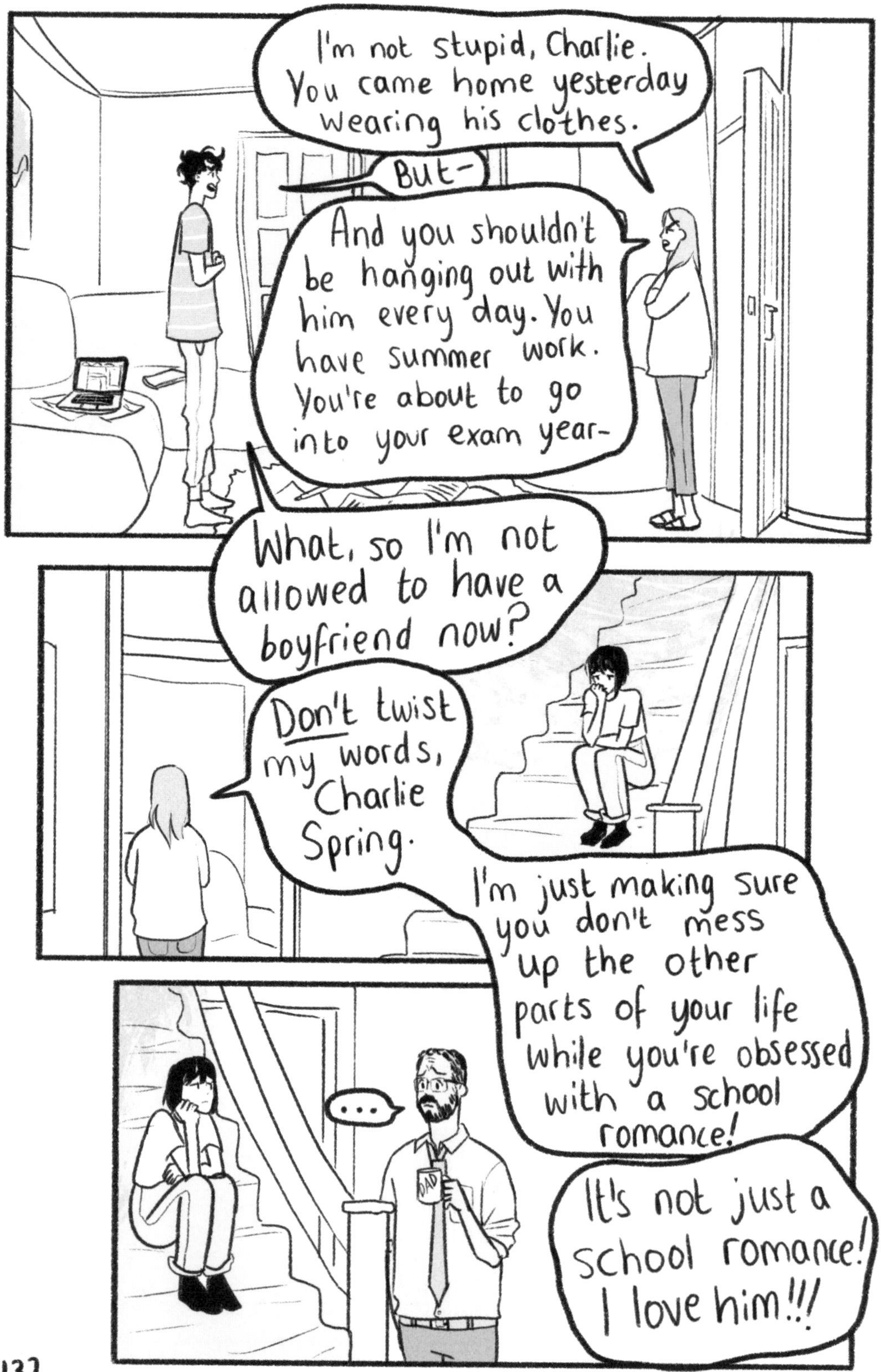
I'm not stupid, Charlie. You came home yesterday wearing his clothes.
But-
And you shouldn't be hanging out with him every day. You have summer work. You're about to go into your exam year-
What, so I'm not allowed to have a boyfriend now?
Don't twist my words, Charlie Spring.
I'm just making sure you don't mess up the other parts of your life while you're obsessed with a school romance!
...
DAD
It's not just a school romance! I love him!!!

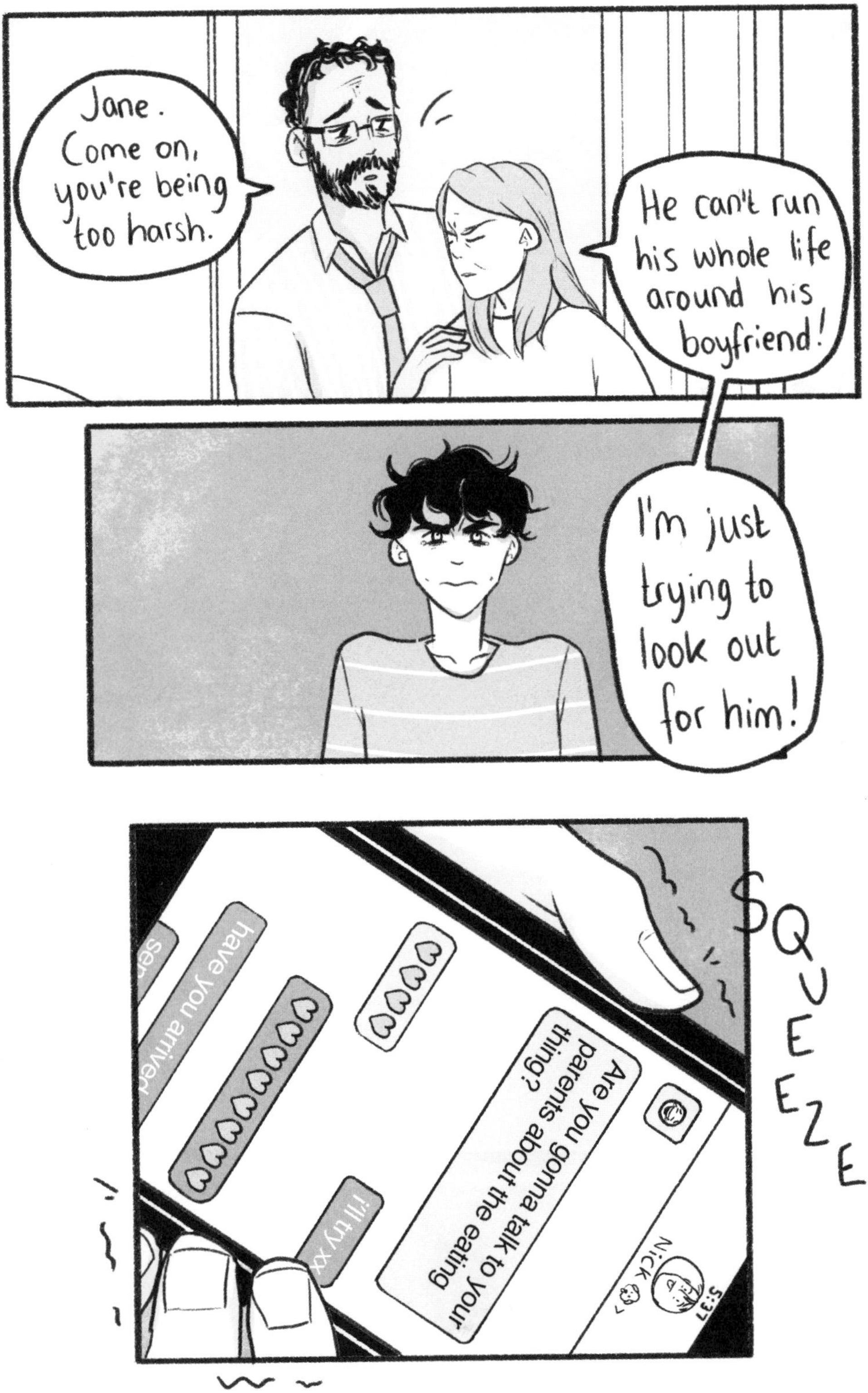
Jane. Come on, you're being too harsh.
He can't run his whole life around his boyfriend!
I'm just trying to look out for him!
have you arrived
Nick
Are you gonna talk to your parents about the eating thing?
i'll try xx
SQUEEZE

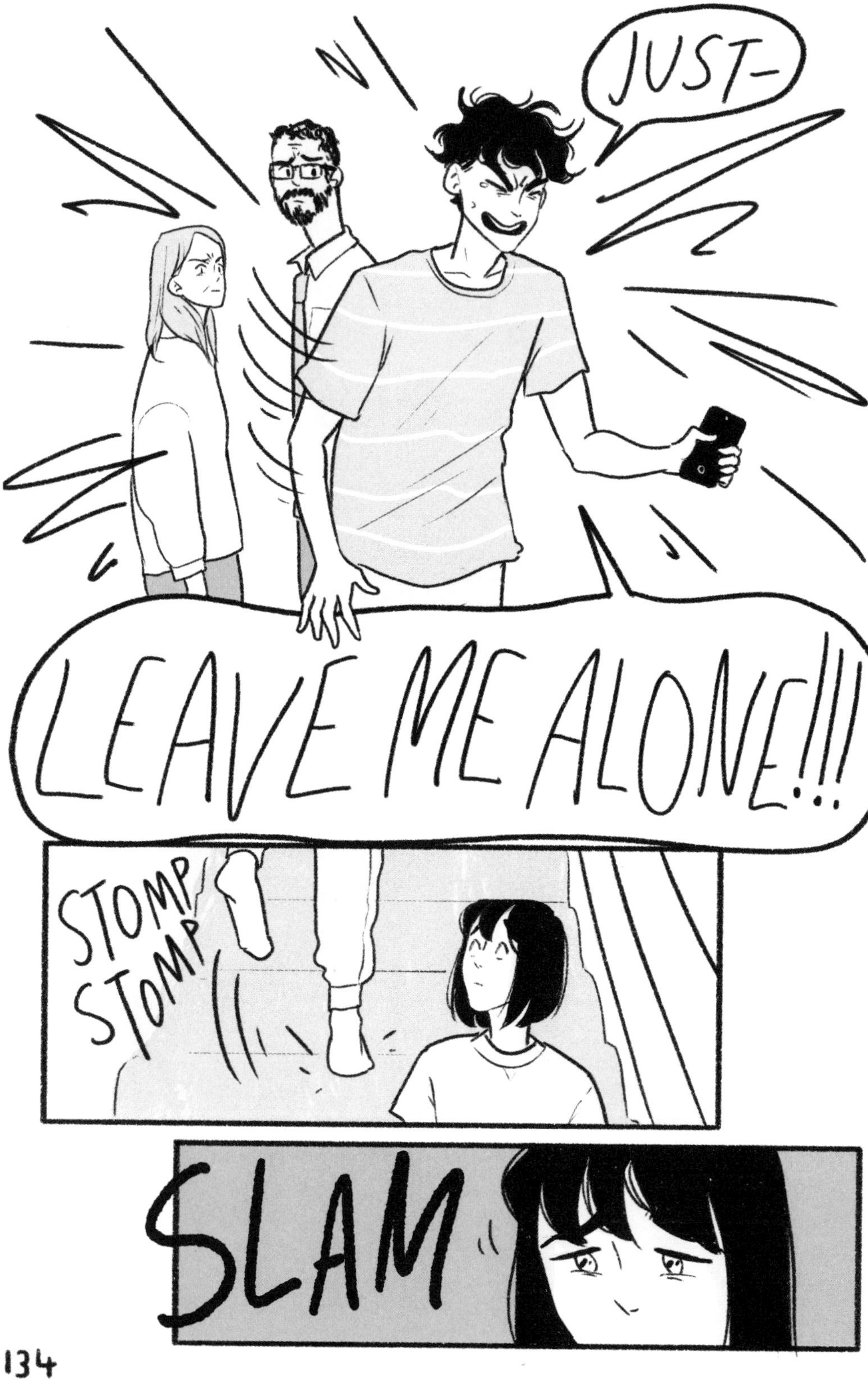
JUST–
LEAVE ME ALONE!!!
STOMP
STOMP
SLAM

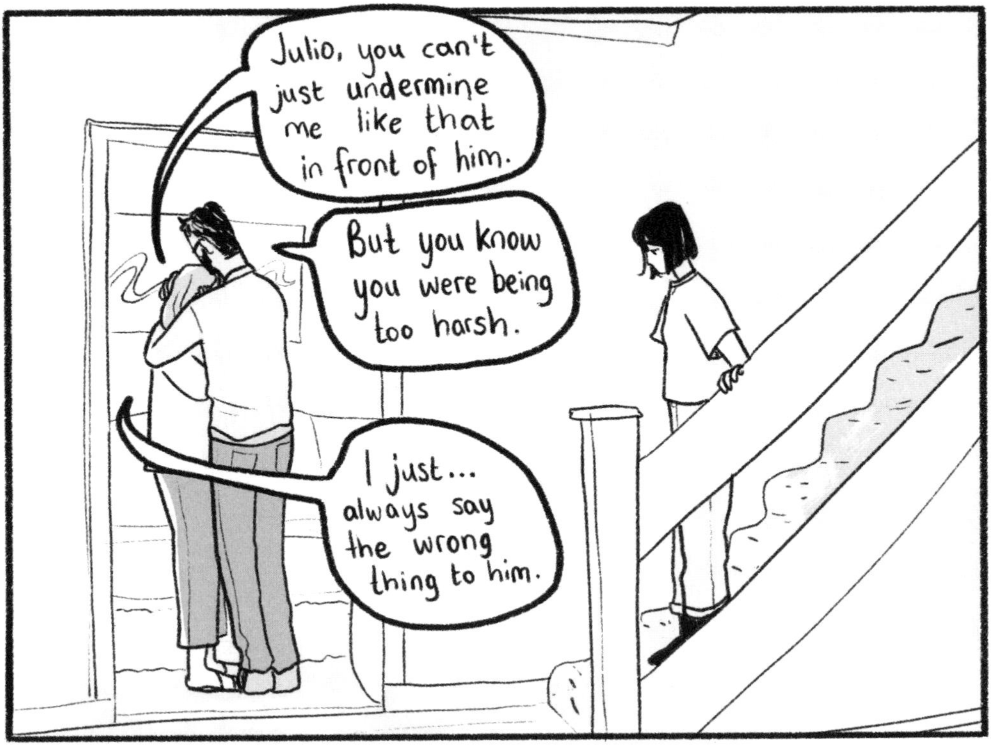
Julio, you can't just undermine me like that in front of him.
But you know you were being too harsh.
I just... always say the wrong thing to him.

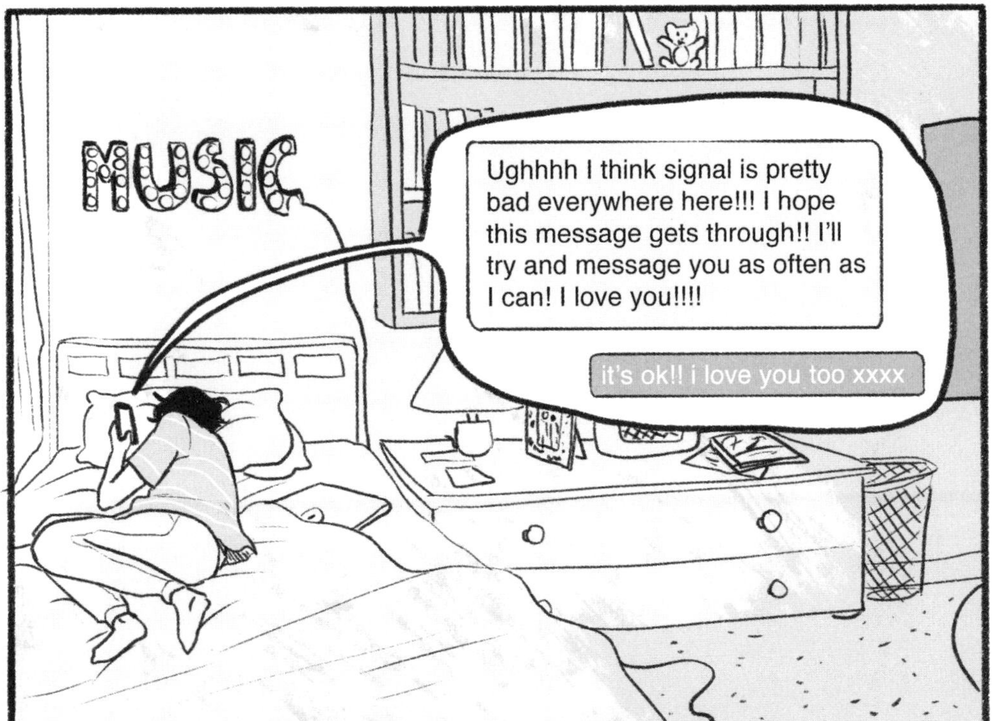
MUSIC
Ughhhh I think signal is pretty bad everywhere here!!! I hope this message gets through!! I'll try and message you as often as I can! I love you!!!!
it's ok!! i love you too xxxx

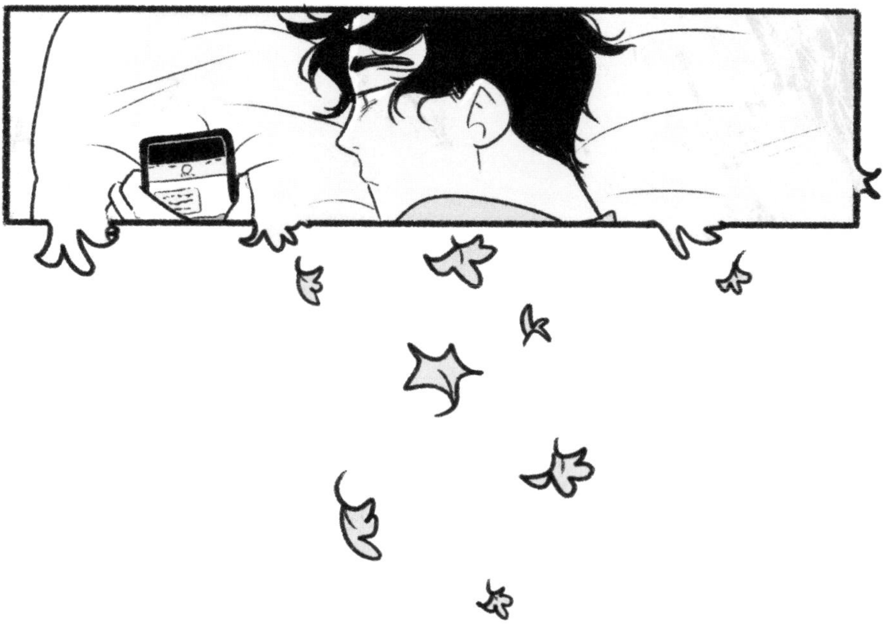

The first week.

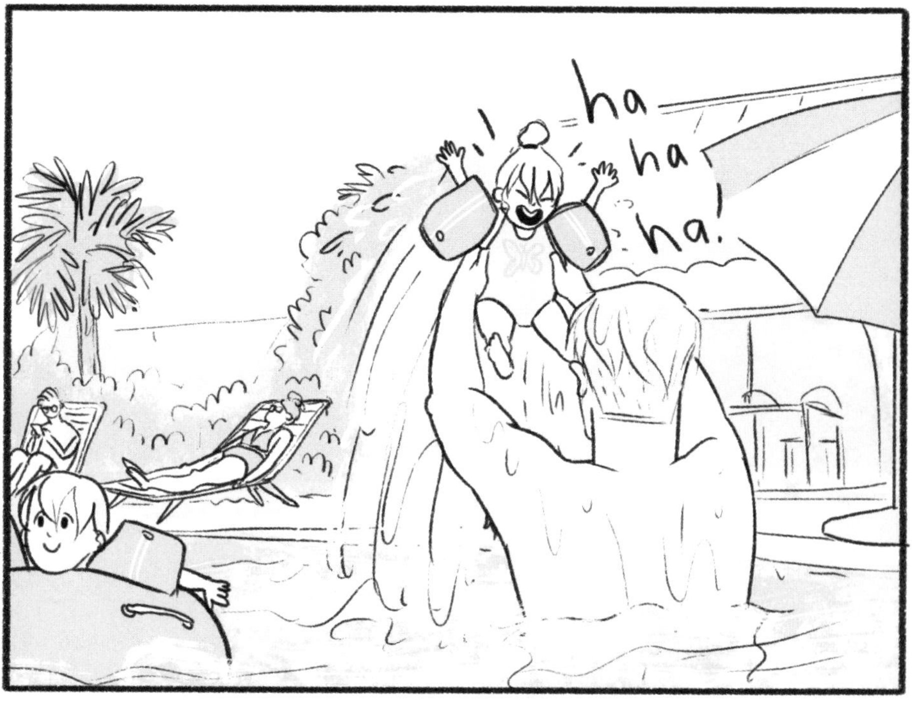
ha
ha
ha!

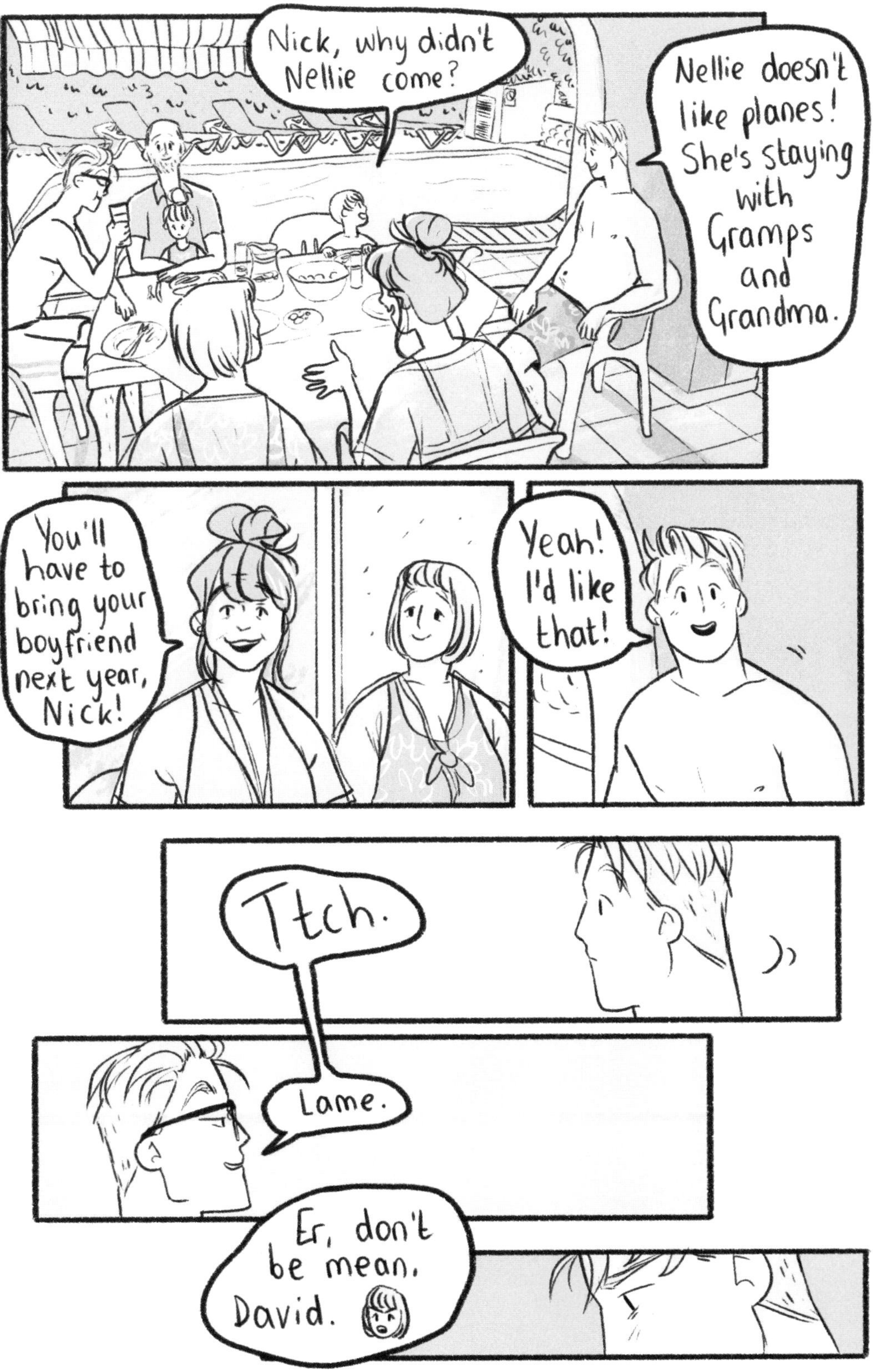
Nick, why didn't Nellie come?
Nellie doesn't like planes! She's staying with Gramps and Grandma.
You'll have to bring your boyfriend next year, Nick!
Yeah! I'd like that!
Ttch.
Lame.
Er, don't be mean, David.

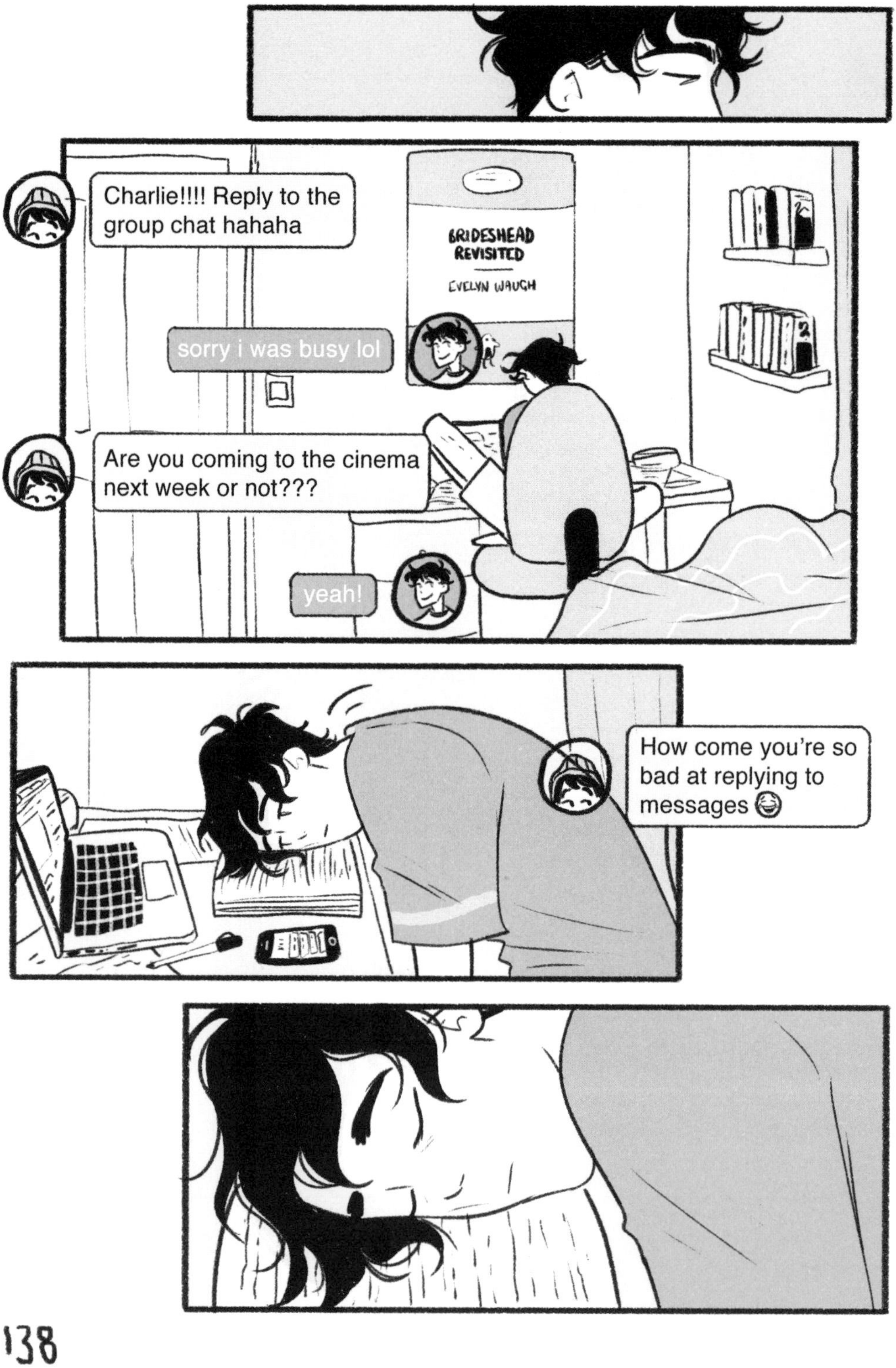

Charlie!!!! Reply to the group chat hahaha
BRIDESHEAD REVISITED
EVELYN WAUGH
sorry i was busy lol
Are you coming to the cinema next week or not???
yeah!
How come you're so bad at replying to messages 😂

The second week.

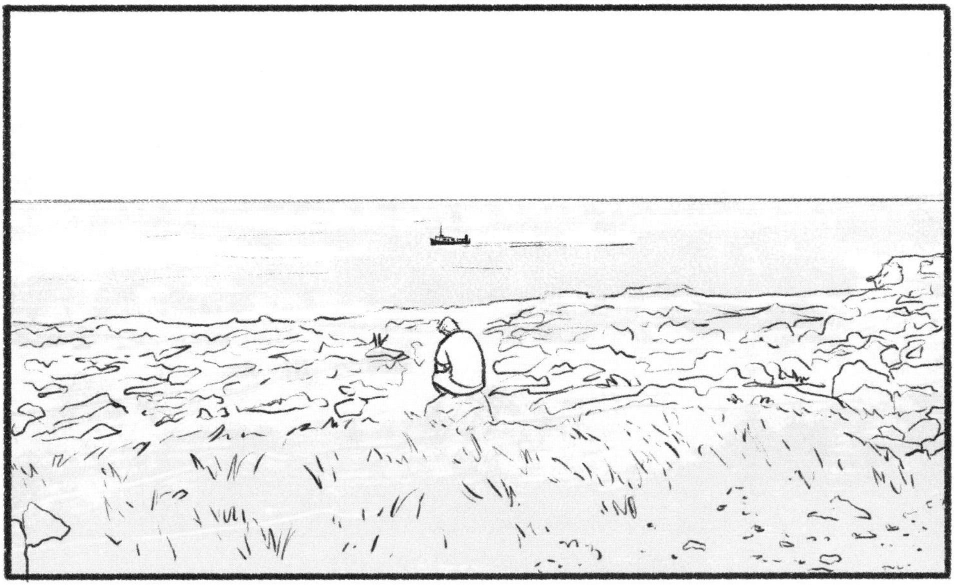

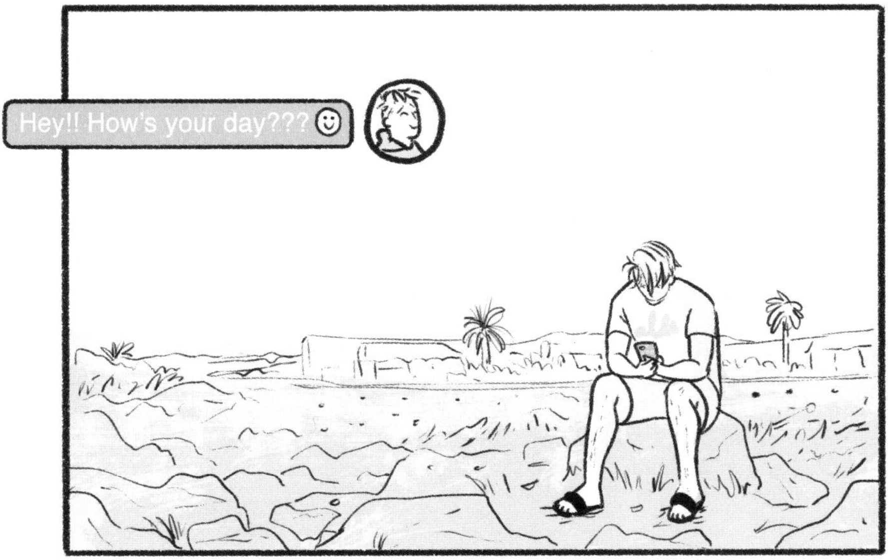
Hey!! How's your day???

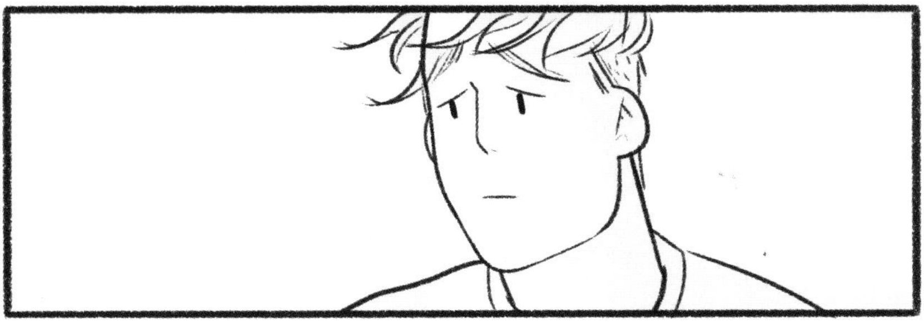

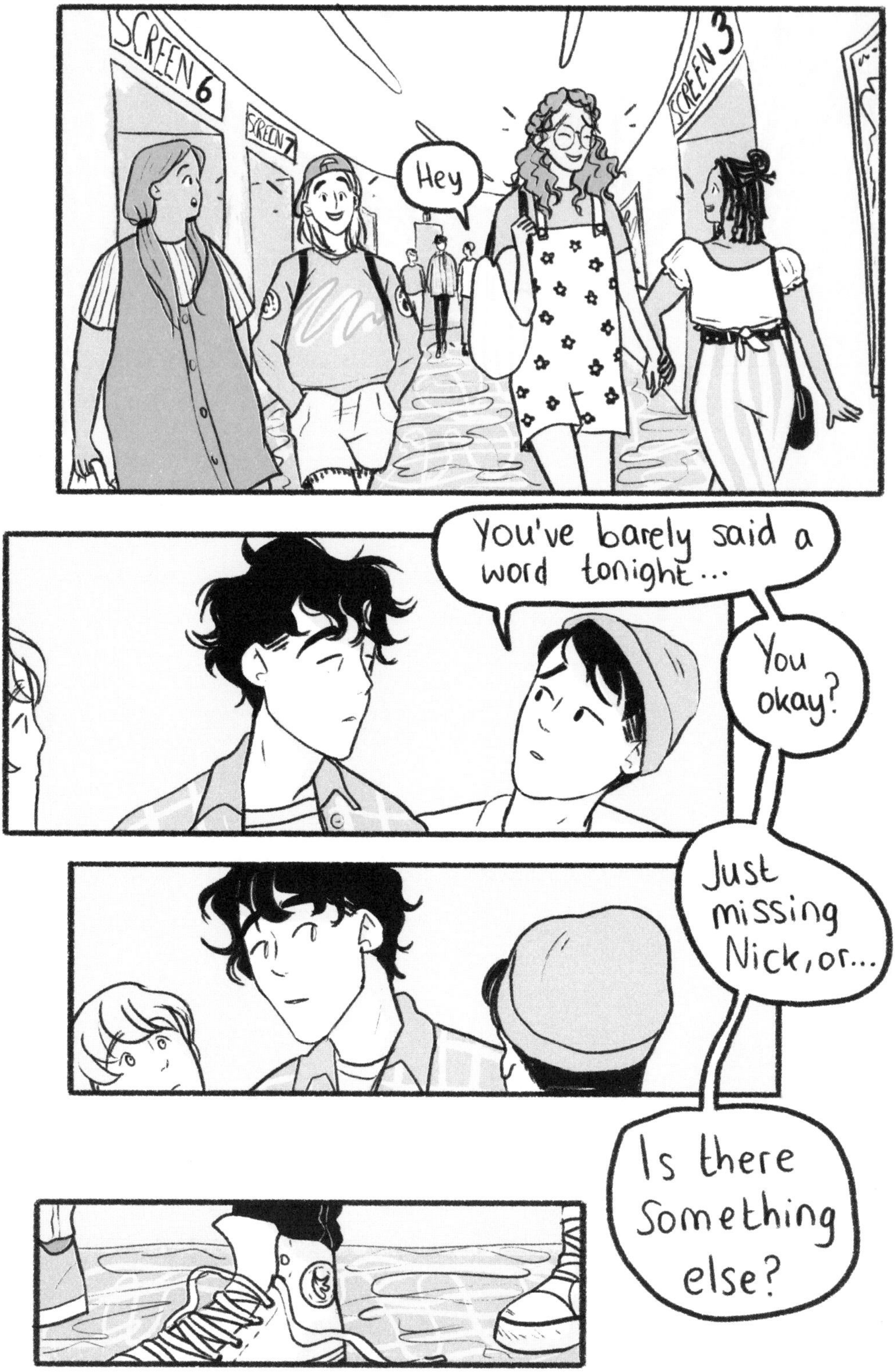
SCREEN 6
SCREEN 7
Hey
SCREEN 3
You've barely said a word tonight...
You okay?
Just missing Nick, or...
Is there something else?

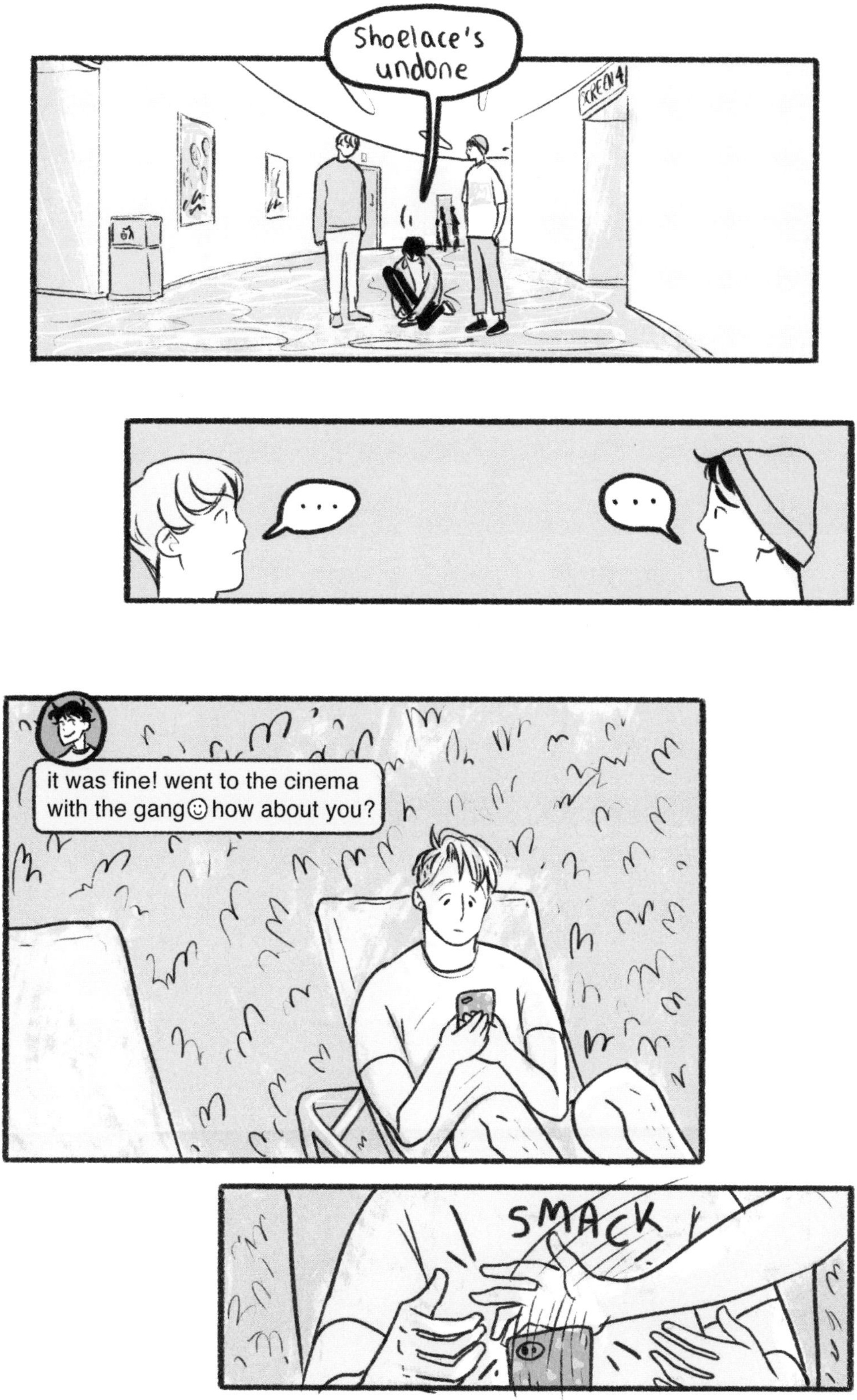
Shoelace's undone
SCREEN 4
...
...
it was fine! went to the cinema with the gang☺ how about you?
SMACK

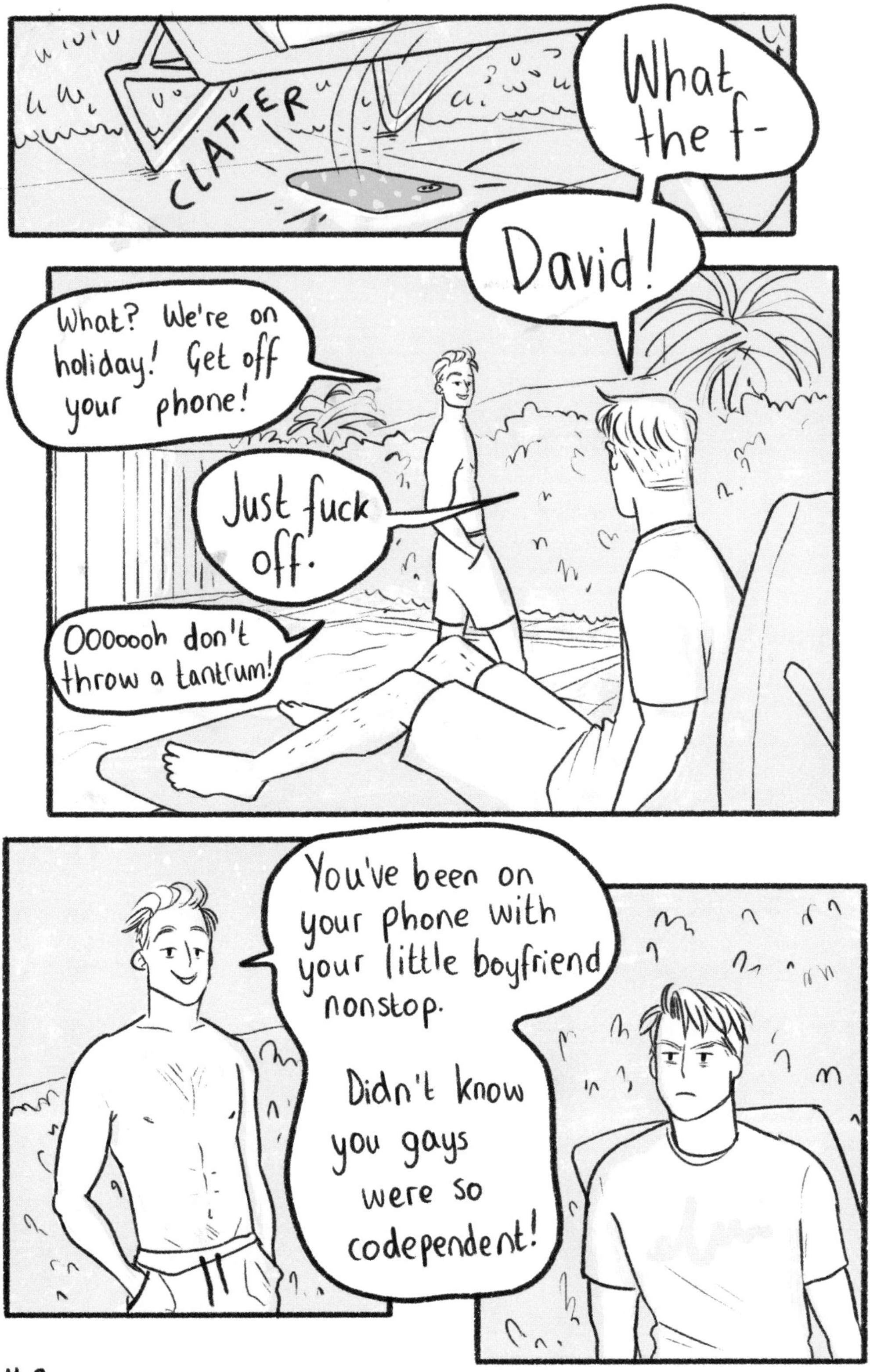
CLATTER
What the f-
David!
What? We're on holiday! Get off your phone!
Just fuck off.
Ooooooh don't throw a tantrum!
You've been on your phone with your little boyfriend nonstop.
Didn't know you gays were so codependent!

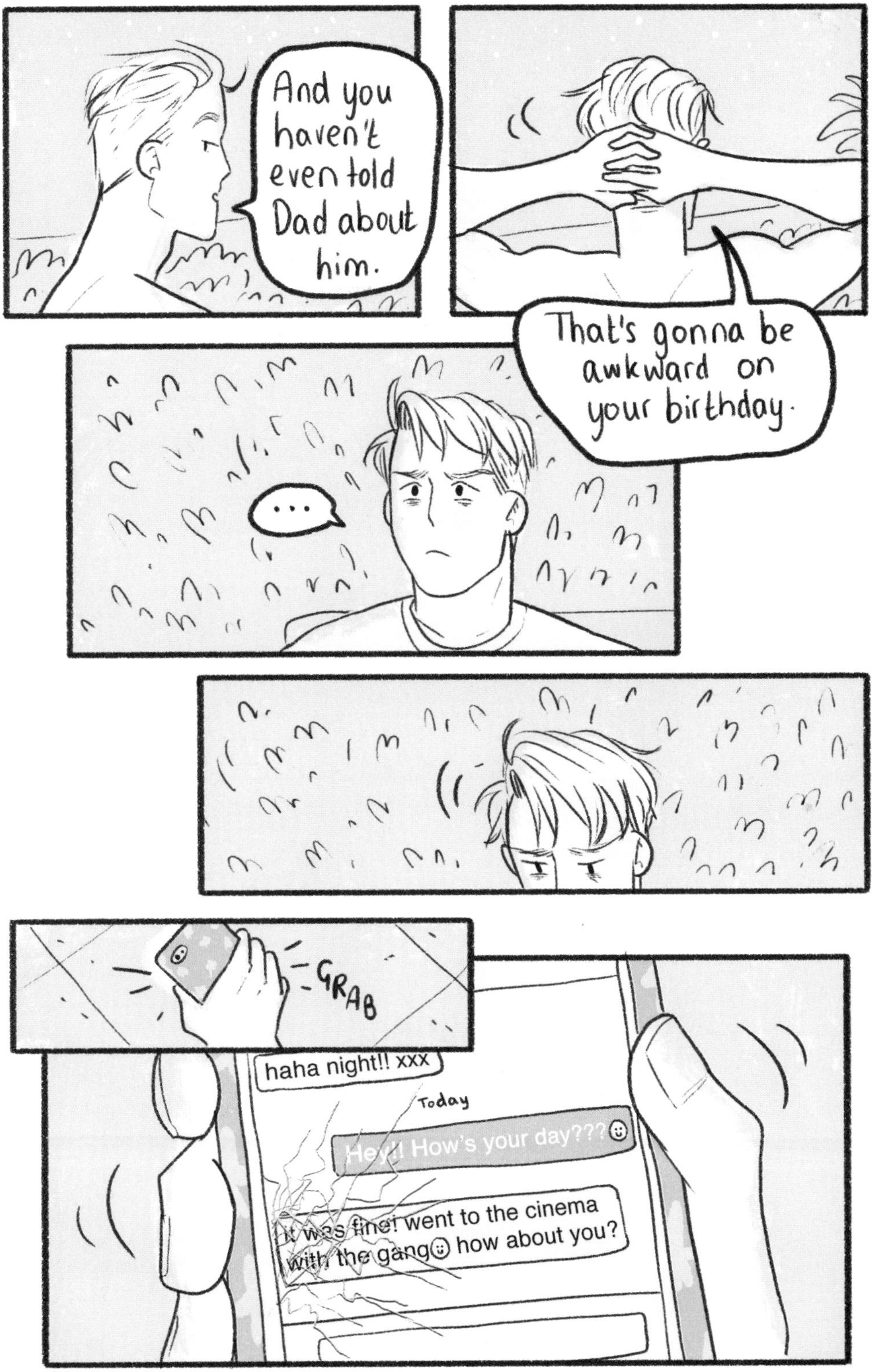
And you haven't even told Dad about him.
That's gonna be awkward on your birthday.
...
GRAB
haha night!! xxx
Today
Hey!! How's your day???
it was fine! went to the cinema with the gang how about you?

The third week.

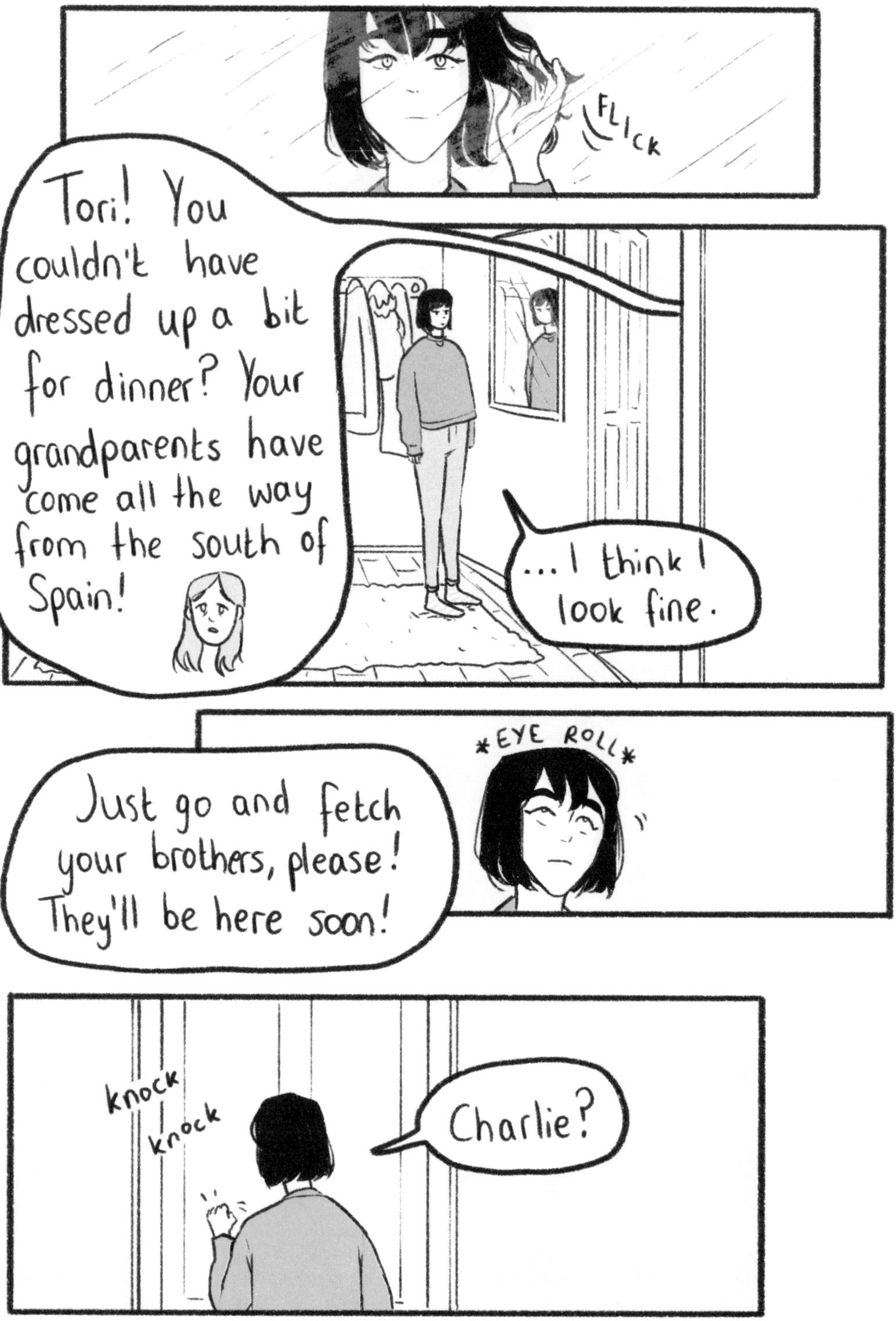
FLICK
Tori! You couldn't have dressed up a bit for dinner? Your grandparents have come all the way from the south of Spain!
...I think I look fine.
EYE ROLL
Just go and fetch your brothers, please! They'll be here soon!
knock
knock
Charlie?

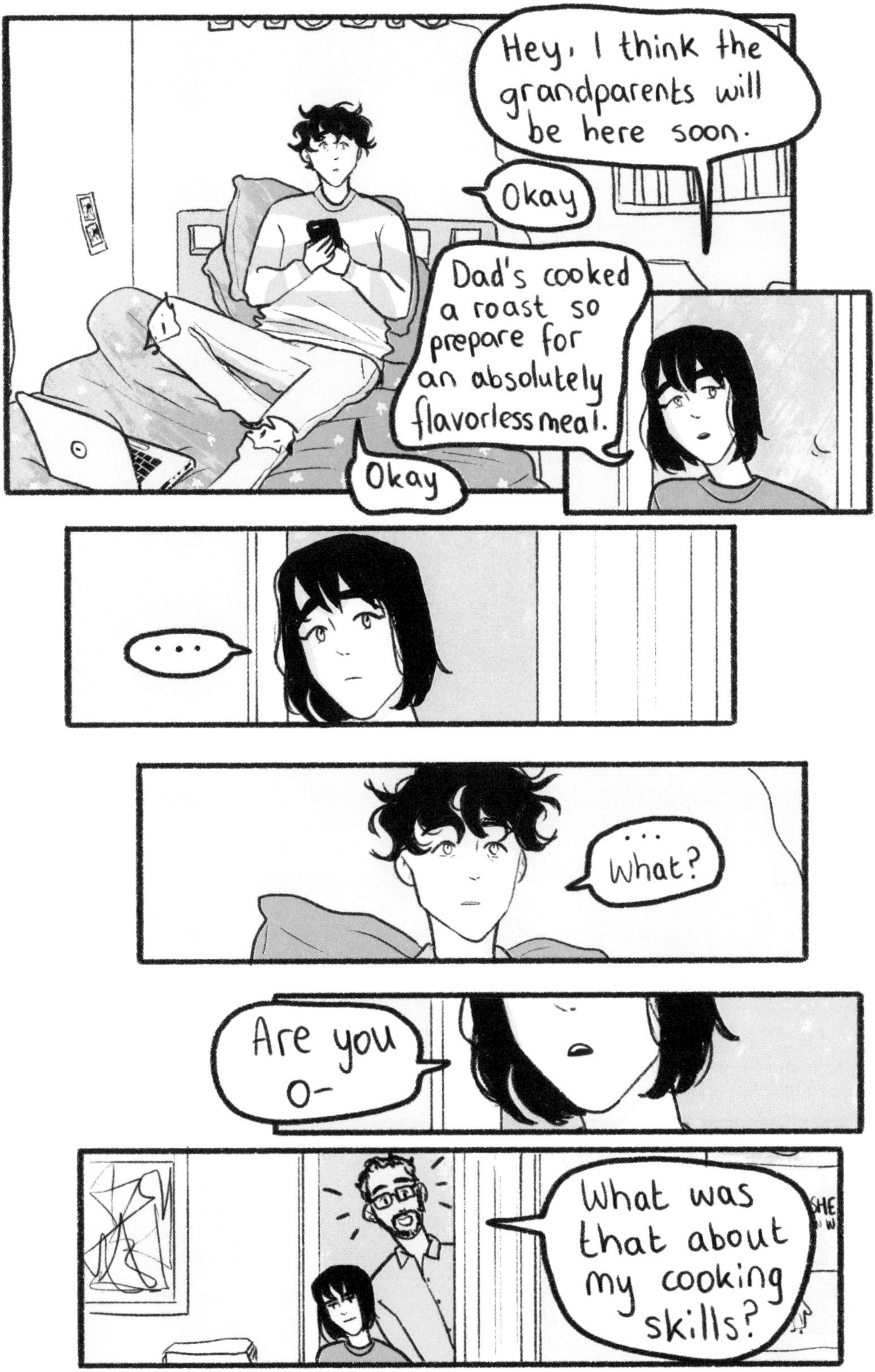
Hey, I think the grandparents will be here soon.
Okay
Dad's cooked a roast so prepare for an absolutely flavorless meal.
Okay
...
... What?
Are you o-
What was that about my cooking skills?

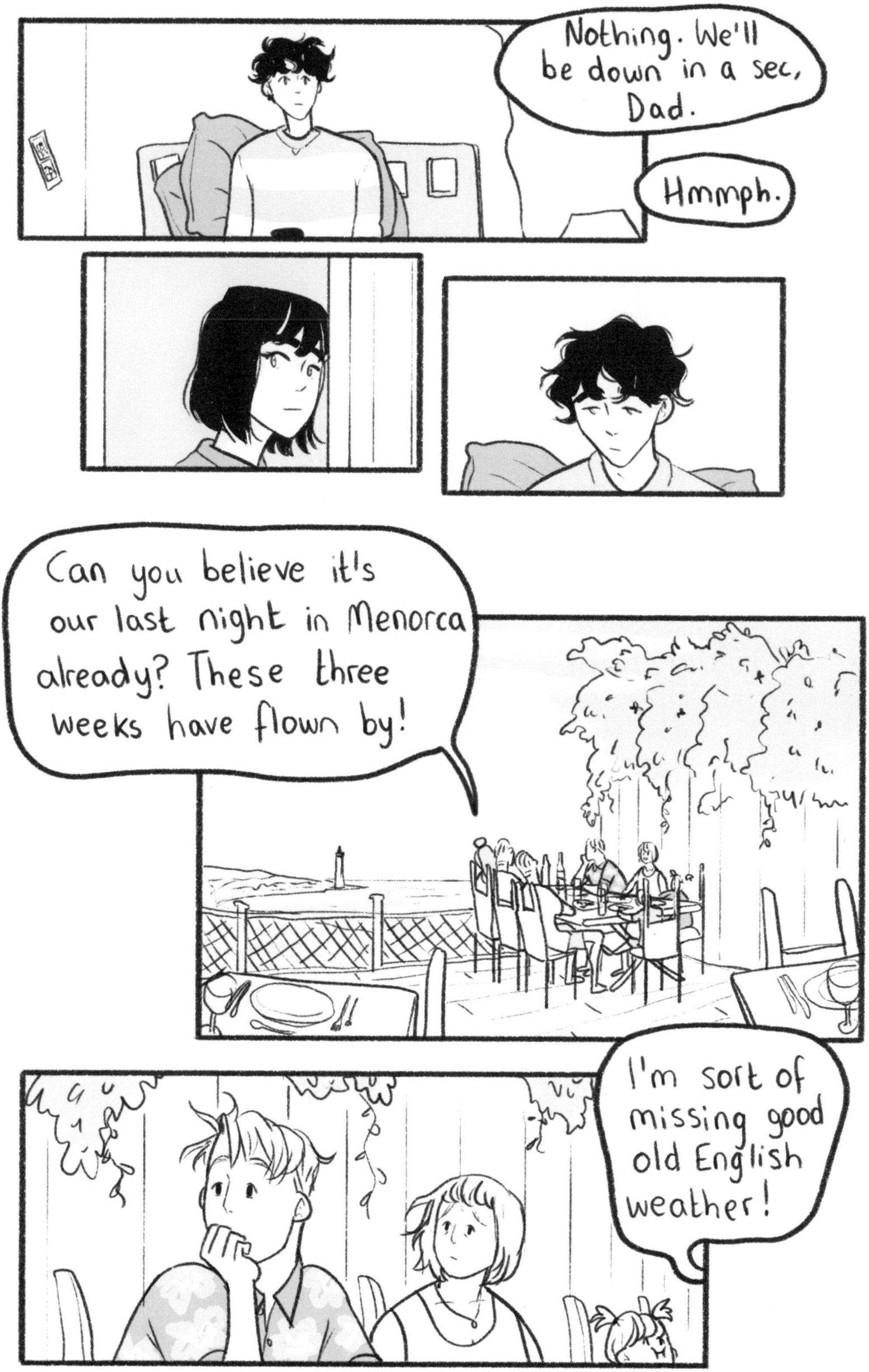
Nothing. We'll be down in a sec, Dad.
Hmmph.
Can you believe it's our last night in Menorca already? These three weeks have flown by!
I'm sort of missing good old English weather!

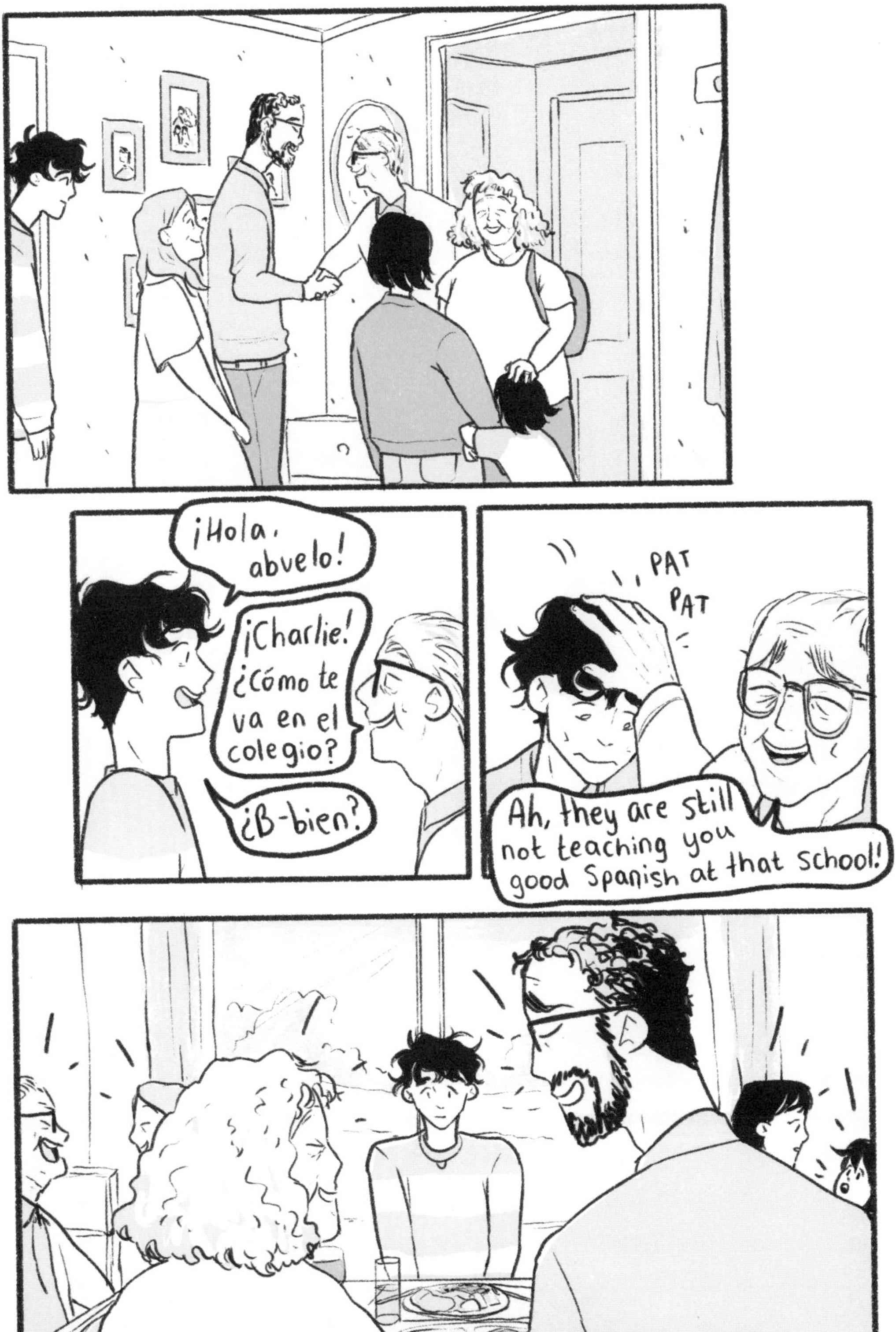
¡Hola, abuelo!
¡Charlie! ¿Cómo te va en el colegio?
¿B-bien?
PAT PAT
Ah, they are still not teaching you good Spanish at that school!

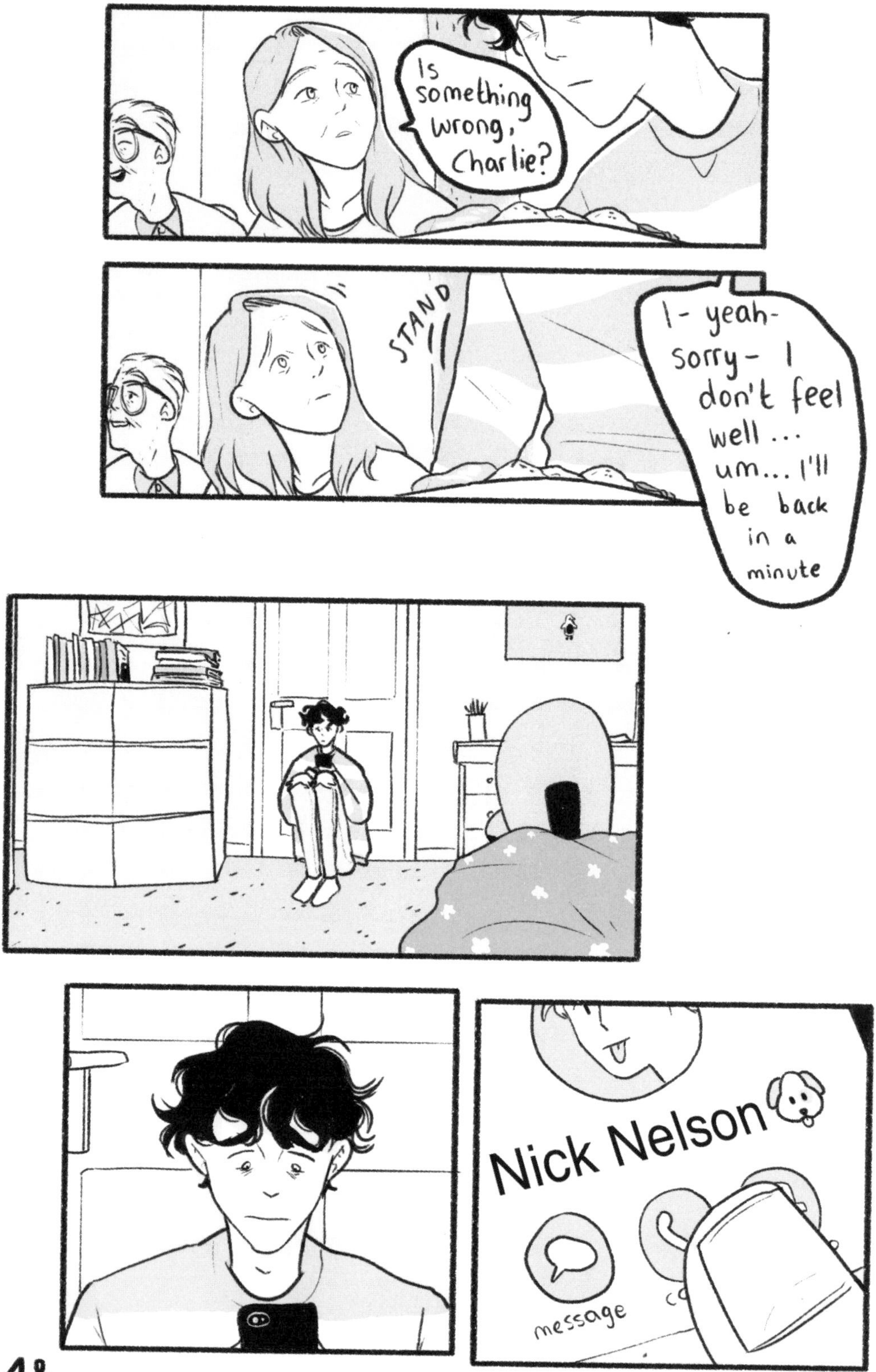

Is something wrong, Charlie?
STAND
I- yeah- sorry- I don't feel well... um... I'll be back in a minute
Nick Nelson
message

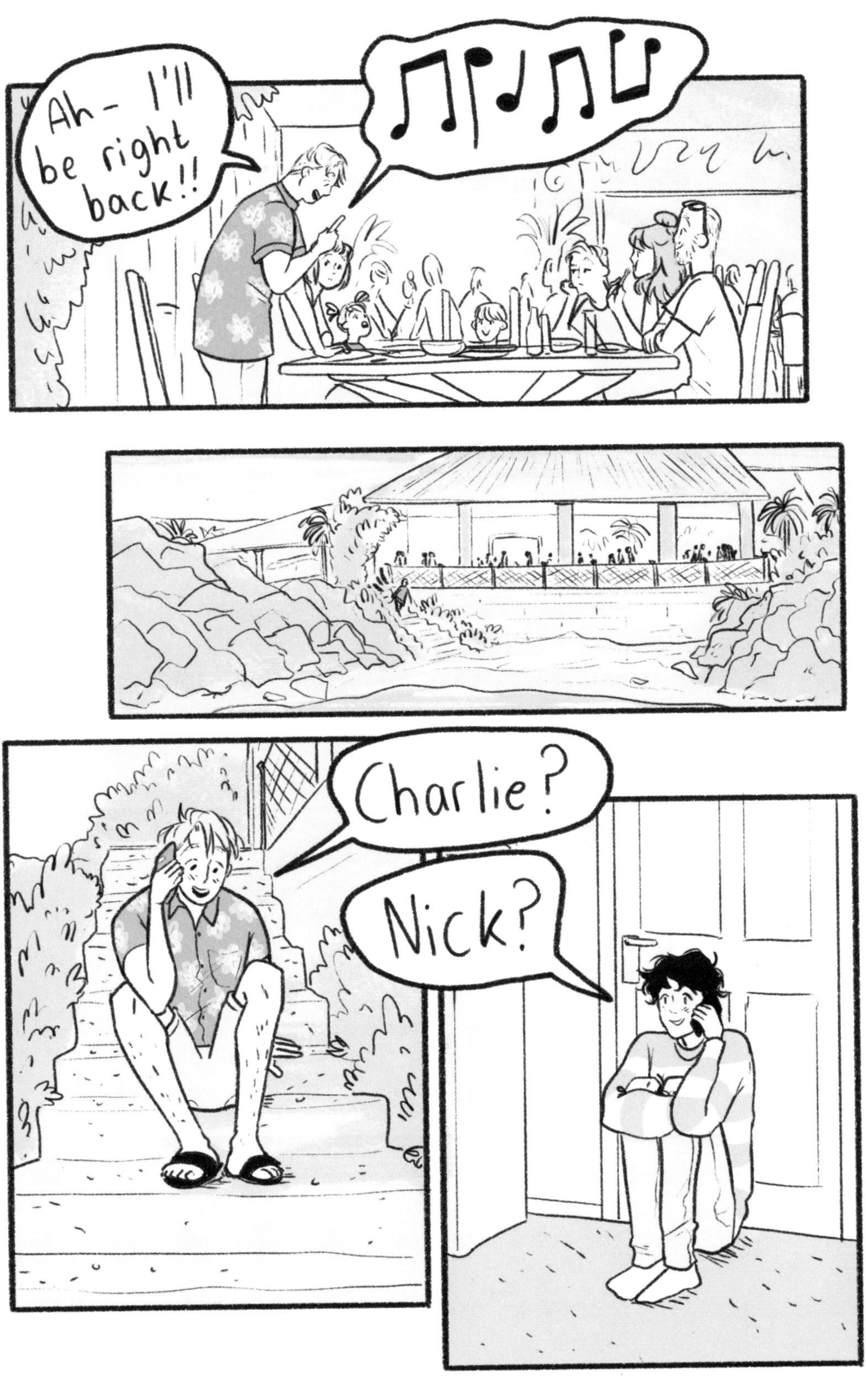
Ah - I'll be right back!!
Charlie?
Nick?

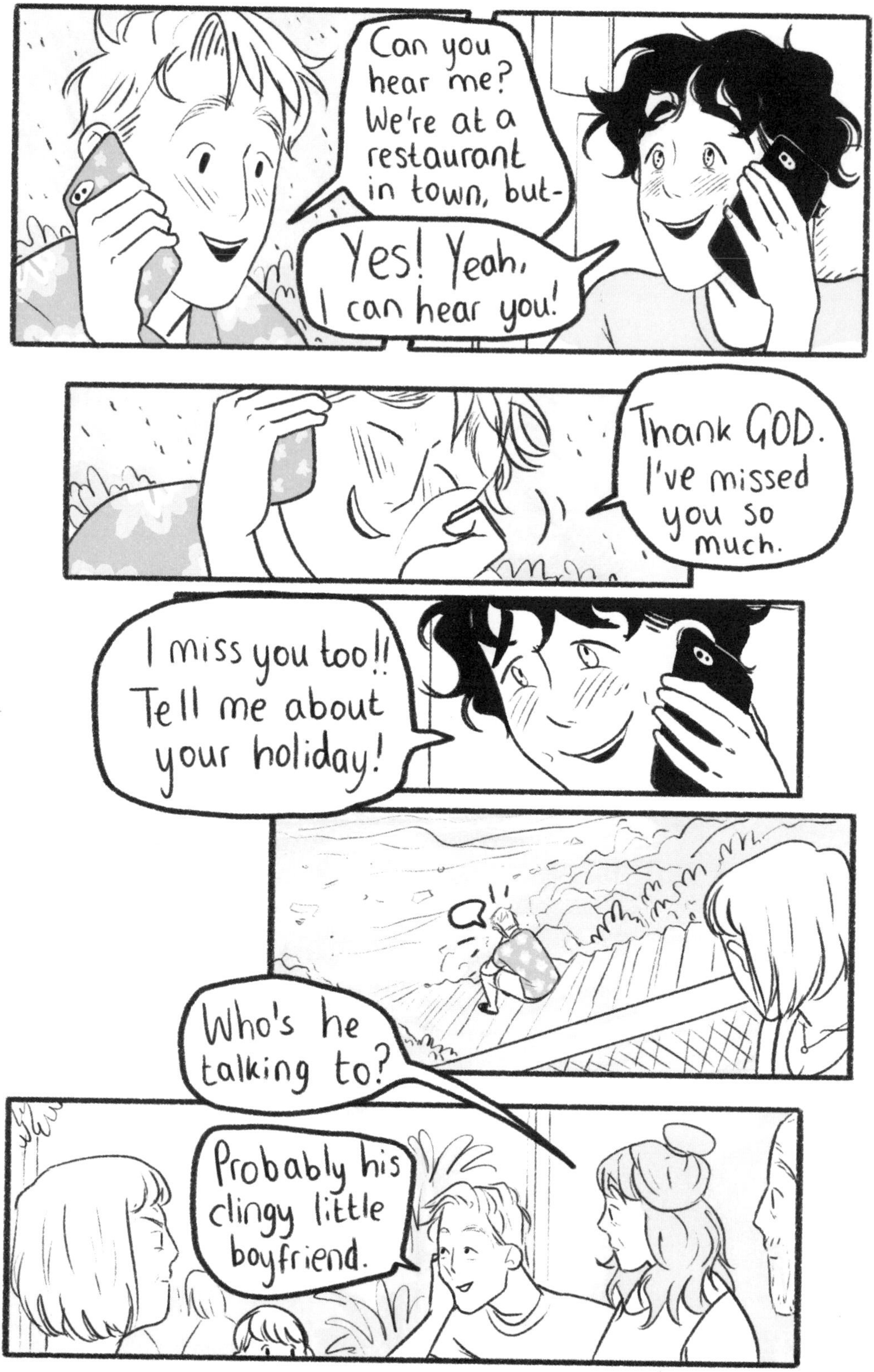
Can you hear me? We're at a restaurant in town, but-
Yes! Yeah, I can hear you!
Thank GOD. I've missed you so much.
I miss you too!! Tell me about your holiday!
Who's he talking to?
Probably his clingy little boyfriend.

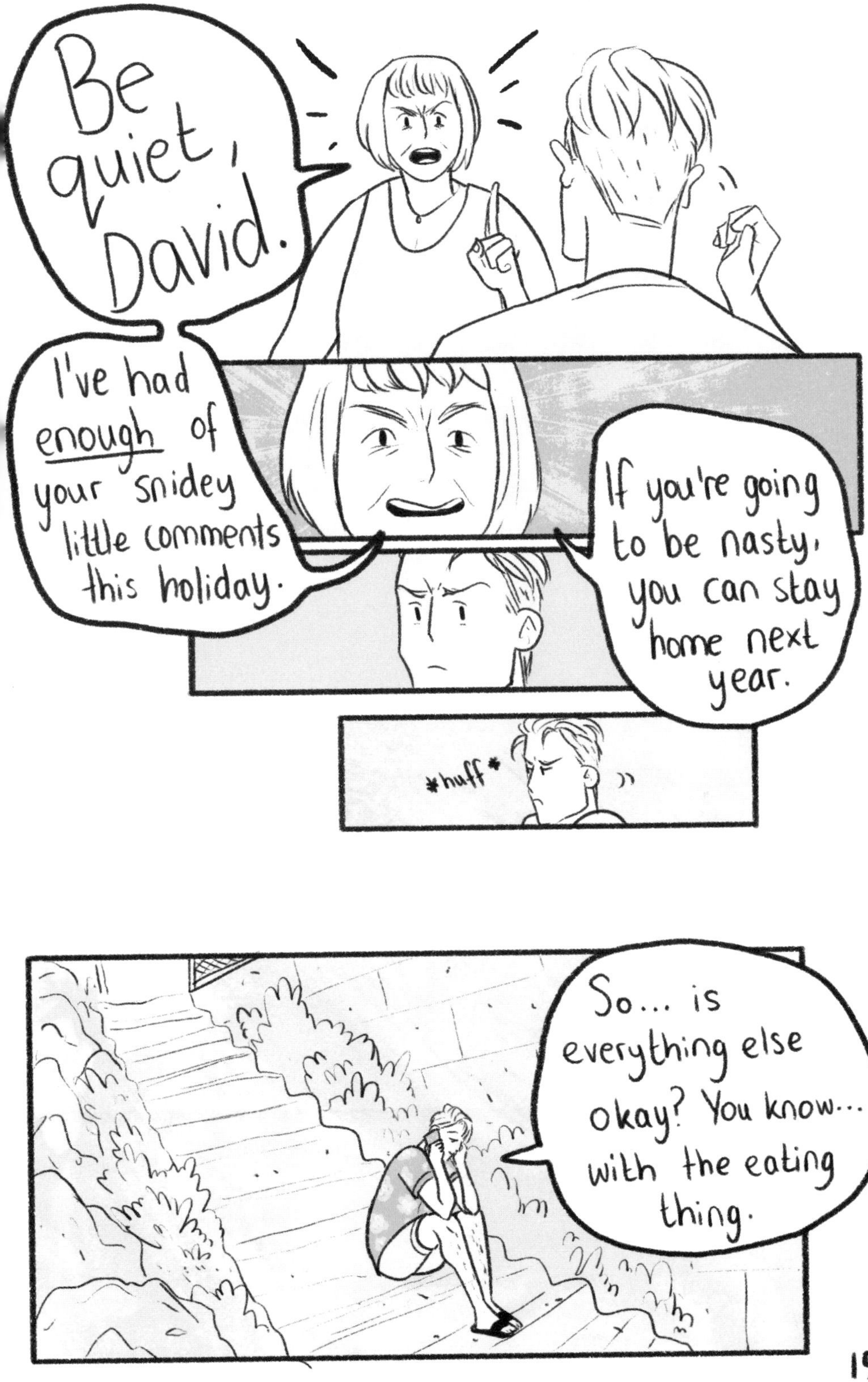
Be quiet, David.
I've had enough of your snidey little comments this holiday.
If you're going to be nasty, you can stay home next year.
huff
So... is everything else okay? You know... with the eating thing.

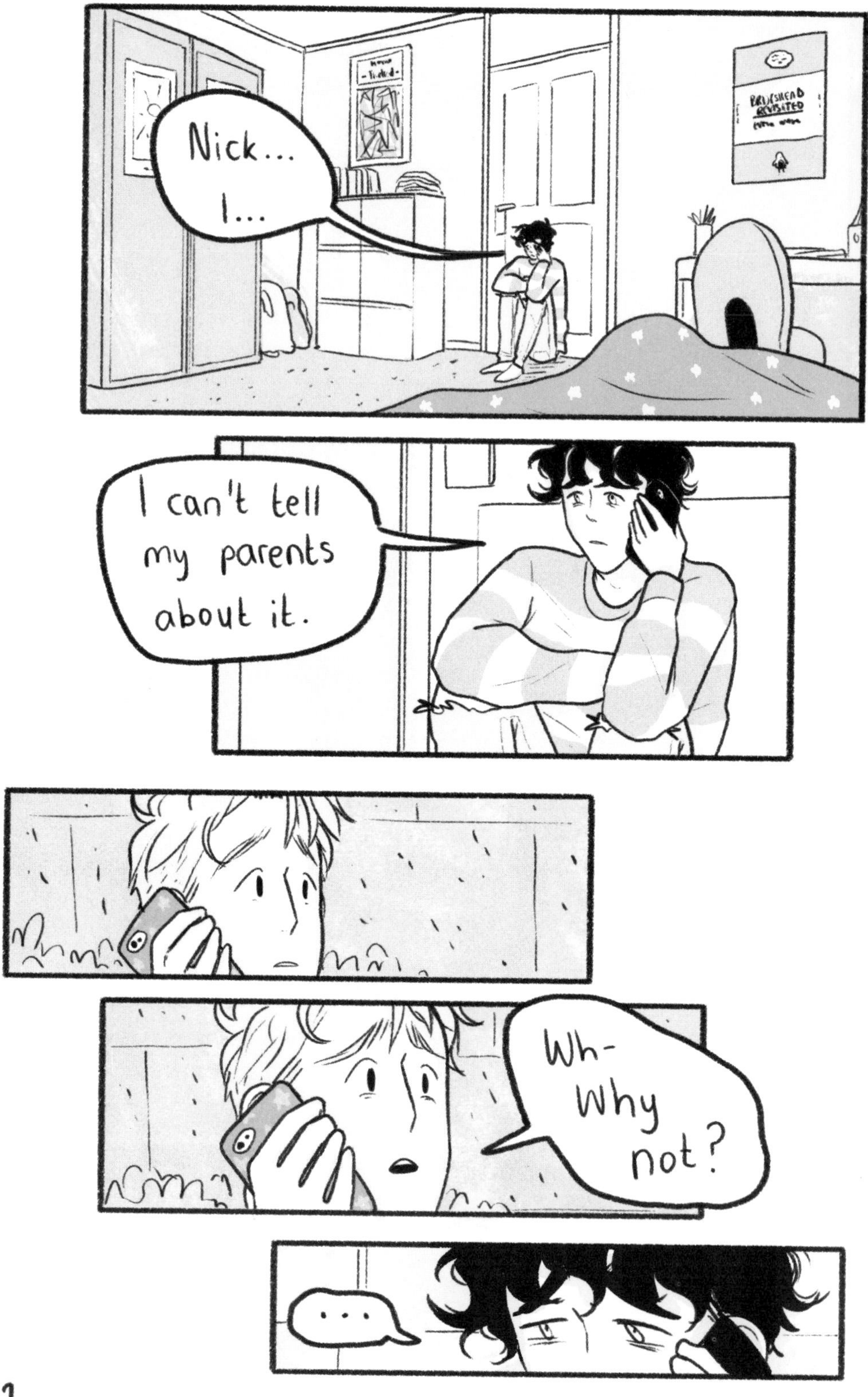
Nick... I...
I can't tell my parents about it.
Wh- Why not?
...

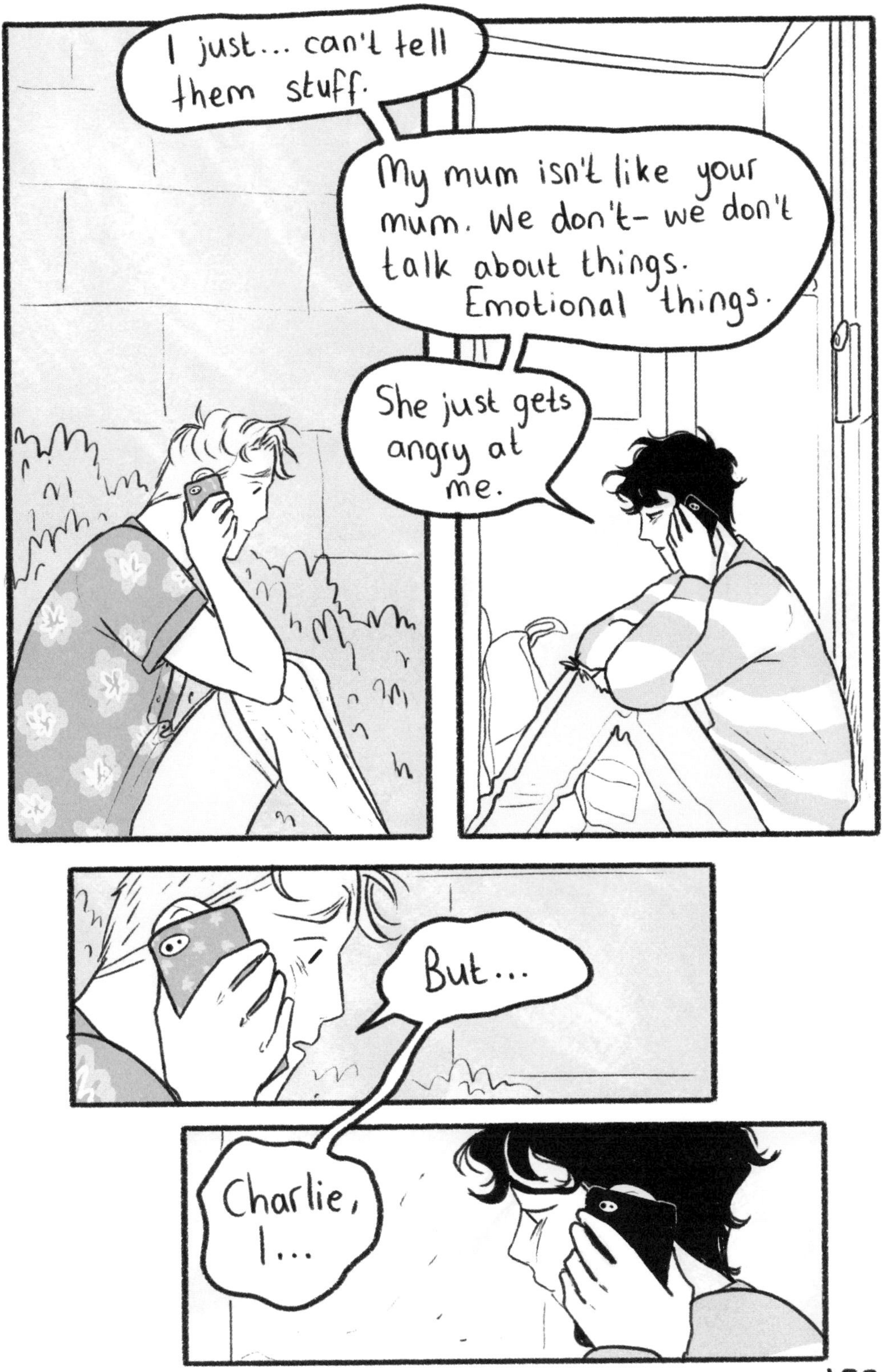
I just... can't tell them stuff.
My mum isn't like your mum. We don't- we don't talk about things. Emotional things.
She just gets angry at me.
But...
Charlie, I...

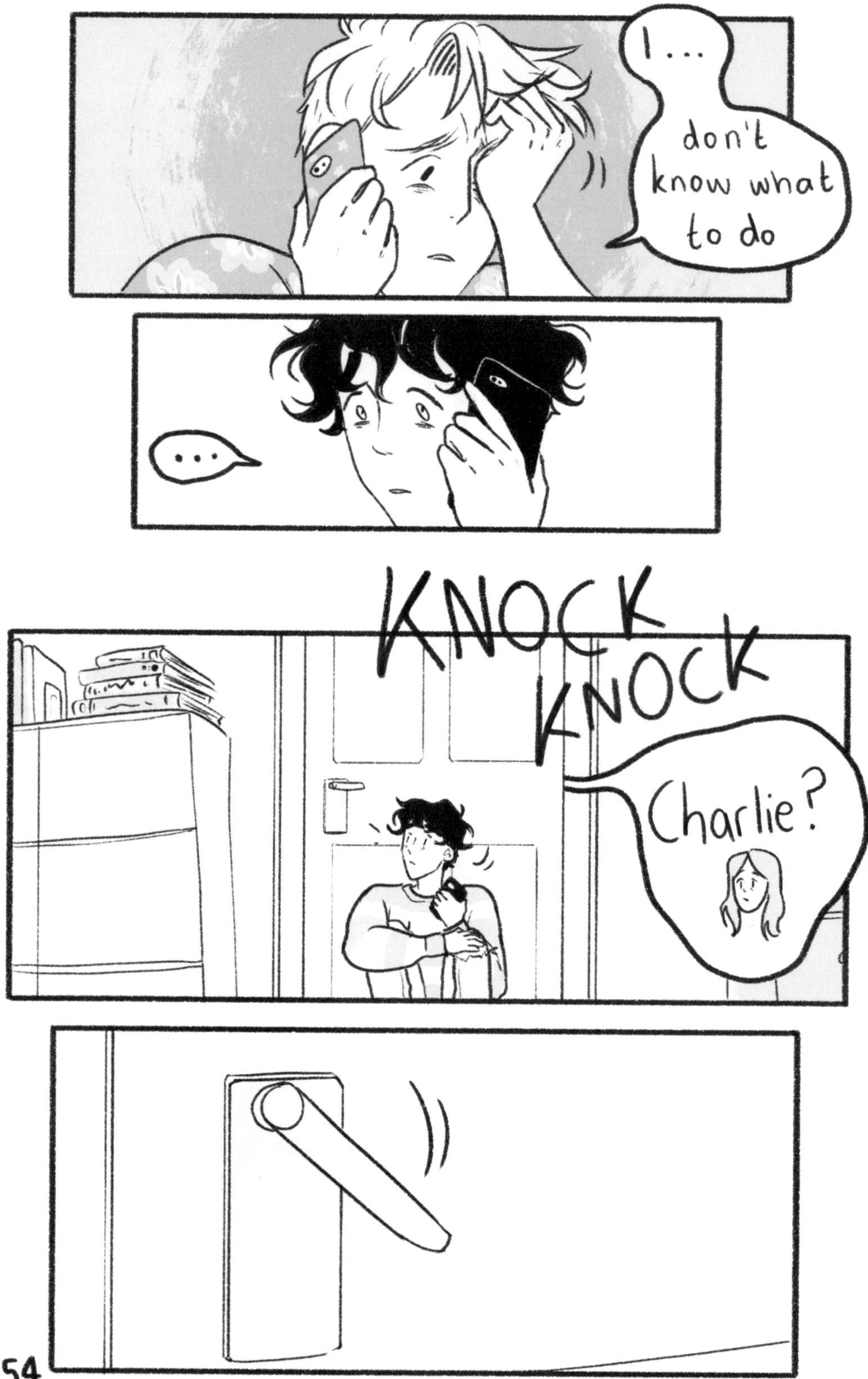
I...
don't know what to do
...
KNOCK KNOCK
Charlie?

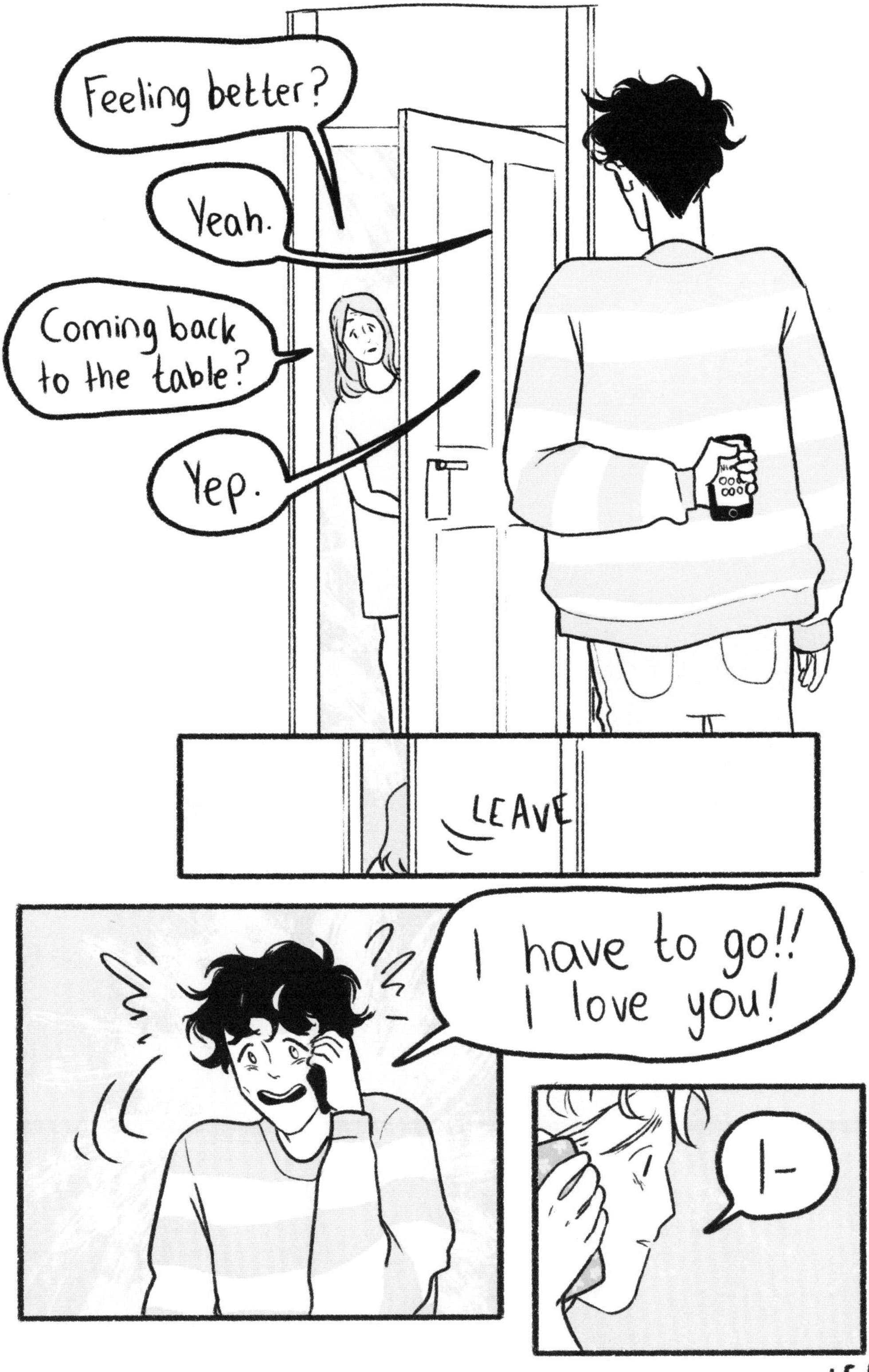
Feeling better?
Yeah.
Coming back to the table?
Yep.
LEAVE
I have to go!! I love you!
I-

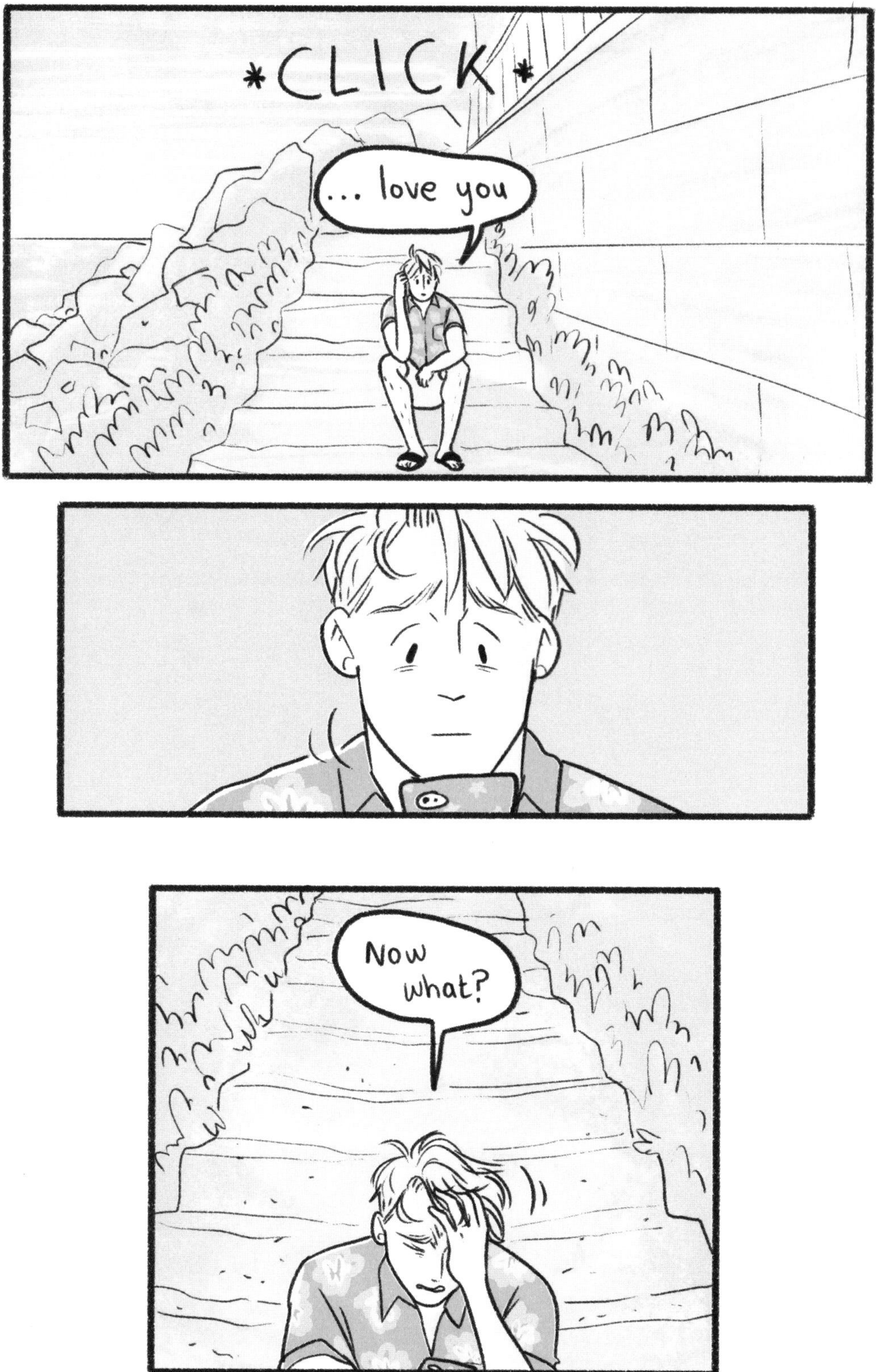
CLICK
... love you
Now what?

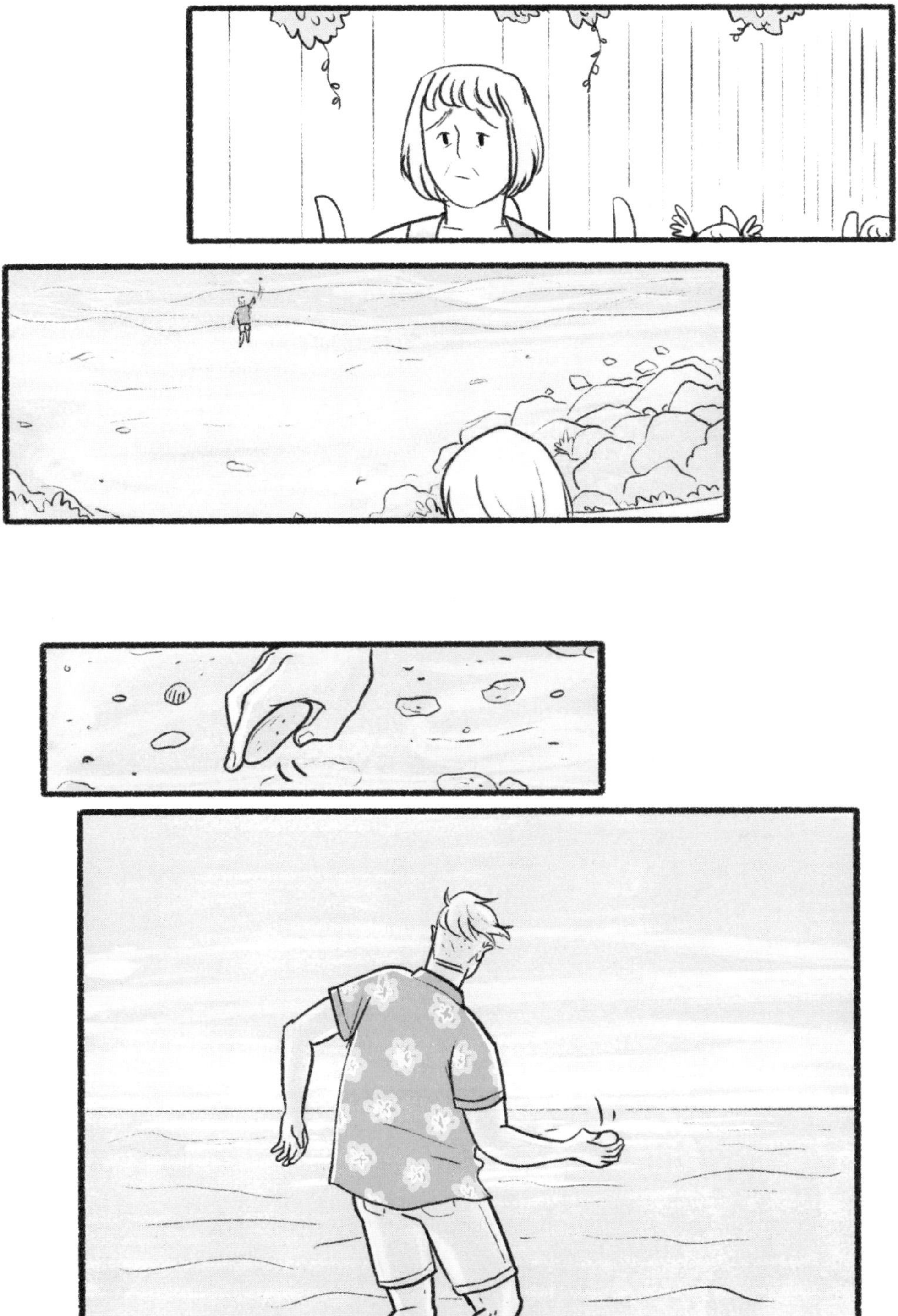

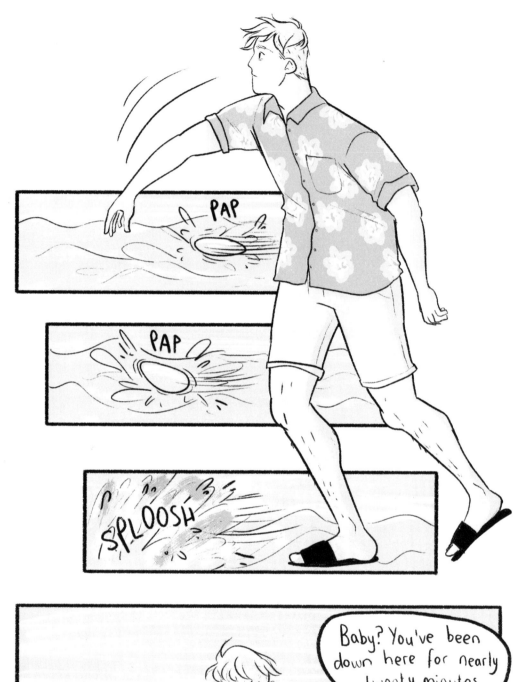

PAP

PAP

SPLOOSH

Baby? You've been down here for nearly twenty minutes.

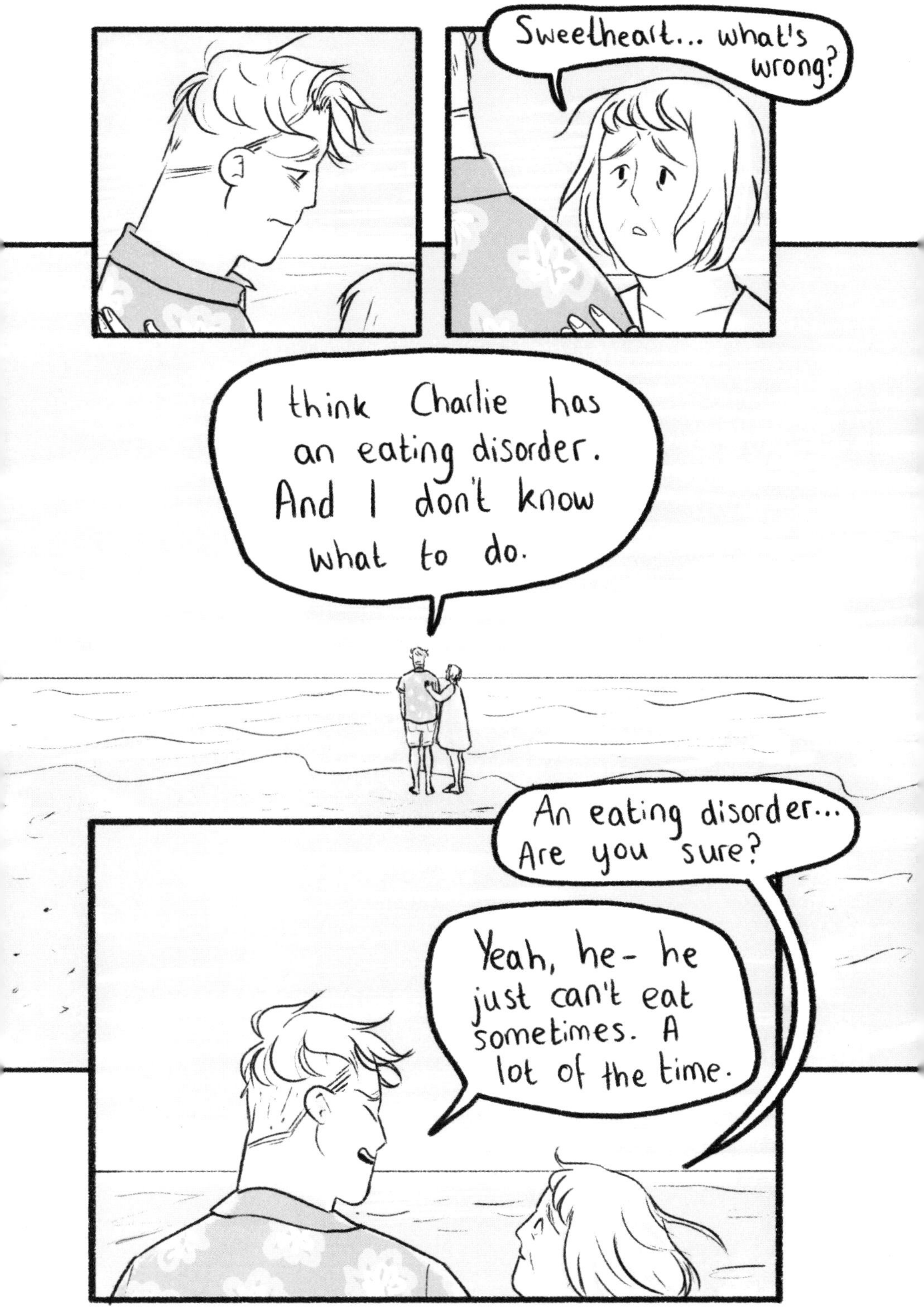
Sweetheart... what's wrong?
I think Charlie has an eating disorder. And I don't know what to do.
An eating disorder... Are you sure?
Yeah, he- he just can't eat sometimes. A lot of the time.

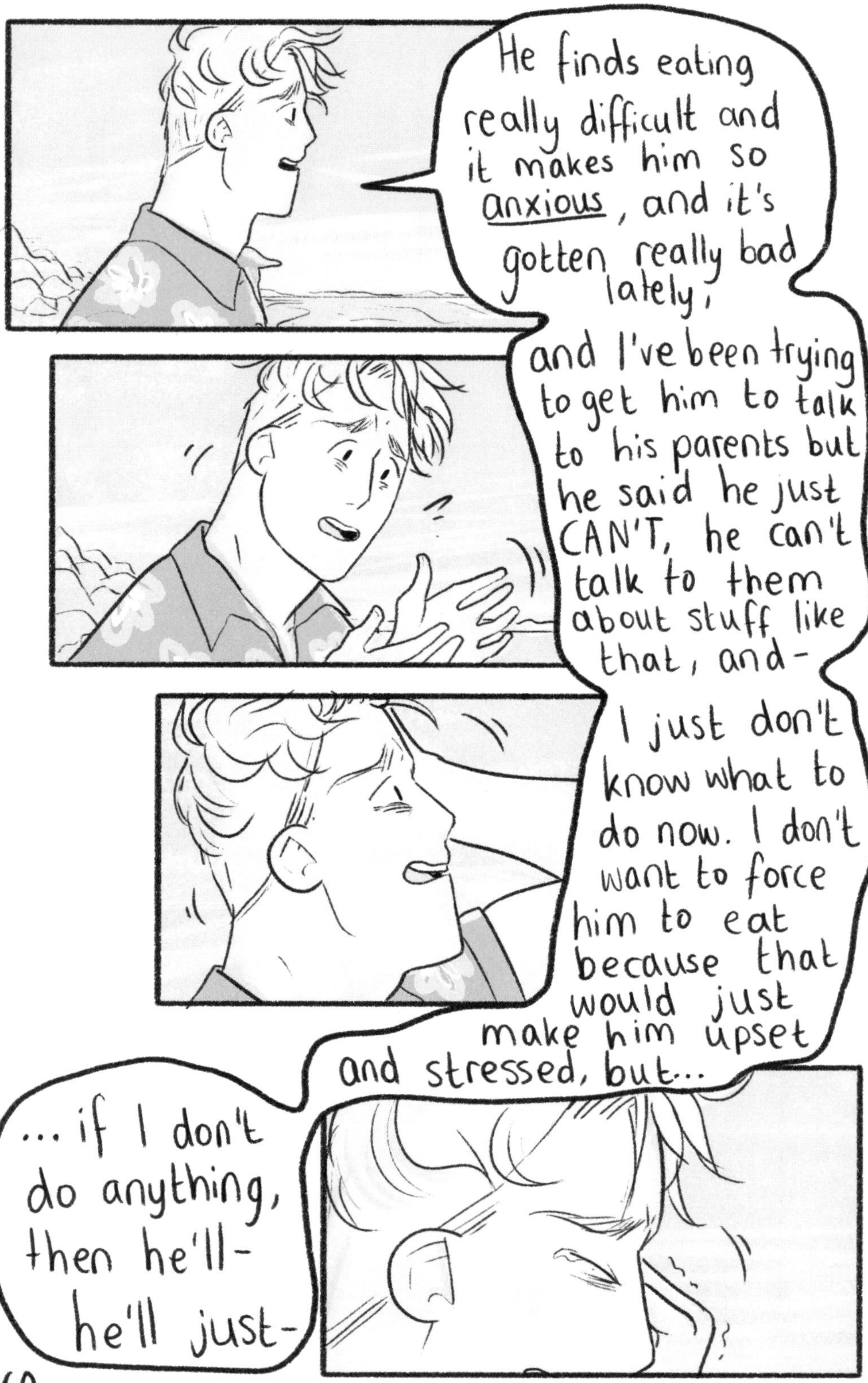
He finds eating really difficult and it makes him so anxious, and it's gotten really bad lately,
and I've been trying to get him to talk to his parents but he said he just CAN'T, he can't talk to them about stuff like that, and-
I just don't know what to do now. I don't want to force him to eat because that would just make him upset and stressed, but...
... if I don't do anything, then he'll- he'll just-

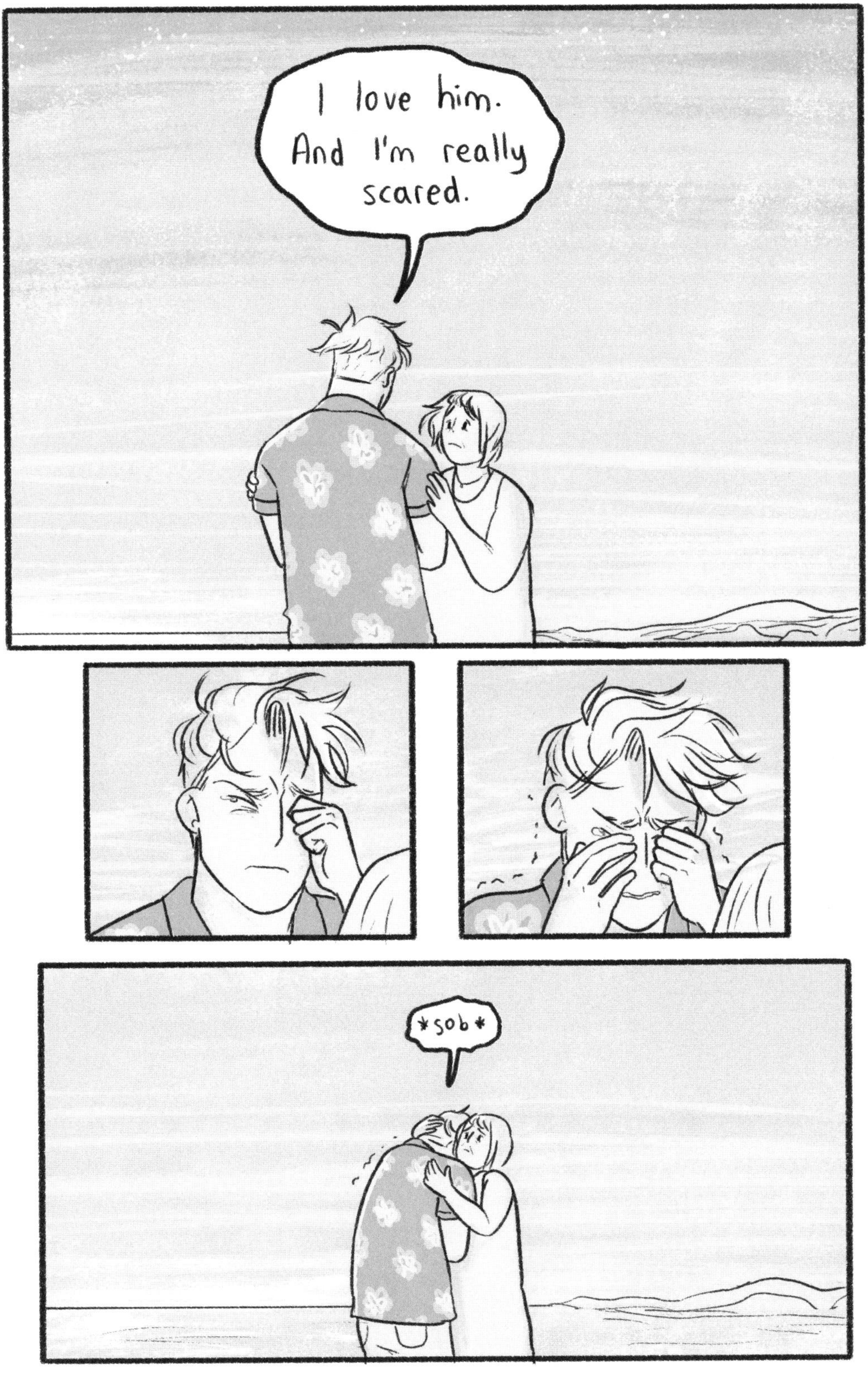
I love him. And I'm really scared.
sob

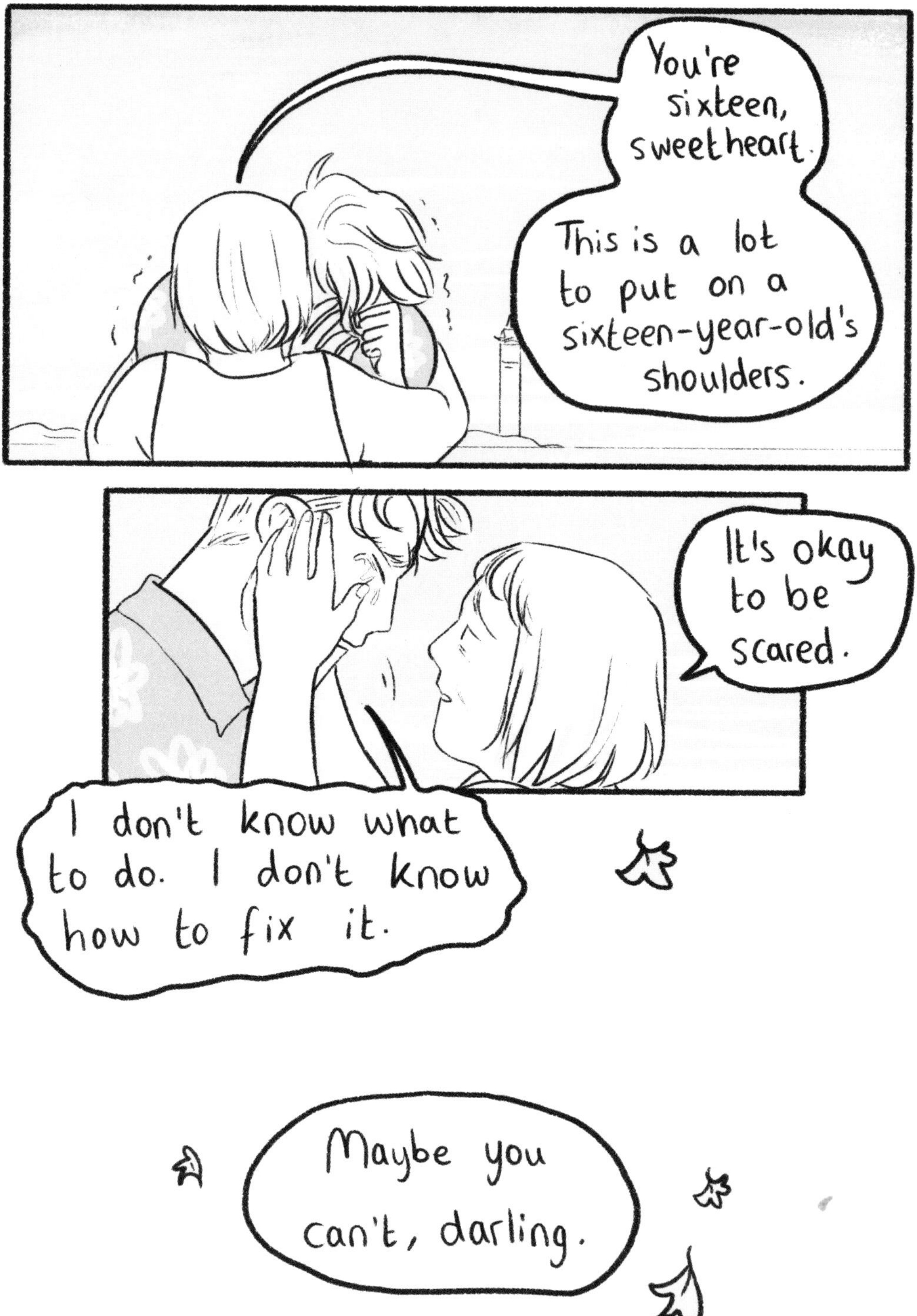

You're sixteen, sweetheart.
This is a lot to put on a sixteen-year-old's shoulders.
It's okay to be scared.
I don't know what to do. I don't know how to fix it.
Maybe you can't, darling.

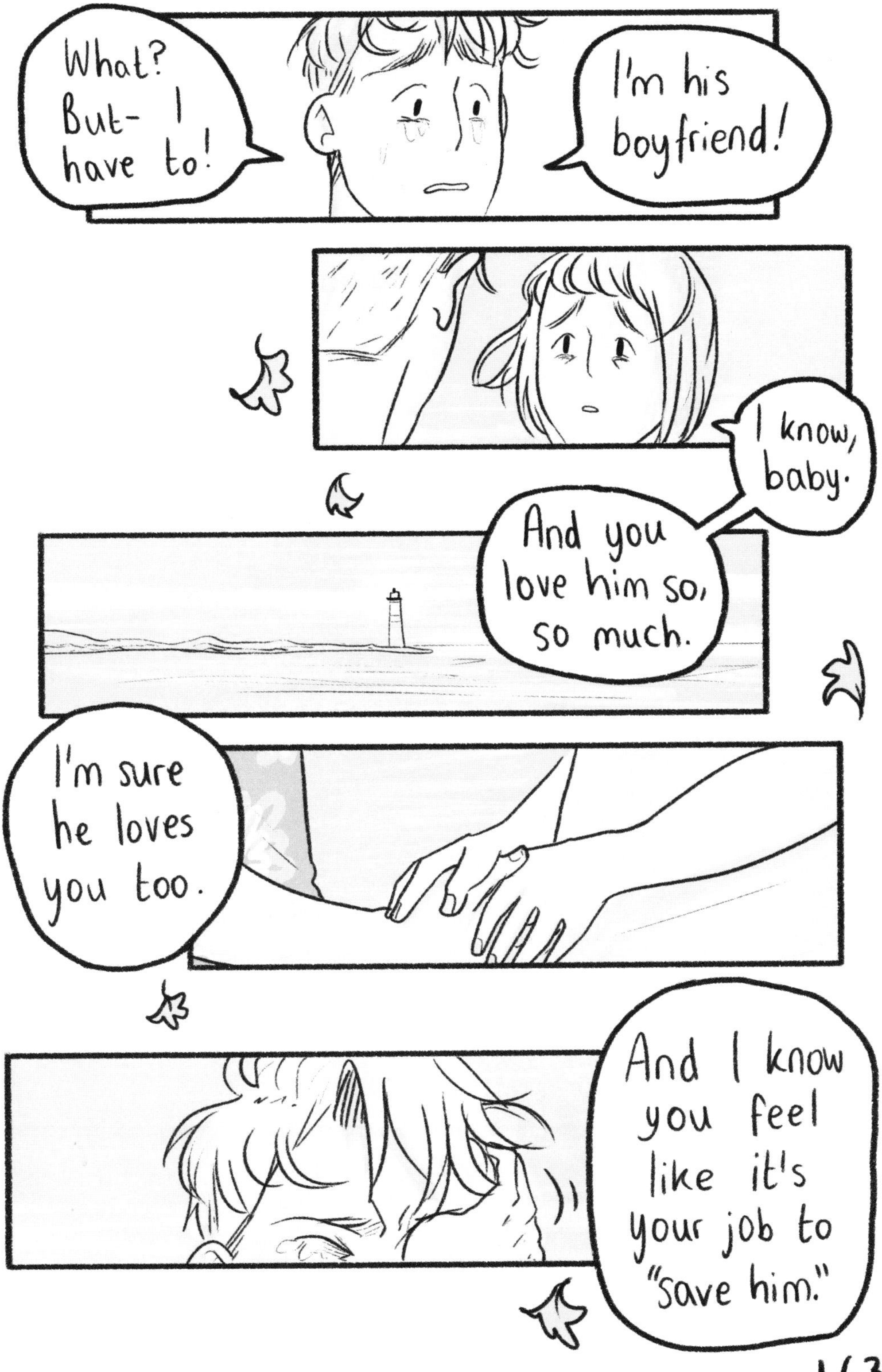
What? But- I have to!
I'm his boyfriend!
I know, baby.
And you love him so, so much.
I'm sure he loves you too.
And I know you feel like it's your job to "save him."

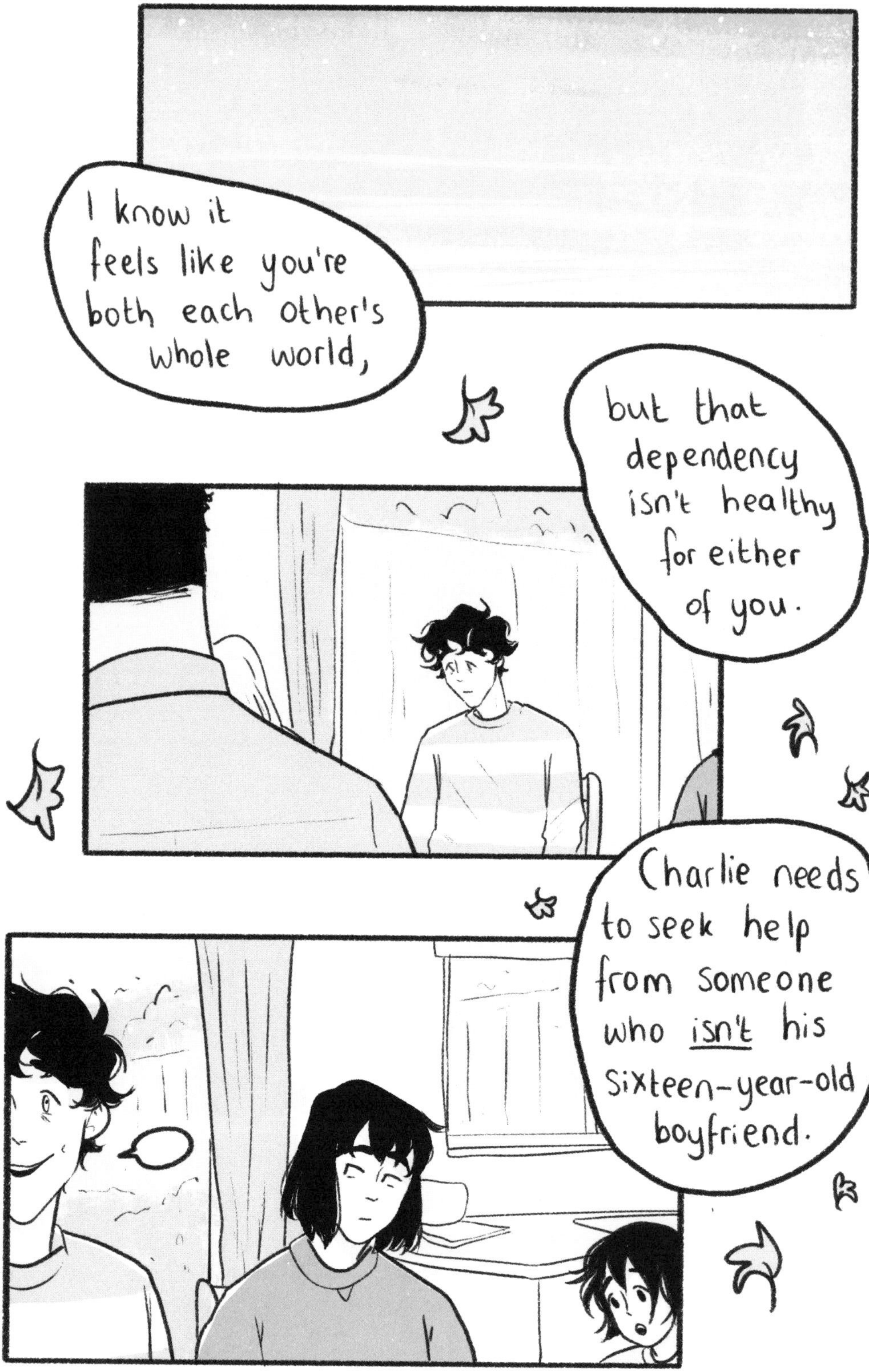
I know it feels like you're both each other's whole world,
but that dependency isn't healthy for either of you.
Charlie needs to seek help from someone who isn't his sixteen-year-old boyfriend.

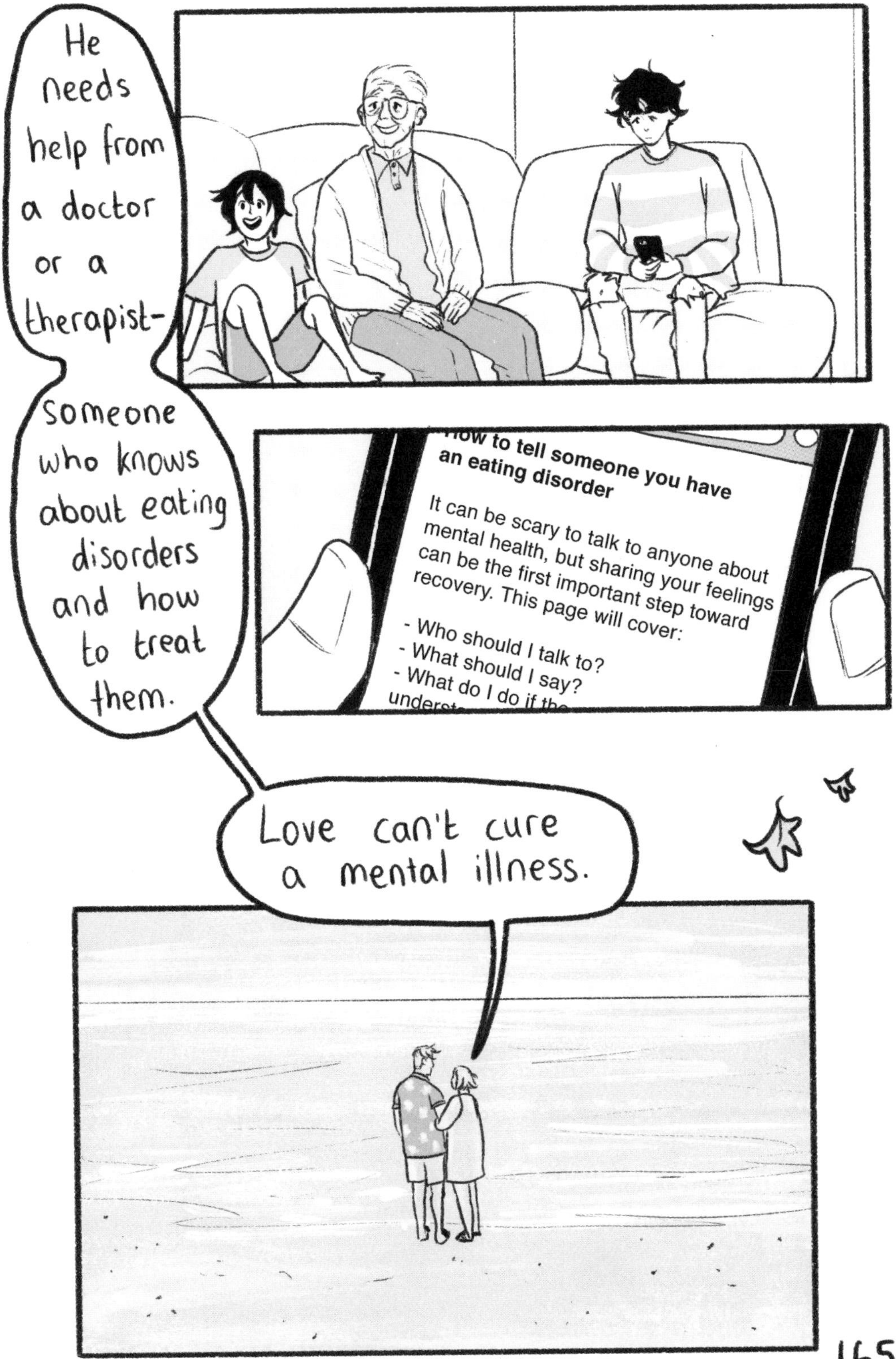
He needs help from a doctor or a therapist-
someone who knows about eating disorders and how to treat them.
How to tell someone you have an eating disorder
It can be scary to talk to anyone about mental health, but sharing your feelings can be the first important step toward recovery. This page will cover:
- Who should I talk to?
- What should I say?
Love can't cure a mental illness.

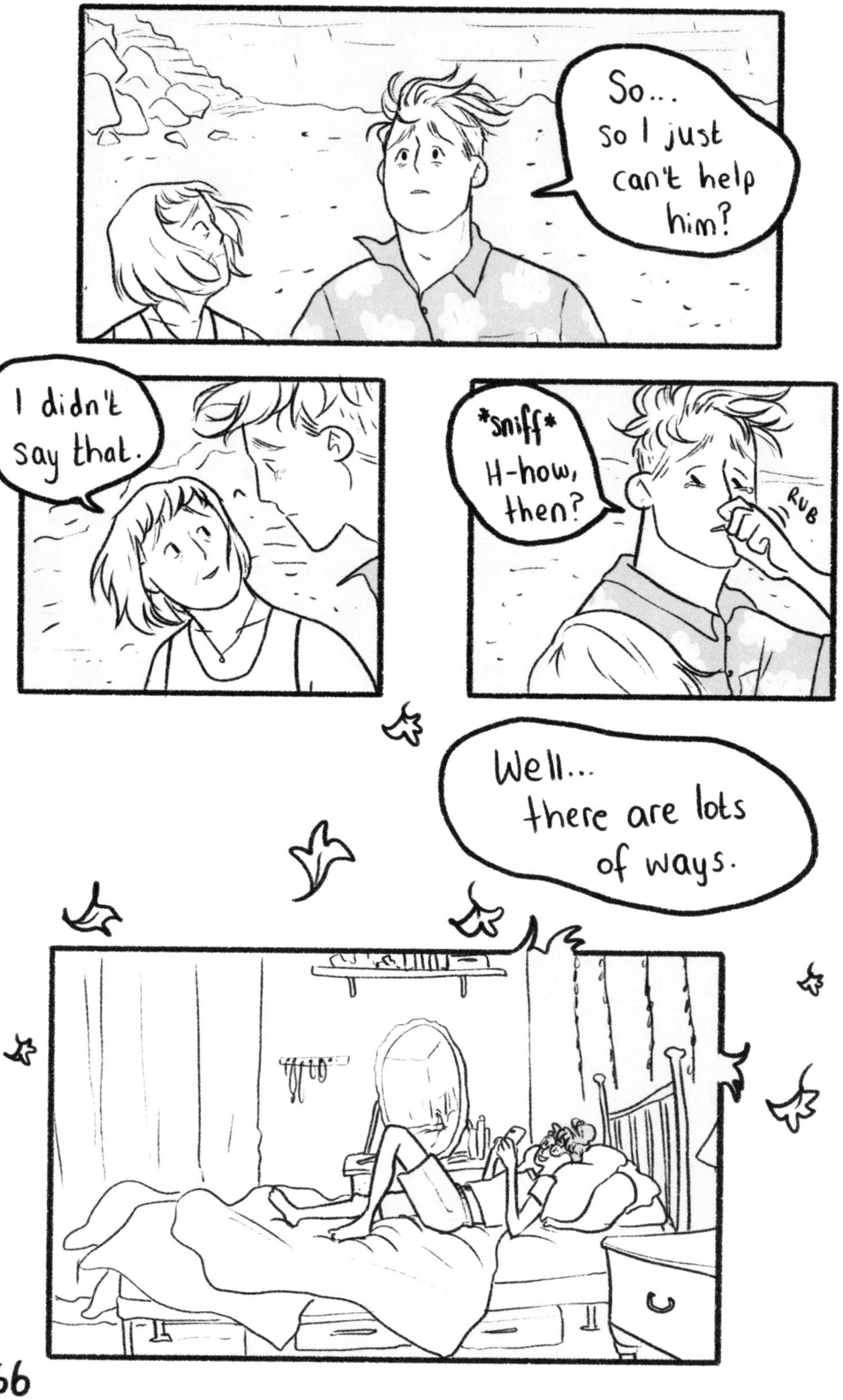
So... so I just can't help him?
I didn't say that.
sniff H-how, then?
RUB
Well... there are lots of ways.

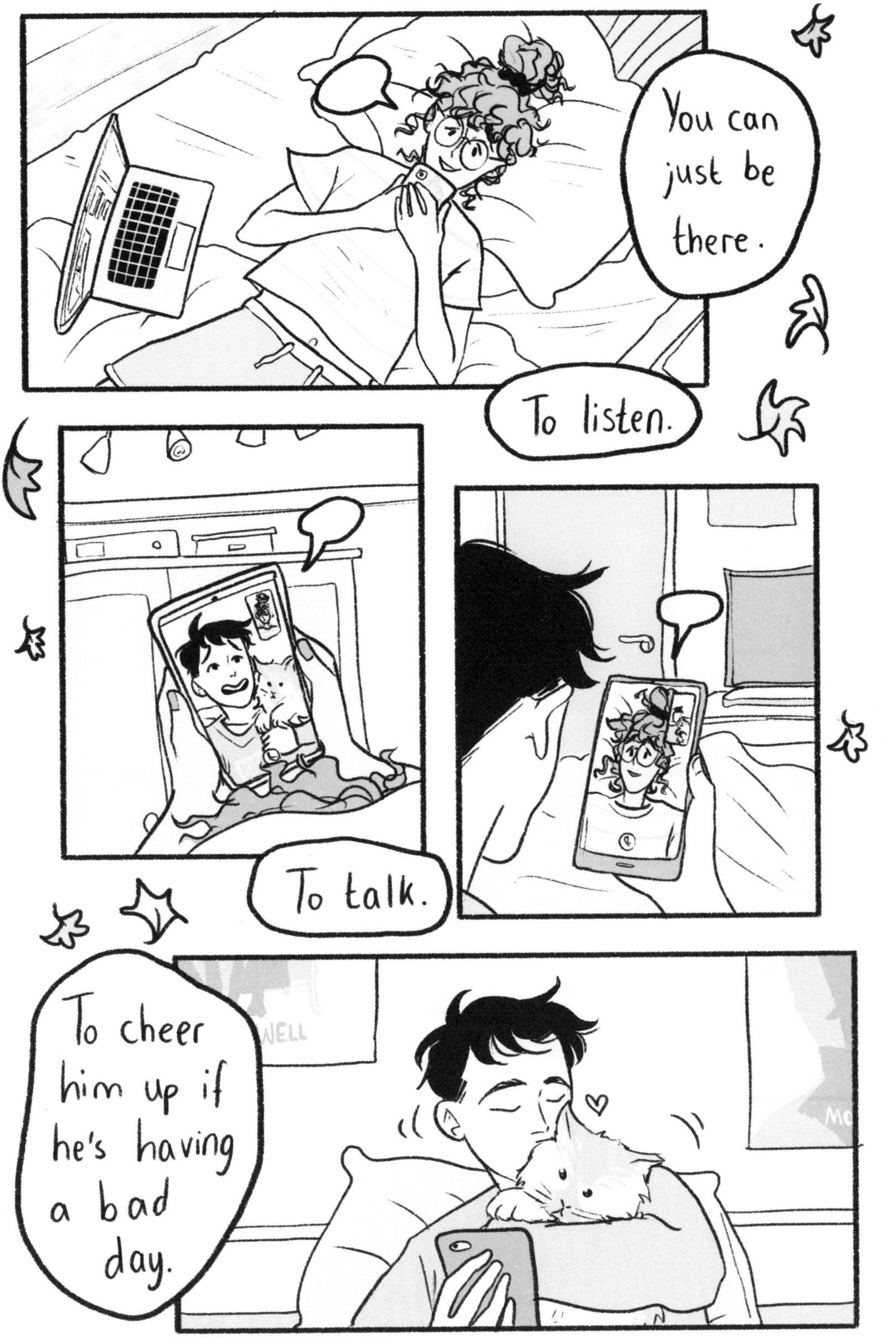
You can just be there.
To listen.
To talk.
To cheer him up if he's having a bad day.

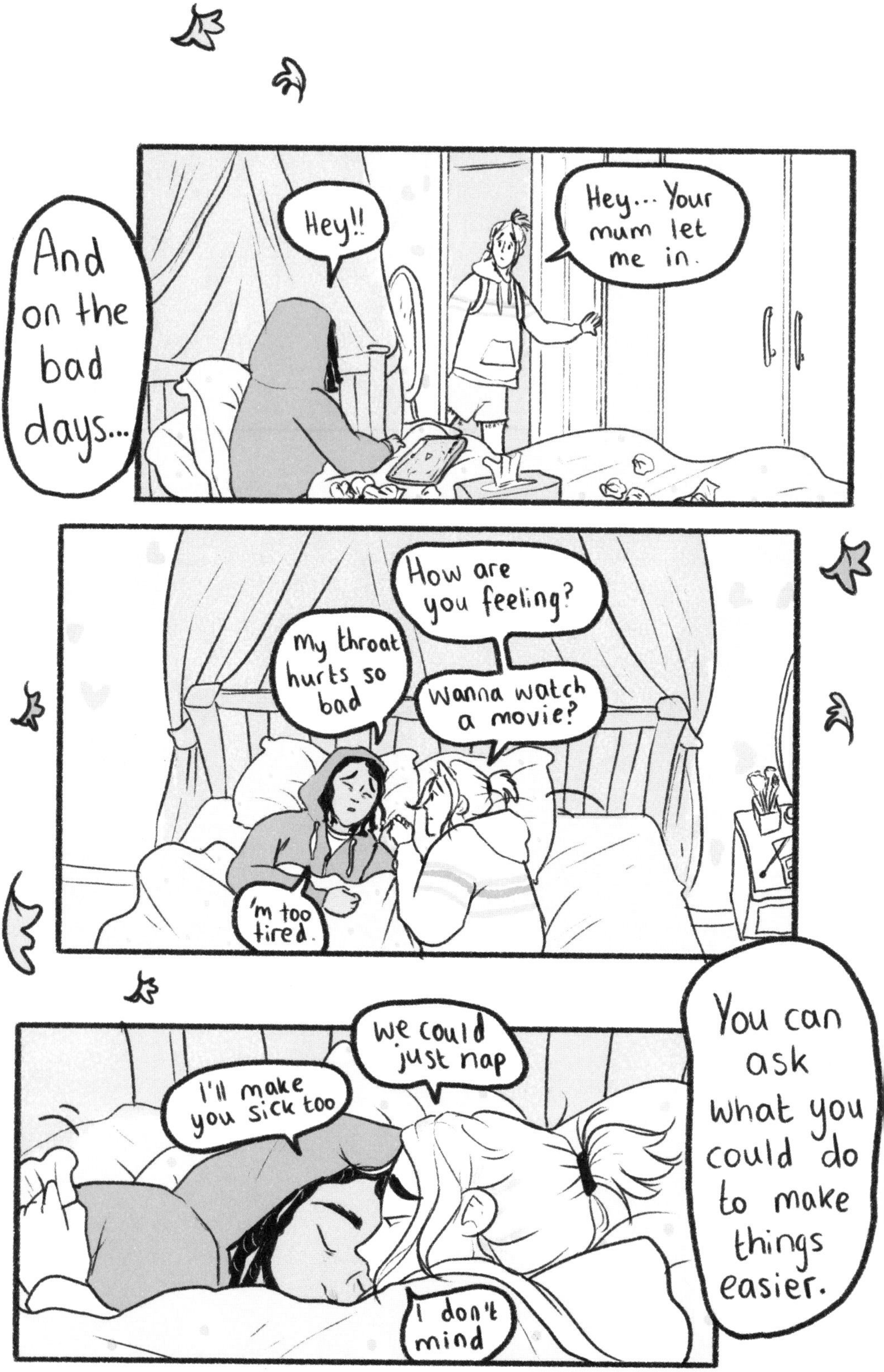

And on the bad days...
Hey!!
Hey... Your mum let me in.
How are you feeling?
My throat hurts so bad
Wanna watch a movie?
'm too tired.
You can ask what you could do to make things easier.
I'll make you sick too
We could just nap
I don't mind

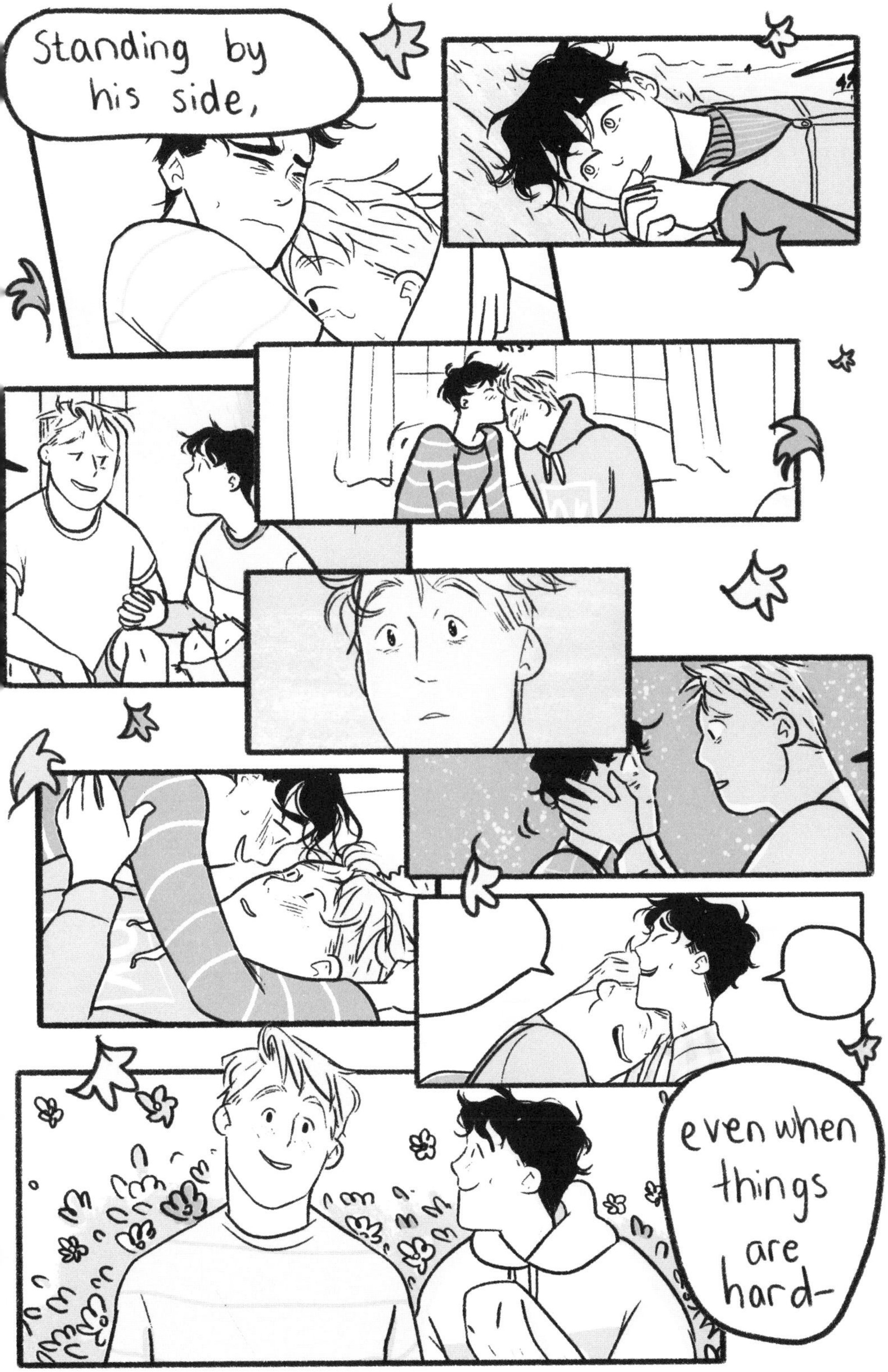
Standing by his side,
even when things are hard-

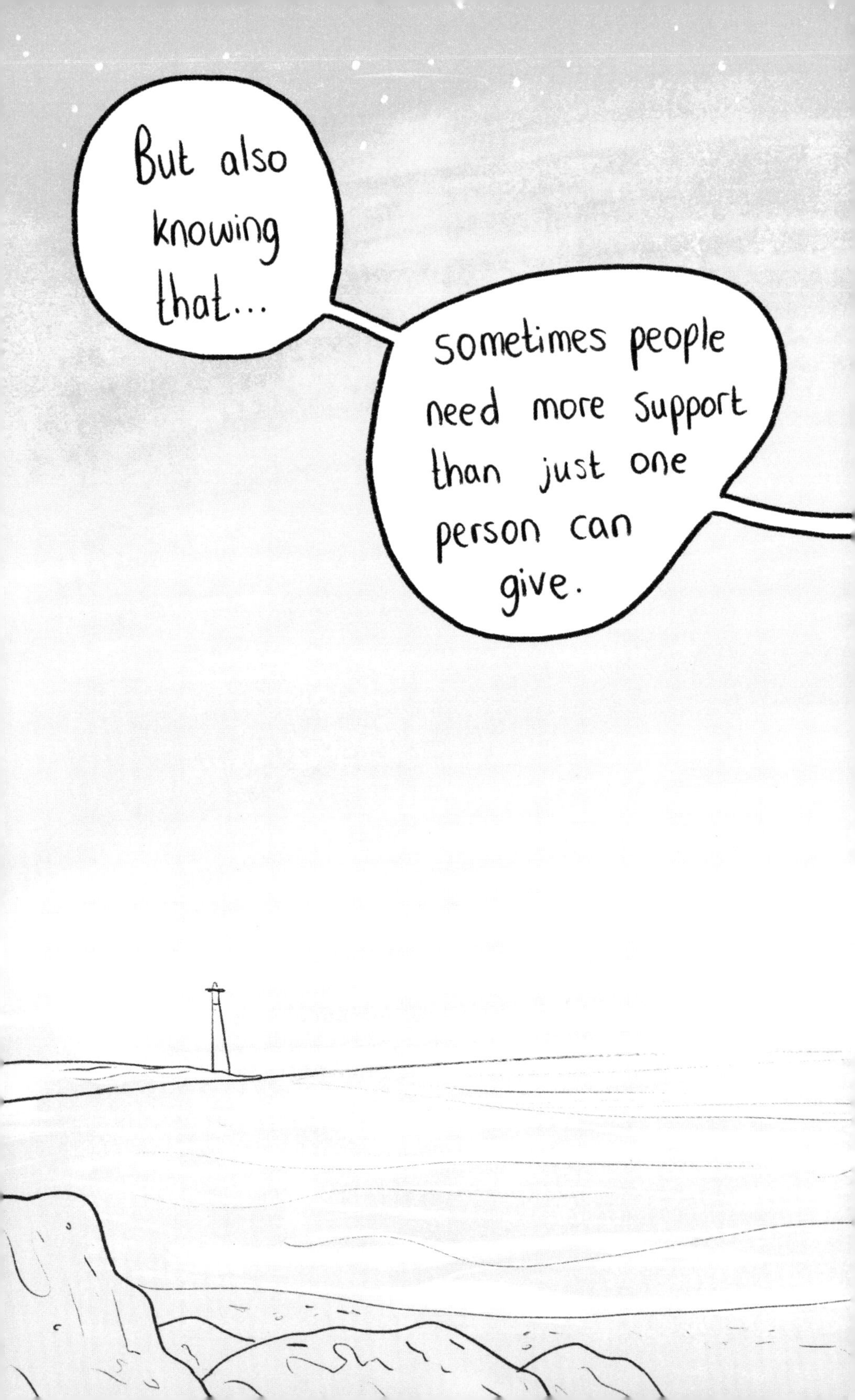
But also knowing that...
sometimes people need more support than just one person can give.

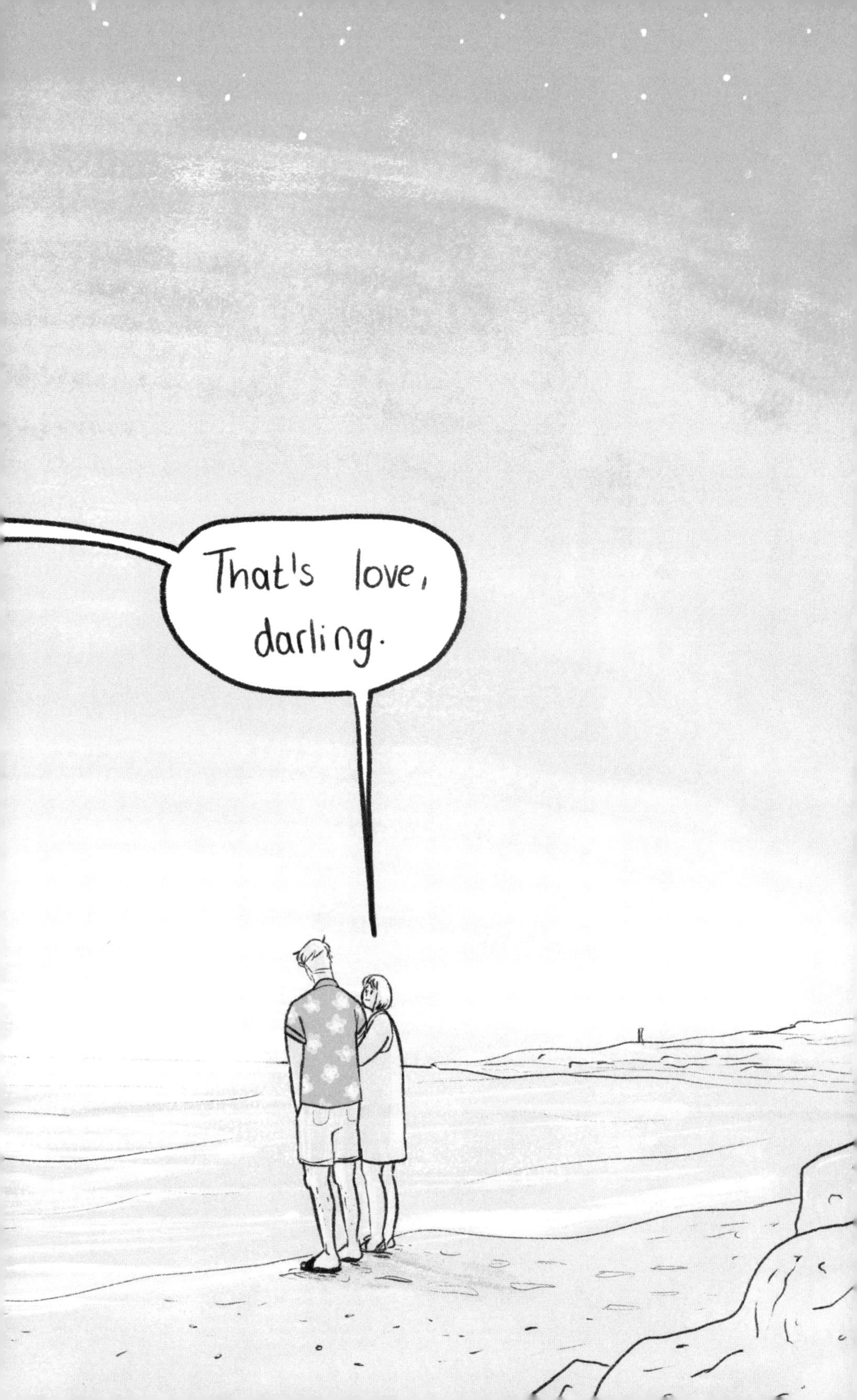
That's love, darling.

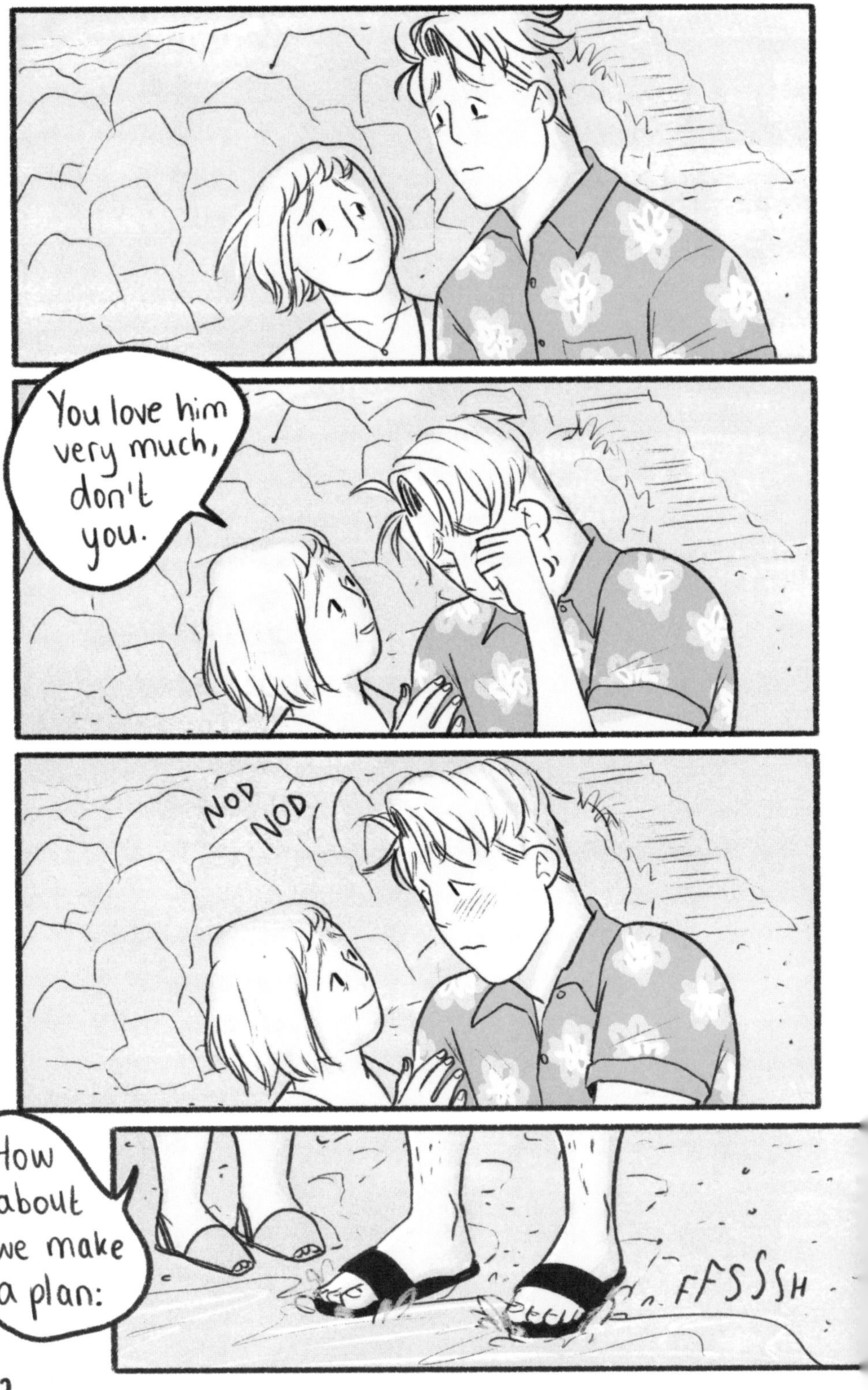

You love him very much, don't you.
NOD NOD
How about we make a plan:
FFSSSH

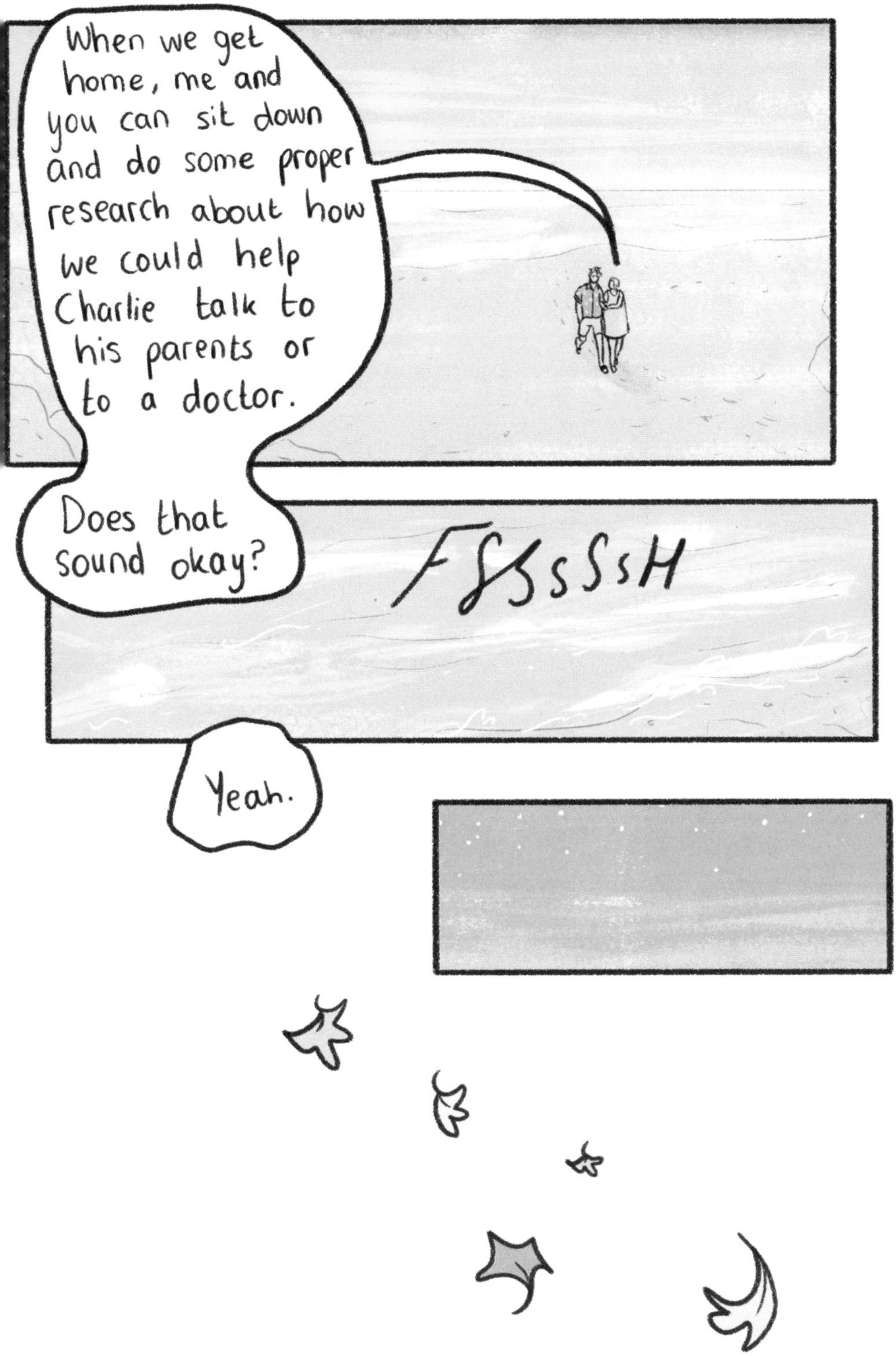
When we get home, me and you can sit down and do some proper research about how we could help Charlie talk to his parents or to a doctor.
Does that sound okay?
FSSsSsH
Yeah.

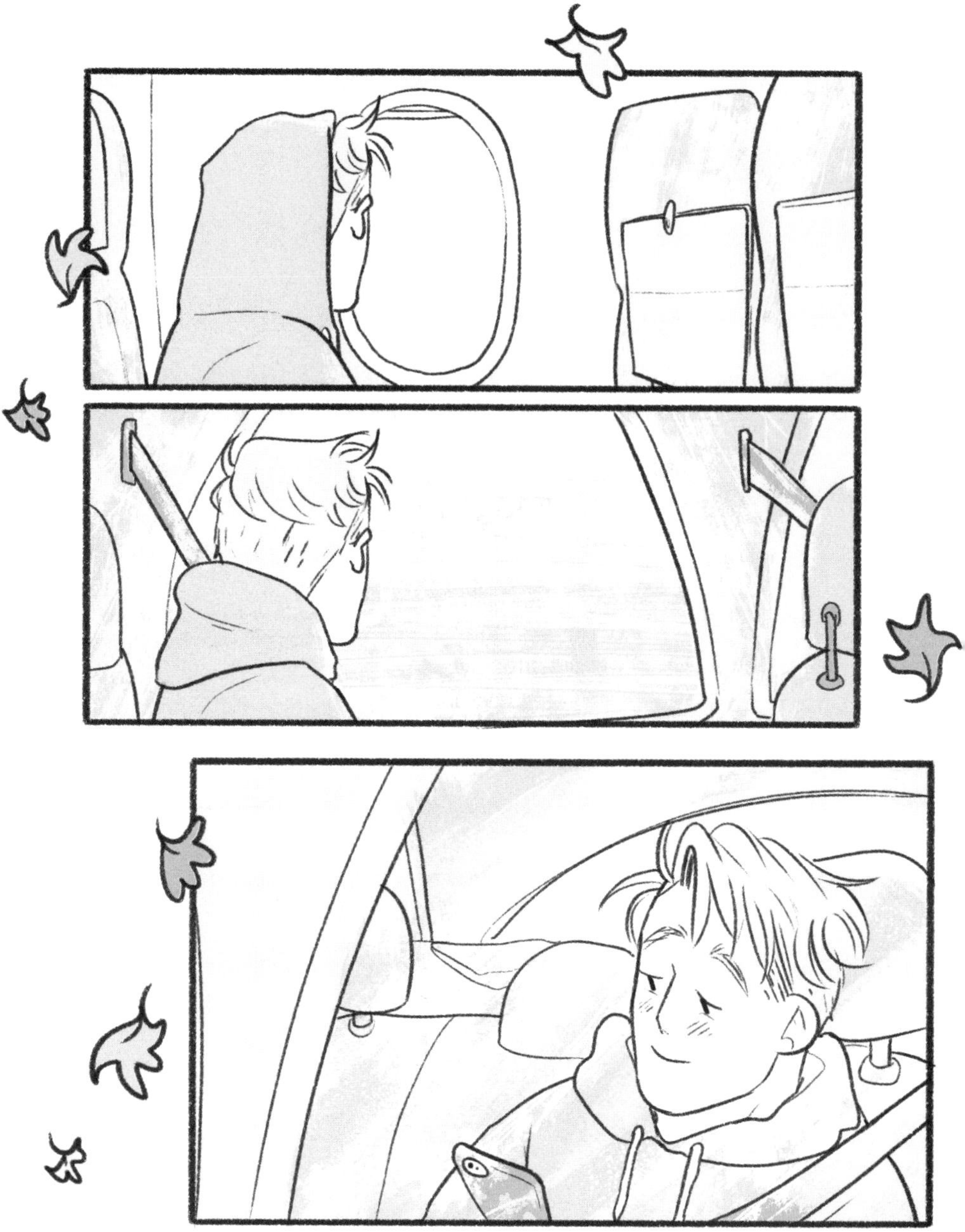

i can't wait to see you at school tomorrow!!!!!!!!

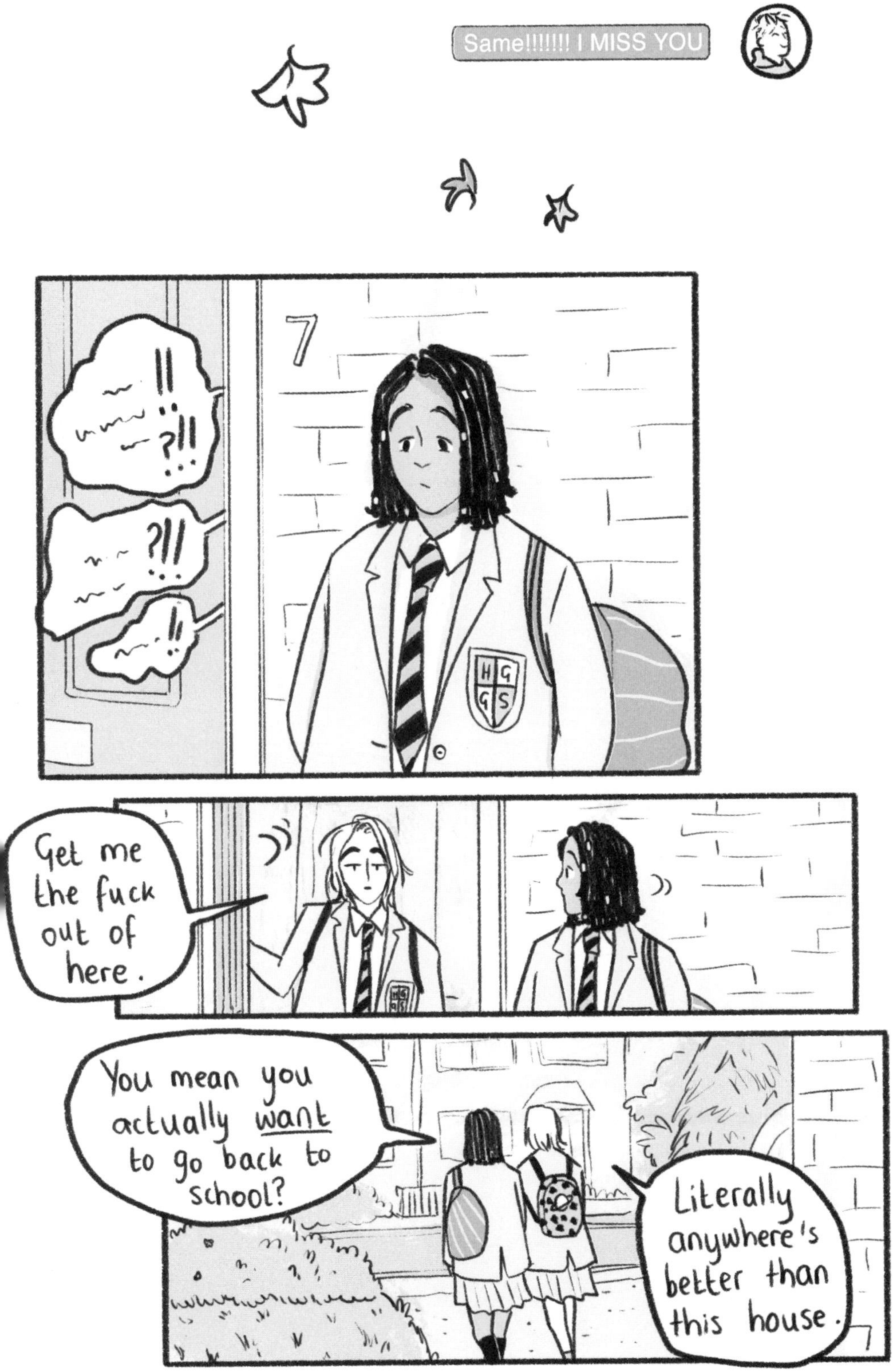
Same!!!!!!! I MISS YOU
7
Get me the fuck out of here.
You mean you actually want to go back to school?
Literally anywhere's better than this house.

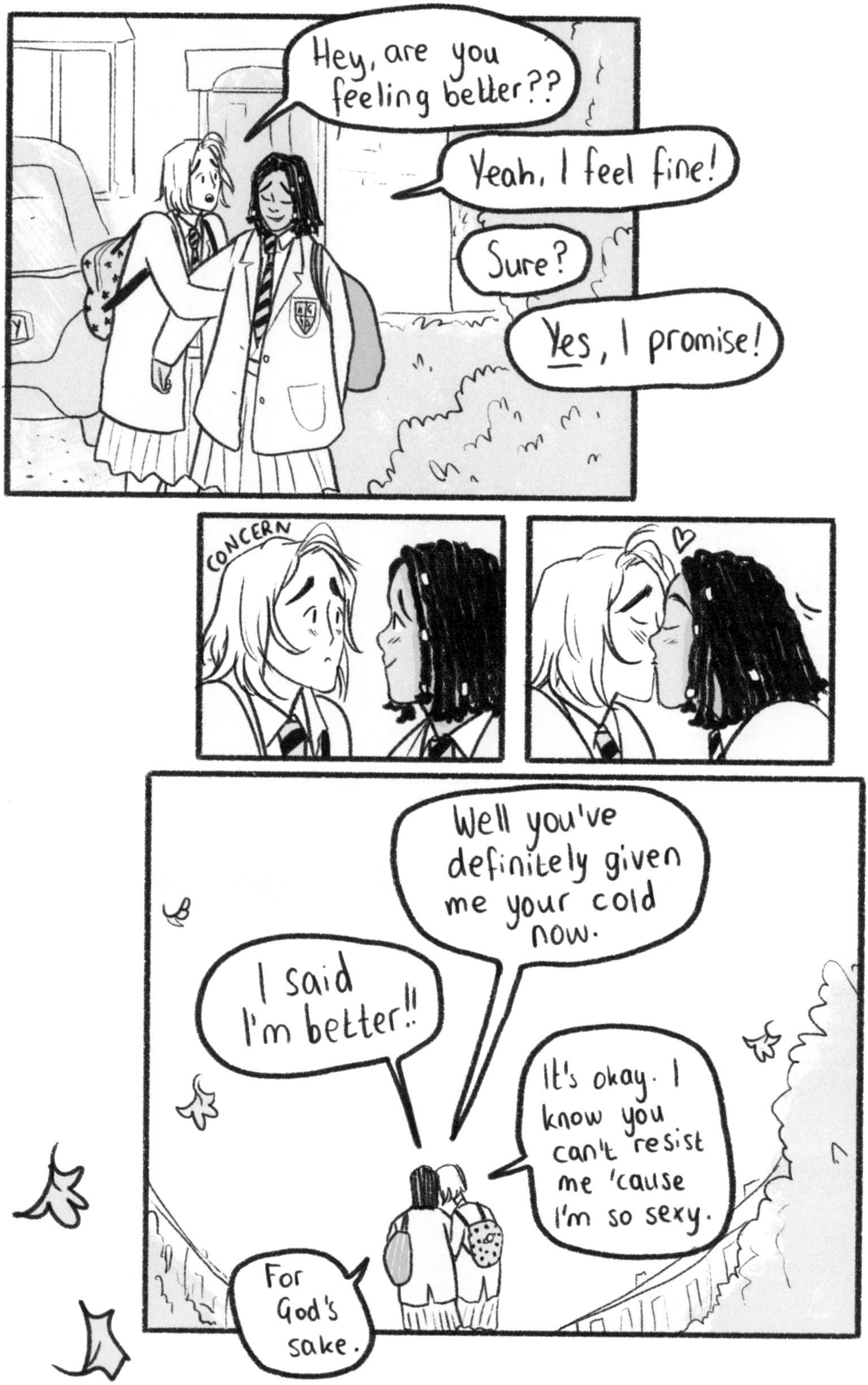
Hey, are you feeling better??
Yeah, I feel fine!
Sure?
Yes, I promise!
CONCERN
Well you've definitely given me your cold now.
I said I'm better!!
It's okay. I know you can't resist me 'cause I'm so sexy.
For God's sake.

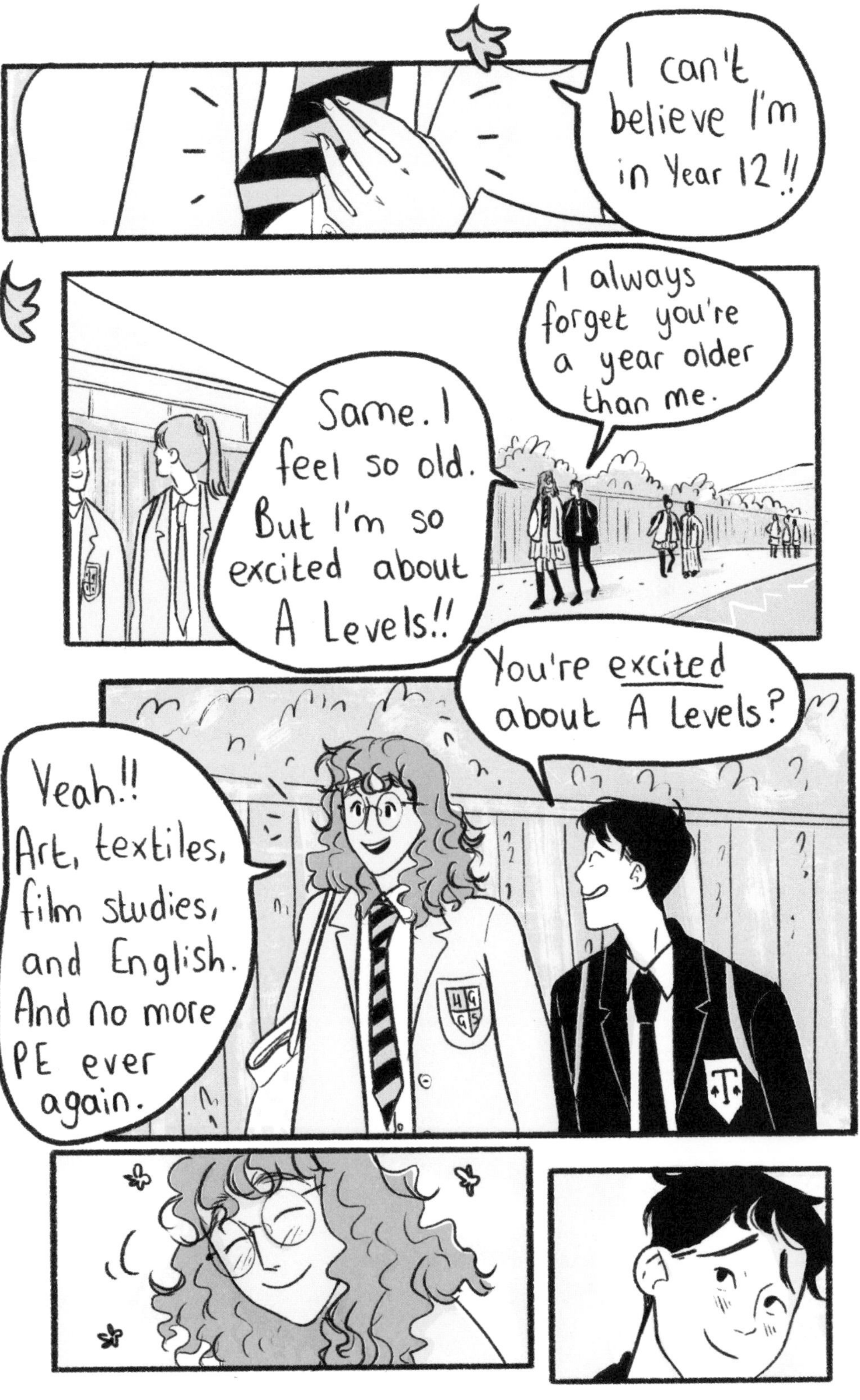
I can't believe I'm in Year 12!!
Same. I feel so old. But I'm so excited about A Levels!!
I always forget you're a year older than me.
You're excited about A Levels?
Yeah!! Art, textiles, film studies, and English. And no more PE ever again.

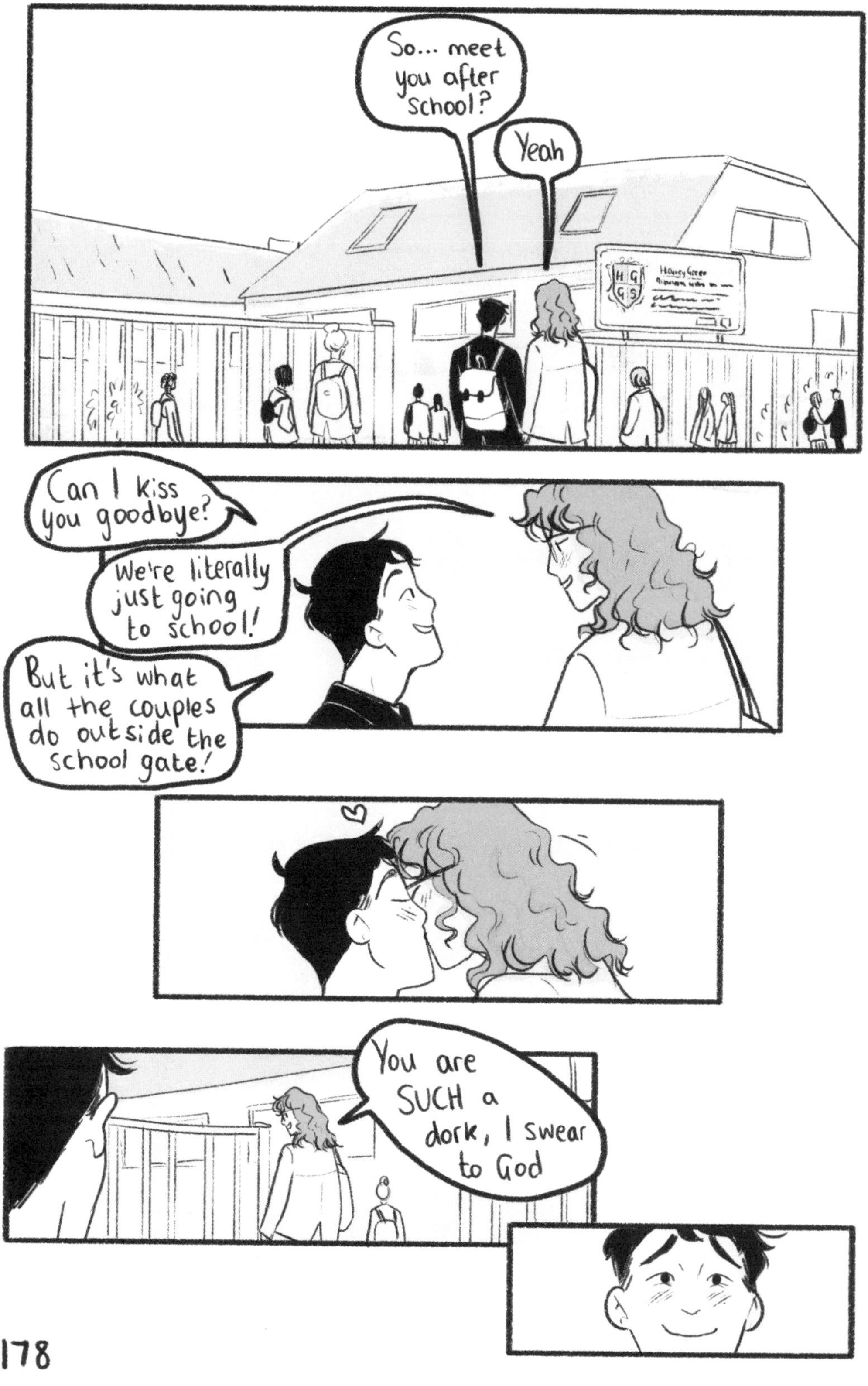
So... meet you after school?
Yeah
Can I kiss you goodbye?
We're literally just going to school!
But it's what all the couples do outside the school gate!
You are SUCH a dork, I swear to God

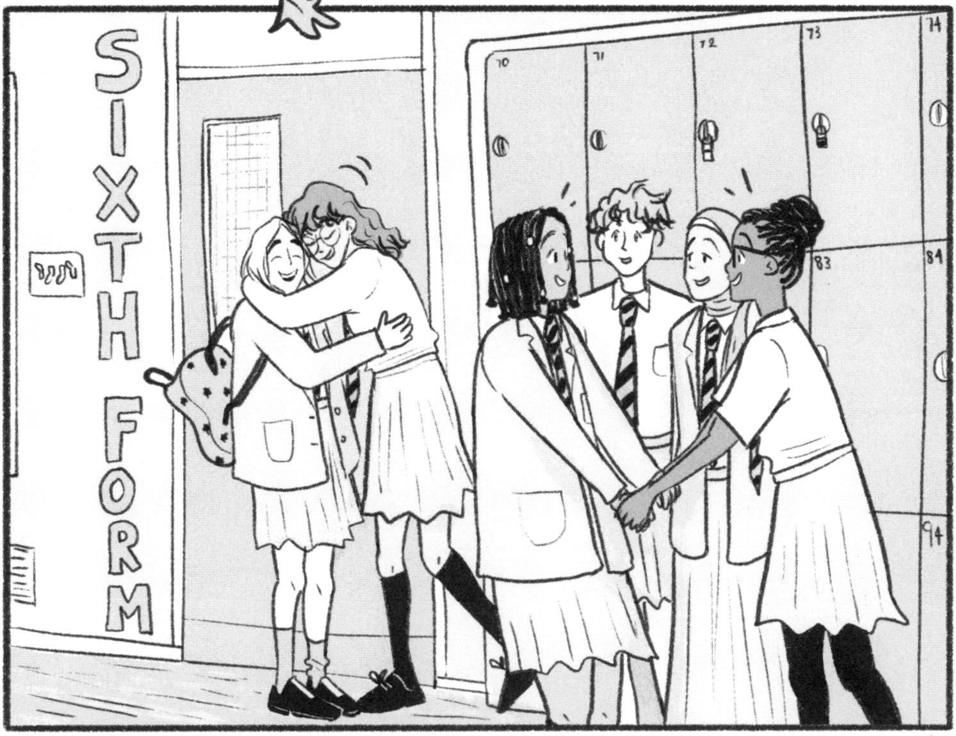
SIXTH FORM

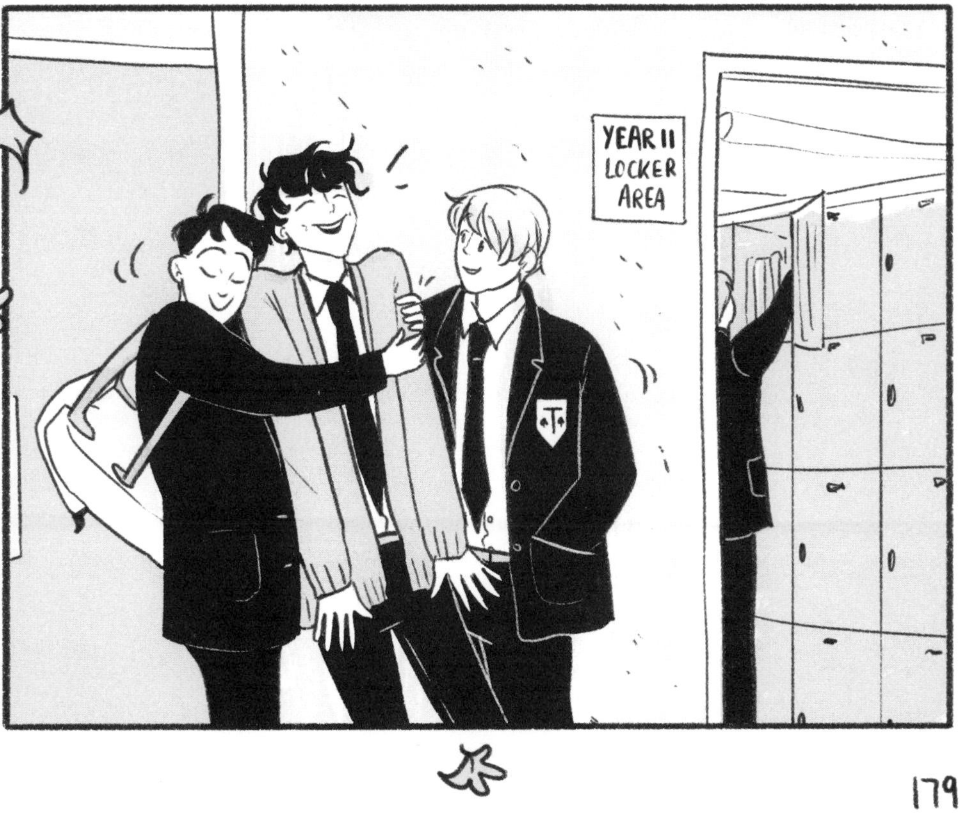
YEAR 11
LOCKER
AREA

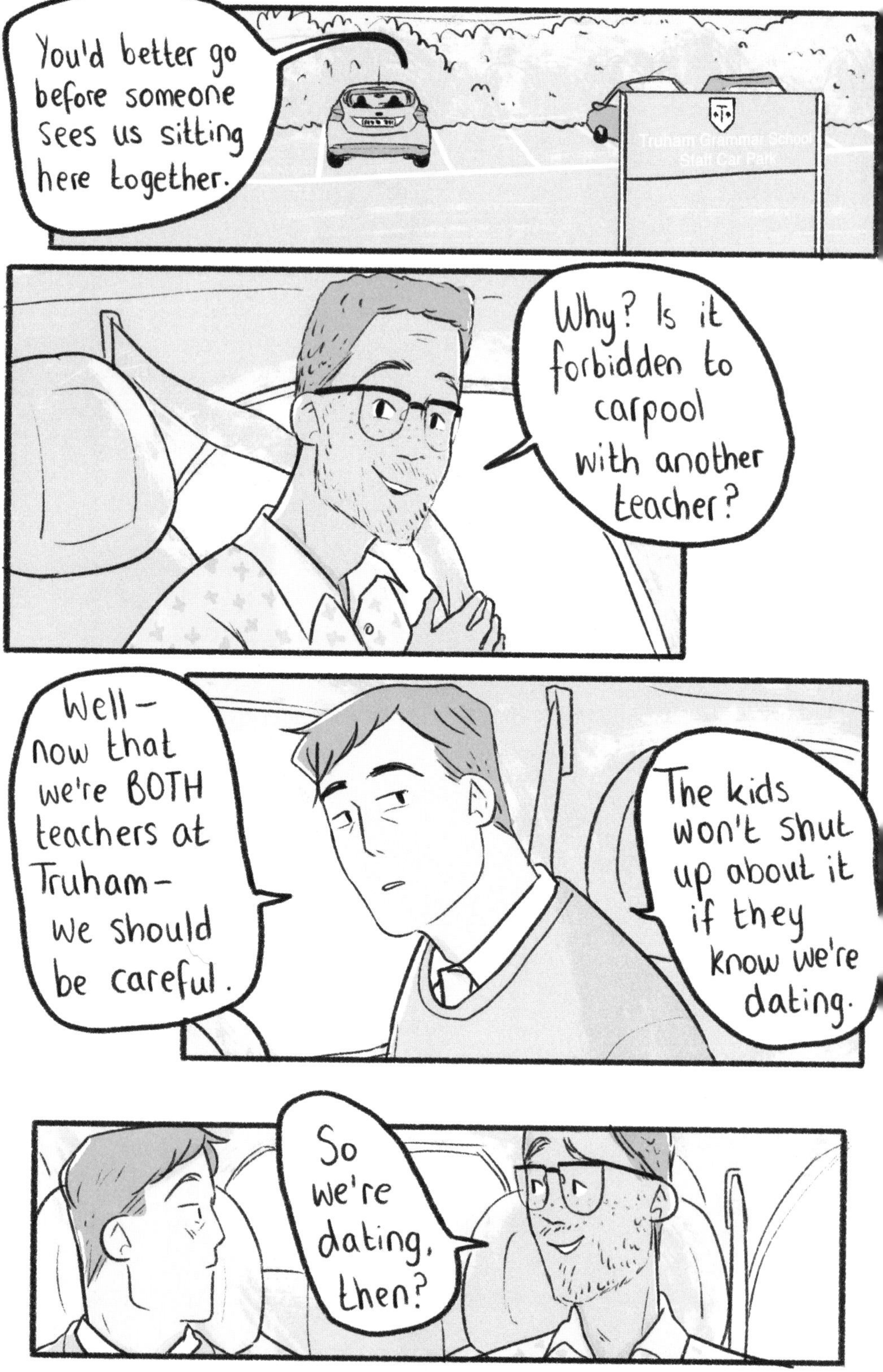
You'd better go before someone sees us sitting here together.
Truham Grammar School Staff Car Park
Why? Is it forbidden to carpool with another teacher?
Well- now that we're BOTH teachers at Truham- we should be careful.
The kids won't shut up about it if they know we're dating.
So we're dating, then?

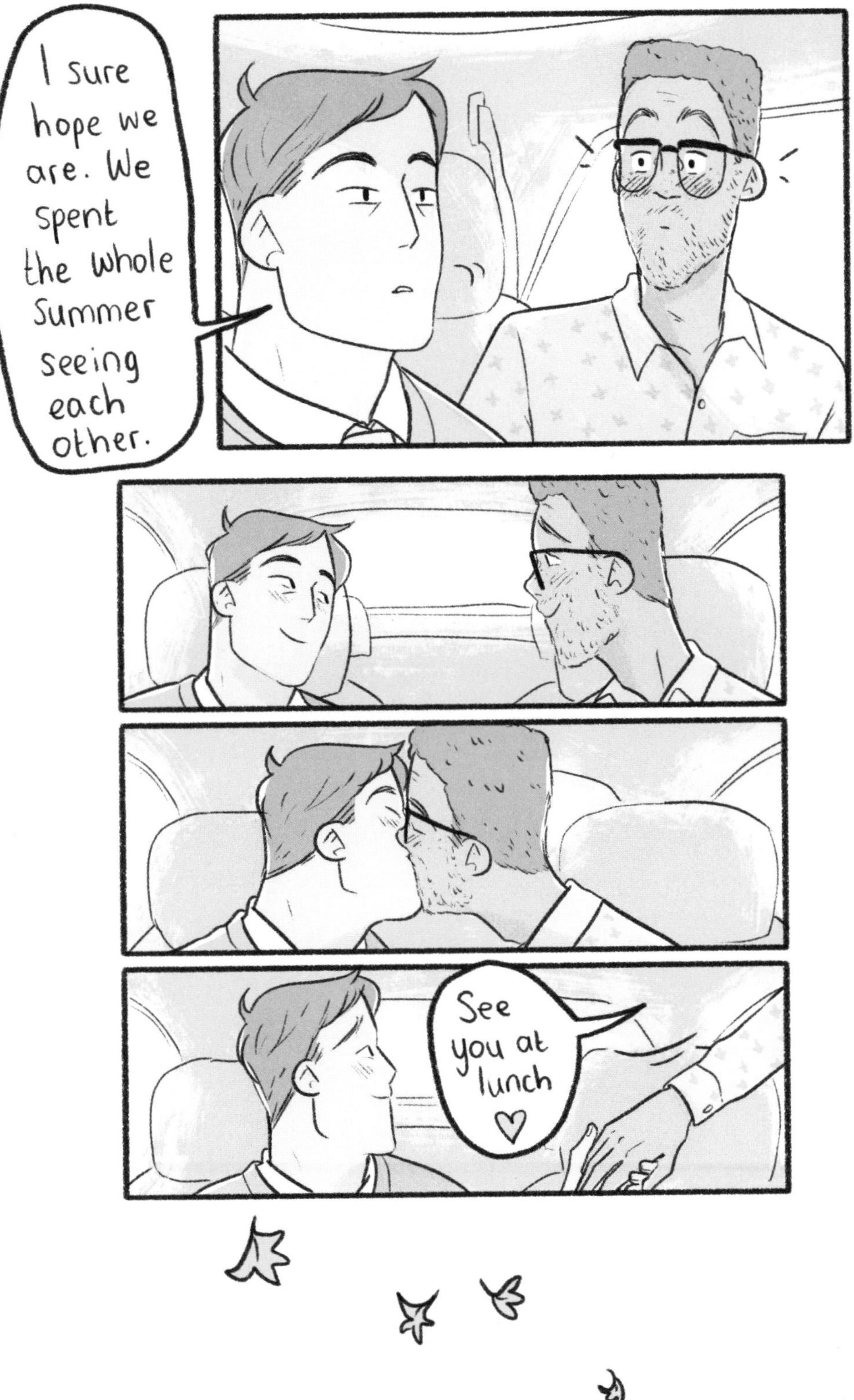
I sure hope we are. We spent the whole summer seeing each other.
See you at lunch ♡

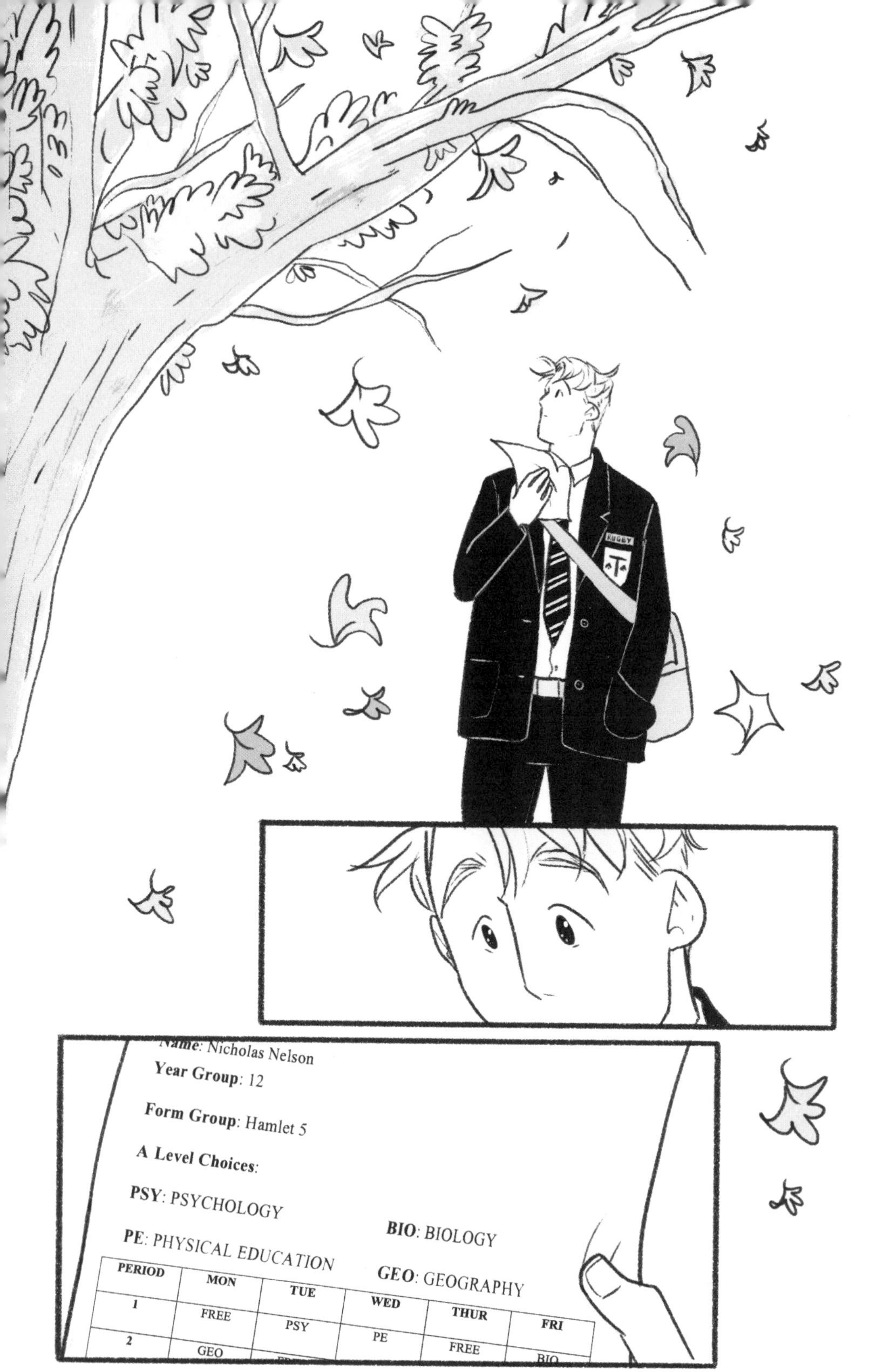

RUGBY
Nicholas Nelson
Year Group: 12
Form Group: Hamlet 5
A Level Choices:
PSY: PSYCHOLOGY
PE: PHYSICAL EDUCATION
BIO: BIOLOGY
GEO: GEOGRAPHY
PERIOD MON TUE WED THUR FRI
1 FREE PSY PE FREE
2 GEO BIO

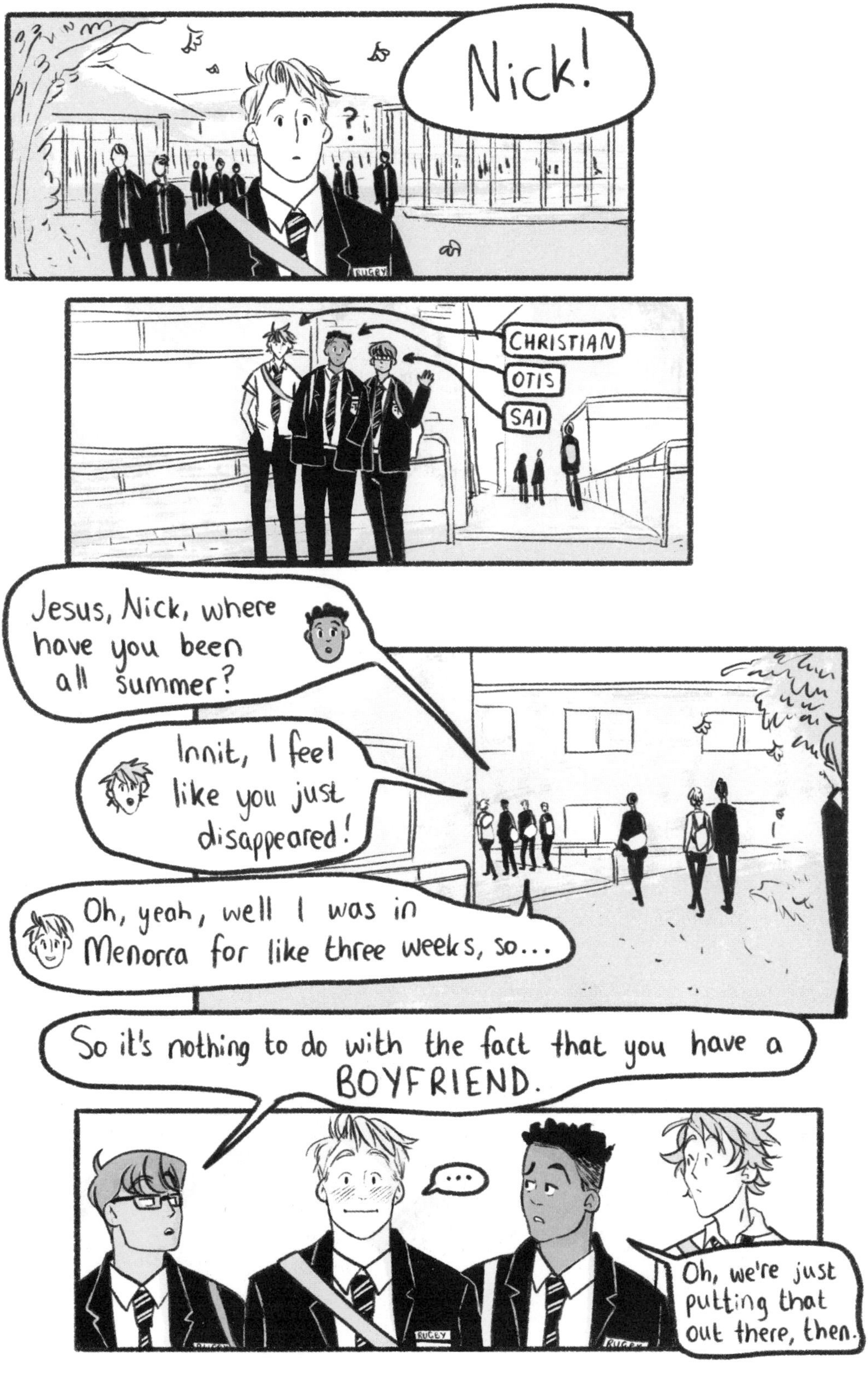
Nick!
RUGBY
CHRISTIAN
OTIS
SAI
Jesus, Nick, where have you been all summer?
Innit, I feel like you just disappeared!
Oh, yeah, well I was in Menorca for like three weeks, so...
So it's nothing to do with the fact that you have a BOYFRIEND.
...
RUGBY
RUGBY
Oh, we're just putting that out there, then.

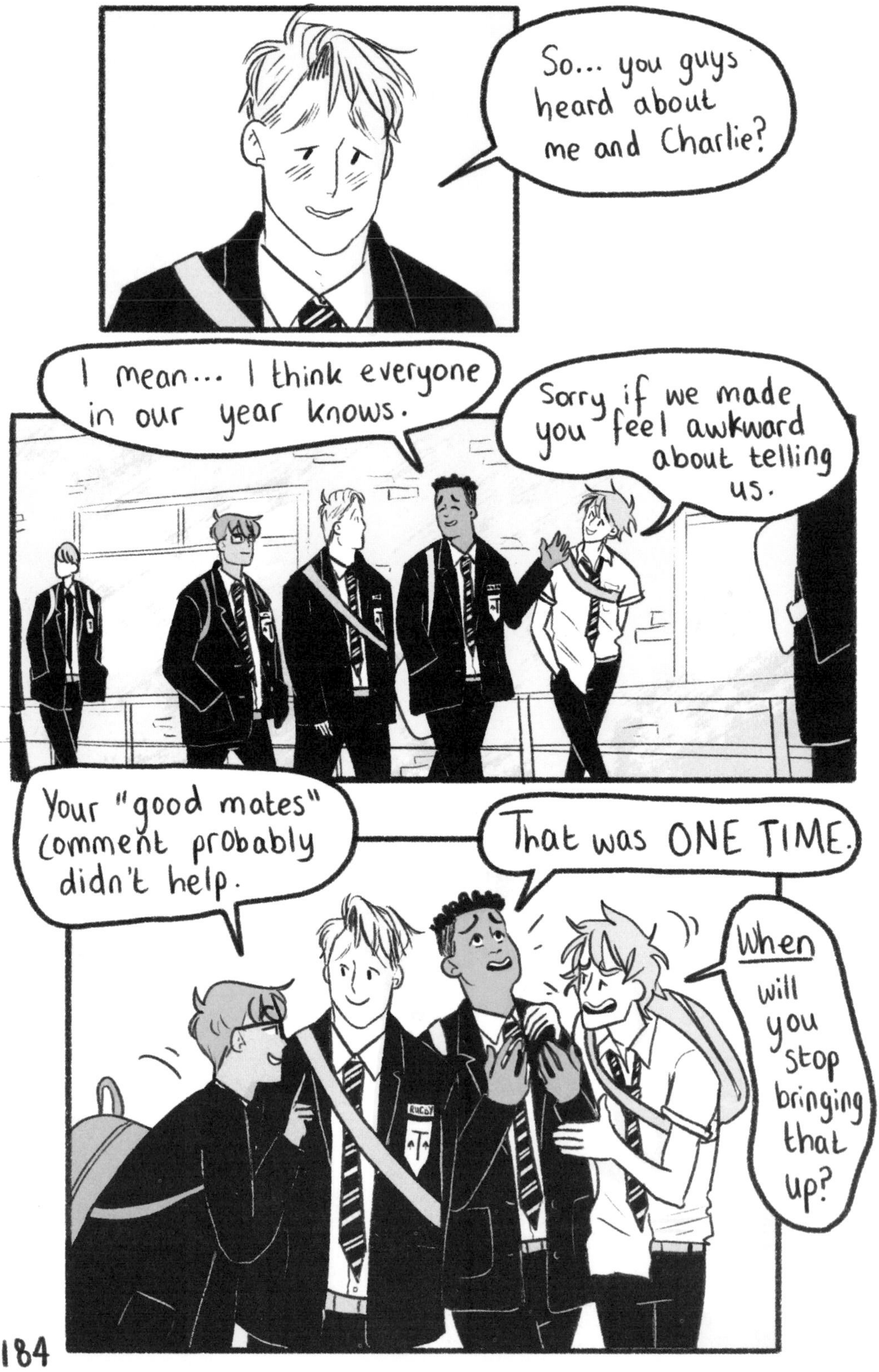
So... you guys heard about me and Charlie?
I mean... I think everyone in our year knows.
Sorry if we made you feel awkward about telling us.
Your "good mates" comment probably didn't help.
That was ONE TIME.
When will you stop bringing that up?

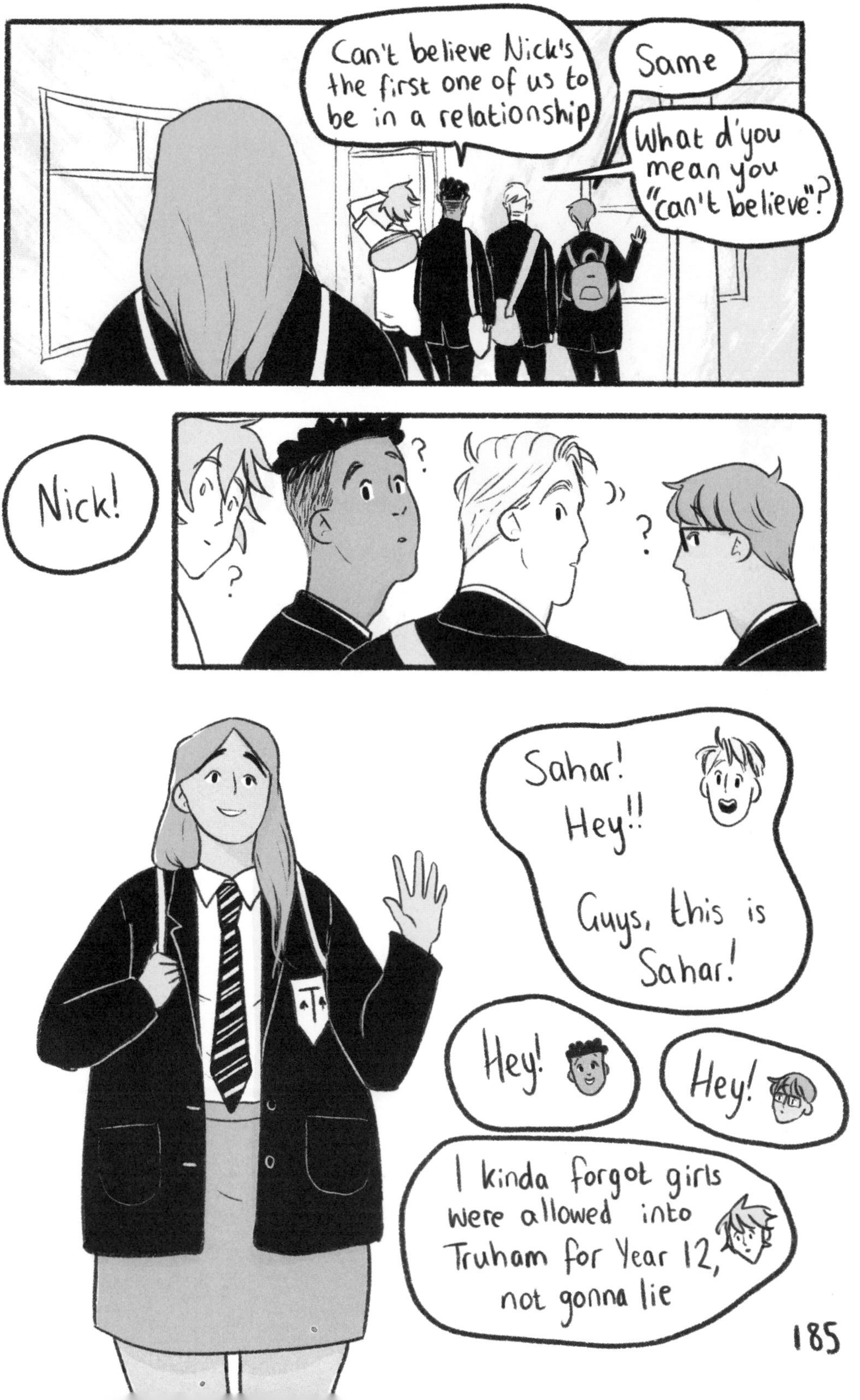
Can't believe Nick's the first one of us to be in a relationship
Same
What d'you mean you "can't believe"?
Nick!
Sahar! Hey!!
Guys, this is Sahar!
Hey!
Hey!
I kinda forgot girls were allowed into Truham for Year 12, not gonna lie

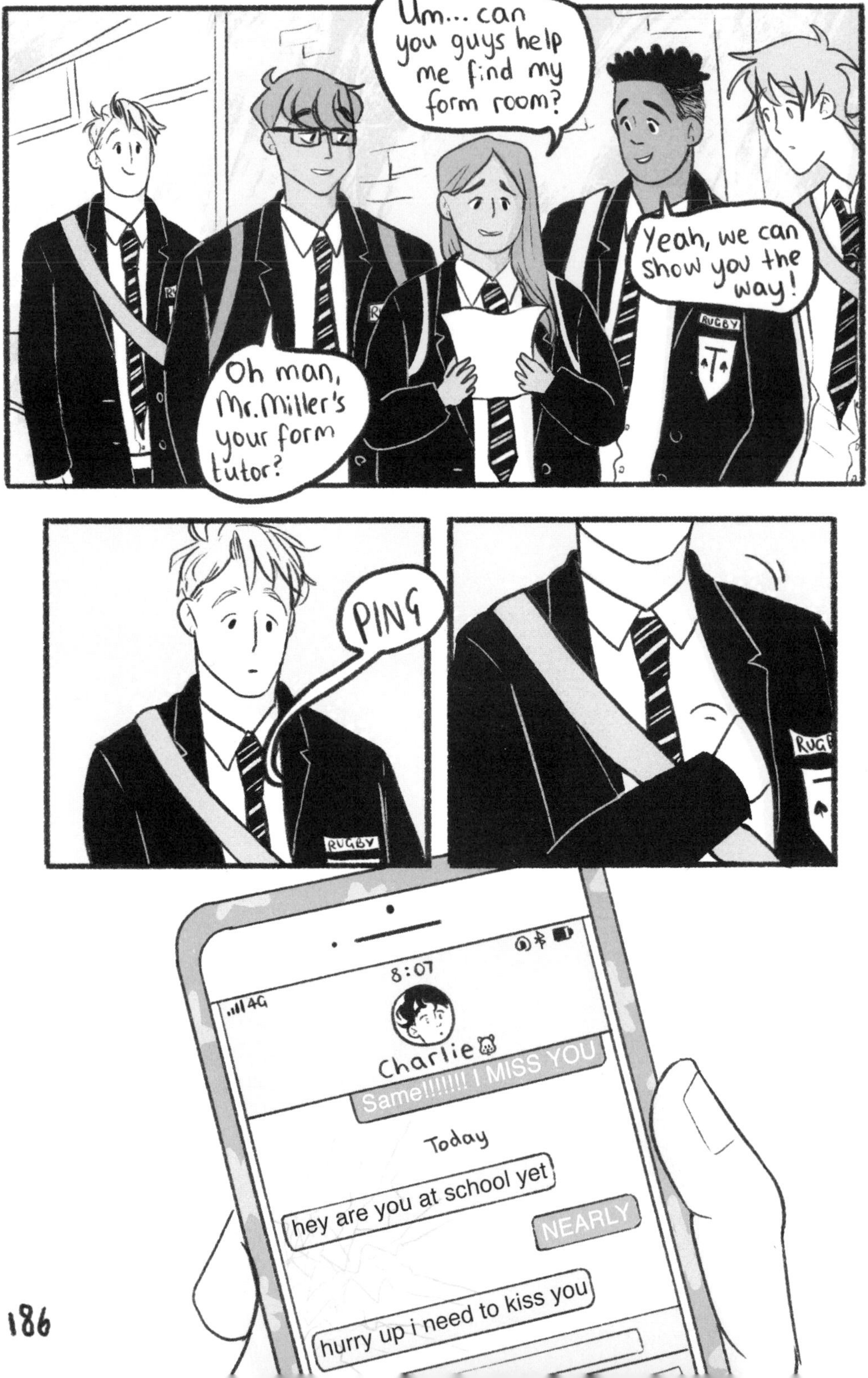
Um... can you guys help me find my form room?
Oh man, Mr. Miller's your form tutor?
Yeah, we can show you the way!
RUGBY
PING
RUGBY
8:07
4G
Charlie
Same!!!!!!! I MISS YOU
Today
hey are you at school yet
NEARLY
hurry up i need to kiss you

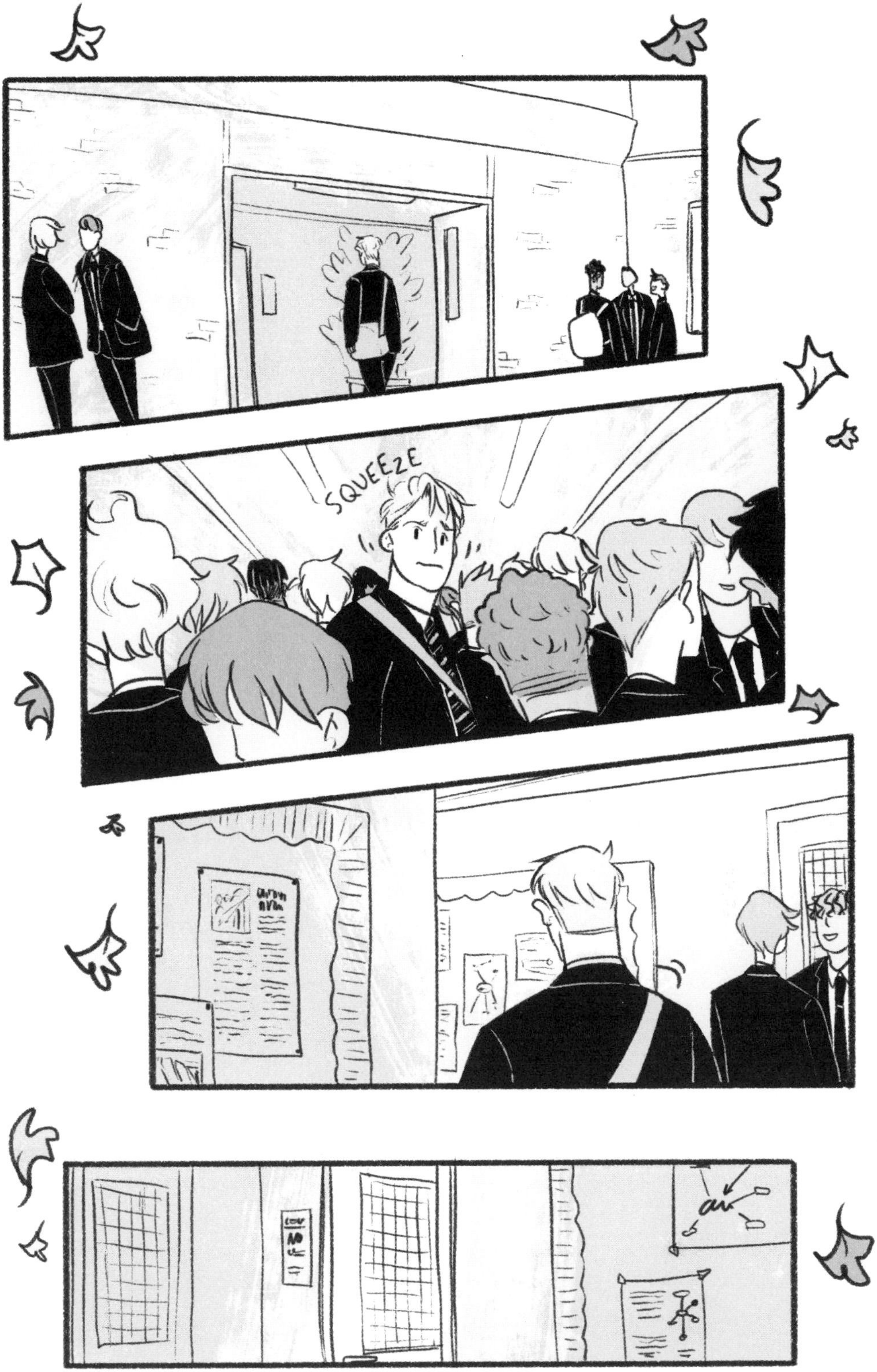
SQUEEZE

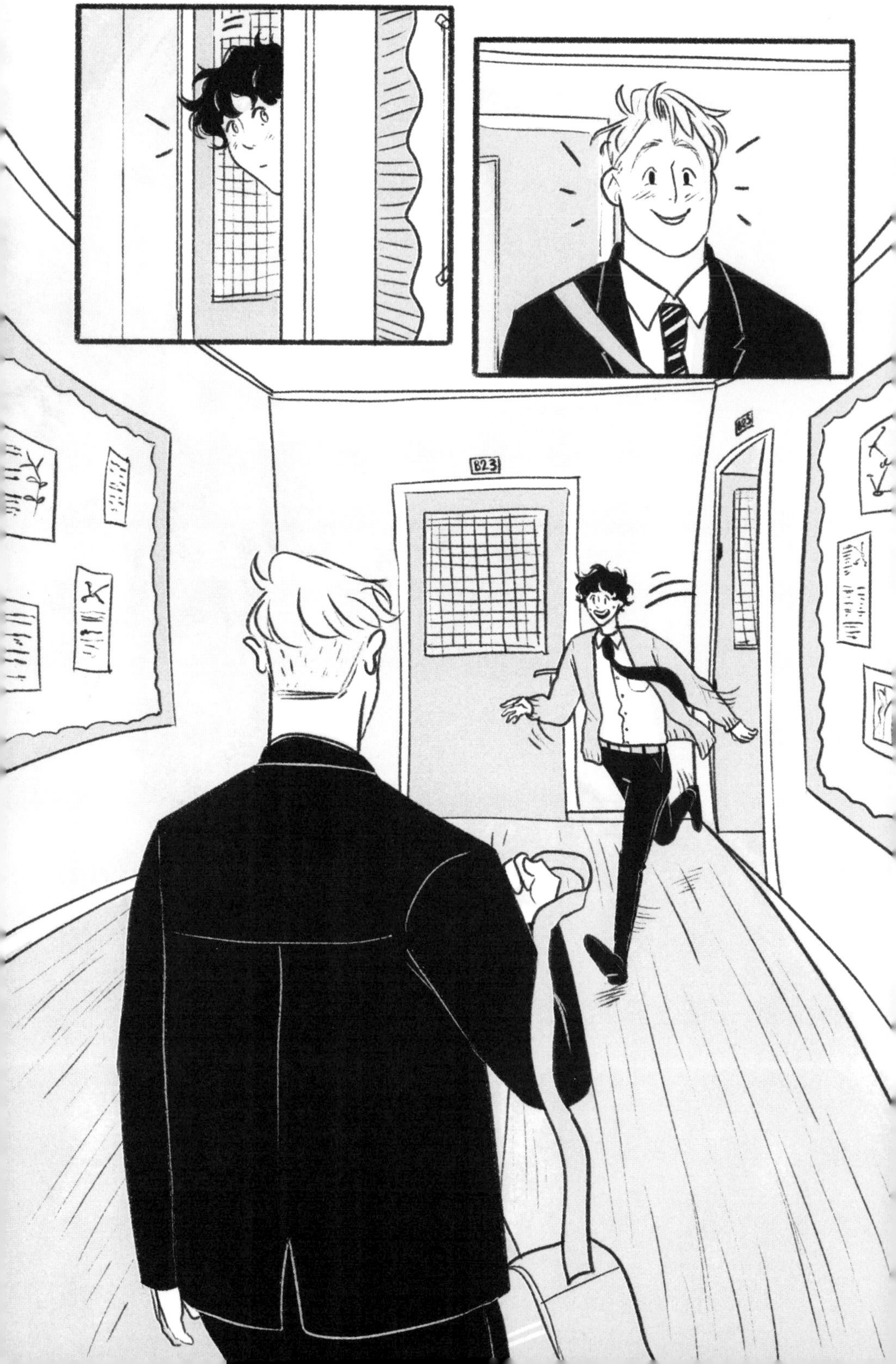
B23

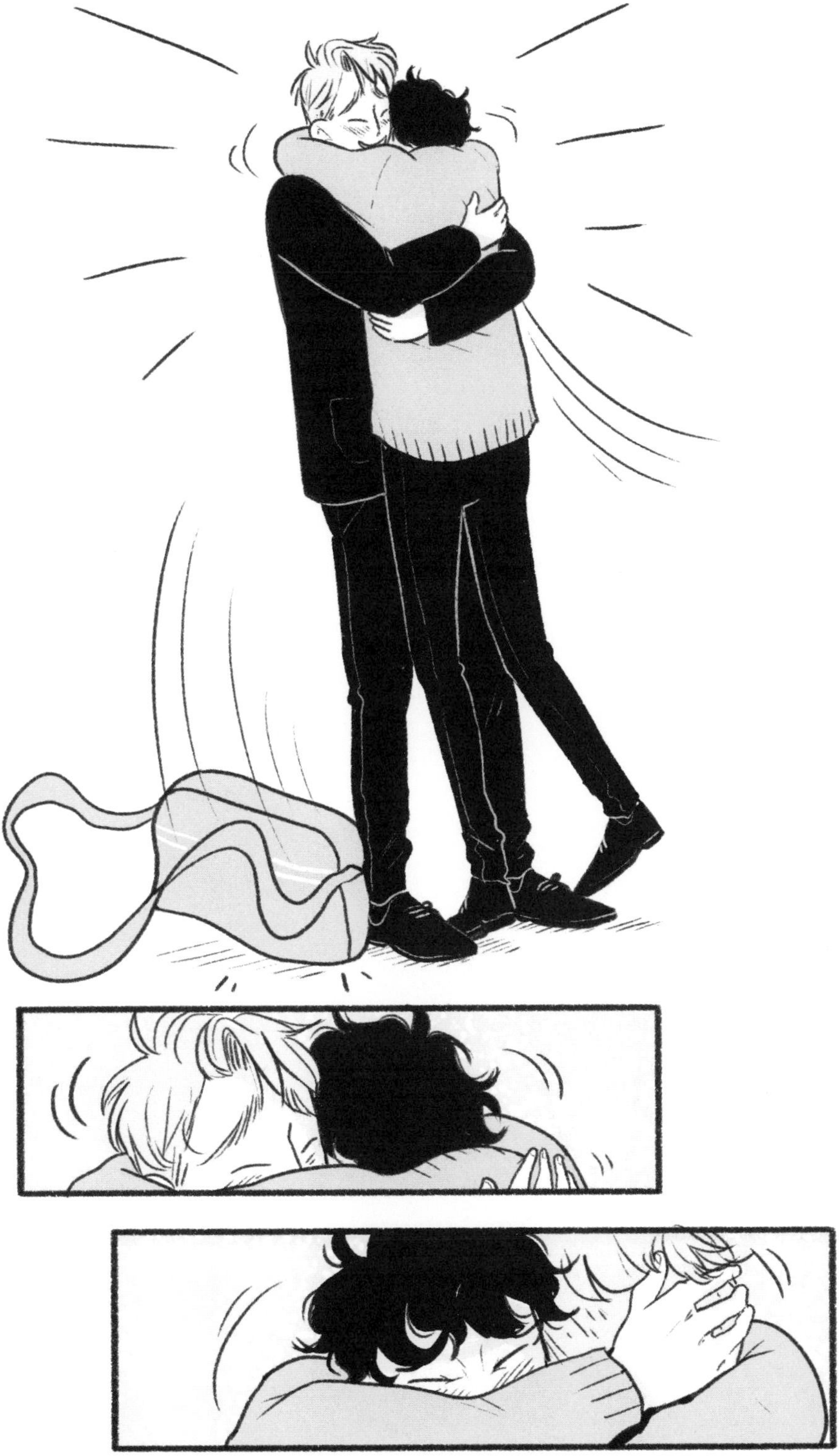

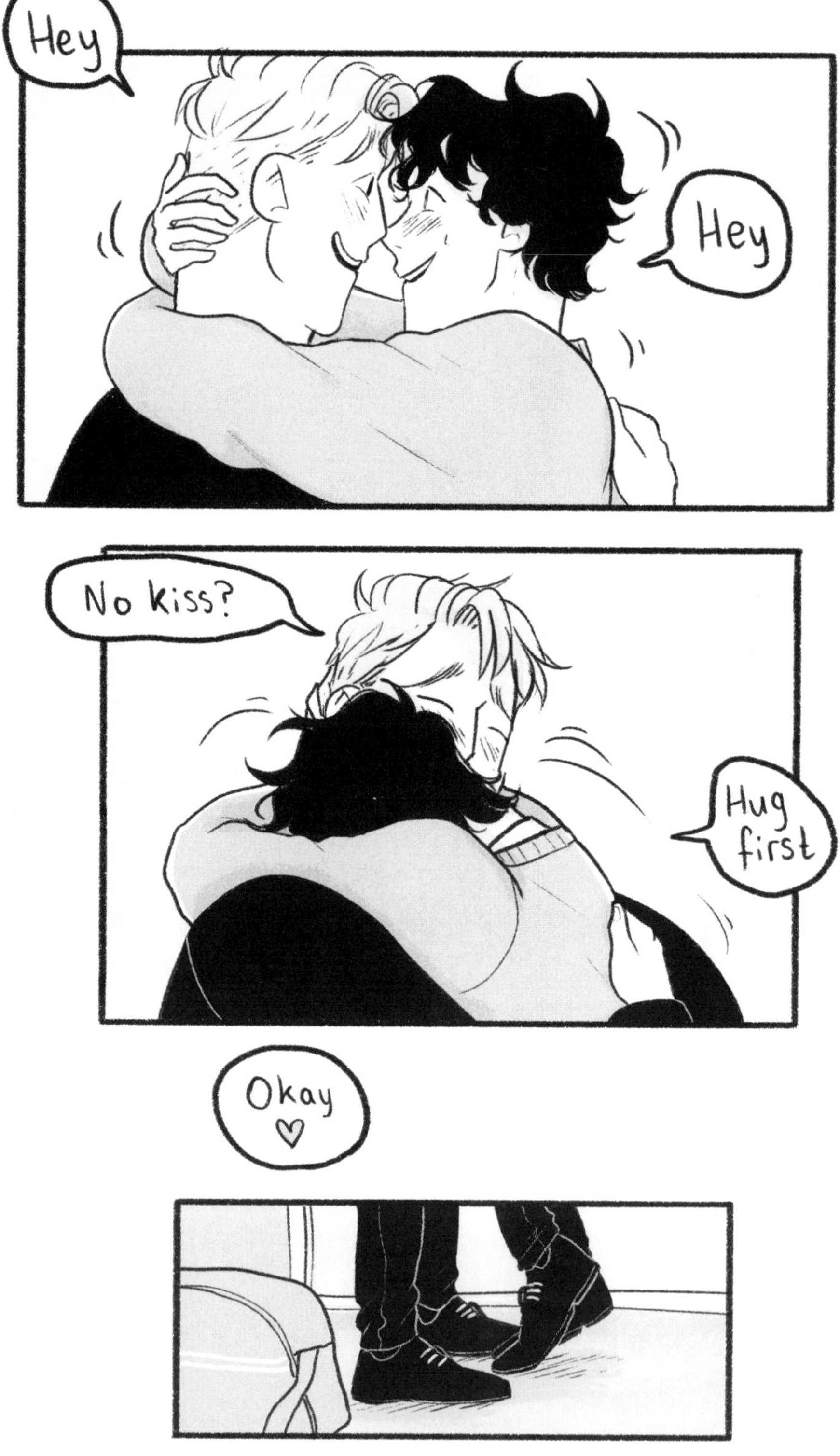
Hey
Hey
No kiss?
Hug first
Okay ♥

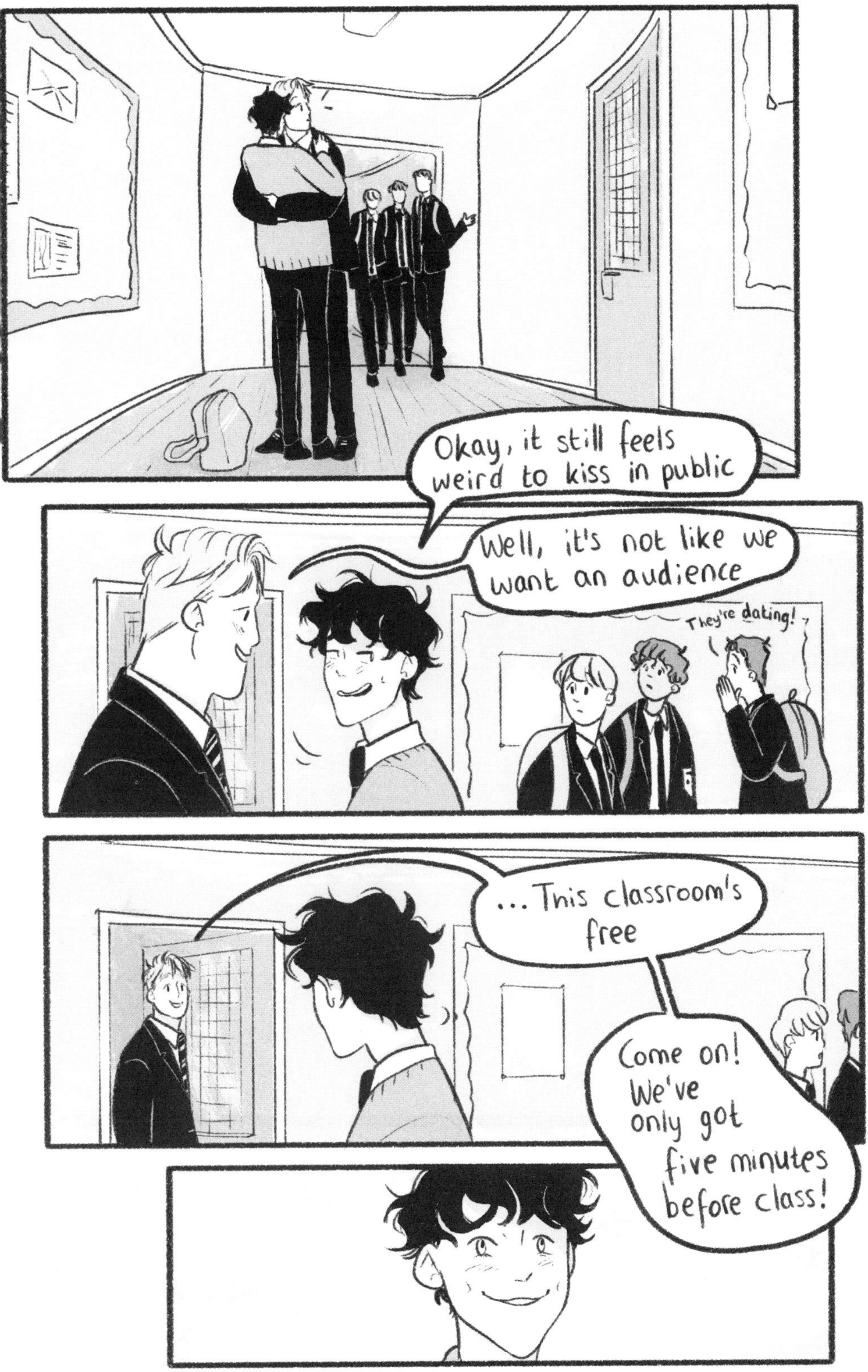
Okay, it still feels weird to kiss in public
Well, it's not like we want an audience
They're dating!
...This classroom's free
Come on! We've only got five minutes before class!

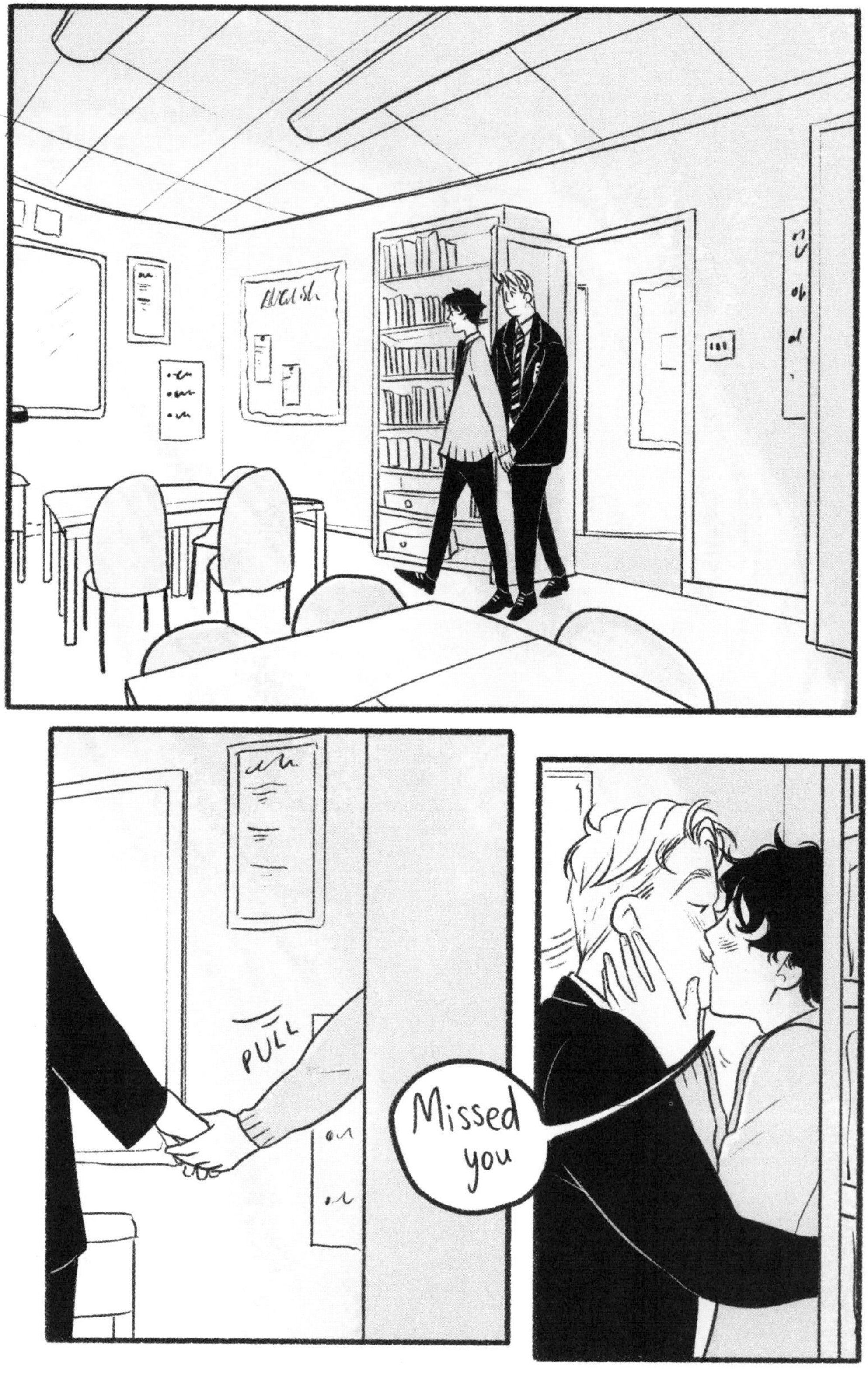
PULL
Missed you

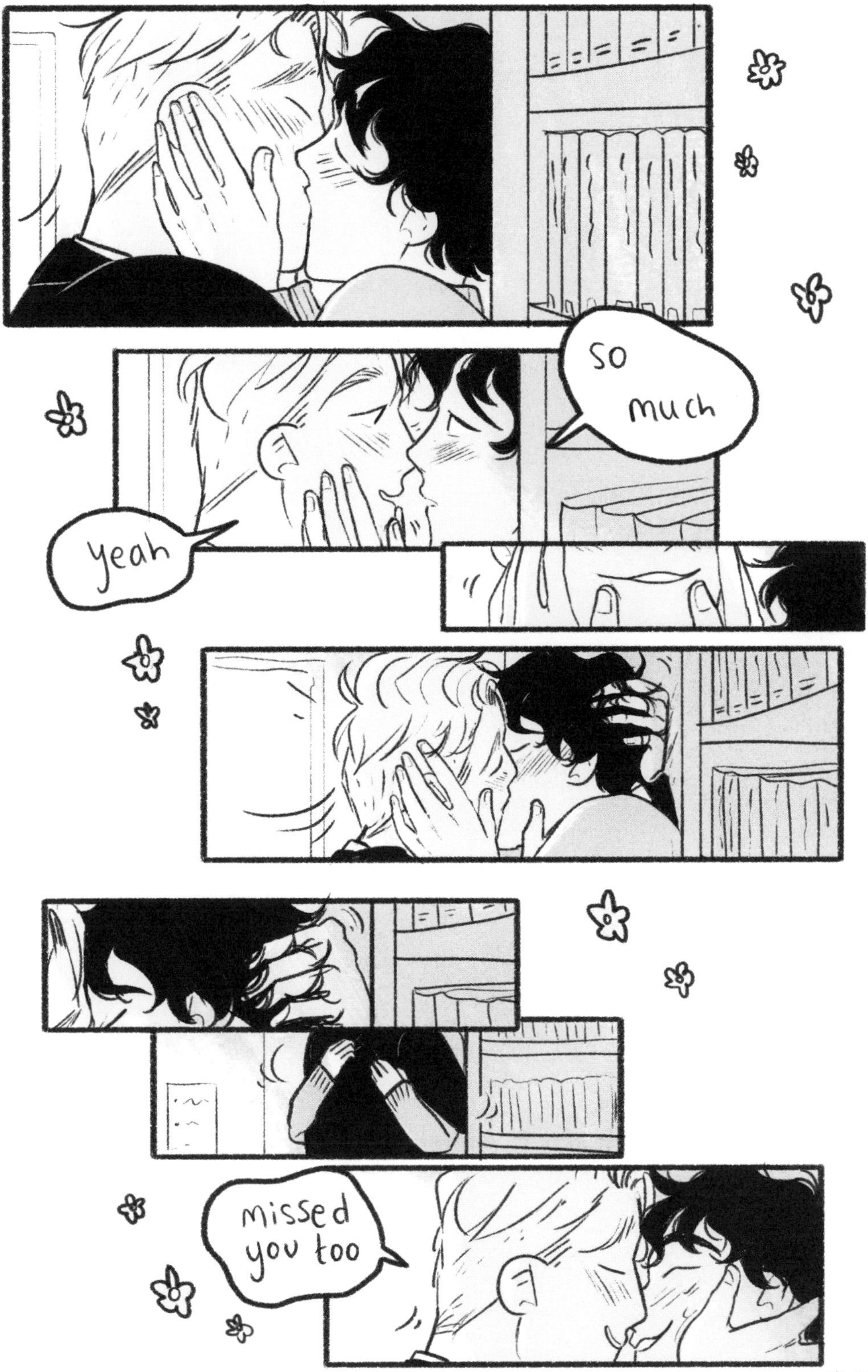
so much
yeah
missed you too

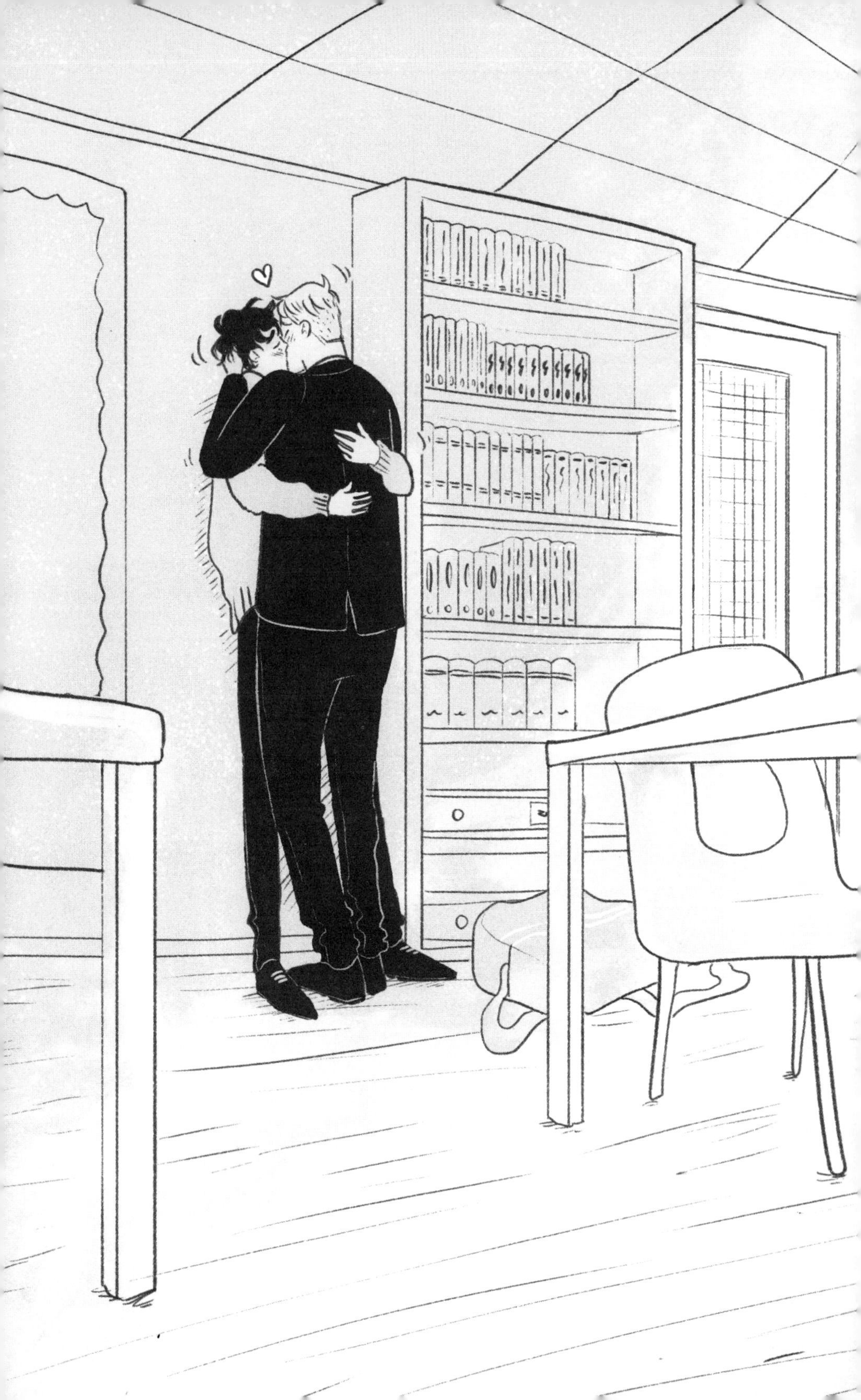

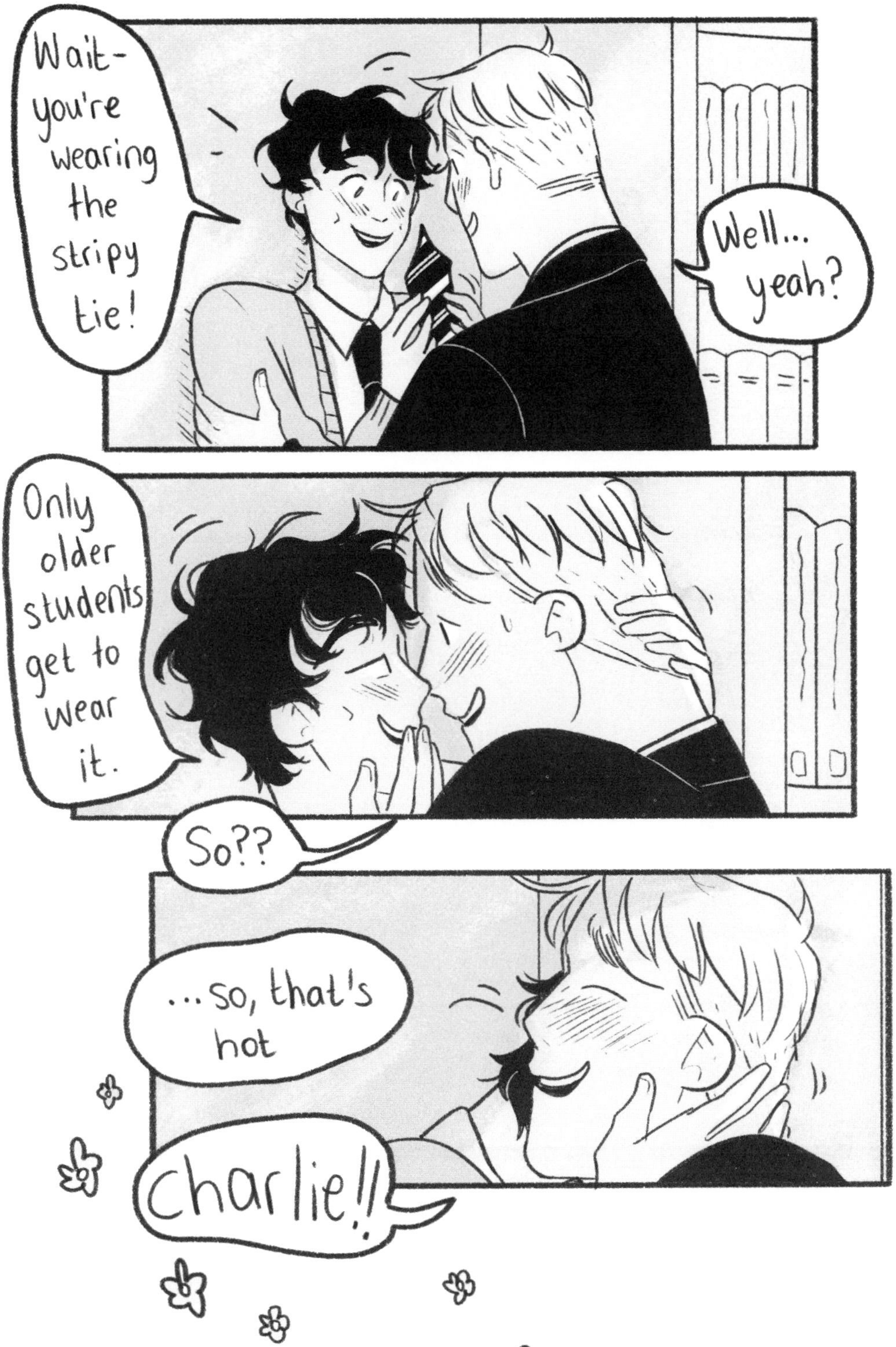
Wait- you're wearing the stripy tie!
Well... yeah?
Only older students get to wear it.
So??
...so, that's hot
Charlie!!

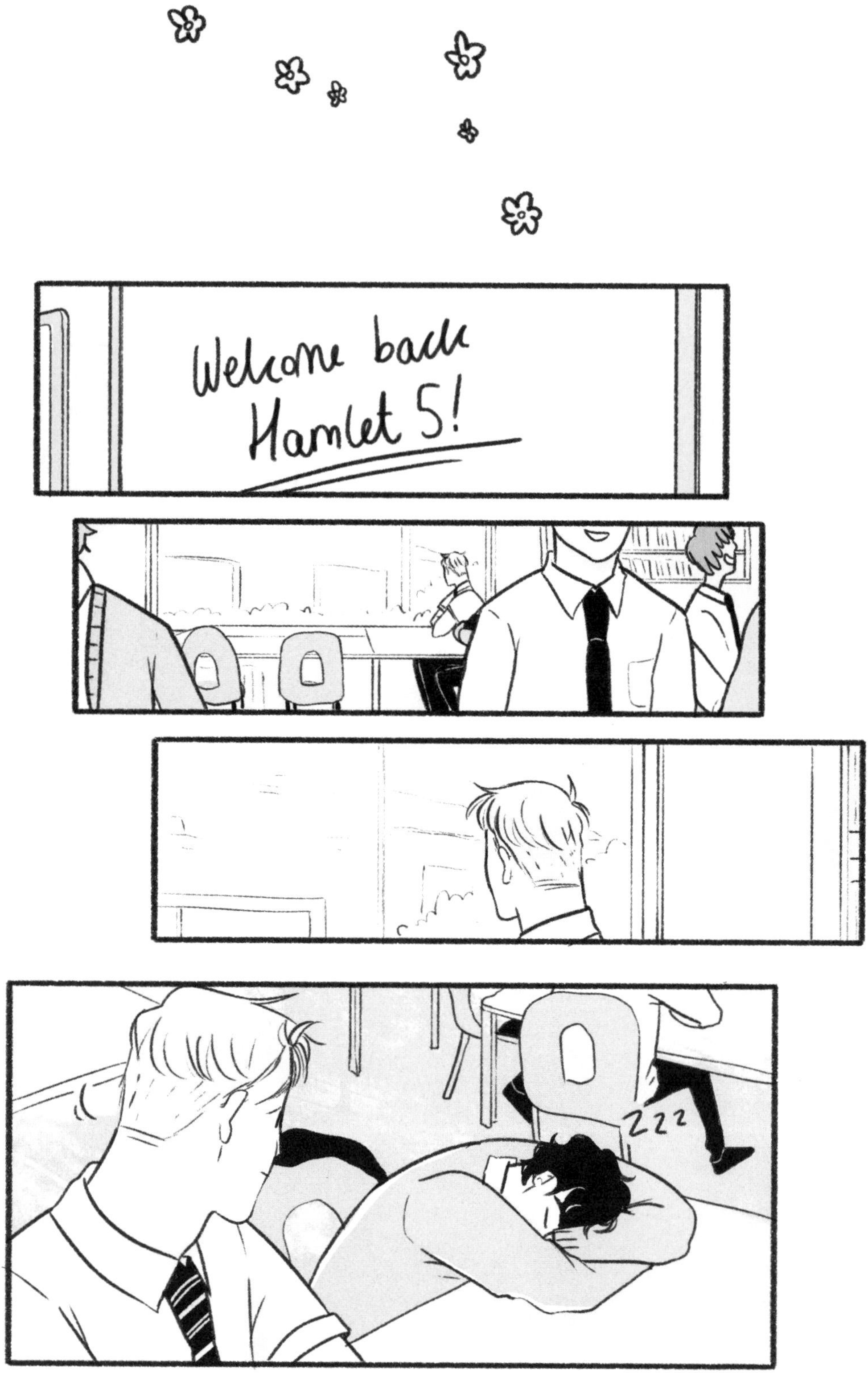
Welcome back
Hamlet 5!
ZZZ

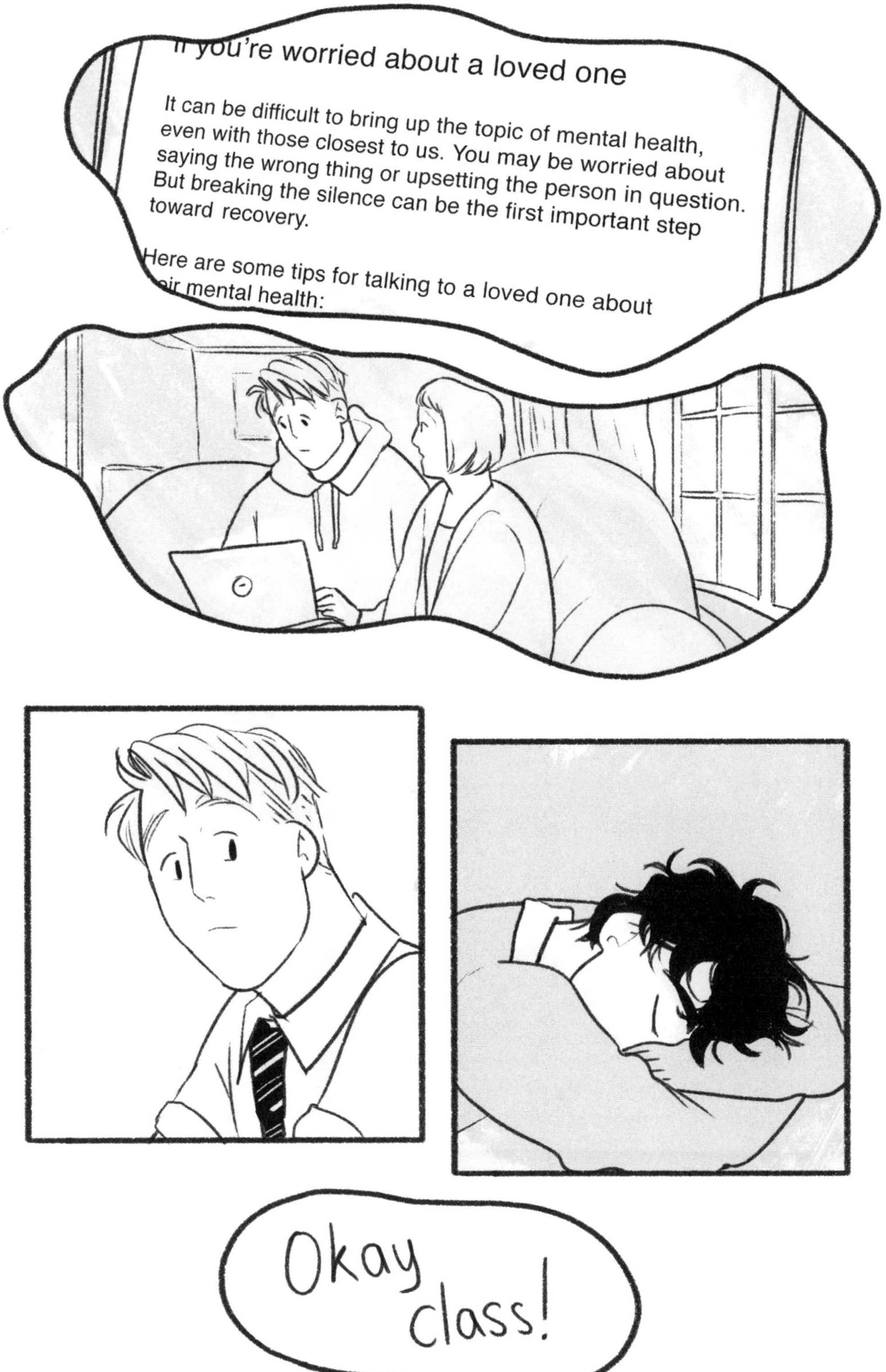
you're worried about a loved one
It can be difficult to bring up the topic of mental health, even with those closest to us. You may be worried about saying the wrong thing or upsetting the person in question. But breaking the silence can be the first important step toward recovery.
Here are some tips for talking to a loved one about
mental health:
Okay class!

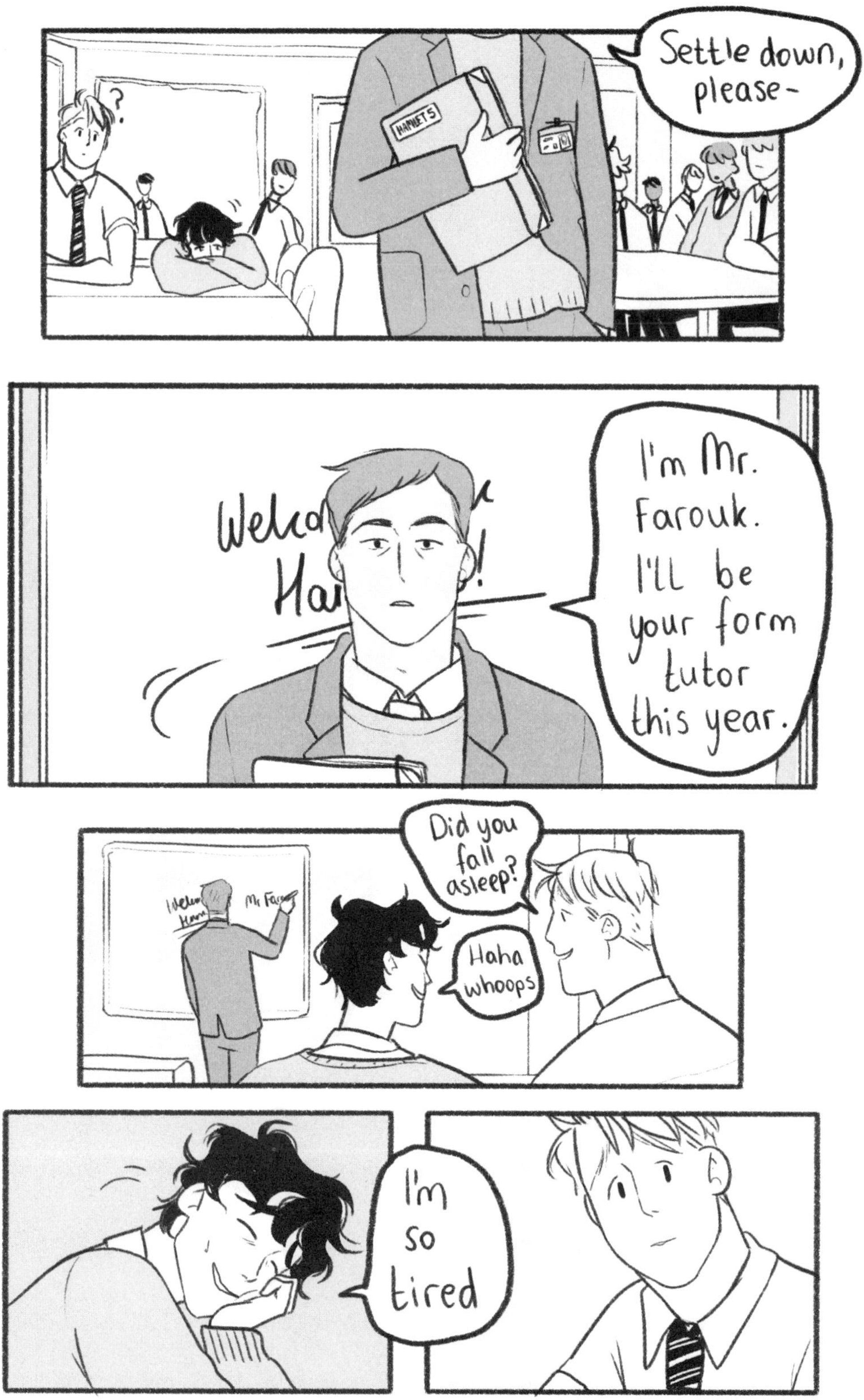
Settle down, please-
I'm Mr. Farouk. I'll be your form tutor this year.
Did you fall asleep?
Haha whoops
I'm so tired

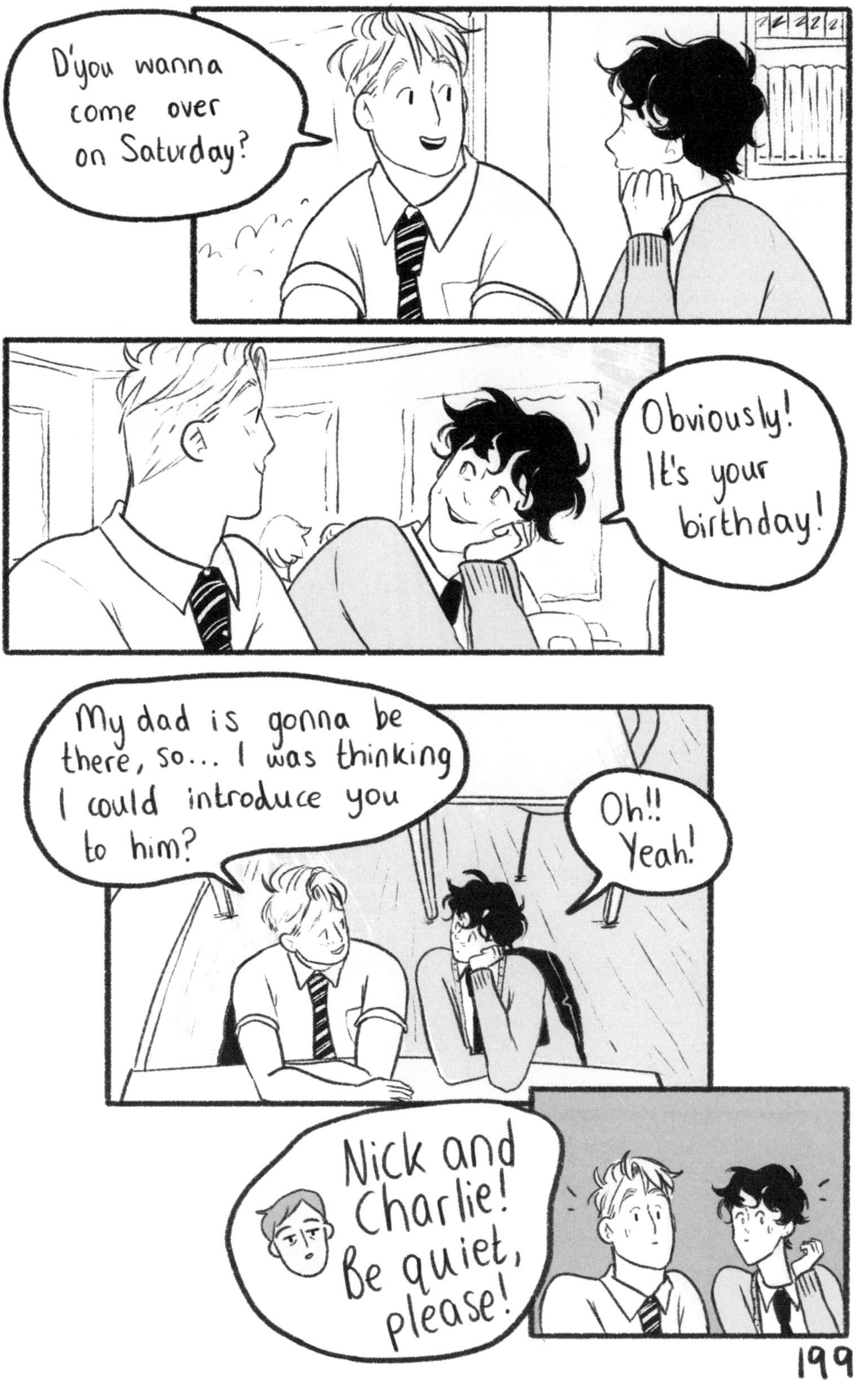
D'you wanna come over on Saturday?
Obviously! It's your birthday!
My dad is gonna be there, so... I was thinking I could introduce you to him?
Oh!! Yeah!
Nick and Charlie! Be quiet, please!

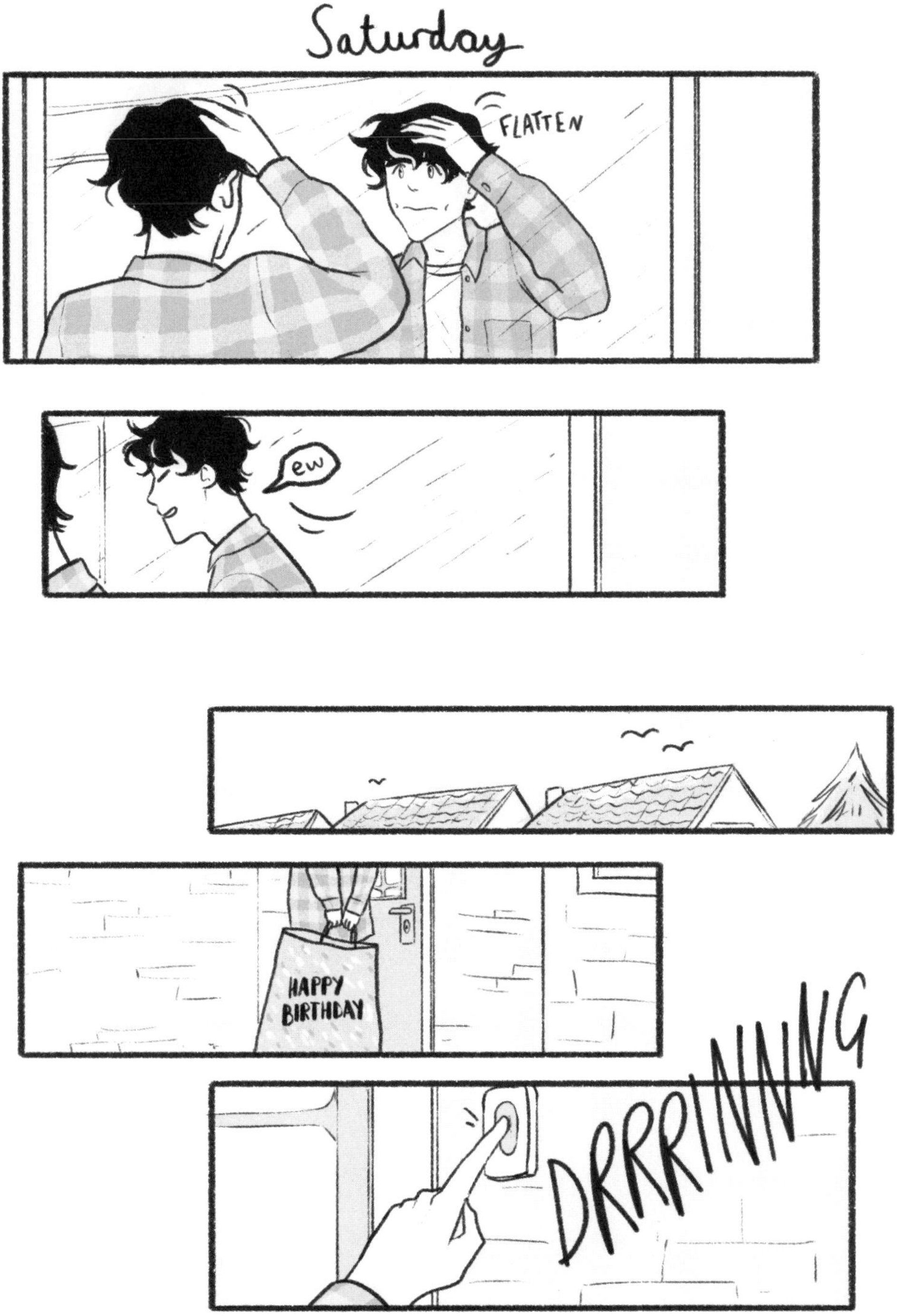
Saturday
FLATTEN
ew
HAPPY BIRTHDAY
DRRRINNNG

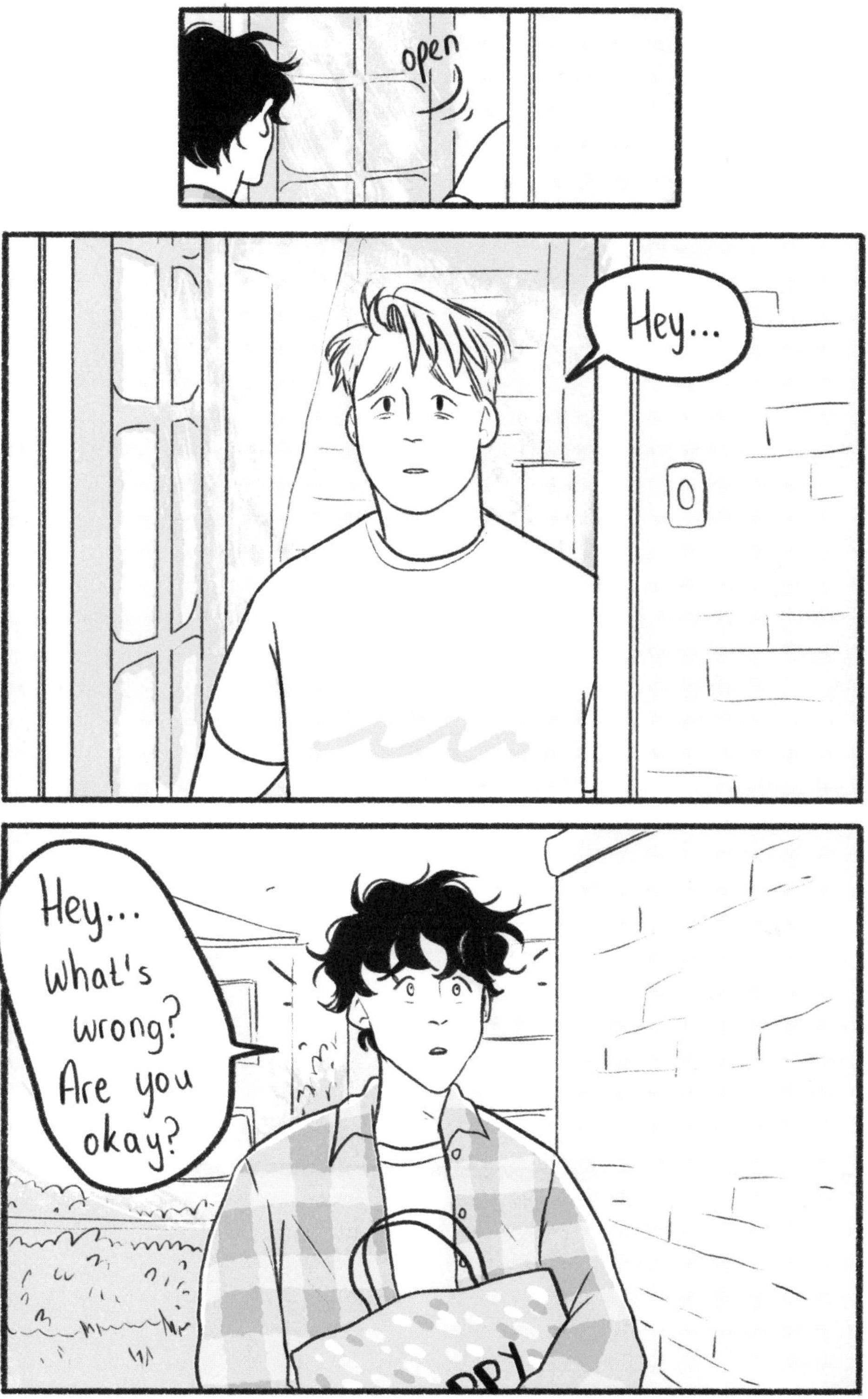
open
Hey...
Hey... what's wrong? Are you okay?

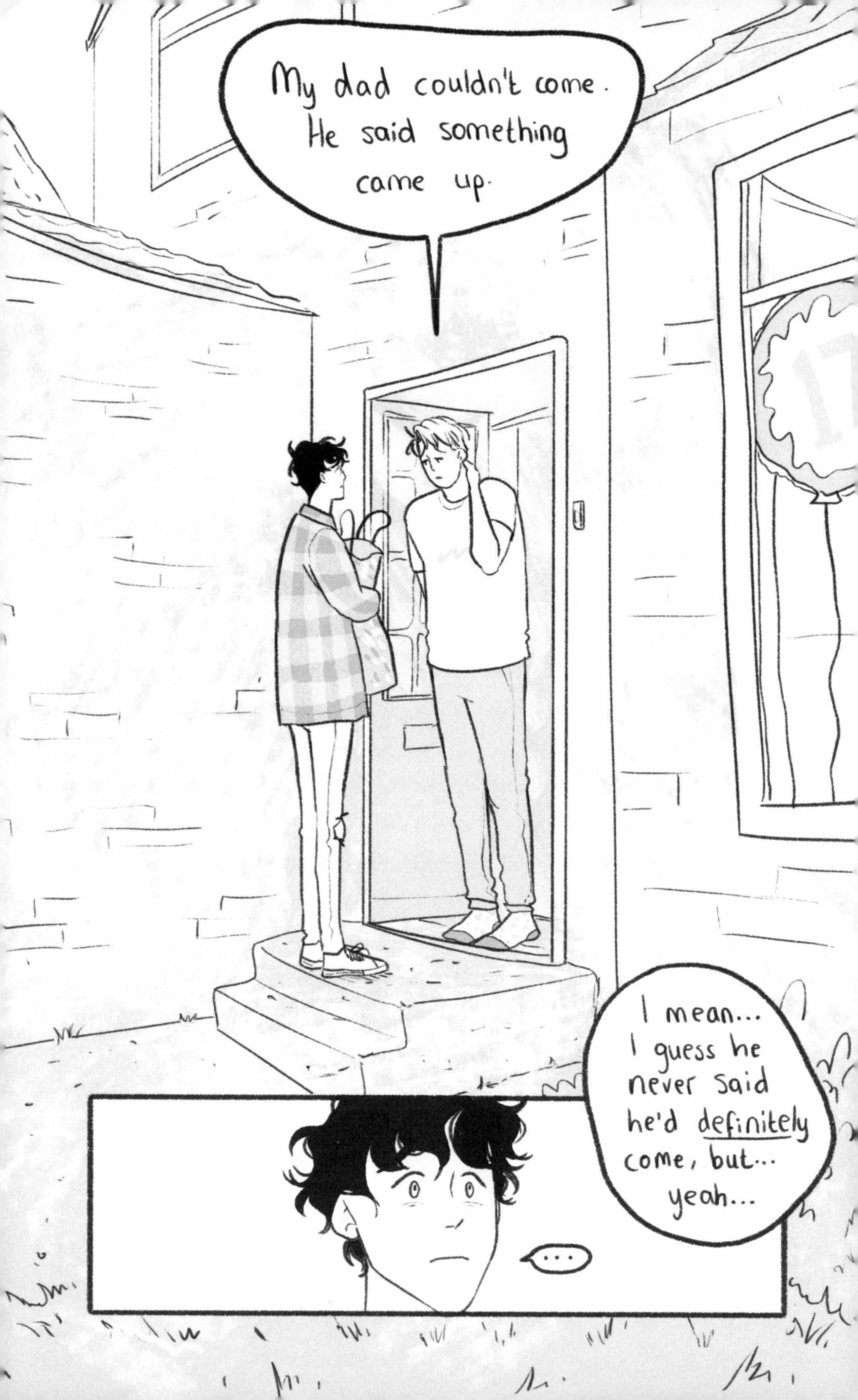
My dad couldn't come. He said something came up.
I mean... I guess he never said he'd definitely come, but... yeah...
...

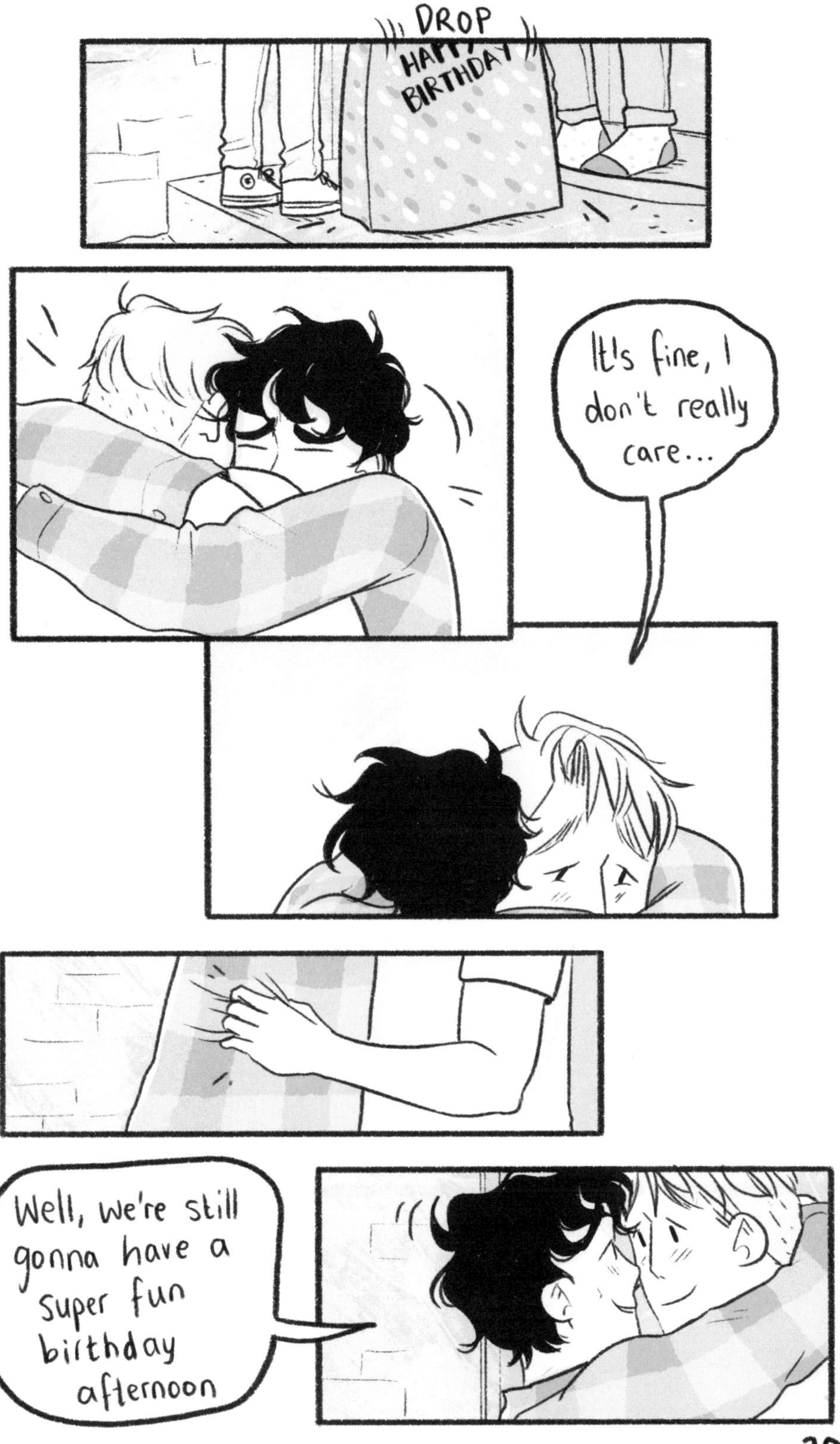
DROP
HAPPY BIRTHDAY
It's fine, I don't really care...
Well, we're still gonna have a super fun birthday afternoon

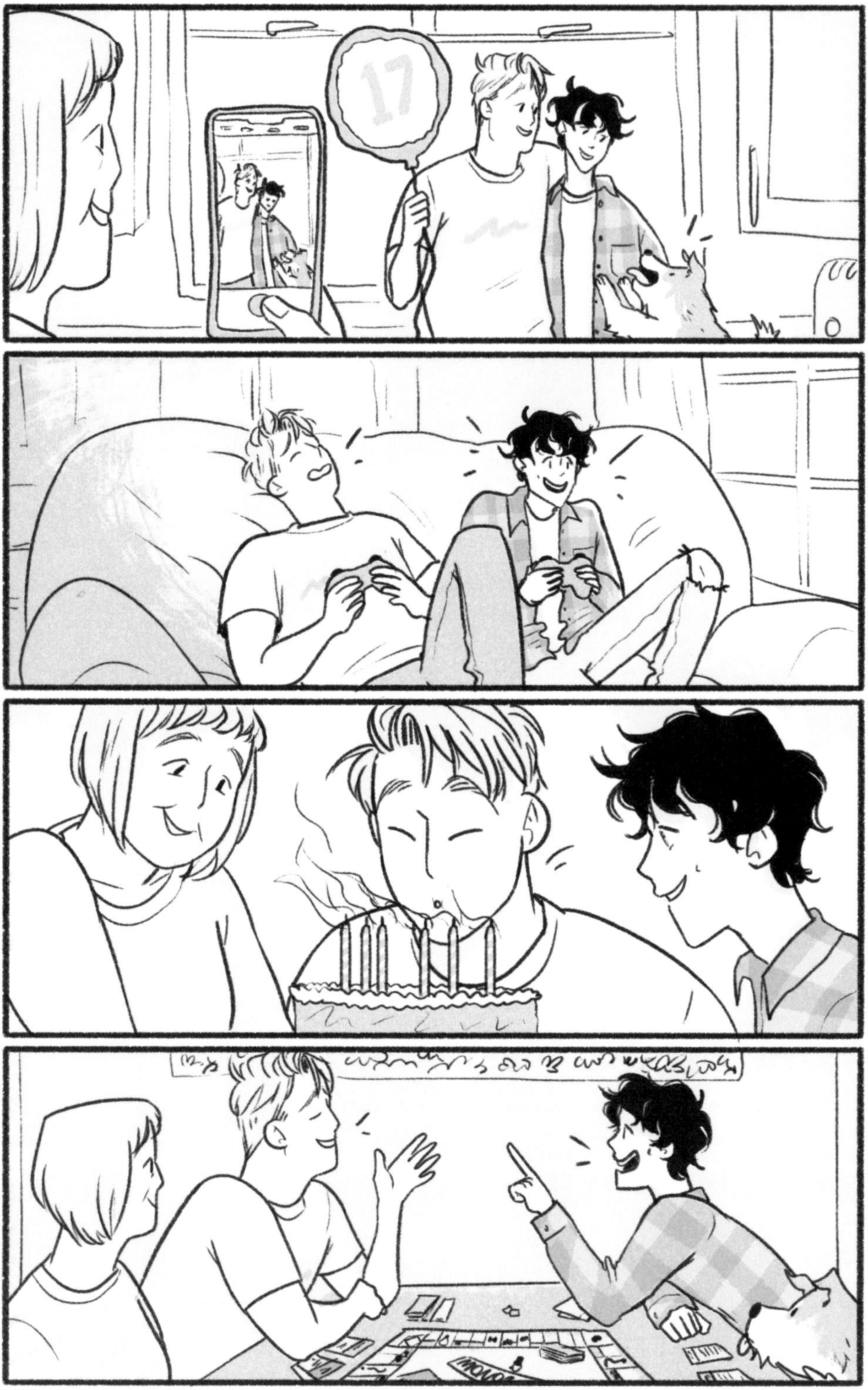
17

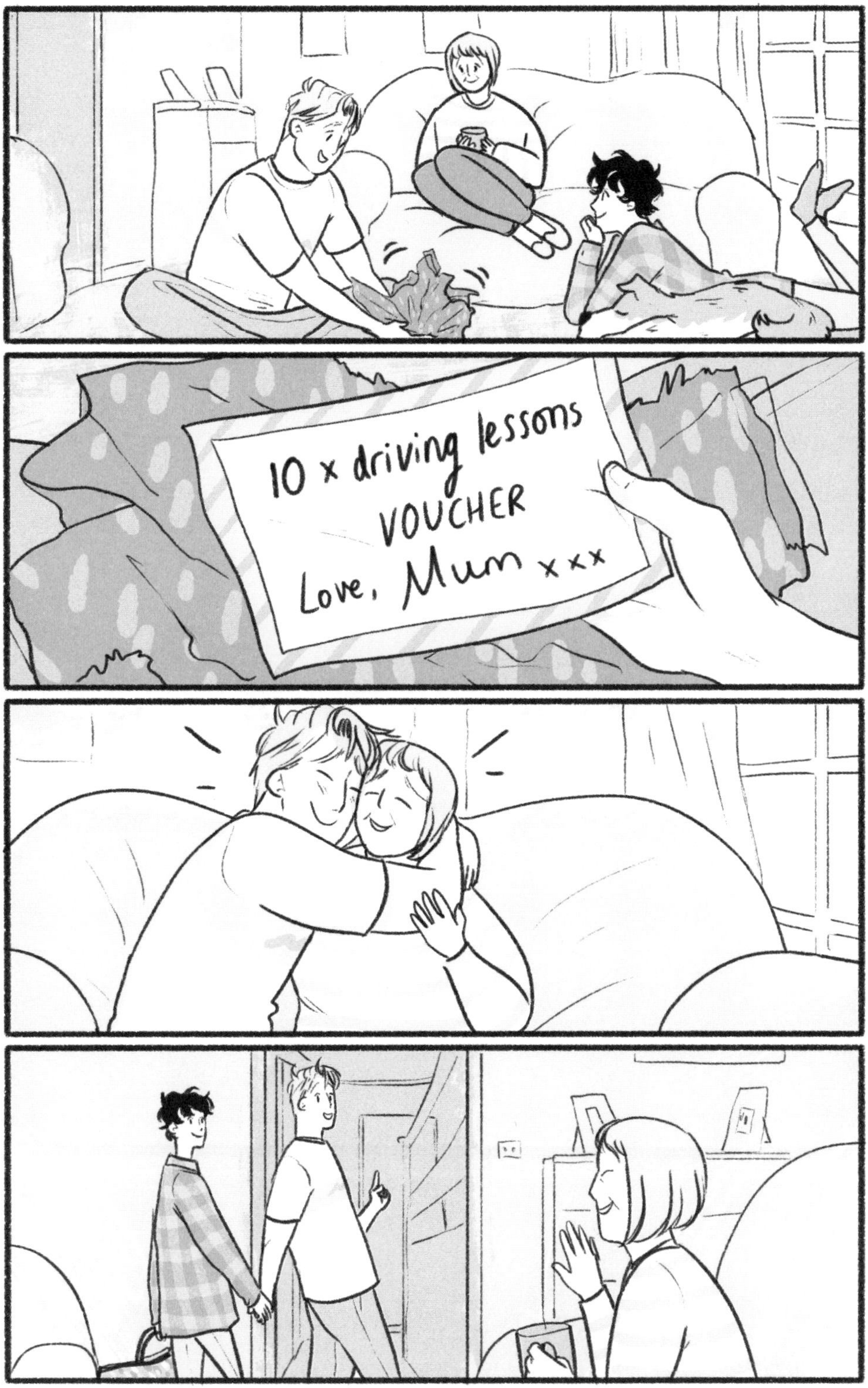
10 x driving lessons
VOUCHER
Love, Mum xxx

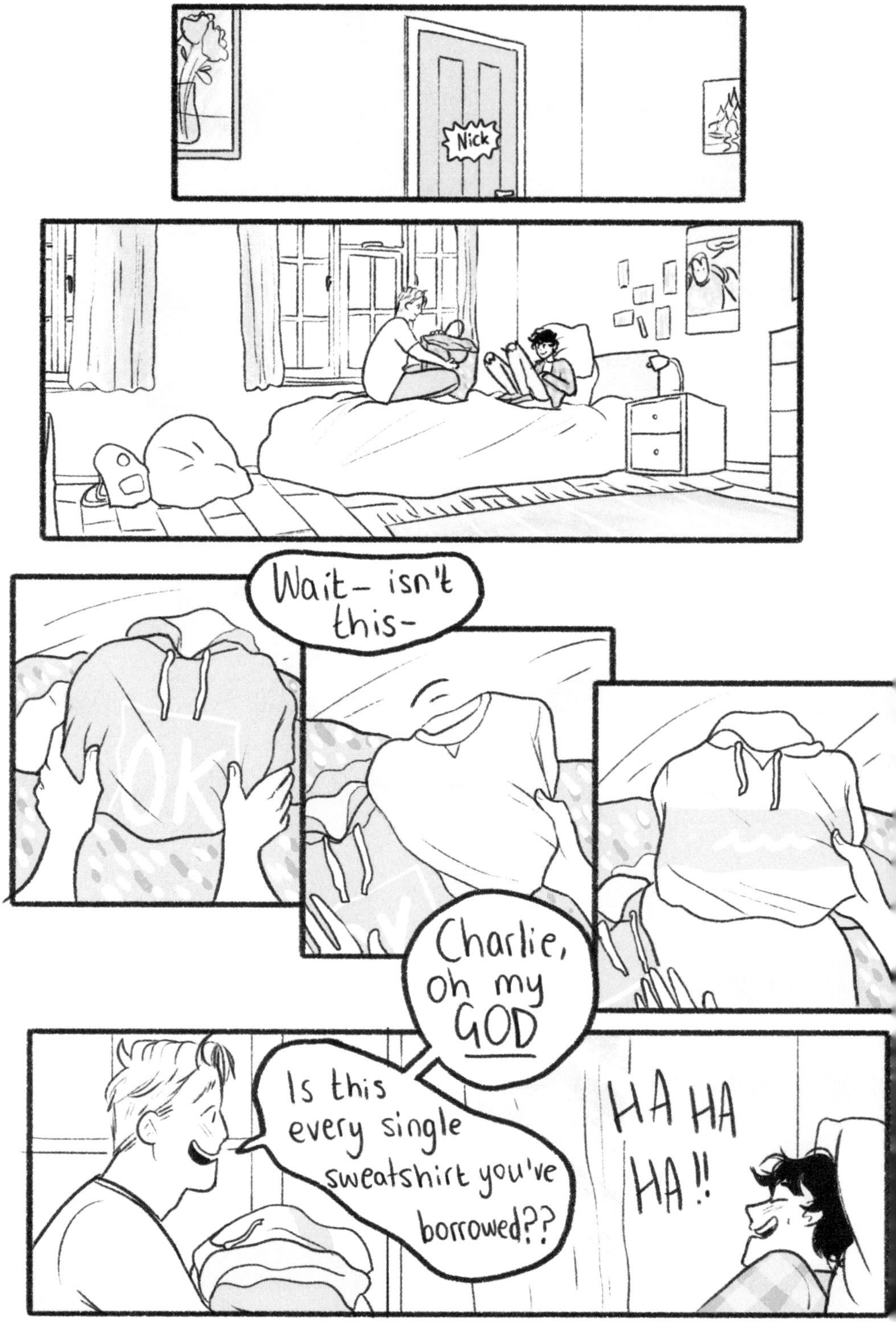
Nick
Wait- isn't this-
OK
Charlie, oh my GOD
Is this every single sweatshirt you've borrowed??
HA HA HA!!

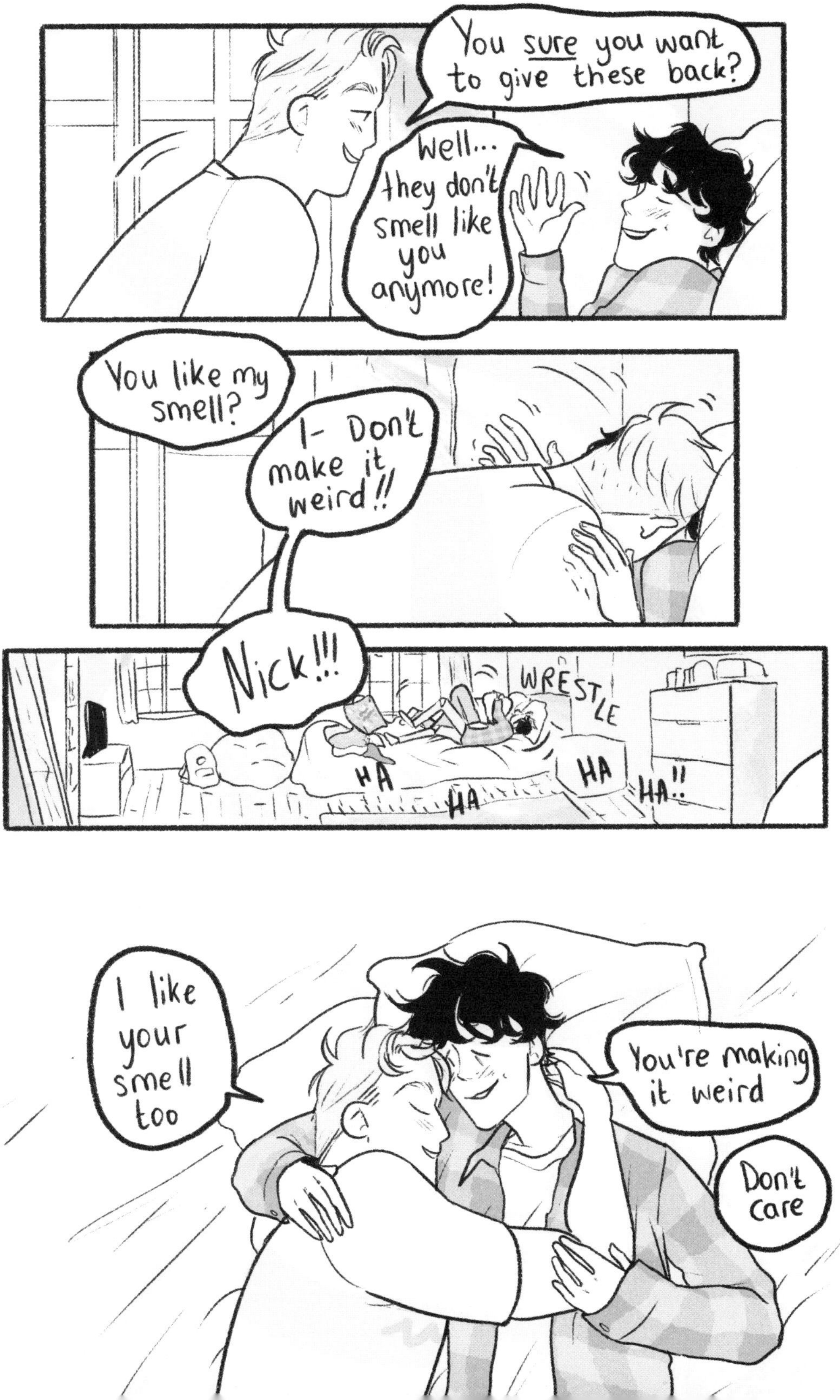
You sure you want to give these back?
Well... they don't smell like you anymore!
You like my smell?
I- Don't make it weird!!
Nick!!!
WRESTLE
HA
HA
HA
HA!!
I like your smell too
You're making it weird
Don't care

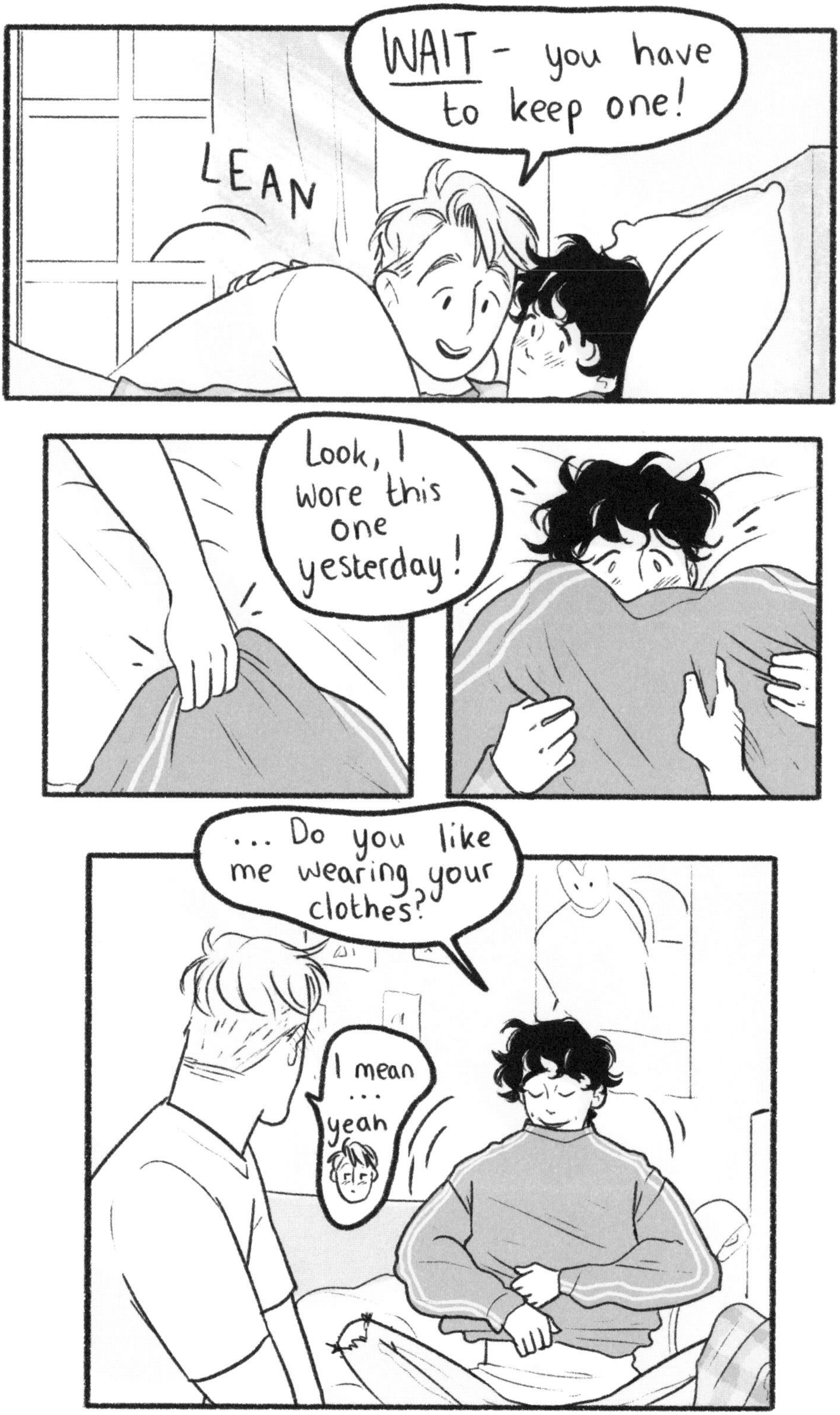
WAIT - you have to keep one!
LEAN
Look, I wore this one yesterday!
... Do you like me wearing your clothes?
I mean ... yeah

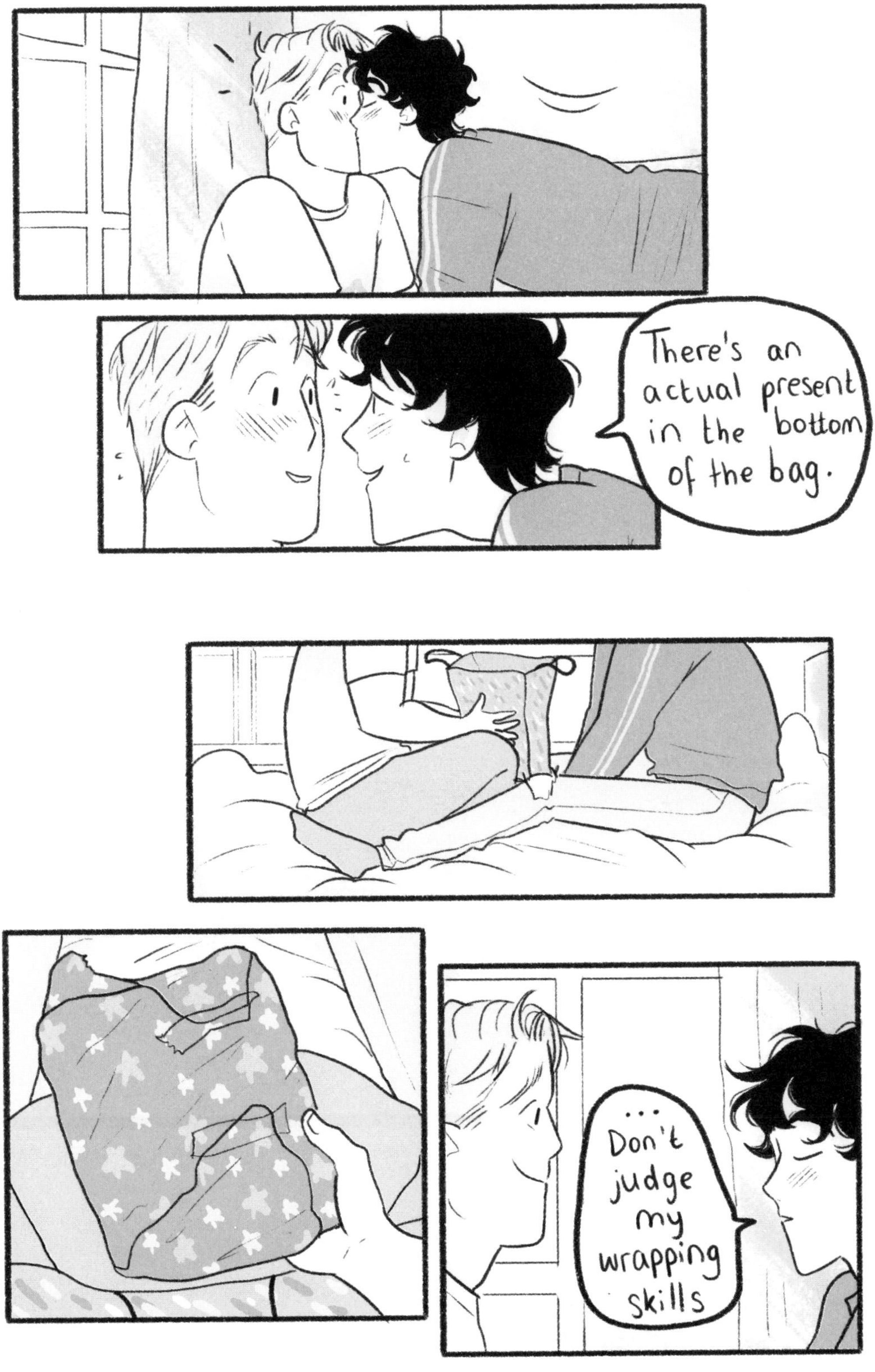
There's an actual present in the bottom of the bag.
... Don't judge my wrapping skills

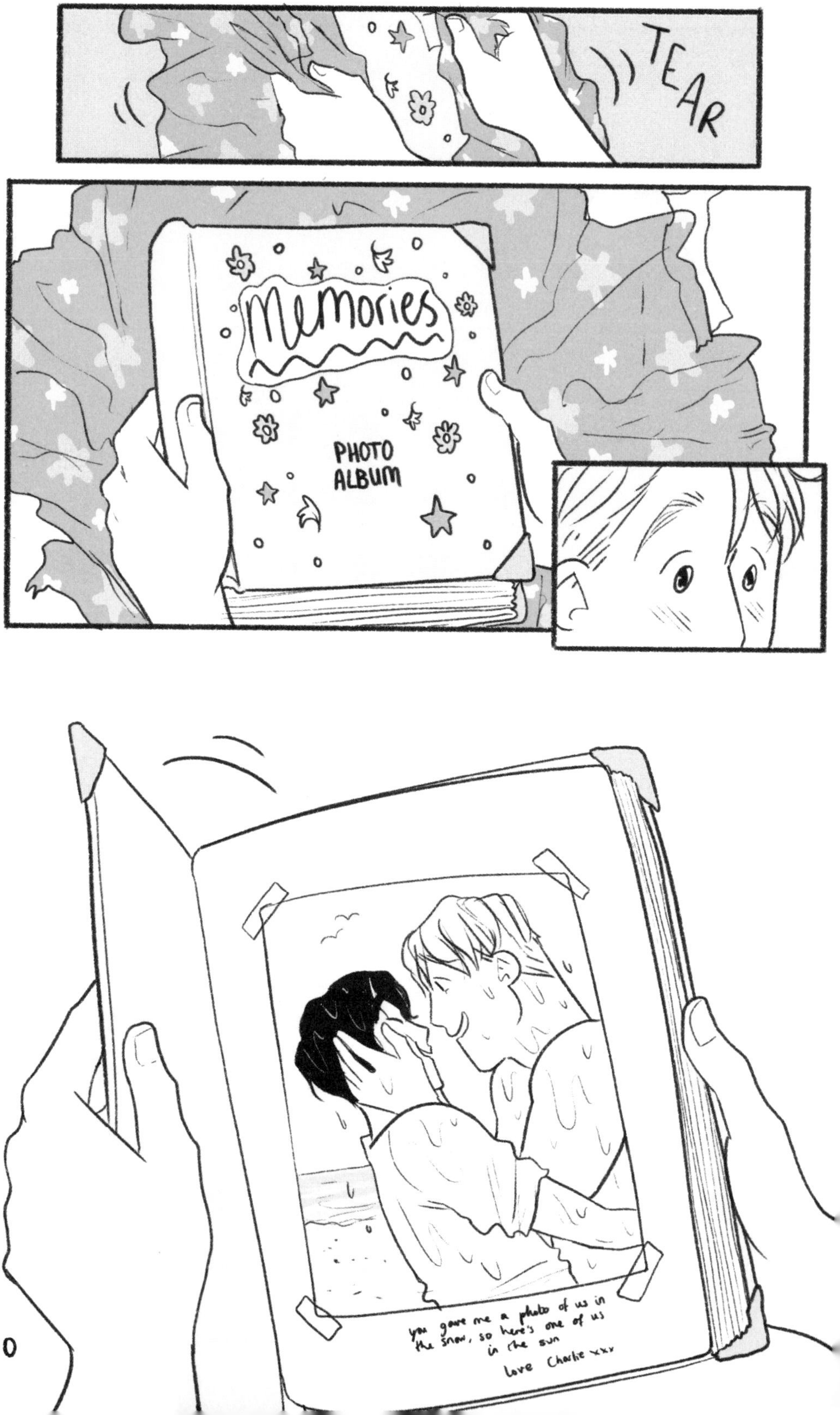
TEAR
Memories
PHOTO ALBUM
you gave me a photo of us in the snow, so here's one of us in the sun
love Charlie xxx

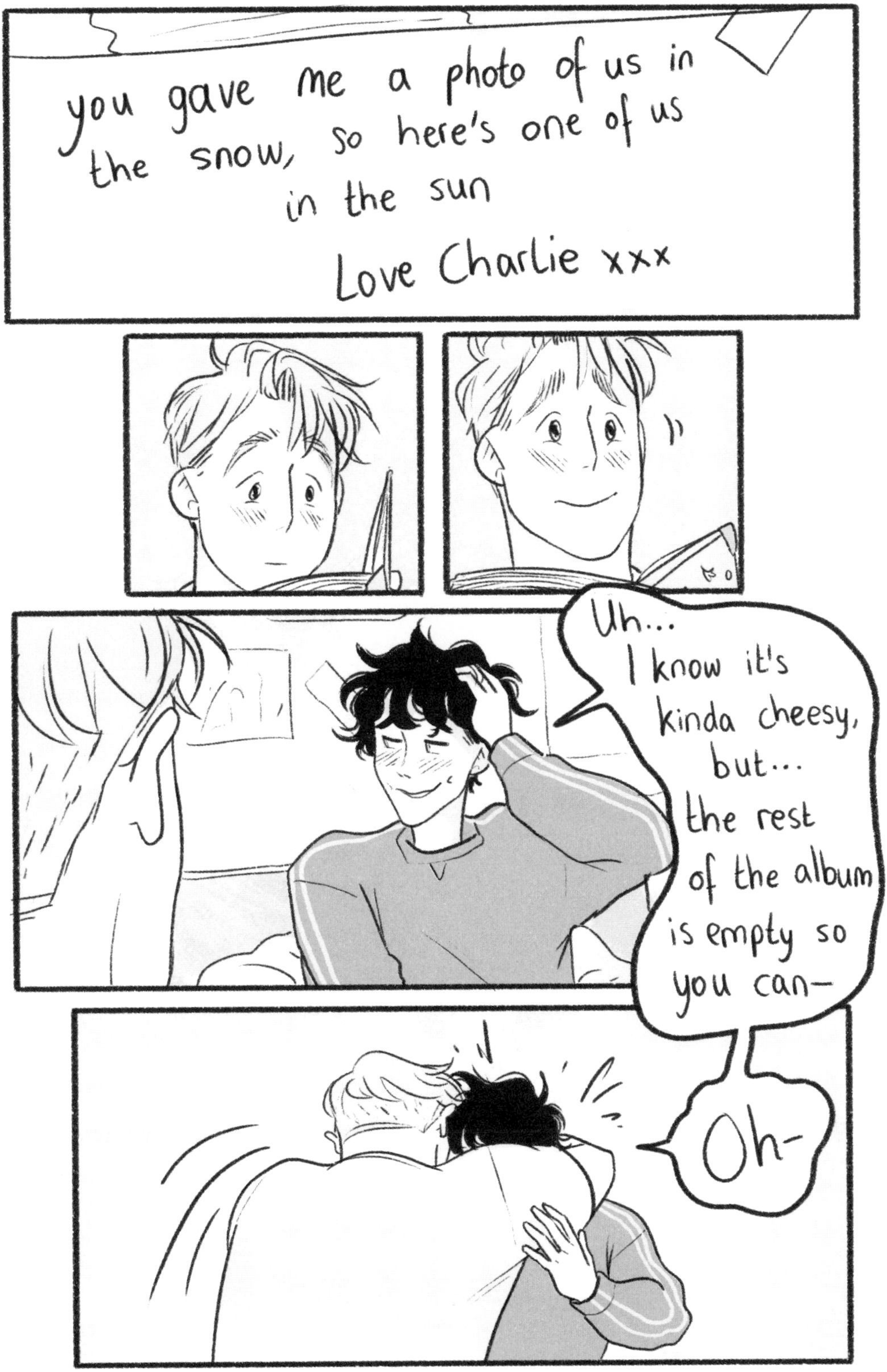
you gave me a photo of us in the snow, so here's one of us in the sun
Love Charlie xxx
Uh...
I know it's kinda cheesy, but... the rest of the album is empty so you can-
Oh-

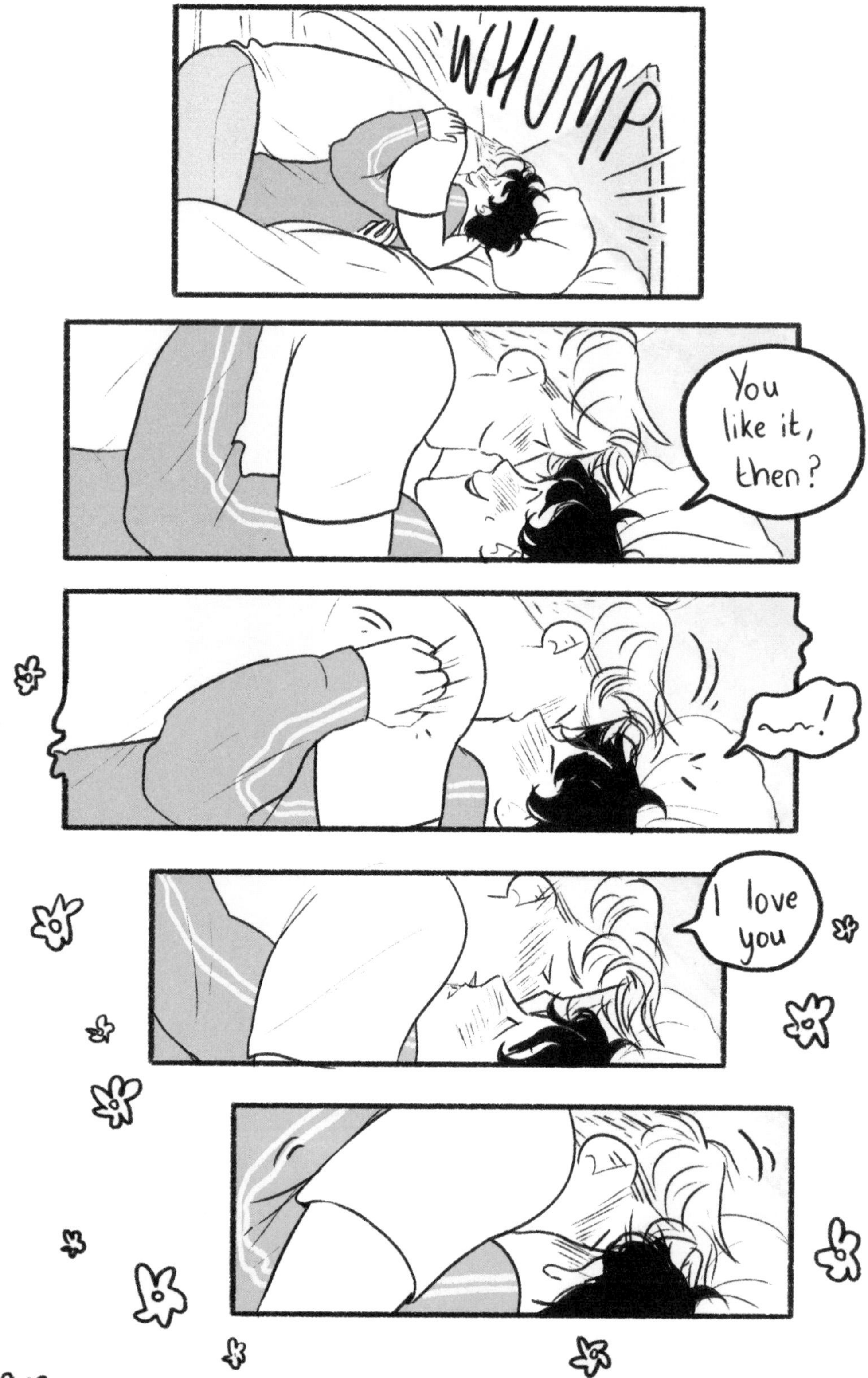
WHUMP
You like it, then?
~~!
I love you

h-huh?
Char... you said wake you up at eight

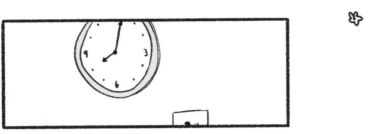

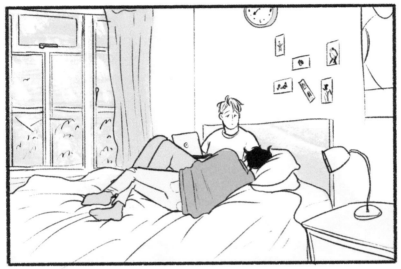

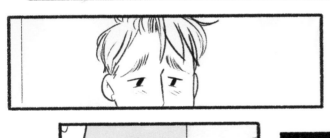

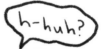

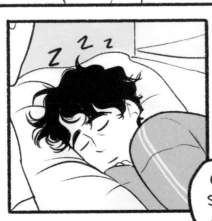

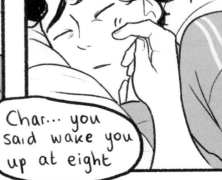

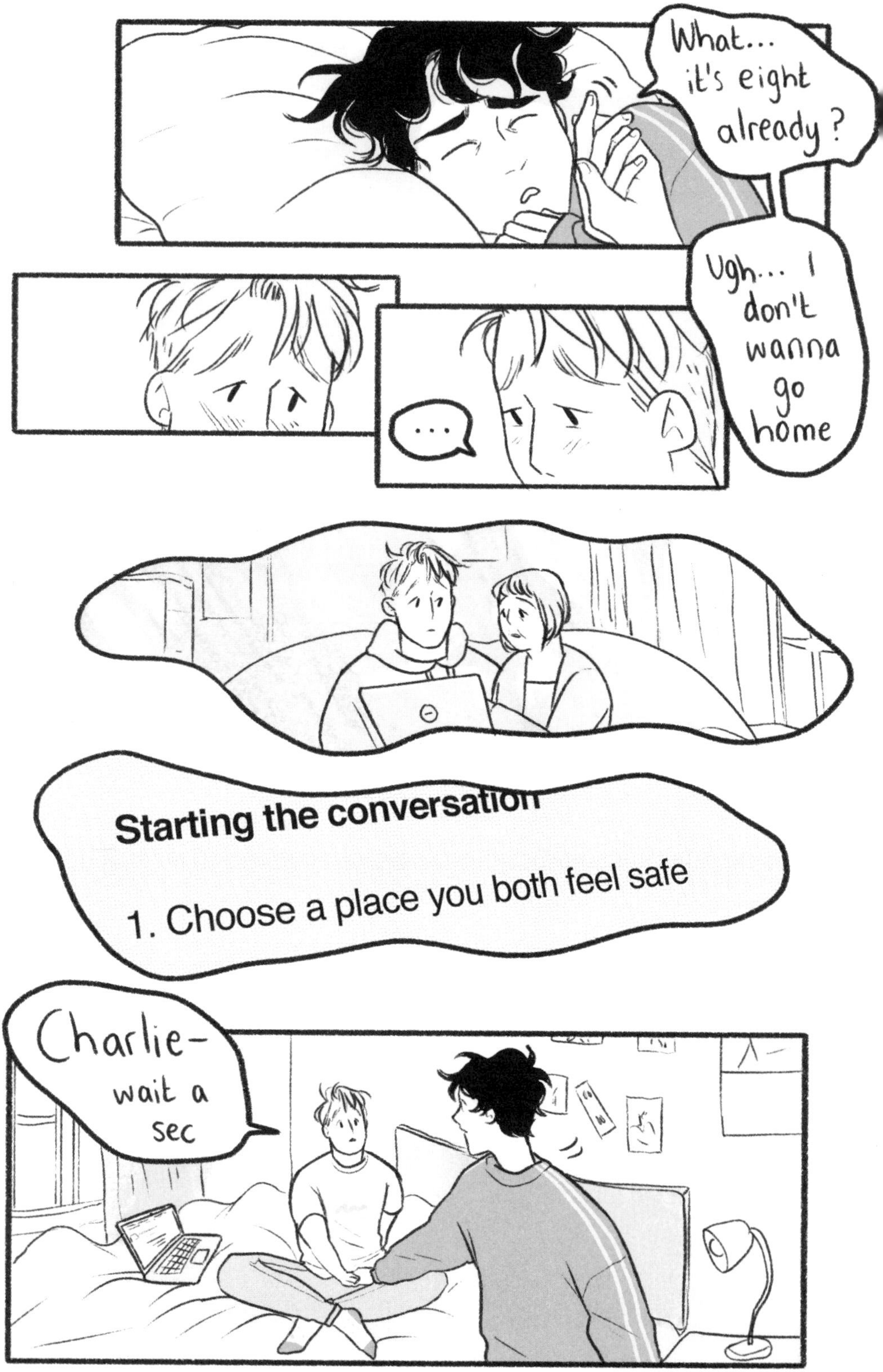
What... it's eight already?
Ugh... I don't wanna go home
...
Starting the conversation
1. Choose a place you both feel safe
Charlie- wait a sec

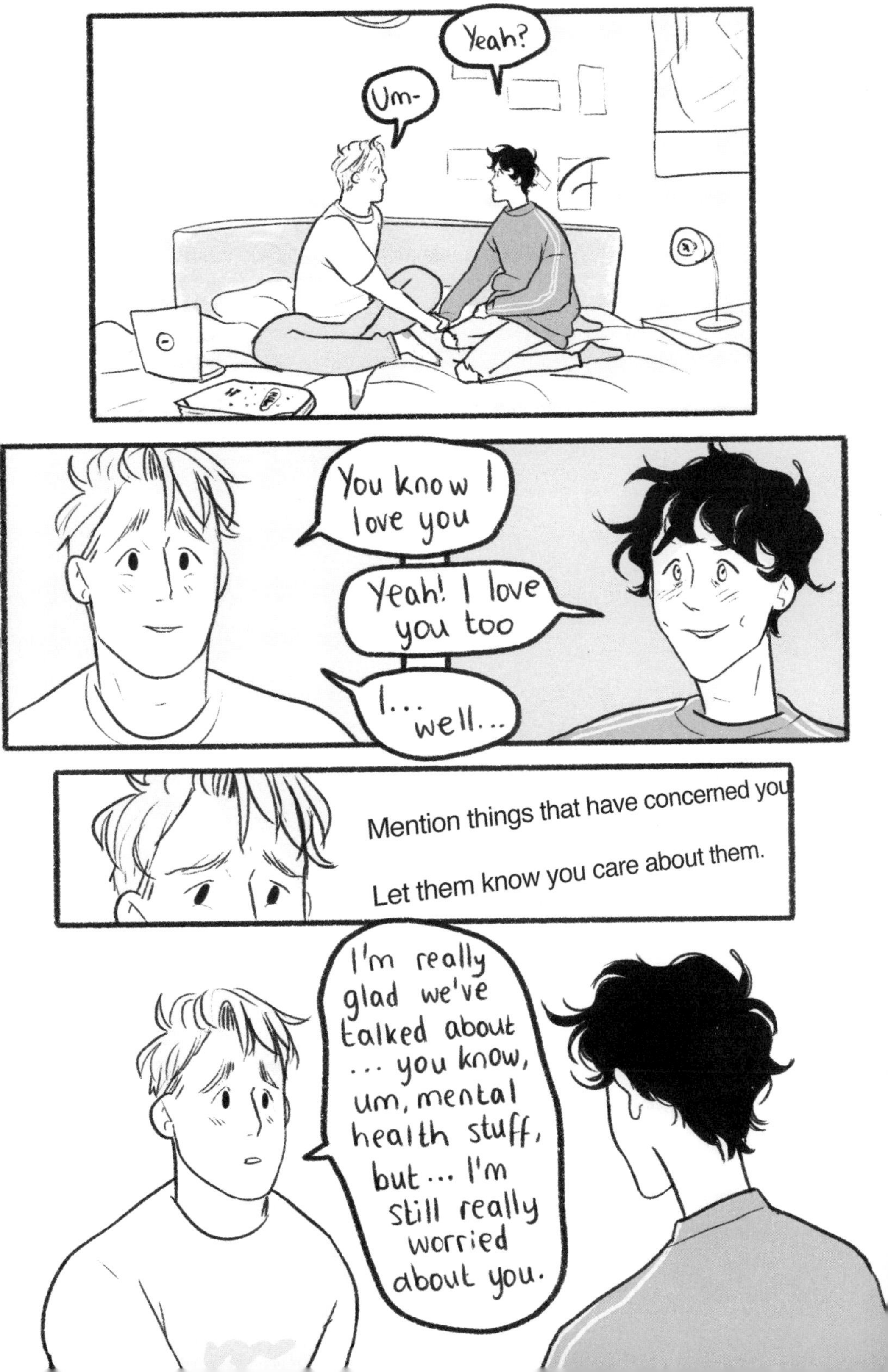
Um-
Yeah?
You know I love you
Yeah! I love you too
I... well...
Mention things that have concerned you
Let them know you care about them.
I'm really glad we've talked about ... you know, um, mental health stuff, but... I'm still really worried about you.

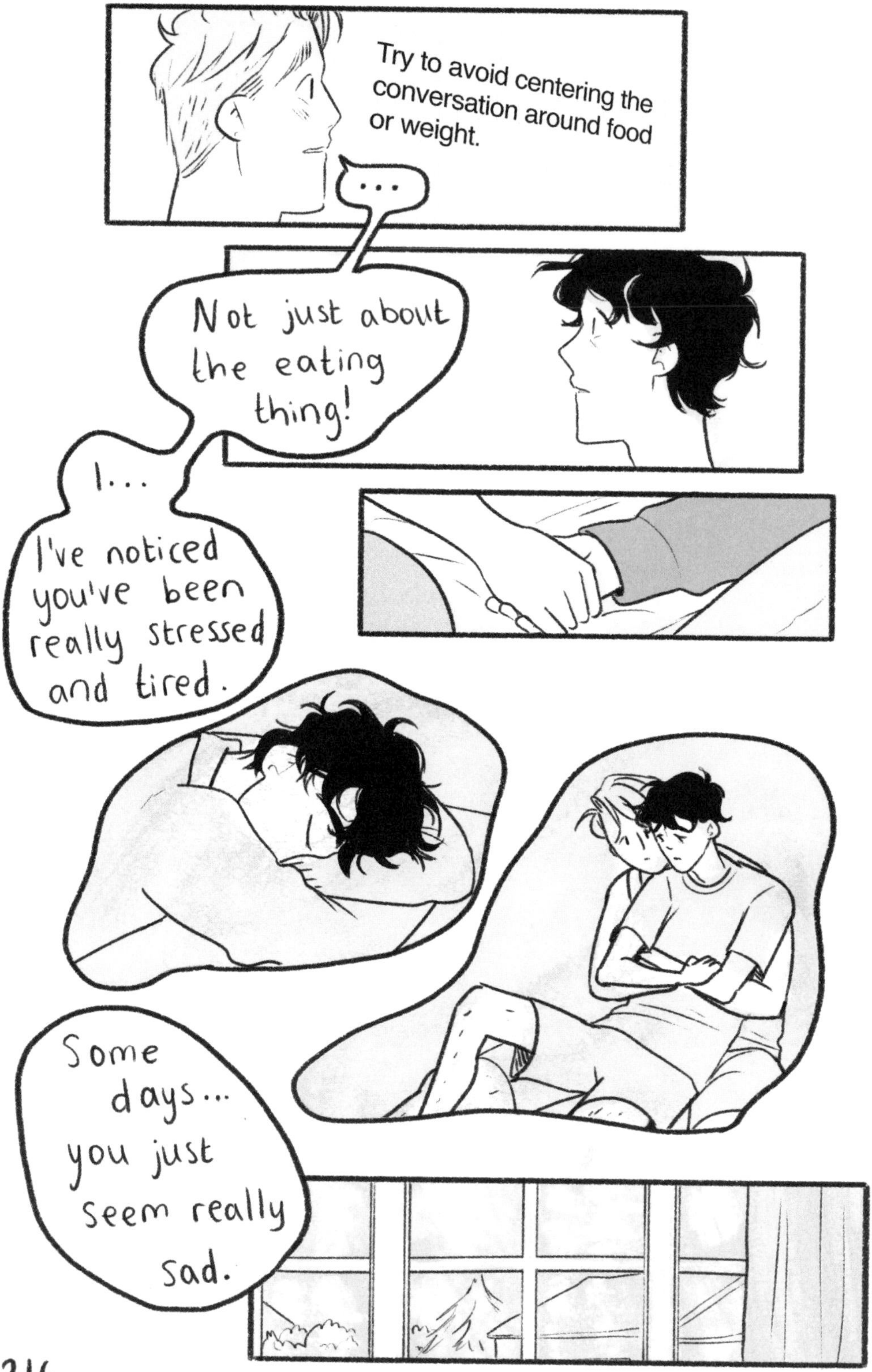
Try to avoid centering the conversation around food or weight.
...
Not just about the eating thing!
I...
I've noticed you've been really stressed and tired.
Some days... you just seem really sad.

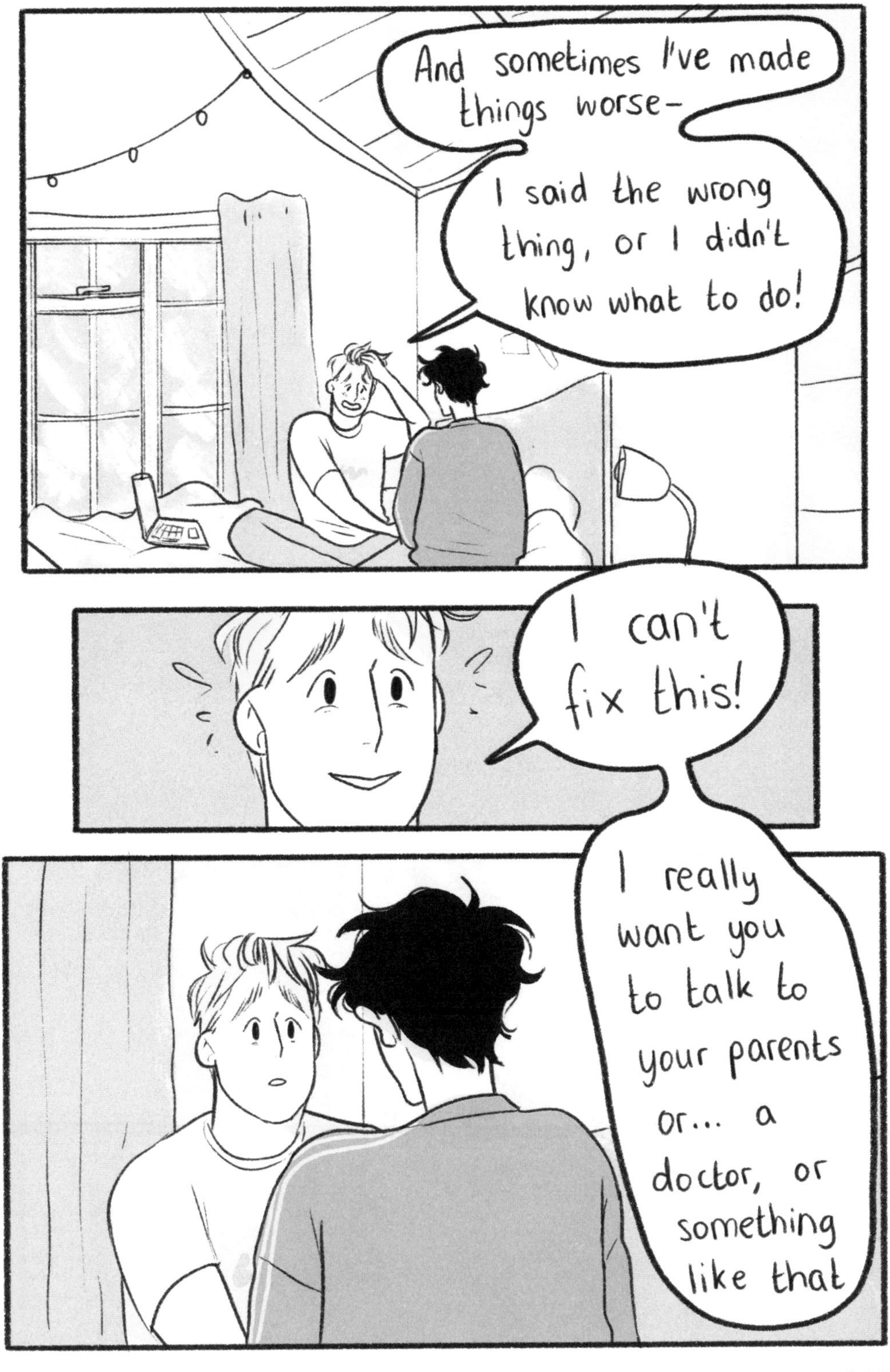
And sometimes I've made things worse-
I said the wrong thing, or I didn't know what to do!
I can't fix this!
I really want you to talk to your parents or... a doctor, or something like that

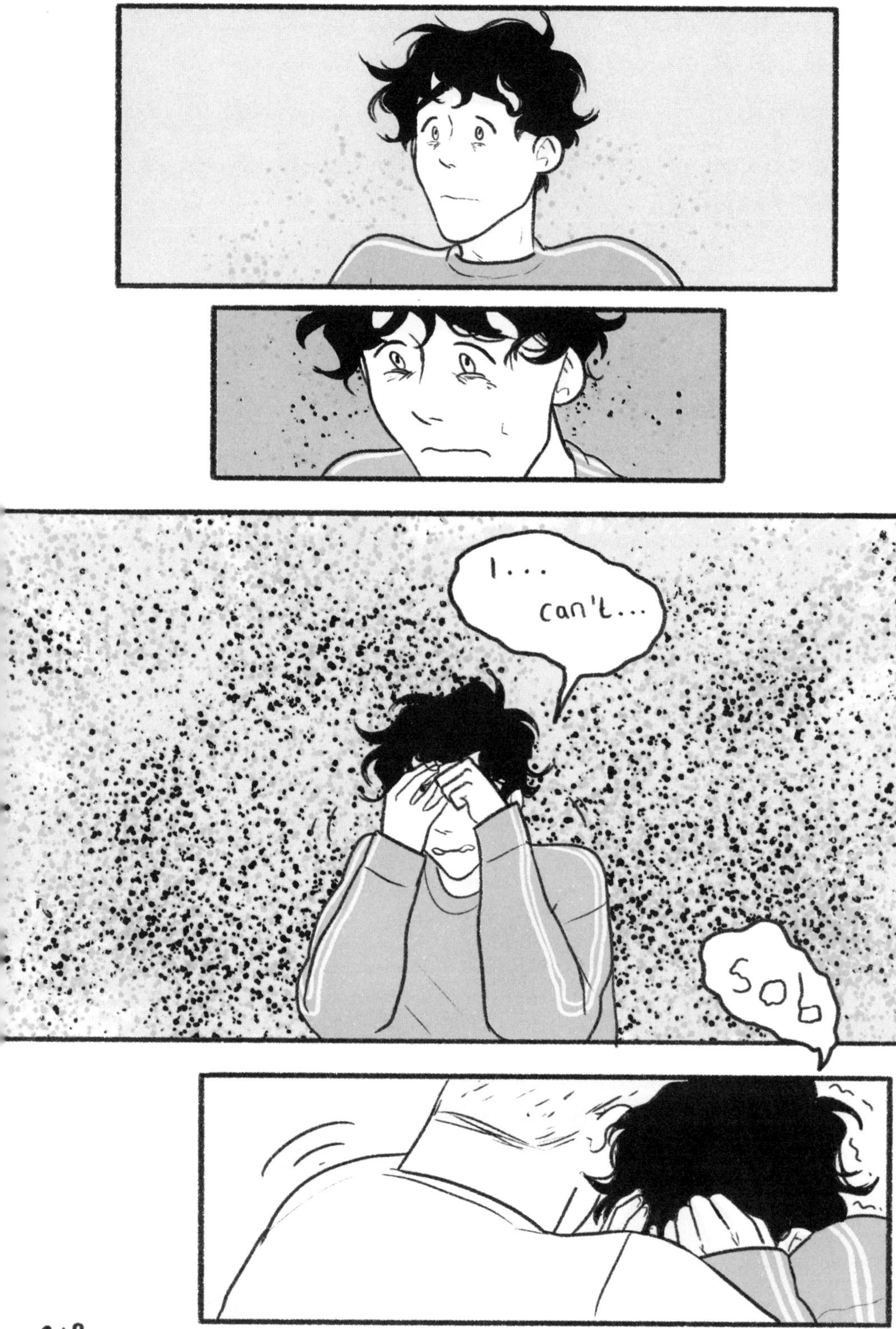
I...
can't...
Sob

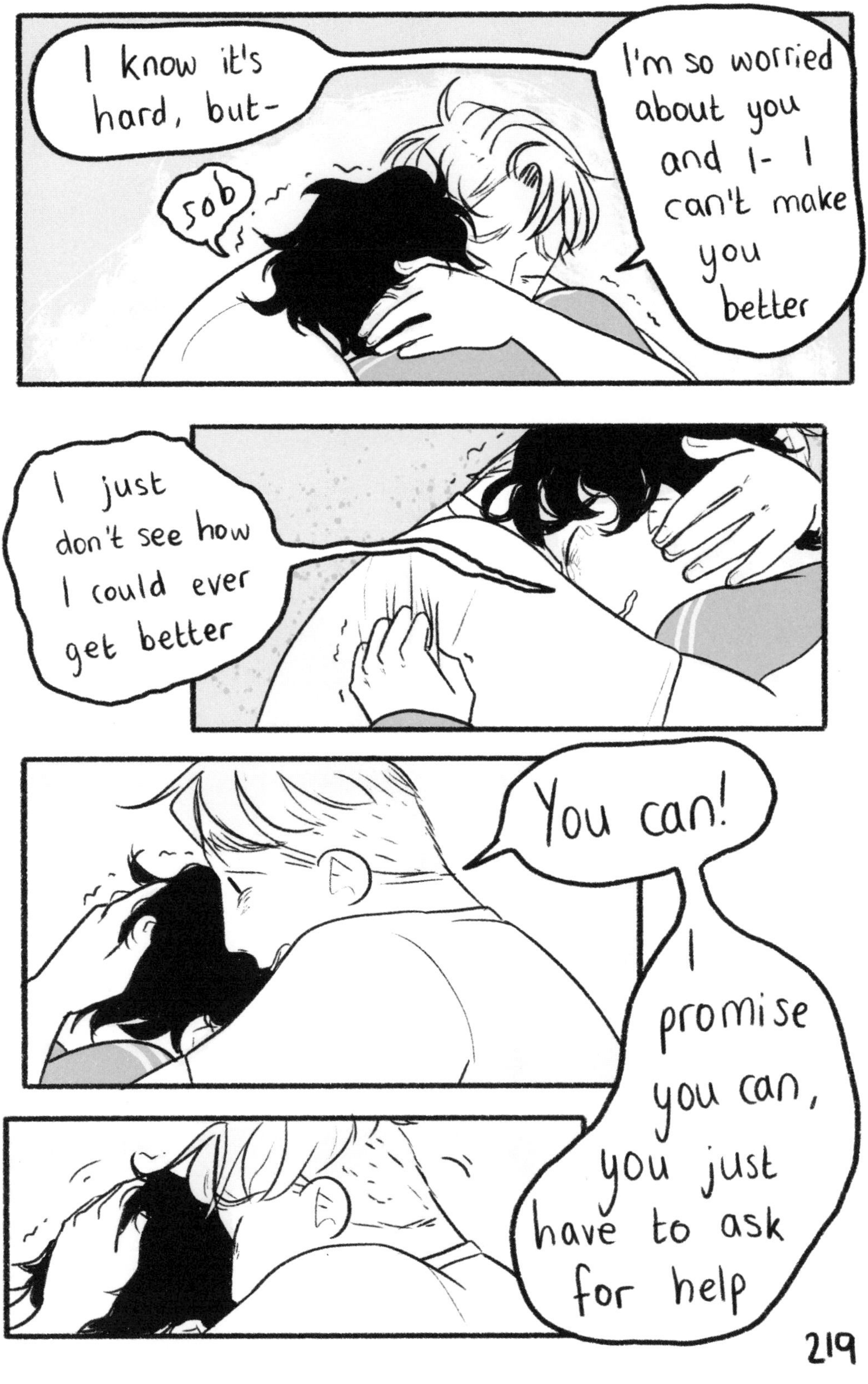
I know it's hard, but-
I'm so worried about you and I- I can't make you better
sob
I just don't see how I could ever get better
You can!
I promise you can, you just have to ask for help

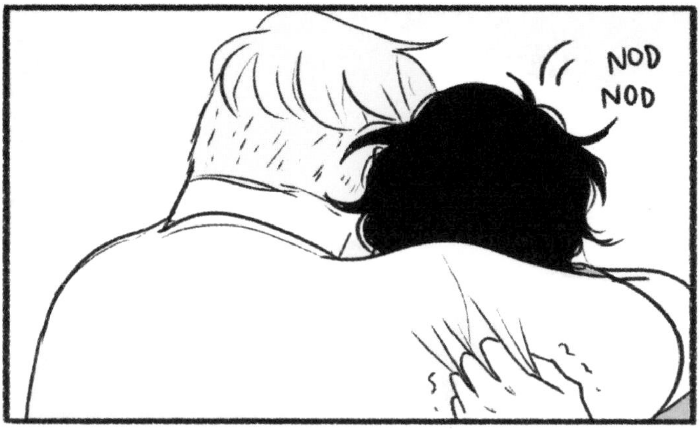
NOD
NOD

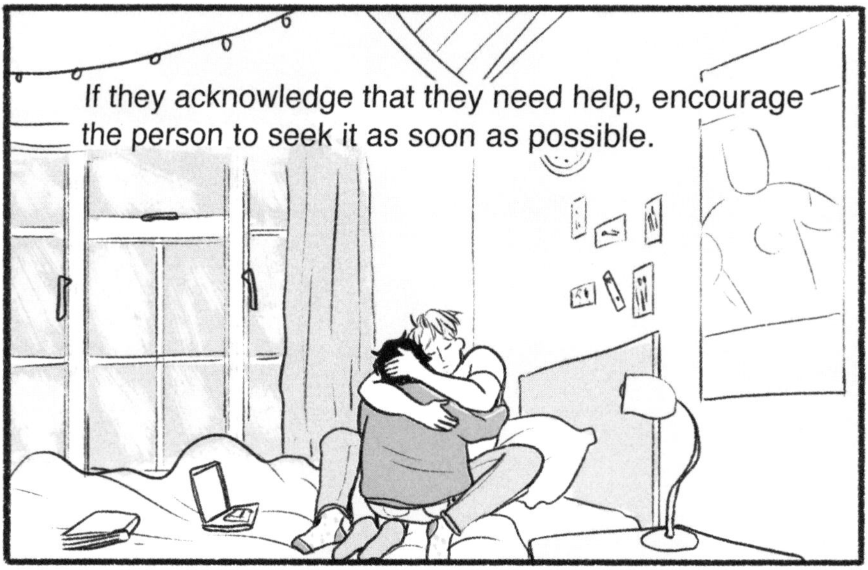
If they acknowledge that they need help, encourage the person to seek it as soon as possible.

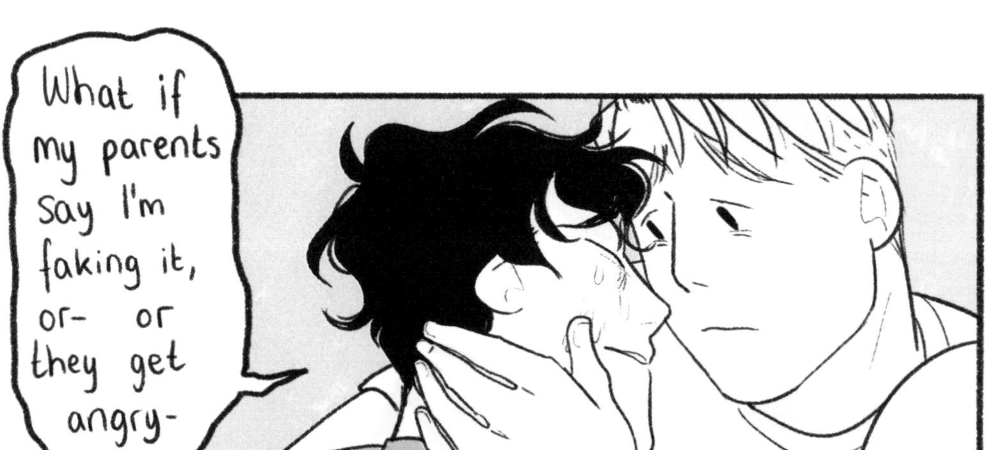
What if my parents say I'm faking it, or- or they get angry-

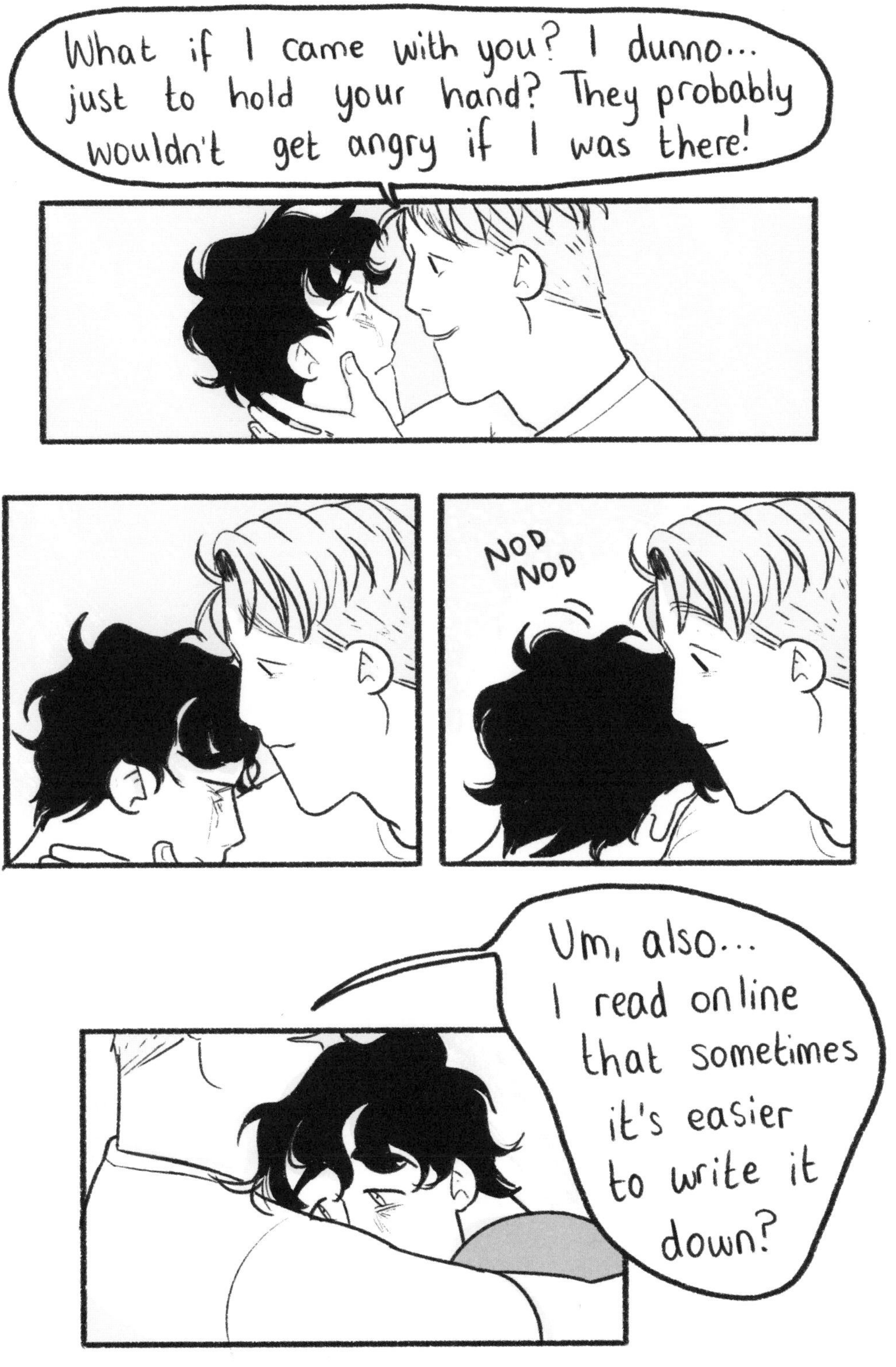
What if I came with you? I dunno... just to hold your hand? They probably wouldn't get angry if I was there!
NOD NOD
Um, also... I read online that sometimes it's easier to write it down?

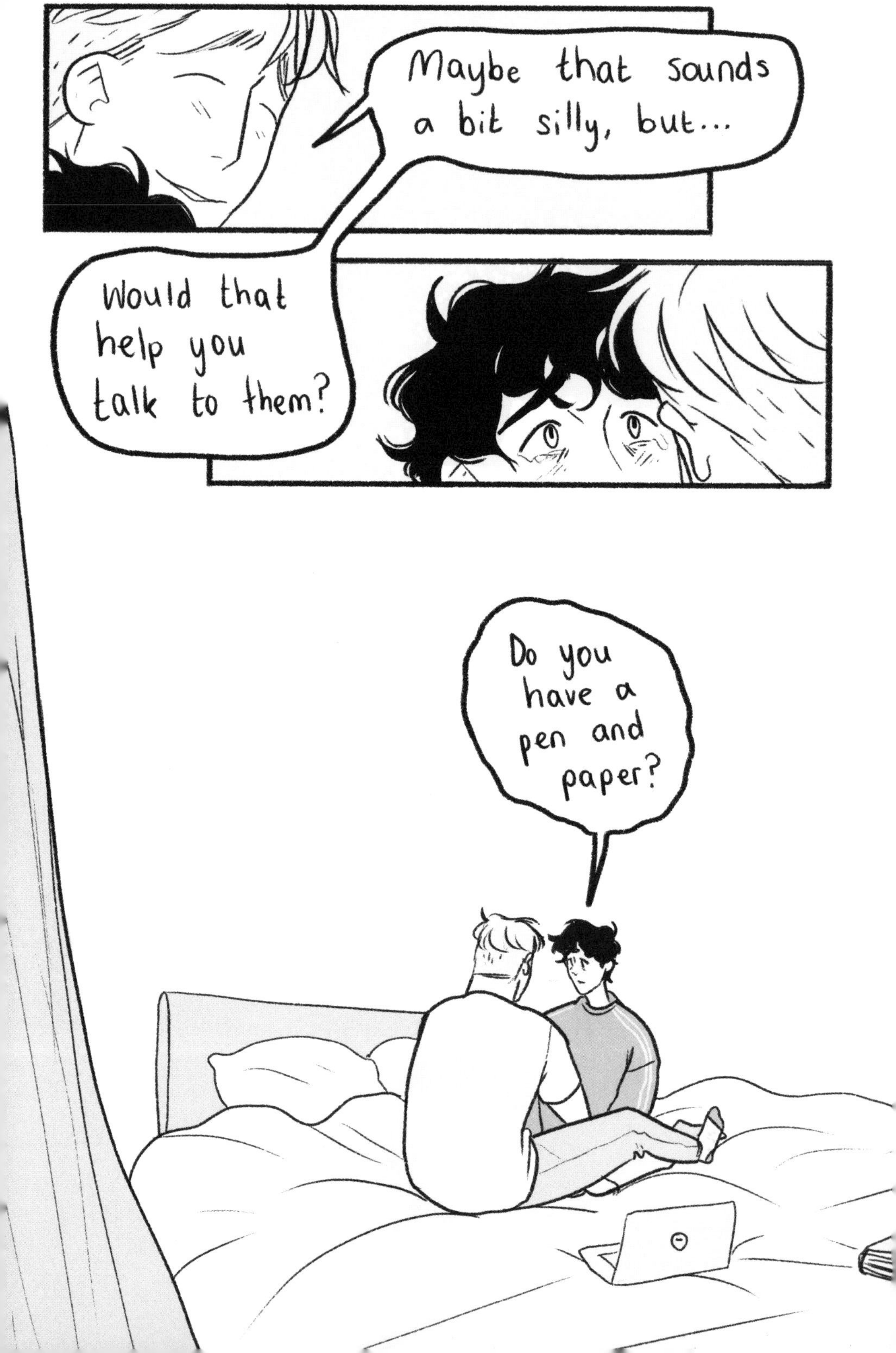
Maybe that sounds a bit silly, but...
Would that help you talk to them?
Do you have a pen and paper?

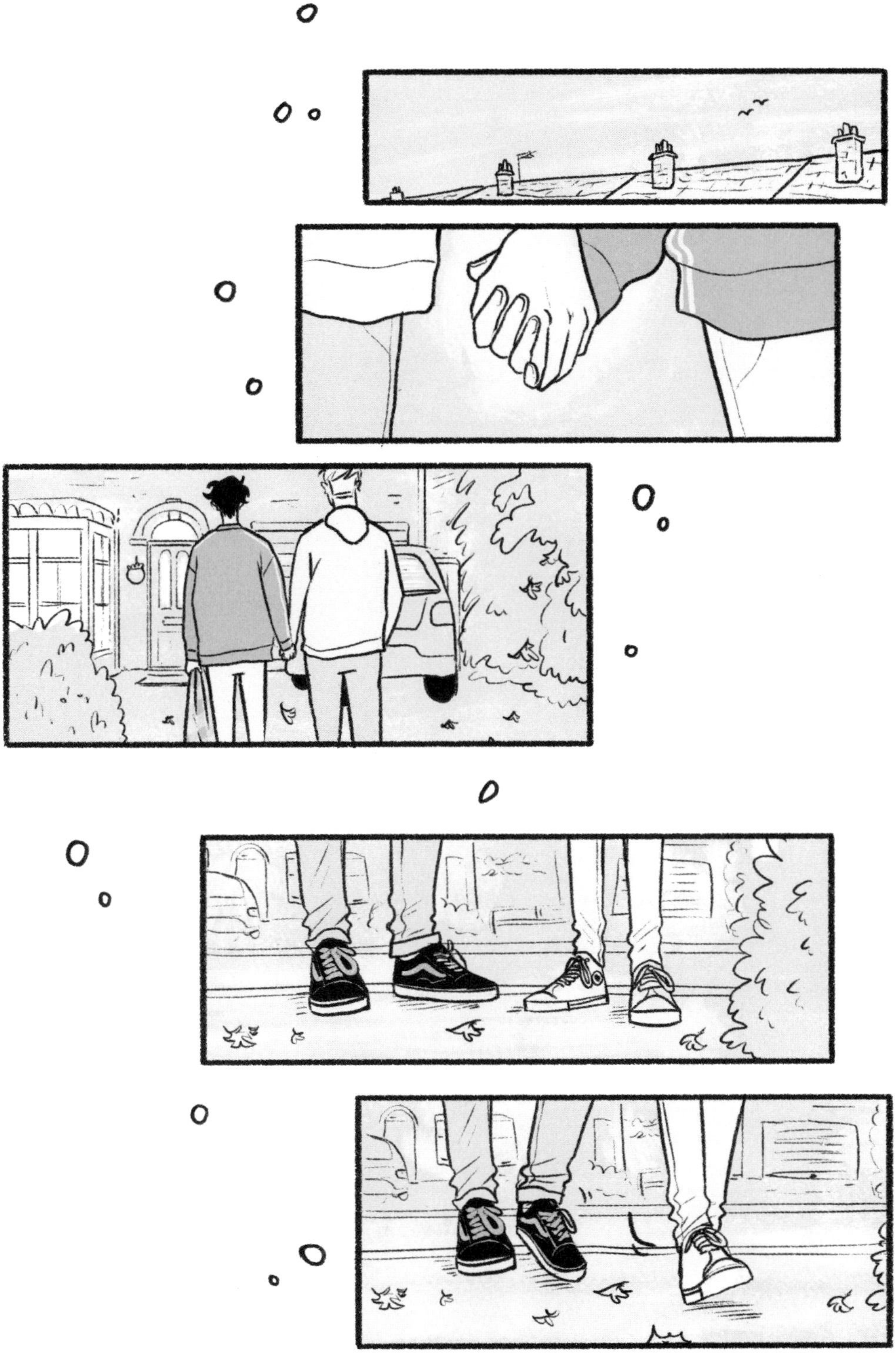

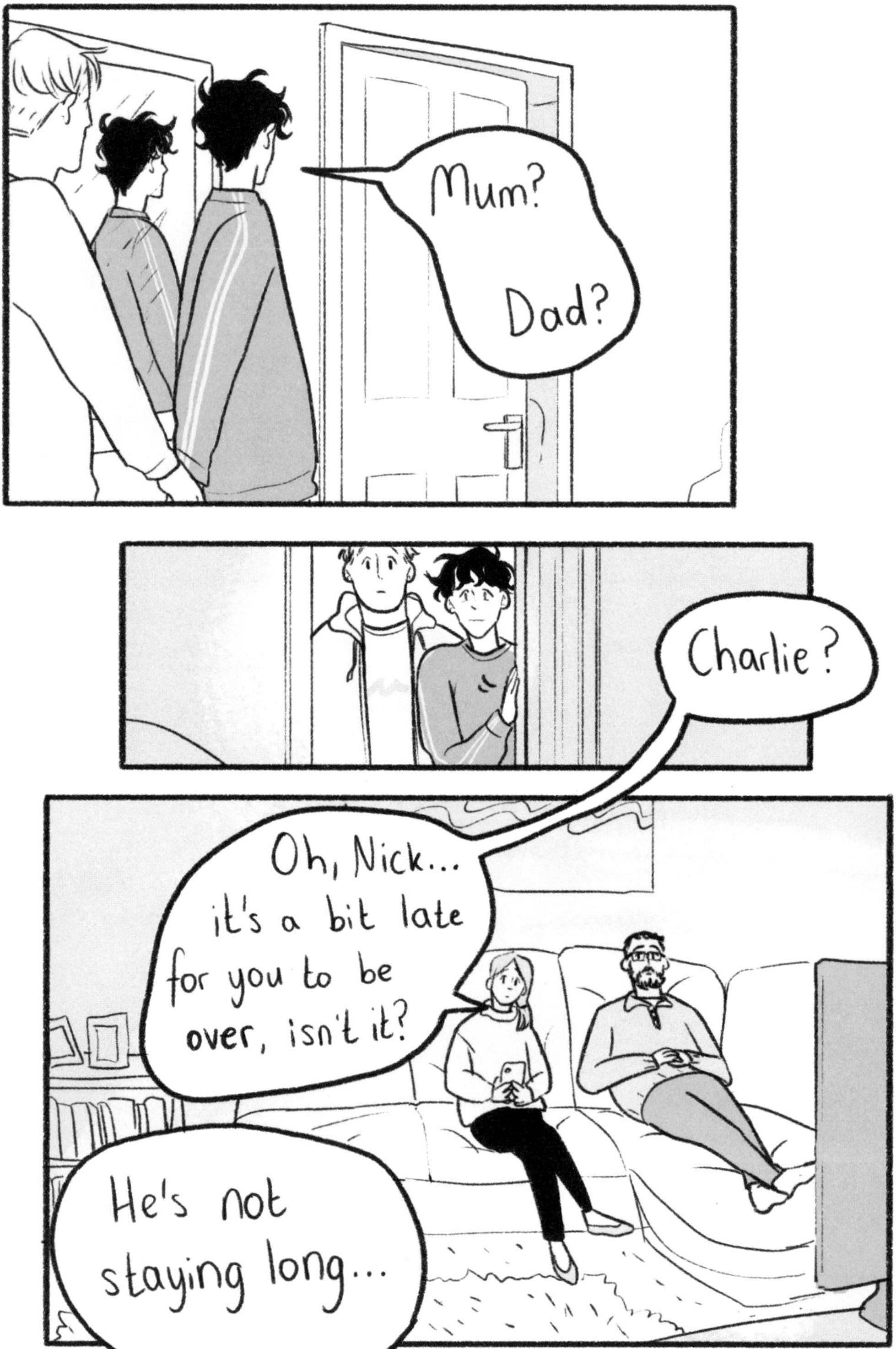
Mum?
Dad?
Charlie?
Oh, Nick... it's a bit late for you to be over, isn't it?
He's not staying long...

I...

...need to talk to you about something.

What's up?

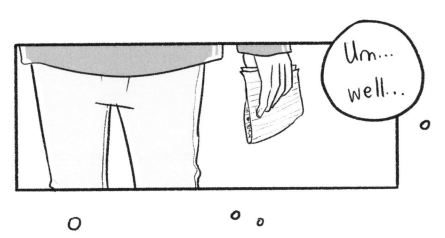

Um... well...

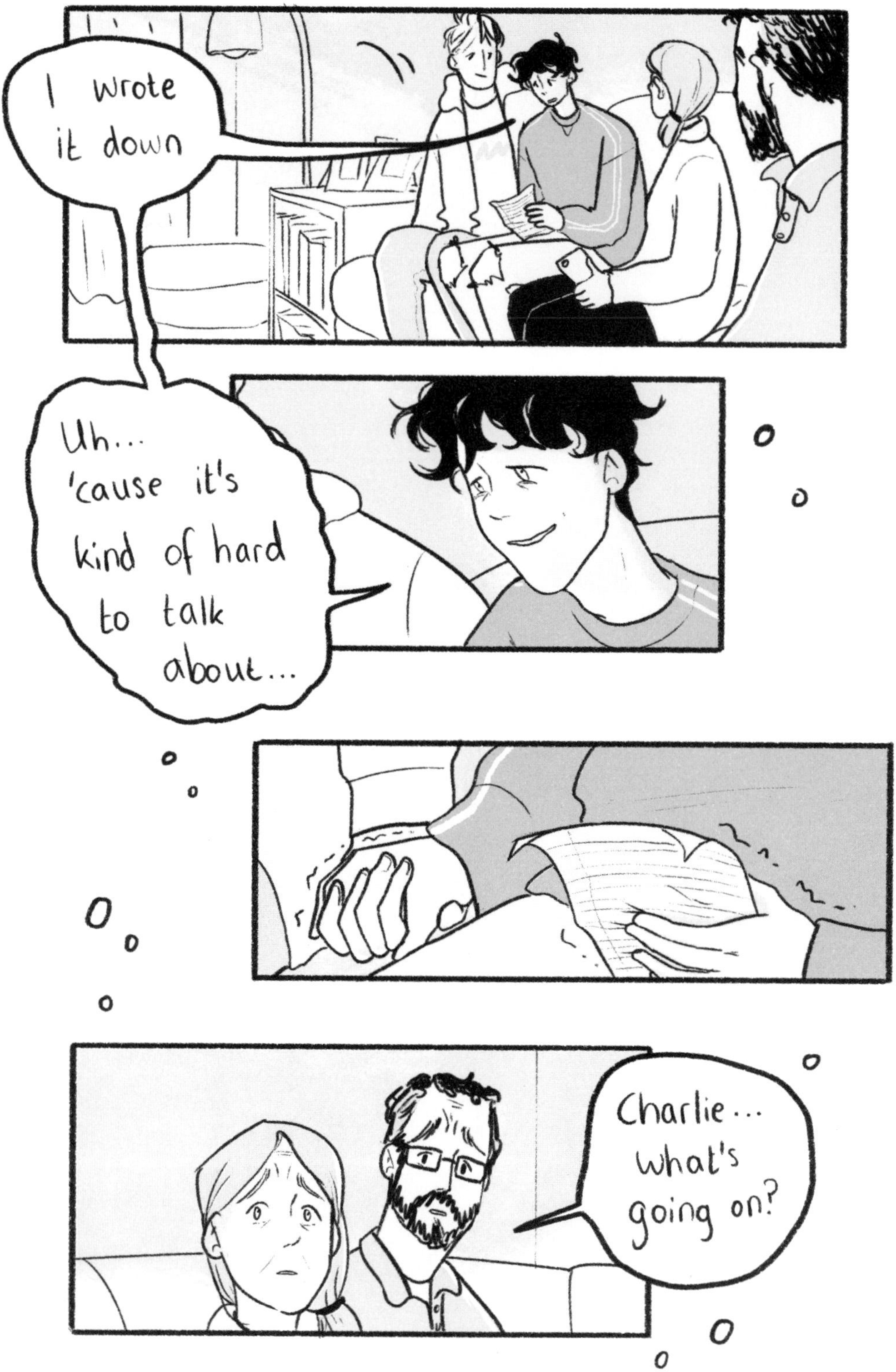
I wrote it down
Uh... 'cause it's kind of hard to talk about...
Charlie... what's going on?

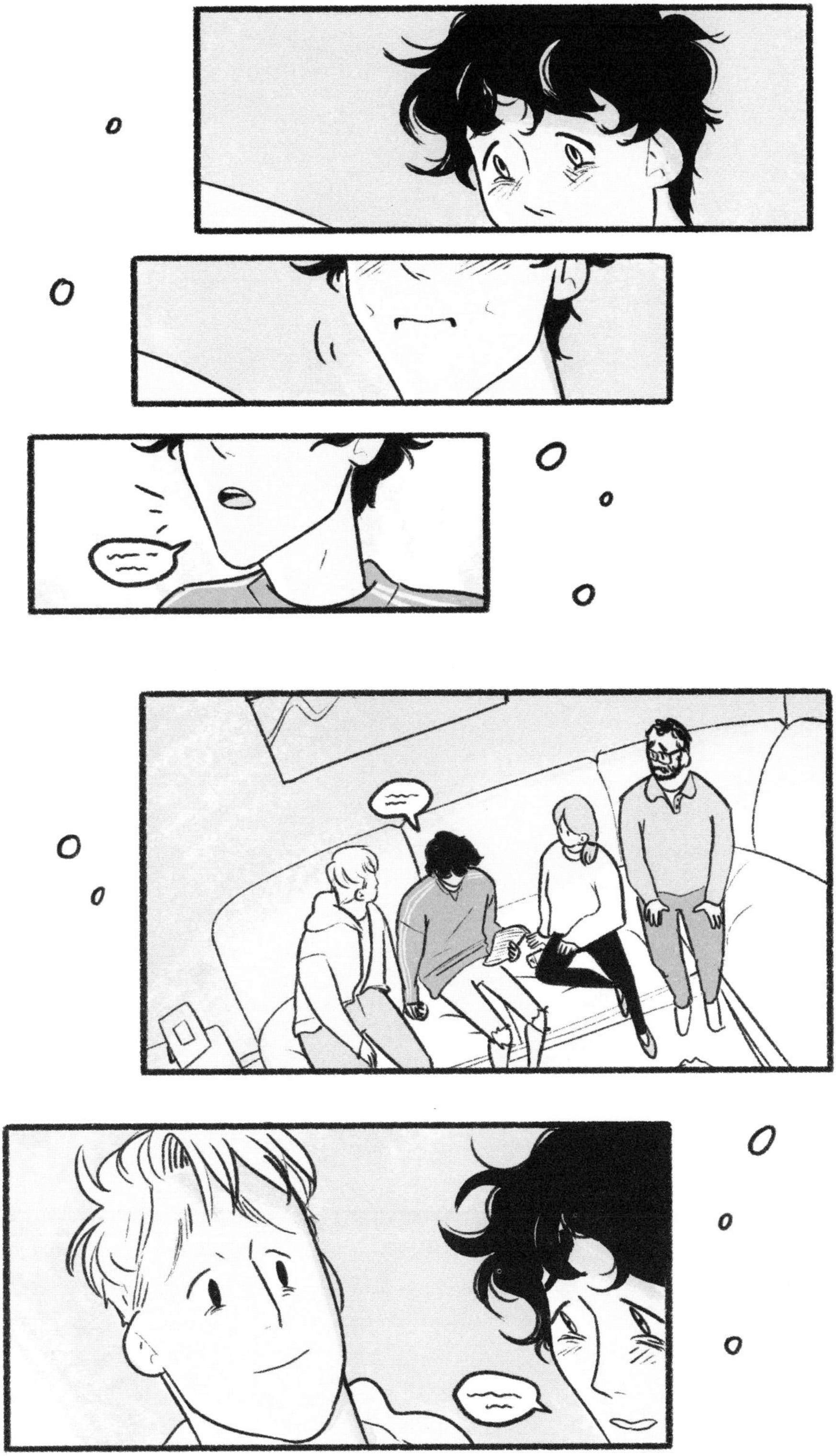

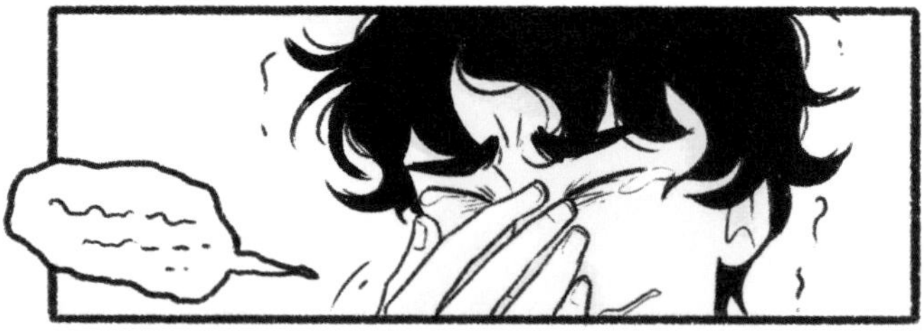

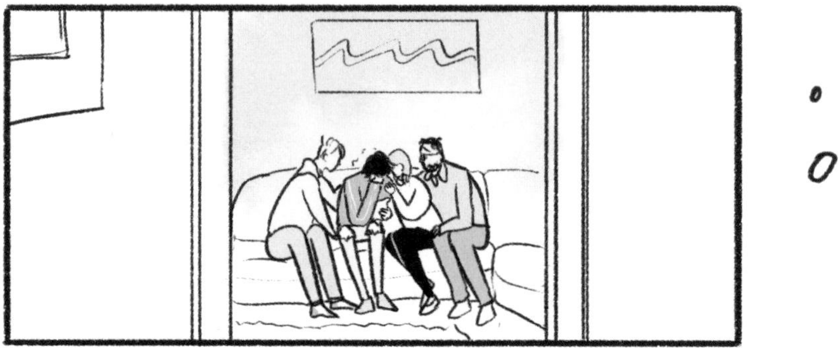

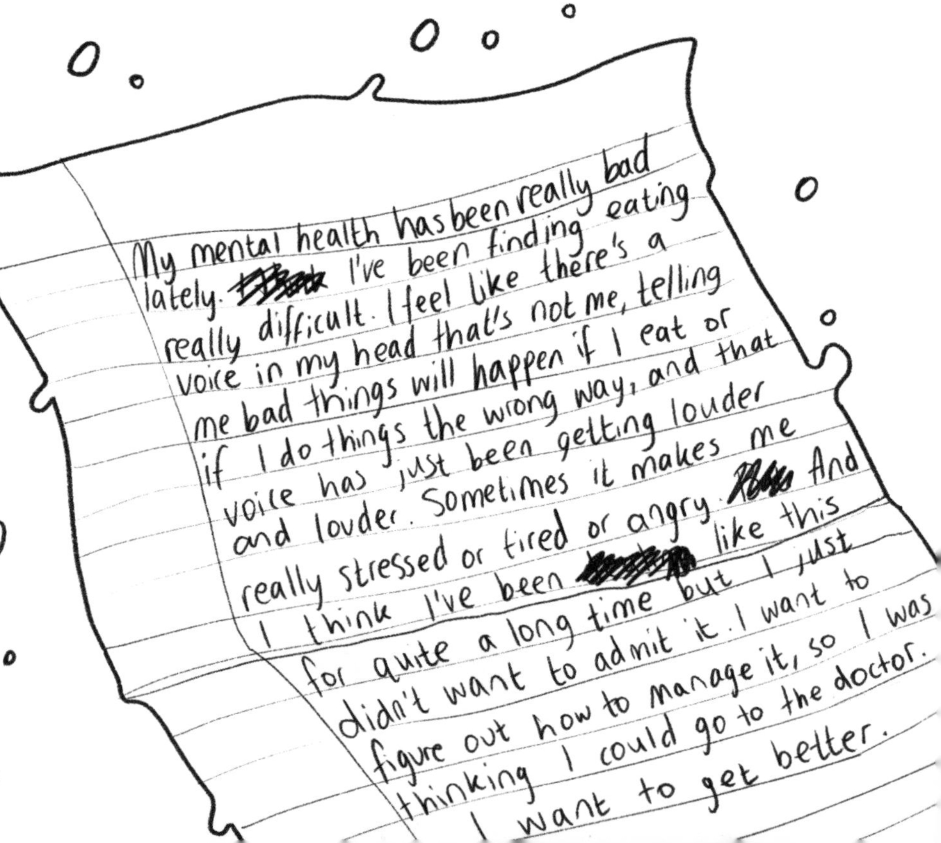
My mental health has been really bad
lately. I've been finding eating
really difficult. I feel like there's a
voice in my head that's not me, telling
me bad things will happen if I eat or
if I do things the wrong way, and that
voice has just been getting louder
and louder. Sometimes it makes me
really stressed or tired or angry. And
I think I've been like this
for quite a long time but I just
didn't want to admit it. I want to
figure out how to manage it, so I was
thinking I could go to the doctor.
I want to get better.

6. JOURNEY

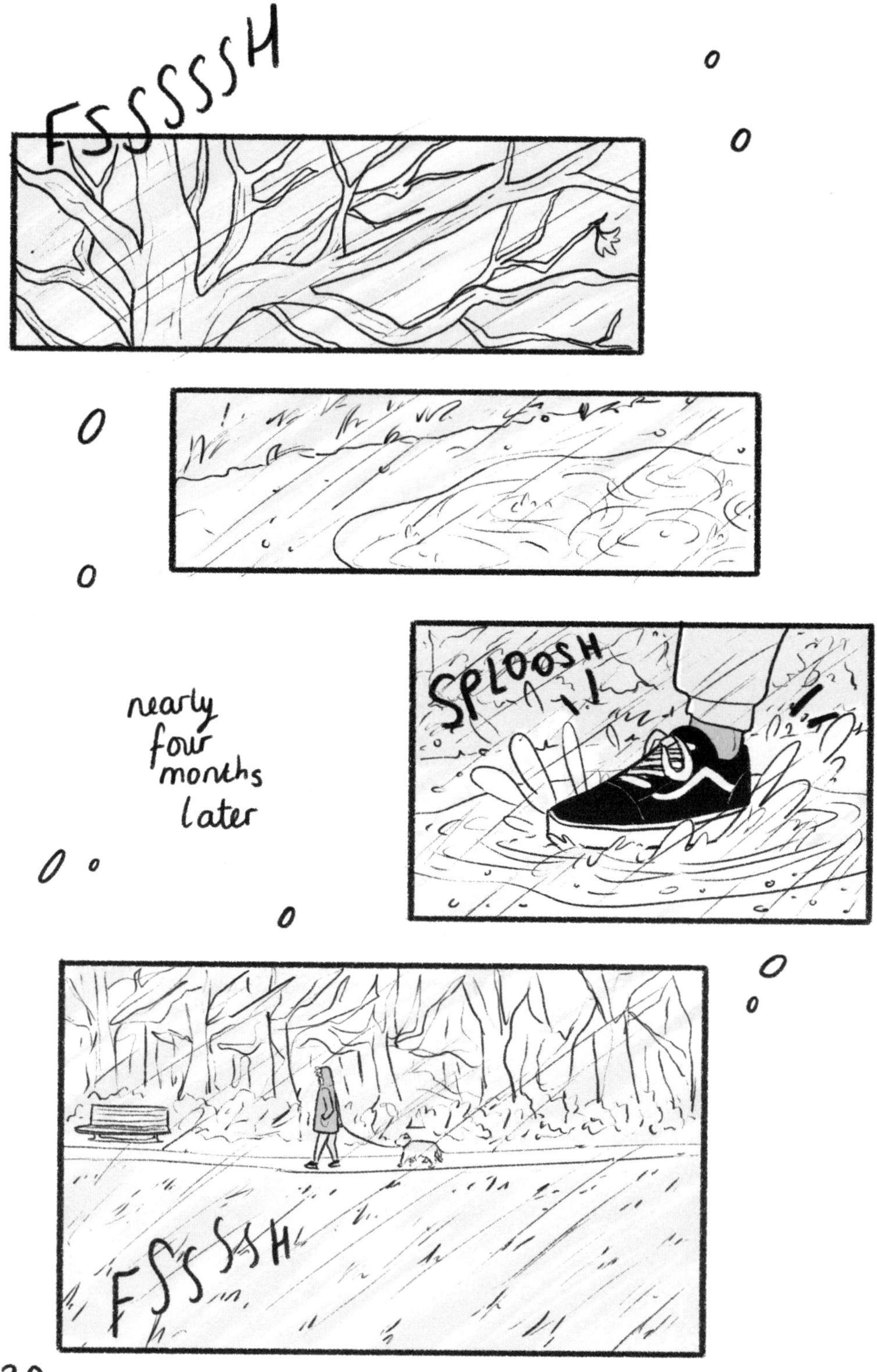
FSSSSSH
nearly four months later
SPLOOSH
FSSSSH

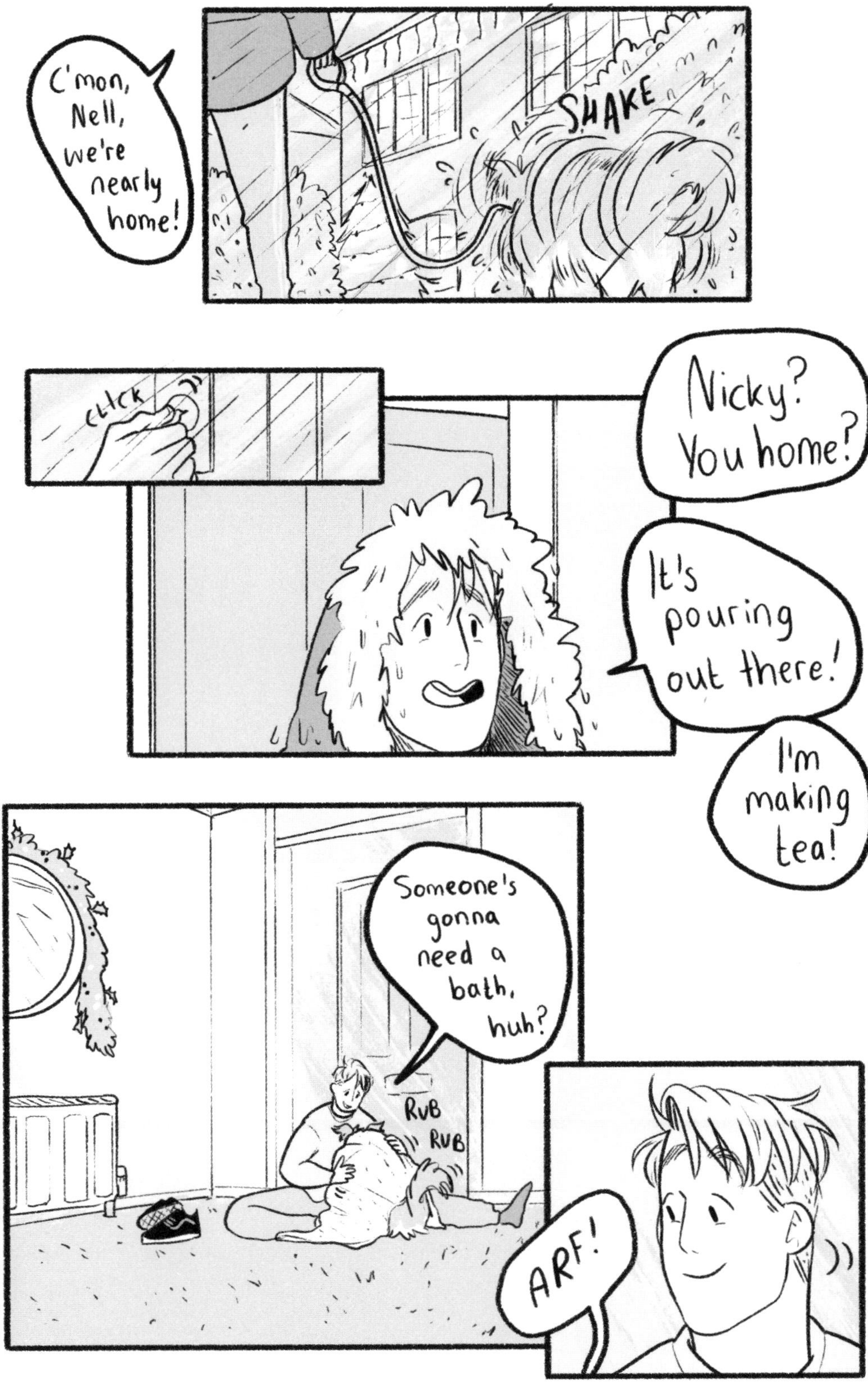
C'mon, Nell, we're nearly home!
SHAKE
CLICK
Nicky? You home?
It's pouring out there!
I'm making tea!
Someone's gonna need a bath, huh?
RUB RUB
ARF!

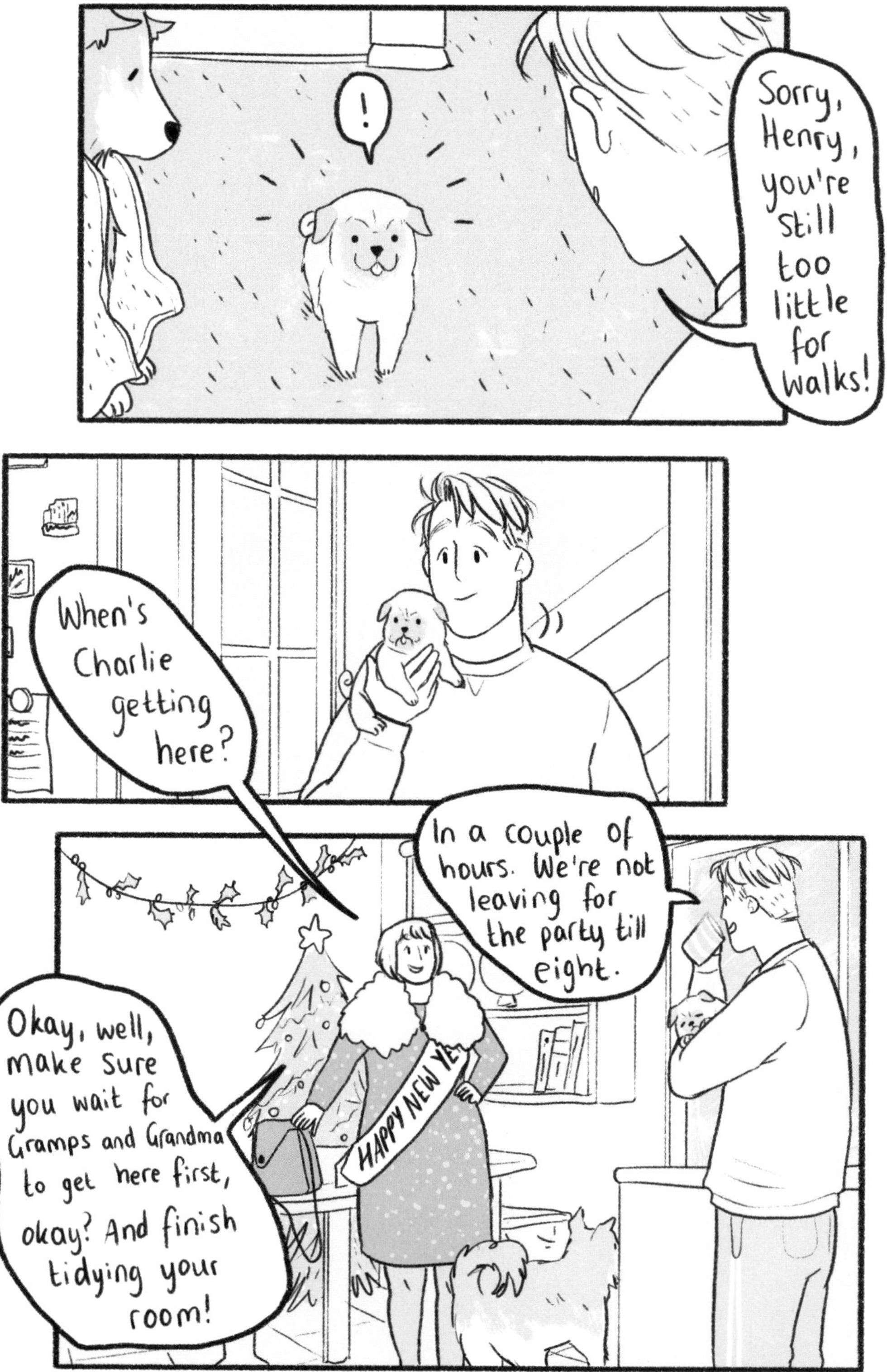
!
Sorry, Henry, you're still too little for walks!
When's Charlie getting here?
In a couple of hours. We're not leaving for the party till eight.
HAPPY NEW YE
Okay, well, make sure you wait for Gramps and Grandma to get here first, okay? And finish tidying your room!

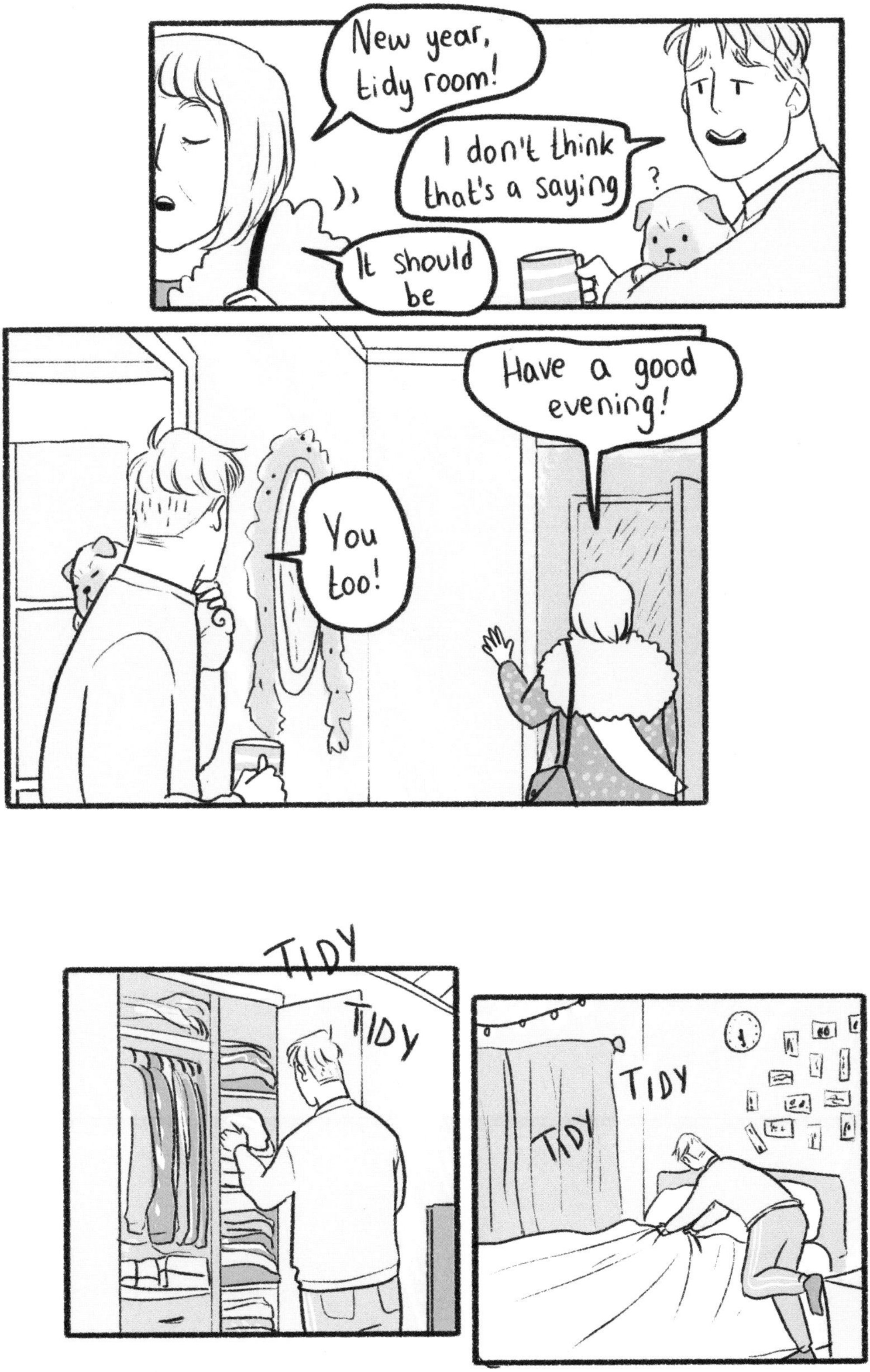
New year, tidy room!
I don't think that's a saying
It should be
Have a good evening!
You too!
TIDY
TIDY
TIDY
TIDY

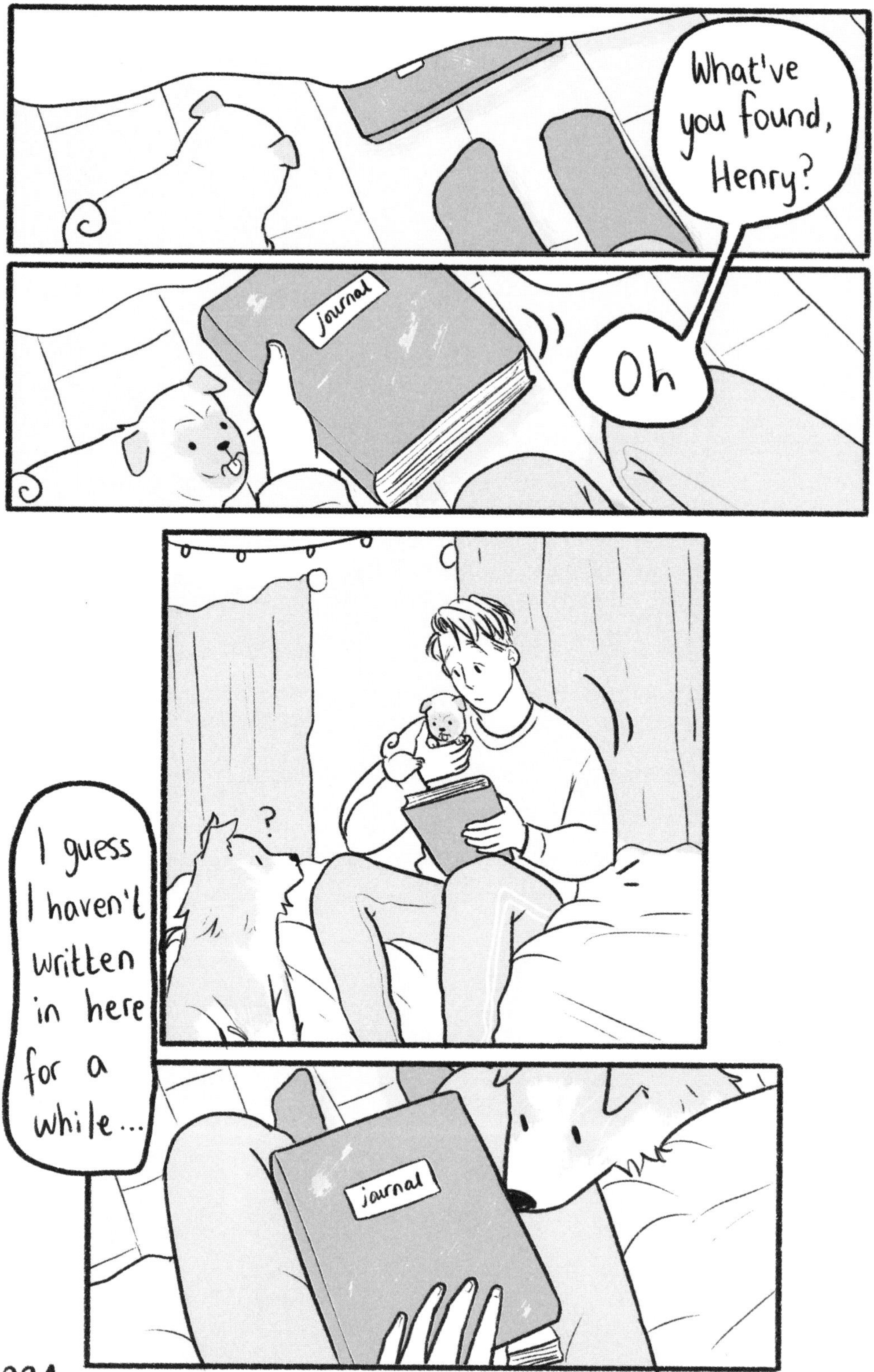
What've you found, Henry?
Oh
journal
?
I guess I haven't written in here for a while...
journal

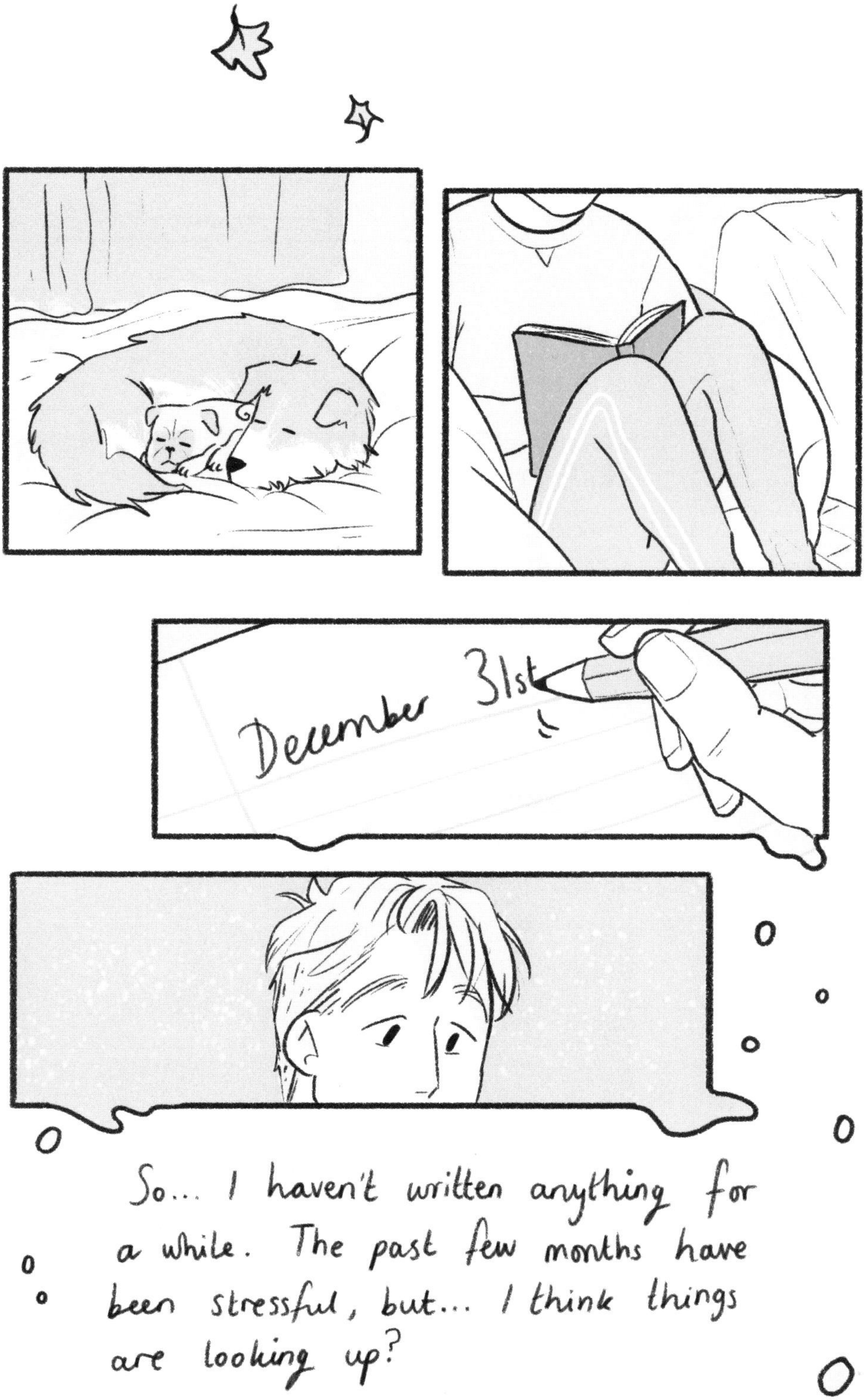
December 31st
So... I haven't written anything for a while. The past few months have been stressful, but... I think things are looking up?

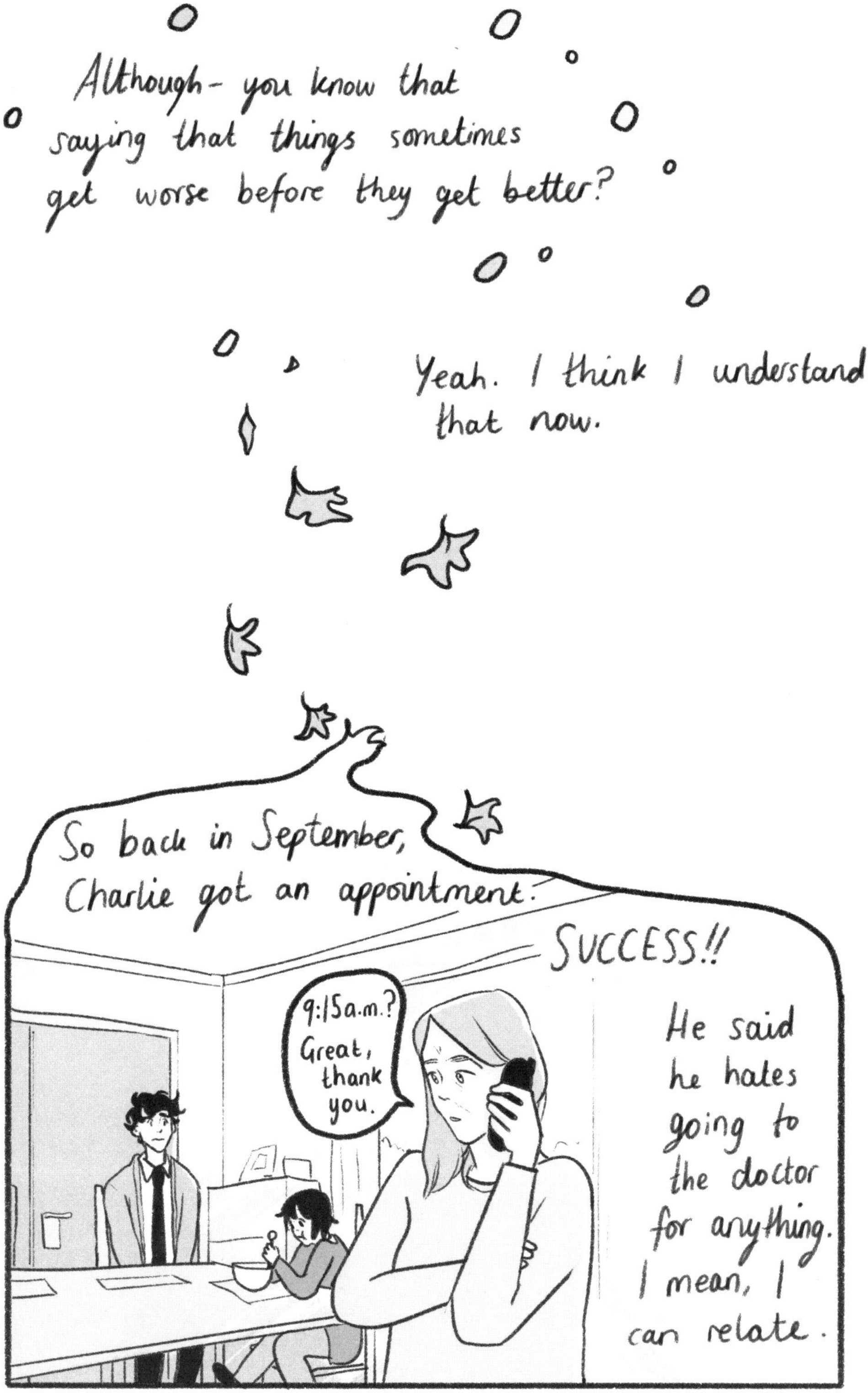
Although - you know that saying that things sometimes get worse before they get better?
Yeah. I think I understand that now.
So back in September, Charlie got an appointment.
SUCCESS!!
9:15a.m.? Great, thank you.
He said he hates going to the doctor for anything. I mean, I can relate.

But this was extra scary.

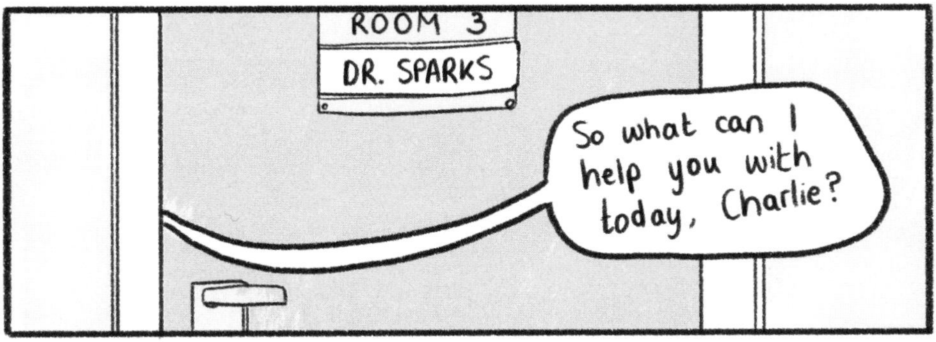
ROOM 3
DR. SPARKS
So what can I help you with today, Charlie?

For obvious reasons.

The doctor was helpful, and referred Charlie to an eating disorder service, but the waiting list was so long.

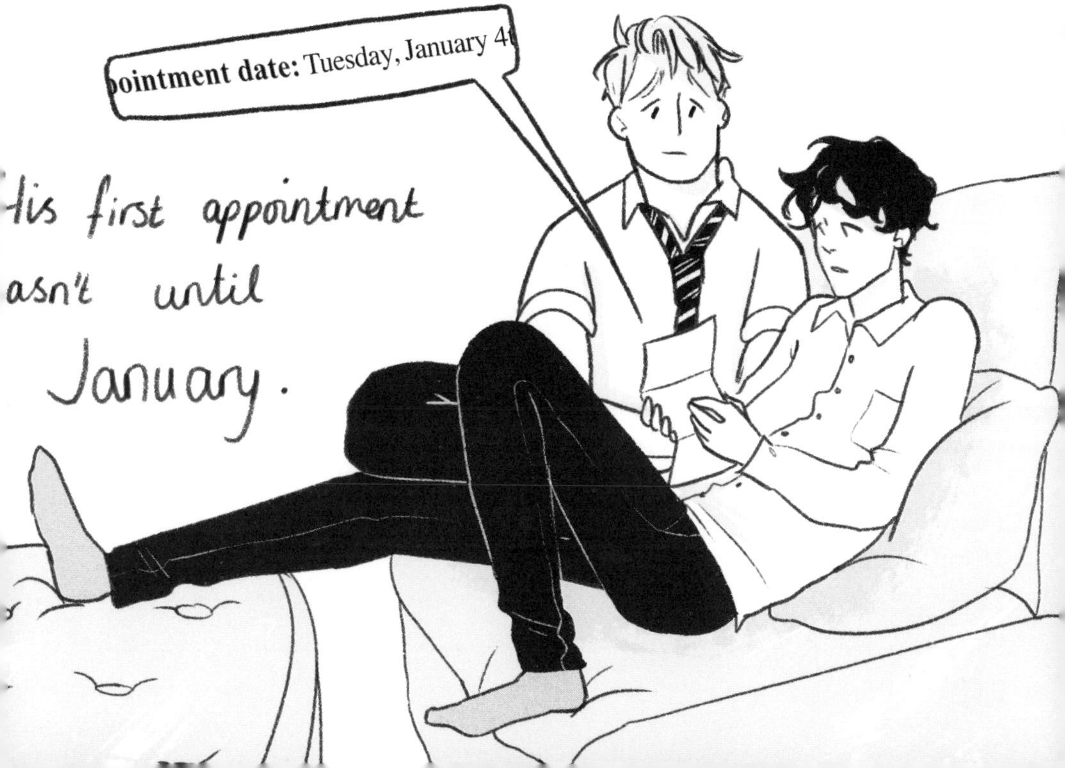
pointment date: Tuesday, January 4
lis first appointment
asn't until
January.

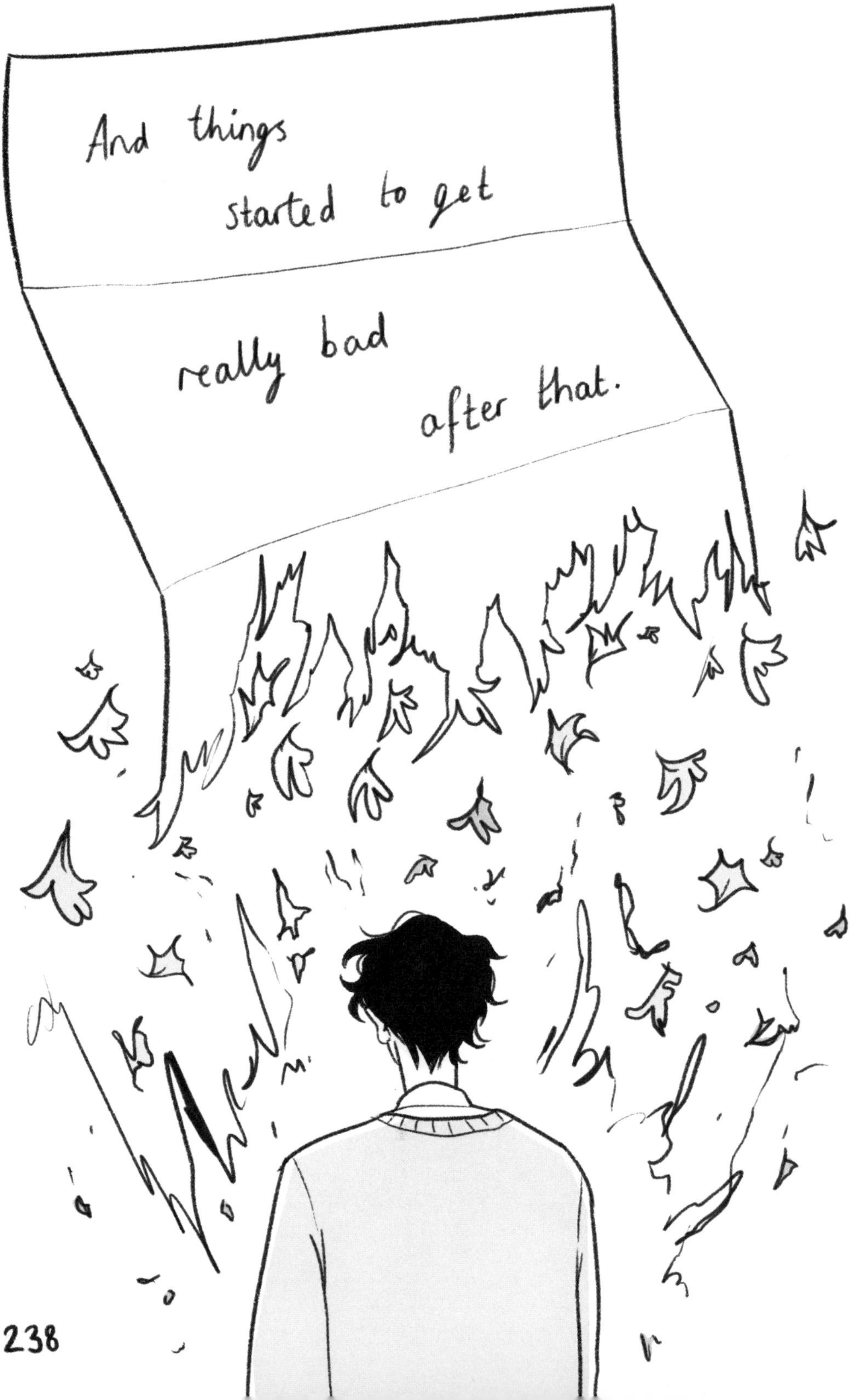
And things started to get
really bad after that.

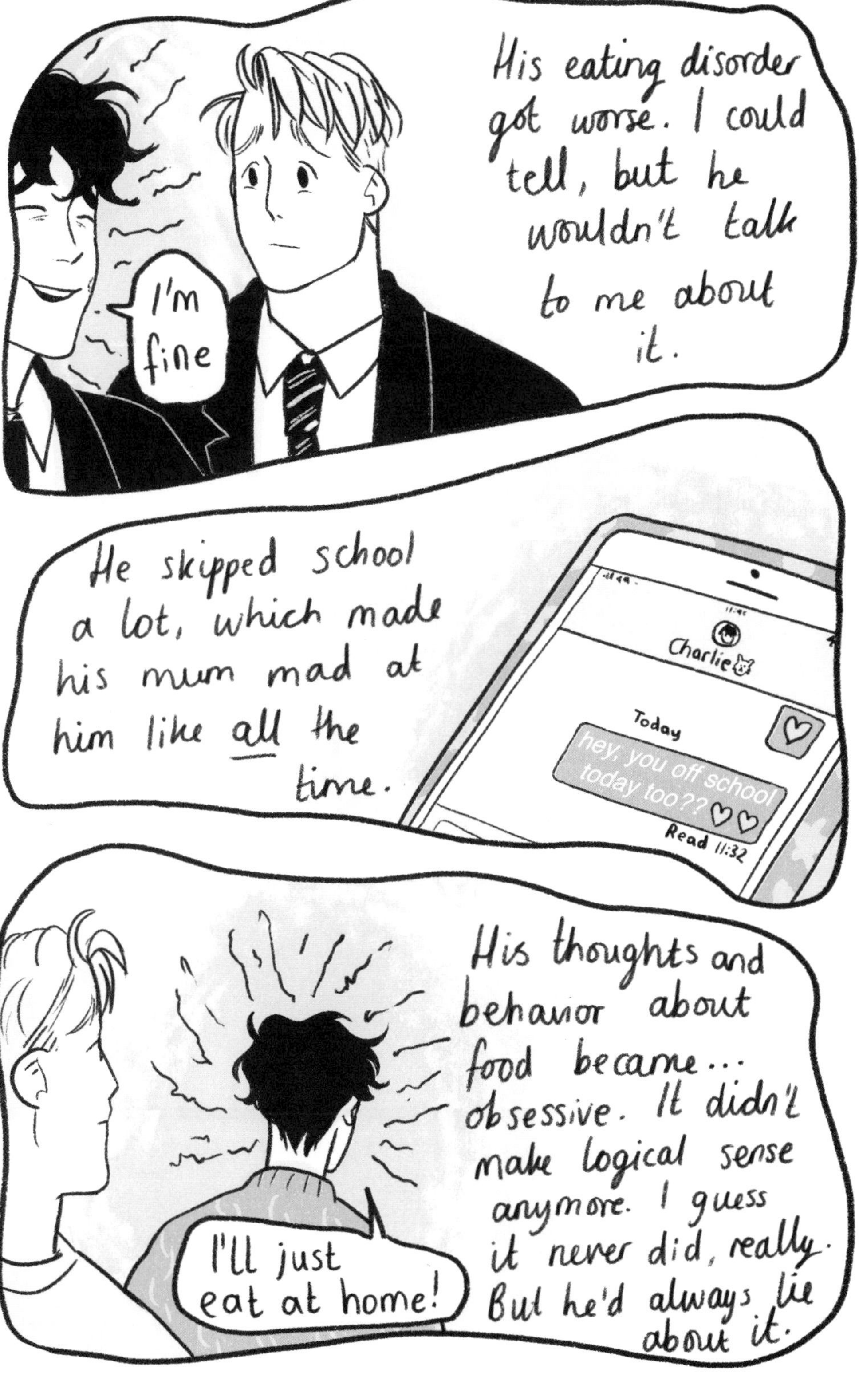
His eating disorder got worse. I could tell, but he wouldn't talk to me about it.
I'm fine
He skipped school a lot, which made his mum mad at him like all the time.
Charlie
Today
hey, you off school today too?? ♡♡
Read 11:32
His thoughts and behavior about food became... obsessive. It didn't make logical sense anymore. I guess it never did, really. But he'd always lie about it.
I'll just eat at home!

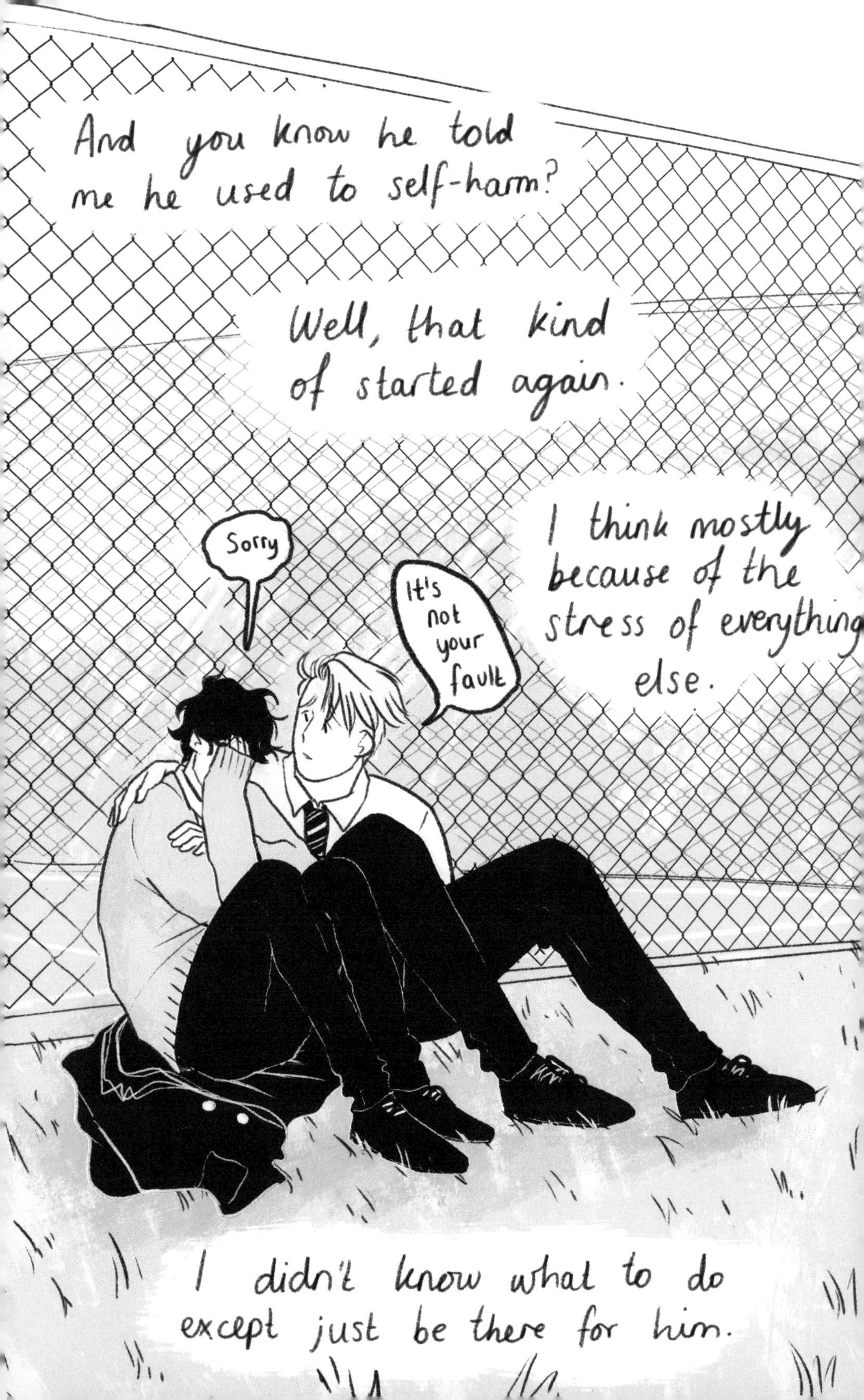
And you know he told me he used to self-harm?
Well, that kind of started again.
Sorry
It's not your fault
I think mostly because of the stress of everything else.
I didn't know what to do except just be there for him.

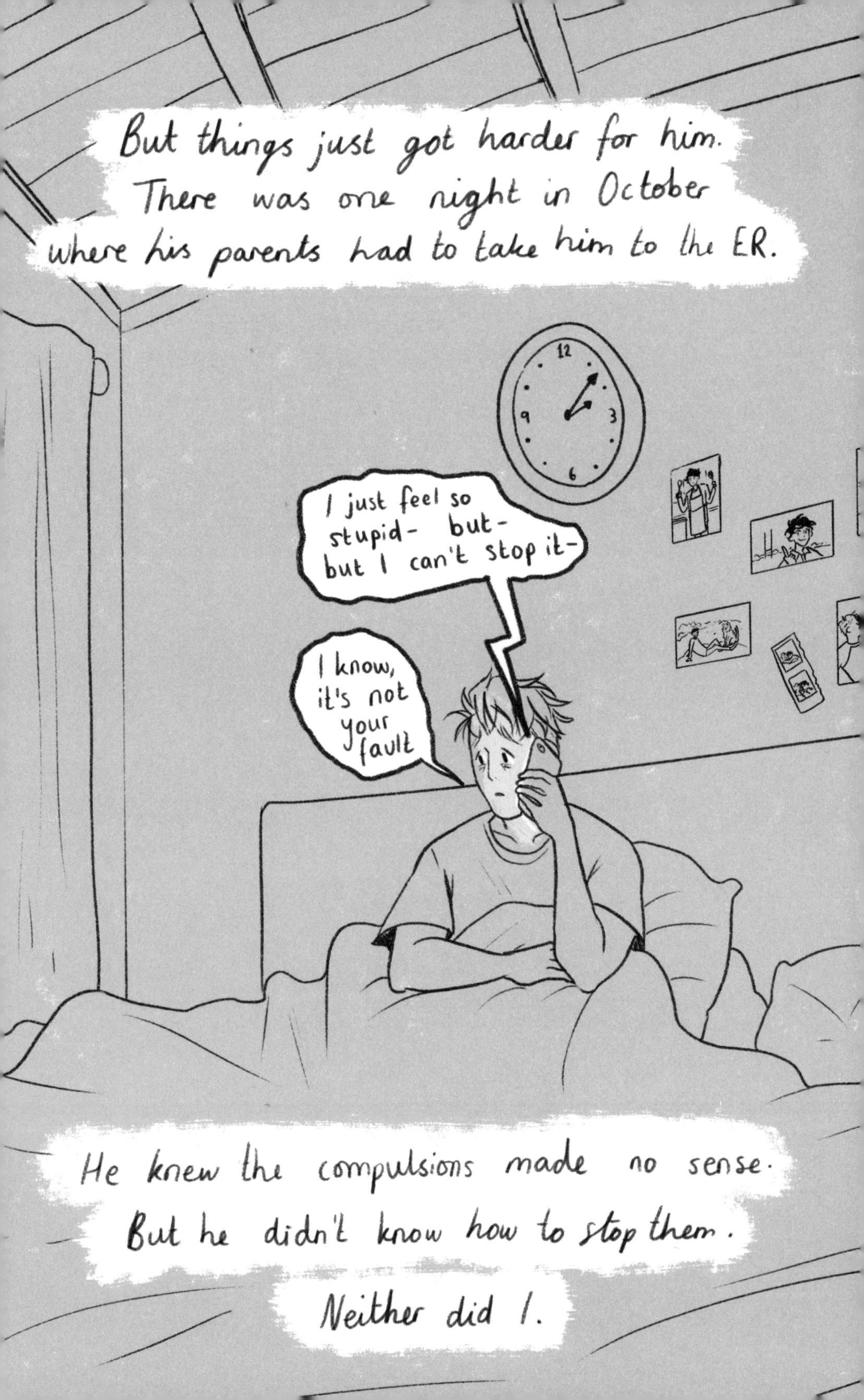
But things just got harder for him. There was one night in October where his parents had to take him to the ER.
I just feel so stupid- but- but I can't stop it-
I know, it's not your fault
He knew the compulsions made no sense. But he didn't know how to stop them.
Neither did I.

Charlie's mental health was assessed while he was there, and they told him that it'd be best if he spent some time as an inpatient.

But it was his choice.

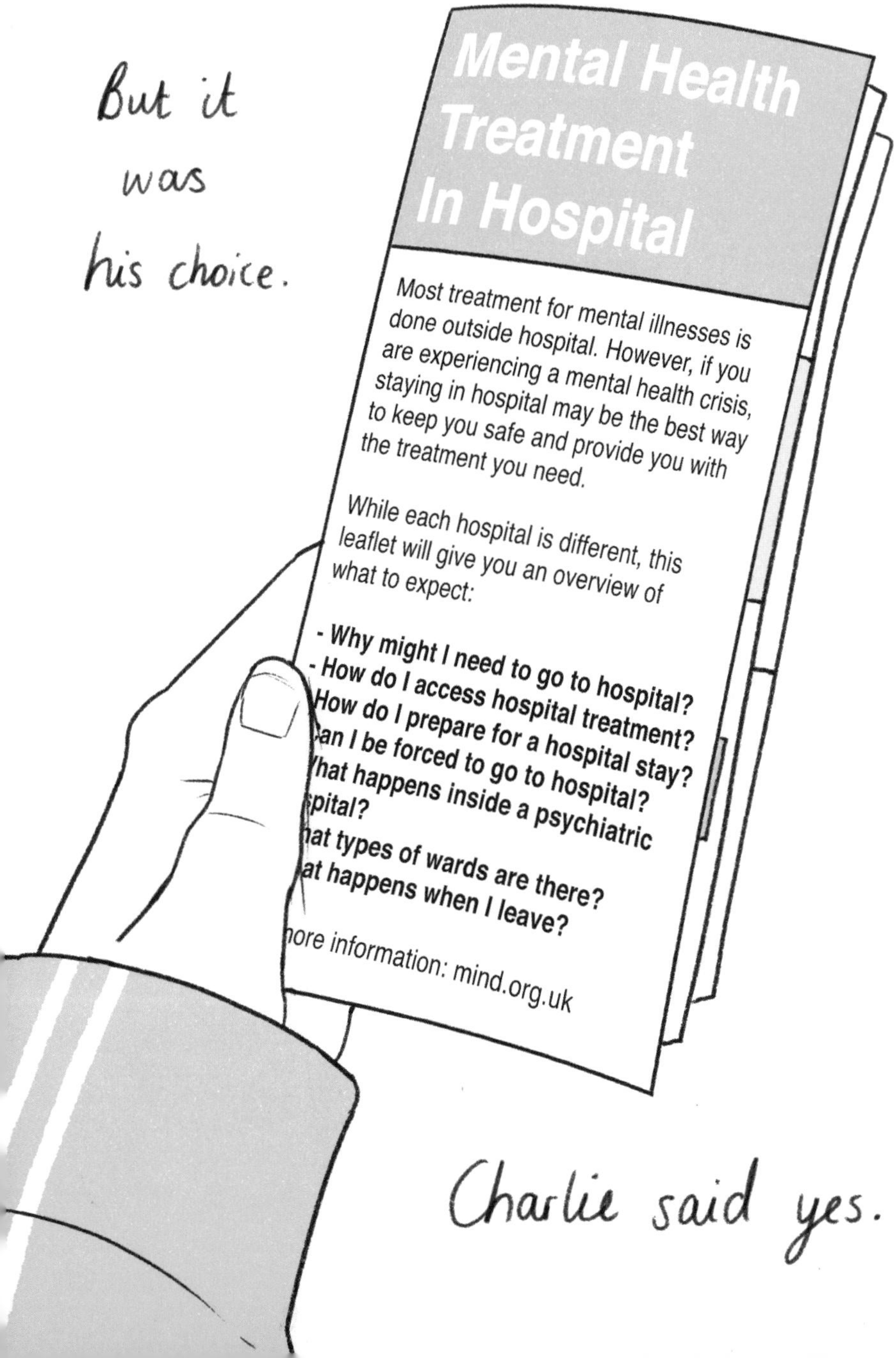

Mental Health Treatment In Hospital
Most treatment for mental illnesses is done outside hospital. However, if you are experiencing a mental health crisis, staying in hospital may be the best way to keep you safe and provide you with the treatment you need.
While each hospital is different, this leaflet will give you an overview of what to expect:
- Why might I need to go to hospital?
- How do I access hospital treatment?
How do I prepare for a hospital stay?
an I be forced to go to hospital?
hat happens inside a psychiatric
spital?
at types of wards are there?
at happens when I leave?
ore information: mind.org.uk

Charlie said yes.

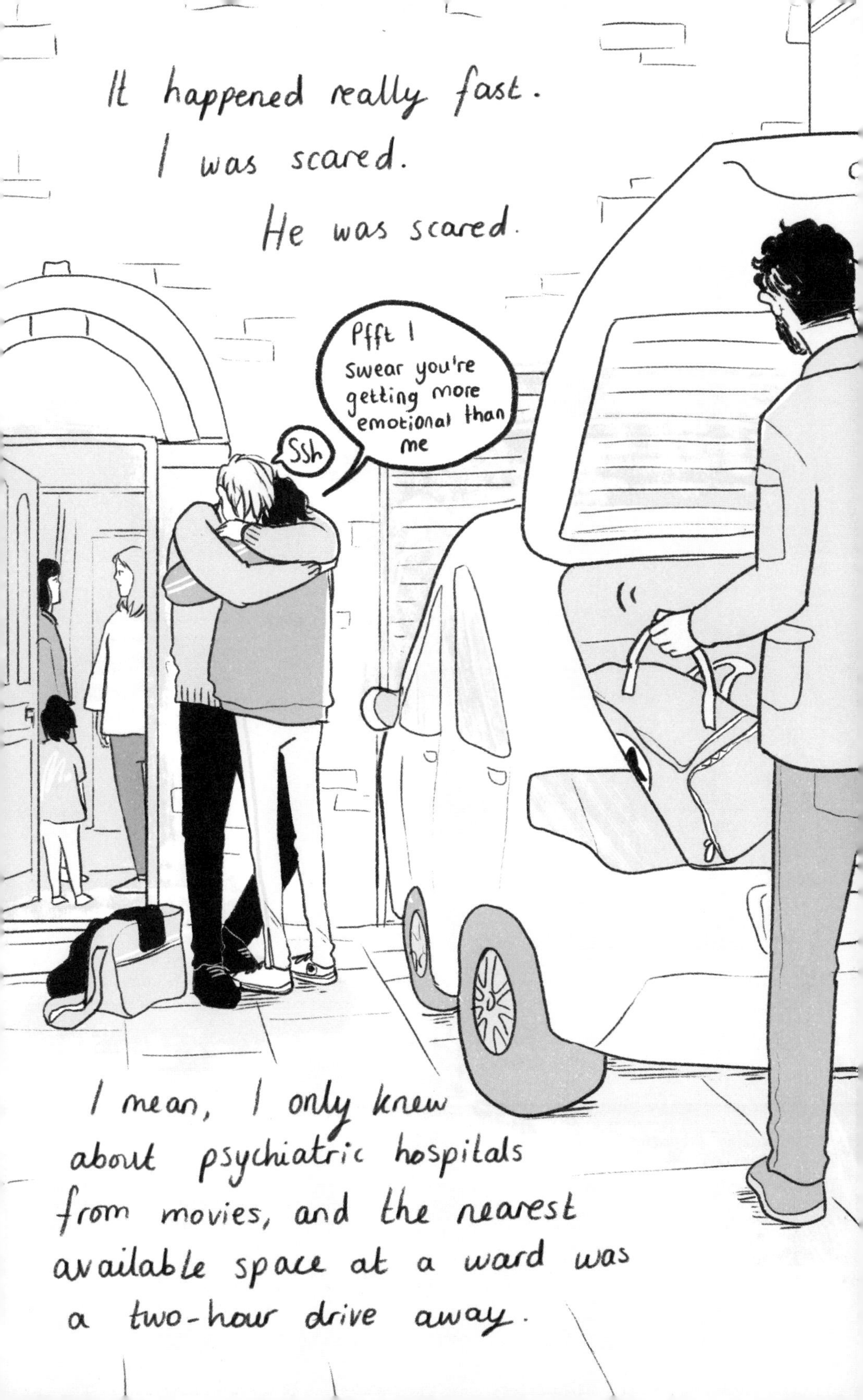
It happened really fast.
I was scared.
He was scared.
Ssh
Pffft I swear you're getting more emotional than me
I mean, I only knew about psychiatric hospitals from movies, and the nearest available space at a ward was a two-hour drive away.

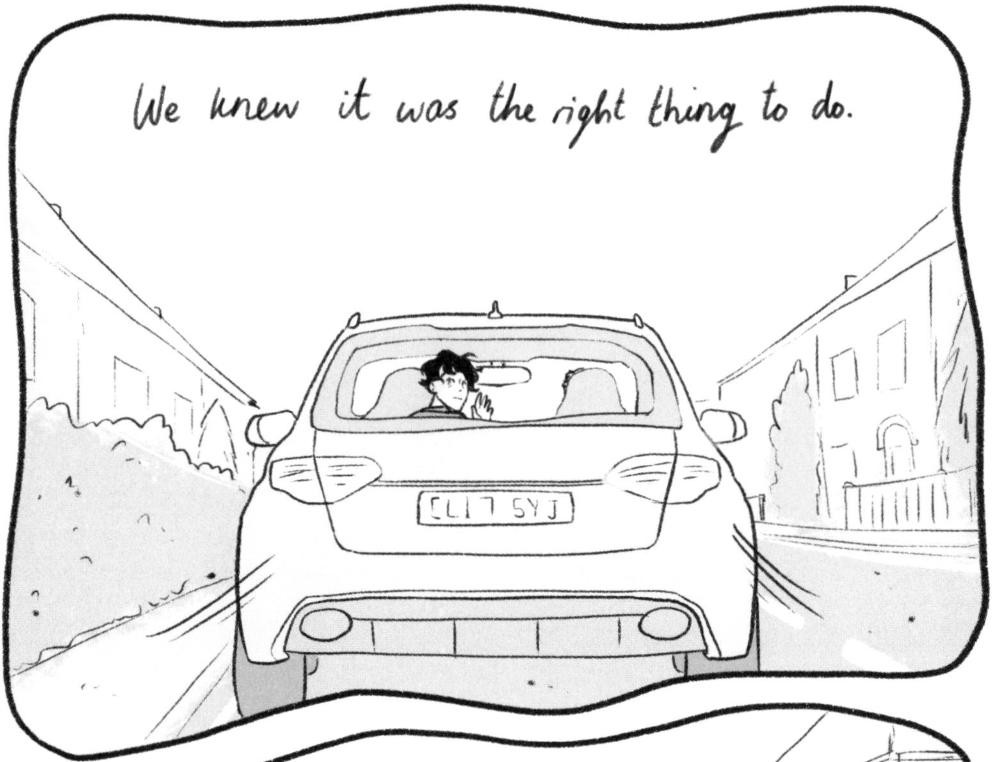
We knew it was the right thing to do.
CL17 SYJ

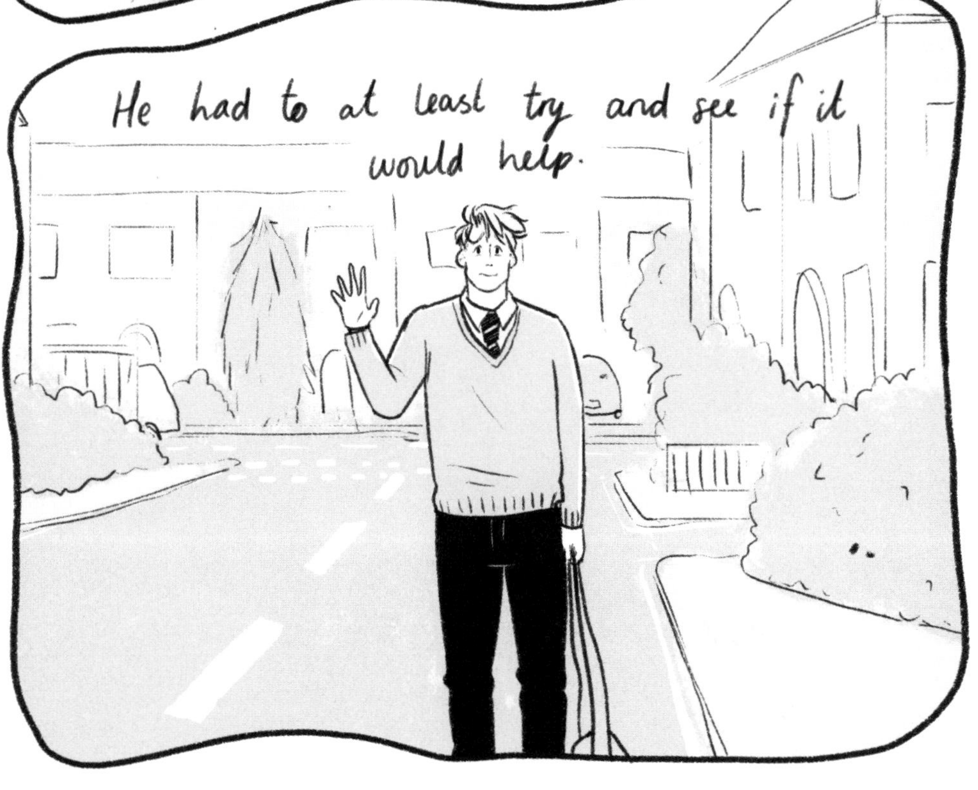
He had to at least try and see if it would help.

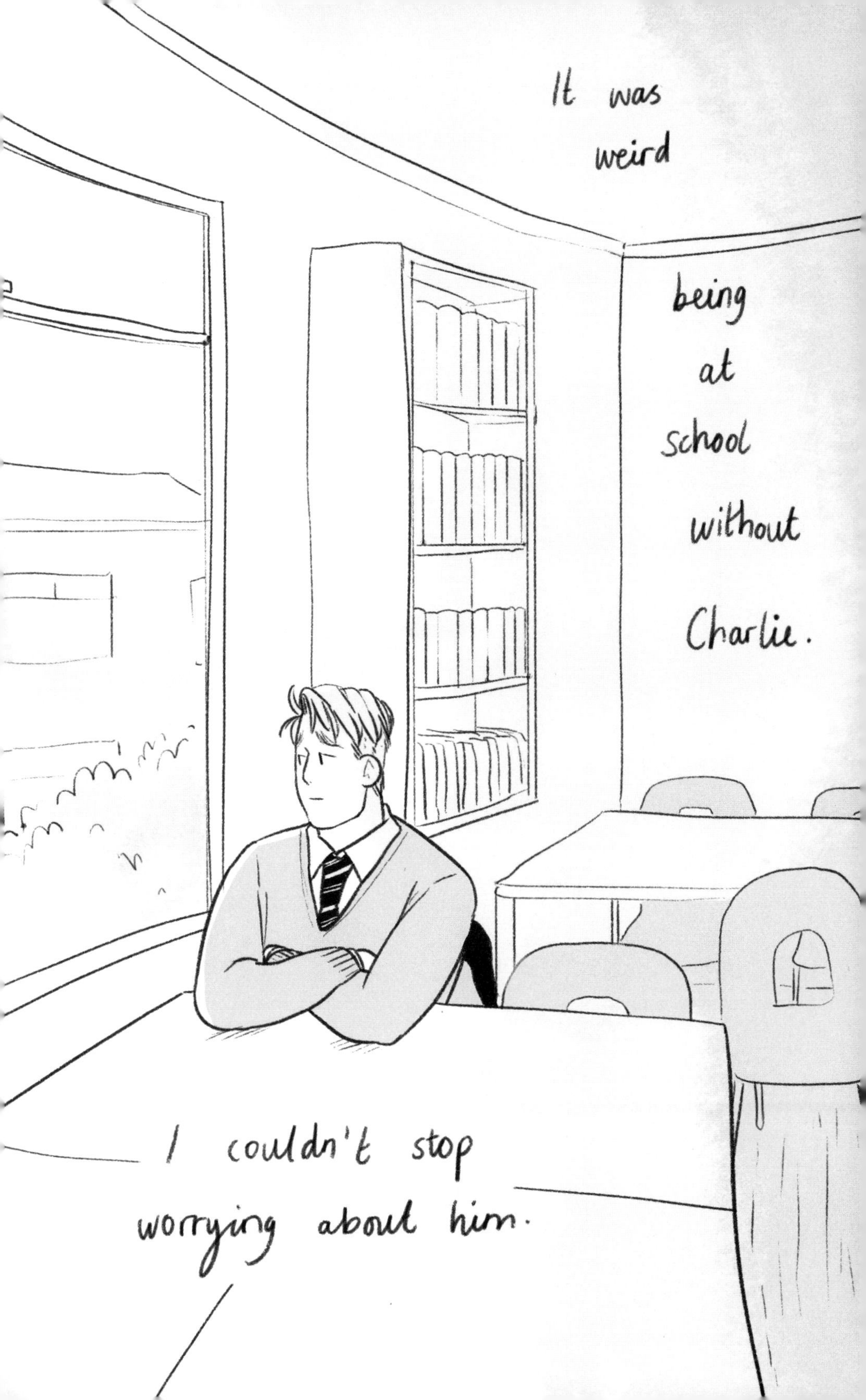
It was weird
being at school without Charlie.
I couldn't stop worrying about him.

We spoke on the phone when we could, and obviously I visited a lot too, but—

—I kept wishing I knew how he was feeling all the time.

Was he homesick?

Was the treatment helping?

Was it making things worse?

Was he lonely?

Was he bored?

Had he made some friends?

What is it like in a psychiatric hospital?

Your experience can depend on the hospital you stay at, what kind of treatment you receive, and your feelings about being in hospital.

However, some common aspects of psychiatric hospitals include:
- access to talking therapies and medication
- trained staff on-site to support you
- a daily routine/structure

There are also some potential disadvantages:
- you will be away from family and friends, and visits might only be permitted at set times
- you can't always decide how you spend your time
- staff may need to search you if they

It feels so awful to complain about my feelings when Charlie's been going through all of that, but I guess I've been pretty anxious these past few months.

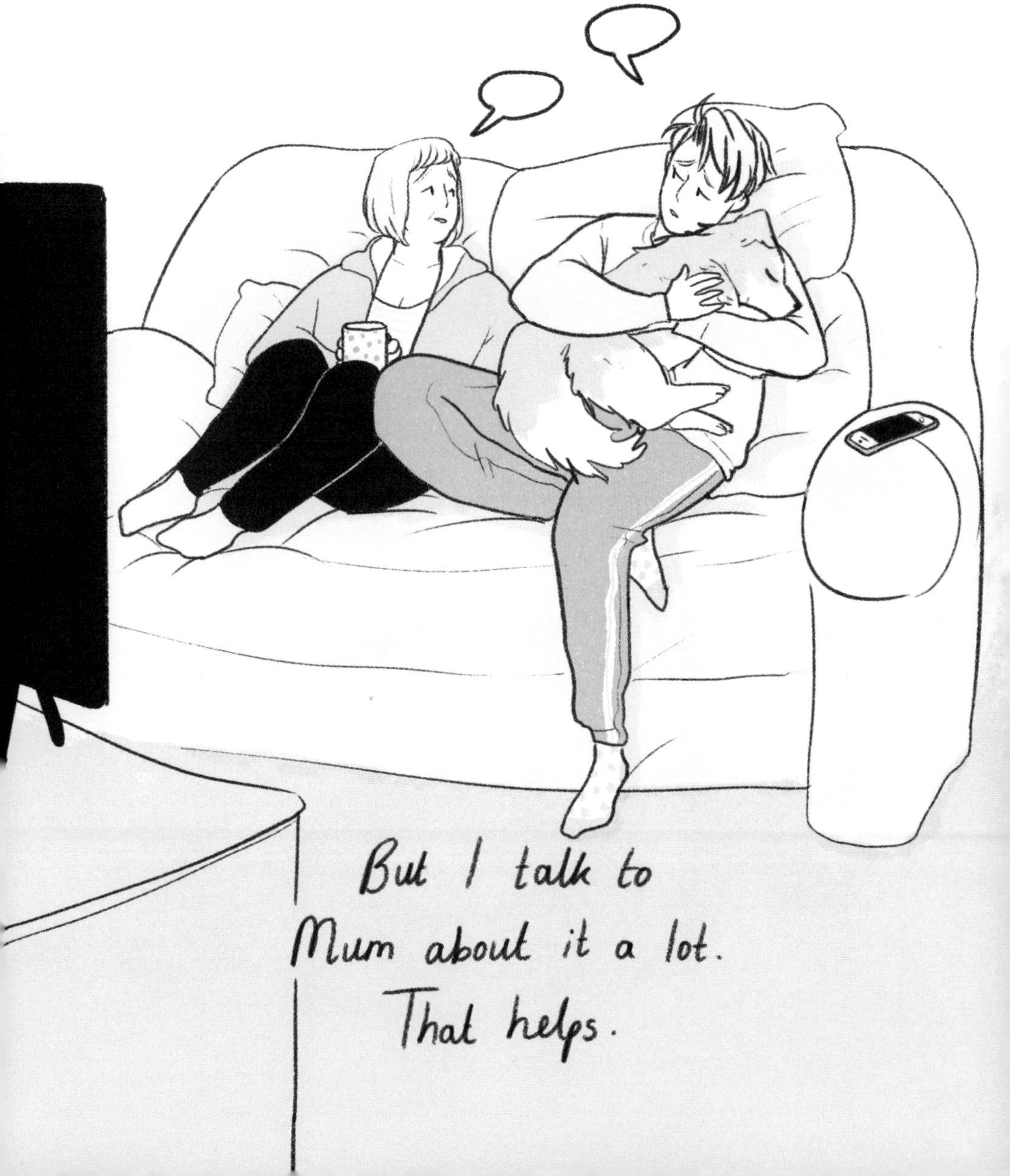
But I talk to
Mum about it a lot.
That helps.

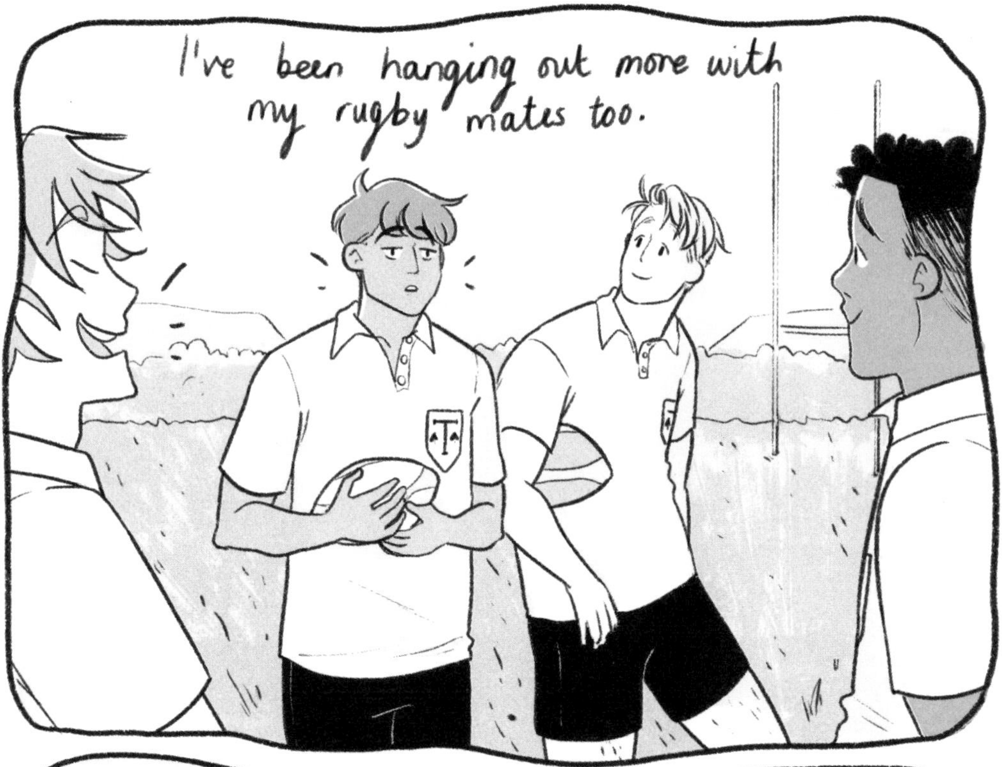
I've been hanging out more with my rugby mates too.

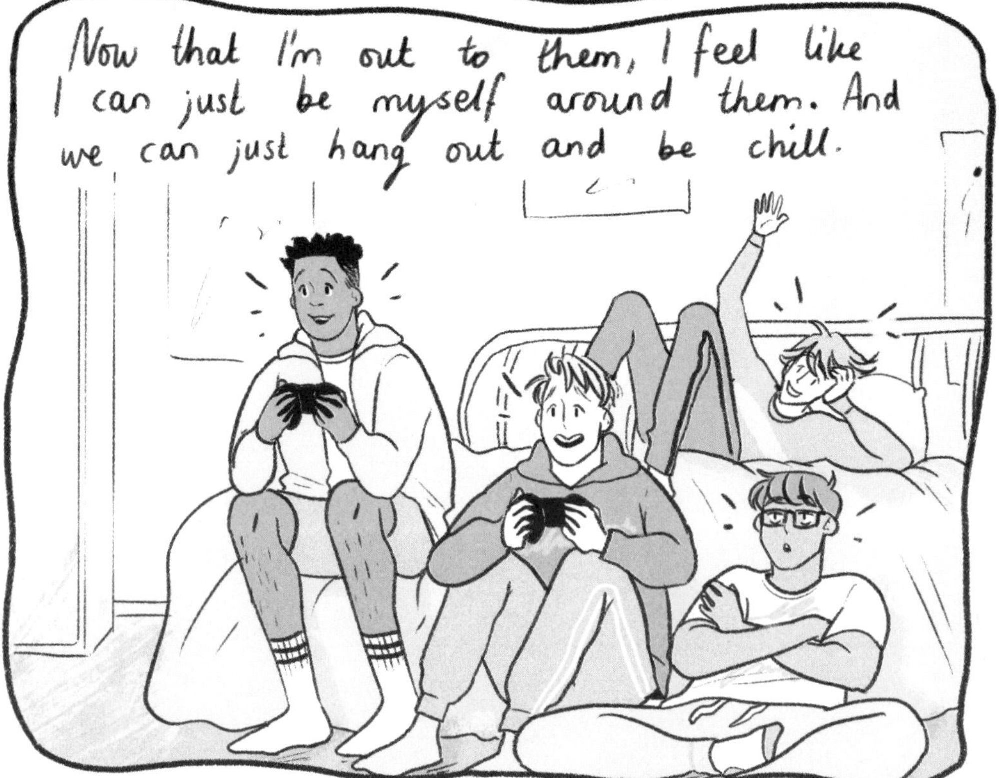
Now that I'm out to them, I feel like I can just be myself around them. And we can just hang out and be chill.

Charlie asked me not to tell them what was going on with him.

He was kinda scared of it spreading around school.

They knew he was off school because he was unwell, though, so they've been supportive in their own way.

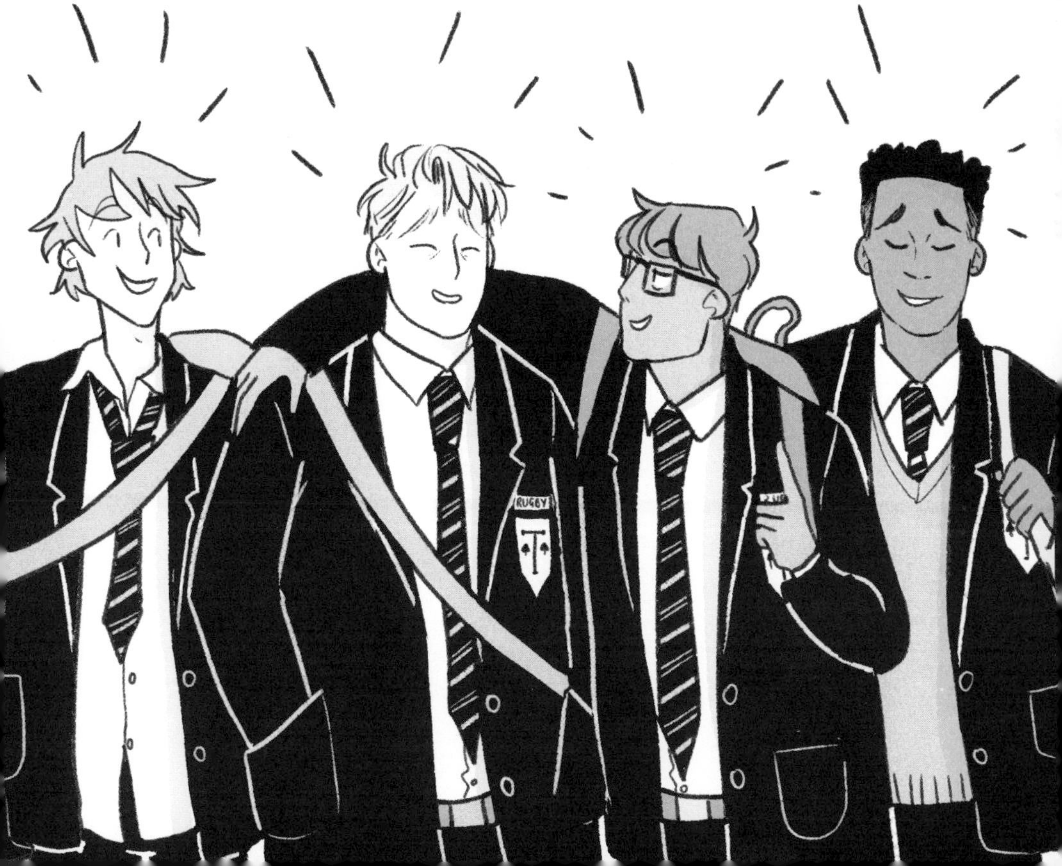
RUGBY

Charlie said I could keep the
Paris Squad updated.

Elle Argent
darcy did you get the card for charlie?

Darcy Olsson
YEP i got a giant one, it's the length of my arm

Tara Jones
omg

Tao Xu
Nick does Charlie have access to a DVD player???
I was thinking we could send him some fun films to watch

Nick Nelson
yeah he does!!! Good idea, he literally said
they don't have Netflix or anything and
they've only got movies from like 2005 haha

Tara Jones
I got the gift basket! And some
stickers and stuff to make it pretty

Aled Last
i got him some art stuff!

Sahar Zahid
I got him a couple of books!! He said he
likes to read so I hope that's okay

Nick Nelson
Do you all wanna come back to mine after school
tomorrow?? You can sign the card and we can
decorate the gift basket and stuff! also you can
come on a walk with Nellie and me if you want!!

Darcy Olsson
I WOULD LIKE TO MEET NELLIE

Elle Argent
i also would like to meet nellie!!!!

Tao Xu
I think we all would like to meet Nellie tbh

He didn't want them all visiting — I think
it would have been too overwhelming.
But they still found ways to help.

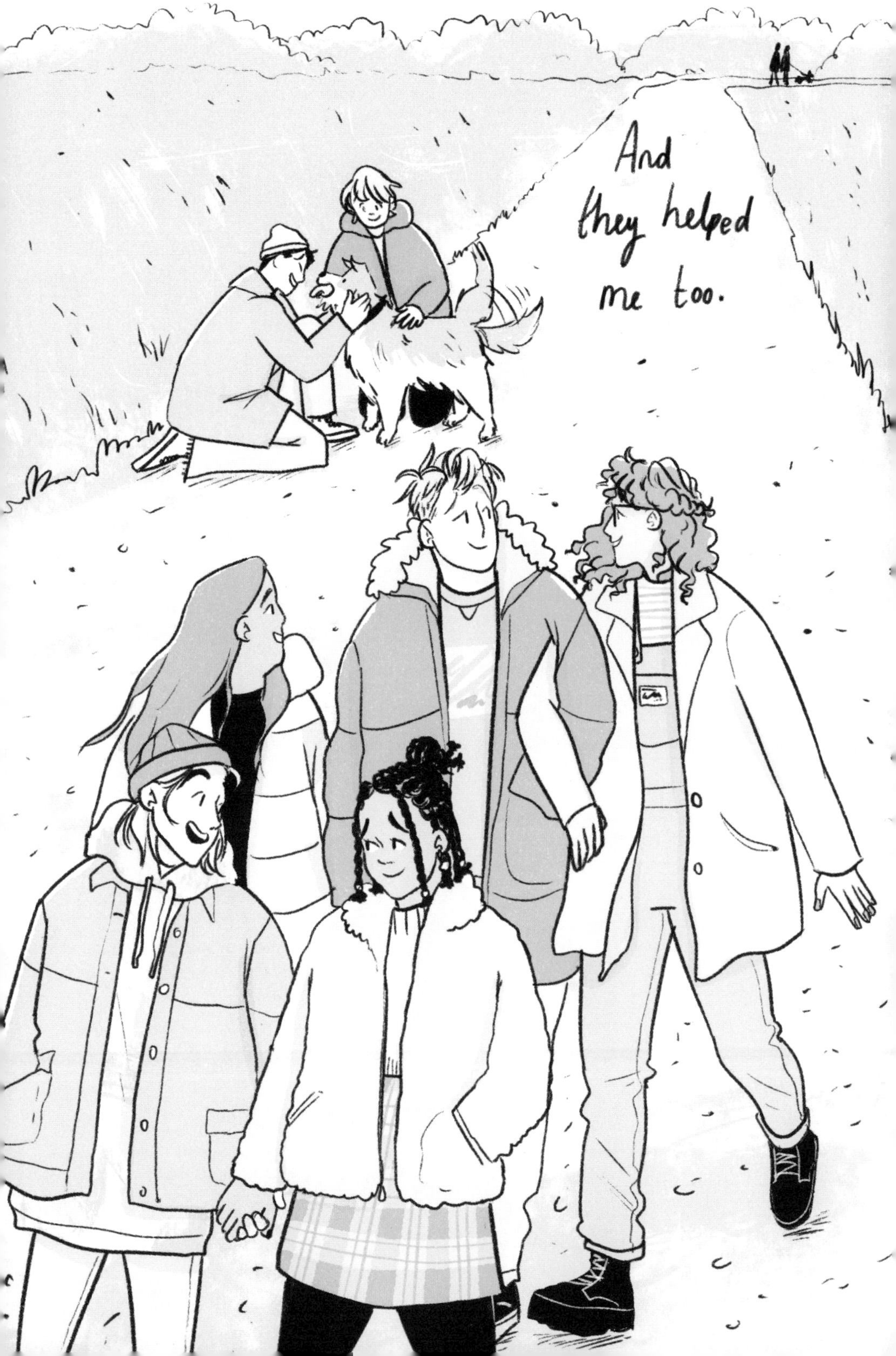
And they helped me too.

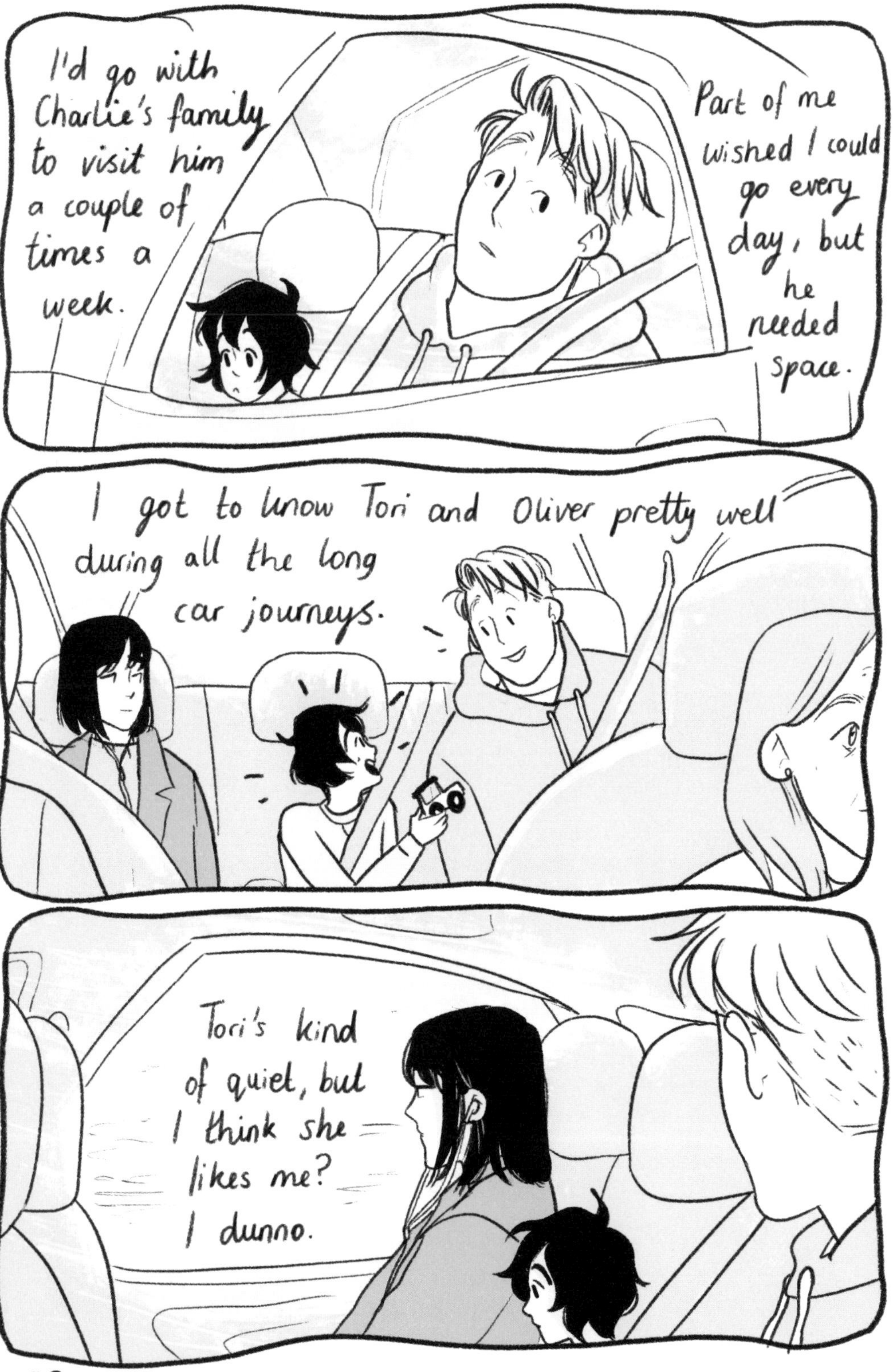
I'd go with Charlie's family to visit him a couple of times a week.
Part of me wished I could go every day, but he needed space.
I got to know Tori and Oliver pretty well during all the long car journeys.
Tori's kind of quiet, but I think she likes me? I dunno.

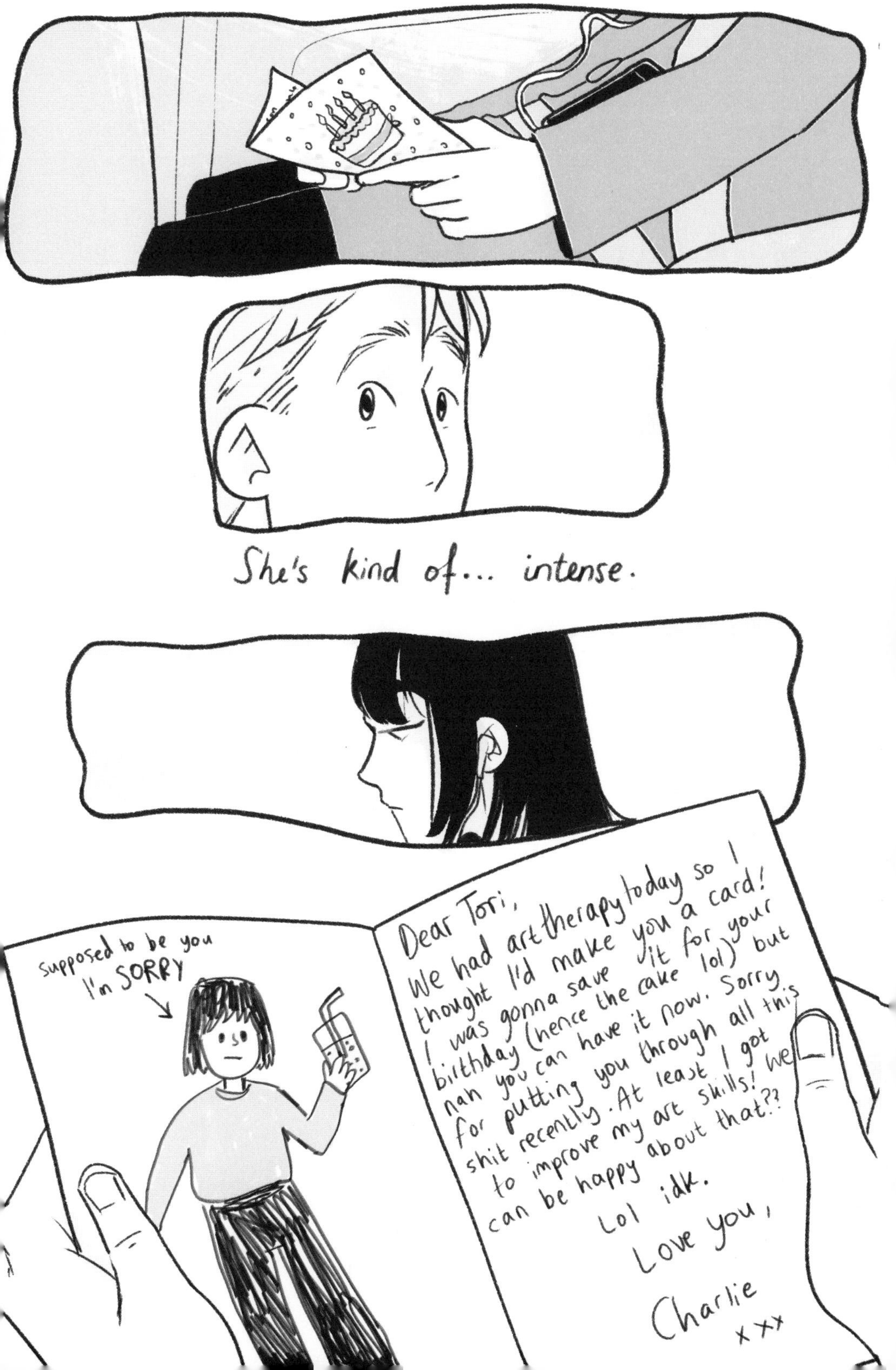
She's kind of... intense.
supposed to be you I'm SORRY
Dear Tori,
We had art therapy today so I thought I'd make you a card! I was gonna save it for your birthday (hence the cake lol) but nah you can have it now. Sorry for putting you through all this shit recently. At least I got to improve my art skills! We can be happy about that??
Lol idk.
Love you,
Charlie
xxx

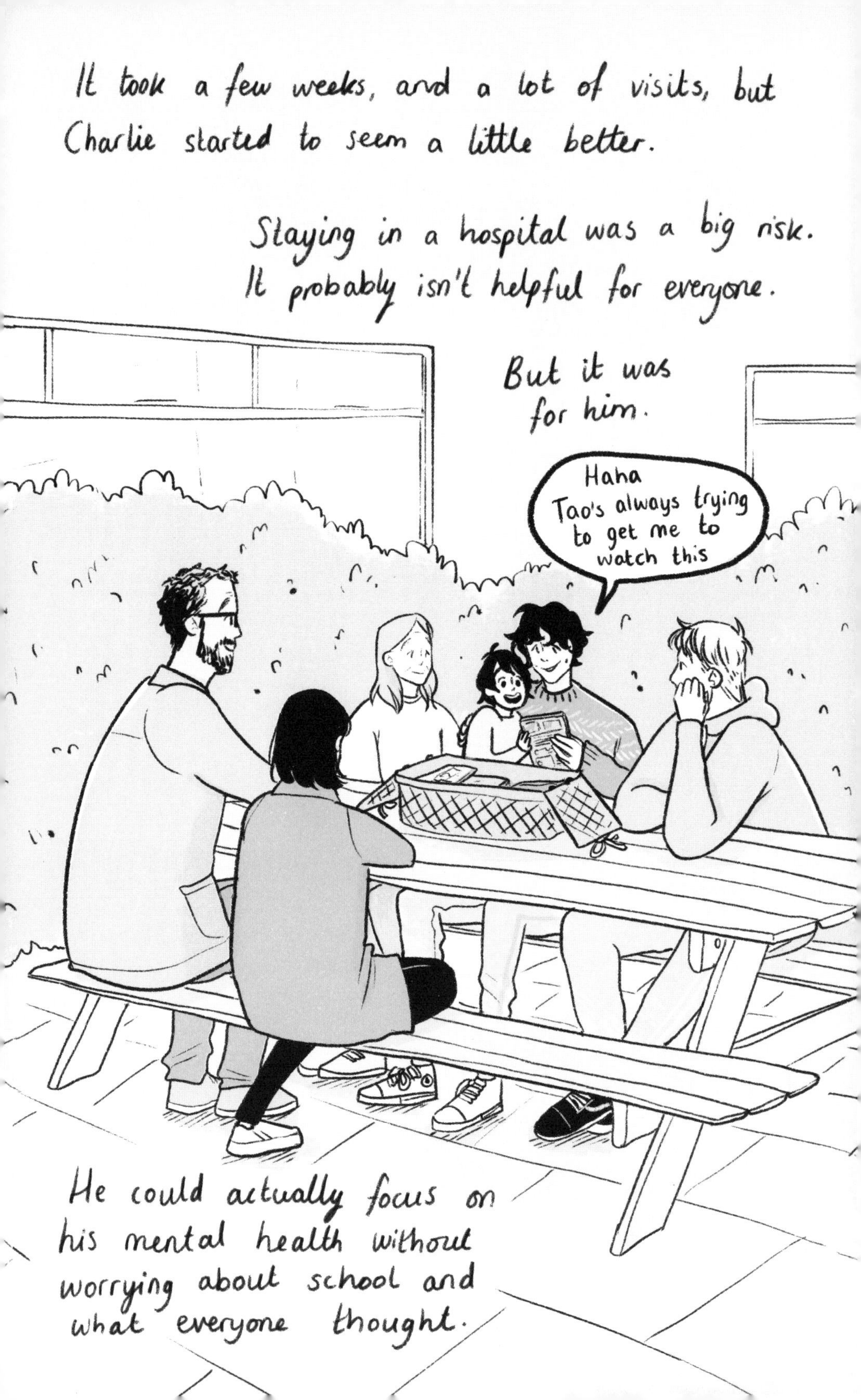
It took a few weeks, and a lot of visits, but Charlie started to seem a little better.
Staying in a hospital was a big risk. It probably isn't helpful for everyone.
But it was for him.
Haha Tao's always trying to get me to watch this
He could actually focus on his mental health without worrying about school and what everyone thought.

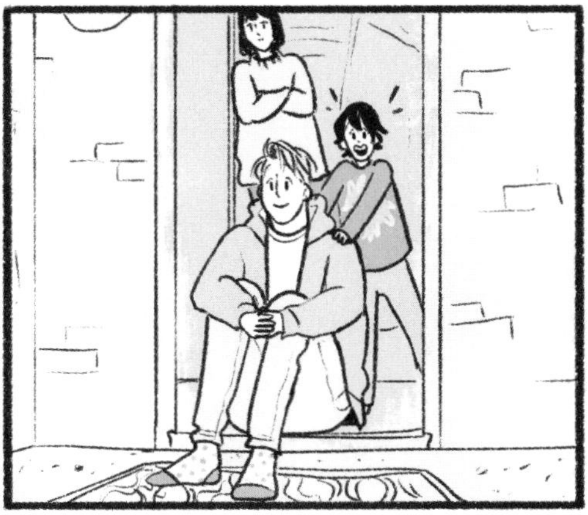

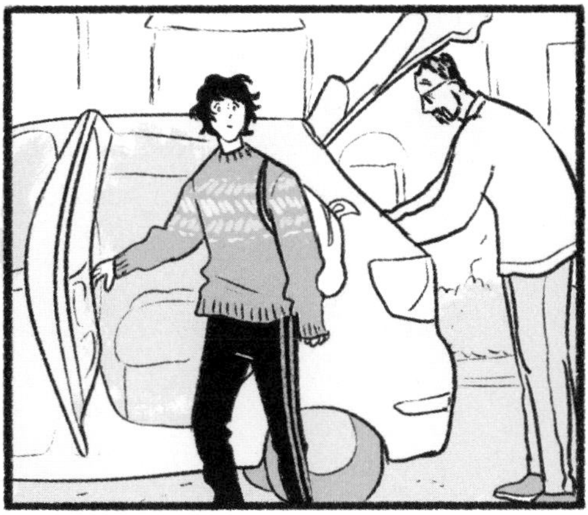

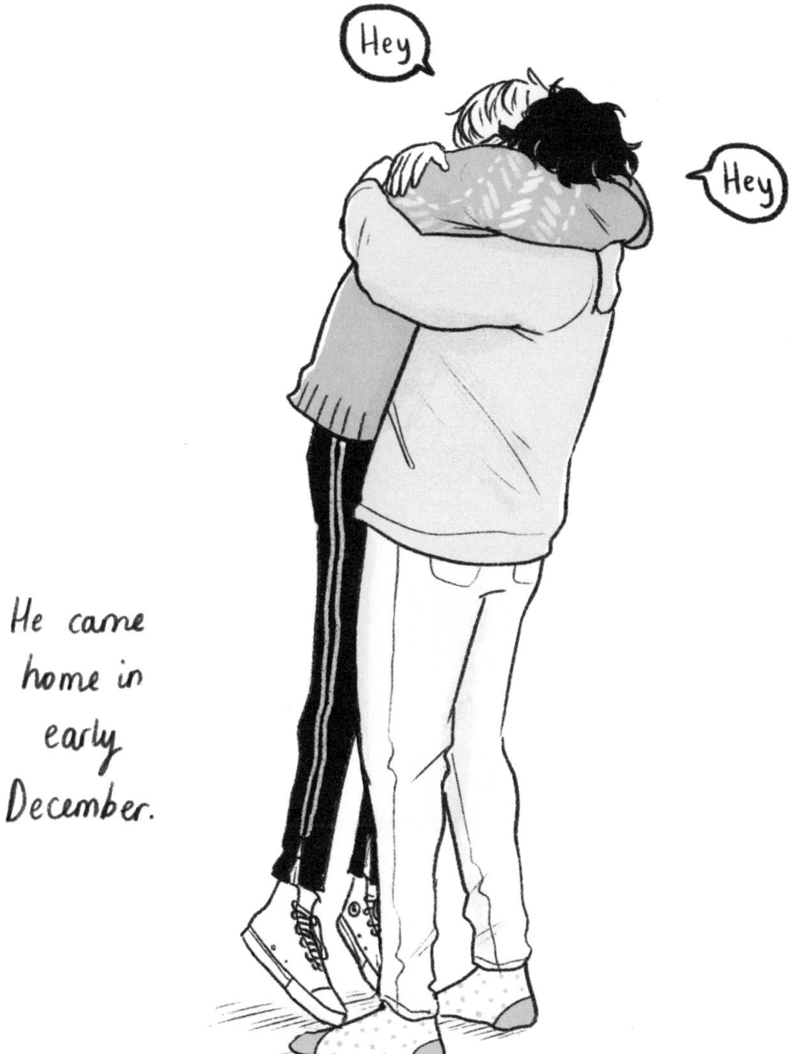
Hey
Hey
He came home in early December.

Just in time for the Christmas season.

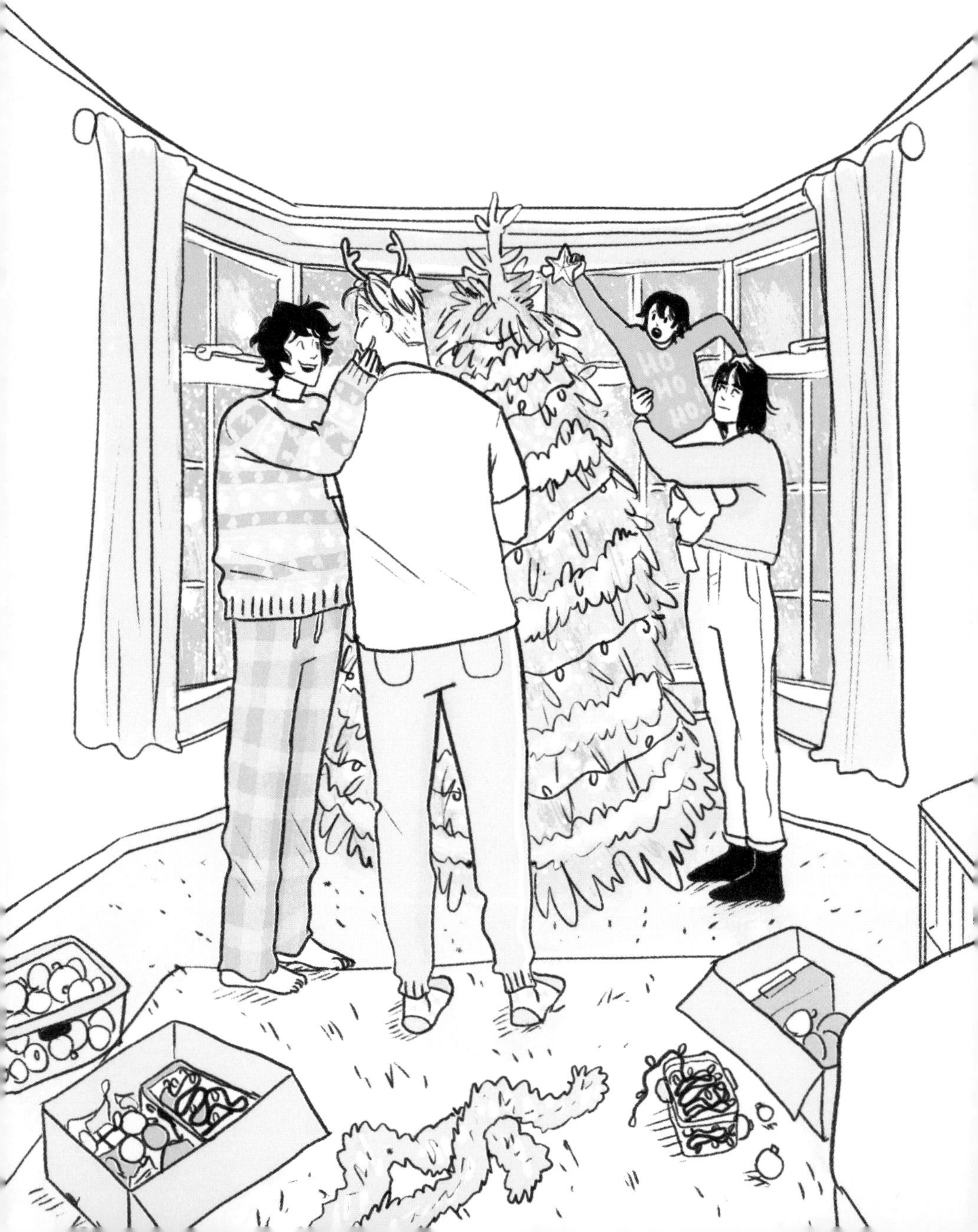
HO HO HO!

He's still dealing with a lot, so he stayed off school for the rest of term.

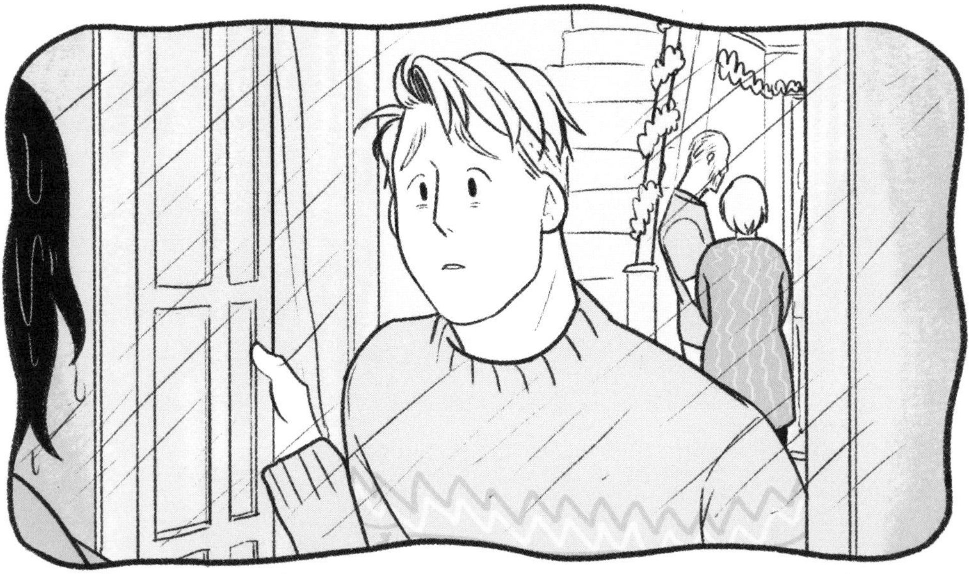

Christmas Day was especially hard. He came over after a big argument with his mum.

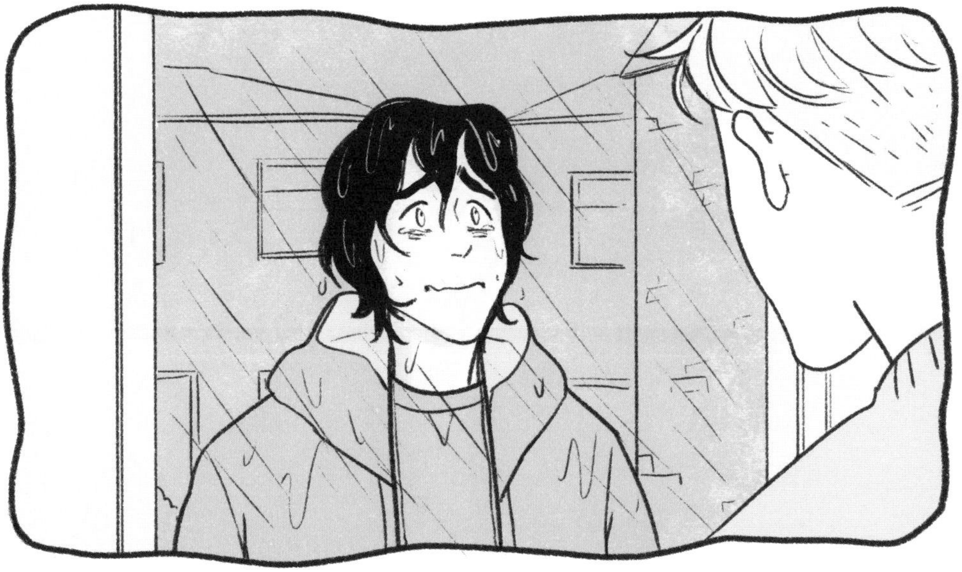

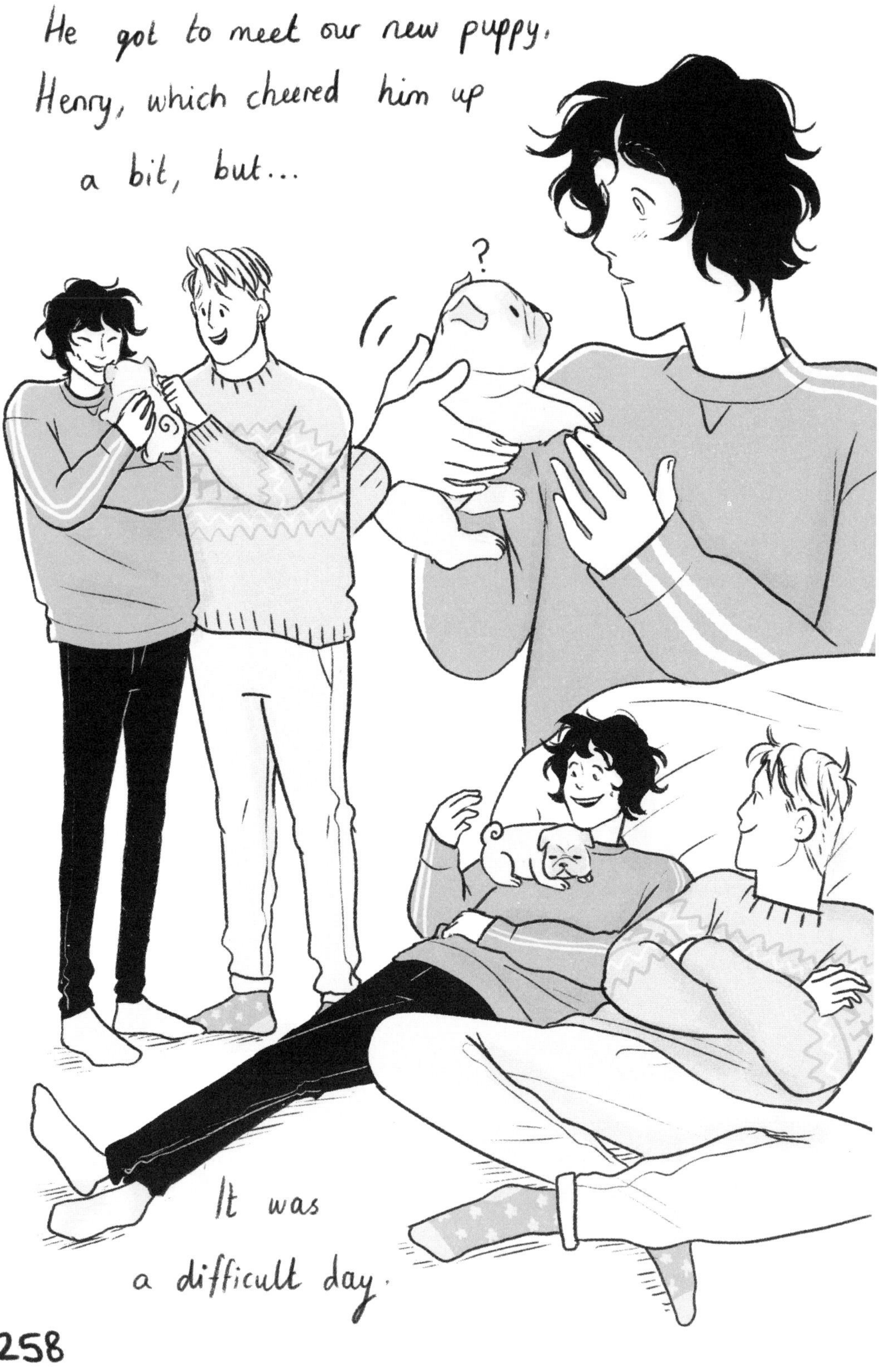
He got to meet our new puppy, Henry, which cheered him up a bit, but...
?
It was a difficult day.

It's not like seven weeks in hospital made him magically okay again.

I know I'm not an expert or anything, but from what I've learned over the past few months, mental illnesses take a long time to go away completely... if they ever do.

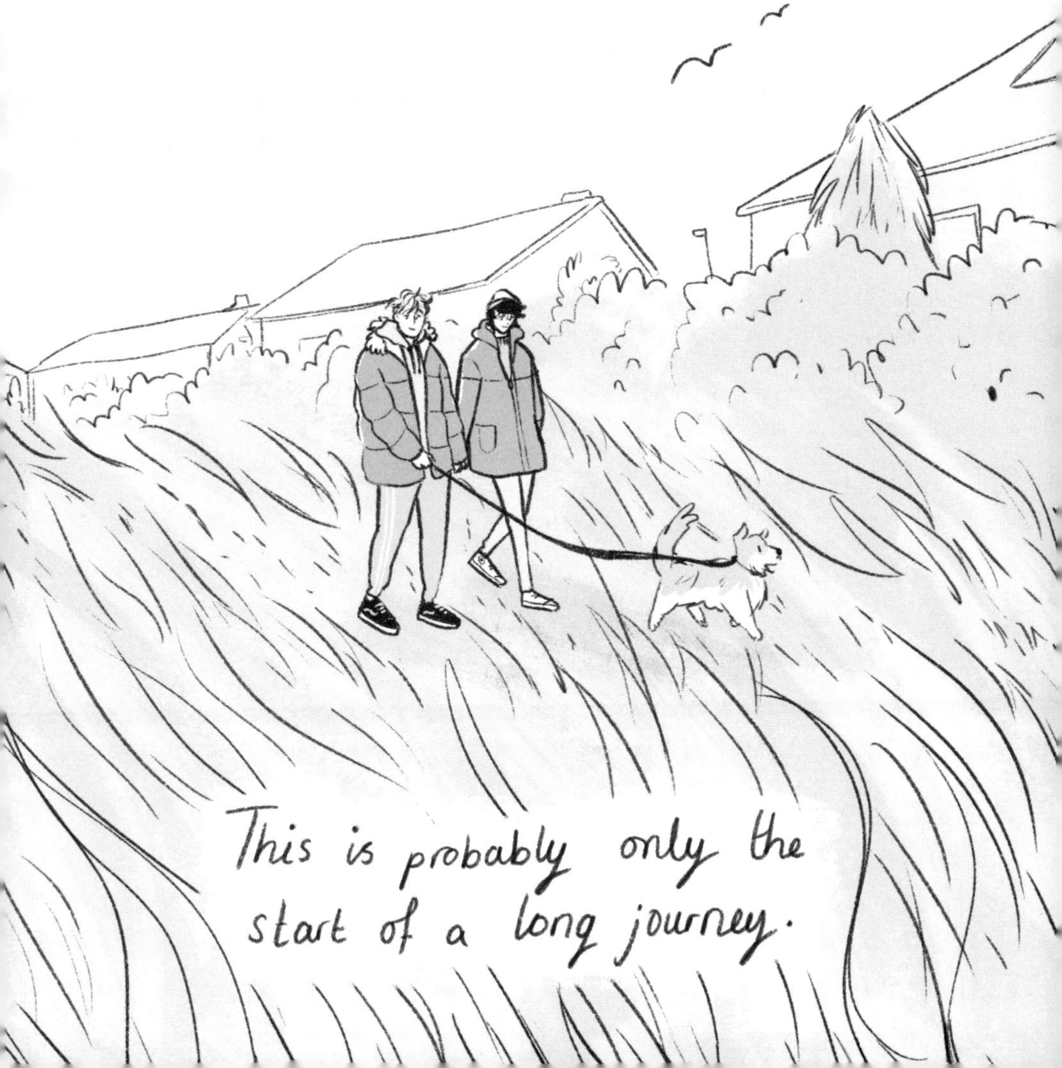
This is probably only the start of a long journey.

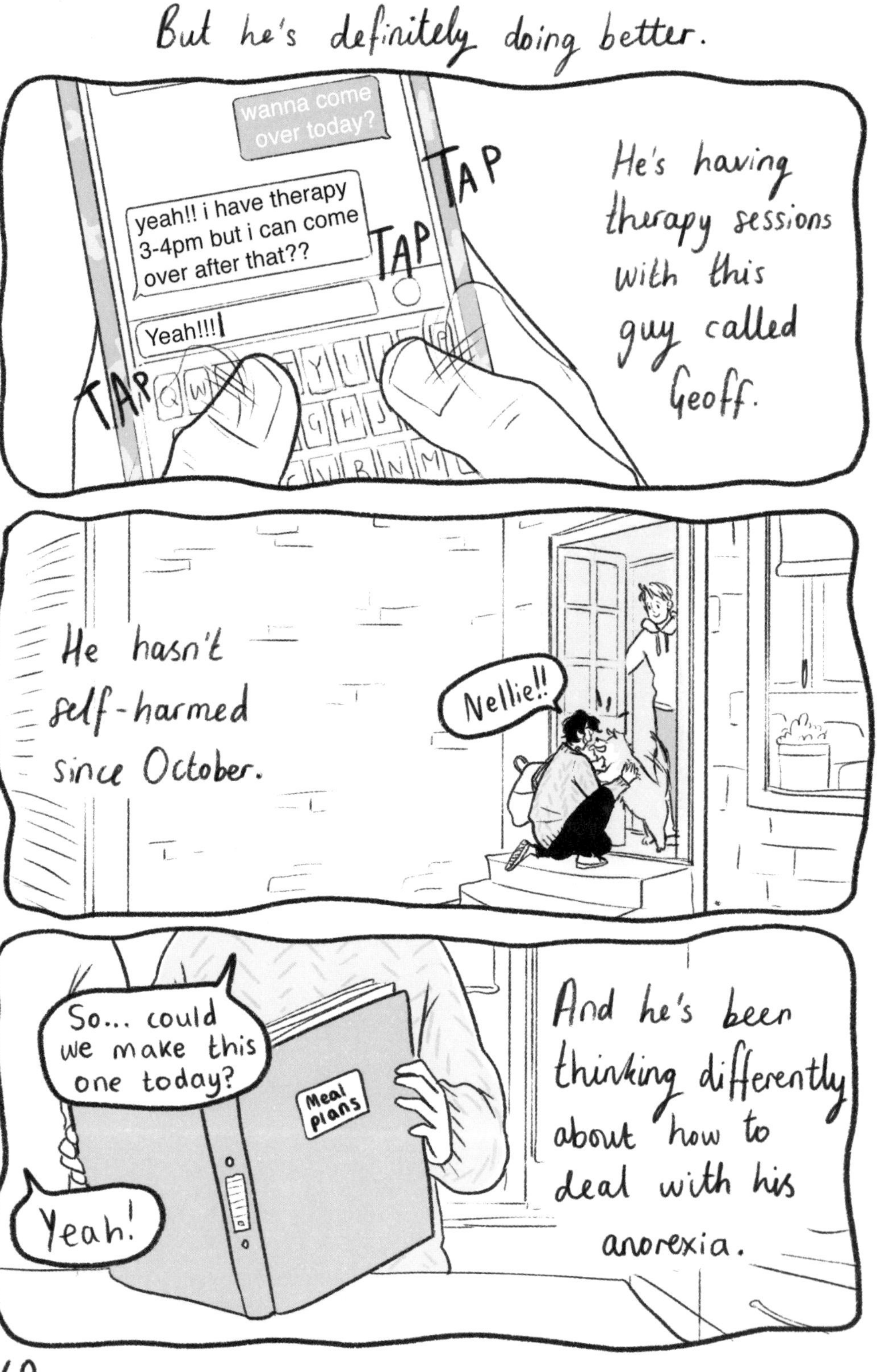
But he's definitely doing better.
wanna come over today?
yeah!! i have therapy 3-4pm but i can come over after that??
Yeah!!!
TAP
TAP
TAP
He's having therapy sessions with this guy called Geoff.
He hasn't self-harmed since October.
Nellie!!
So... could we make this one today?
Meal plans
Yeah!
And he's been thinking differently about how to deal with his anorexia.

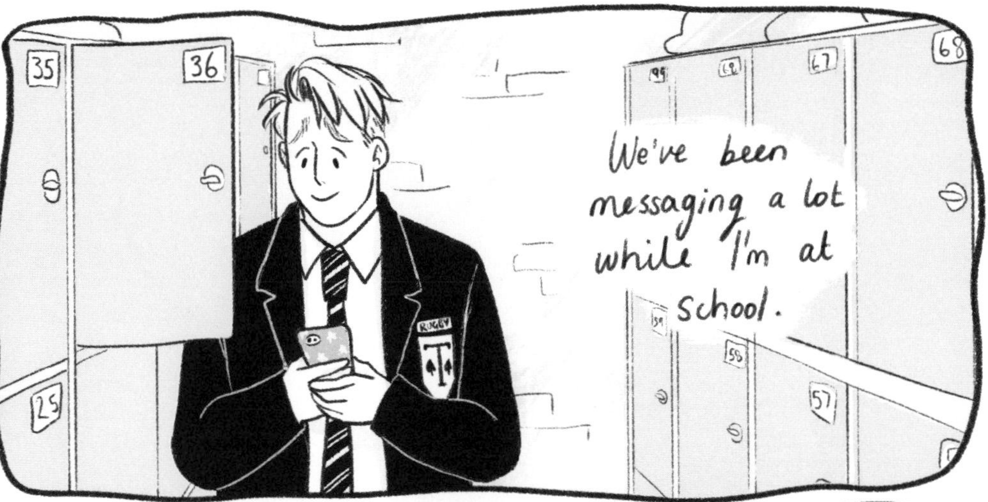
We've been messaging a lot while I'm at school.
RUGBY

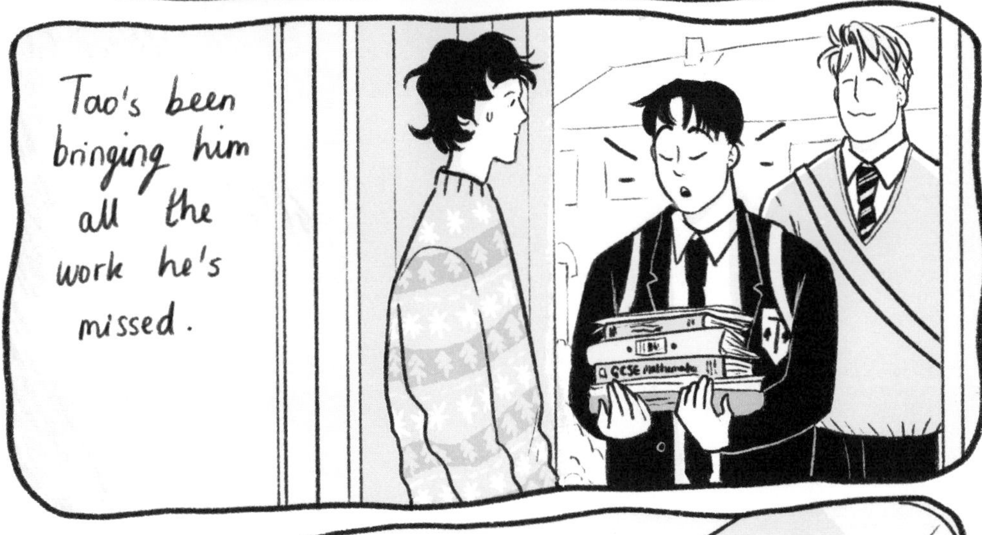
Tao's been bringing him all the work he's missed.
GCSE Mathematics

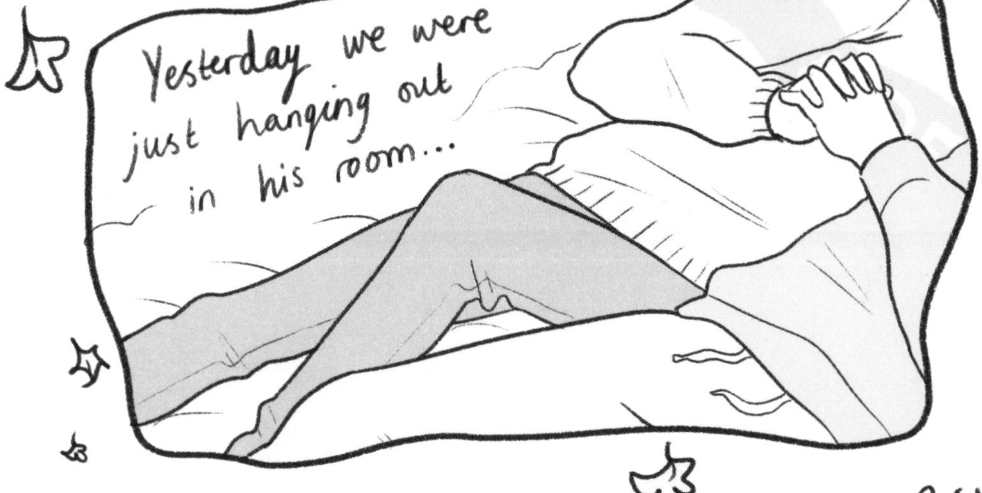
Yesterday we were just hanging out in his room...

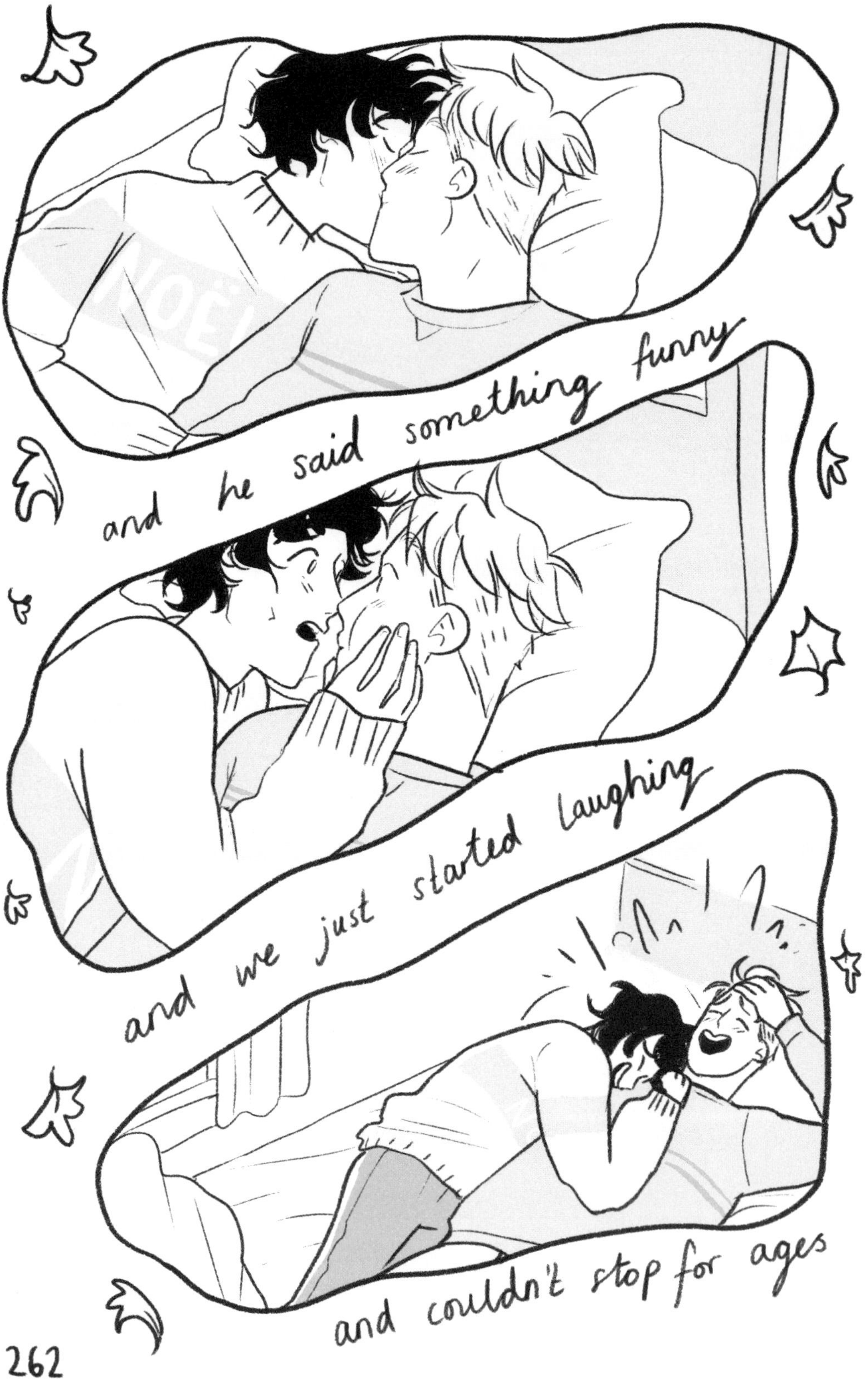
NOEL
and he said something funny
and we just started laughing
and couldn't stop for ages

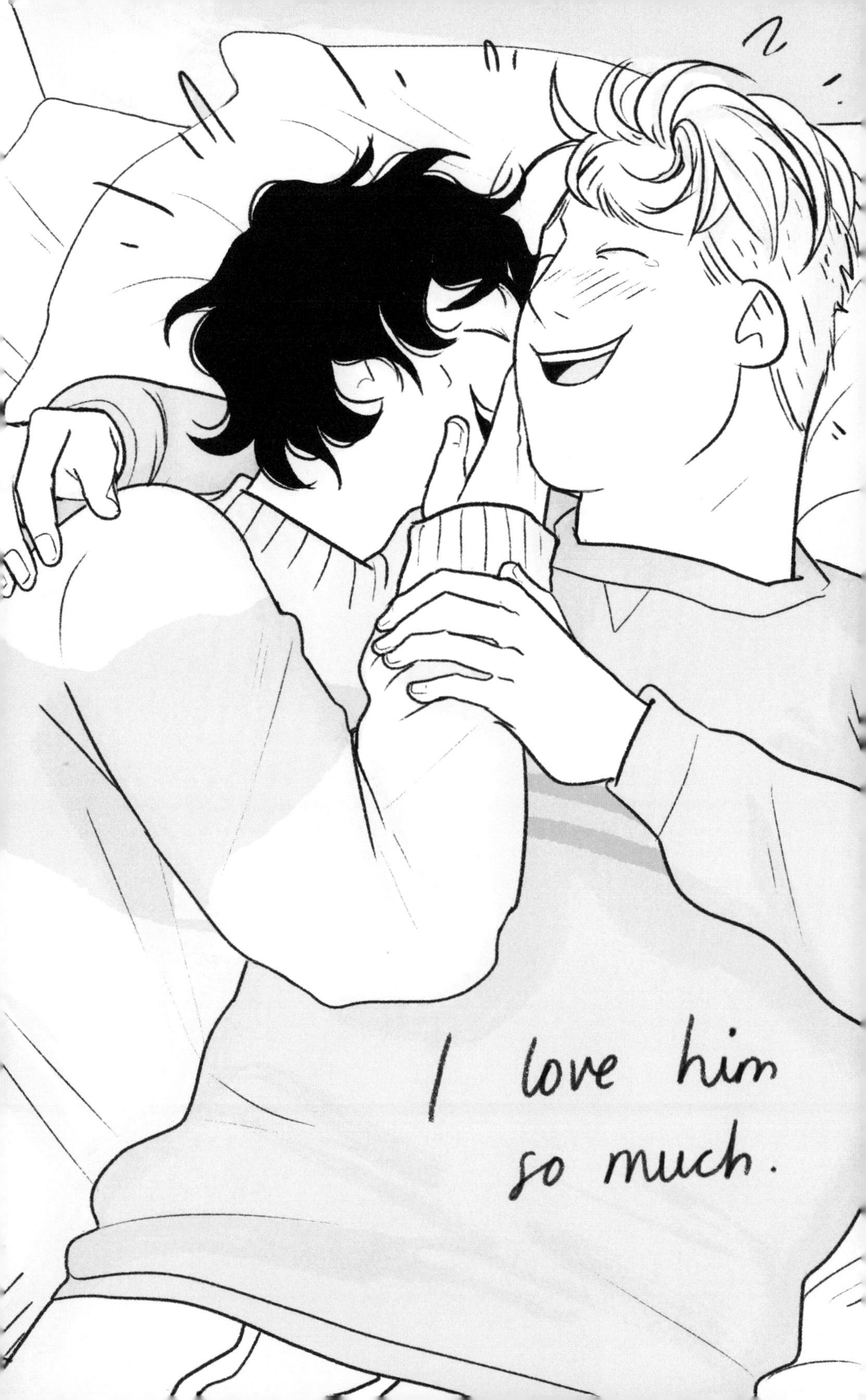
I love him
so much.

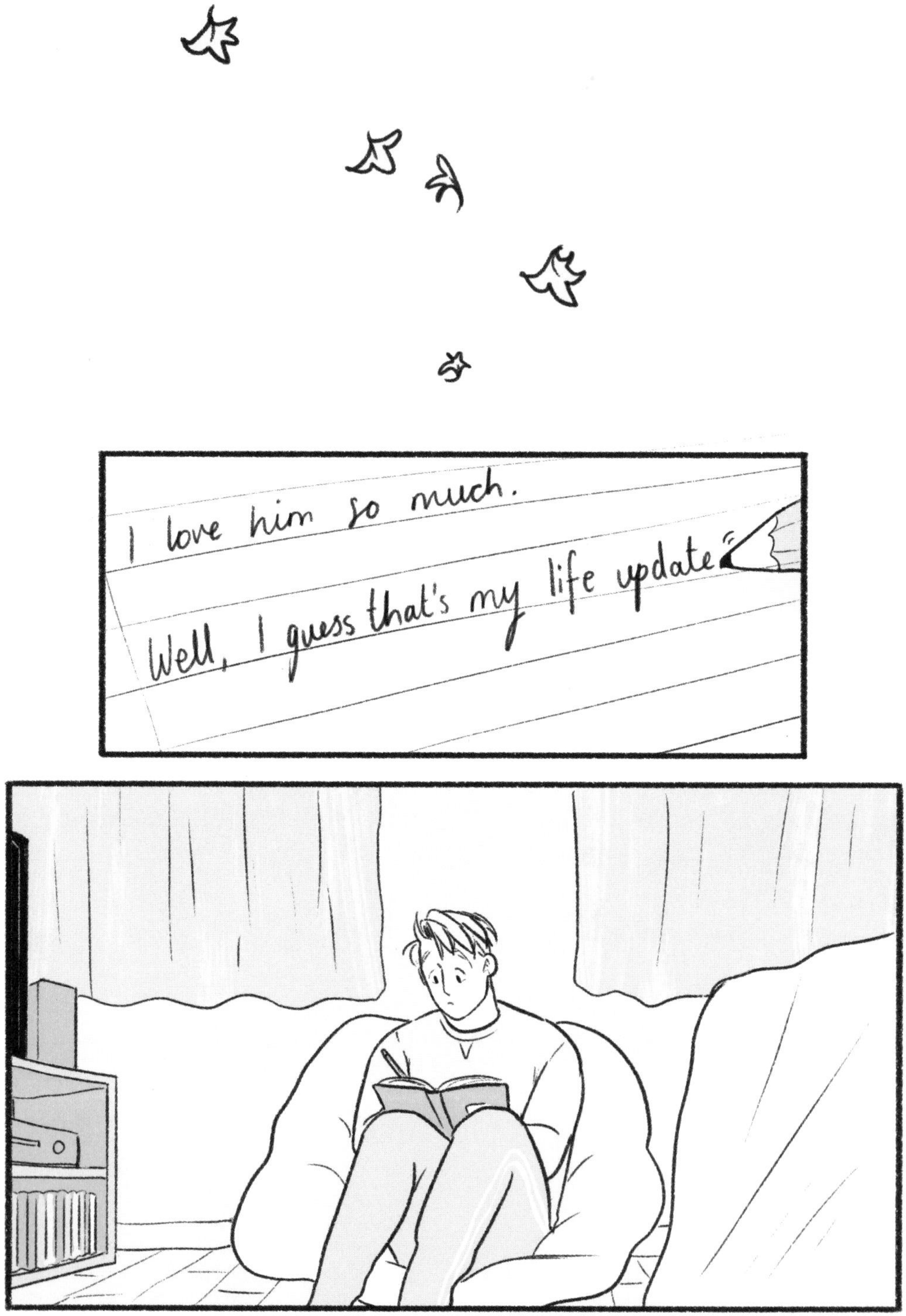
I love him so much.
Well, I guess that's my life update

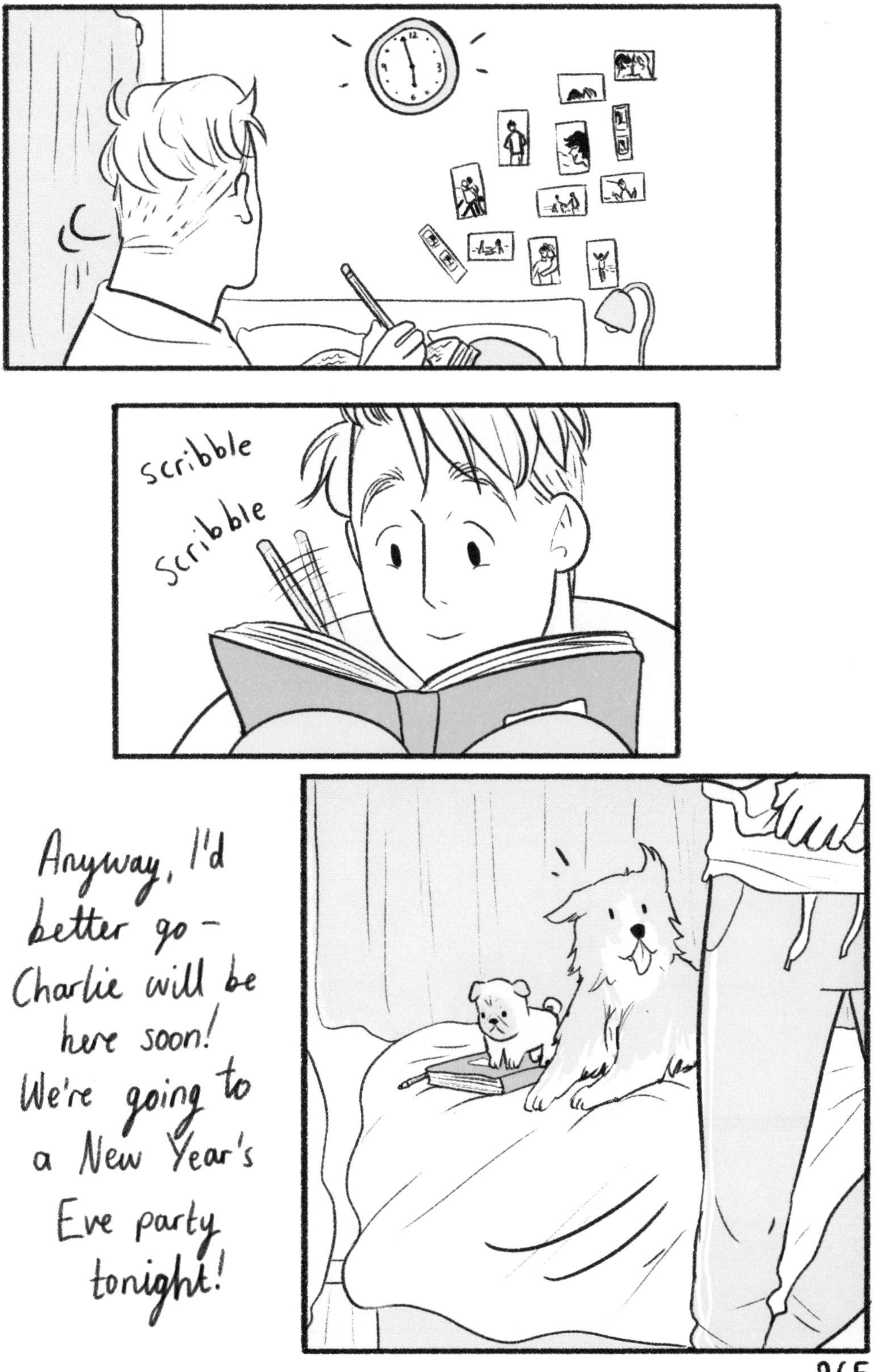
scribble
scribble
Anyway, I'd better go - Charlie will be here soon! We're going to a New Year's Eve party tonight!

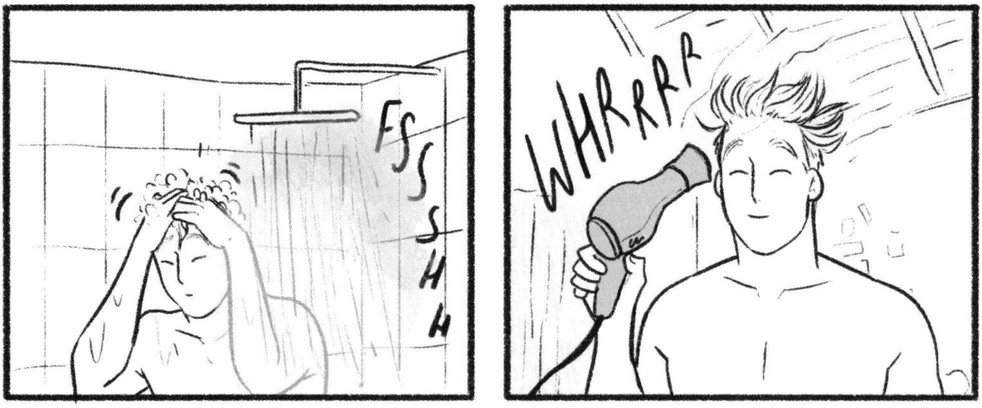
FSSSHH
WHRRRR

A guy in my year is having a big house party with fireworks and stuff.

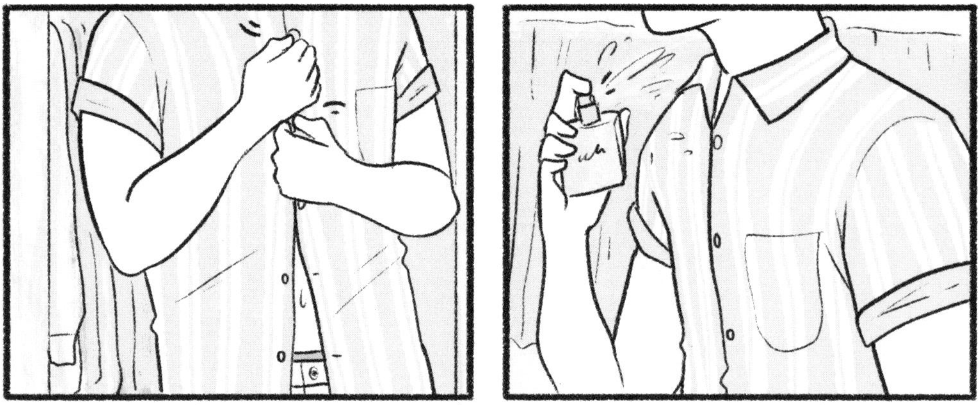

It's the first time Charlie will have been back with a bunch of people from school. We can always leave if it's awful, but I'm excited.

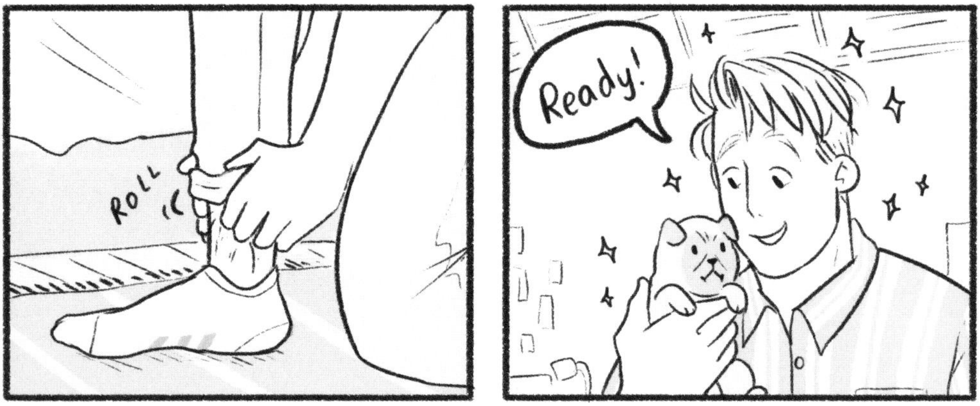
ROLL
Ready!

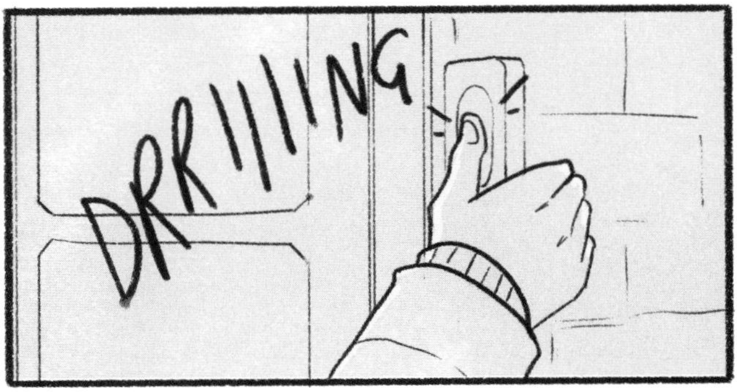
DRRIIIING

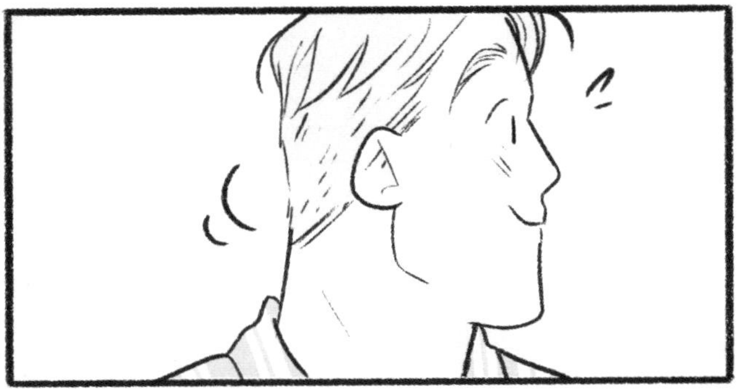

I'm excited to just hang out at a party with my boyfriend.

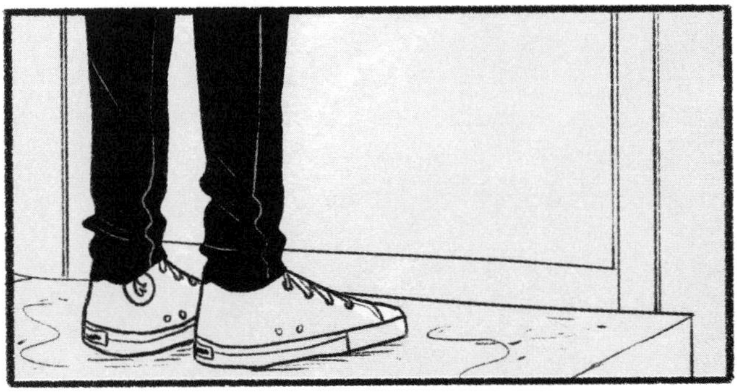

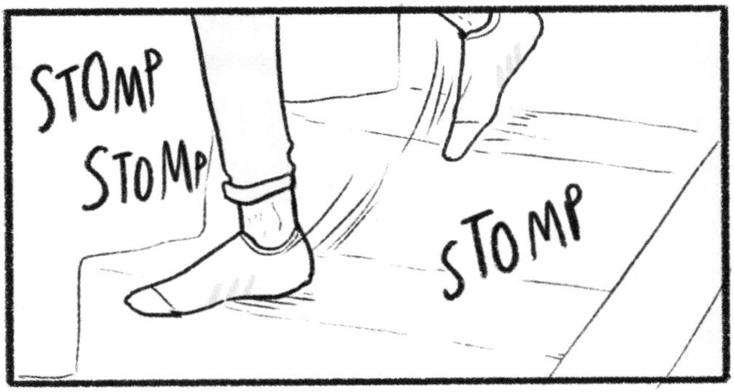
STOMP
STOMP
STOMP

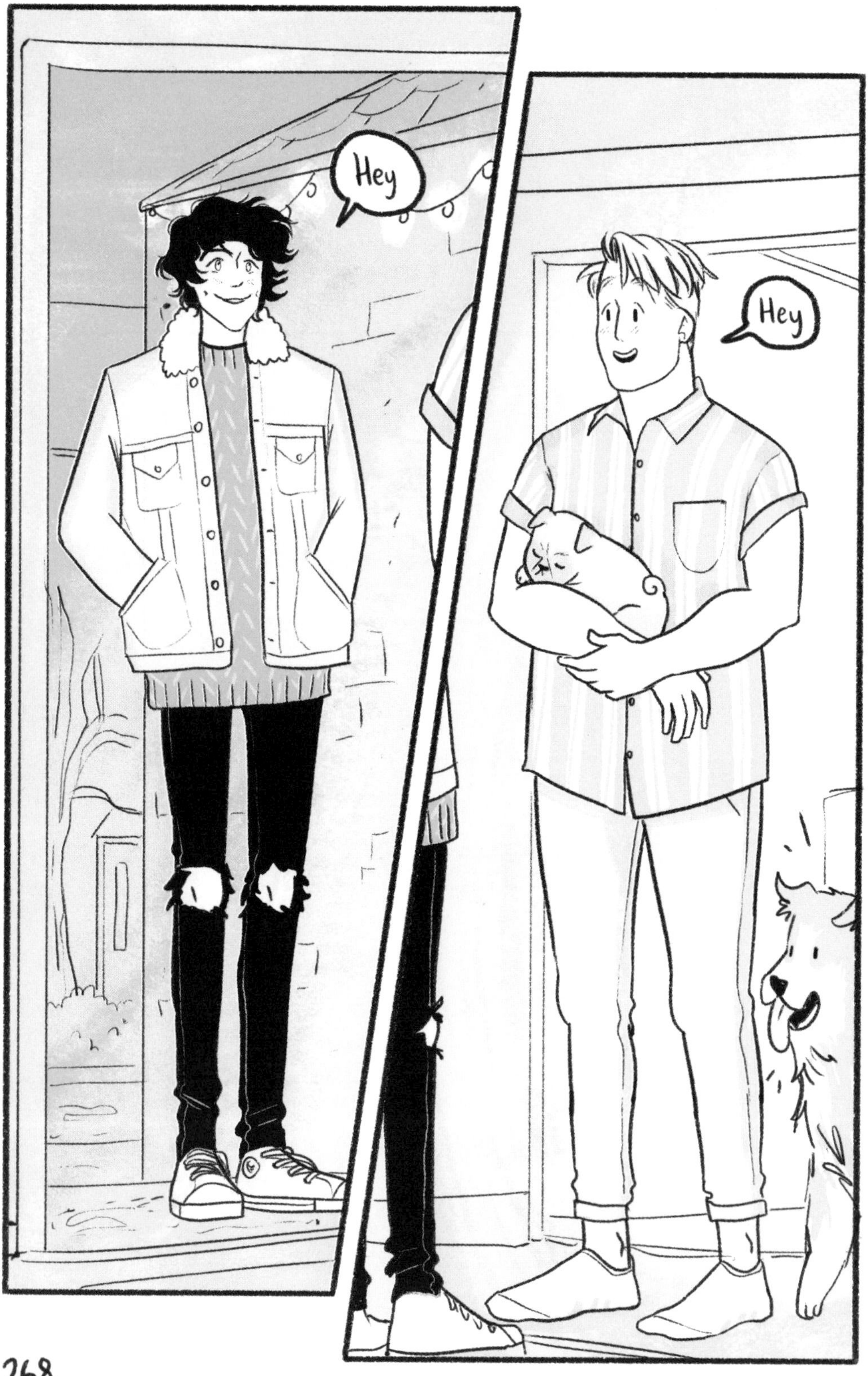
Hey
Hey

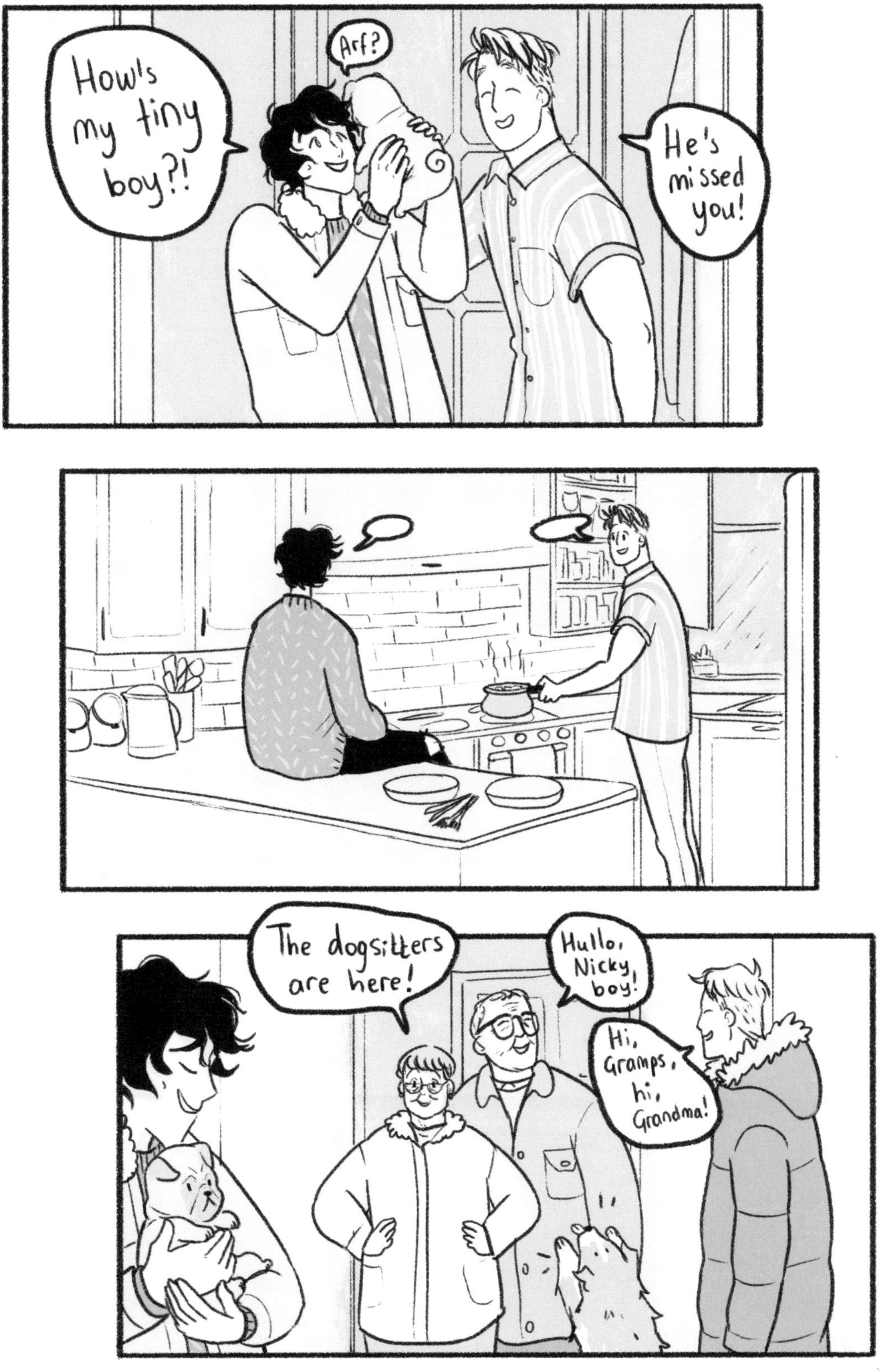
How's my tiny boy?!
Arf?
He's missed you!
The dogsitters are here!
Hullo, Nicky boy!
Hi, Gramps, hi, Grandma!

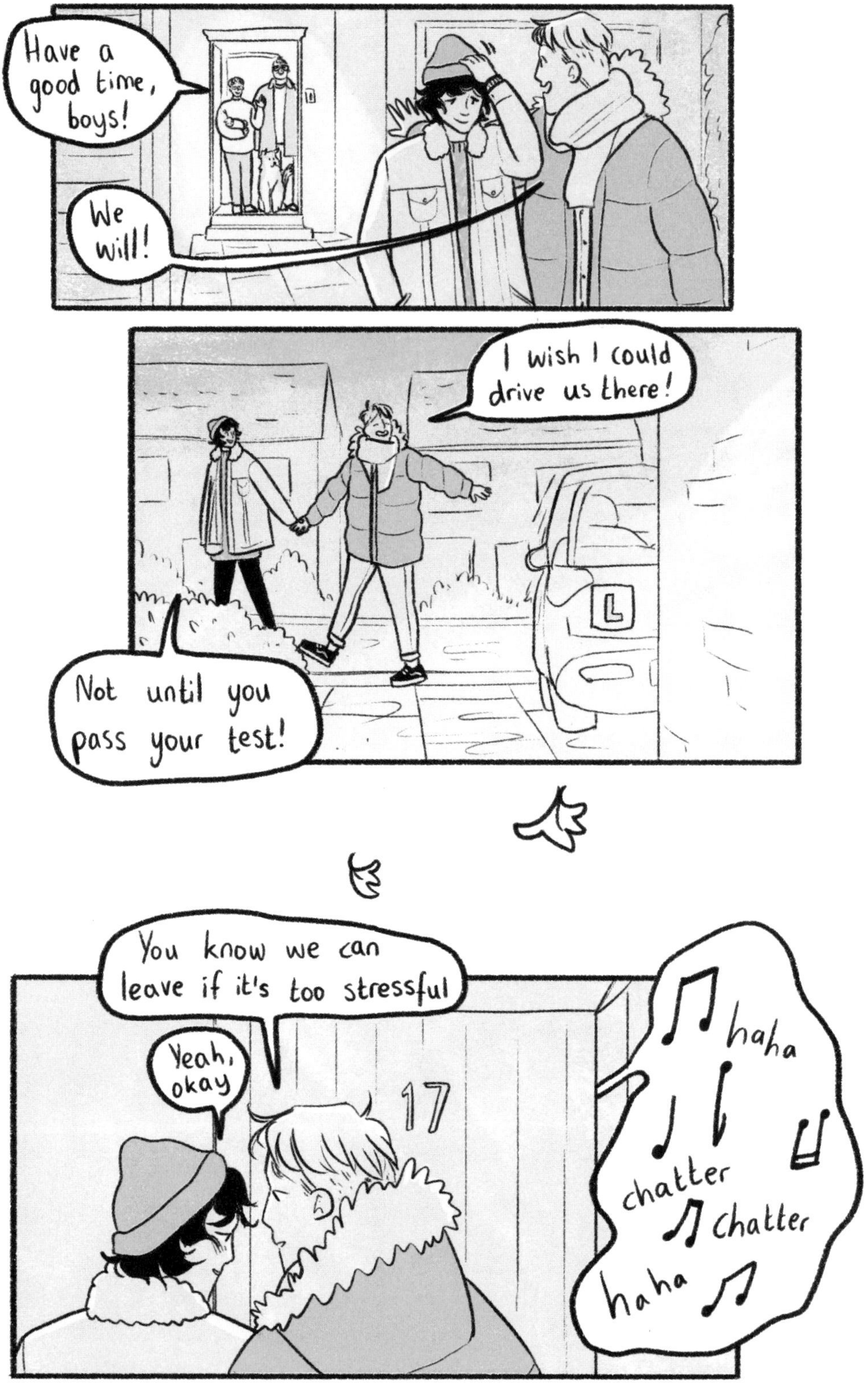
Have a good time, boys!
We will!
I wish I could drive us there!
Not until you pass your test!
You know we can leave if it's too stressful
Yeah, okay
17
haha
chatter
chatter
haha

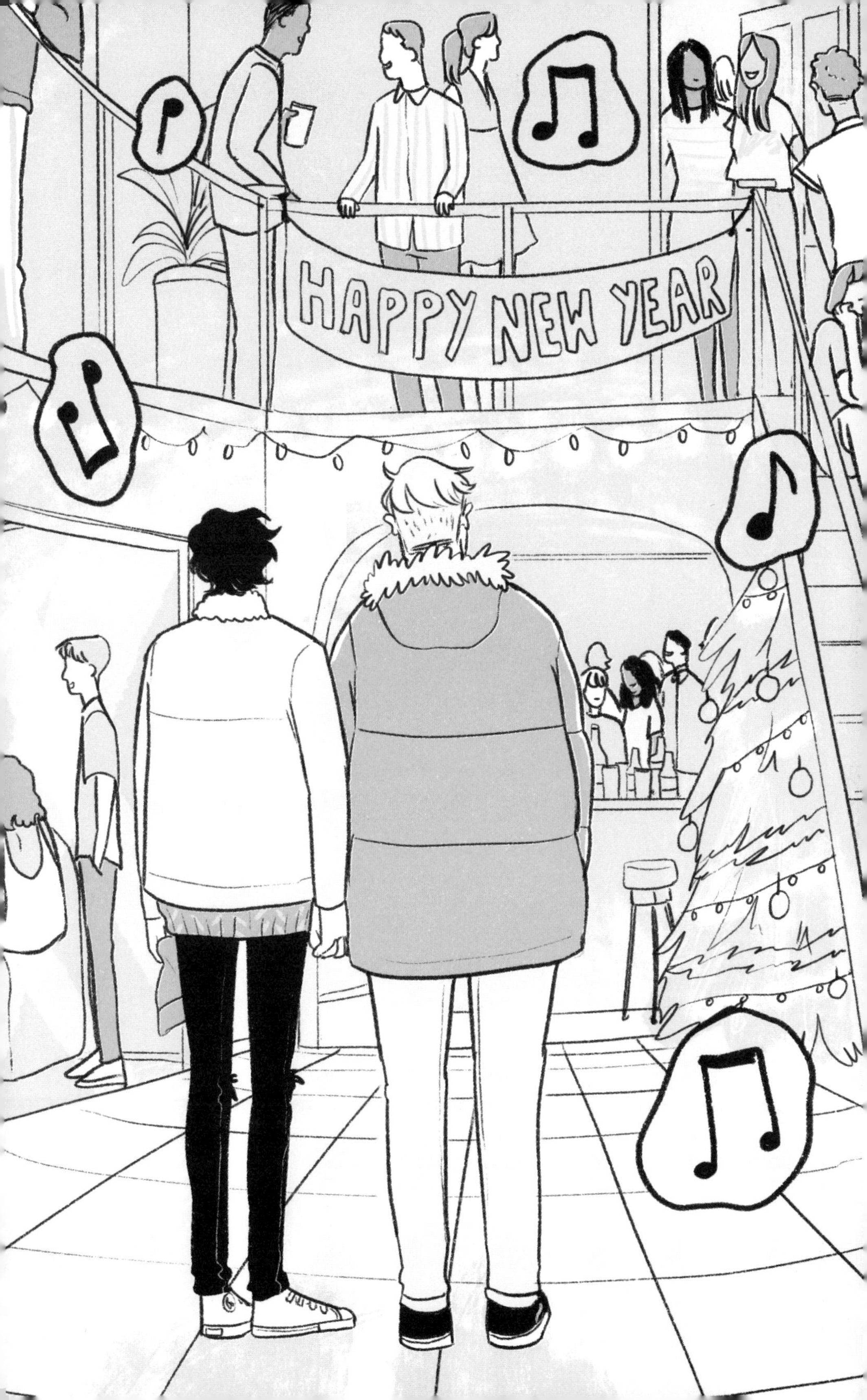
HAPPY NEW YEAR

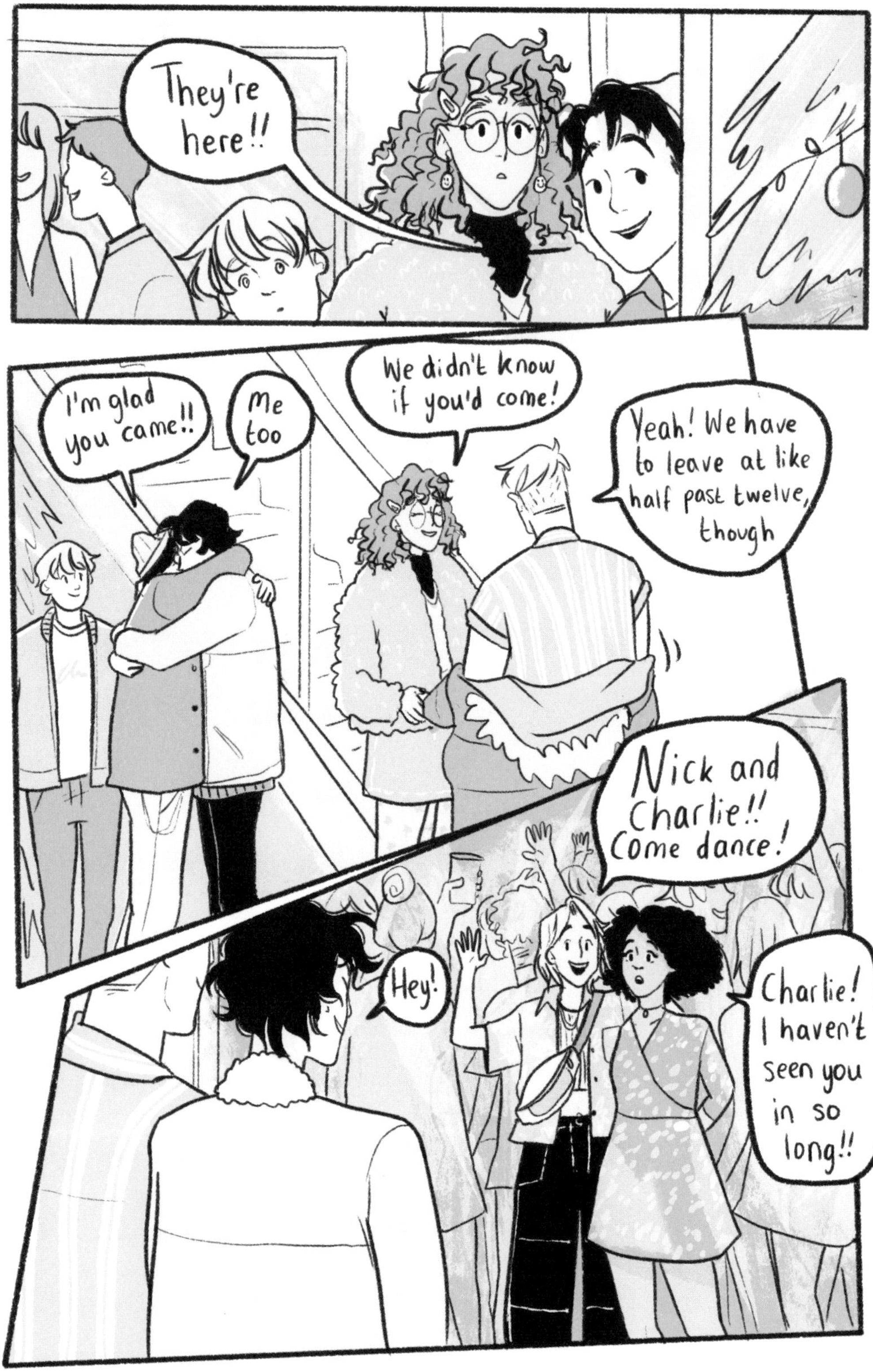
They're here!!
I'm glad you came!!
Me too
We didn't know if you'd come!
Yeah! We have to leave at like half past twelve, though
Nick and Charlie!! Come dance!
Hey!
Charlie! I haven't seen you in so long!!

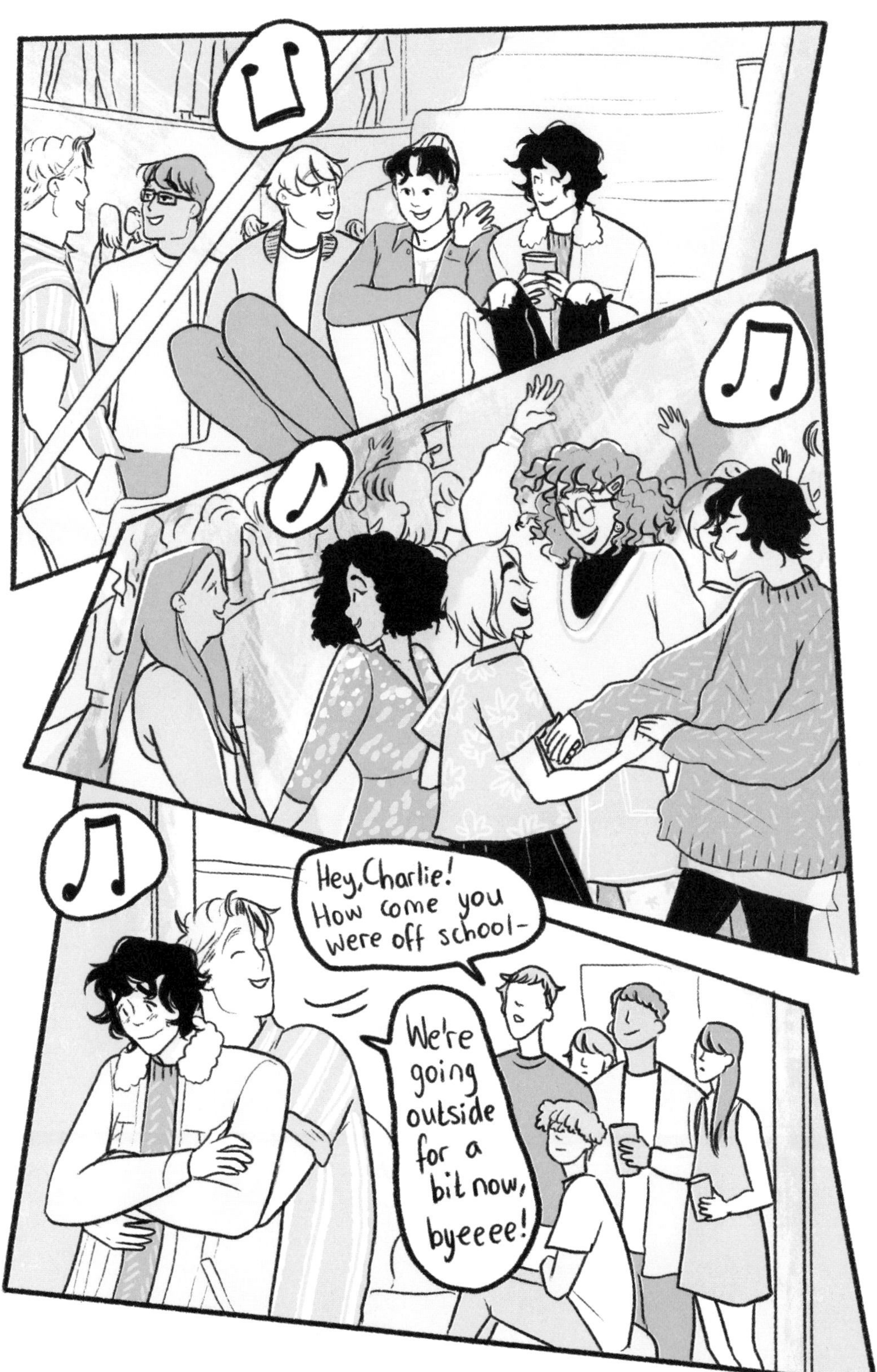
Hey, Charlie! How come you were off school-
We're going outside for a bit now, byeeee!

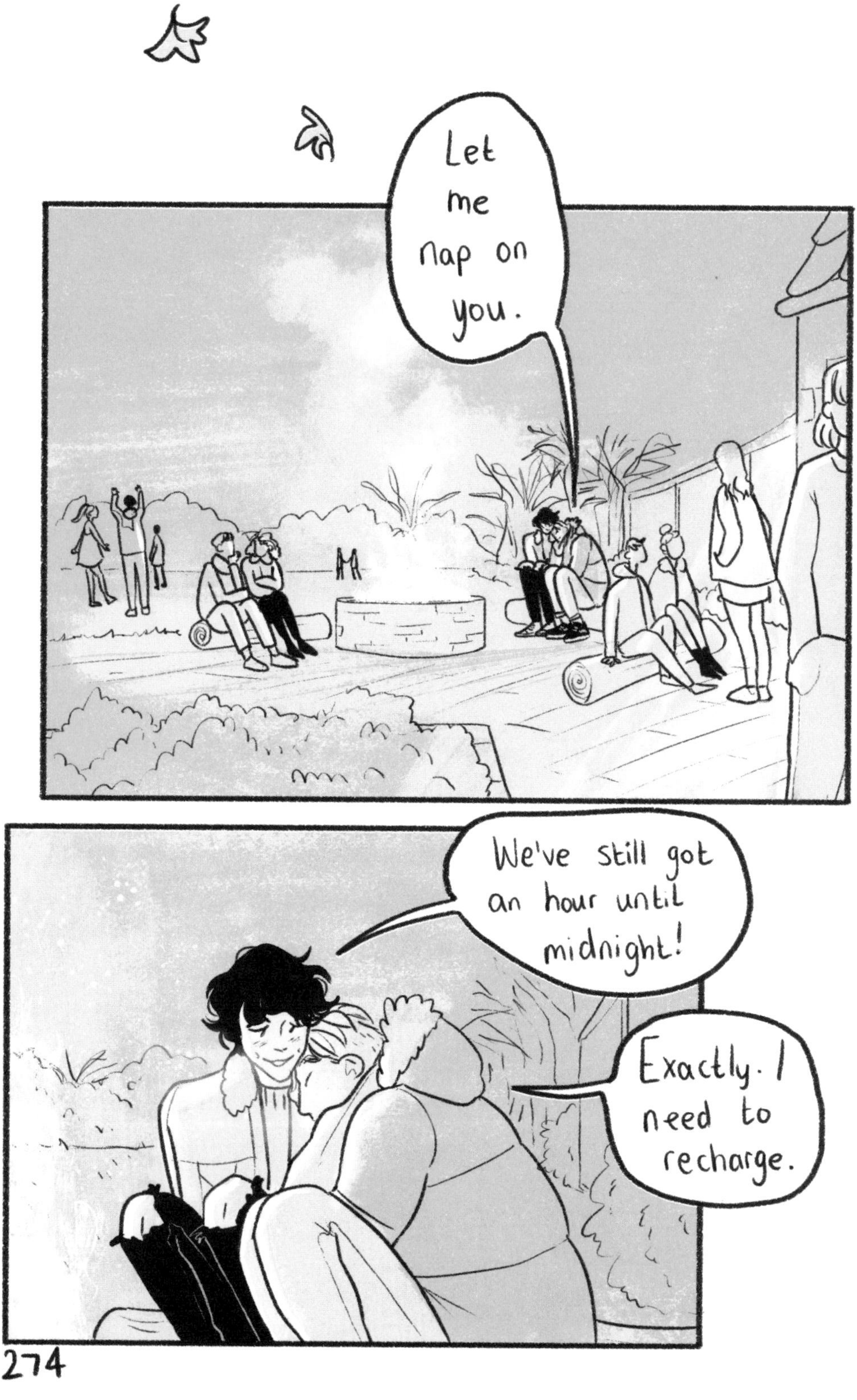
Let me nap on you.
We've still got an hour until midnight!
Exactly. I need to recharge.

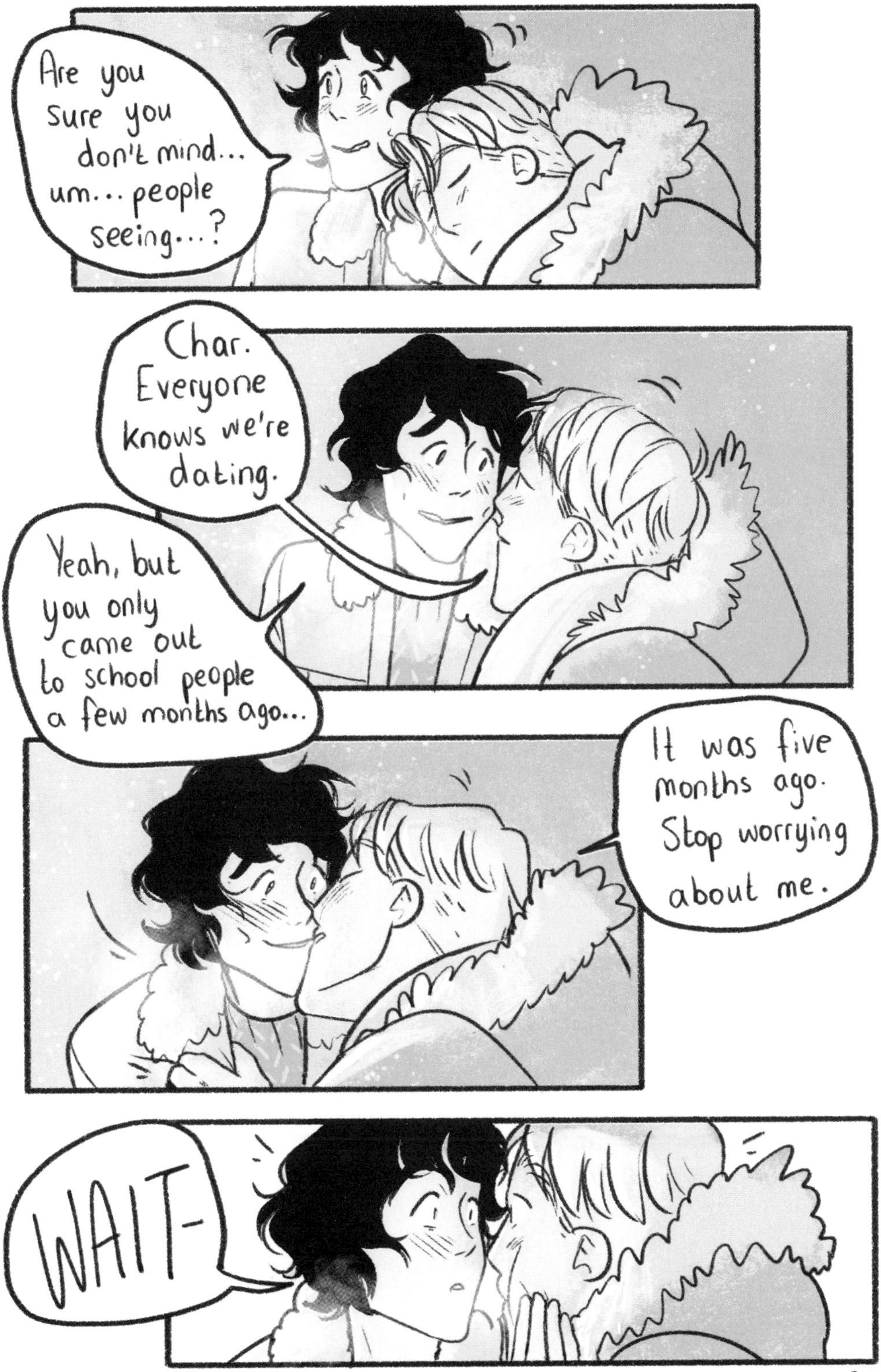
Are you sure you don't mind... um... people seeing...?
Char. Everyone knows we're dating.
Yeah, but you only came out to school people a few months ago...
It was five months ago. Stop worrying about me.
WAIT-

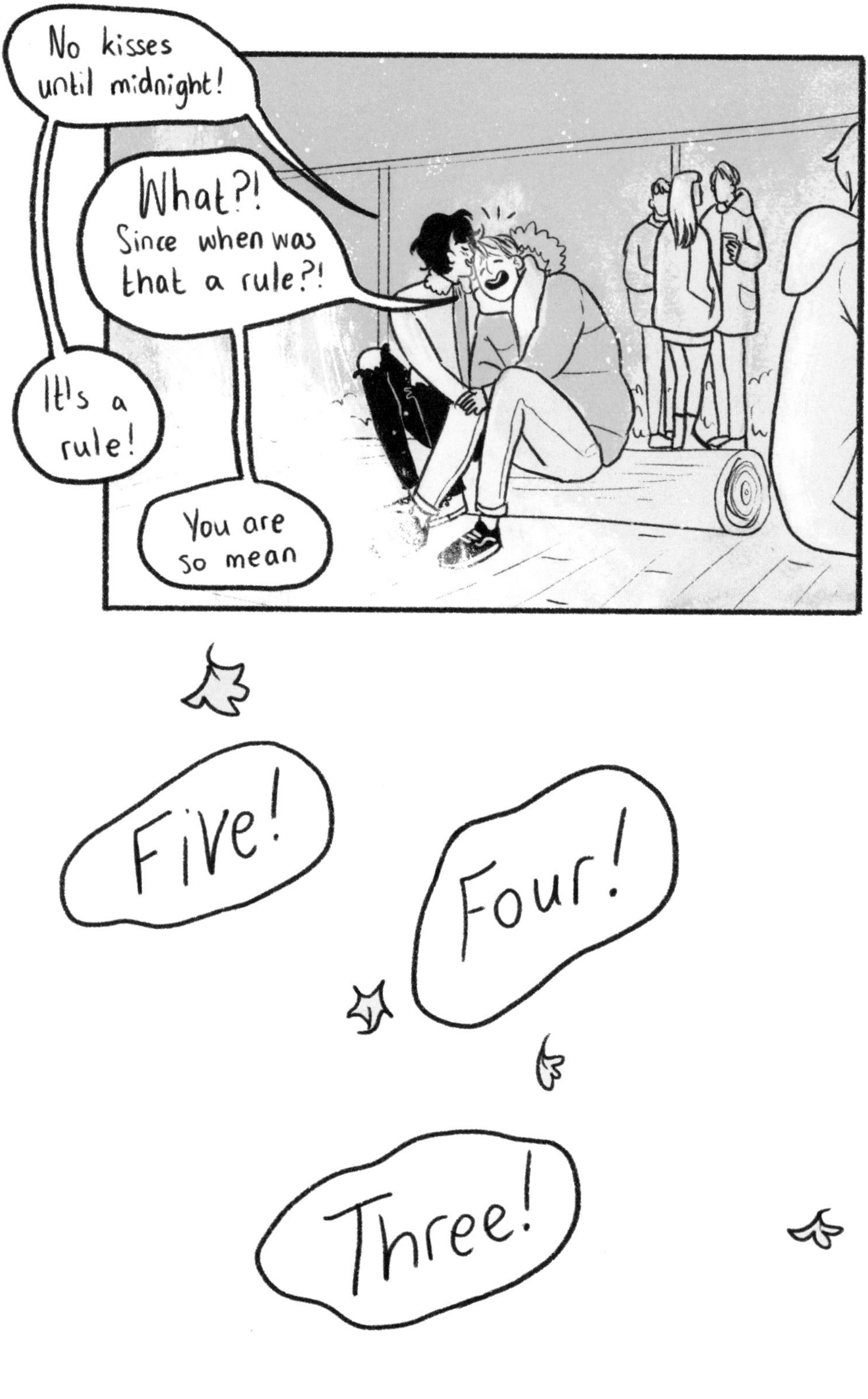
No kisses until midnight!
What?! Since when was that a rule?!
It's a rule!
You are so mean
Five!
Four!
Three!

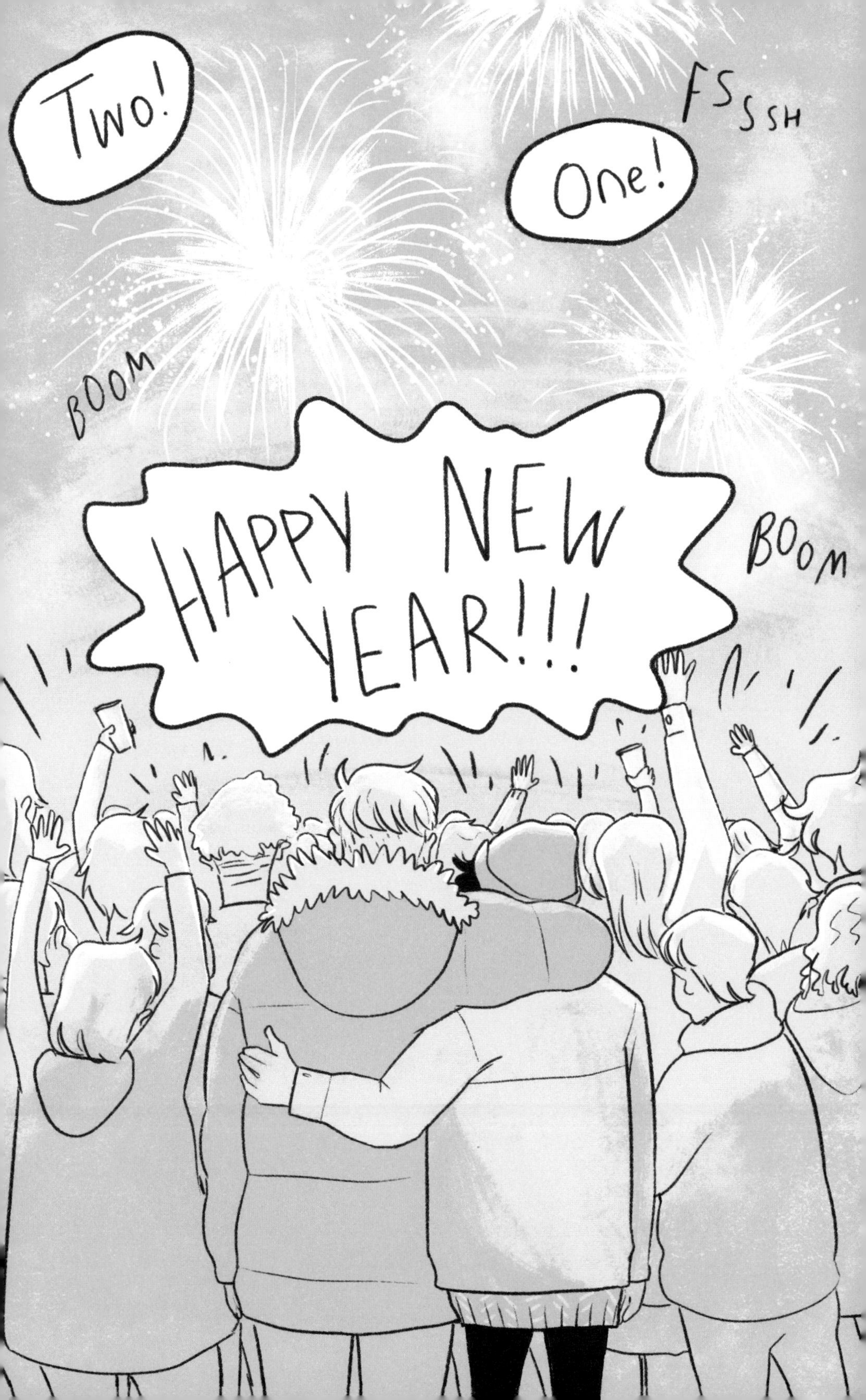
Two!
FSSSH
One!
BOOM
HAPPY NEW YEAR!!!
BOOM

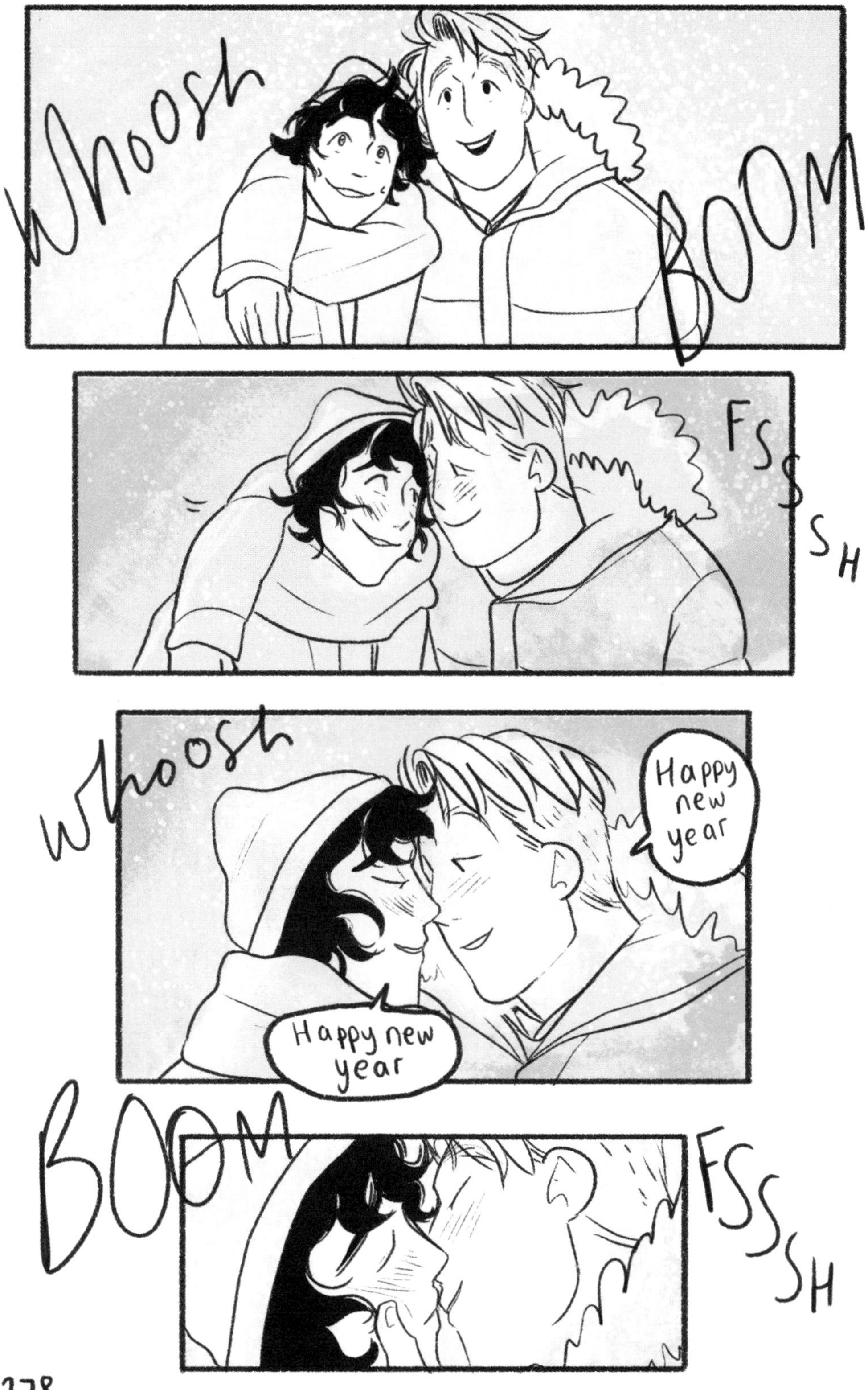
Whoosh
BOOM
FSSSH
Whoosh
Happy new year
Happy new year
BOOM
FSSSH

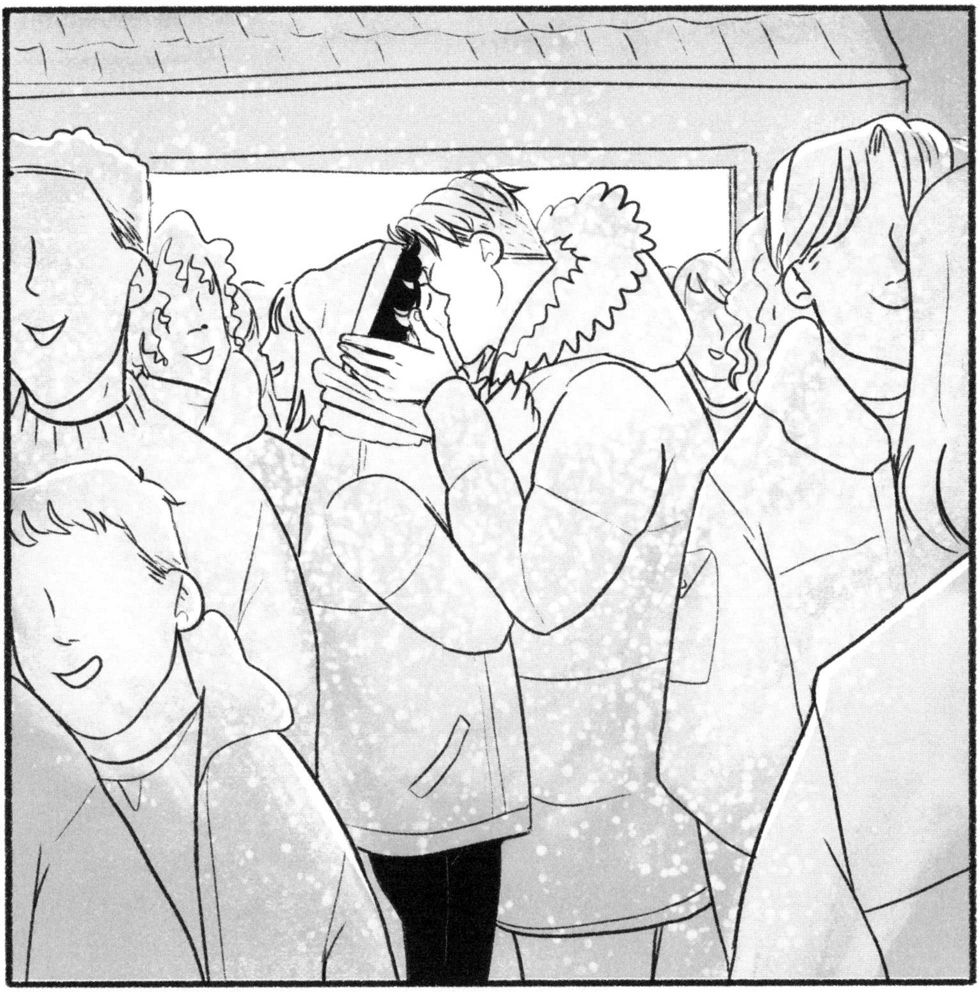

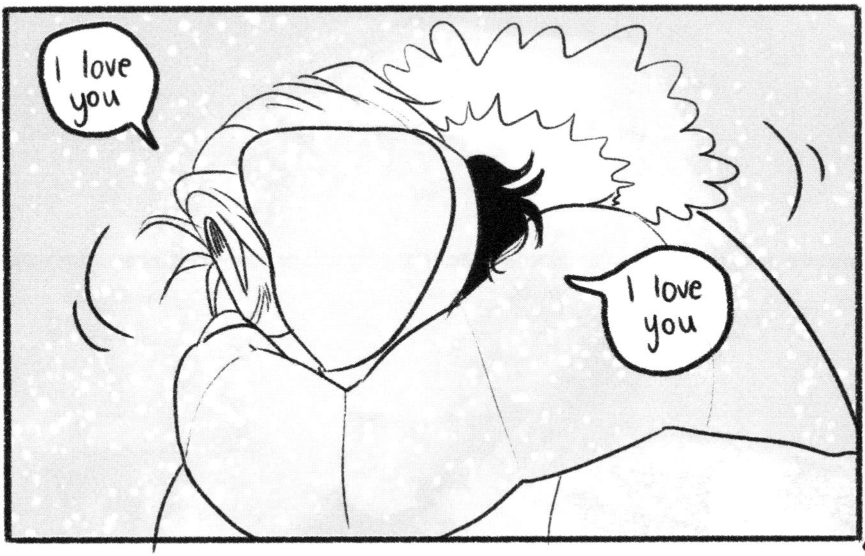
I love you
I love you

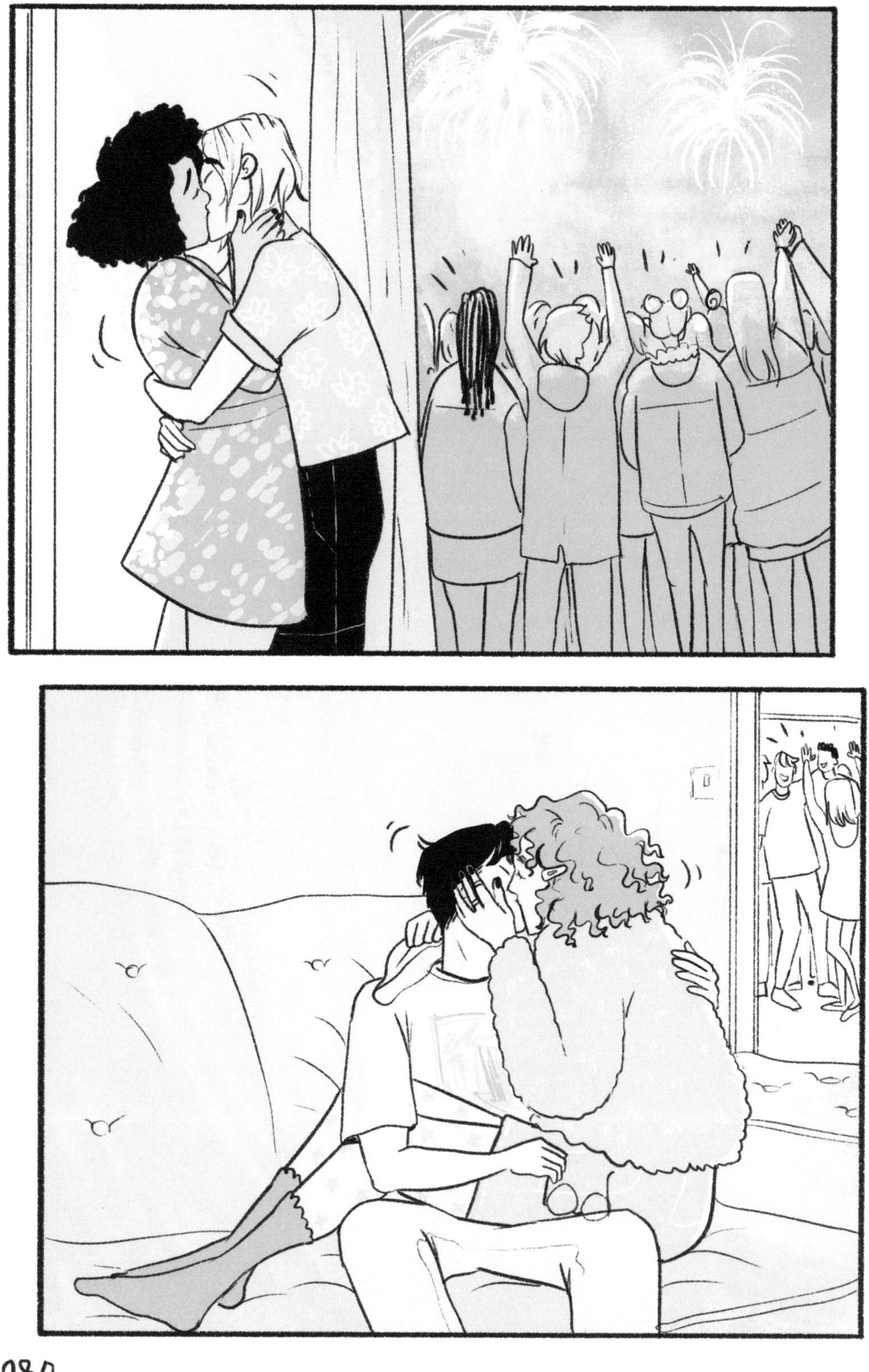

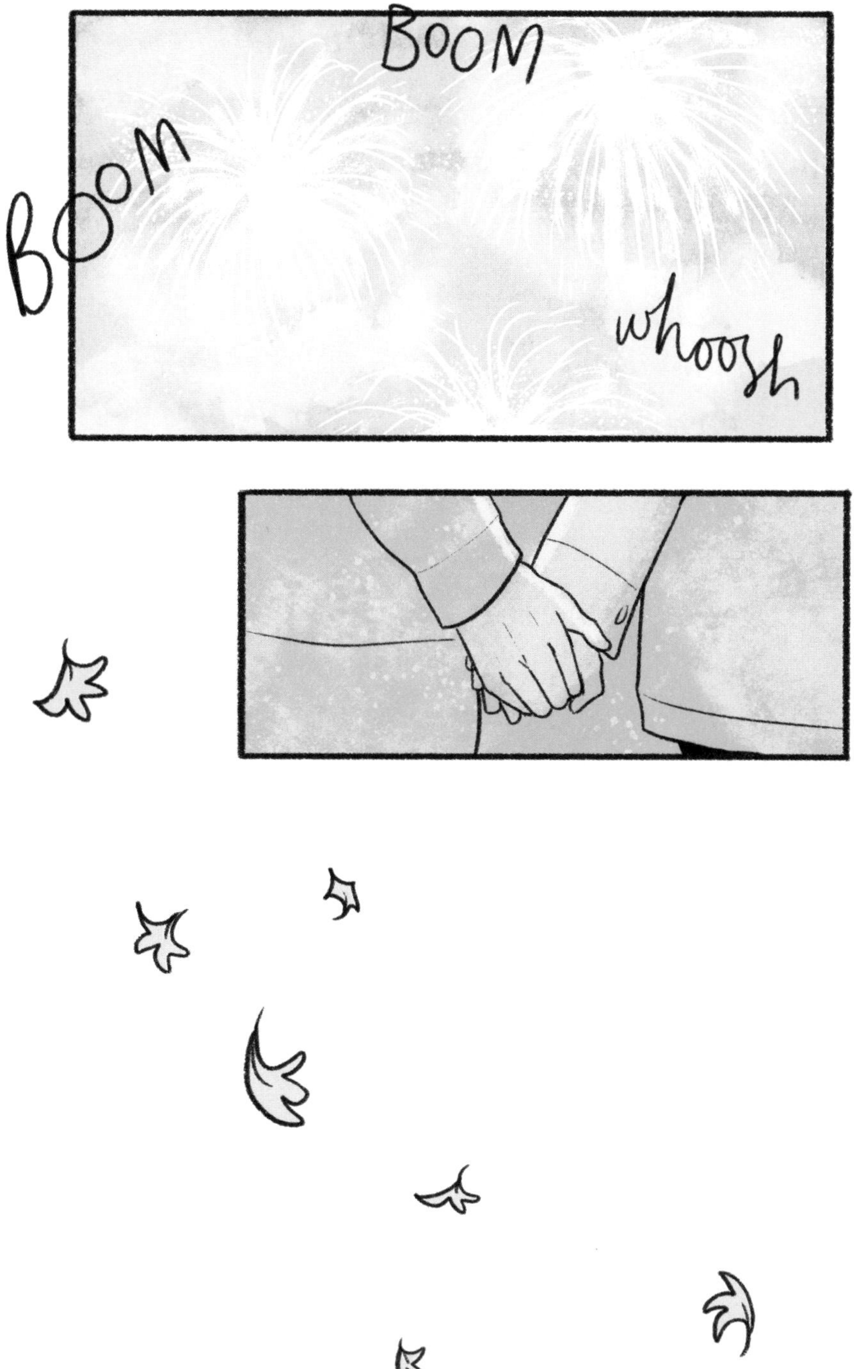
BOOM
BOOM
whoosh

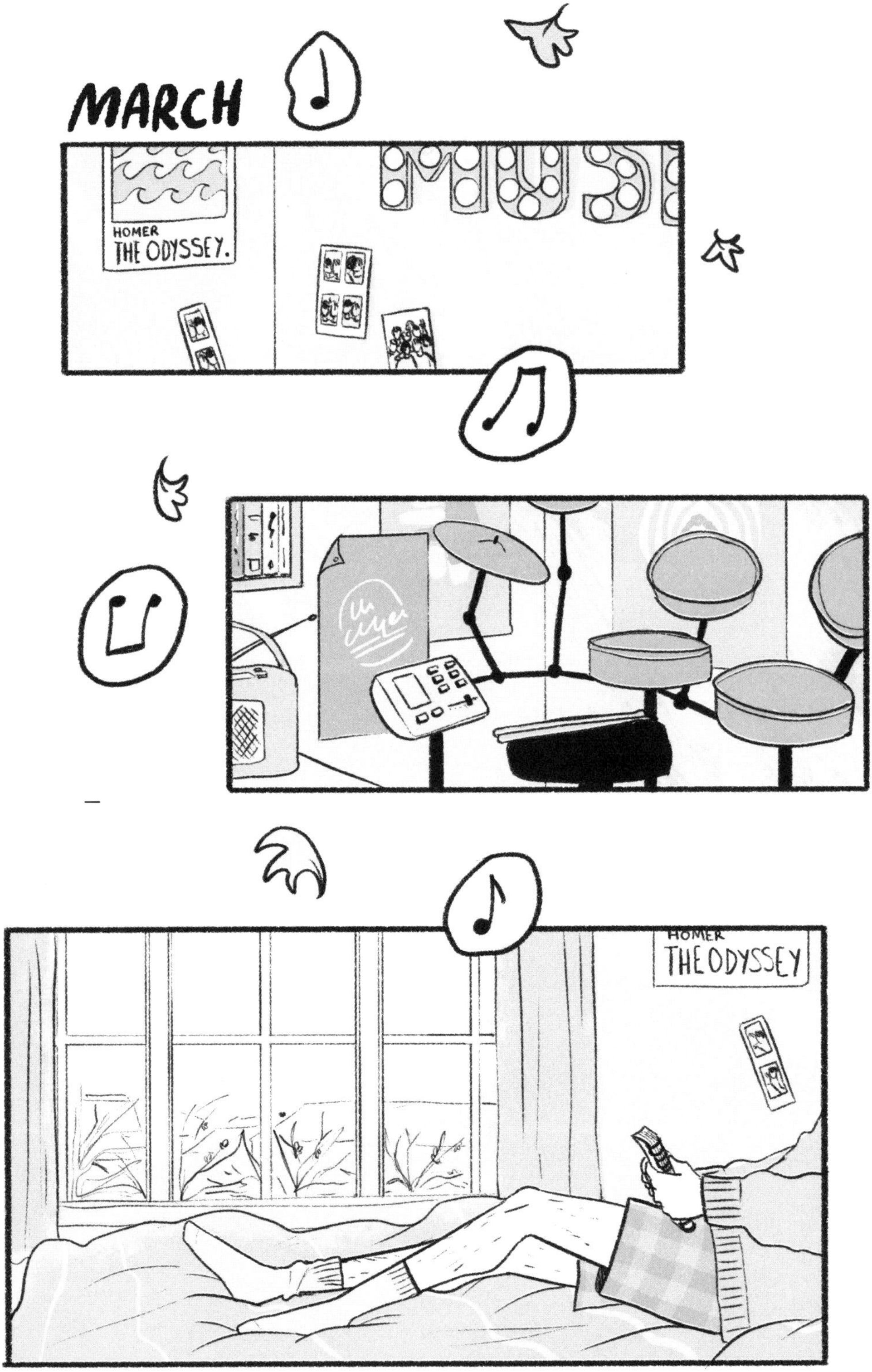
MARCH
HOMER
THE ODYSSEY.
HOMER
THE ODYSSEY

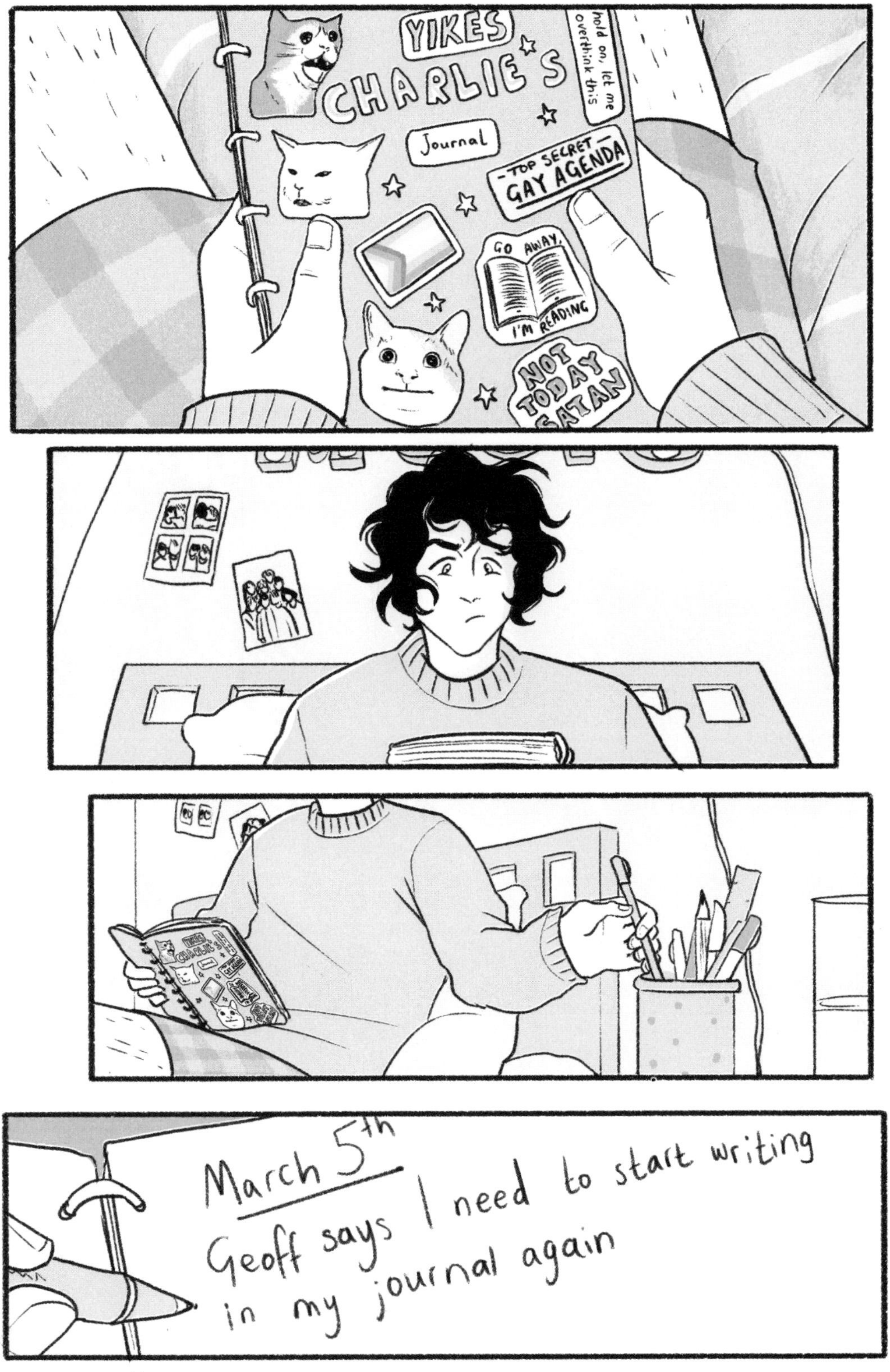
YIKES
CHARLIE'S
Journal
hold on, let me overthink this
TOP SECRET GAY AGENDA
GO AWAY, I'M READING
NOT TODAY SATAN
March 5th
Geoff says I need to start writing in my journal again

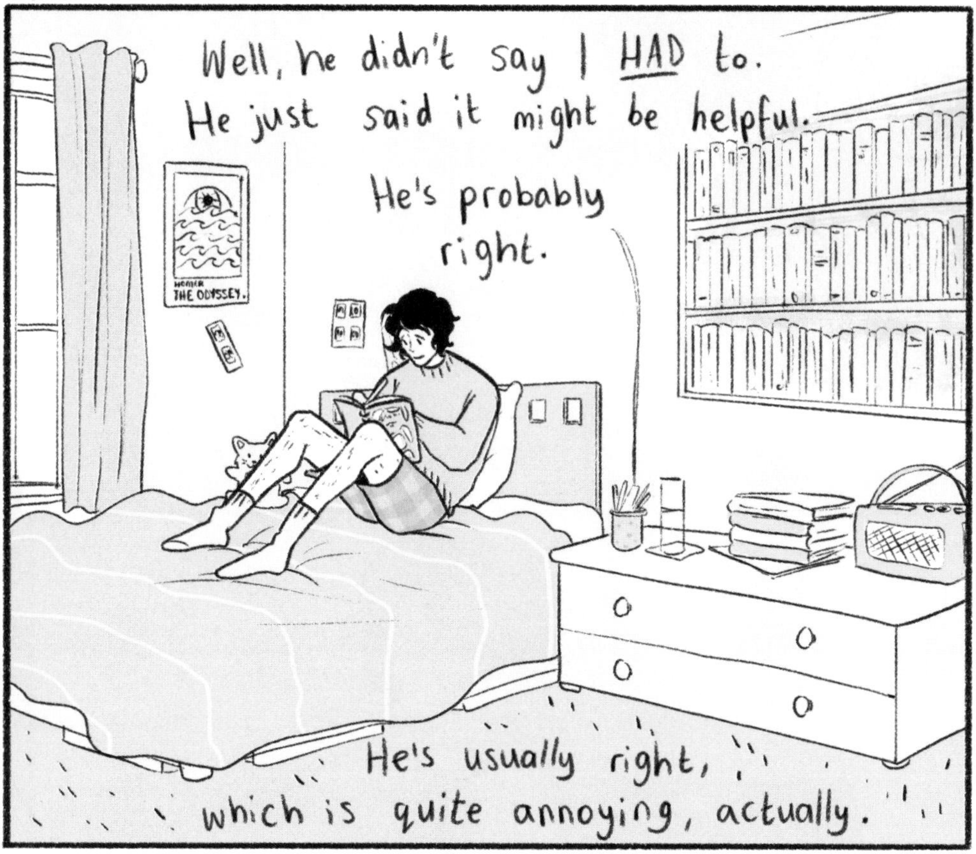
Well, he didn't say I HAD to. He just said it might be helpful.
He's probably right.
HOMER
THE ODYSSEY.
He's usually right, which is quite annoying, actually.

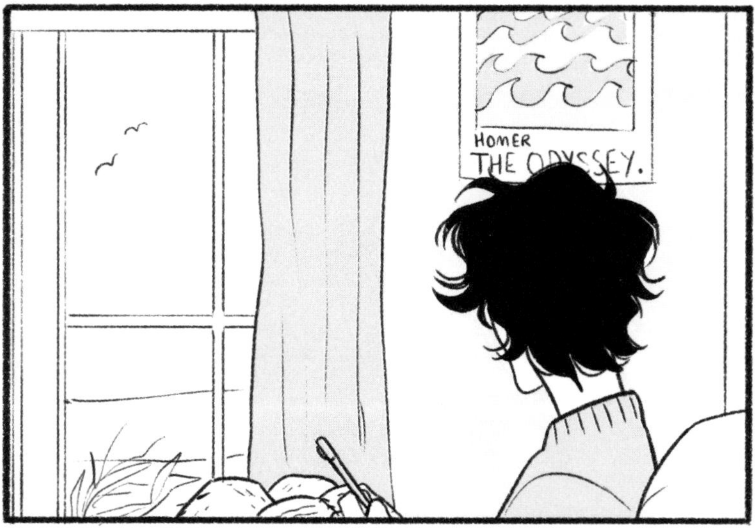
HOMER
THE ODYSSEY.

But I haven't written in here since last summer, and a lot has happened since then.

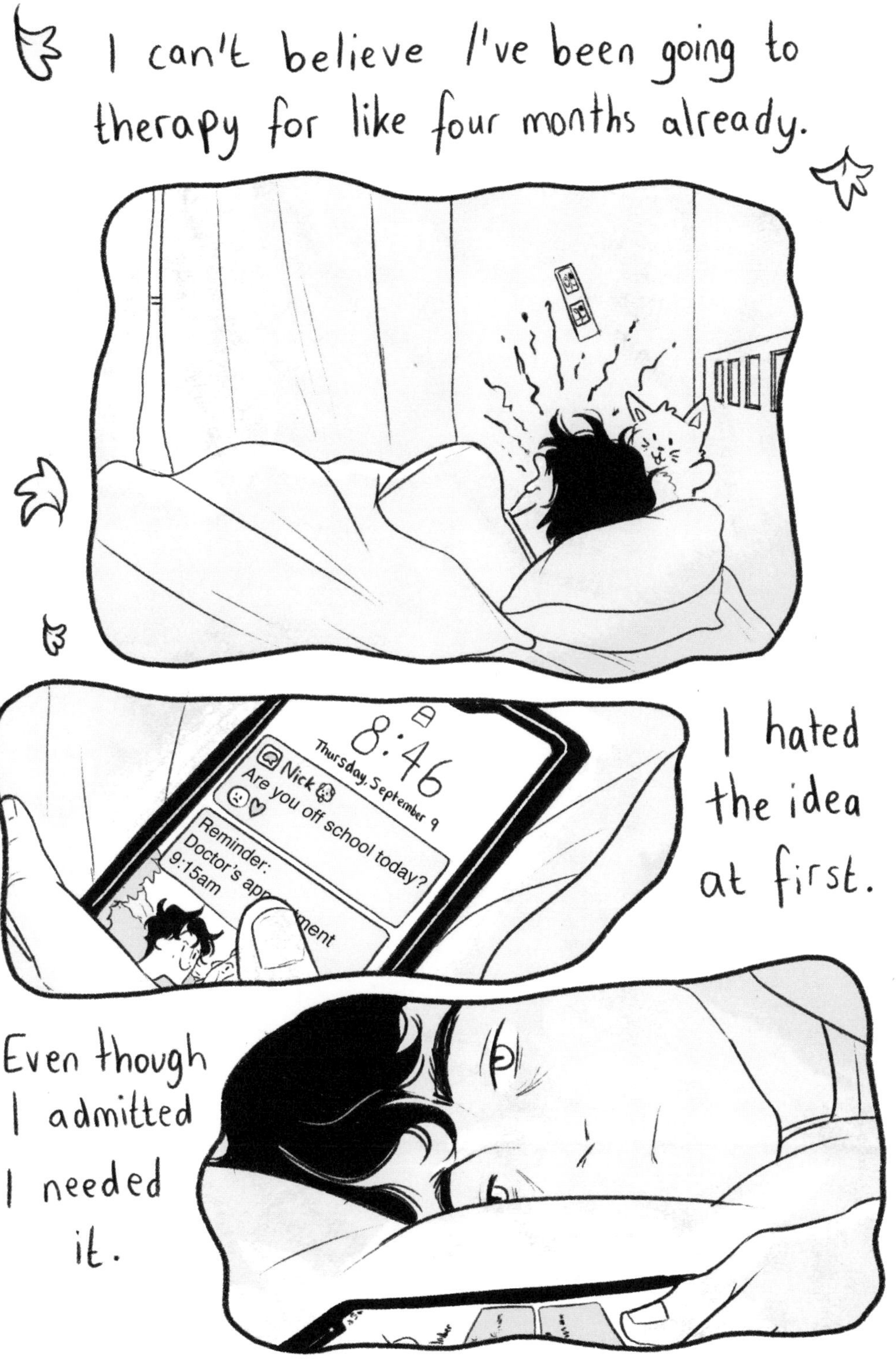
I can't believe I've been going to therapy for like four months already.
8:46
Thursday, September 9
Nick
Are you off school today?
Reminder:
9:15am
I hated the idea at first.
Even though I admitted I needed it.

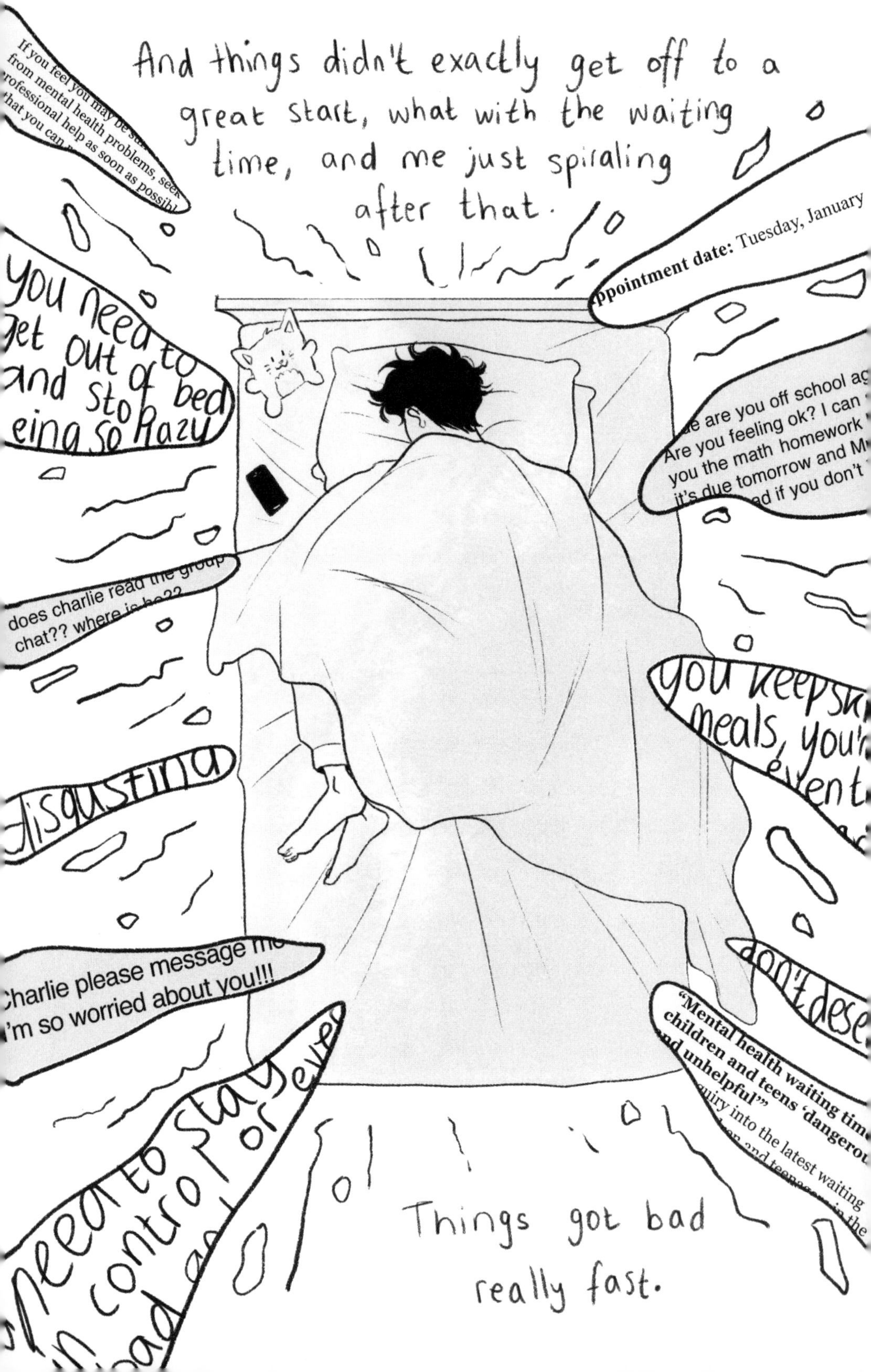
And things didn't exactly get off to a great start, what with the waiting time, and me just spiraling after that.
If you feel you may be
from mental health problems, seek
professional help as soon as
that you can
you need to get out of bed and stop being so lazy
ppointment date: Tuesday, January
are you off school ag
Are you feeling ok? I can
you the math homework
tomorrow and M
it's due
if you don't
does charlie read the group chat?? where is he??
disgusting
you keep sk
meals, you'r
charlie please message me
I'm so worried about you!!!
don't dese
"Mental health waiting tim
children and teens 'dangerou
and unhelpful'"
into the latest waiting
need to stay in control or ever
Things got bad really fast.

Spending a few weeks in a psych ward was obviously not my plan.

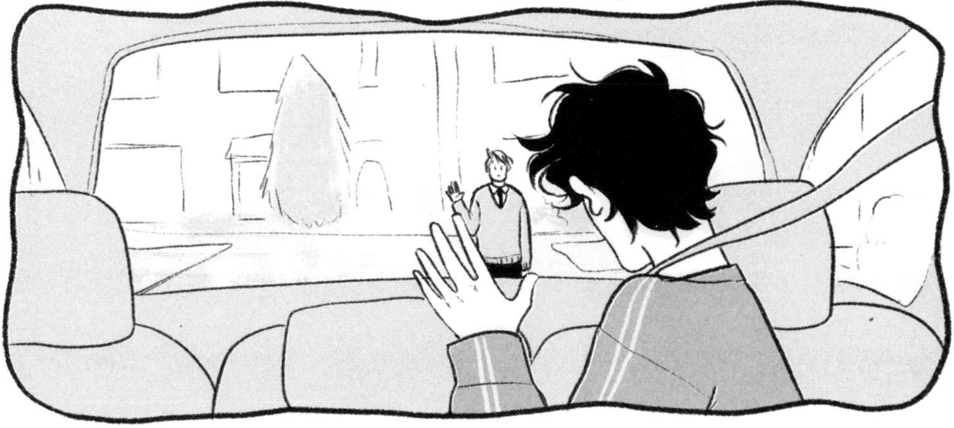

And there were some ups and downs there, sure.

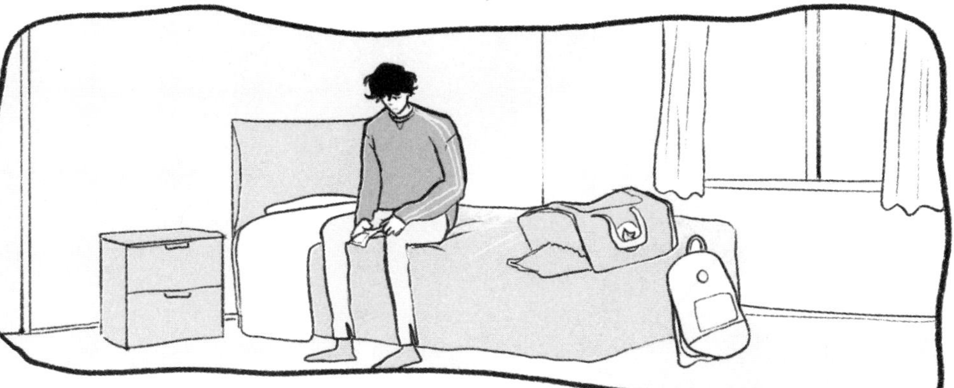

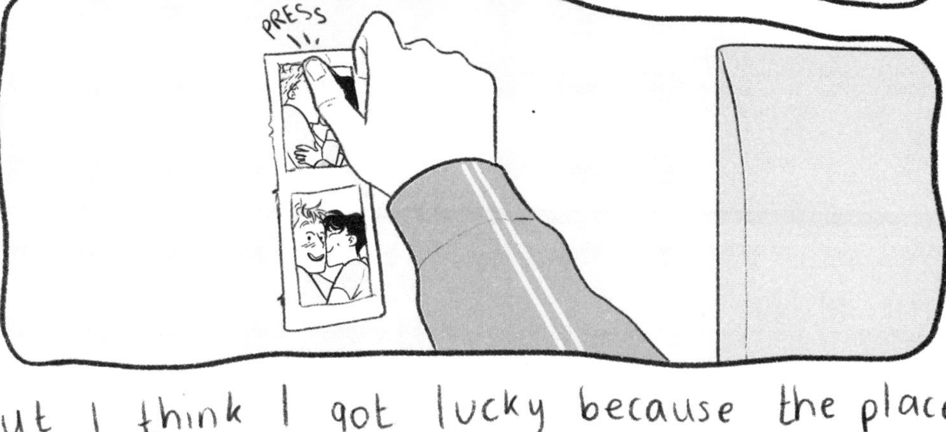
PRESS

But I think I got lucky because the place I went to was actually helpful.

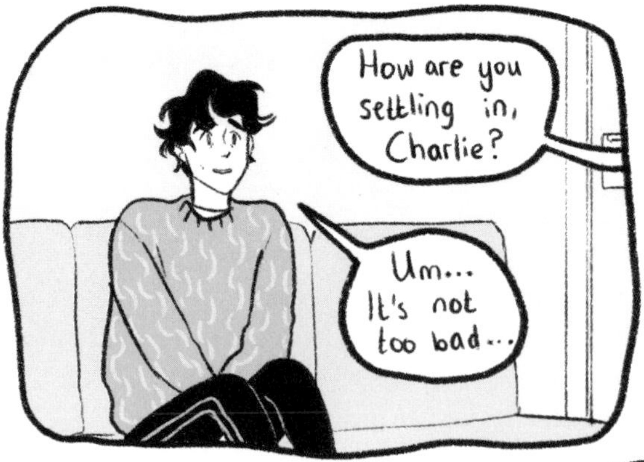
How are you settling in, Charlie?
Um... It's not too bad...

I started therapy there. Not with Geoff, but the therapist was really nice.

I had a nutritionist, too. I know that isn't the case for all psych wards.

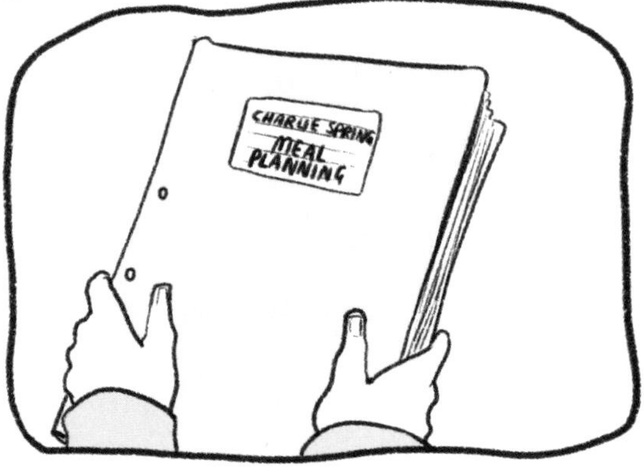
CHARLIE SPRING
MEAL PLANNING

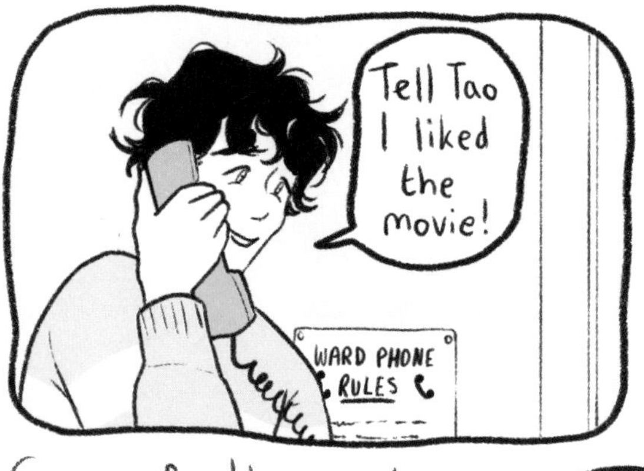
Tell Tao I liked the movie!
WARD PHONE RULES

We weren't allowed cell phones, but I could still call home from the ward phone.

Some of the rules kinda sucked, and some days were awful, but a lot of it was fine. I even made a couple of friends.

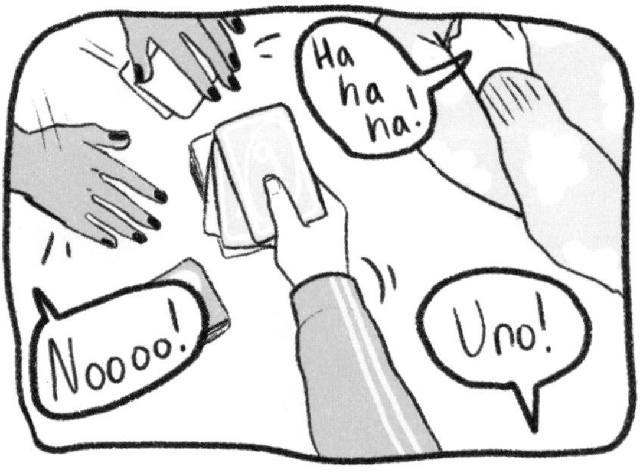
Ha ha ha!
Noooo!
Uno!

At first, I think there was a big part of me that didn't even want to get better. That just wanted to keep pretending I was fine, so I didn't have to put in the effort to change.

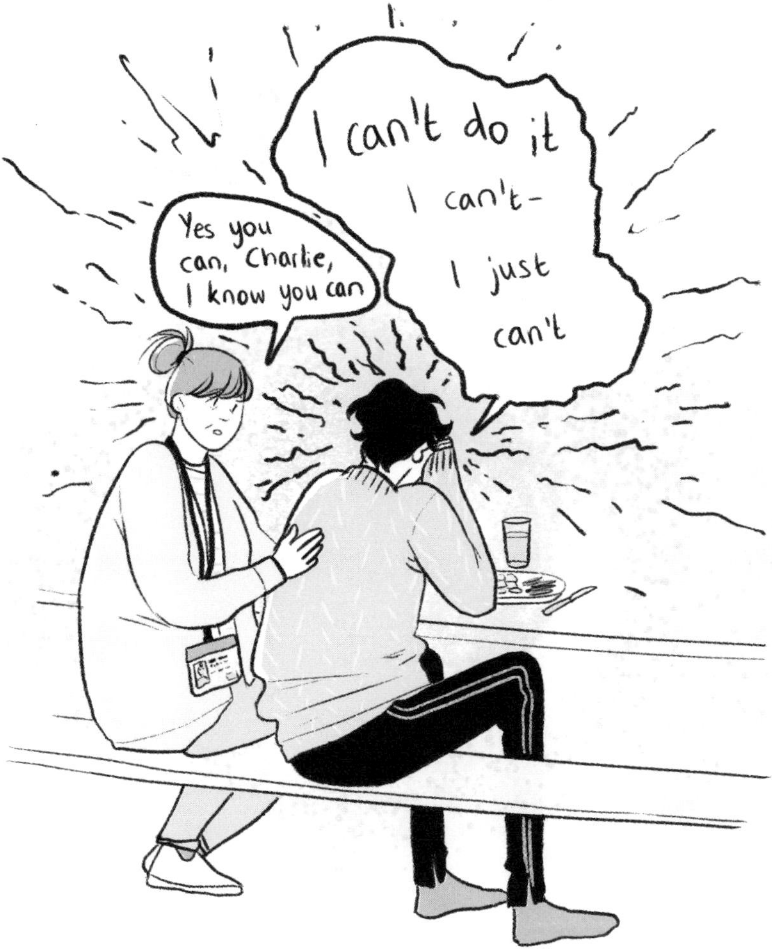
Yes you can, Charlie, I know you can
I can't do it
I can't-
I just can't

I was so scared of losing control.

Eating was something I could control.

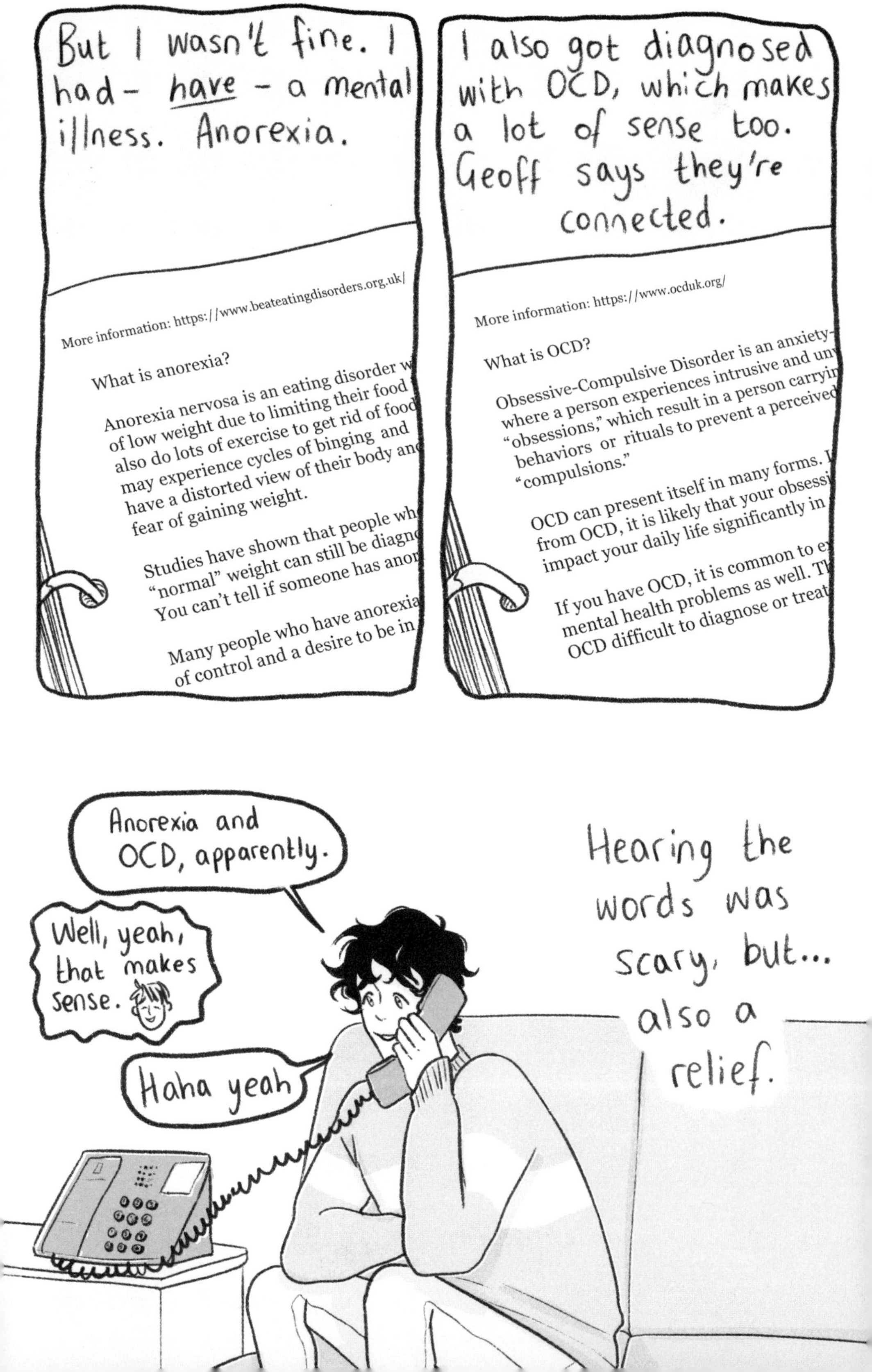

But I wasn't fine. I had- have - a mental illness. Anorexia.
More information: https://www.beateatingdisorders.org.uk/
What is anorexia?
Anorexia nervosa is an eating disorder
of low weight due to limiting their food
also do lots of exercise to get rid of food
may experience cycles of binging and
have a distorted view of their body
fear of gaining weight.
Studies have shown that people
"normal" weight can still be
You can't tell if someone has
Many people who have anorexia
of control and a desire to be in
I also got diagnosed with OCD, which makes a lot of sense too. Geoff says they're connected.
More information: https://www.ocduk.org/
What is OCD?
Obsessive-Compulsive Disorder is an anxiety-
where a person experiences intrusive and
"obsessions," which result in a person
behaviors or rituals to prevent a perceived
"compulsions."
OCD can present itself in many forms.
from OCD, it is likely that your
impact your daily life significantly in
If you have OCD, it is common to
mental health problems as well.
OCD difficult to diagnose or
Anorexia and OCD, apparently.
Well, yeah, that makes sense.
Haha yeah
Hearing the words was scary, but... also a relief.

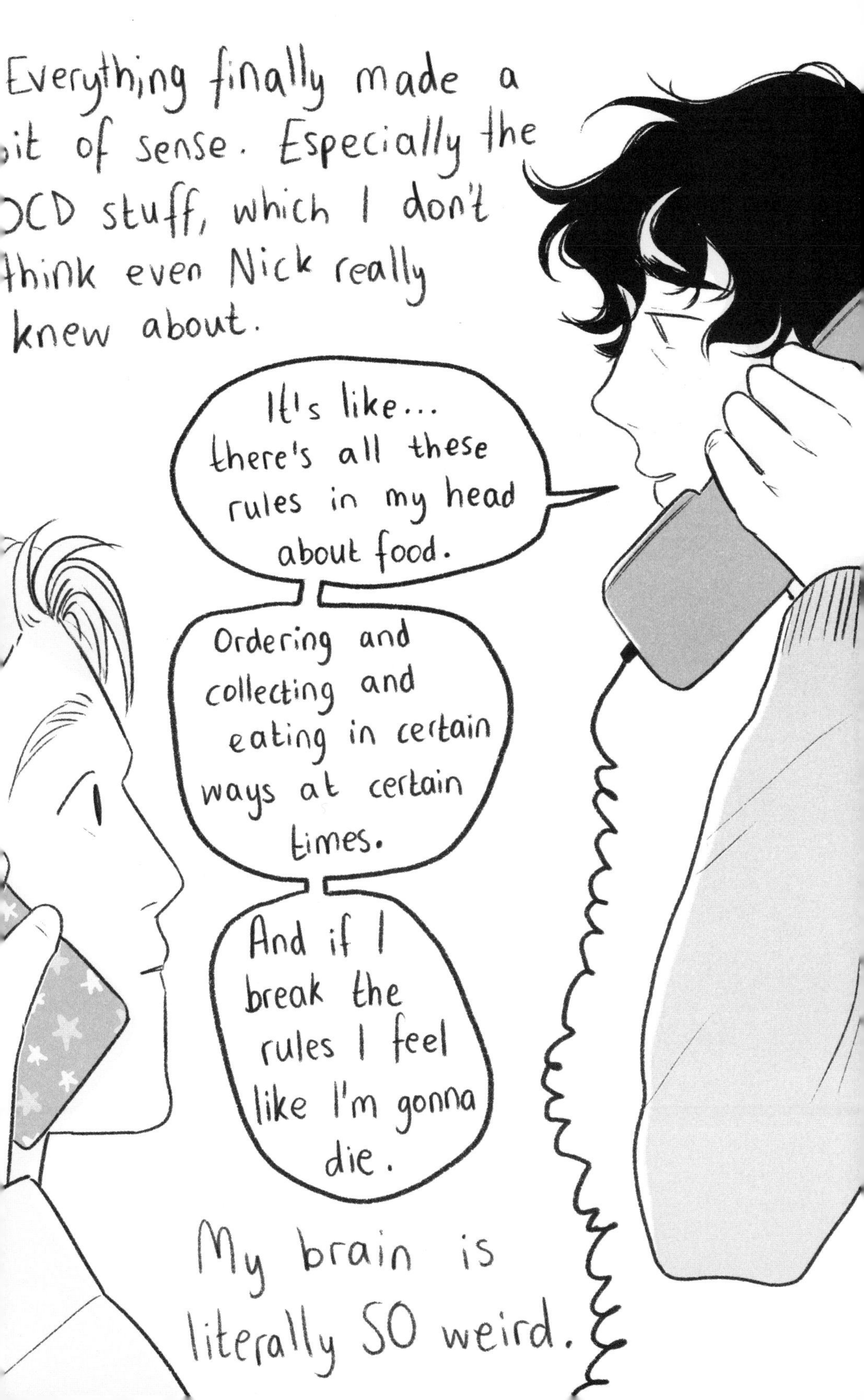
Everything finally made a bit of sense. Especially the OCD stuff, which I don't think even Nick really knew about.
It's like... there's all these rules in my head about food.
Ordering and collecting and eating in certain ways at certain times.
And if I break the rules I feel like I'm gonna die.
My brain is literally SO weird.

Being in hospital didn't make me completely free of mental illness. Not even close.

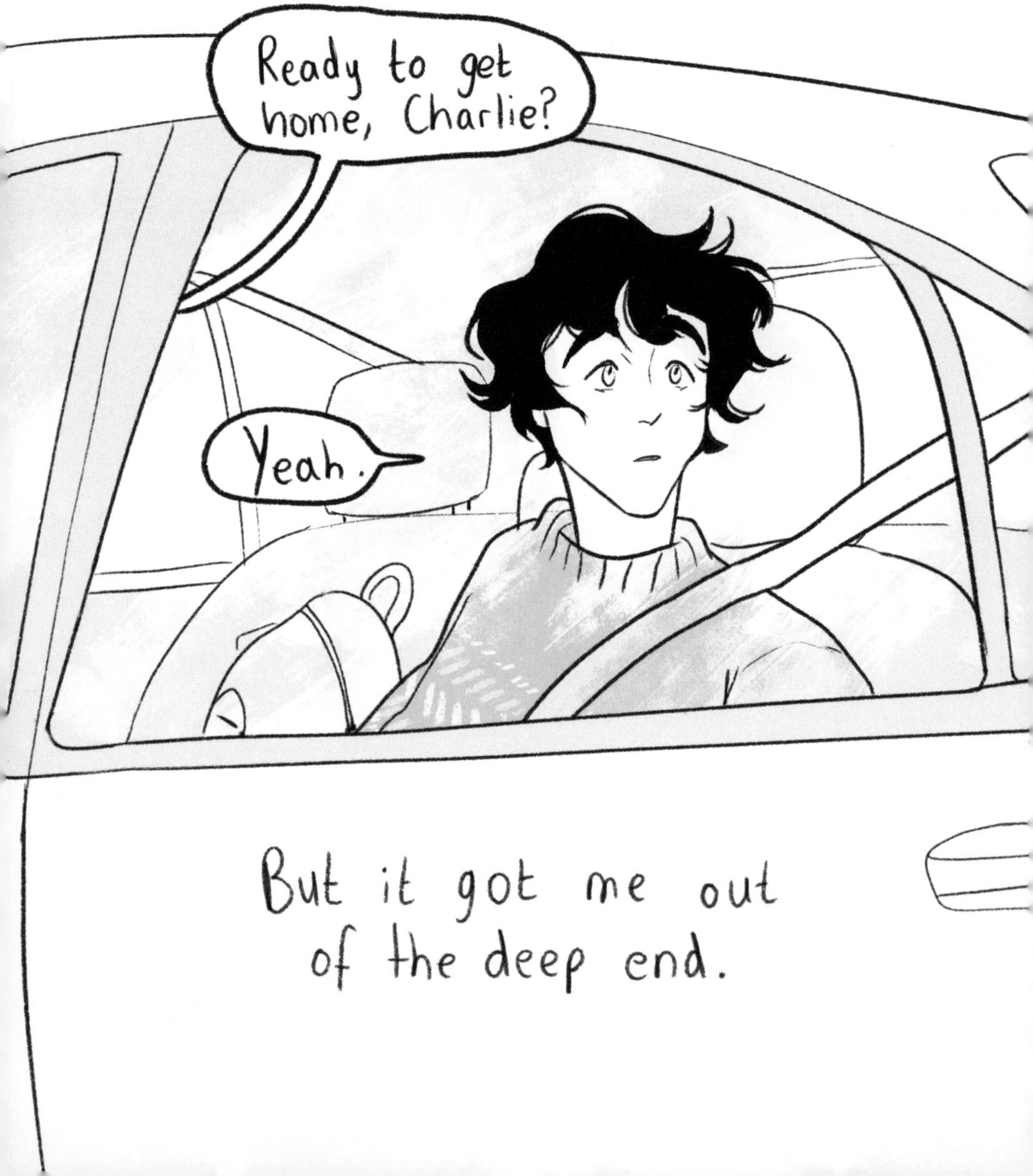
Ready to get home, Charlie?
Yeah.
But it got me out of the deep end.

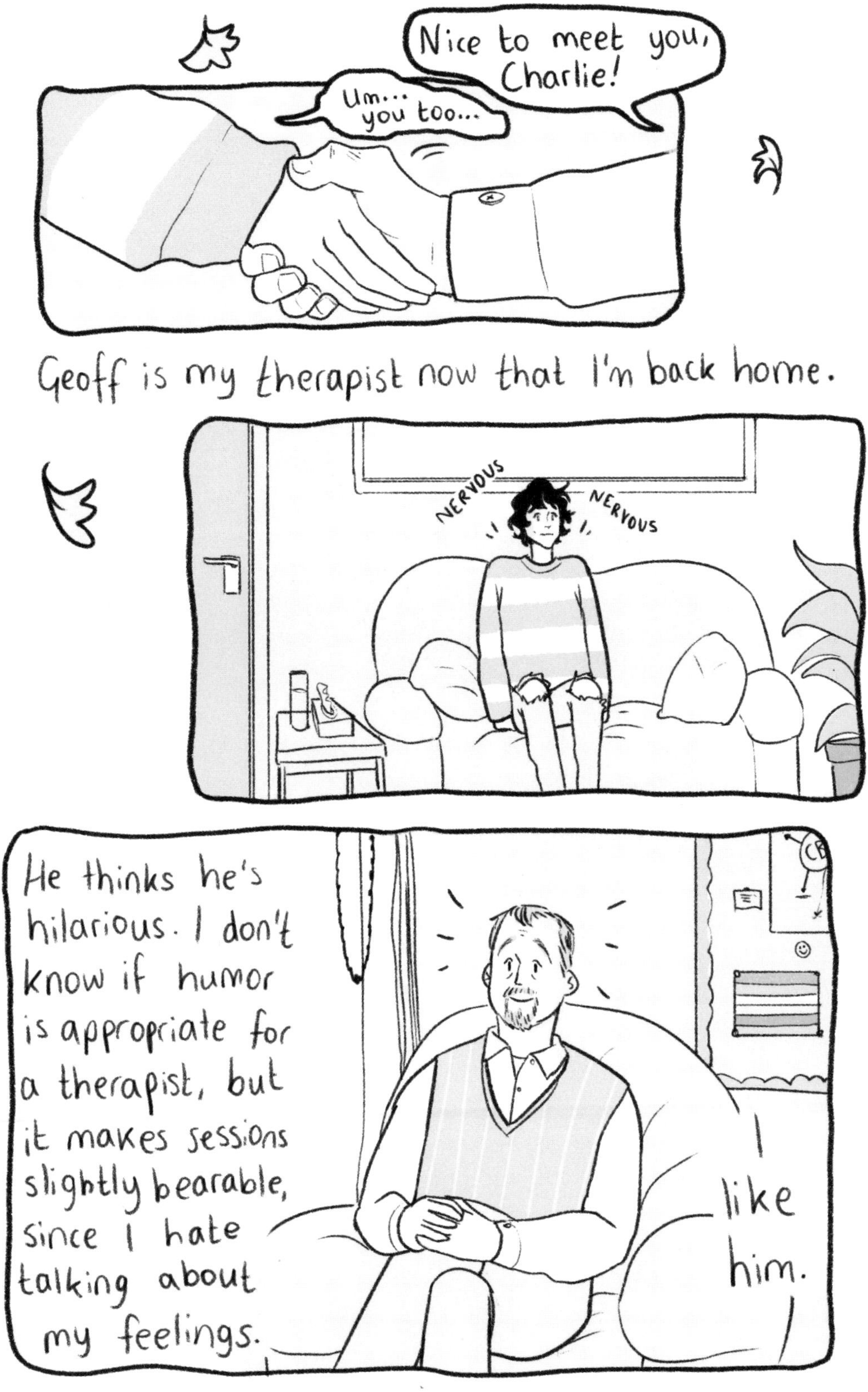
Nice to meet you, Charlie!
Um... you too...
Geoff is my therapist now that I'm back home.
NERVOUS
NERVOUS
He thinks he's hilarious. I don't know if humor is appropriate for a therapist, but it makes sessions slightly bearable, since I hate talking about my feelings.
I like him.

Me and Geoff have talked about what's happened in my life over the past couple of years.

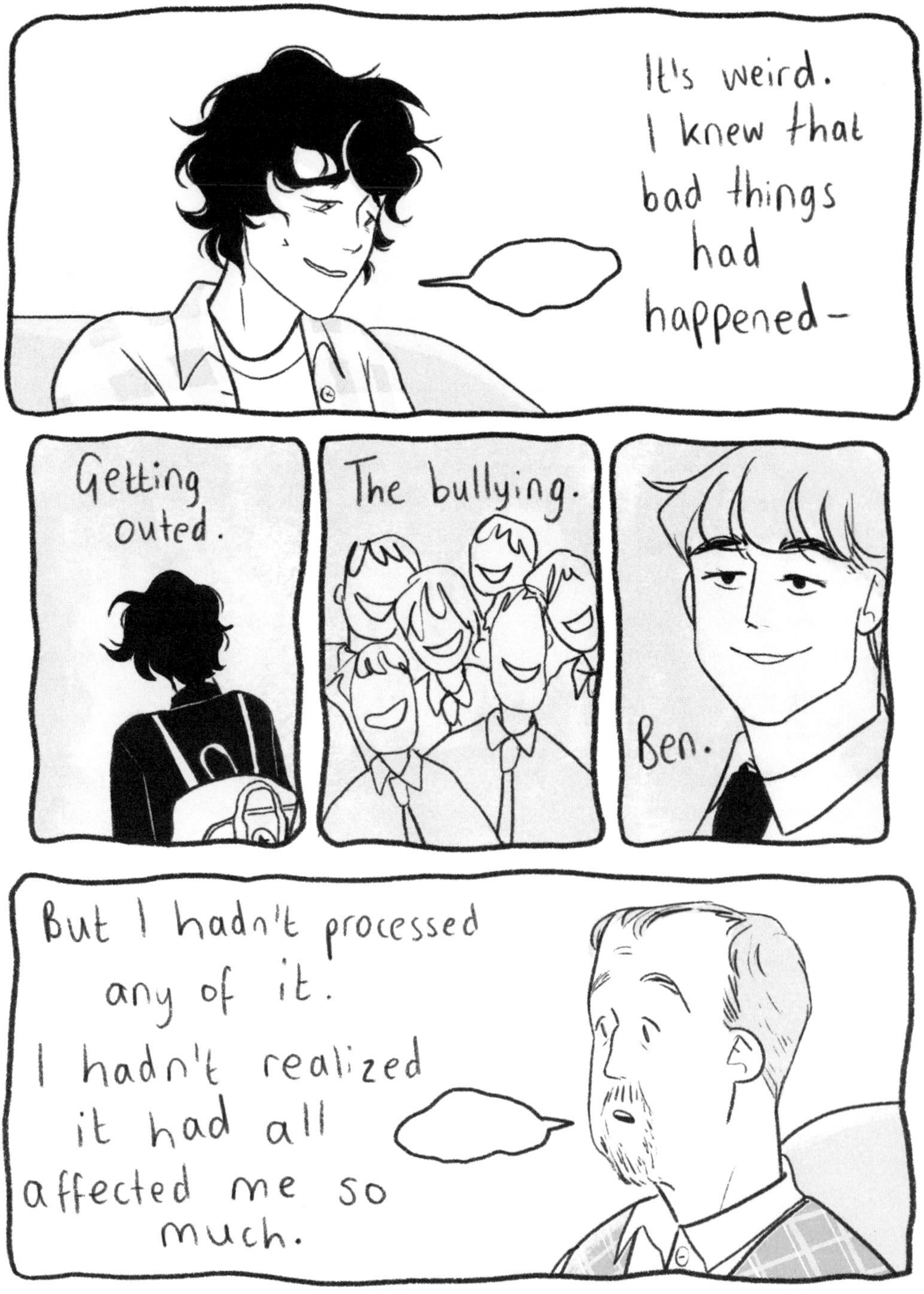
It's weird. I knew that bad things had happened–
Getting outed.
The bullying.
Ben.
But I hadn't processed any of it.
I hadn't realized it had all affected me so much.

Geoff says it's
trauma.

Kind of a dramatic word, I guess,
but Geoff says trauma can come
from all sorts of things.

Geoff says I'm making progress, but I think I'm realizing now that there might never be an "end".

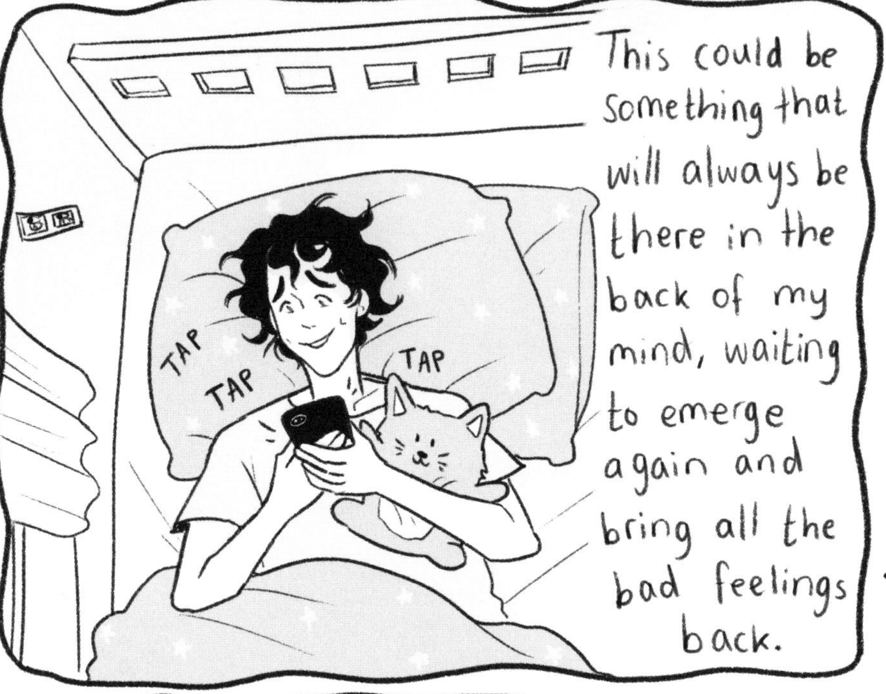
This could be something that will always be there in the back of my mind, waiting to emerge again and bring all the bad feelings back.
TAP
TAP
TAP

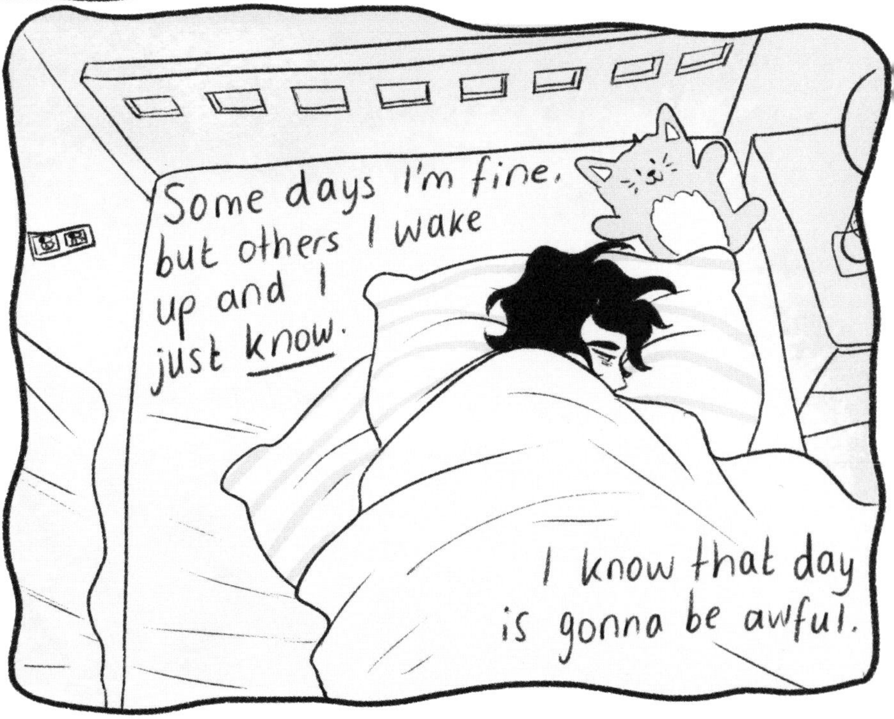
Some days I'm fine, but others I wake up and I just know.
I know that day is gonna be awful.

But Geoff also says the bad days will get less common. And I can just enjoy my life and hardly ever stress out about food.

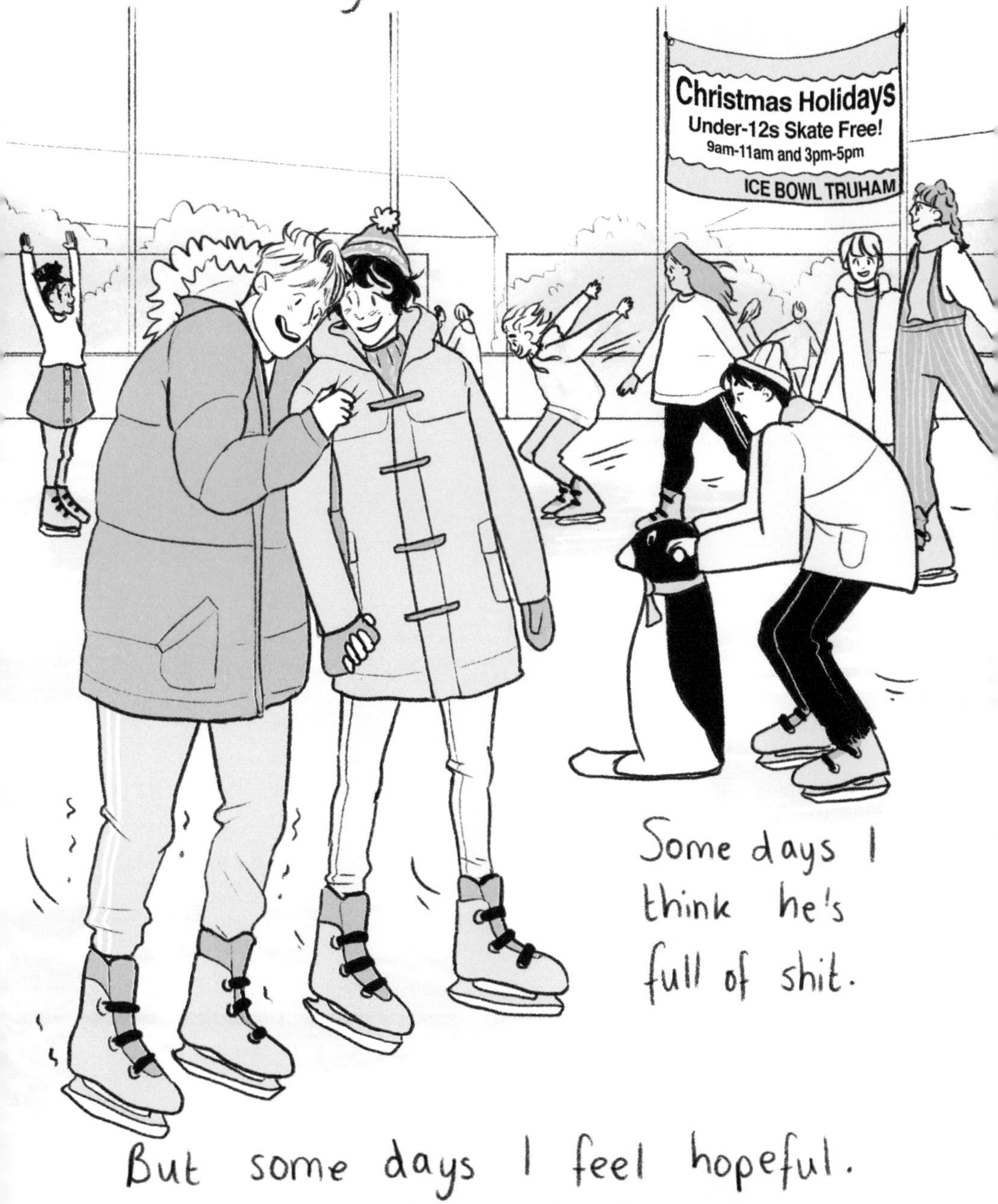
Christmas Holidays
Under-12s Skate Free!
9am-11am and 3pm-5pm
ICE BOWL TRUHAM

Some days I think he's full of shit.

But some days I feel hopeful. I guess I'll have to keep trying.

So I went back to school after the Christmas holidays!

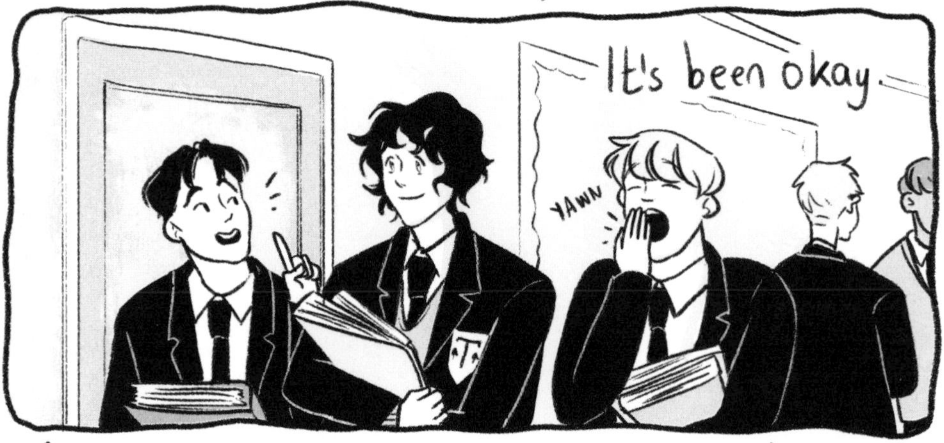
It's been okay.
YAWN

A couple of teachers knew what had happened.

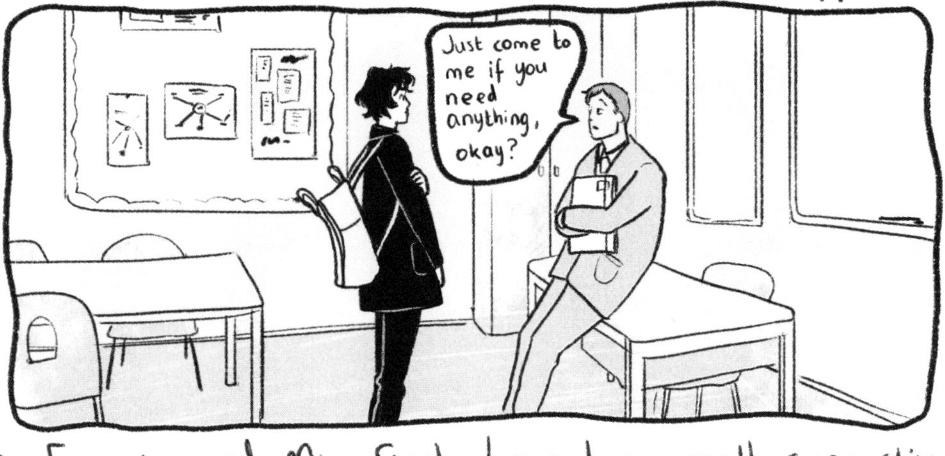
Just come to me if you need anything, okay?

Mr. Farouk and Miss Singh have been really supportive.

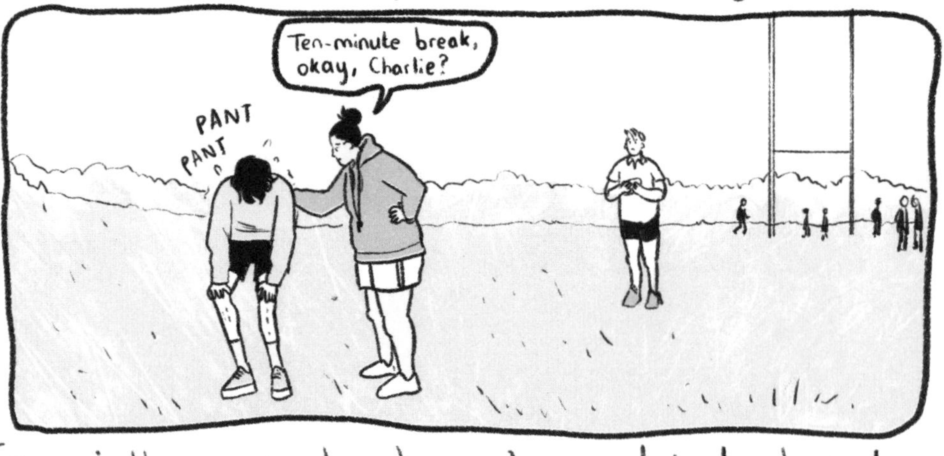
Ten-minute break, okay, Charlie?
PANT
PANT

Especially as rugby has been kinda hard.

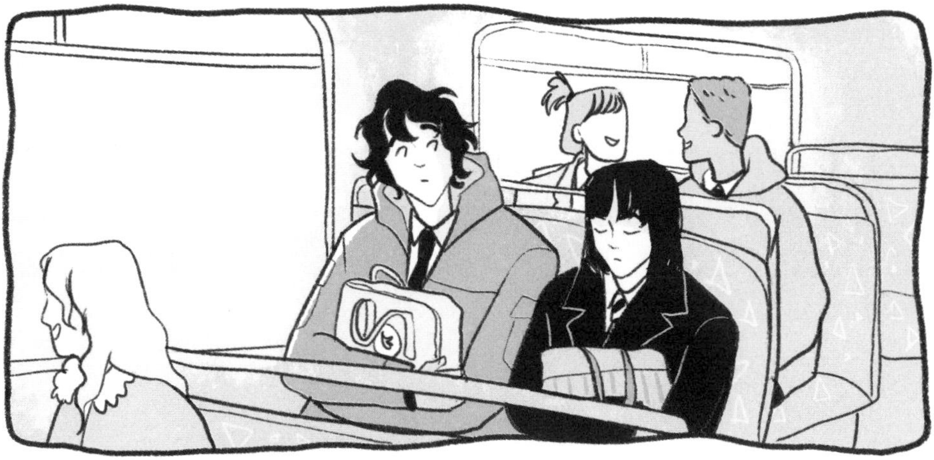

I think Tori feels guilty about everything.

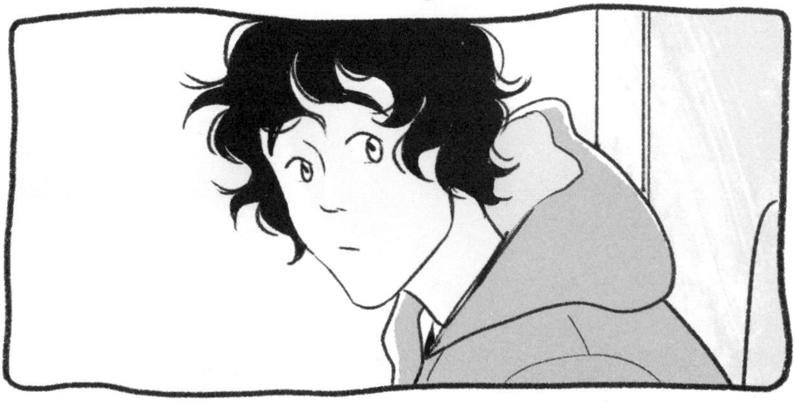

She shouldn't, but...

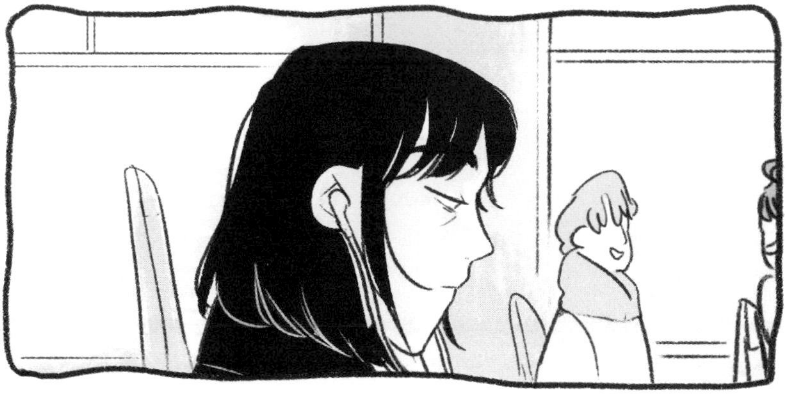

her mental health hasn't been great either.

But she's made this new friend called Michael.

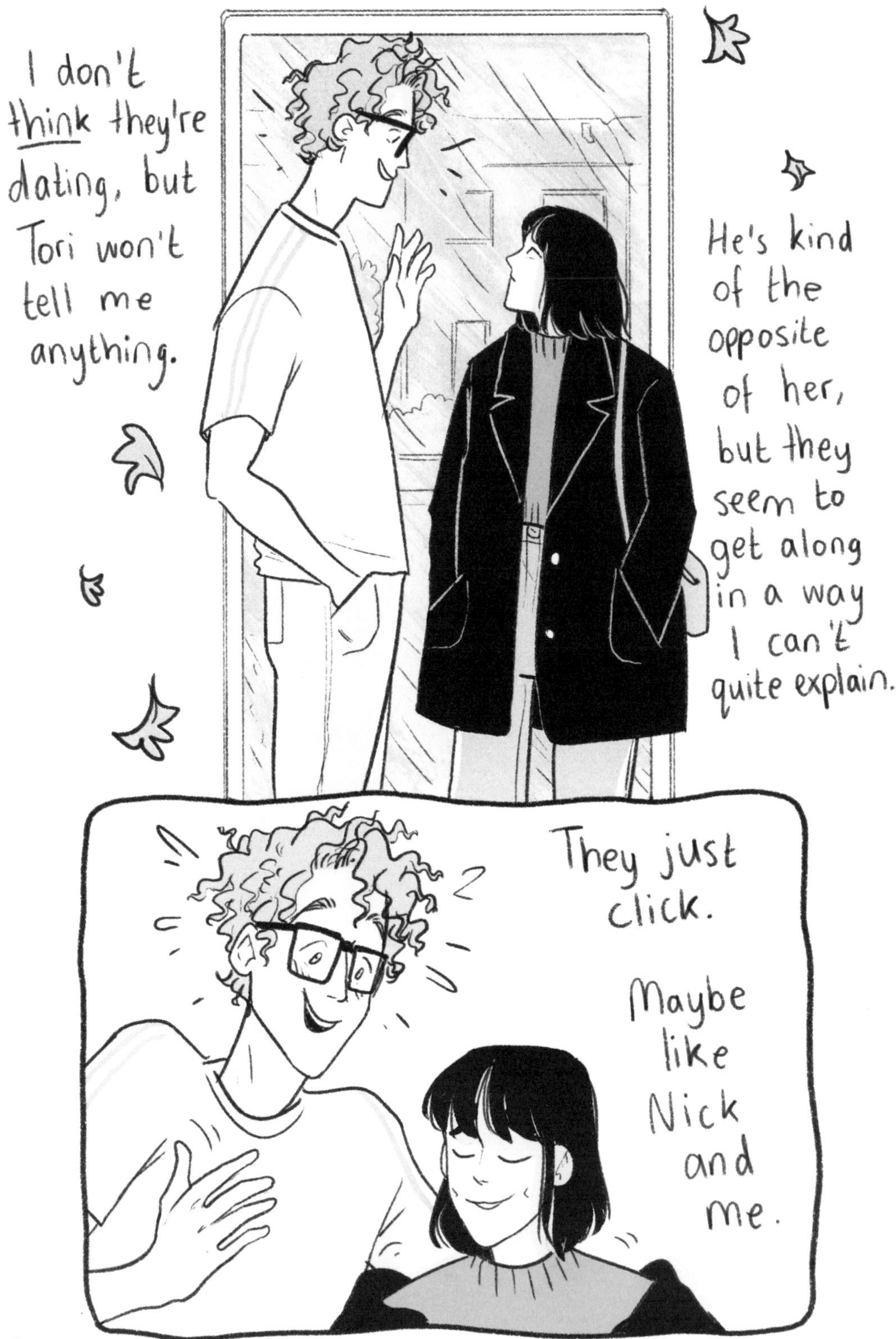
I don't think they're dating, but Tori won't tell me anything.
He's kind of the opposite of her, but they seem to get along in a way I can't quite explain.
They just click.
Maybe like Nick and me.

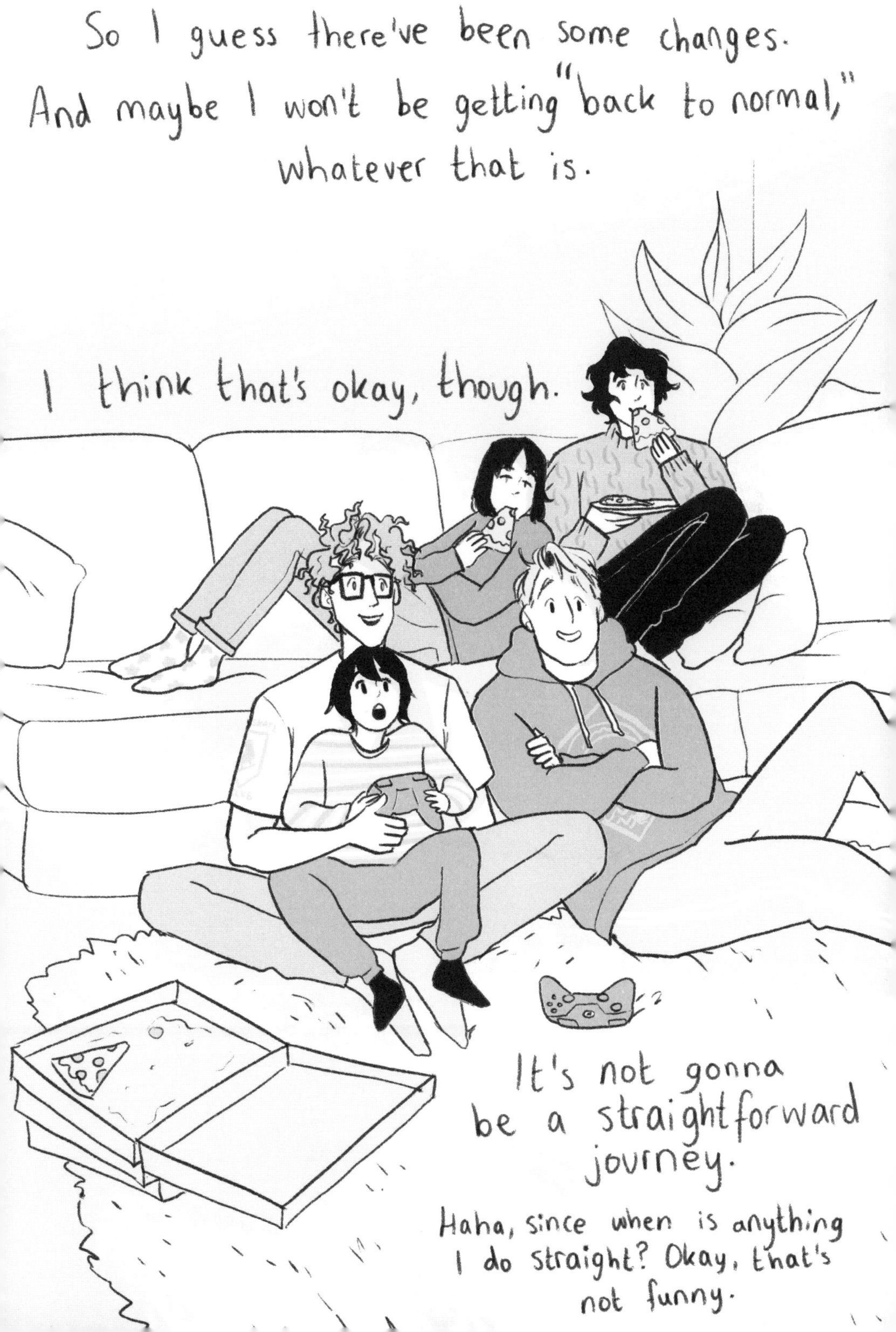
So I guess there've been some changes. And maybe I won't be getting "back to normal," whatever that is.
I think that's okay, though.
It's not gonna be a straightforward journey.
Haha, since when is anything I do straight? Okay, that's not funny.

But really.

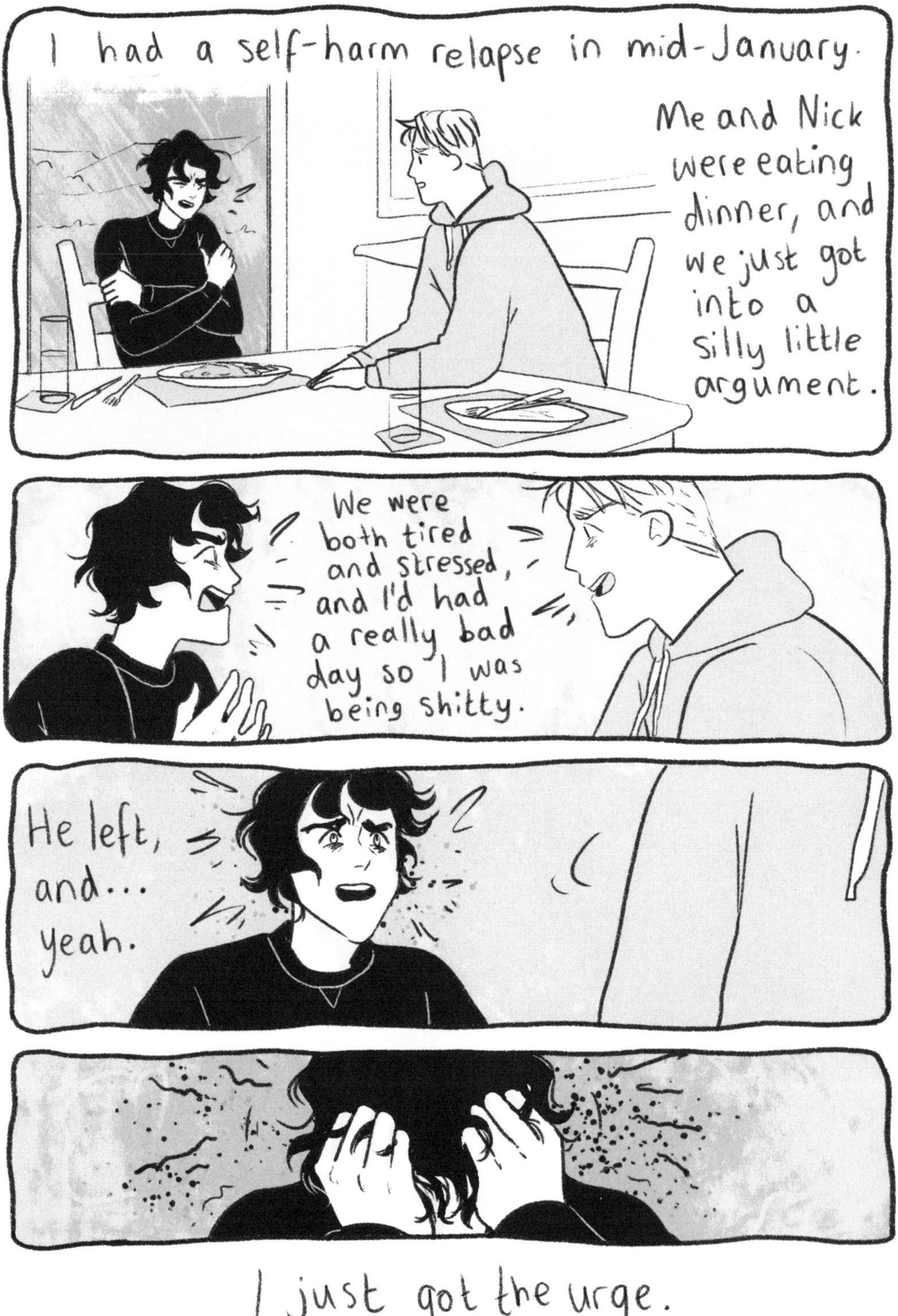
I had a self-harm relapse in mid-January.
Me and Nick were eating dinner, and we just got into a silly little argument.
We were both tired and stressed, and I'd had a really bad day so I was being shitty.
He left, and... yeah.

I just got the urge.

It wasn't anyone's fault. Relapses happen. Tori told Nick what had happened, and he came back later that night.

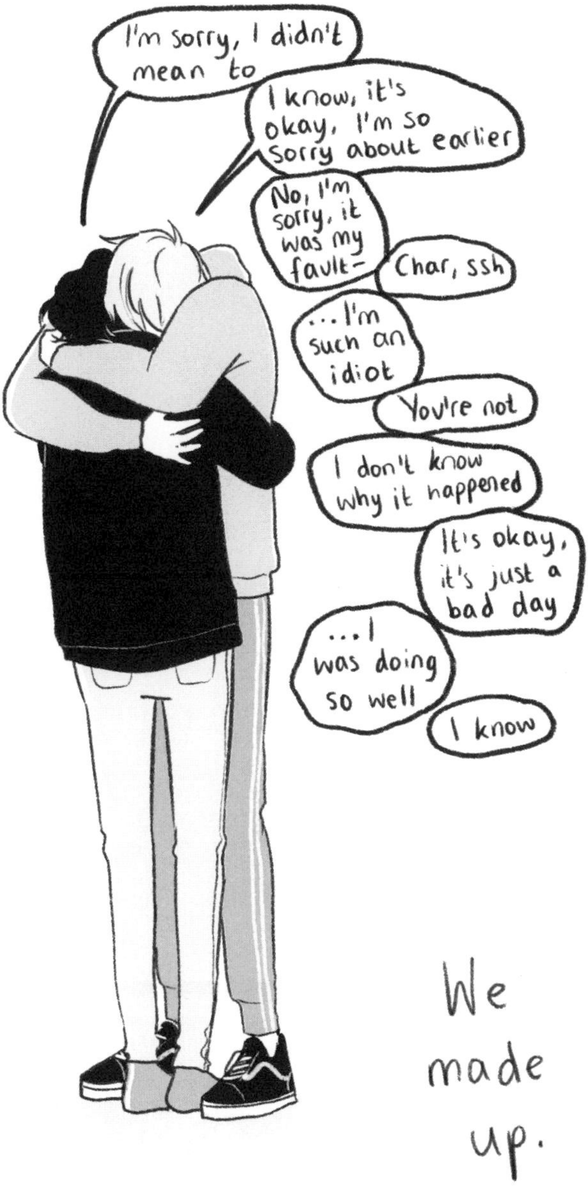
I'm sorry, I didn't mean to
I know, it's okay, I'm so sorry about earlier
No, I'm sorry, it was my fault–
Char, ssh
...I'm such an idiot
You're not
I don't know why it happened
It's okay, it's just a bad day
...I was doing so well
I know

We made up.

Mum and Dad even let him stay over to "keep an eye on me."

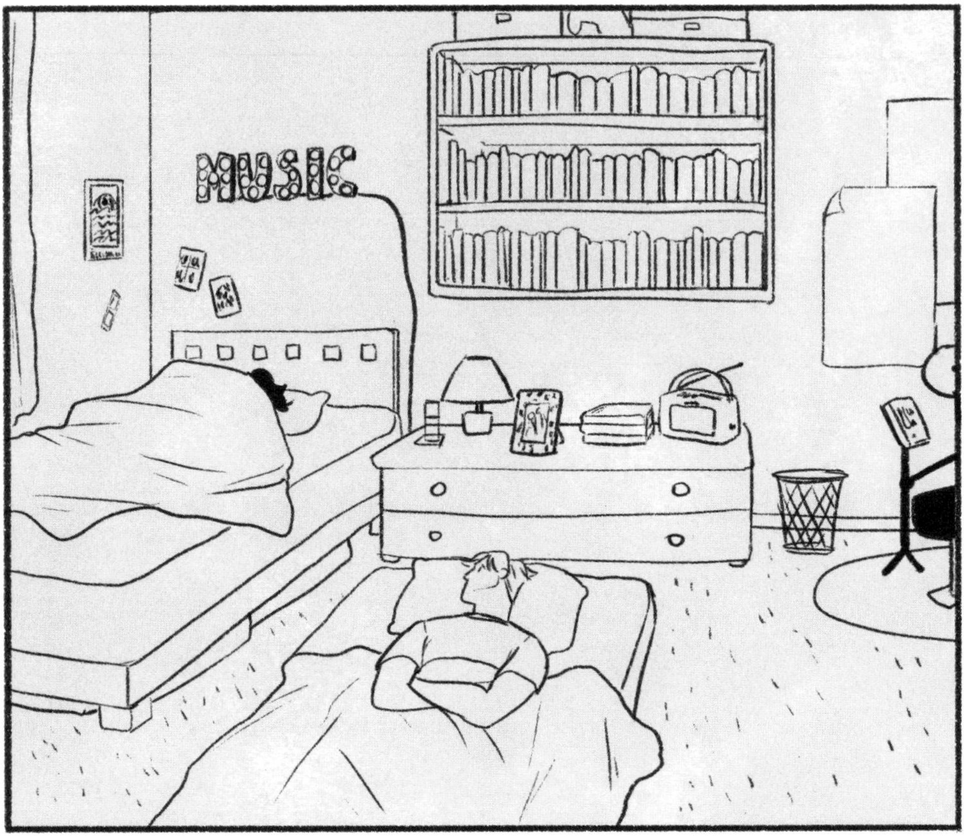
MUSIC

Not really necessary, but I wasn't complaining.

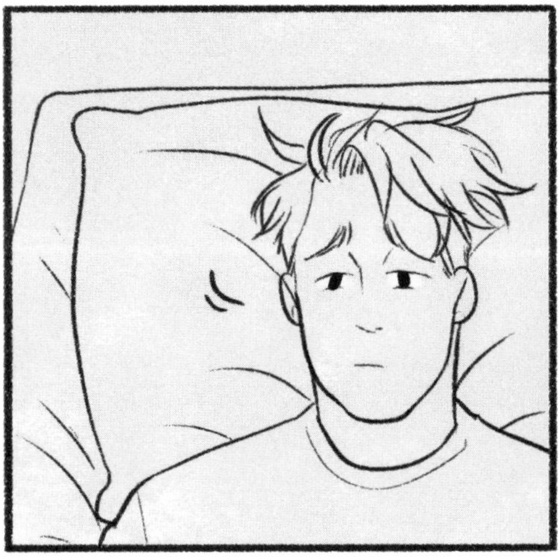

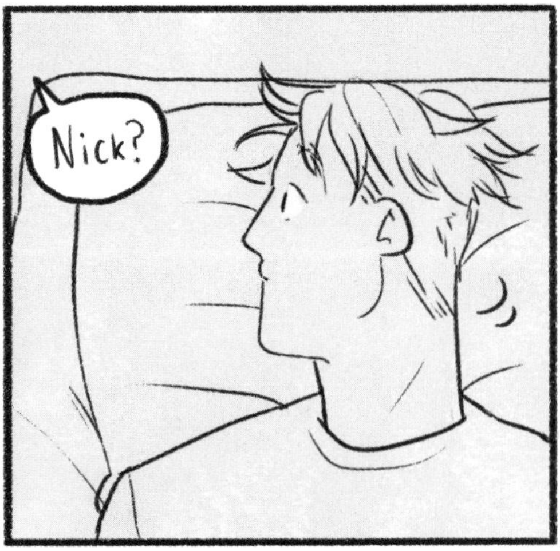
Nick?

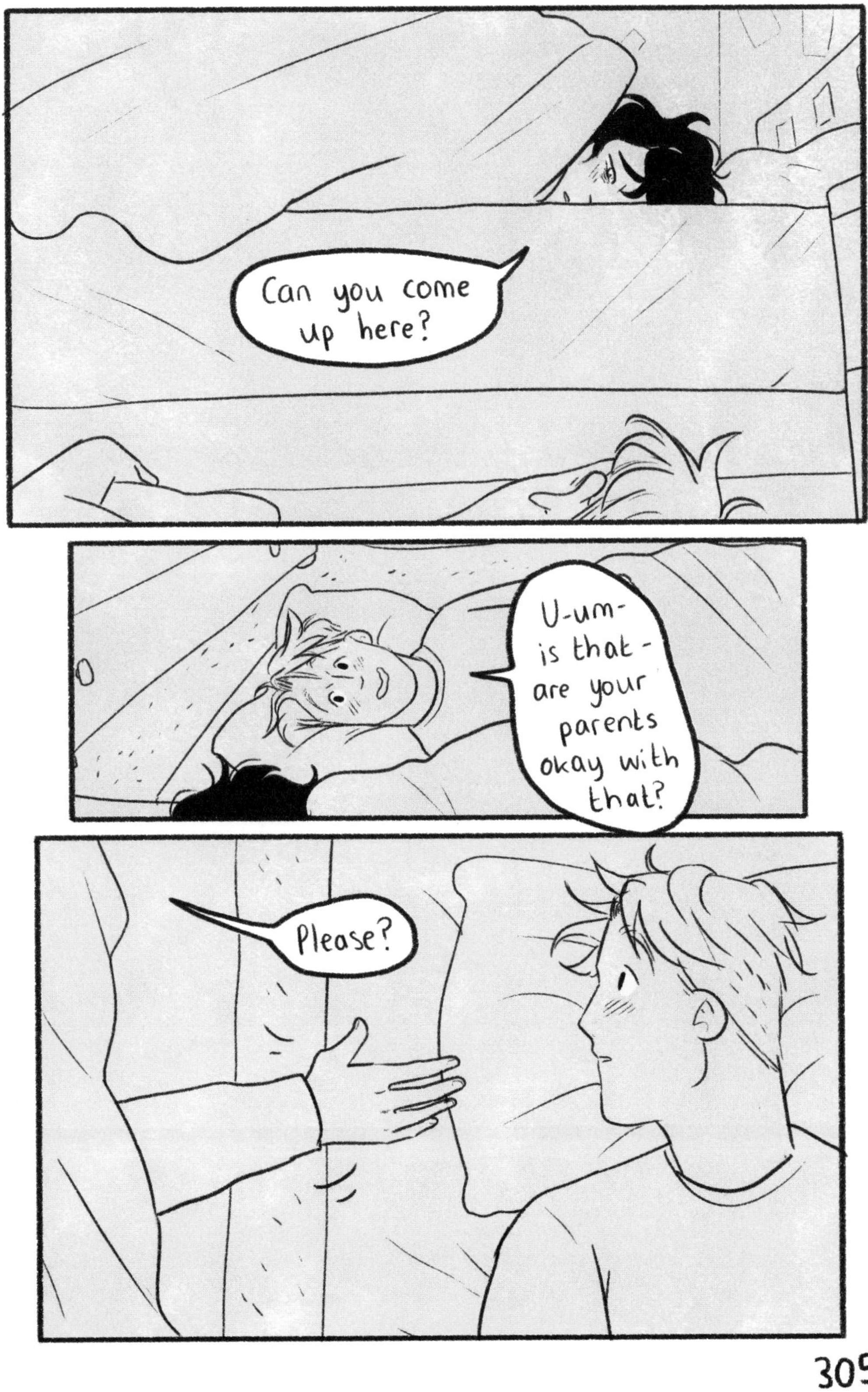
Can you come up here?
U-um- is that - are your parents okay with that?
Please?

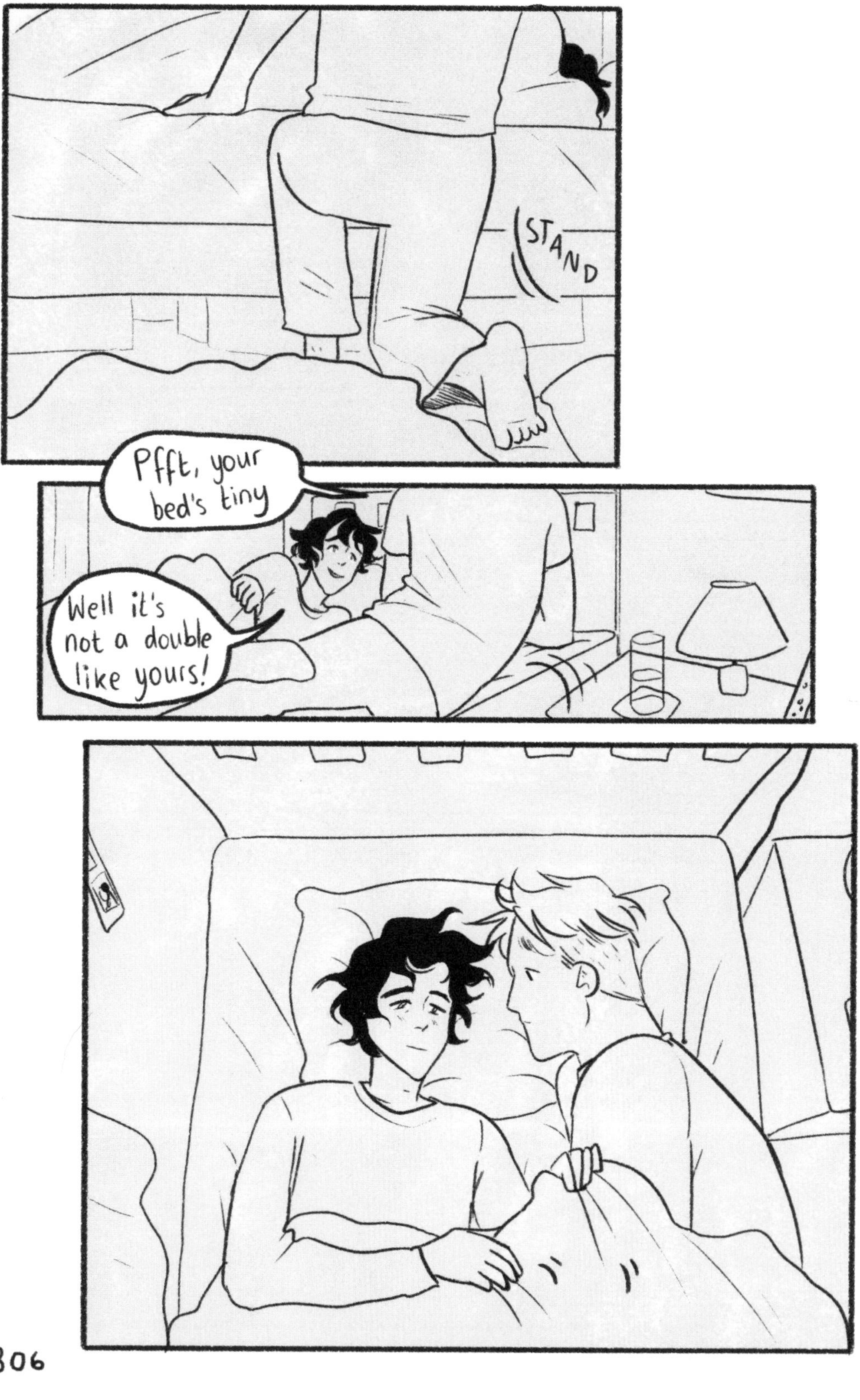
STAND
Pffft, your bed's tiny
Well it's not a double like yours!

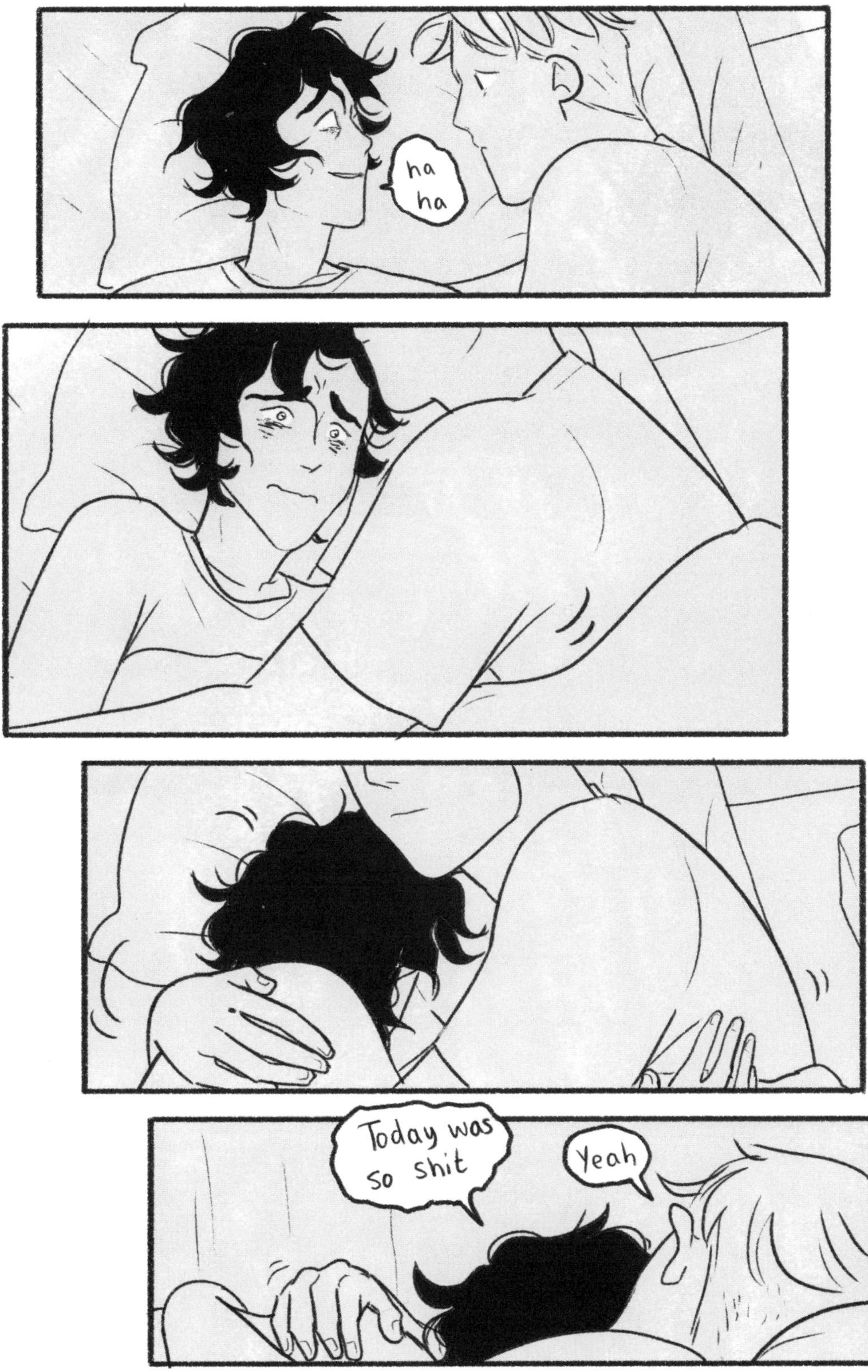
ha ha
Today was so shit
Yeah

I love Nick.

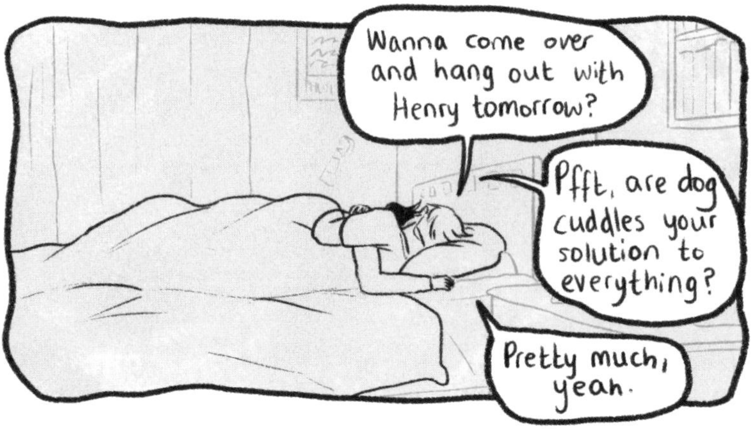
Wanna come over and hang out with Henry tomorrow?
Pfft, are dog cuddles your solution to everything?
Pretty much, yeah.

I love Nick so, so much.

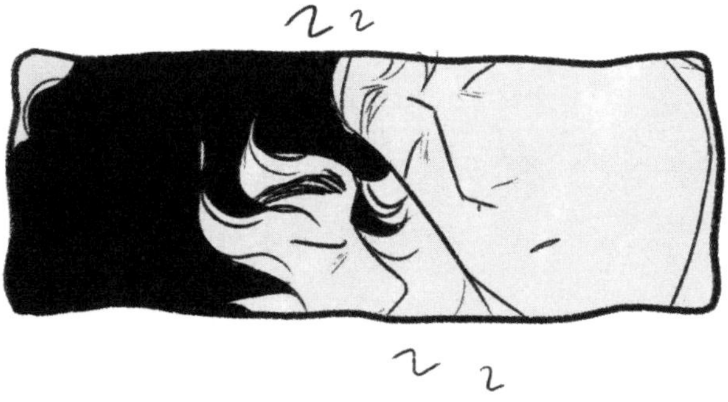

But what I've realized through all of this is that we need <u>other</u> people too.

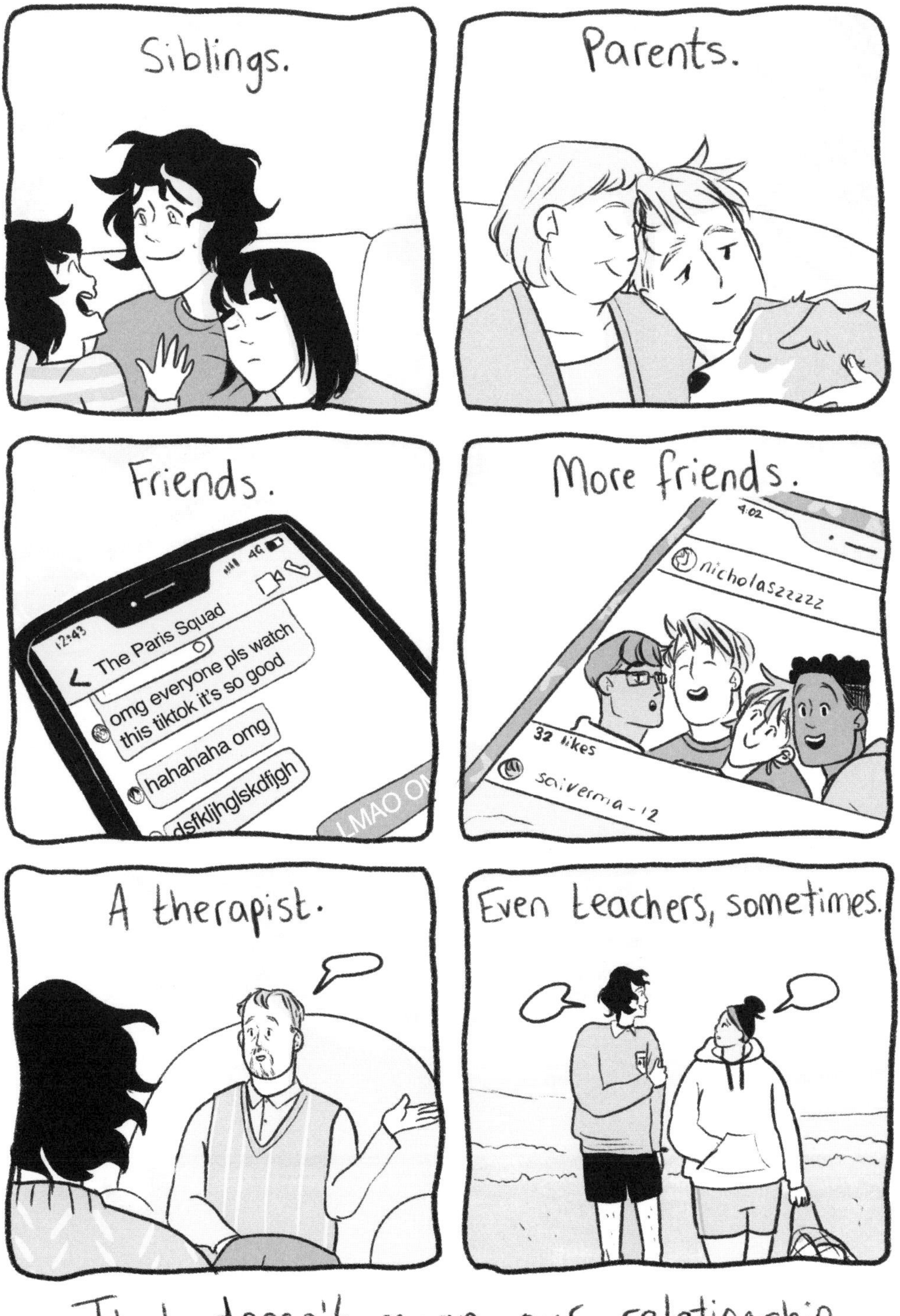
Siblings.
Parents.
Friends.
12:43
The Paris Squad
omg everyone pls watch this tiktok it's so good
hahahaha omg
dsfkljhglskdfjgh
More friends.
4:02
nicholaszzzzz
32 likes
saiverma-12
A therapist.
Even teachers, sometimes.

That doesn't mean our relationship isn't strong.

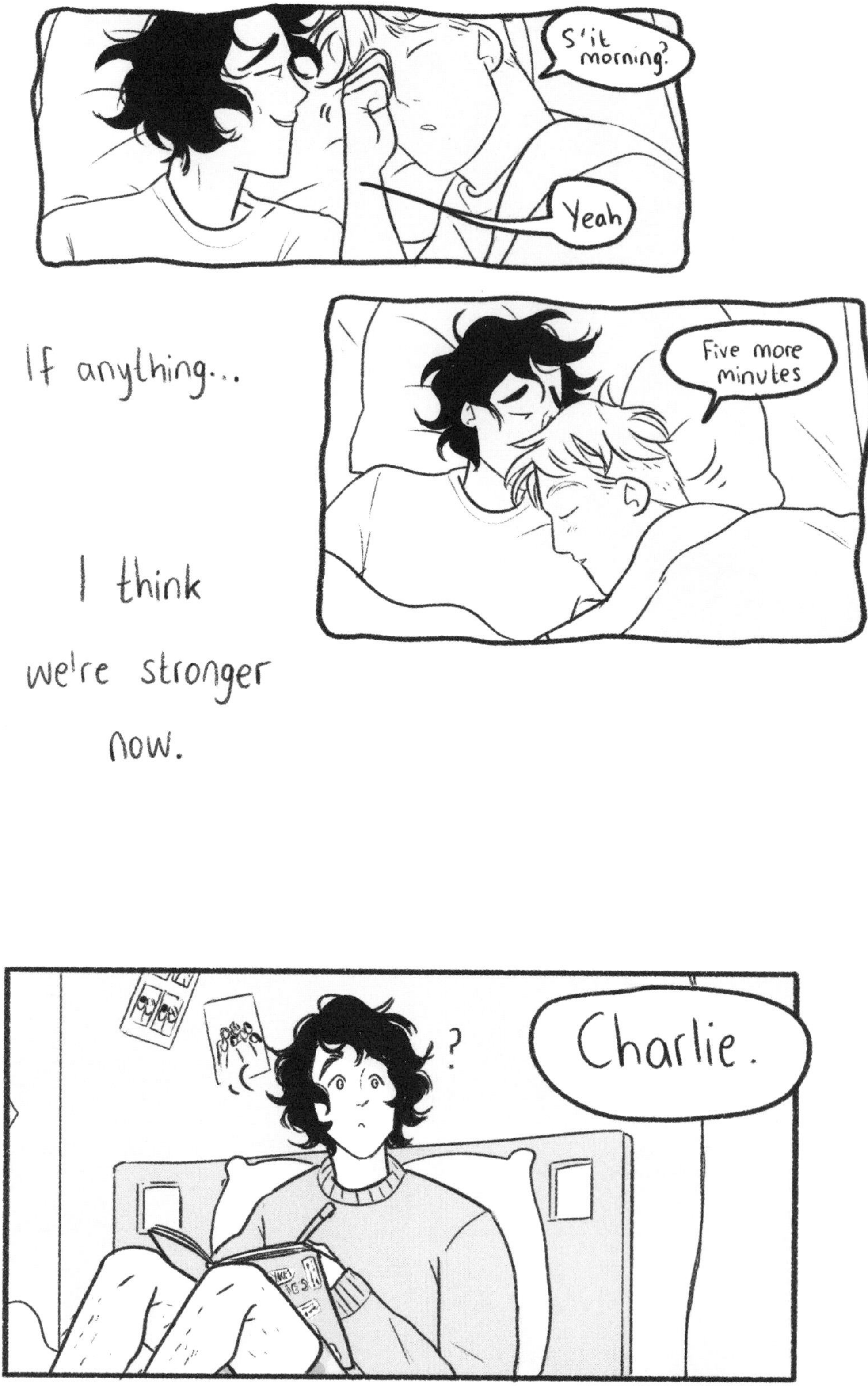
S'it morning?
Yeah
If anything...
Five more minutes
I think
we're stronger
now.
?
Charlie.

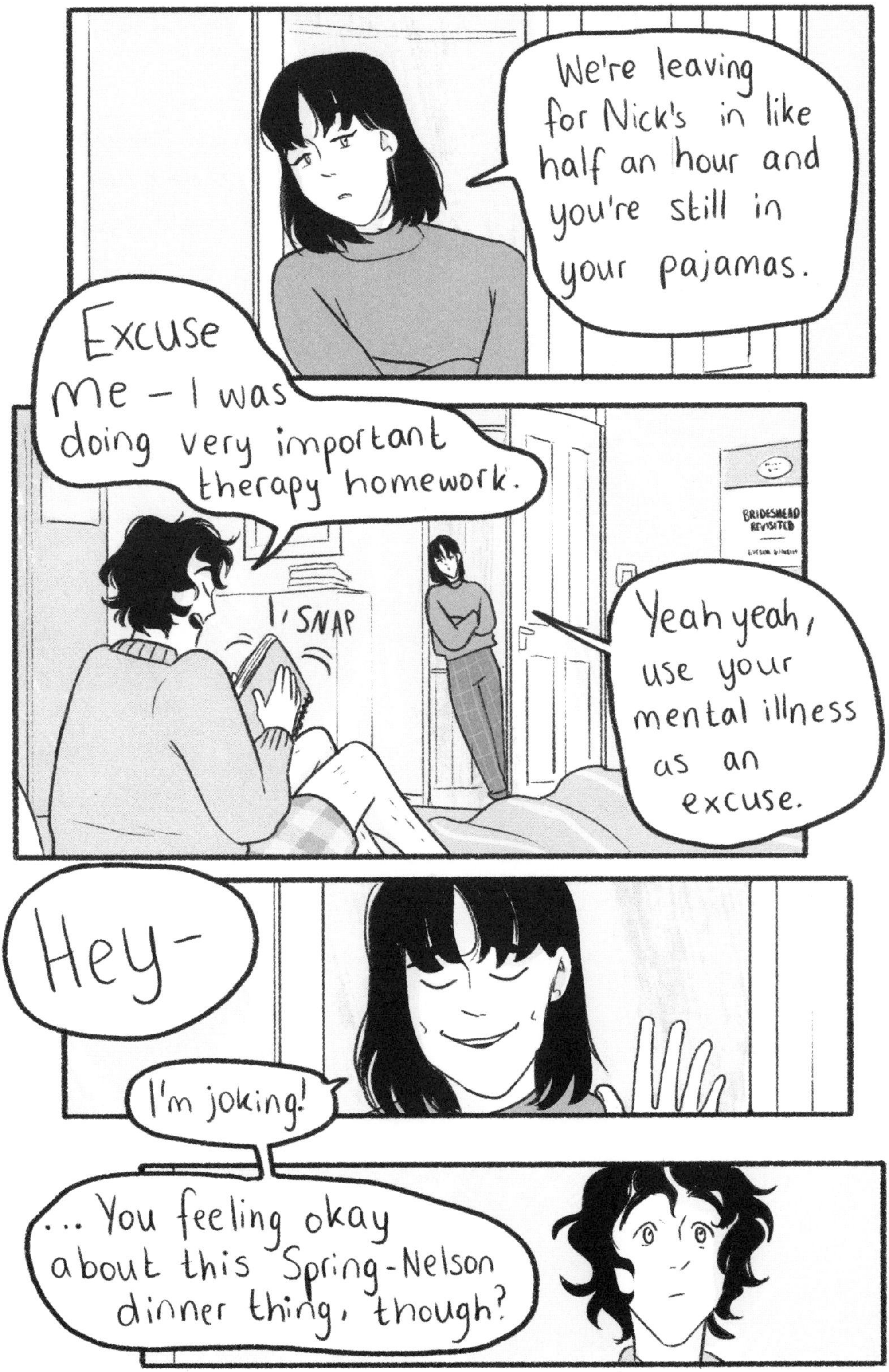
We're leaving for Nick's in like half an hour and you're still in your pajamas.
Excuse me - I was doing very important therapy homework.
SNAP
BRIDESHEAD REVISITED
Yeah yeah, use your mental illness as an excuse.
Hey-
I'm joking!
... You feeling okay about this Spring-Nelson dinner thing, though?

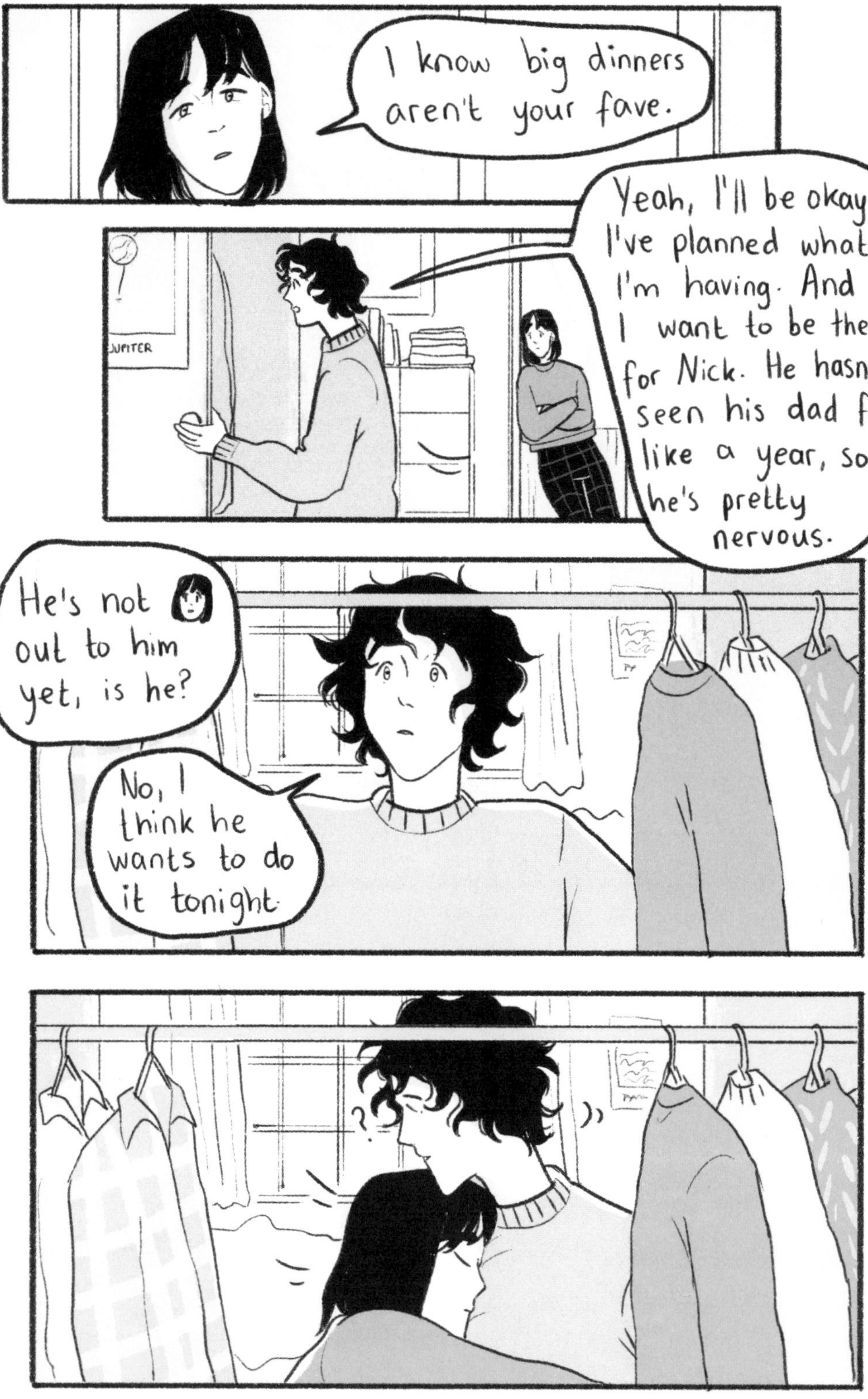
I know big dinners aren't your fave.
Yeah, I'll be okay. I've planned what I'm having. And I want to be there for Nick. He hasn't seen his dad for like a year, so he's pretty nervous.
JUPITER
He's not out to him yet, is he?
No, I think he wants to do it tonight.
?

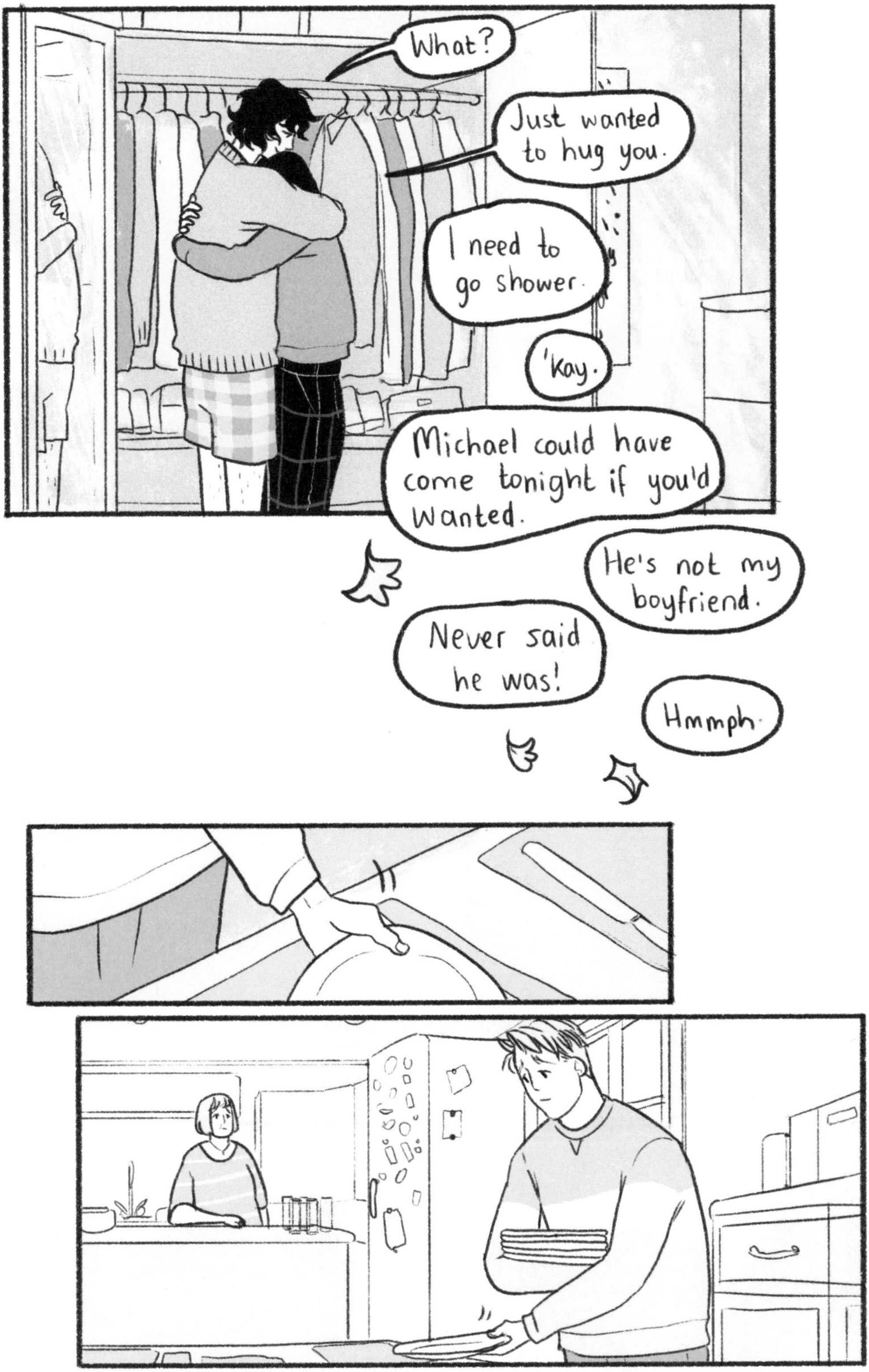
What?
Just wanted to hug you.
I need to go shower.
'Kay.
Michael could have come tonight if you'd wanted.
He's not my boyfriend.
Never said he was!
Hmmph.

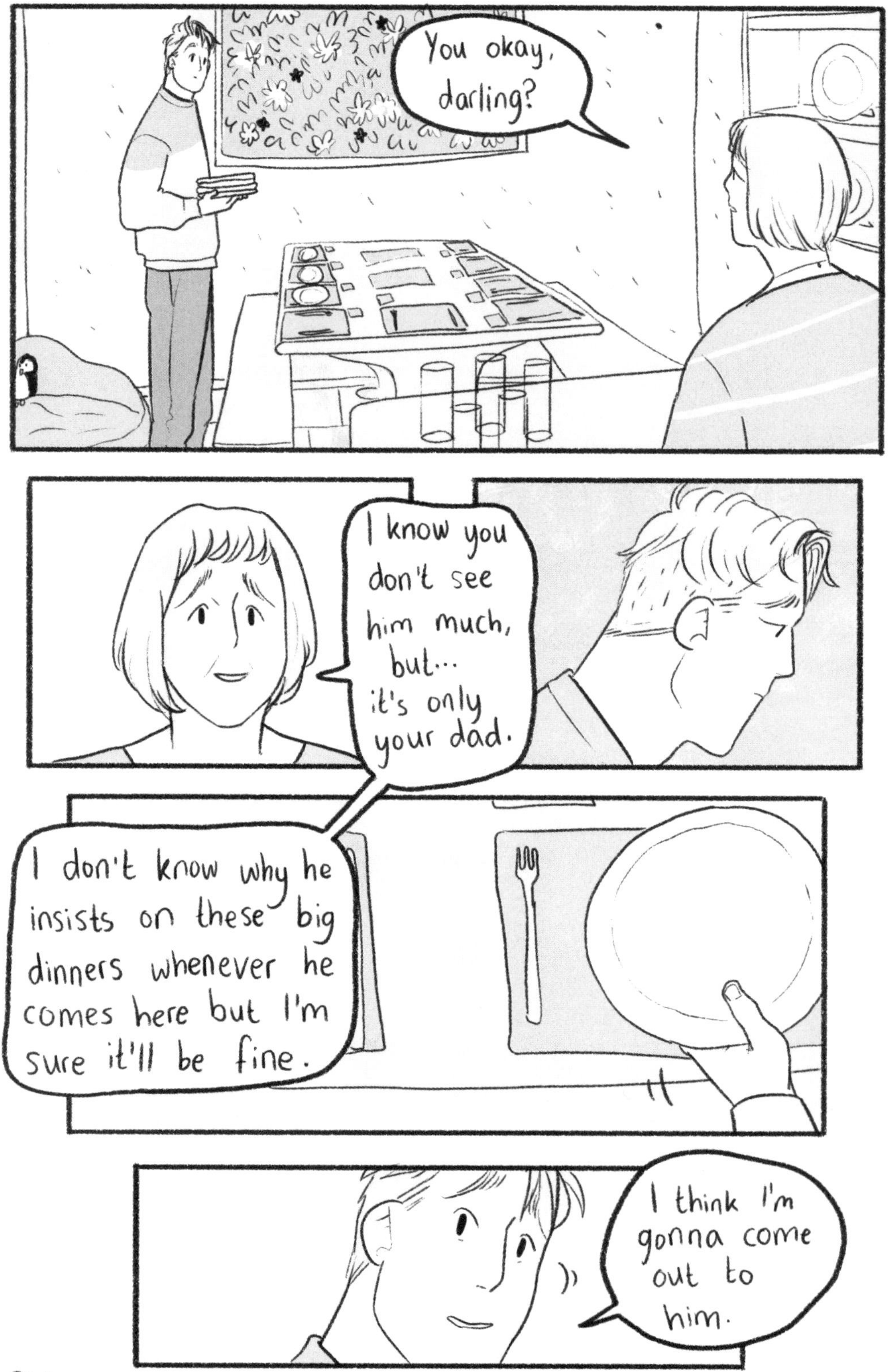
You okay, darling?
I know you don't see him much, but... it's only your dad.
I don't know why he insists on these big dinners whenever he comes here but I'm sure it'll be fine.
I think I'm gonna come out to him.

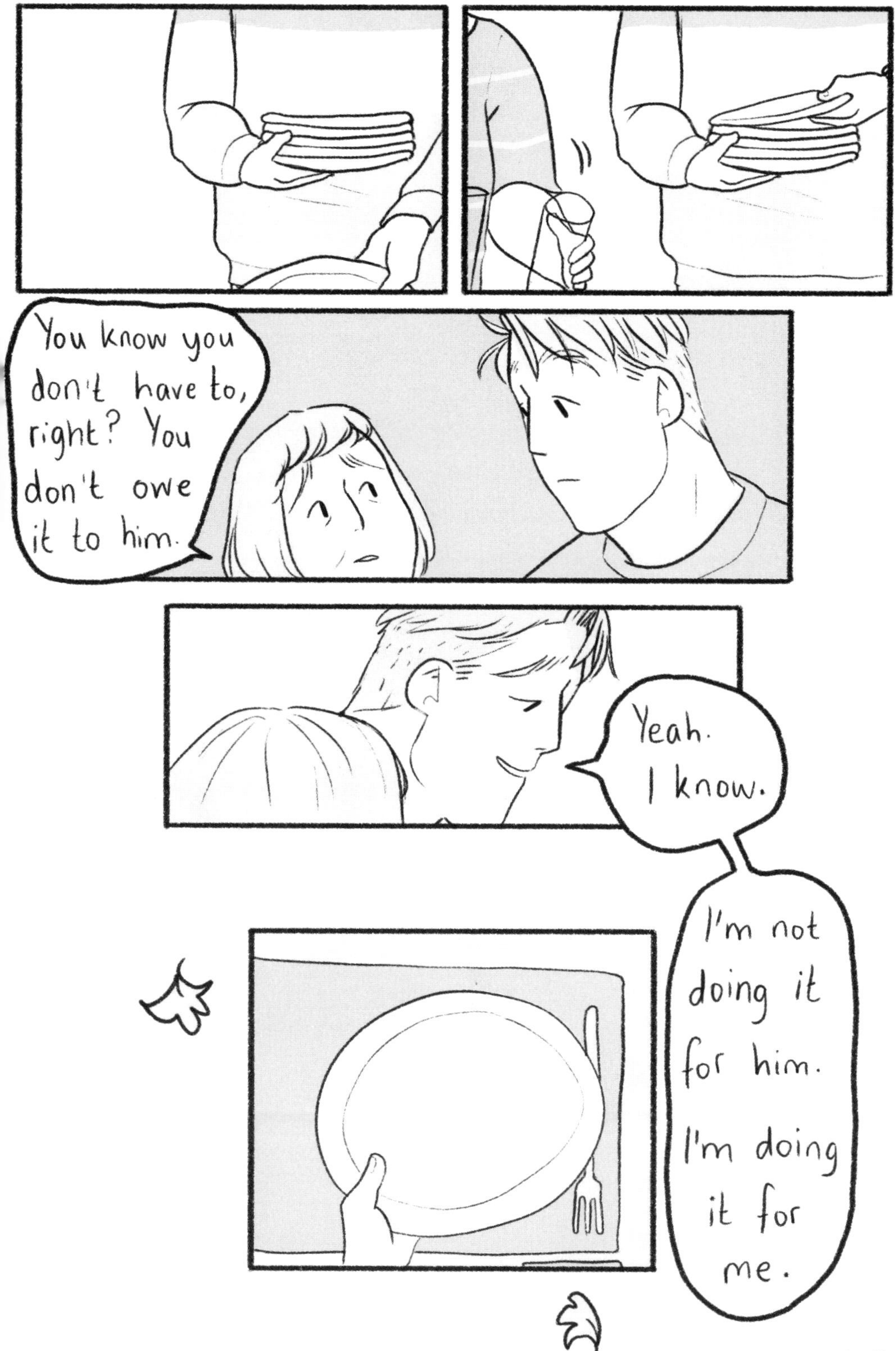
You know you don't have to, right? You don't owe it to him.
Yeah. I know.
I'm not doing it for him.
I'm doing it for me.

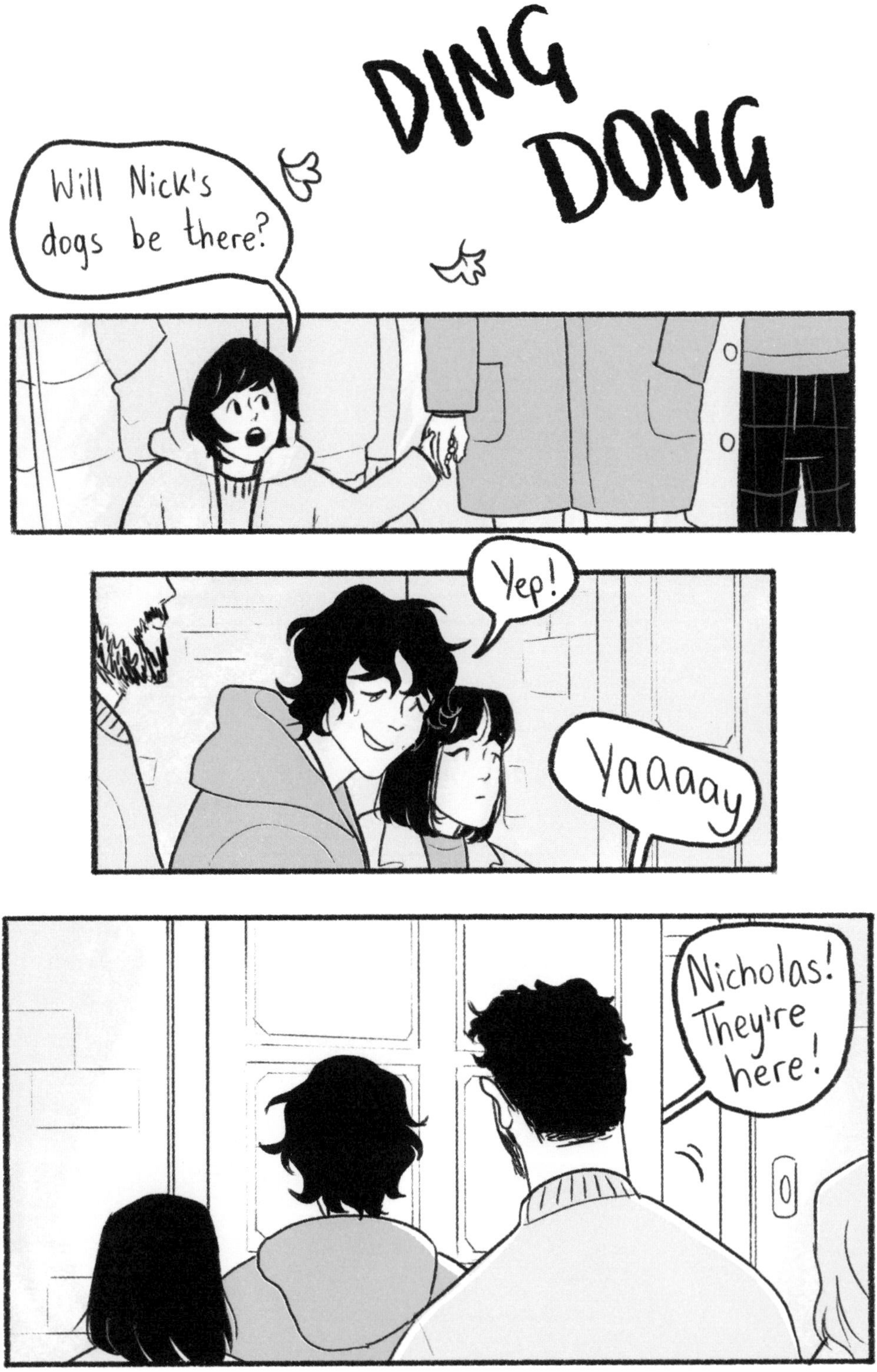
DING DONG
Will Nick's dogs be there?
Yep!
Yaaaay
Nicholas! They're here!

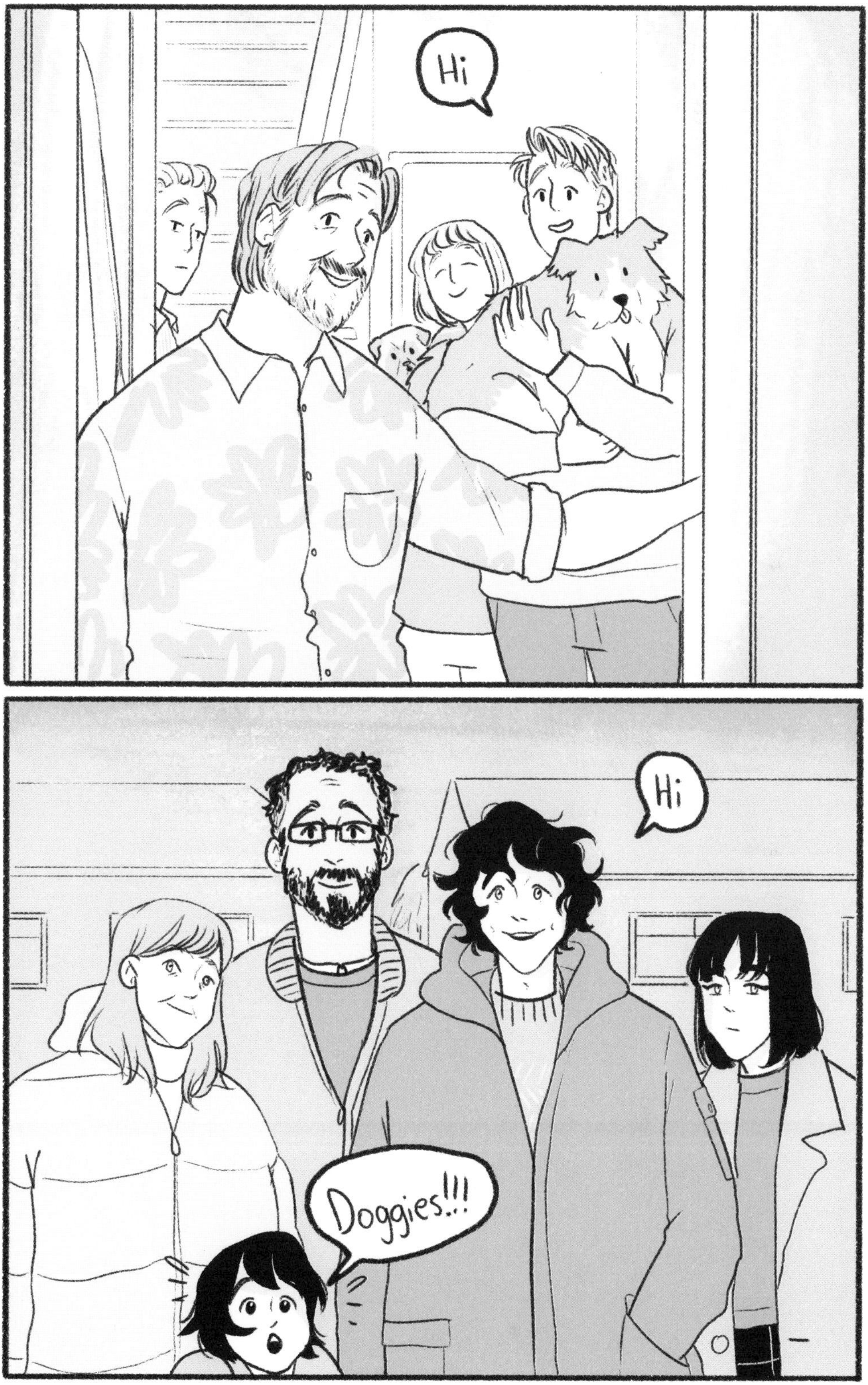
Hi
Hi
Doggies!!!

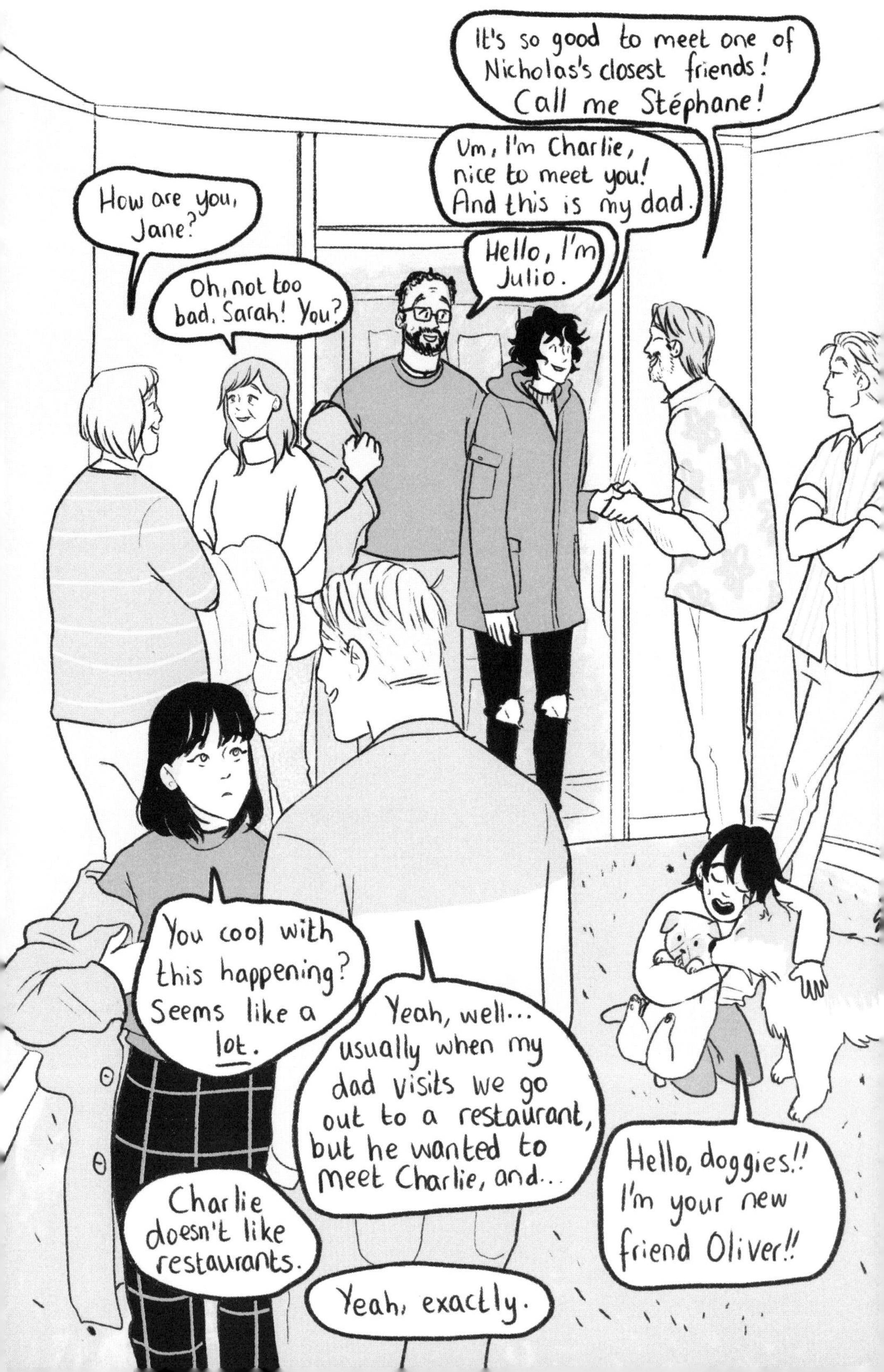
It's so good to meet one of Nicholas's closest friends! Call me Stéphane!
Um, I'm Charlie, nice to meet you! And this is my dad.
Hello, I'm Julio.
How are you, Jane?
Oh, not too bad, Sarah! You?
You cool with this happening? Seems like a lot.
Yeah, well... usually when my dad visits we go out to a restaurant, but he wanted to meet Charlie, and...
Charlie doesn't like restaurants.
Yeah, exactly.
Hello, doggies!! I'm your new friend Oliver!!

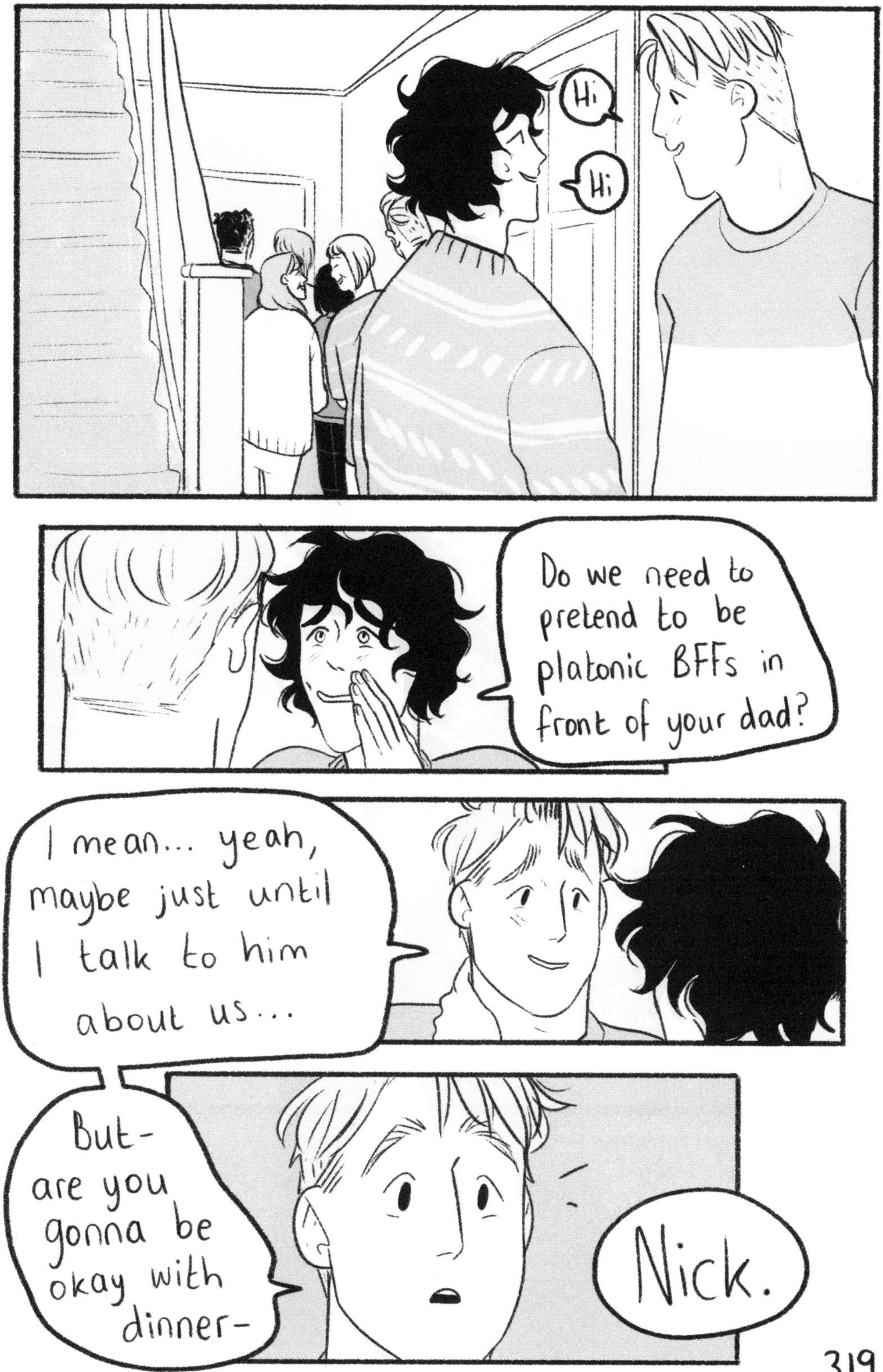
Hi
Hi
Do we need to pretend to be platonic BFFs in front of your dad?
I mean... yeah, maybe just until I talk to him about us...
But- are you gonna be okay with dinner-
Nick.

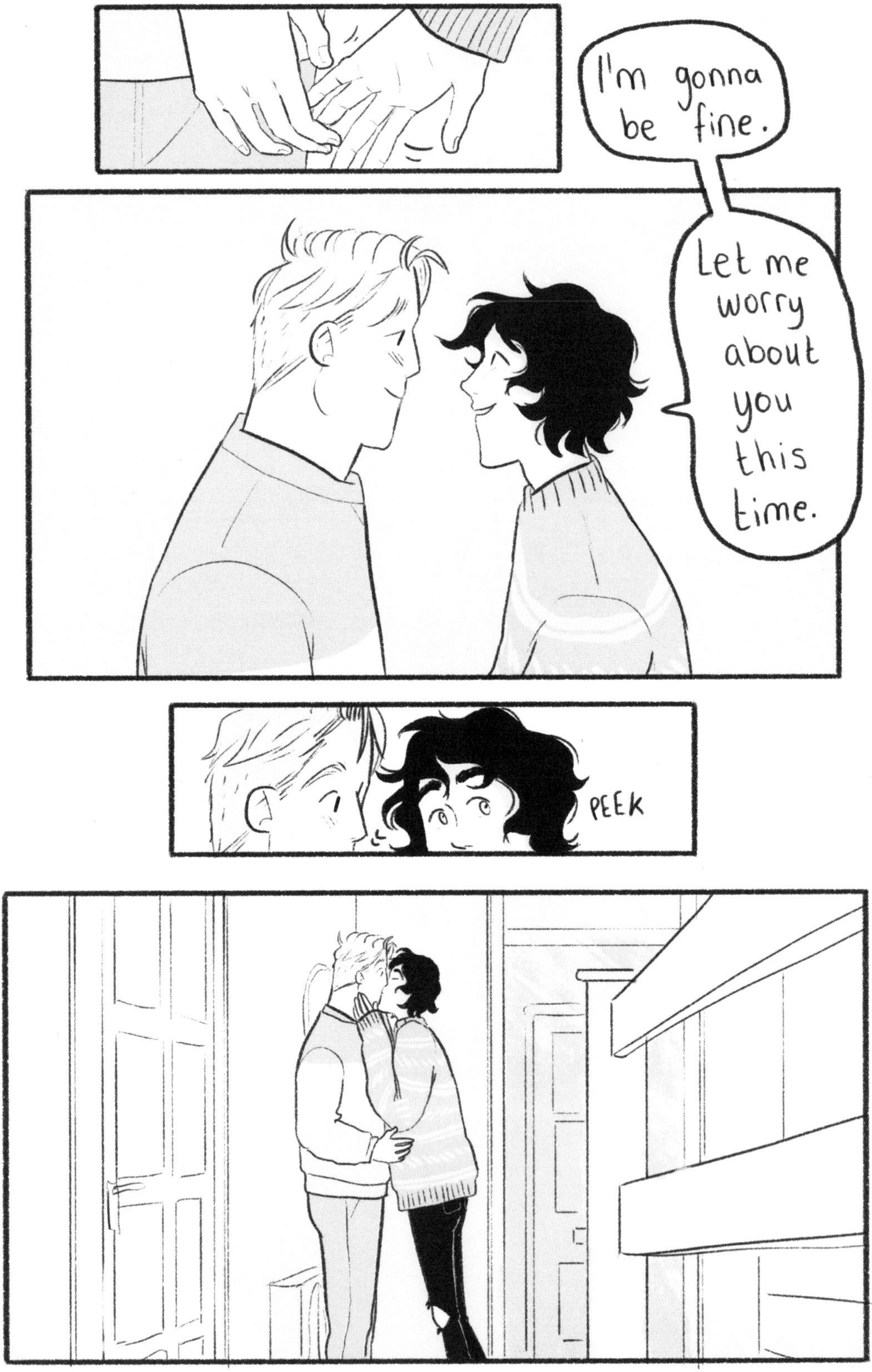
I'm gonna be fine.
Let me worry about you this time.
PEEK

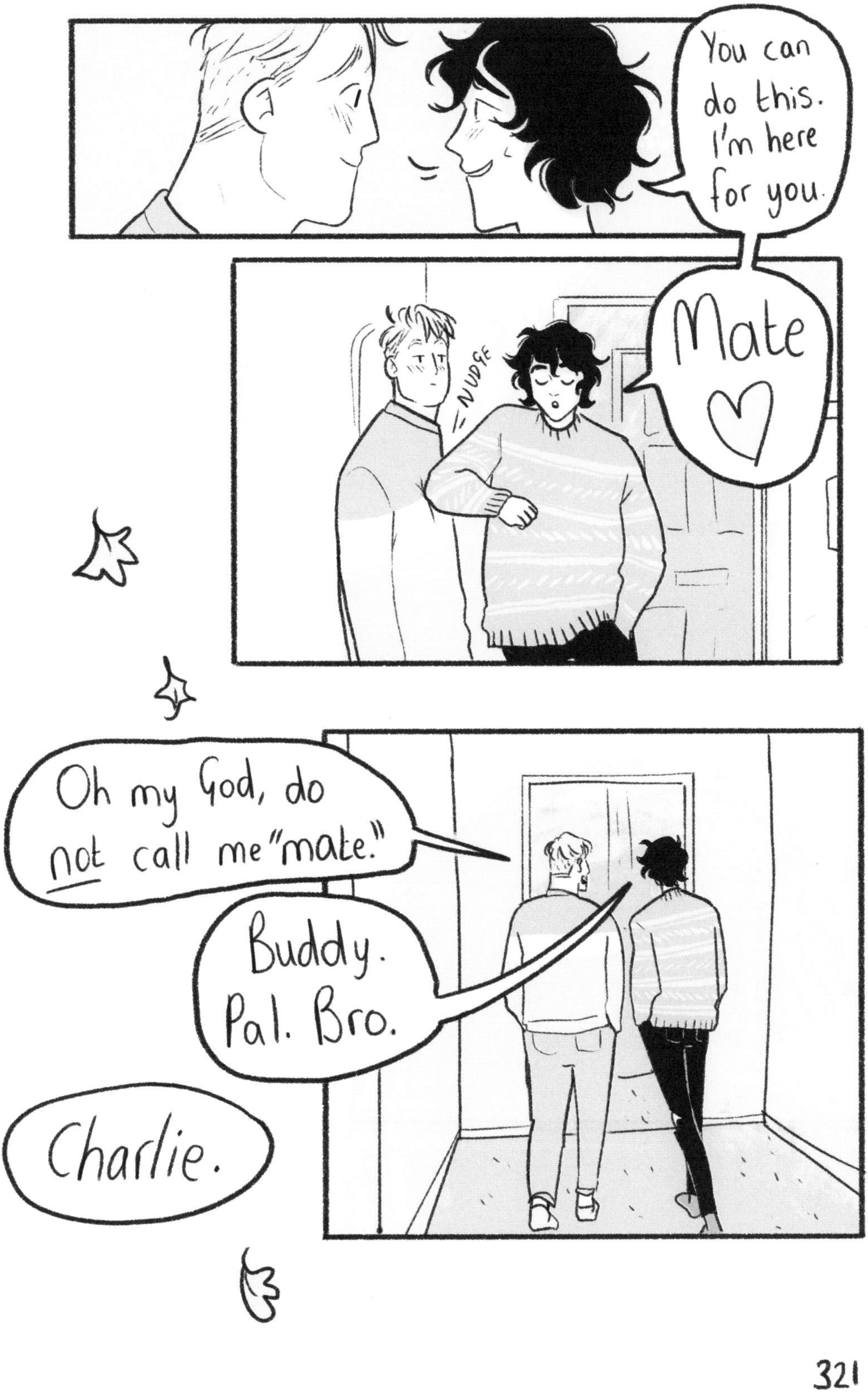
You can do this. I'm here for you.
Mate ♥
NUDGE
Oh my God, do not call me "mate."
Buddy. Pal. Bro.
Charlie.

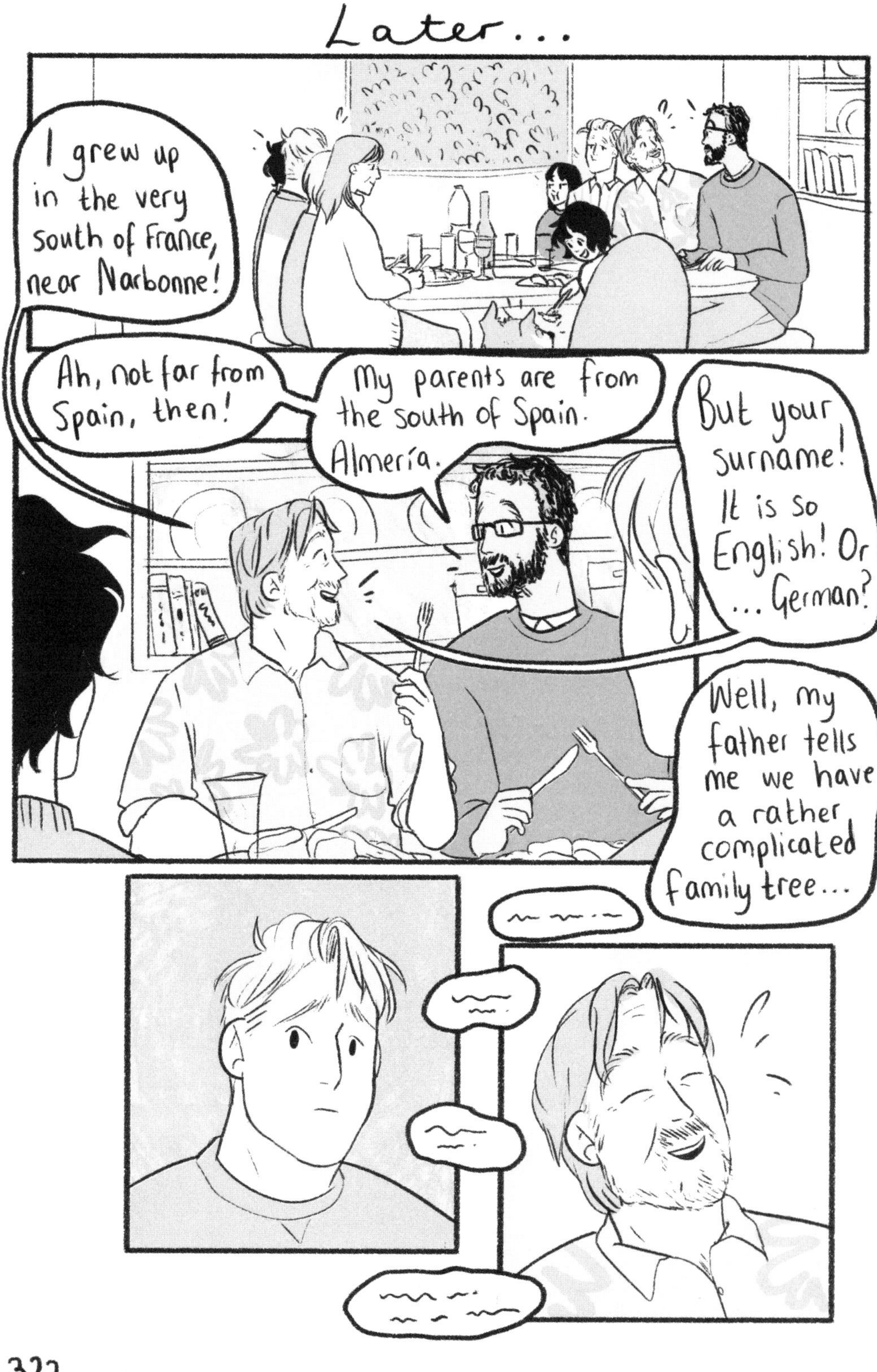
Later...
I grew up in the very south of France, near Narbonne!
Ah, not far from Spain, then!
My parents are from the south of Spain. Almería.
But your surname! It is so English! Or ...German?
Well, my father tells me we have a rather complicated family tree...

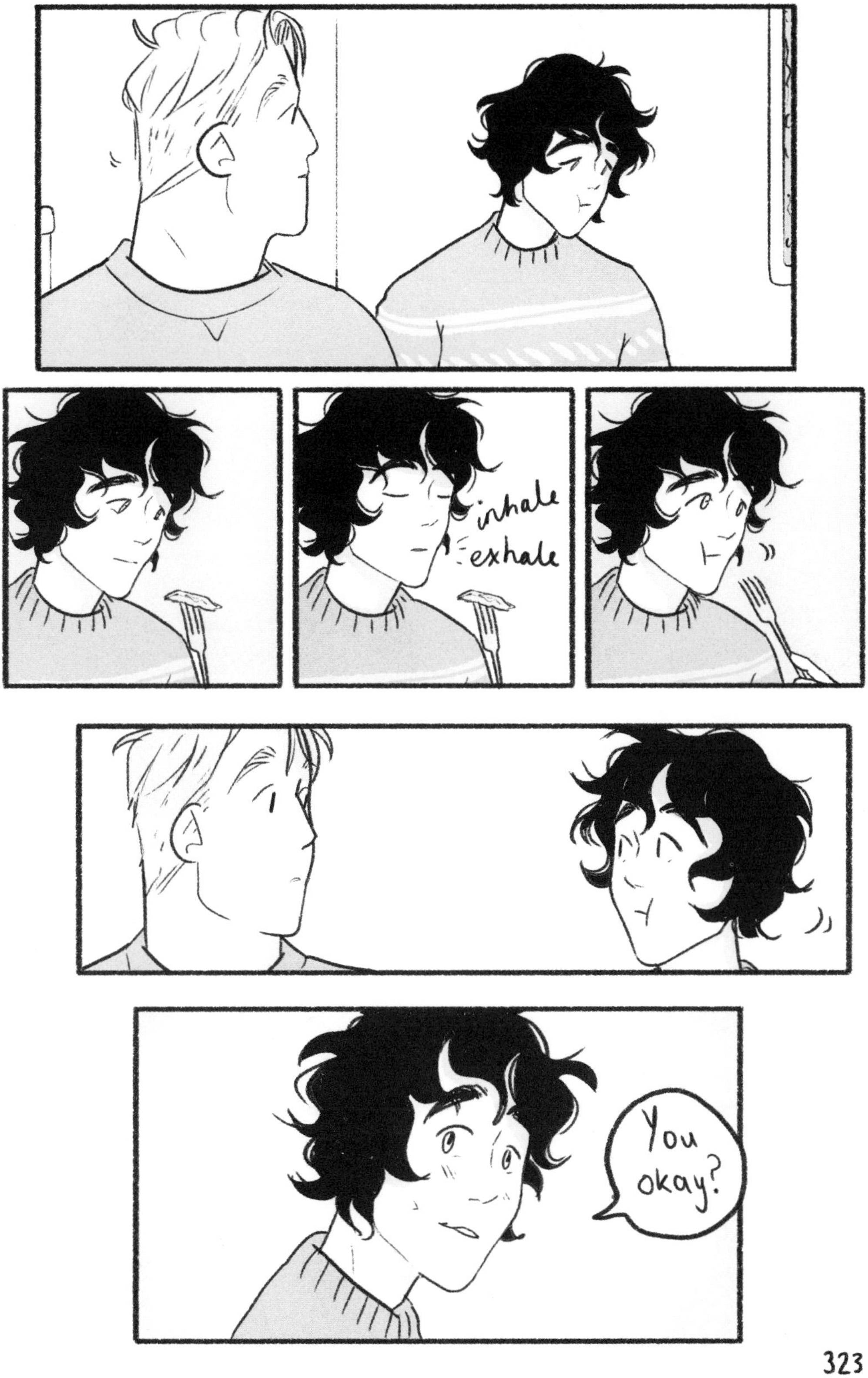
inhale
exhale
You okay?

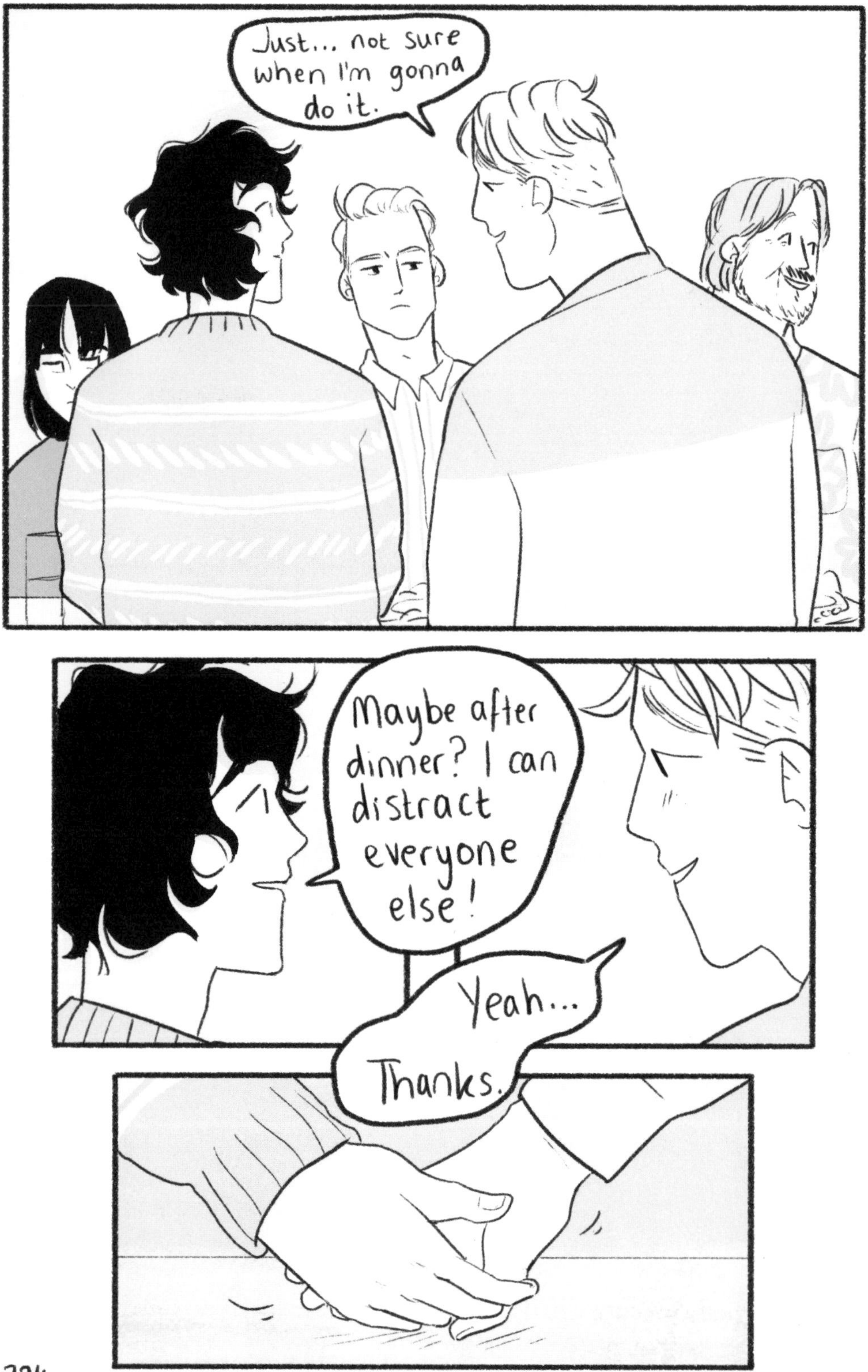
Just... not sure when I'm gonna do it.
Maybe after dinner? I can distract everyone else!
Yeah... Thanks.

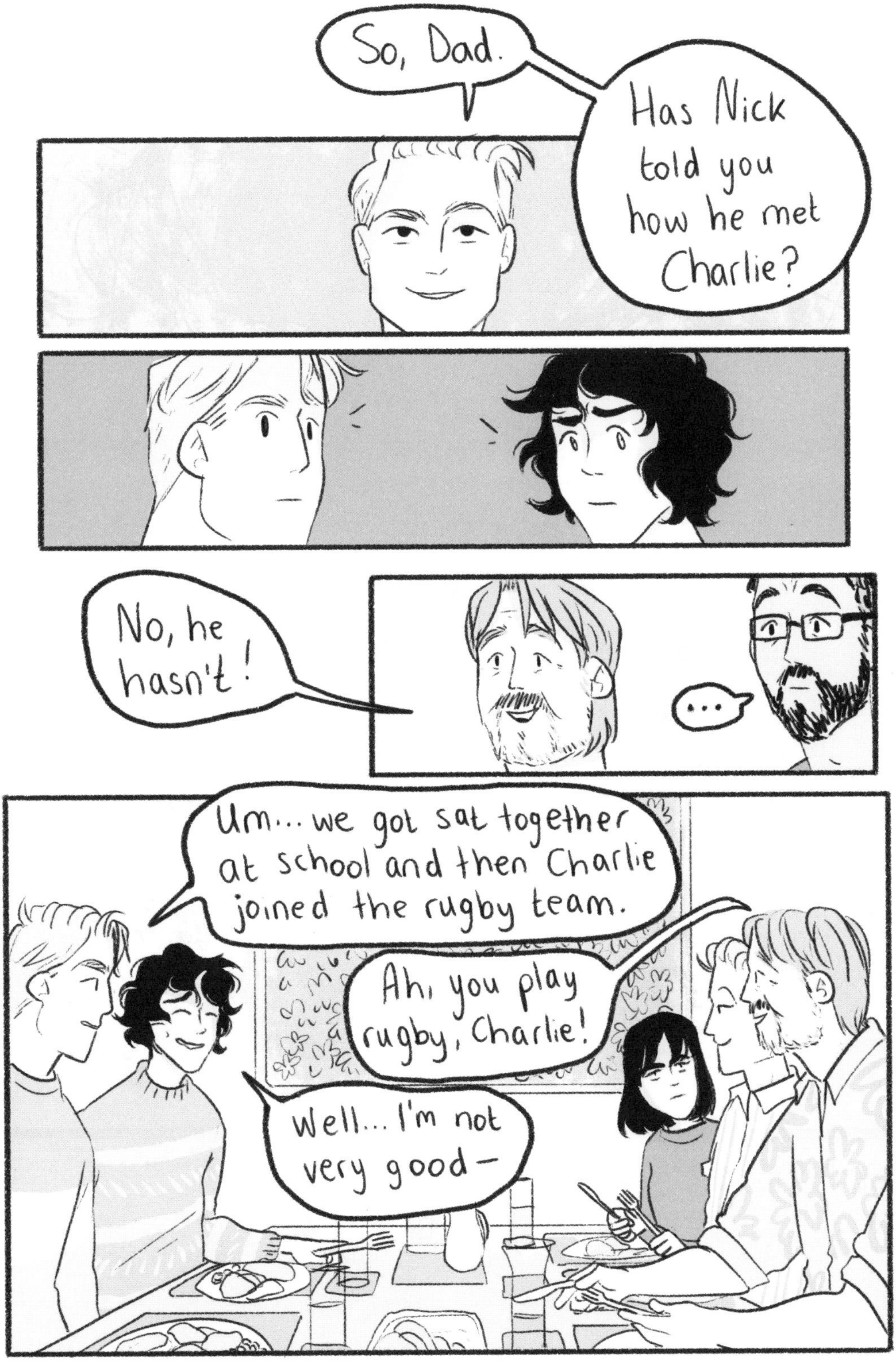
So, Dad.
Has Nick told you how he met Charlie?
No, he hasn't!
...
Um... we got sat together at school and then Charlie joined the rugby team.
Ah, you play rugby, Charlie!
Well... I'm not very good–

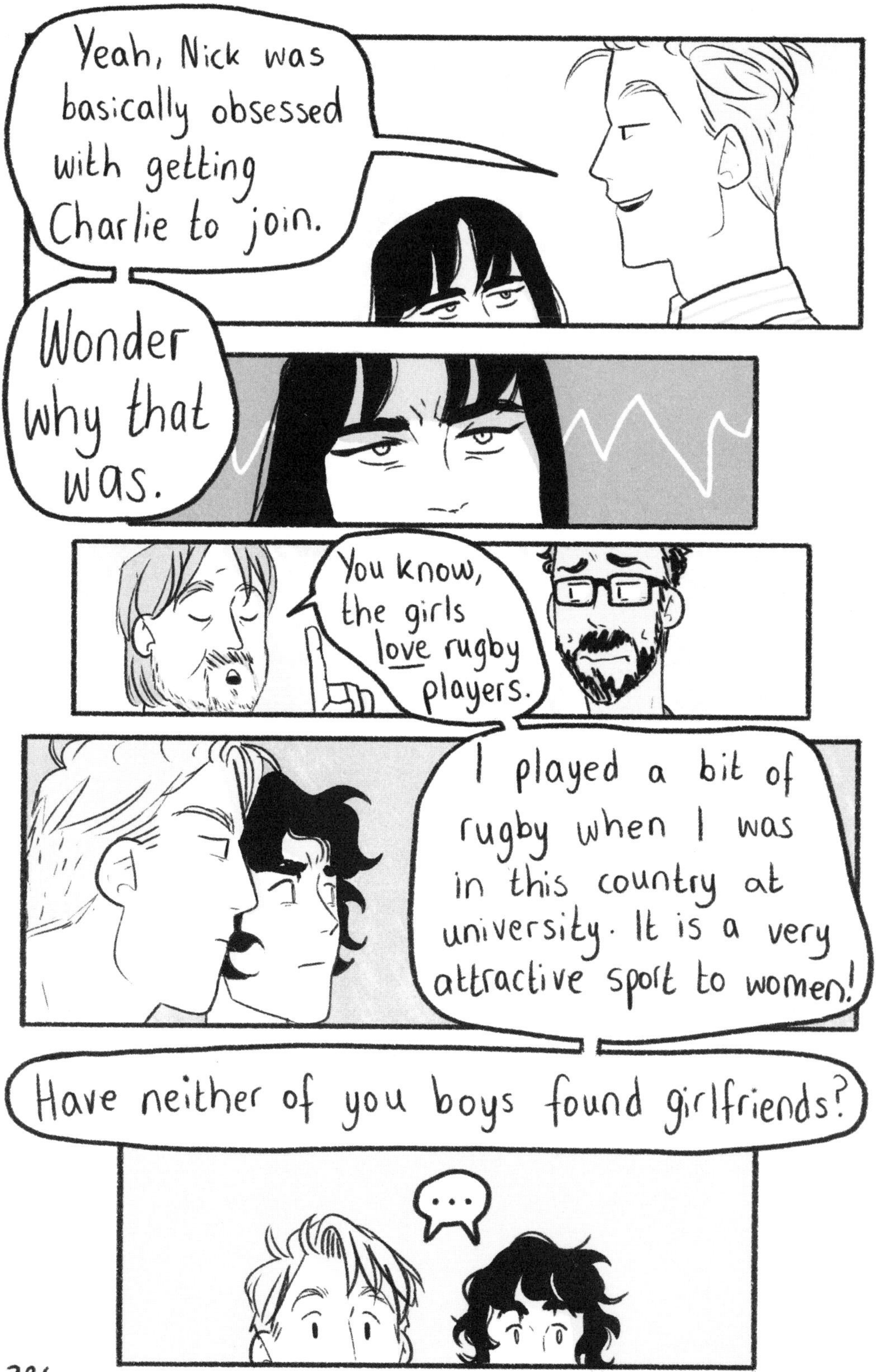

Yeah, Nick was basically obsessed with getting Charlie to join.
Wonder why that was.
You know, the girls love rugby players.
I played a bit of rugby when I was in this country at university. It is a very attractive sport to women!
Have neither of you boys found girlfriends?
...

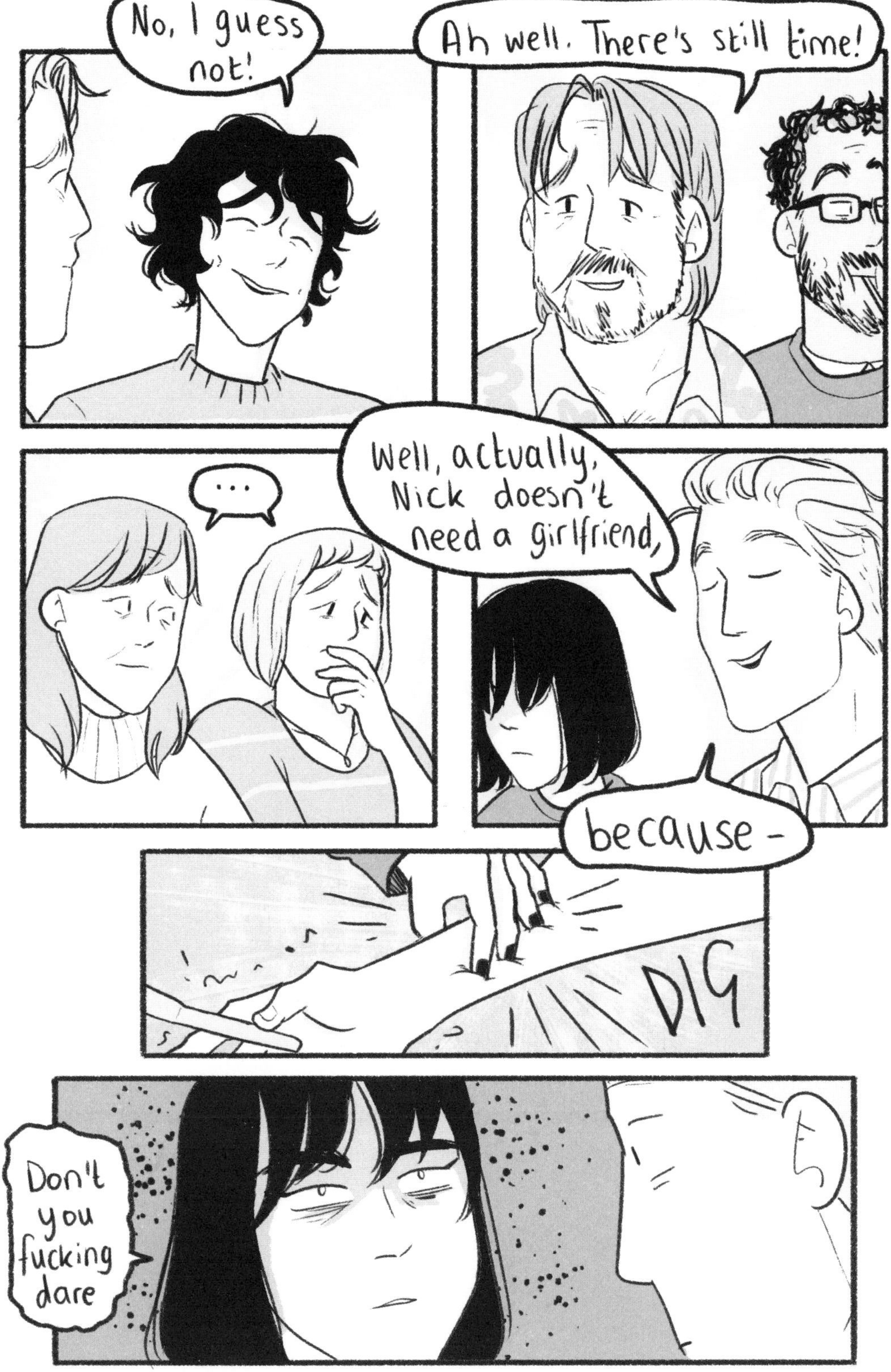
No, I guess not!
Ah well. There's still time!
...
Well, actually, Nick doesn't need a girlfriend,
because -
DIG
Don't you fucking dare

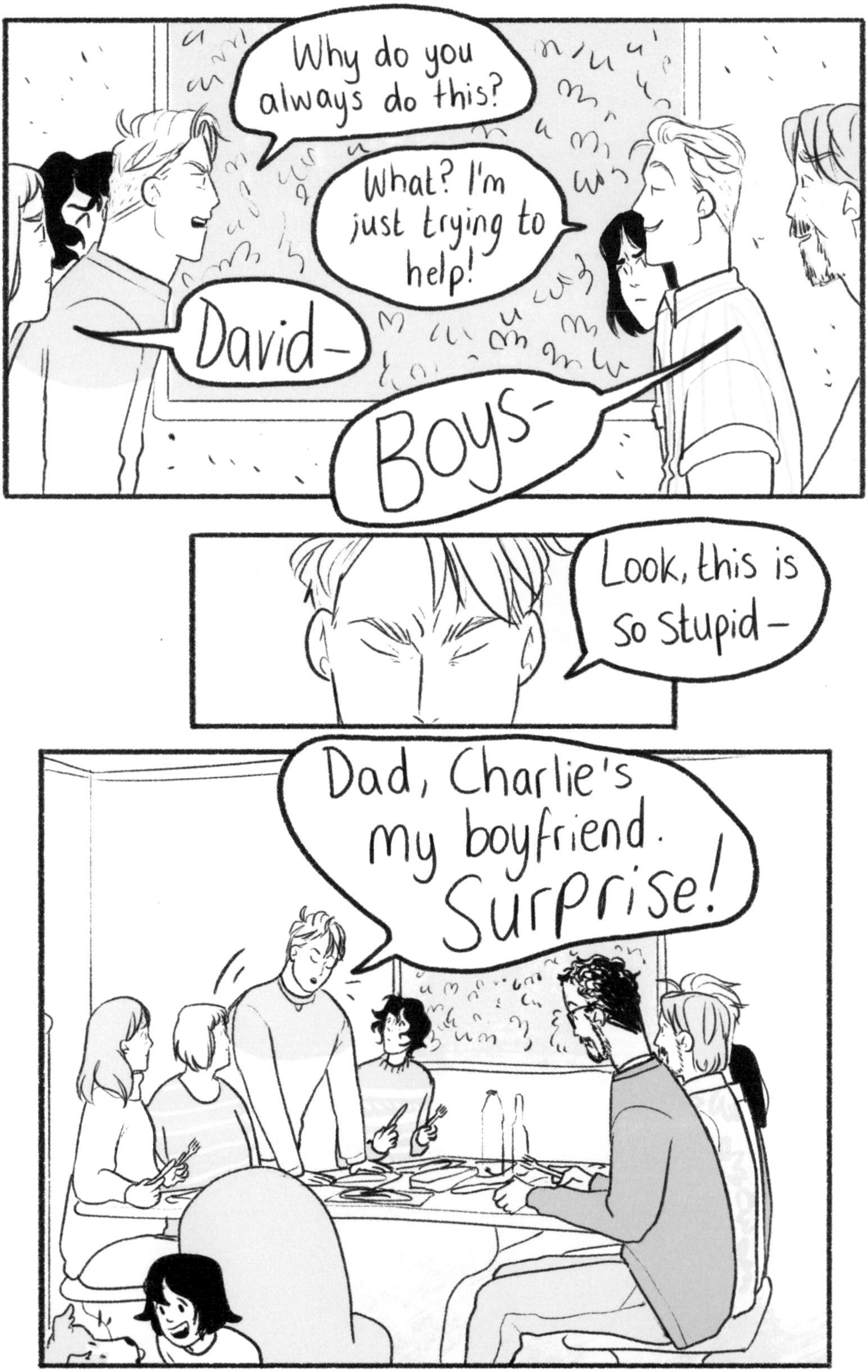
Why do you always do this?
What? I'm just trying to help!
David-
Boys-
Look, this is so stupid-
Dad, Charlie's my boyfriend. Surprise!

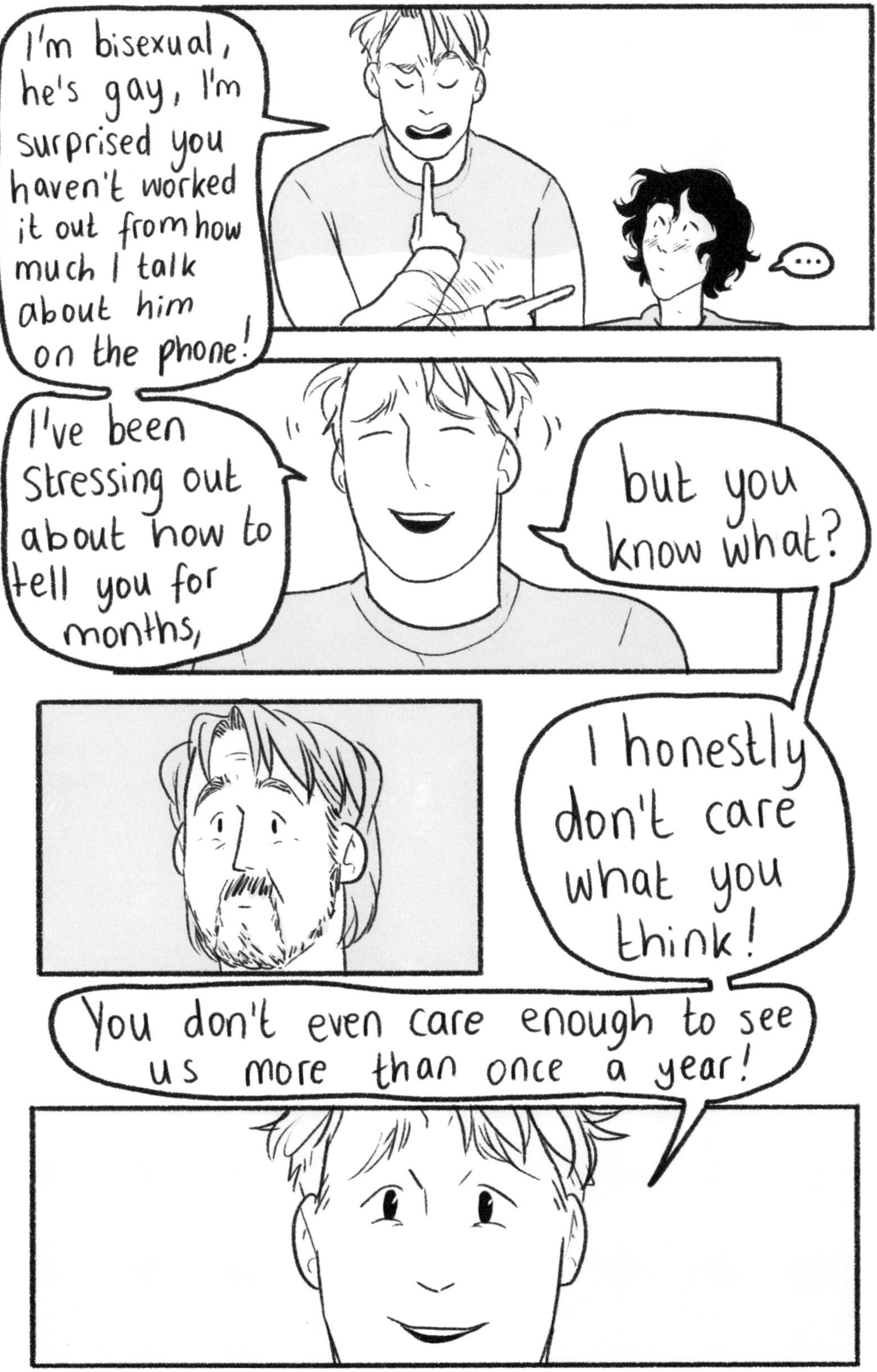
I'm bisexual, he's gay, I'm surprised you haven't worked it out from how much I talk about him on the phone!
...
I've been stressing out about how to tell you for months,
but you know what?
I honestly don't care what you think!
You don't even care enough to see us more than once a year!

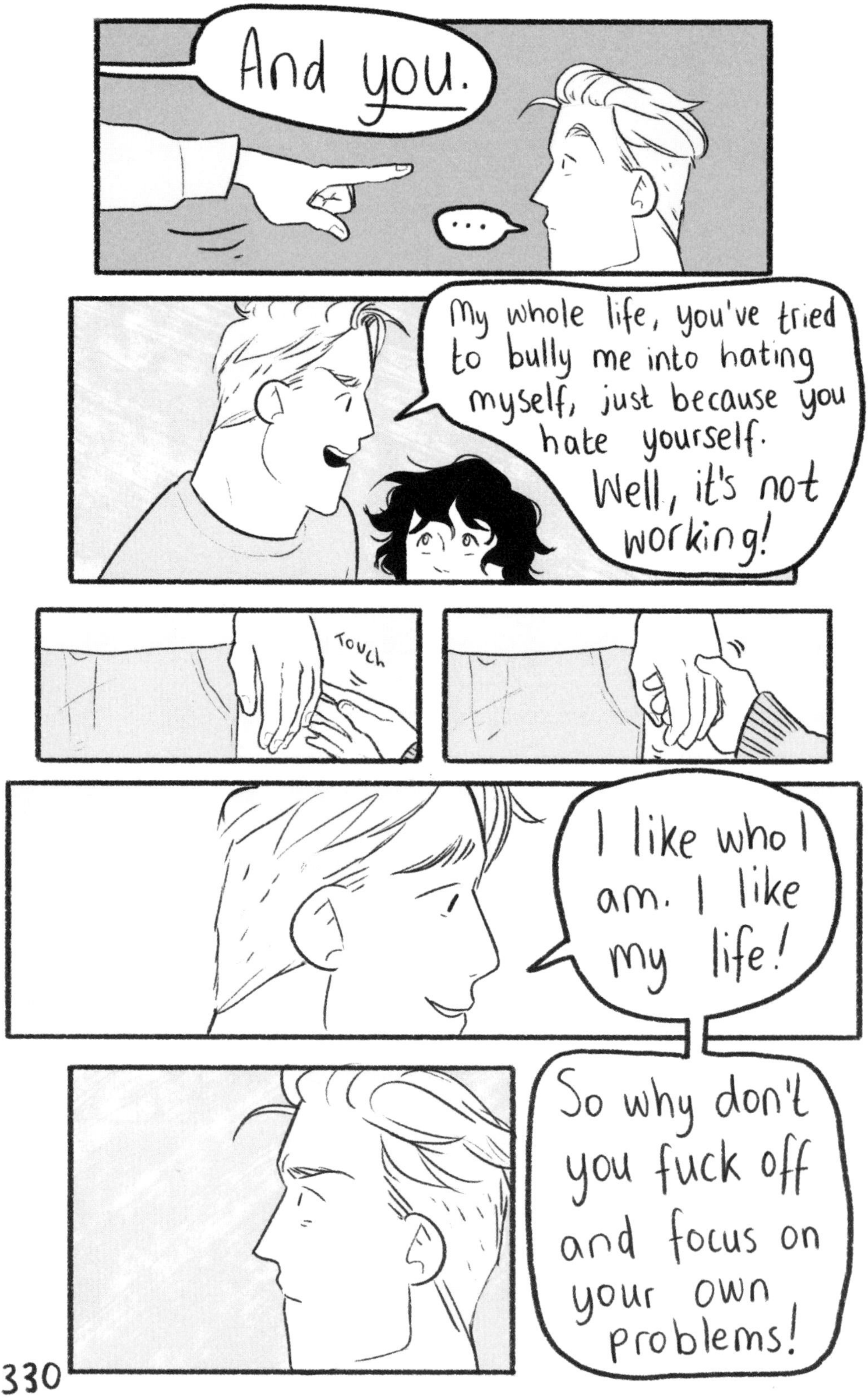
And you.
...
My whole life, you've tried to bully me into hating myself, just because you hate yourself. Well, it's not working!
TOUCH
I like who I am. I like my life!
So why don't you fuck off and focus on your own problems!

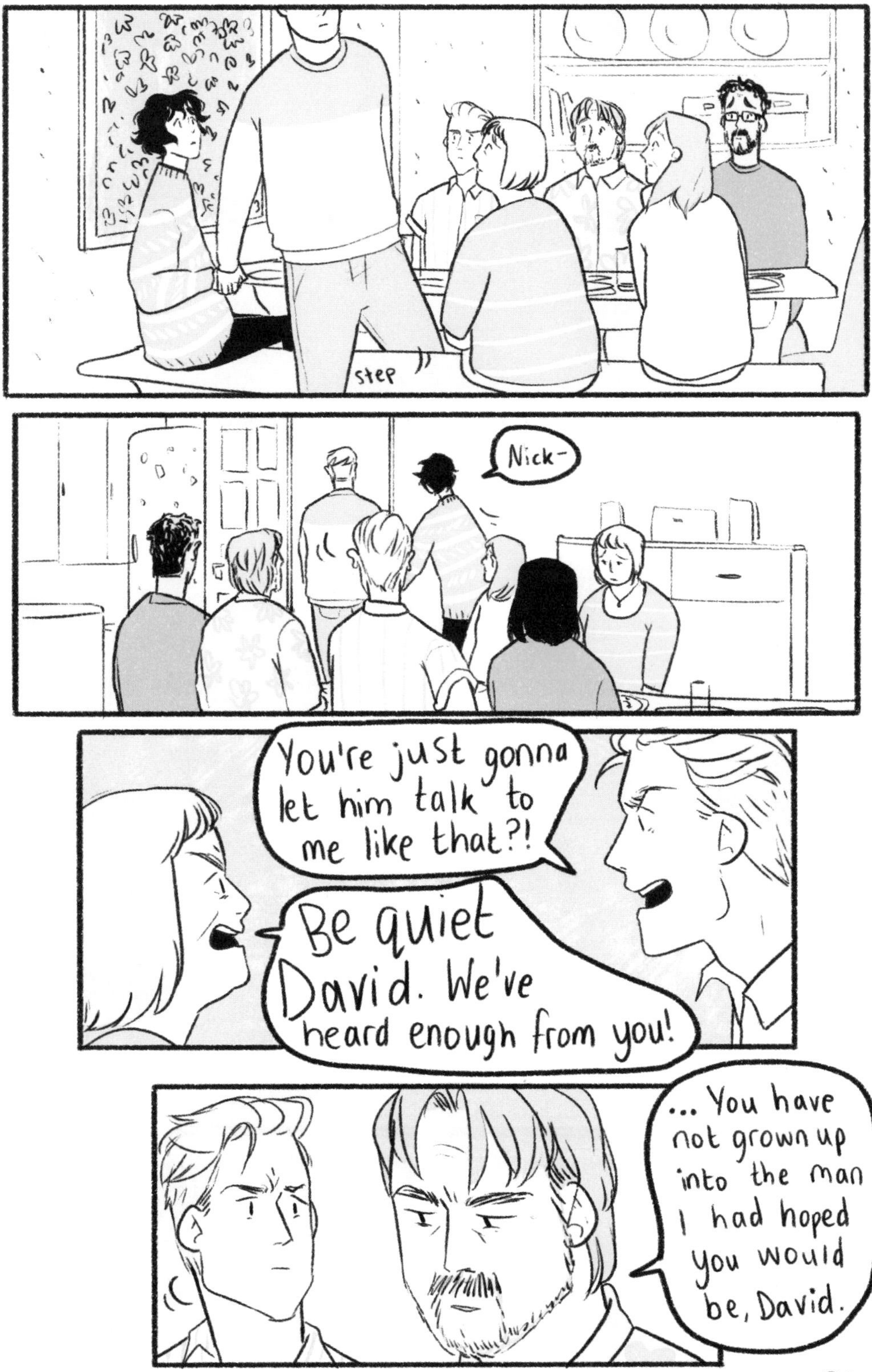
step
Nick-
You're just gonna let him talk to me like that?!
Be quiet David. We've heard enough from you!
... You have not grown up into the man I had hoped you would be, David.

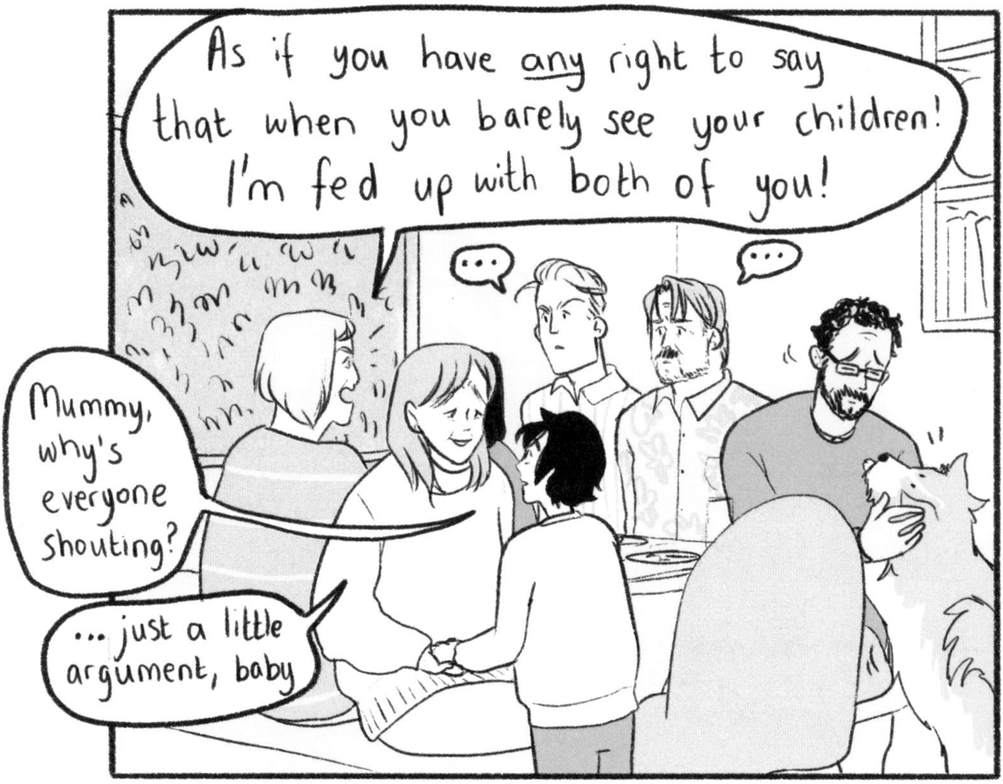
As if you have any right to say that when you barely see your children! I'm fed up with both of you!
...
...
Mummy, why's everyone shouting?
... just a little argument, baby

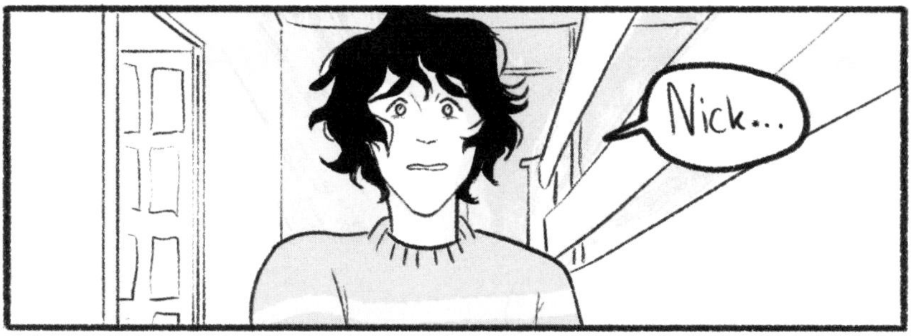
Nick...

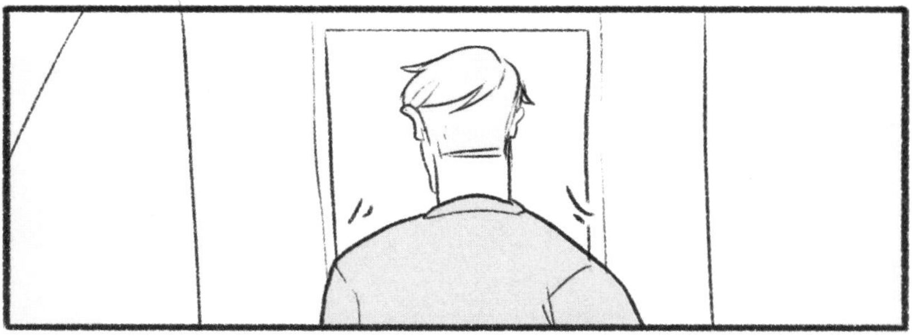

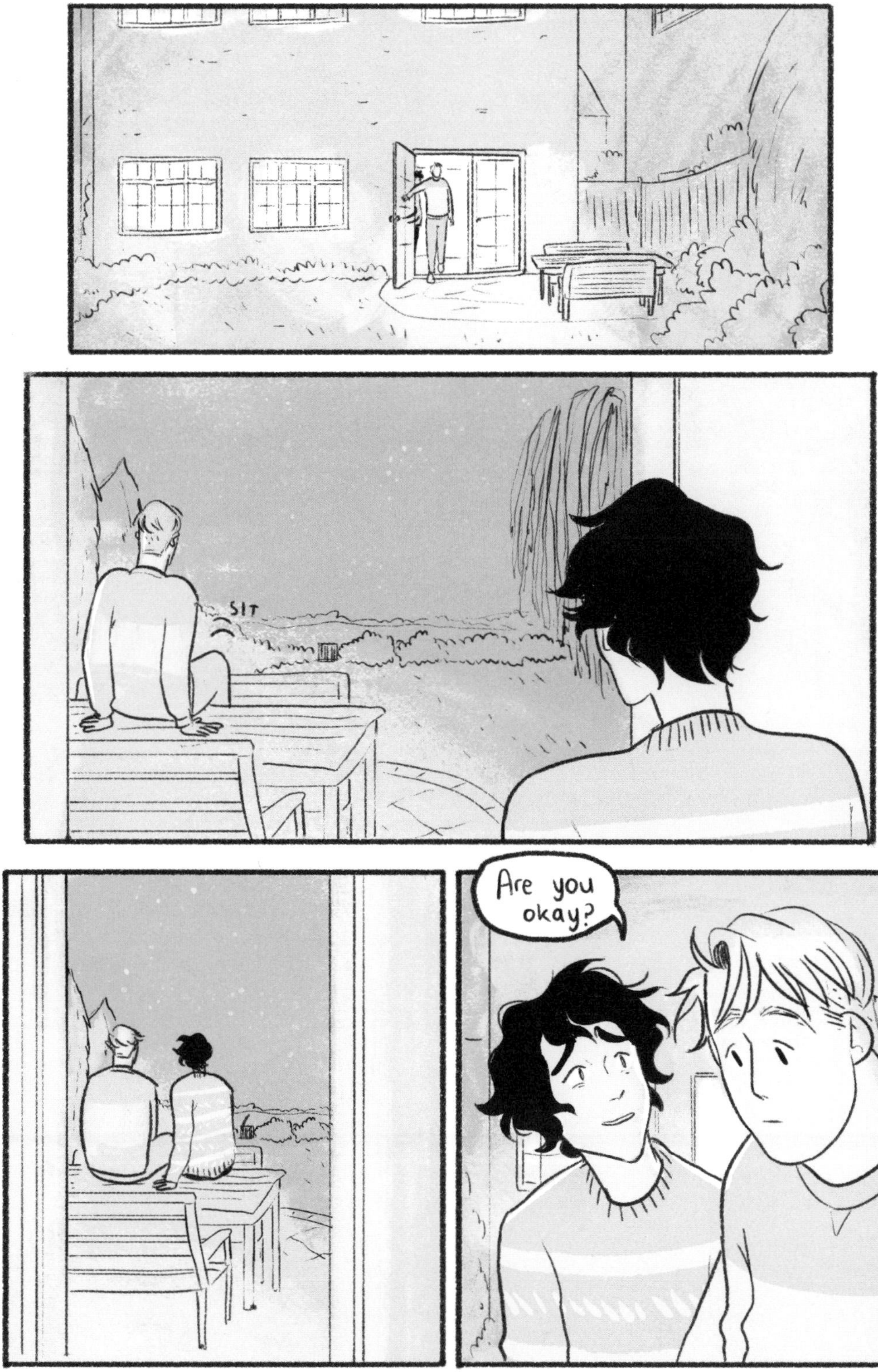
SIT
Are you okay?

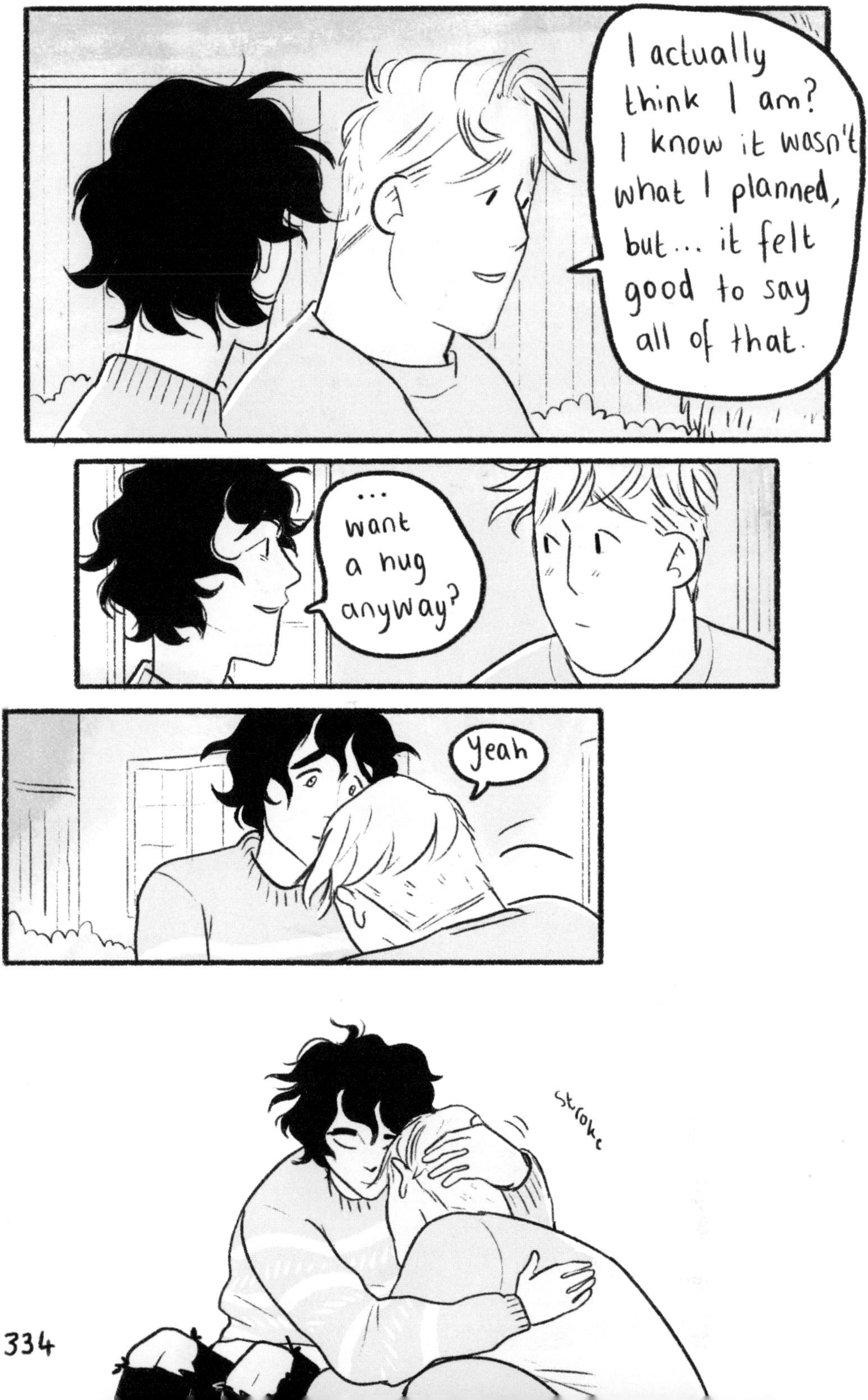
I actually think I am? I know it wasn't what I planned, but... it felt good to say all of that.
... want a hug anyway?
Yeah
stroke

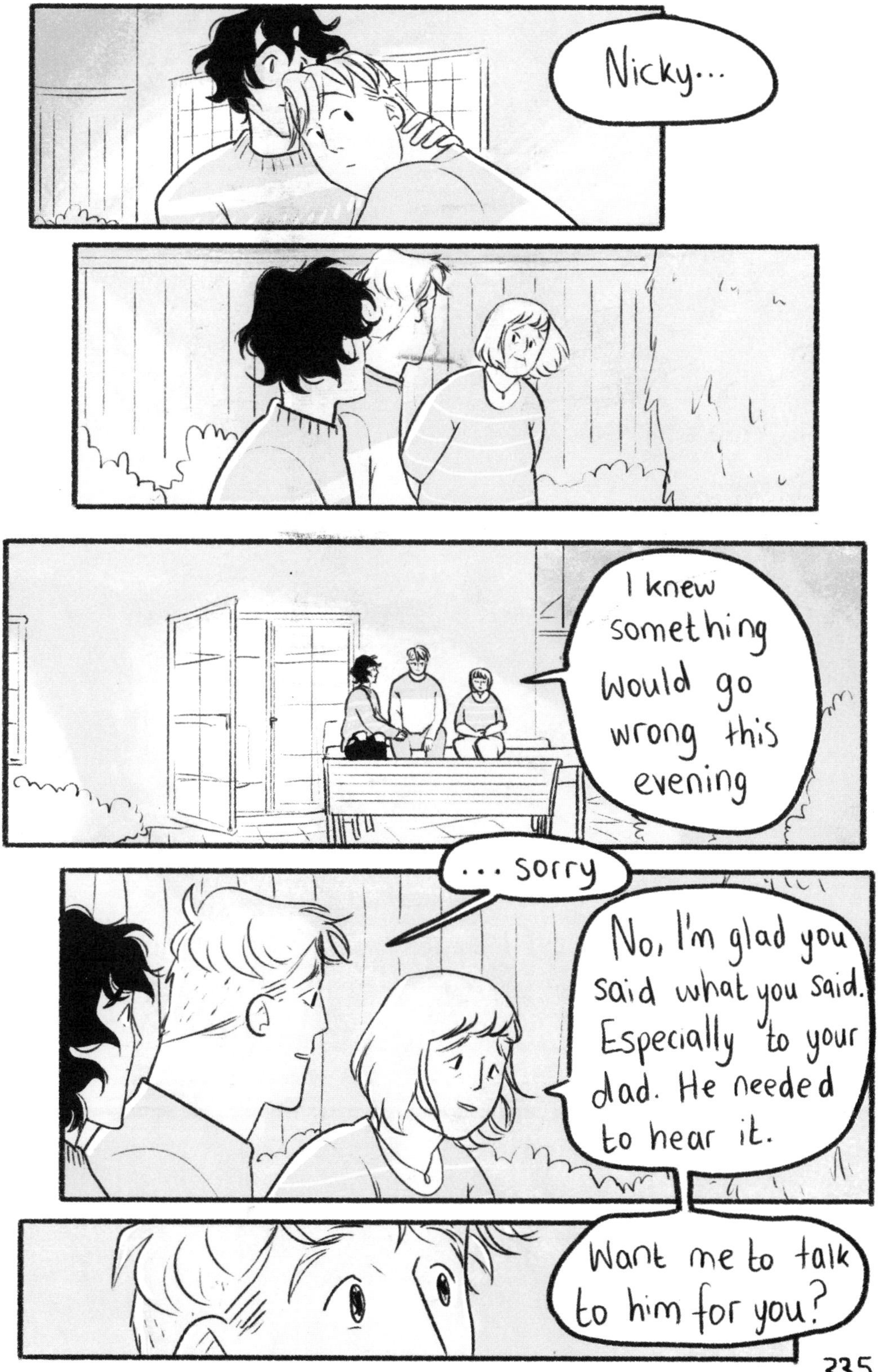
Nicky...
I knew something would go wrong this evening
...sorry
No, I'm glad you said what you said. Especially to your dad. He needed to hear it.
Want me to talk to him for you?

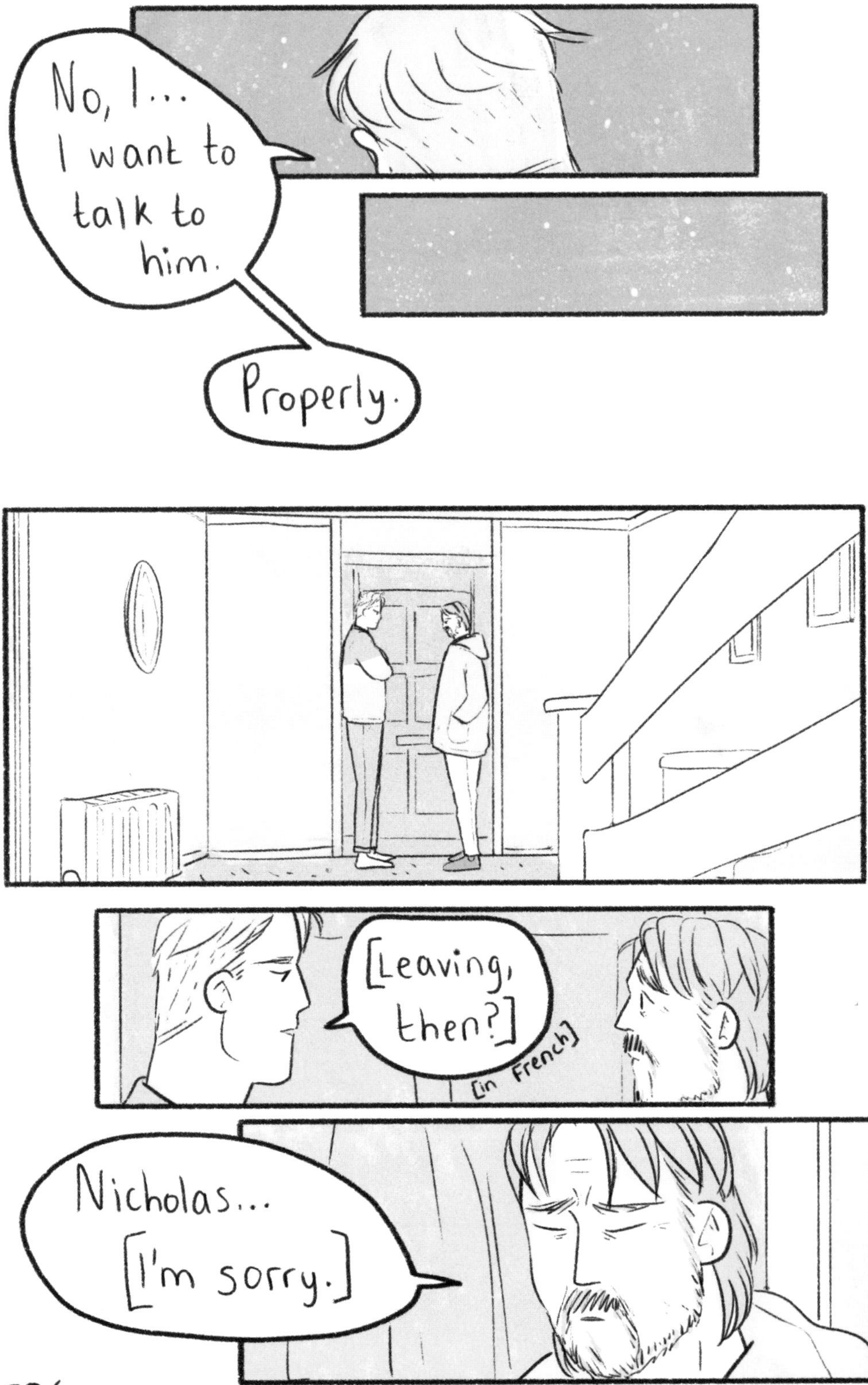
No, I... I want to talk to him.
Properly.
[Leaving, then?]
[in French]
Nicholas... [I'm sorry.]

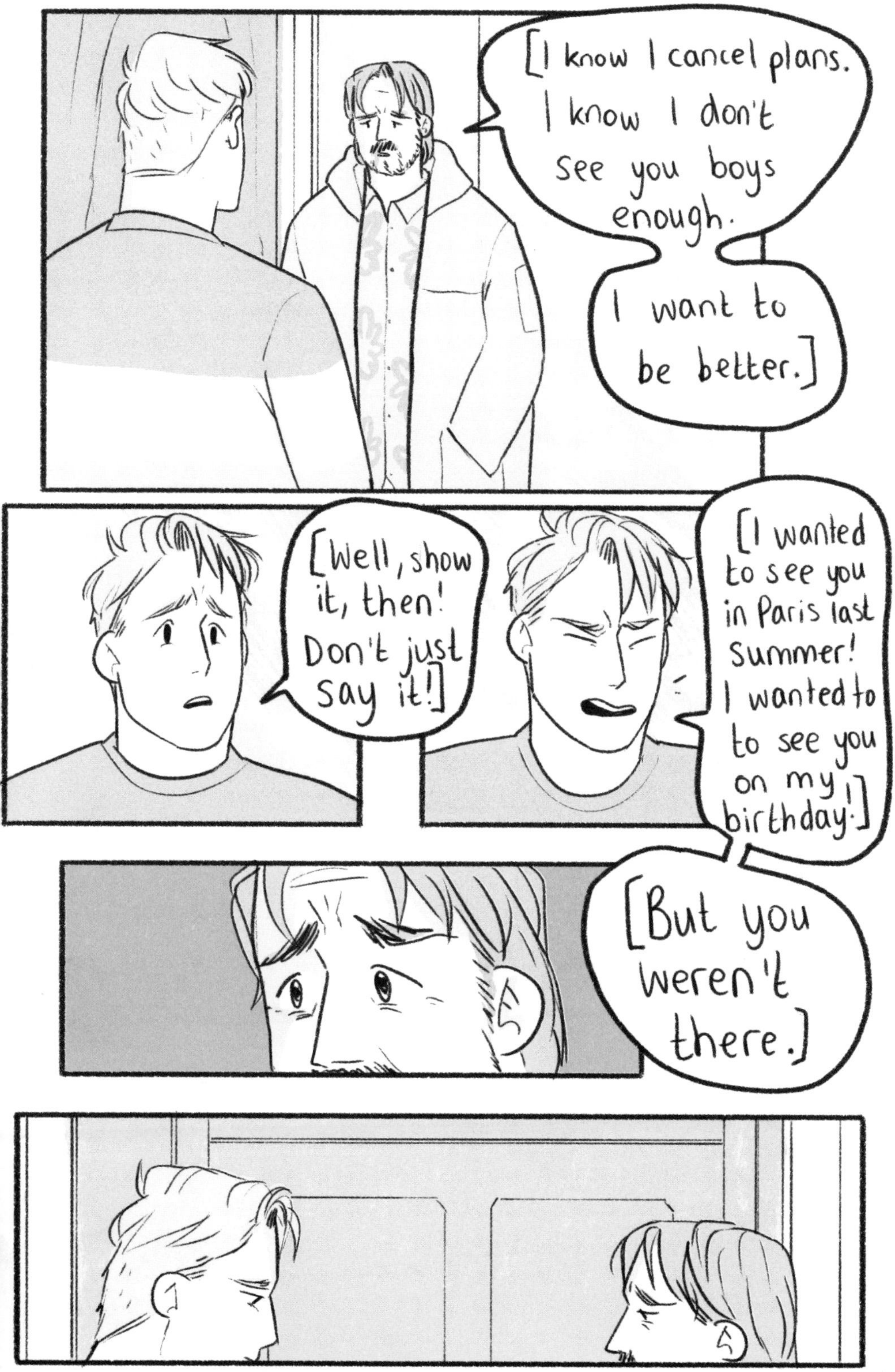
[I know I cancel plans. I know I don't see you boys enough.
I want to be better.]
[Well, show it, then! Don't just say it!]
[I wanted to see you in Paris last summer! I wanted to to see you on my birthday!]
[But you weren't there.]

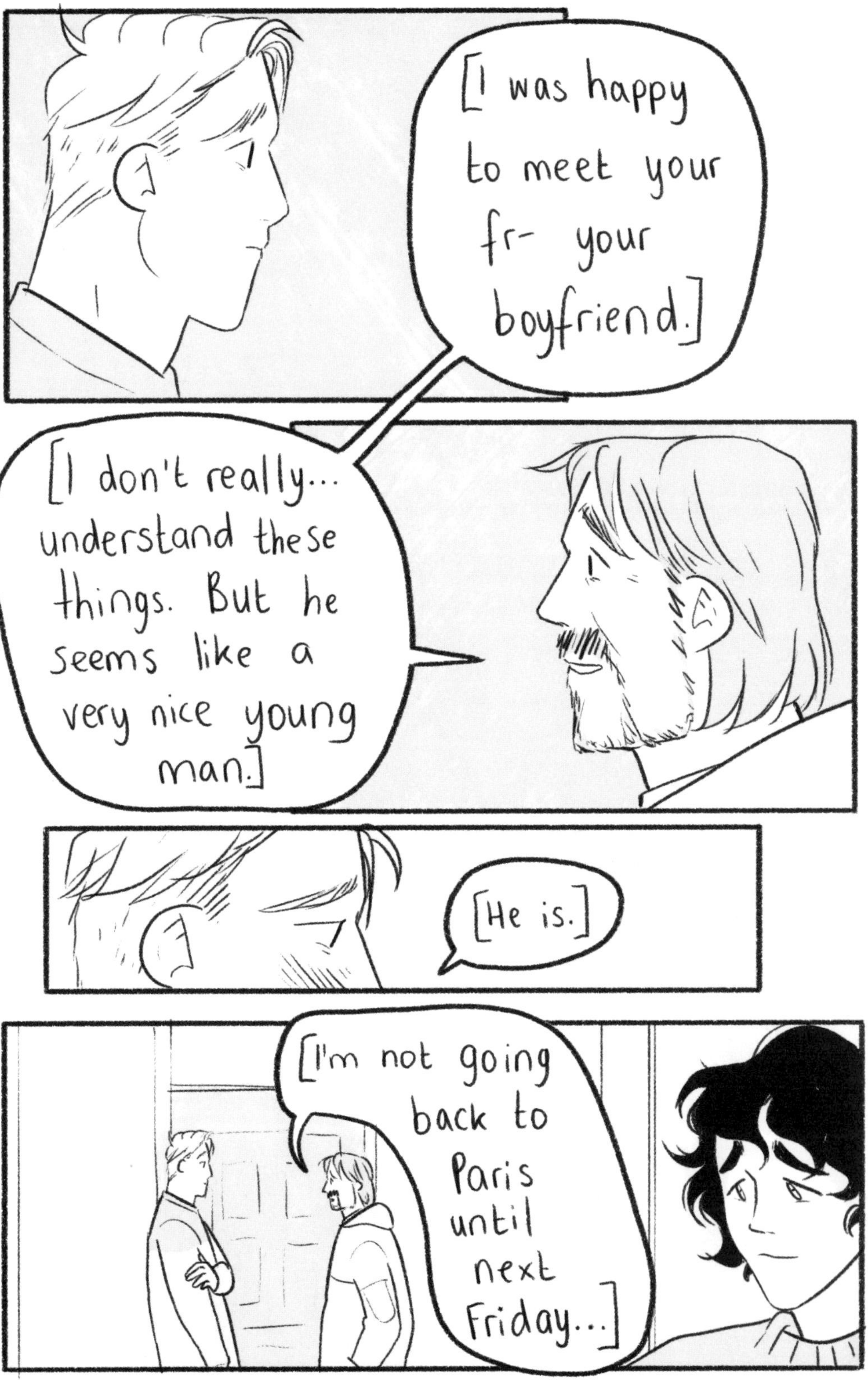
[I was happy to meet your fr- your boyfriend.]
[I don't really... understand these things. But he seems like a very nice young man.]
[He is.]
[I'm not going back to Paris until next Friday...]

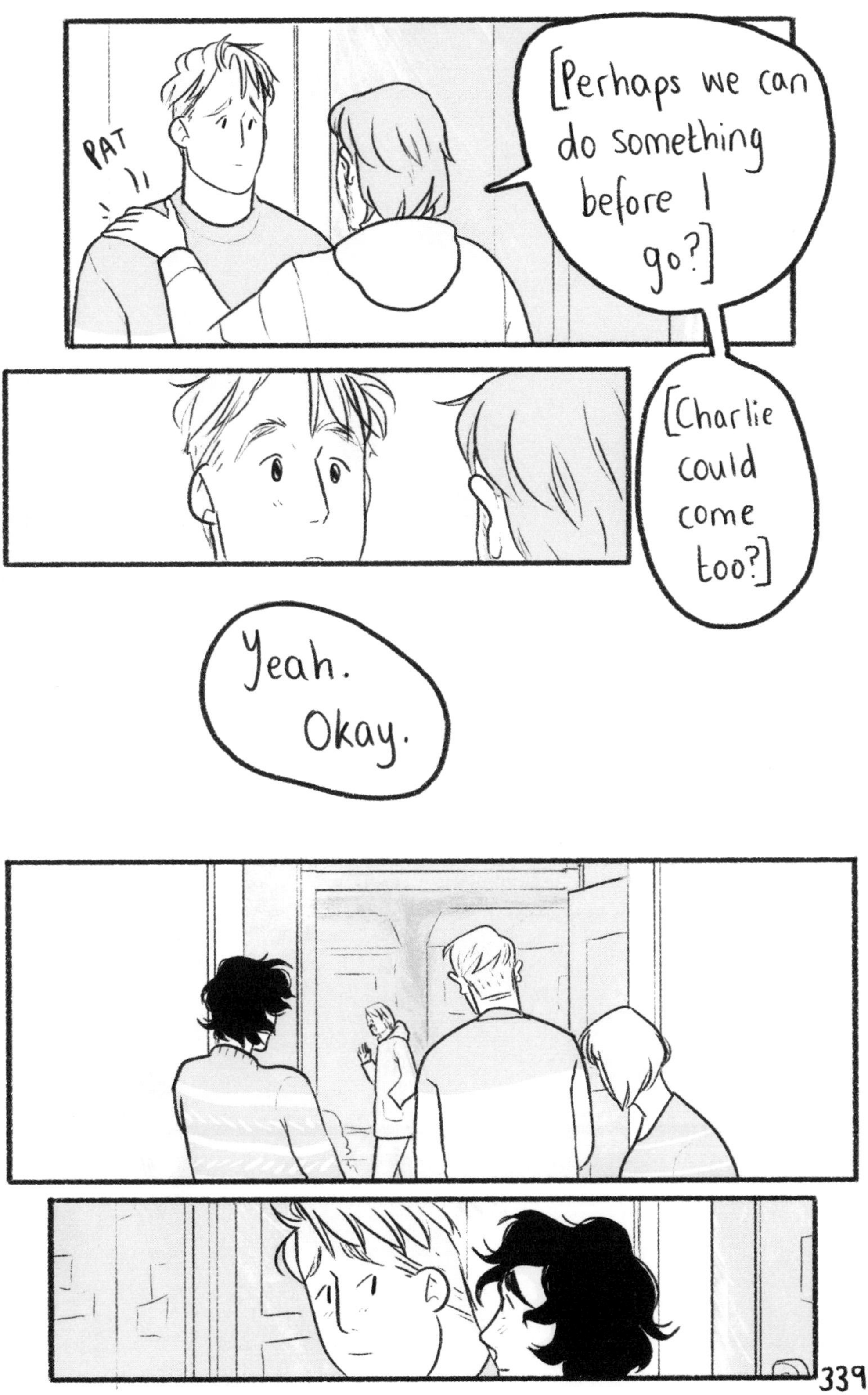
PAT
[Perhaps we can do something before I go?]
[Charlie could come too?]
Yeah. Okay.

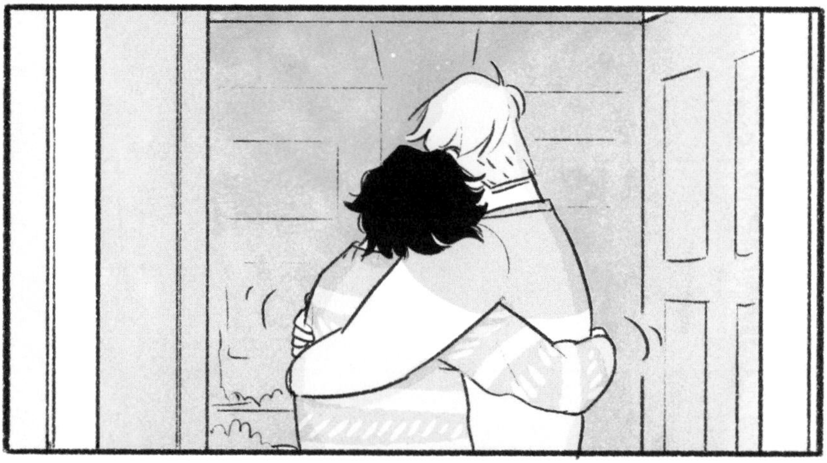

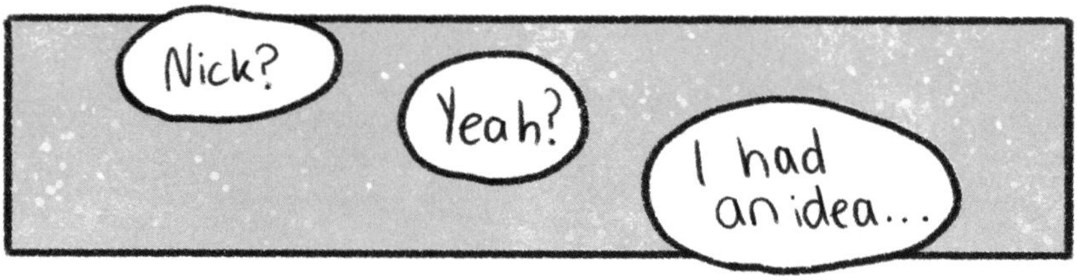
Nick?
Yeah?
I had an idea...

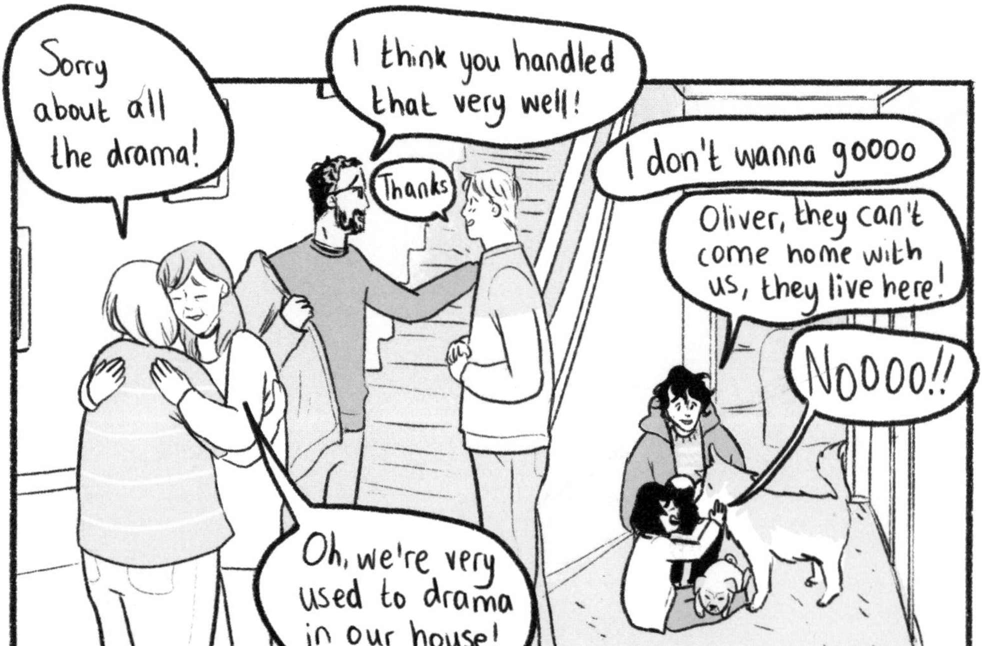
Sorry about all the drama!
I think you handled that very well!
Thanks
I don't wanna goooo
Oliver, they can't come home with us, they live here!
Noooo!!
Oh, we're very used to drama in our house!

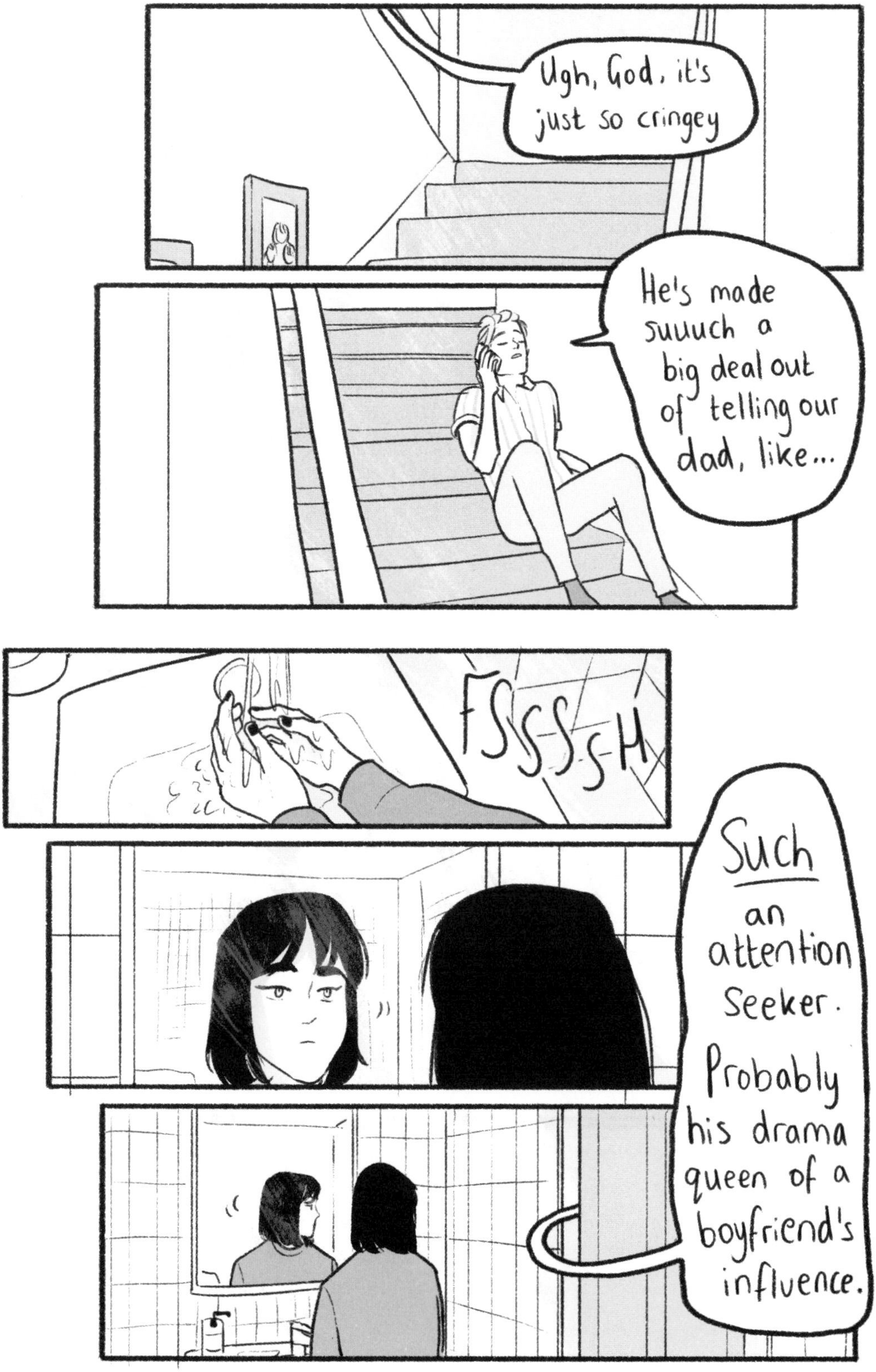
Ugh, God, it's just so cringey
He's made suuuch a big deal out of telling our dad, like...
FSSSSH
Such an attention seeker.
Probably his drama queen of a boyfriend's influence.

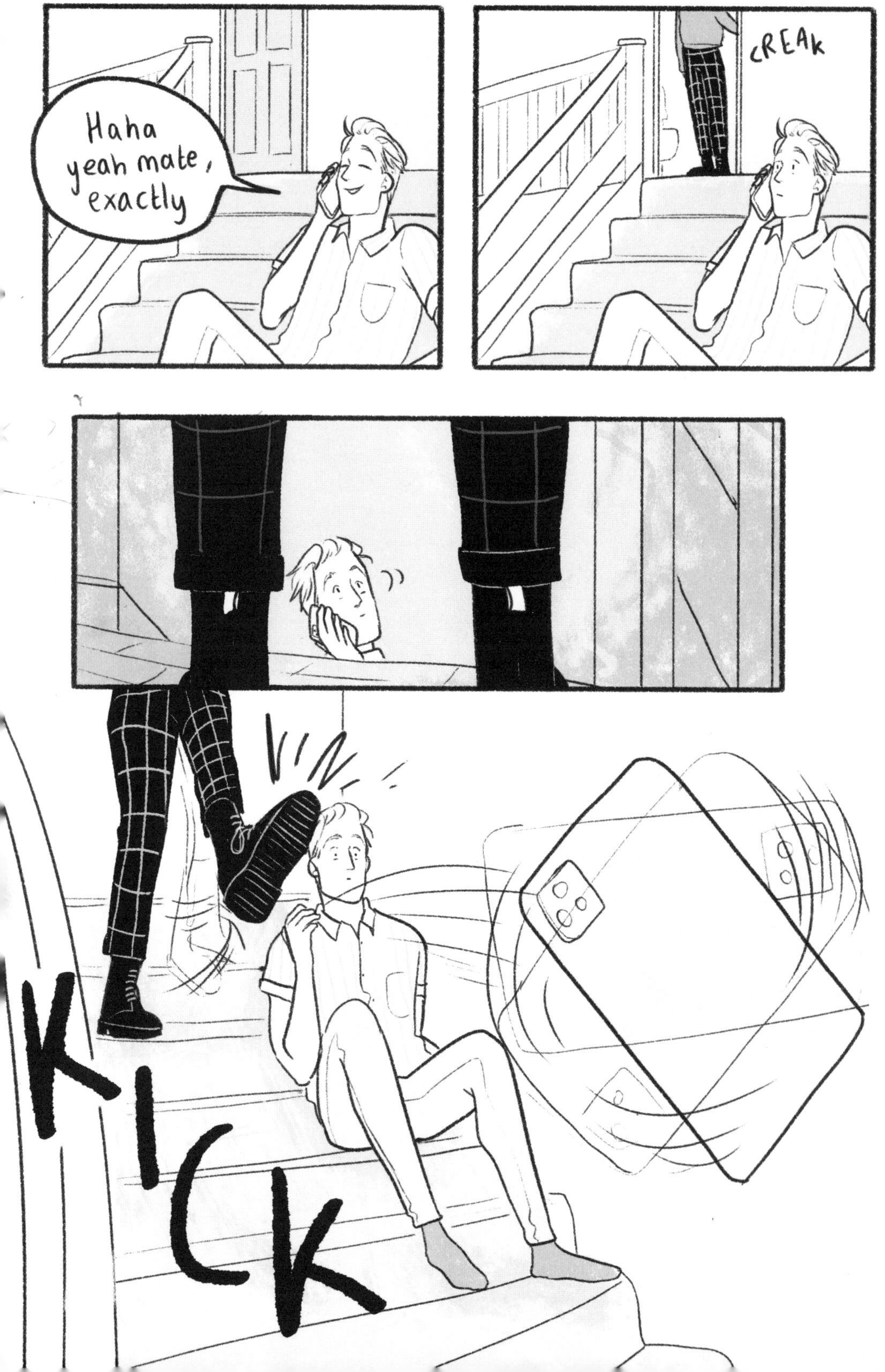

Haha yeah mate, exactly
cREAk
KICK

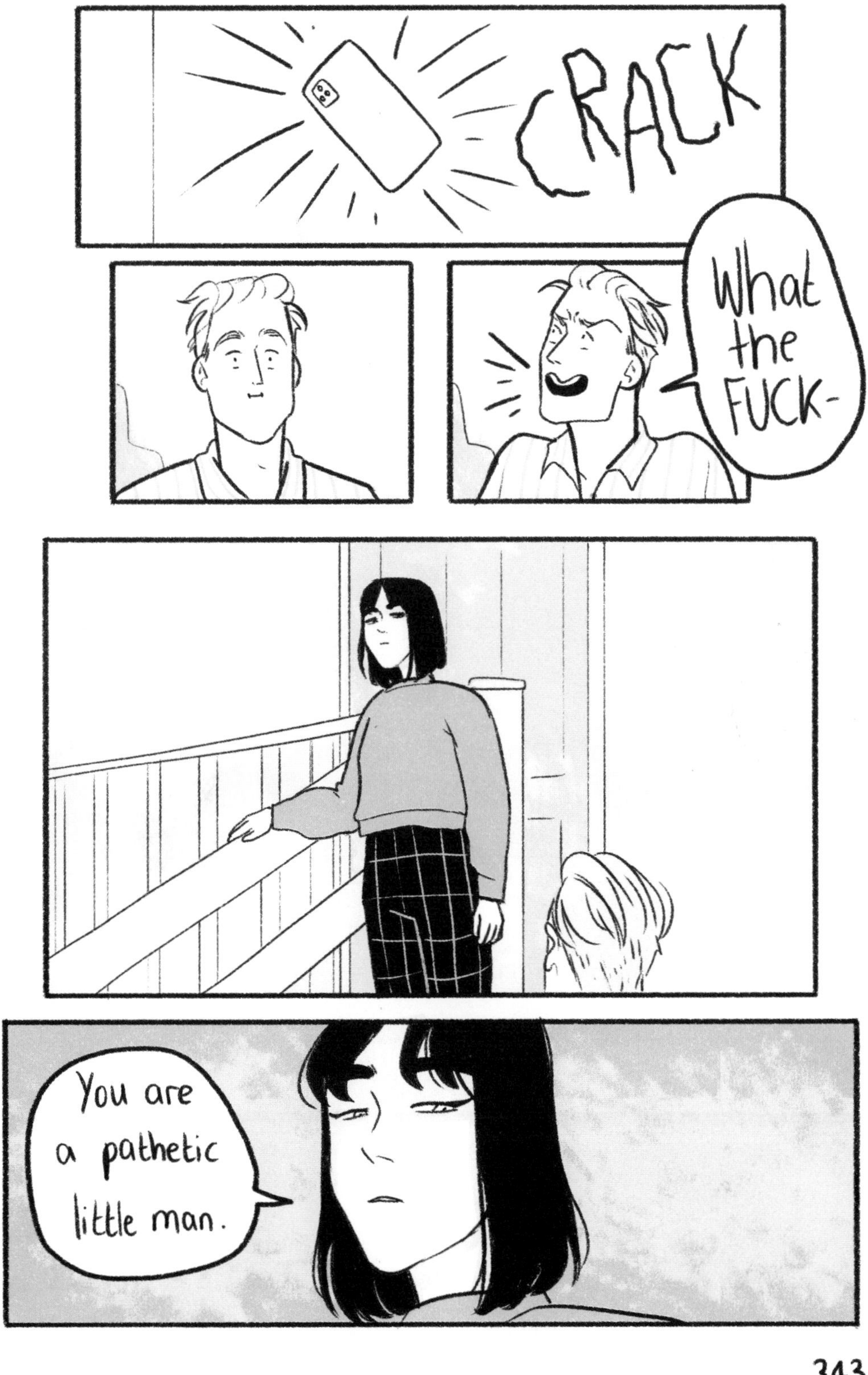
CRACK
What the FUCK-
You are a pathetic little man.

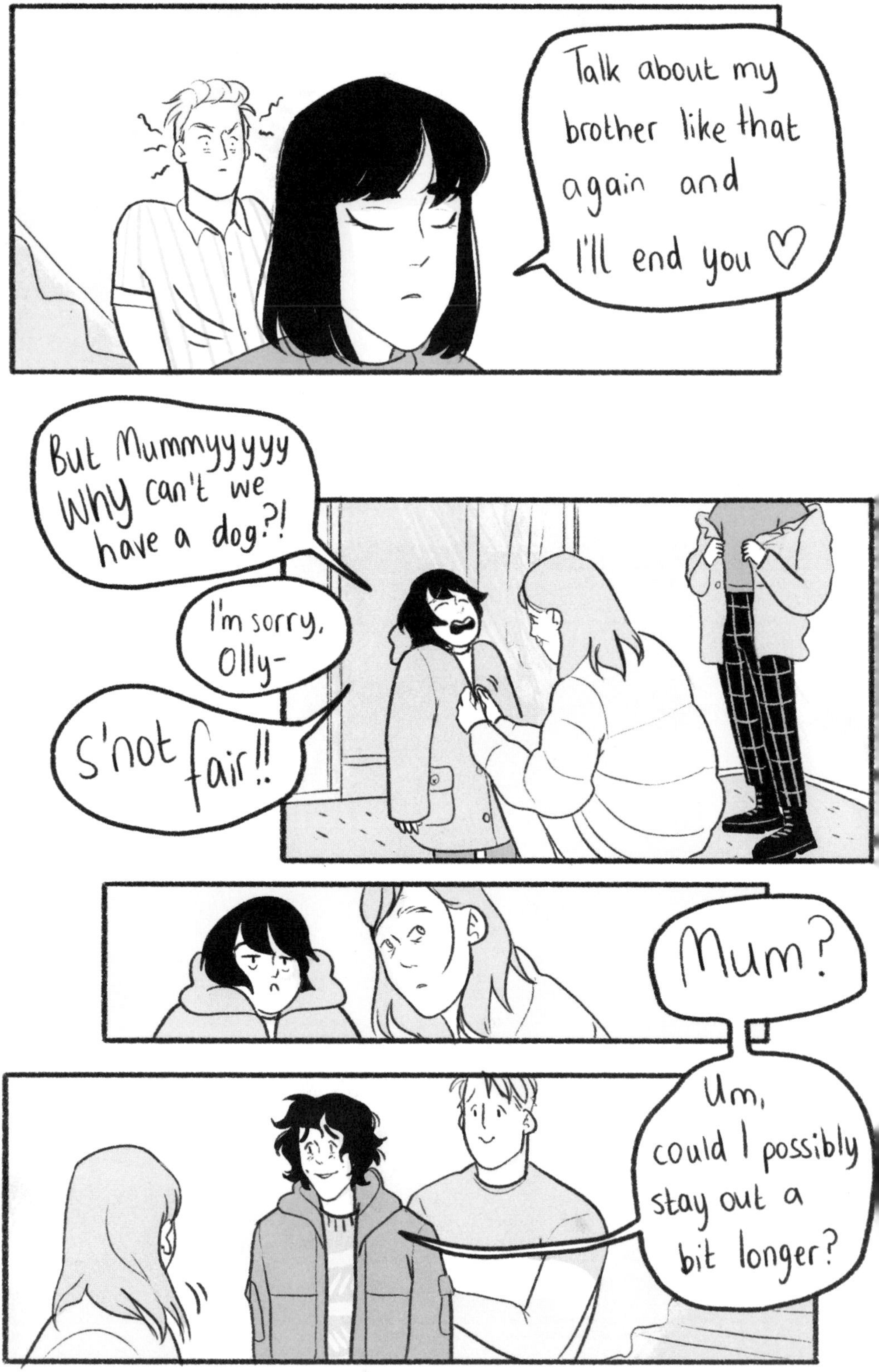
Talk about my brother like that again and I'll end you ♡
But Mummyyyyy WHY can't we have a dog?!
I'm sorry, Olly-
S'not fair!!
Mum?
Um, could I possibly stay out a bit longer?

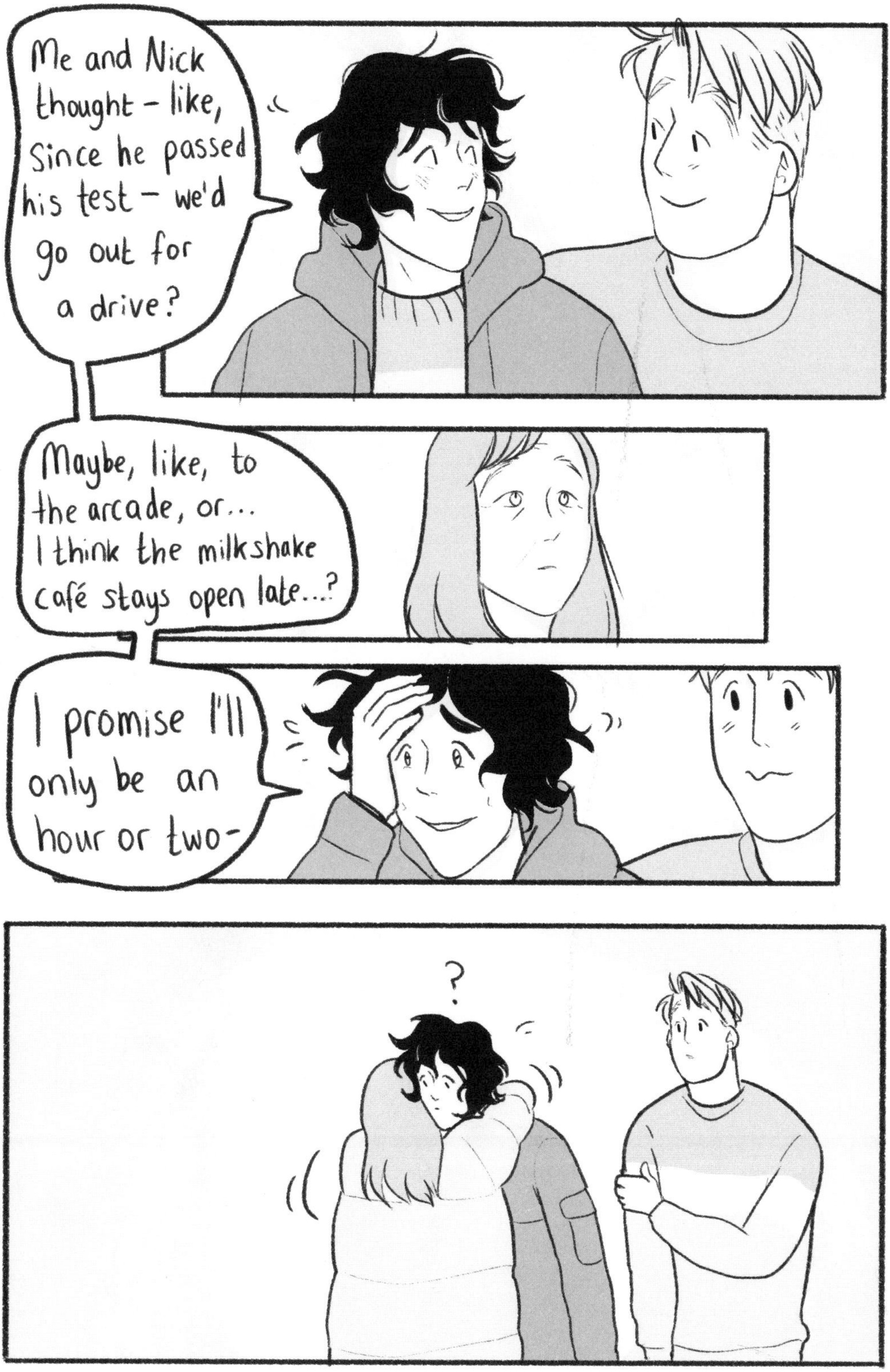
Me and Nick thought - like, since he passed his test - we'd go out for a drive?
Maybe, like, to the arcade, or... I think the milkshake café stays open late...?
I promise I'll only be an hour or two-
?

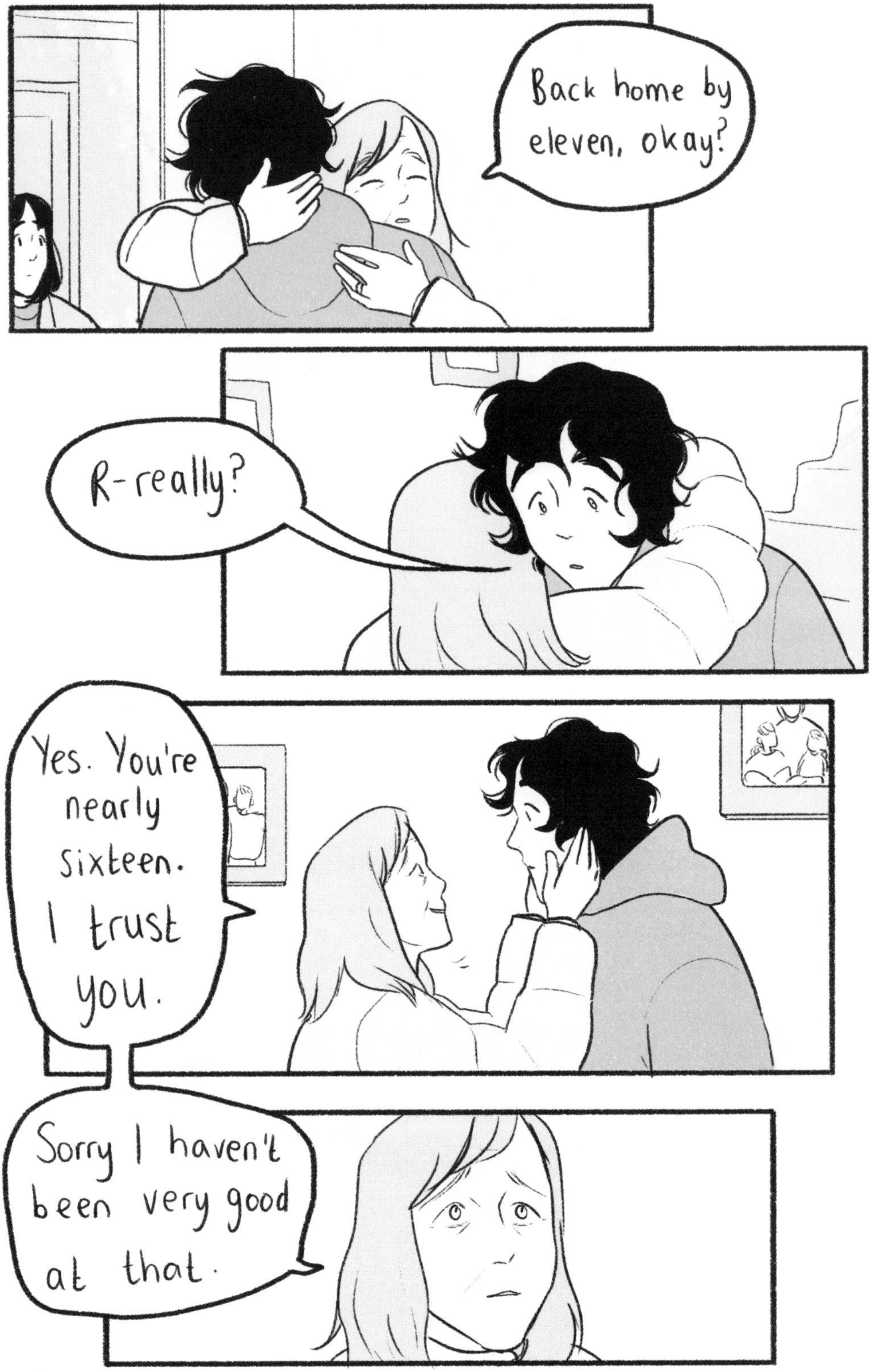
Back home by eleven, okay?
R-really?
Yes. You're nearly sixteen. I trust you.
Sorry I haven't been very good at that.

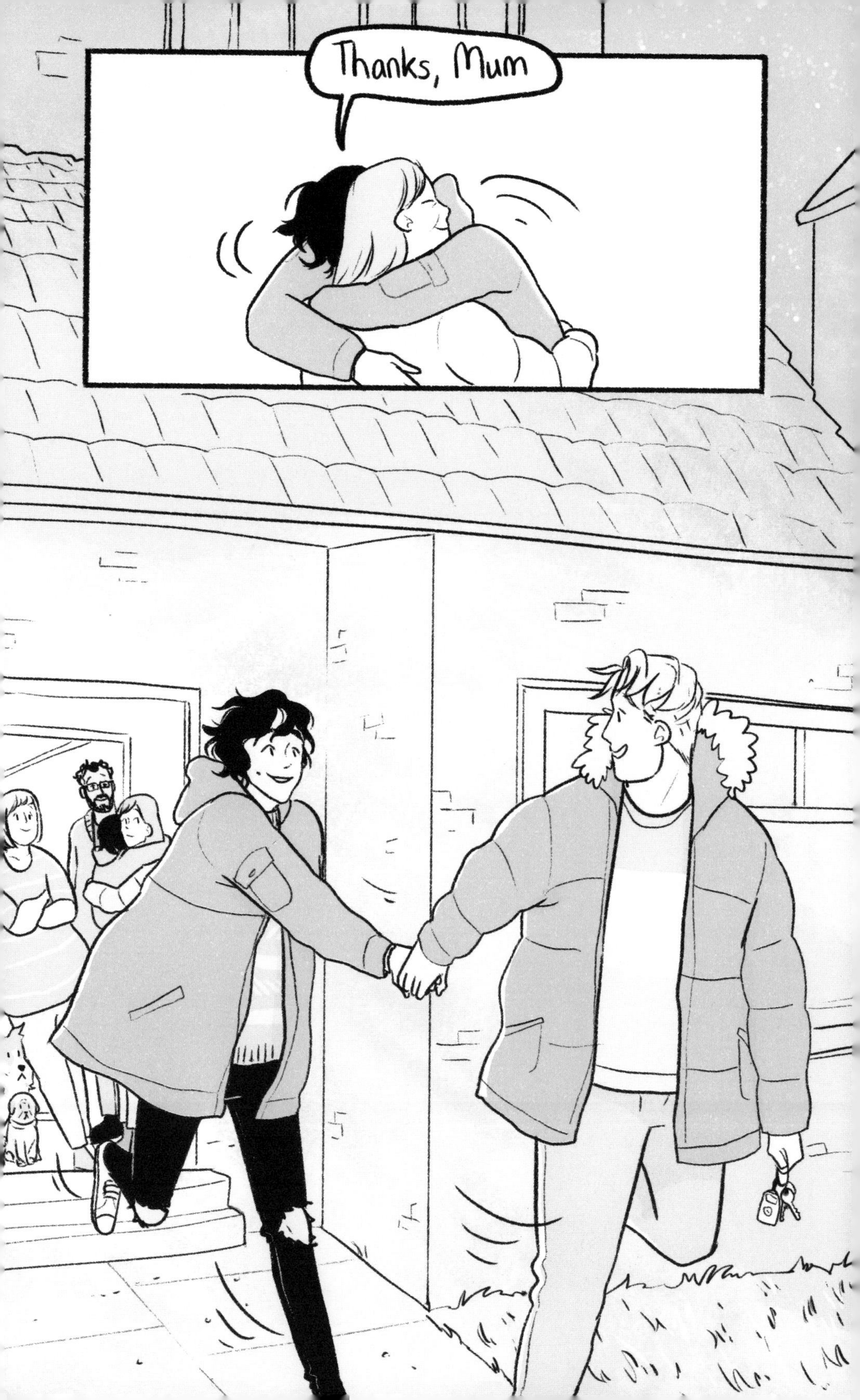
Thanks, Mum

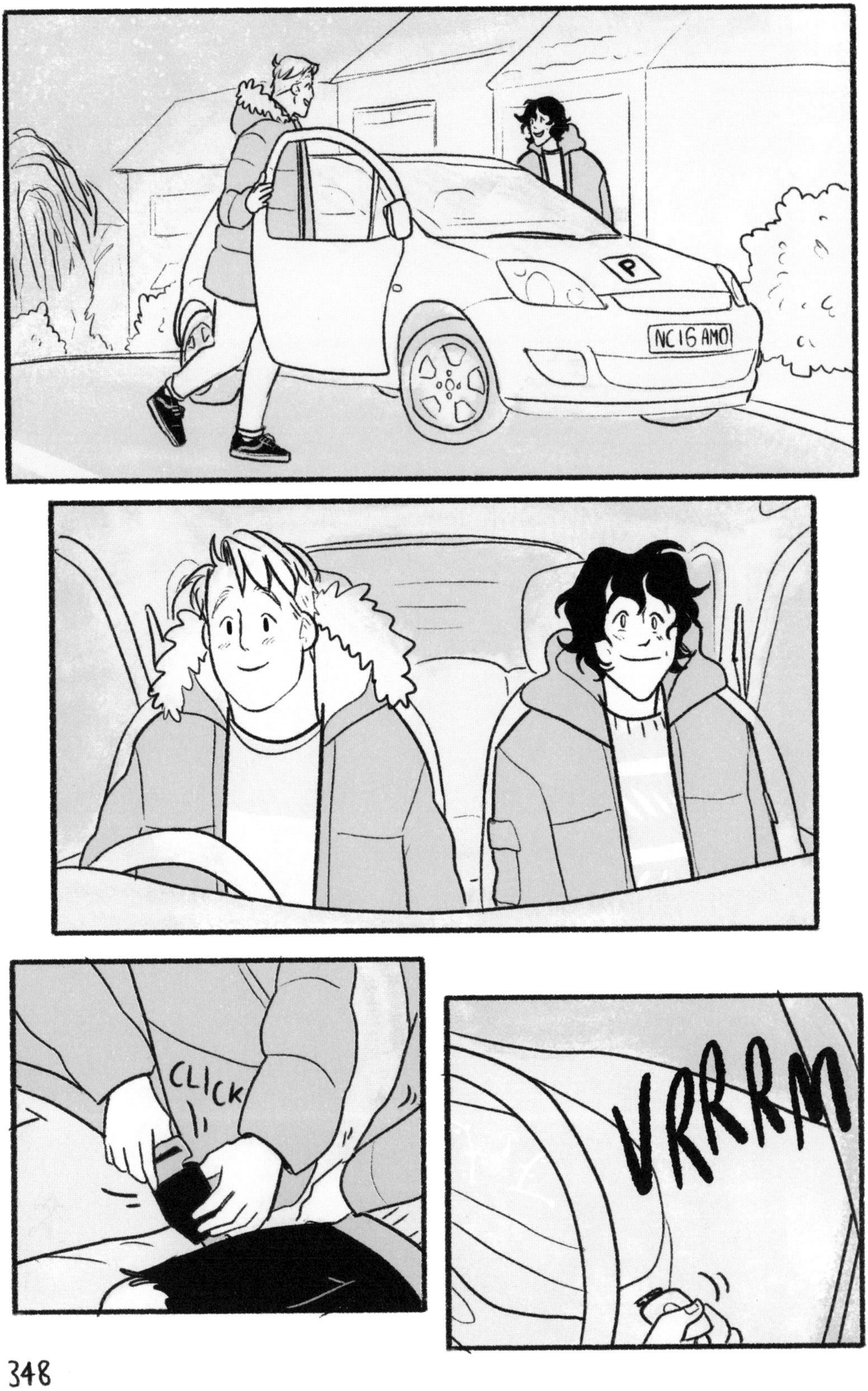
P
NC16 AMO
CLICK
VRRRM

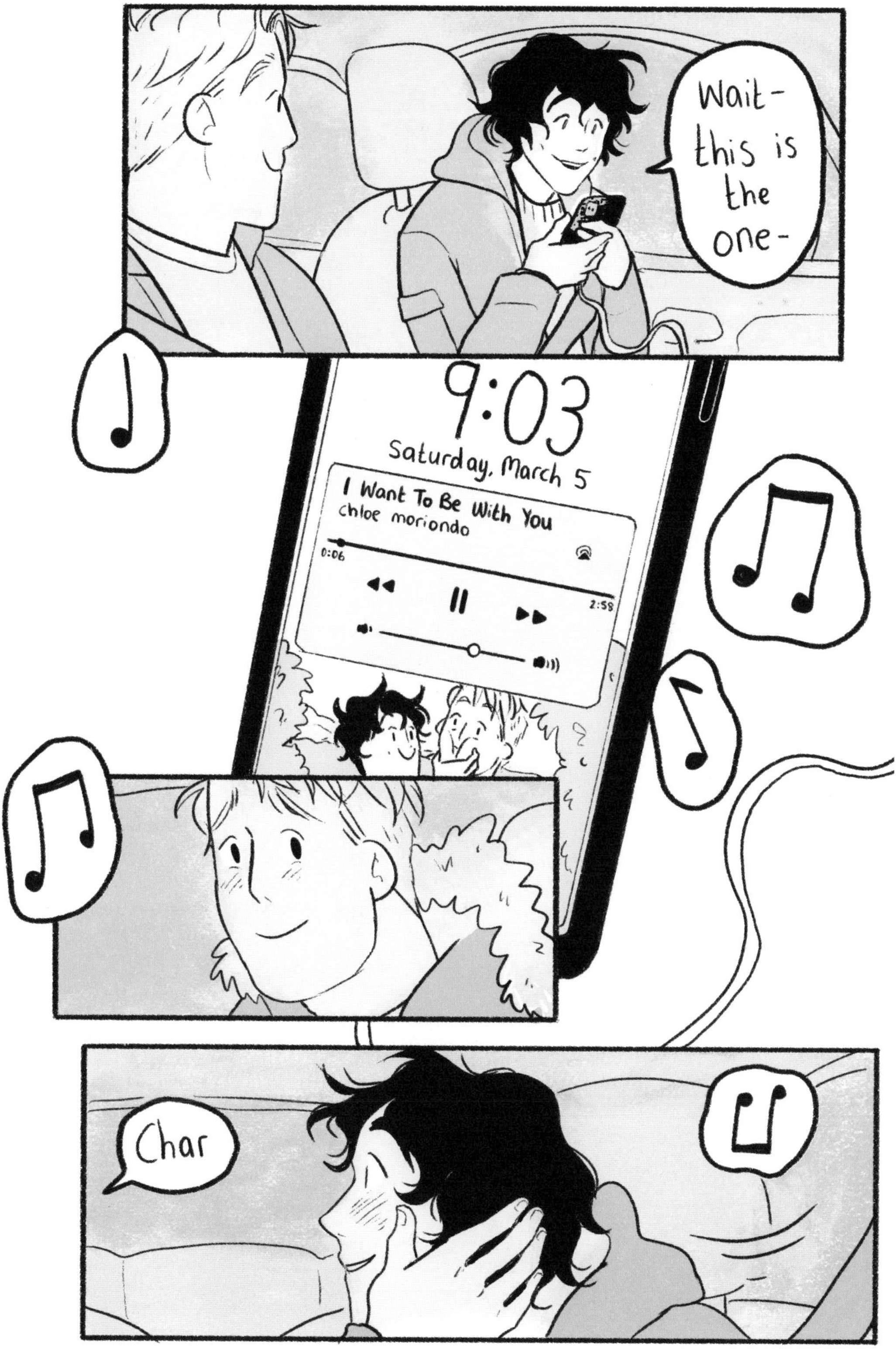
Wait-
this is
the
one-
9:03
Saturday, March 5
I Want To Be With You
chloe moriondo
0:06
2:58
Char

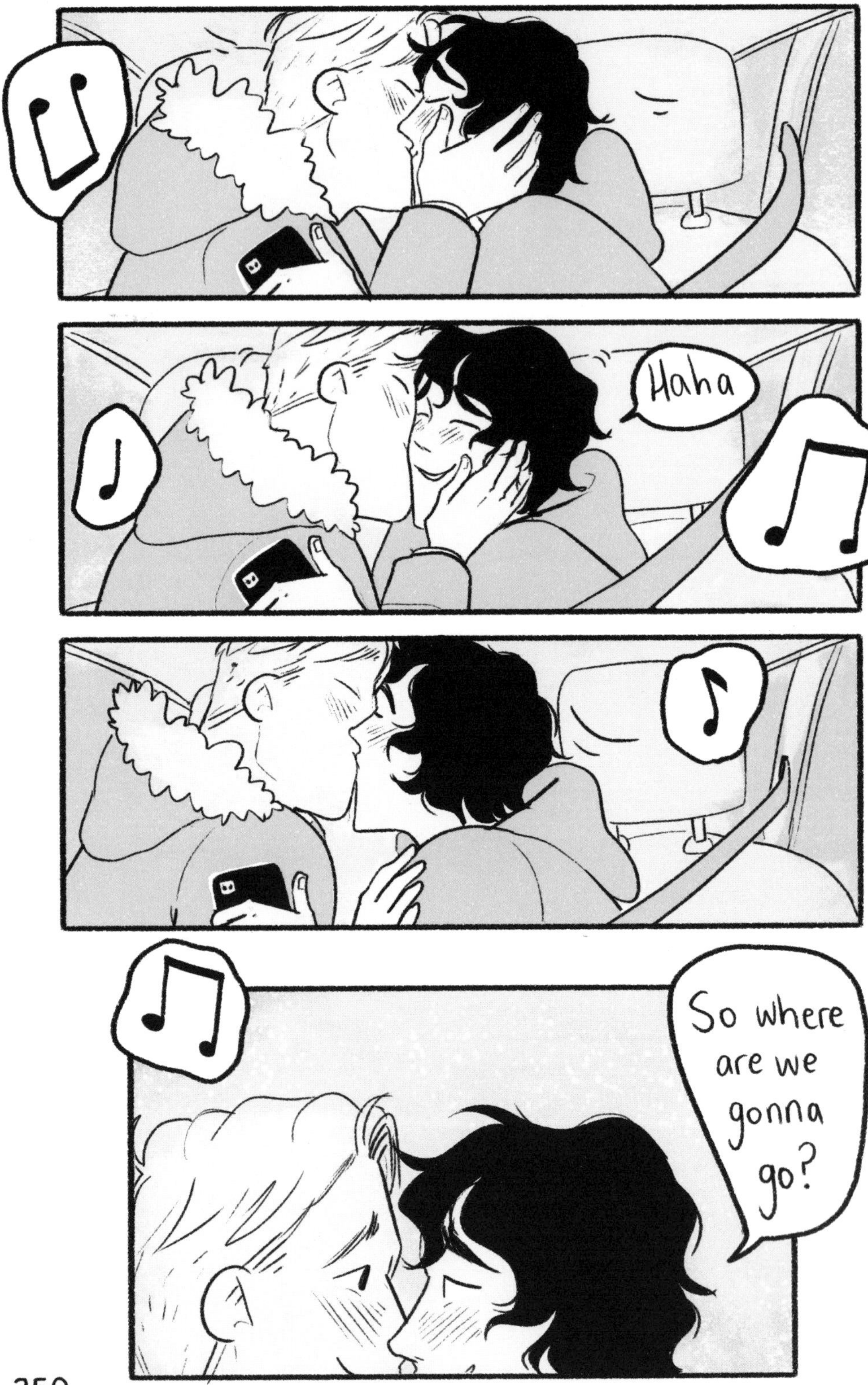
Haha
So where are we gonna go?

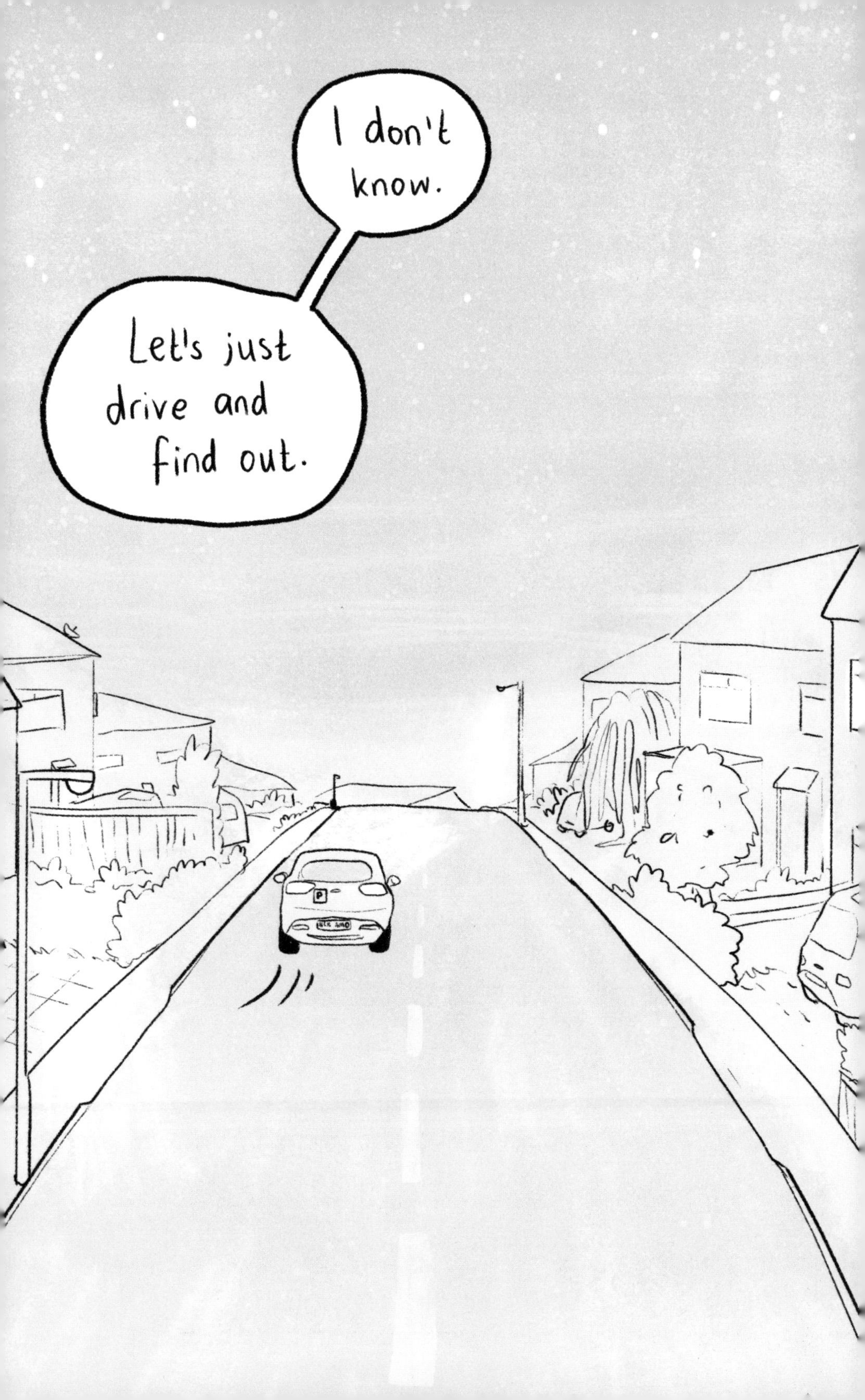
I don't know.
Let's just drive and find out.

Heartstopper will continue in
Volume 5!

Firsts

A HEARTSTOPPER MINI-COMIC

FIRST KISS

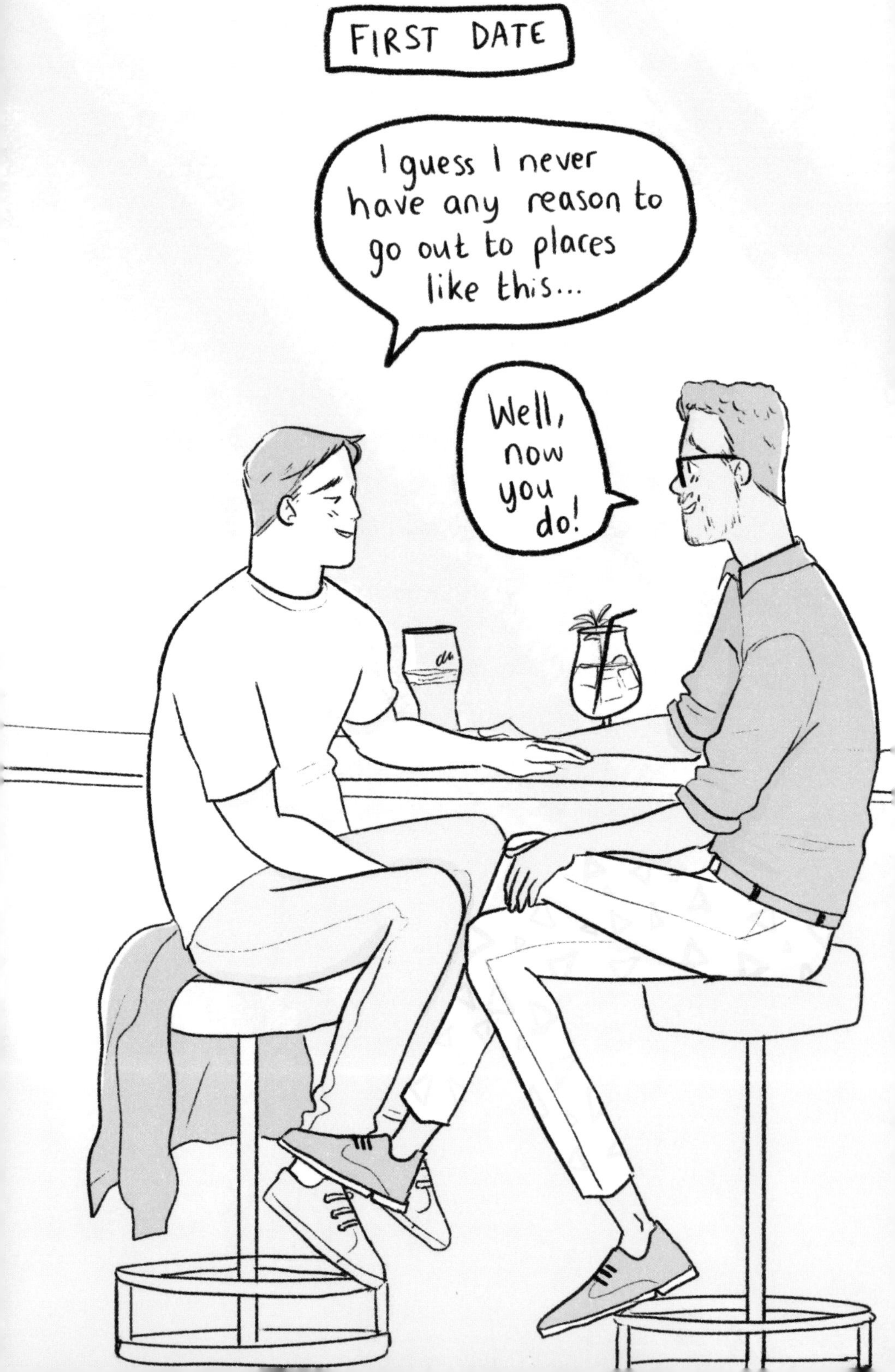
FIRST DATE
I guess I never have any reason to go out to places like this...
Well, now you do!

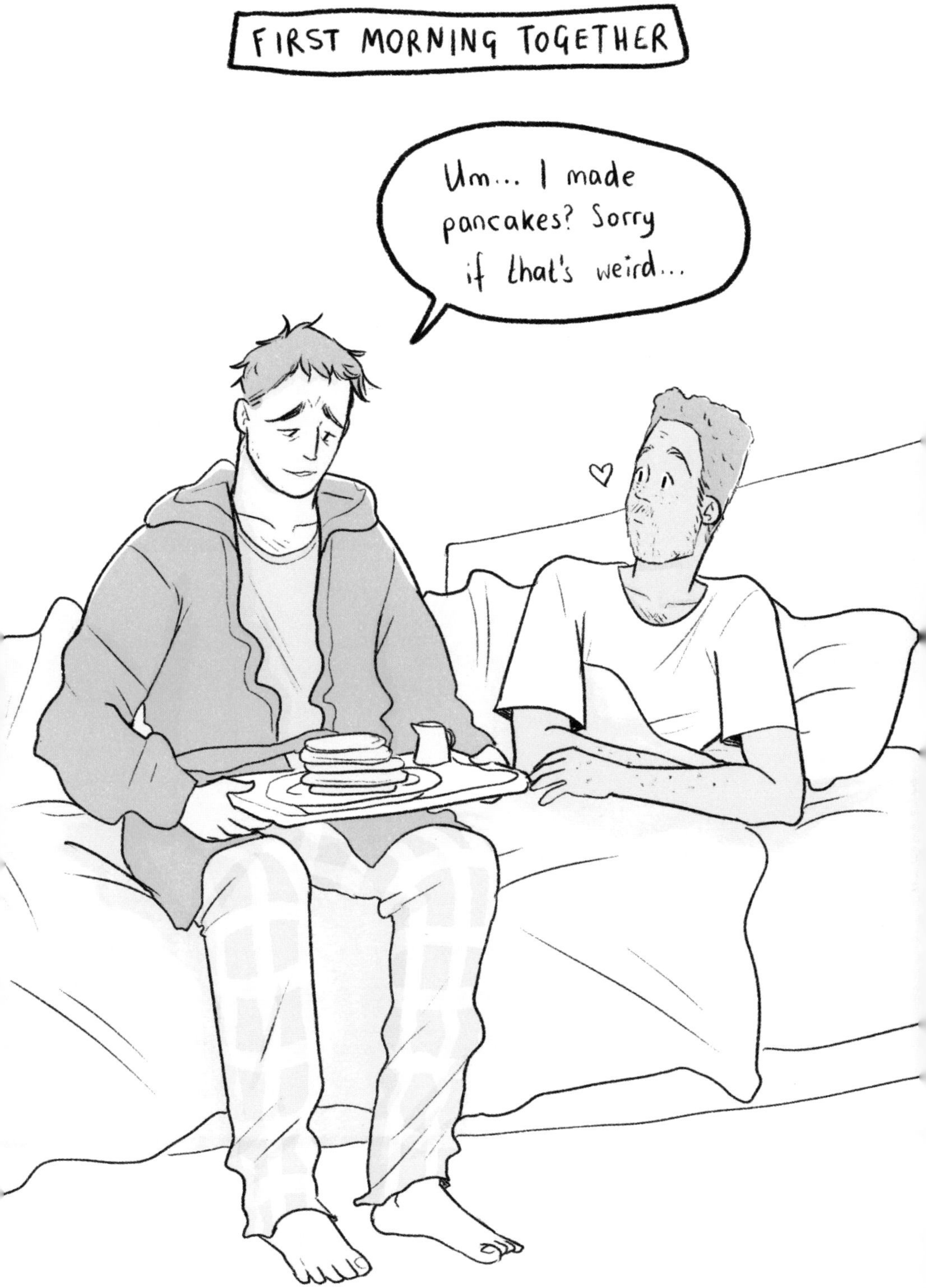
FIRST MORNING TOGETHER
Um... I made pancakes? Sorry if that's weird...

FIRST TIME COOKING TOGETHER

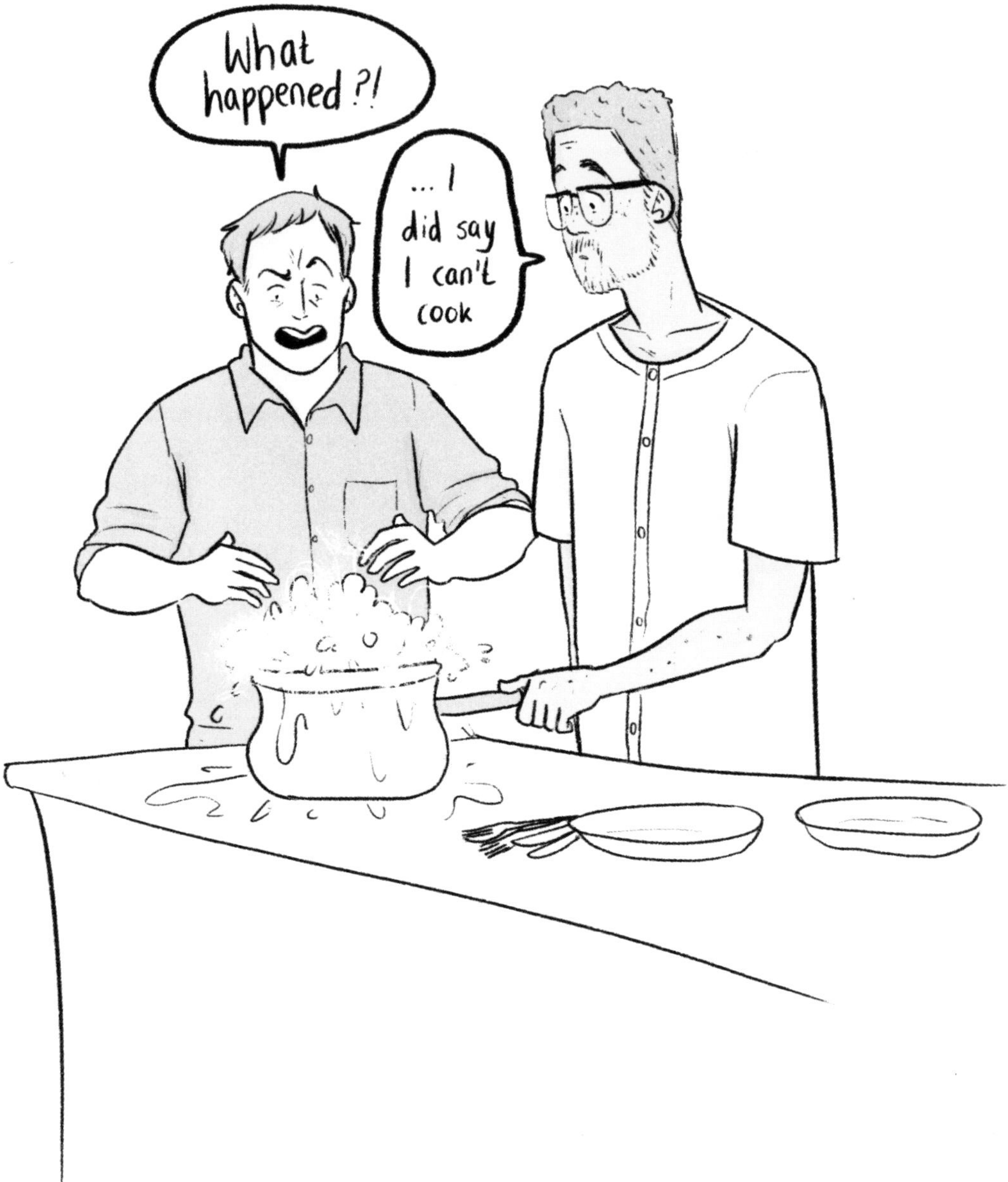
What happened?!
...I did say I can't cook

FIRST SICK DAY

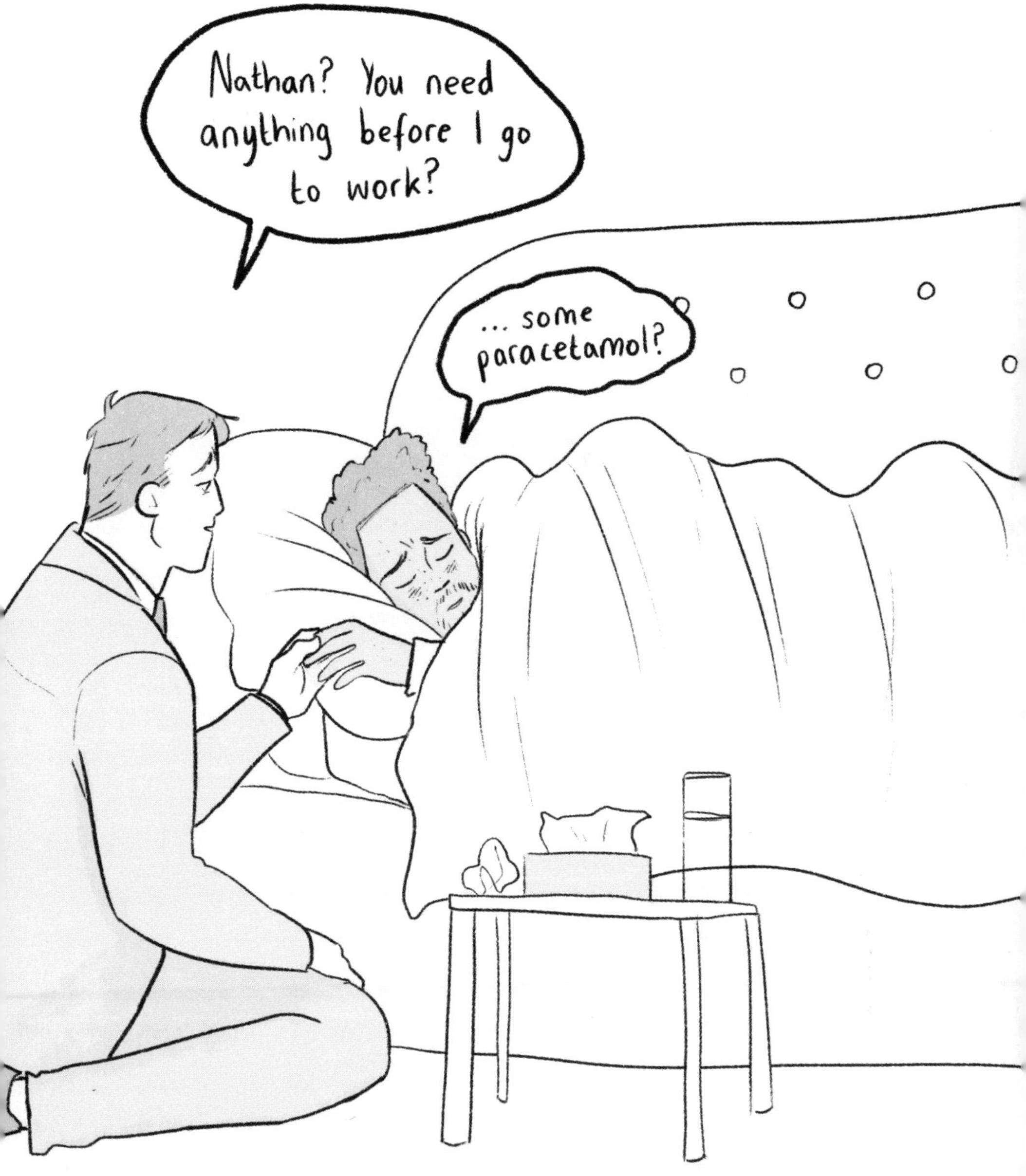

Nathan? You need anything before I go to work?
... some paracetamol?

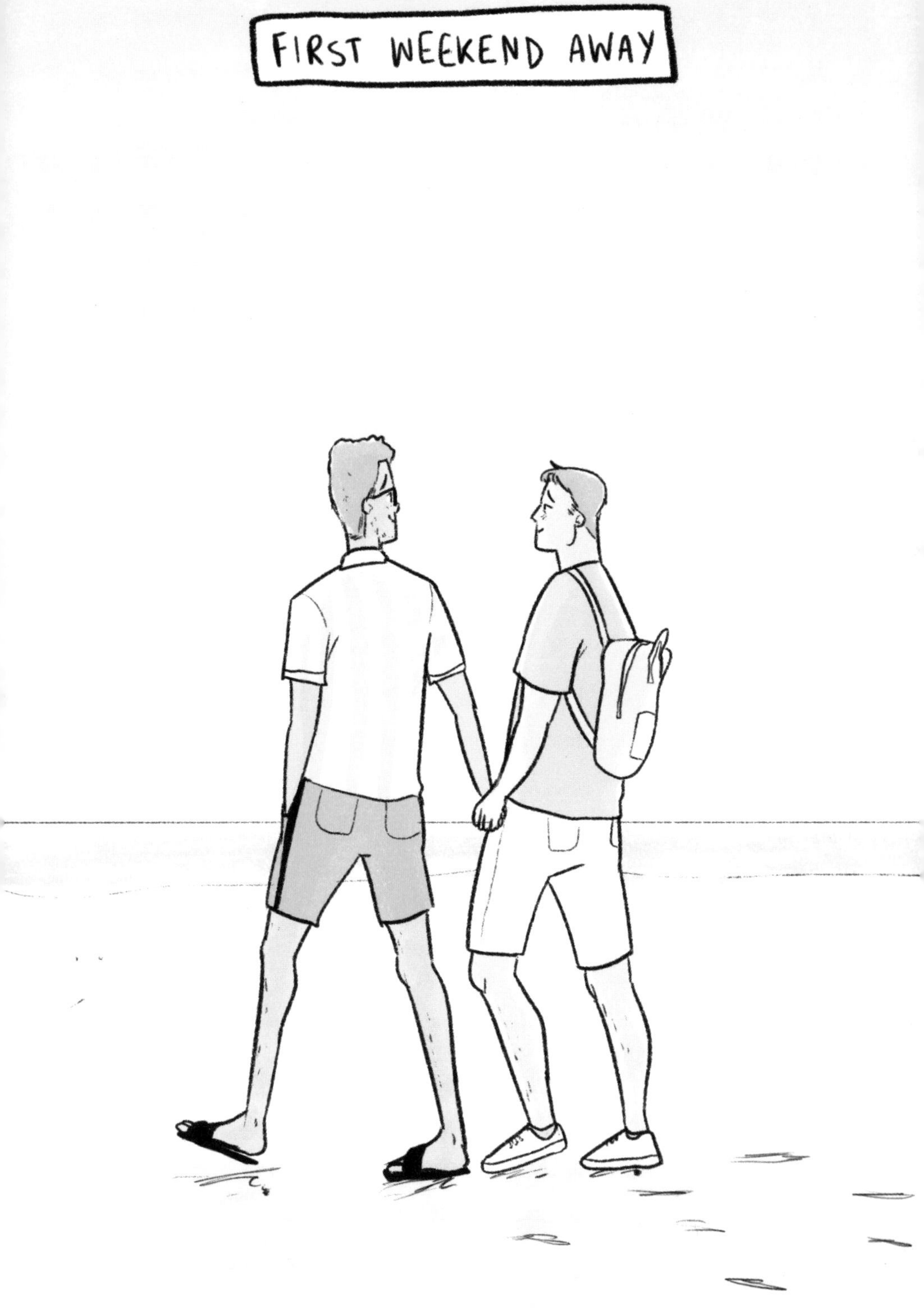
FIRST WEEKEND AWAY

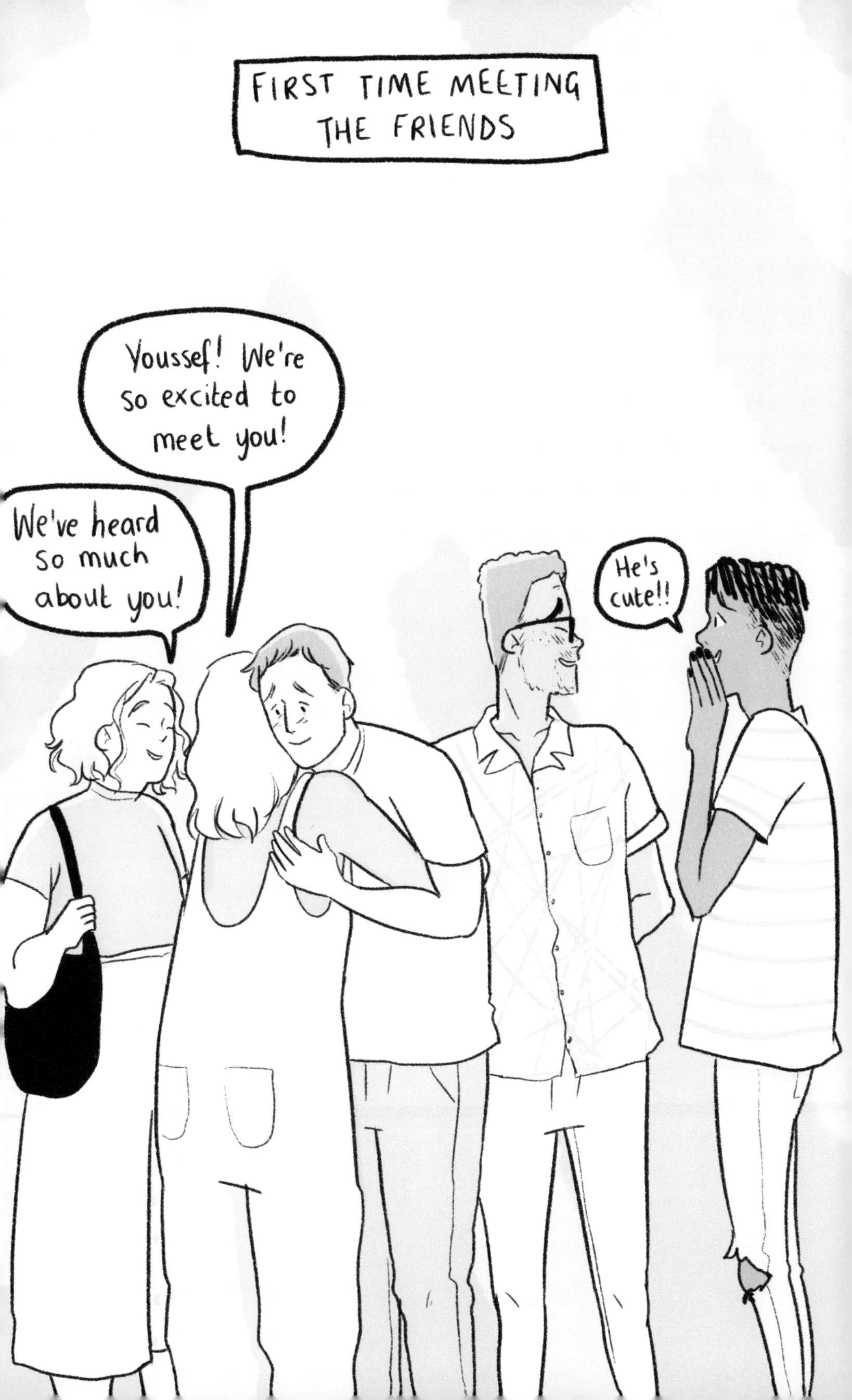
FIRST TIME MEETING THE FRIENDS
We've heard so much about you!
Youssef! We're so excited to meet you!
He's cute!!

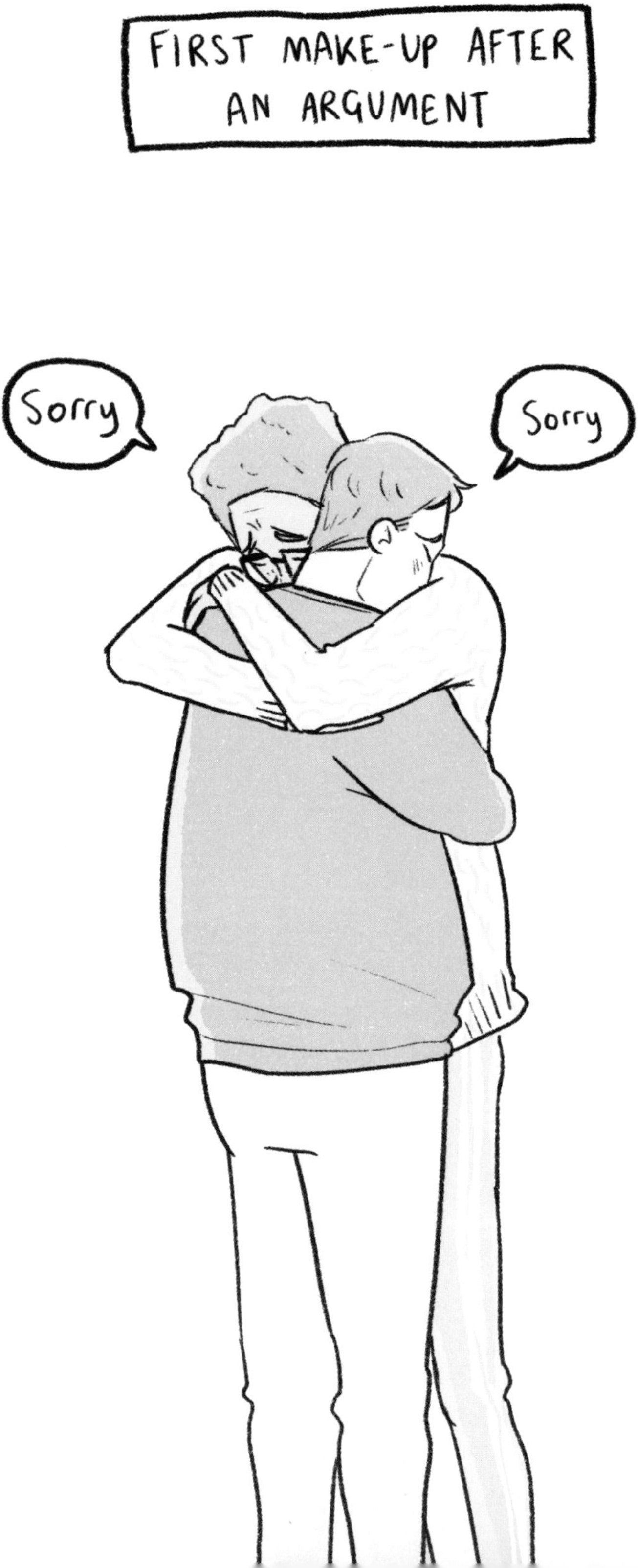
FIRST MAKE-UP AFTER AN ARGUMENT
Sorry
Sorry

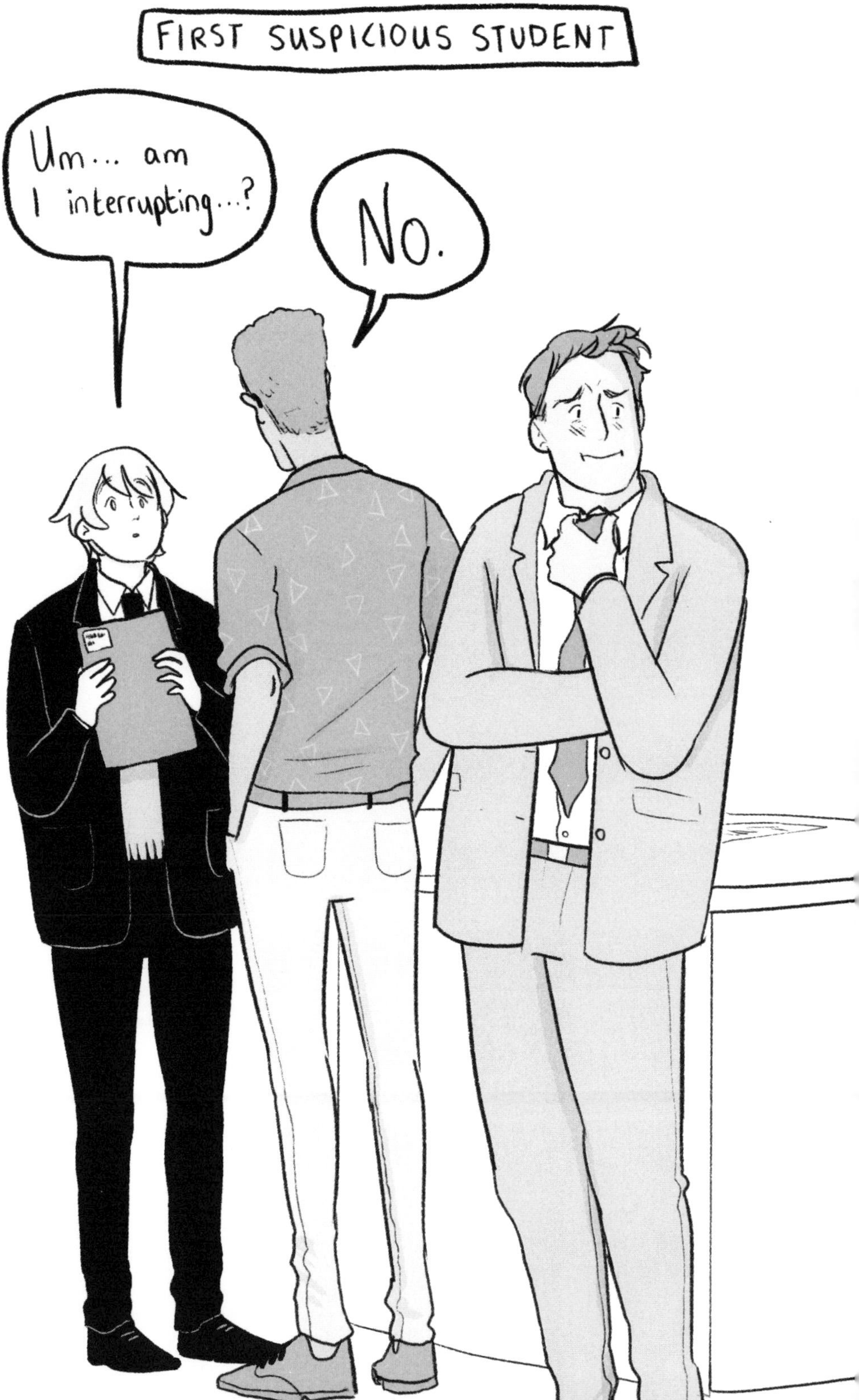
FIRST SUSPICIOUS STUDENT
Um... am I interrupting...?
No.

FIRST "I LOVE YOU"

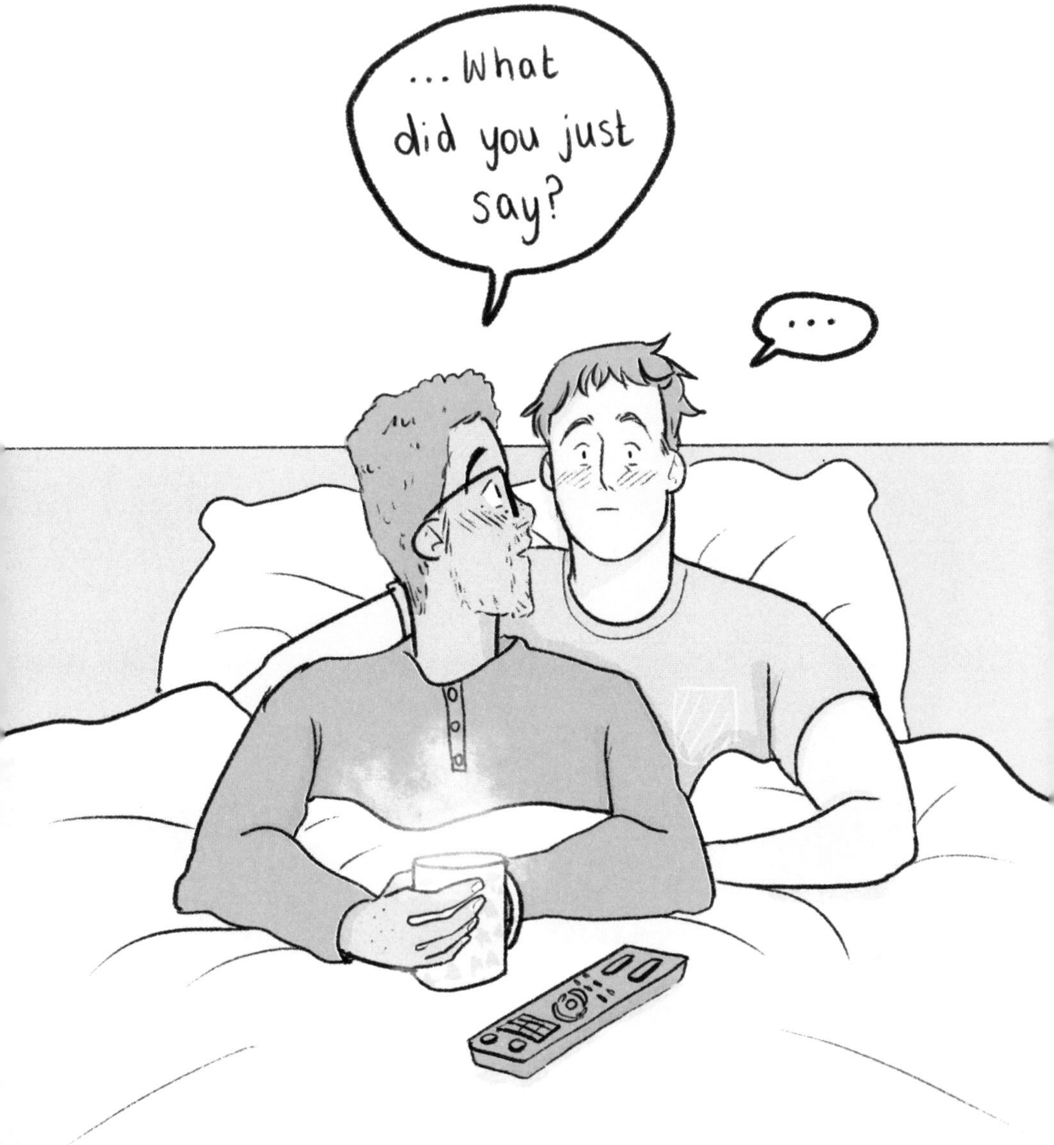
...What did you just say?
...

NAME: CHARLES "CHARLIE" SPRING
WHO ARE YOU: NICK'S BOYFRIEND
SCHOOL YEAR: YEAR 11   **AGE:** 15
BIRTHDAY: APRIL 27TH
FUN FACT: I LOVE TO READ!

NAME: Nicholas "Nick" Nelson
WHO ARE YOU: Charlie's boyfriend
SCHOOL YEAR: Year 12   **AGE:** 17
BIRTHDAY: September 4th
FUN FACT: I'm great at baking cakes

NAME: Tao Xu
WHO ARE YOU: Charlie's friend
SCHOOL YEAR: Year 11   **AGE:** 16
BIRTHDAY: September 23rd
FUN FACT: I have a film review blog

NAME: Victoria "Tori" Spring
WHO ARE YOU: Charlie's sister
SCHOOL YEAR: Year 12   **AGE:** 16
BIRTHDAY: April 5th
FUN FACT: I HATE (ALMOST) EVERYONE

NAME: Elle Argent
WHO ARE YOU: Charlie's friend
SCHOOL YEAR: Year 12   **AGE:** 16
BIRTHDAY: May 4th
FUN FACT: I like making clothes ♡

NAME: Tara Jones
WHO ARE YOU: Darcy's girlfriend
SCHOOL YEAR: Year 12   **AGE:** 16
BIRTHDAY: July 3rd
FUN FACT: I love dance! (especially ballet)

NAME: Darcy Olsson
WHO ARE YOU: Tara's girlfriend
SCHOOL YEAR: Year 12   **AGE:** 17
BIRTHDAY: January 9th
FUN FACT: I once ate a whole jar of mustard for a dare

NAME: Aled Last
WHO ARE YOU: Charlie's friend
SCHOOL YEAR: Year 11   **AGE:** 15
BIRTHDAY: August 15th
FUN FACT: I want to make a podcast

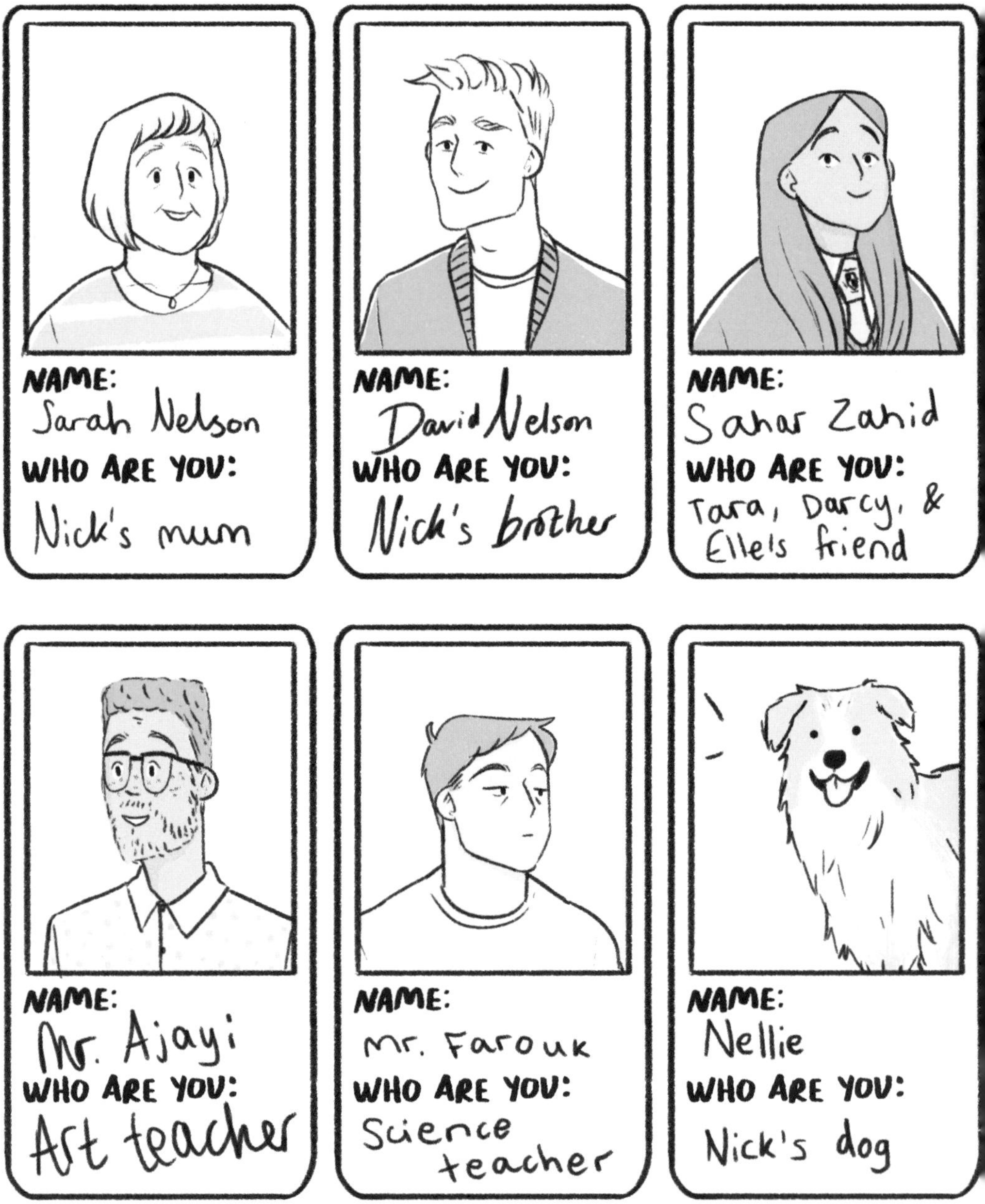
NAME:
Sarah Nelson
WHO ARE YOU:
Nick's mum
NAME:
David Nelson
WHO ARE YOU:
Nick's brother
NAME:
Sahar Zahid
WHO ARE YOU:
Tara, Darcy, & Elle's friend
NAME:
Mr. Ajayi
WHO ARE YOU:
Art teacher
NAME:
Mr. Farouk
WHO ARE YOU:
Science teacher
NAME:
Nellie
WHO ARE YOU:
Nick's dog

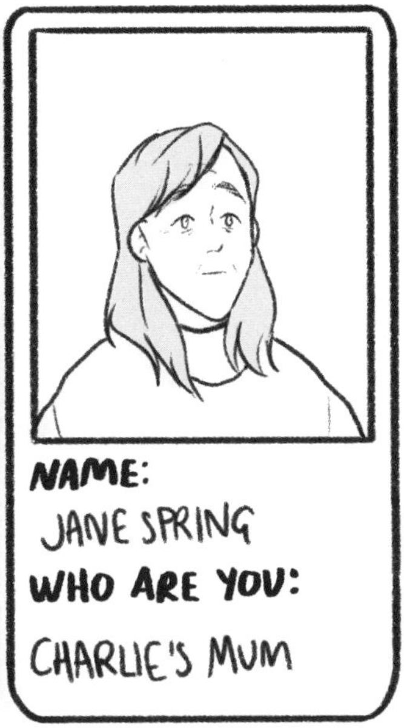
NAME:
JANE SPRING
WHO ARE YOU:
CHARLIE'S MUM

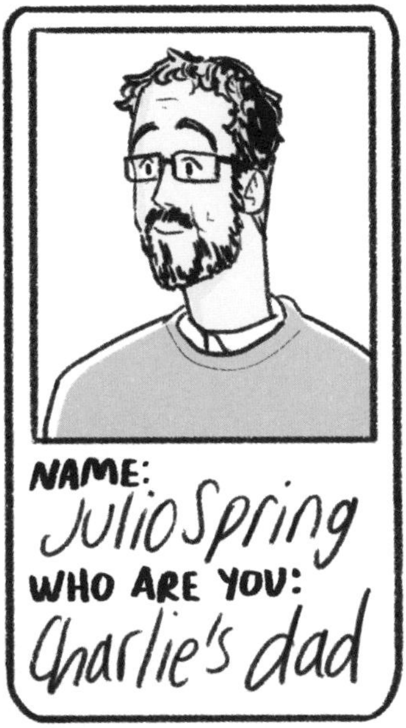
NAME:
Julio Spring
WHO ARE YOU:
Charlie's dad

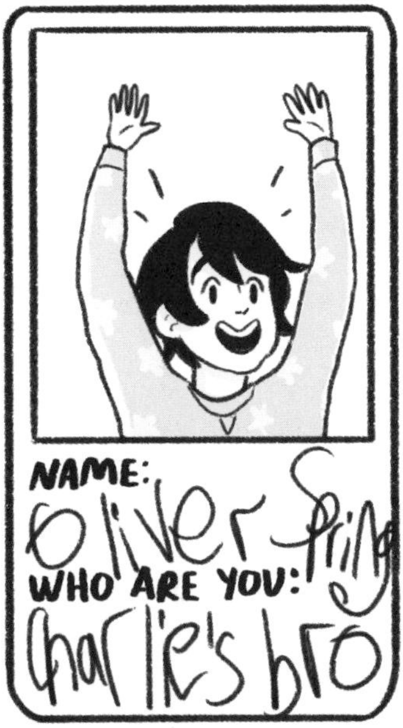
NAME:
Oliver Spring
WHO ARE YOU:
Charlie's bro

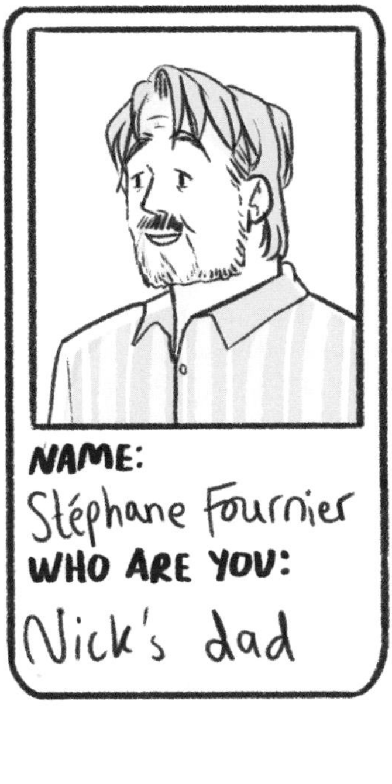
NAME:
Stéphane Fournier
WHO ARE YOU:
Nick's dad

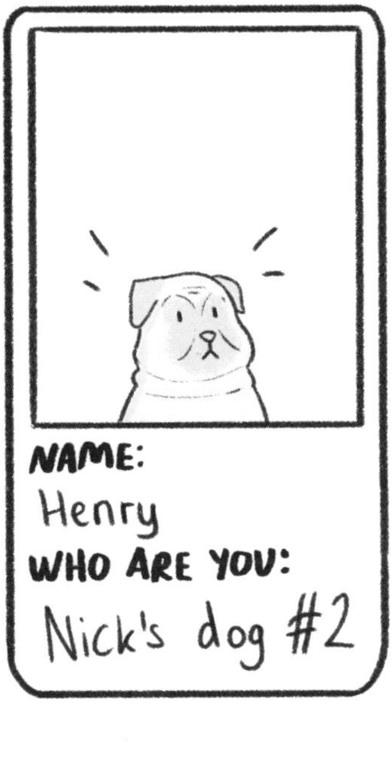
NAME:
Henry
WHO ARE YOU:
Nick's dog #2

 **the.xu.tao**

64 likes

the.xu.tao third wheeling

 **the.xu.tao**

71 likes

the.xu.tao third wheel part 2 (they've been making out for like half an hour)

cfspring why are you so obsessed with me!!!!!
the.xu.tao @cfspring i just ship you two so much
cfspring @the.xu.tao fuck off

 **the.xu.tao**

98 likes

the.xu.tao third wheel part 3. literally just trying to do my math
homework here

cfspring IT WAS JUST A PECK WE WEREN'T EVEN MAKING
OUT
the.xu.tao @cfspring still inappropriate school behavior and i will
report you to the authorities
cfspring @the.xu.tao homophobia

 **cfspring**

102 likes

cfspring NOW who's the third wheel huh **@the.xu.tao**

the.xu.tao ...truce?
cfspring @the.xu.tao truce

Mental Health Resources

For information, help, support, and guidance
about mental health and mental illness,
please check out the following resources:

National Eating Disorders Association
nationaleatingdisorders.org

Anxiety & Depression Association of America
adaa.org

Heard Alliance
heardalliance.org

The Trevor Project
thetrevorproject.org

Author's Note

Hello, everyone! I really hope you enjoyed the fourth volume of Heartstopper. Can you believe we're already on the fourth volume? I certainly can't!

This volume mostly followed Charlie's mental health journey. I wanted to explore some of his struggles with his eating disorder, but to always show that recovery is possible, and that even though it may not be a straightforward journey, things can get better. But romantic love does not "cure" mental illness, as movies often suggest! This is something Nick learns in this volume. Nick can be there for him, but Charlie has to find his own path to recovery.

So much has happened since the last volume. I got to go on a UK book tour in early 2020, release a Heartstopper coloring book, and was finally able to announce that a TV adaptation is in the works with Netflix and See-Saw Films. None of this would have been possible without all you brilliant, passionate readers. I'm so, so grateful for your support and love for the series.

A huge thanks, as always, to the wonderful team working on Heartstopper: my amazing agent, Claire Wilson, my incredible editor, Rachel Wade, my awesome publicist, Emily Thomas, everyone at Hachette who is a part of the Heartstopper journey, and all the international publishers around the world who are now supporting the series, too.

I know that many of you are sad that the next volume will be the final volume of Nick and Charlie's story. I'm sad, too! But I promise that it shall be magical and heartwarming and full of queer joy.

See you in Volume Five!

Collect the Heartstopper series!

"Absolutely delightful. Sweet, romantic, kind. Beautifully paced. I loved this book."
– Rainbow Rowell, author of Carry On
HEARTSTOPPER
VOLUME 1
ALICE OSEMAN

VOLUME
2
HEARTSTOPPER
ALICE OSEMAN

ALICE OSEMAN
VOLUME
3
HEARTSTOPPER

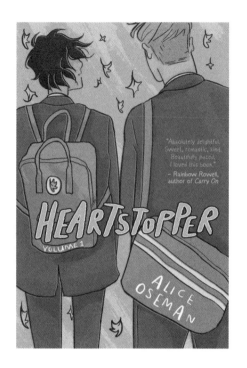

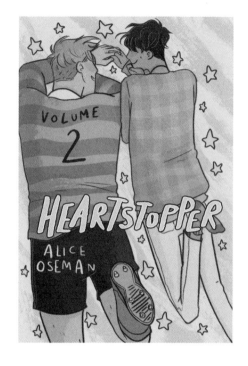

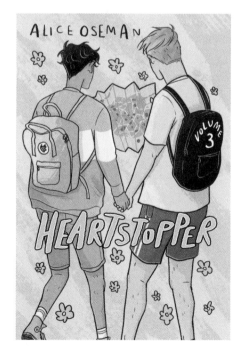

Don't miss this exceptional YA novel about discovering that it's okay not to have romantic feelings for anyone . . . since there are plenty of other ways to find love and connection.

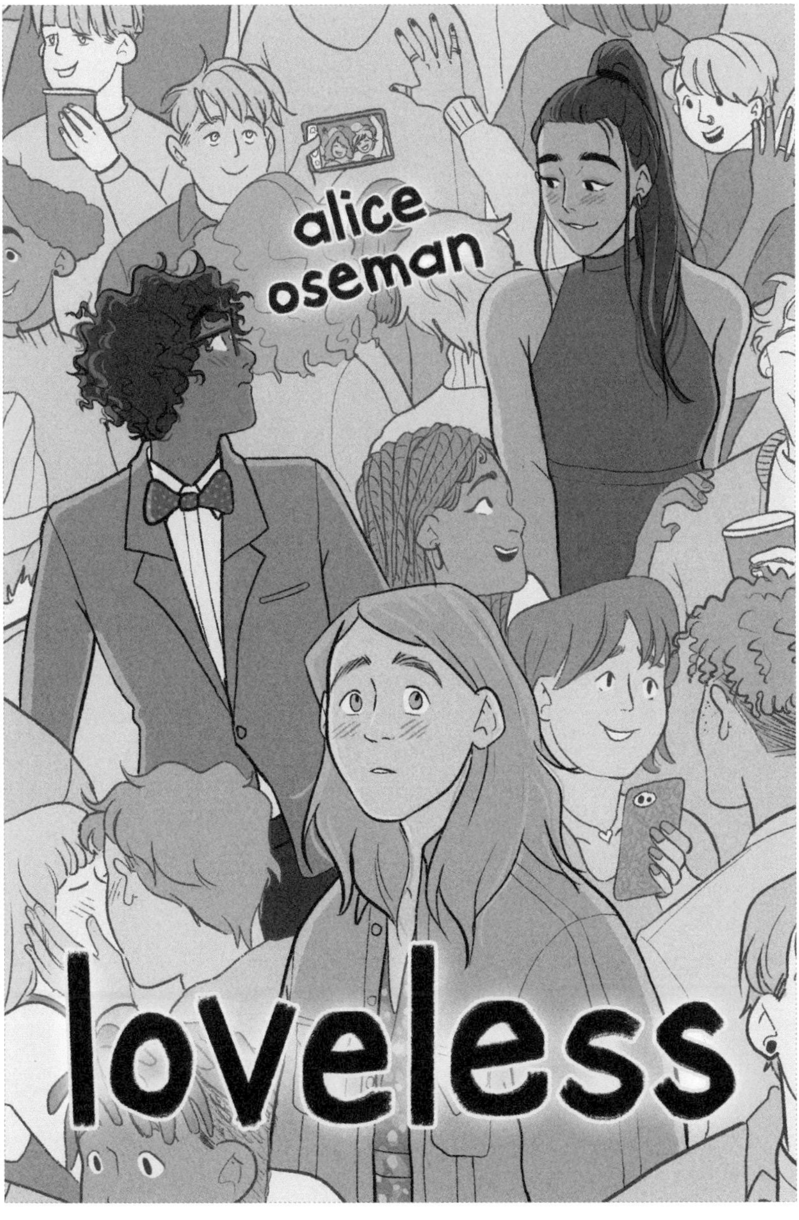
alice oseman
loveless

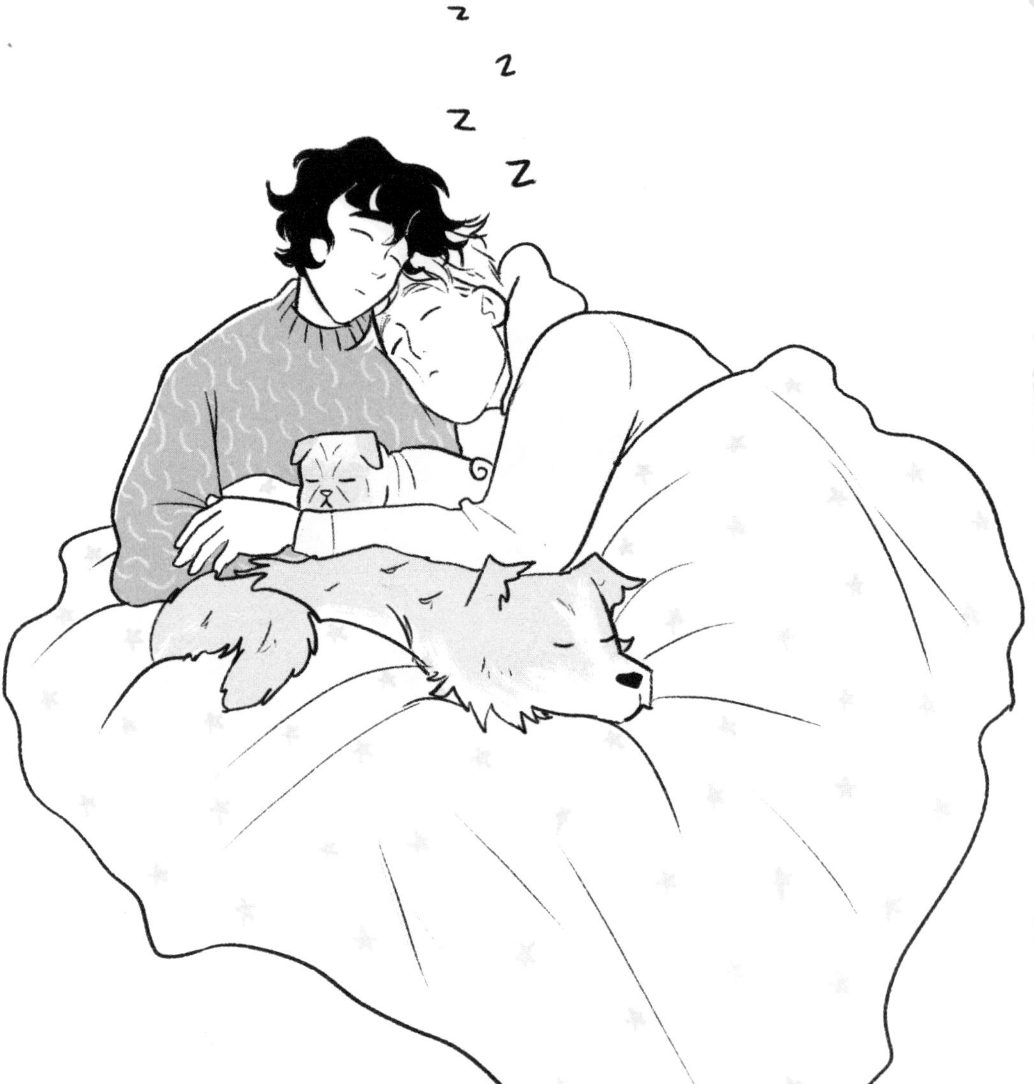
z z Z Z